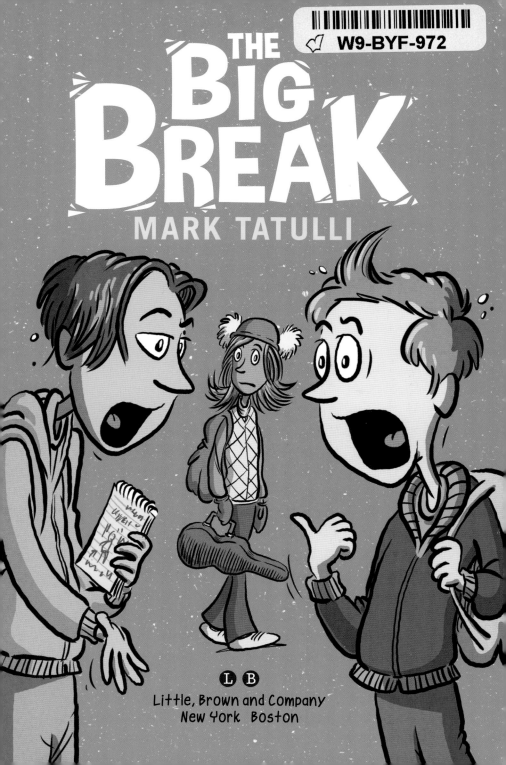

THE BIG BREAK

MARK TATULLI

L B

Little, Brown and Company
New York Boston

About This Book

This book was edited by Pam Gruber and designed by Marcie Lawrence and Carla Weise.
The production was supervised by Bernadette Flinn, and the production editor was
Lindsay Walter-Greaney. The text font and display type were illustrated by Mark Tatulli.

Colors by Caravan Studios

Little, Brown and Company
Hachette Book Group
1290 Avenue of the Americas, New York, NY 10104
Visit us at LBYR.com

First Edition: March 2020

Little, Brown and Company is a division of Hachette Book Group, Inc.
The Little, Brown name and logo are trademarks of Hachette Book Group, Inc.

Library of Congress Cataloging-in-Publication Data

Names: Tatulli, Mark, author, illustrator.
Title: The big break / Mark Tatulli.
Description: First edition. | New York : Little, Brown and Company, 2020. | Audience: Ages 8-12. | Summary: Russ's friendship with Andrew disintegrates when Russ gets a girlfriend, leaving the video they are making without an ending, but a close encounter with the legendary Jersey Devil brings them back together.
Identifiers: LCCN 2019029919 | ISBN 9780316440547 (hardcover) | ISBN 9780316440554 (paperback) | ISBN 9780316440523 (ebook) | ISBN 9780316536912 (library edition ebook)
Subjects: LCSH: Graphic novels. | CYAC: Graphic novels. | Jersey Devil (Monster)—Fiction. | Monsters—Fiction. | Video recordings—Production and direction—Fiction. | Friendship—Fiction. | Best friends—Fiction.
Classification: LCC PZ7.7.T377 Bi 2020 | DDC 741.5/973--dc23
LC record available at https://lccn.loc.gov/2019029919

ISBNs: 978-0-316-44054-7 (hardcover), 978-0-316-44055-4 (paperback),
978-0-316-44052-3 (ebook), 978-0-316-53689-9 (ebook), 978-0-316-53690-5 (ebook)

Printed in China
1010

Hardcover: 10 9 8 7 6 5 4 3 2 1
Paperback: 10 9 8 7 6 5 4 3 2 1

To Bryan Sherman and Stephan Pastis—
the great love/hate frenemies of my life.

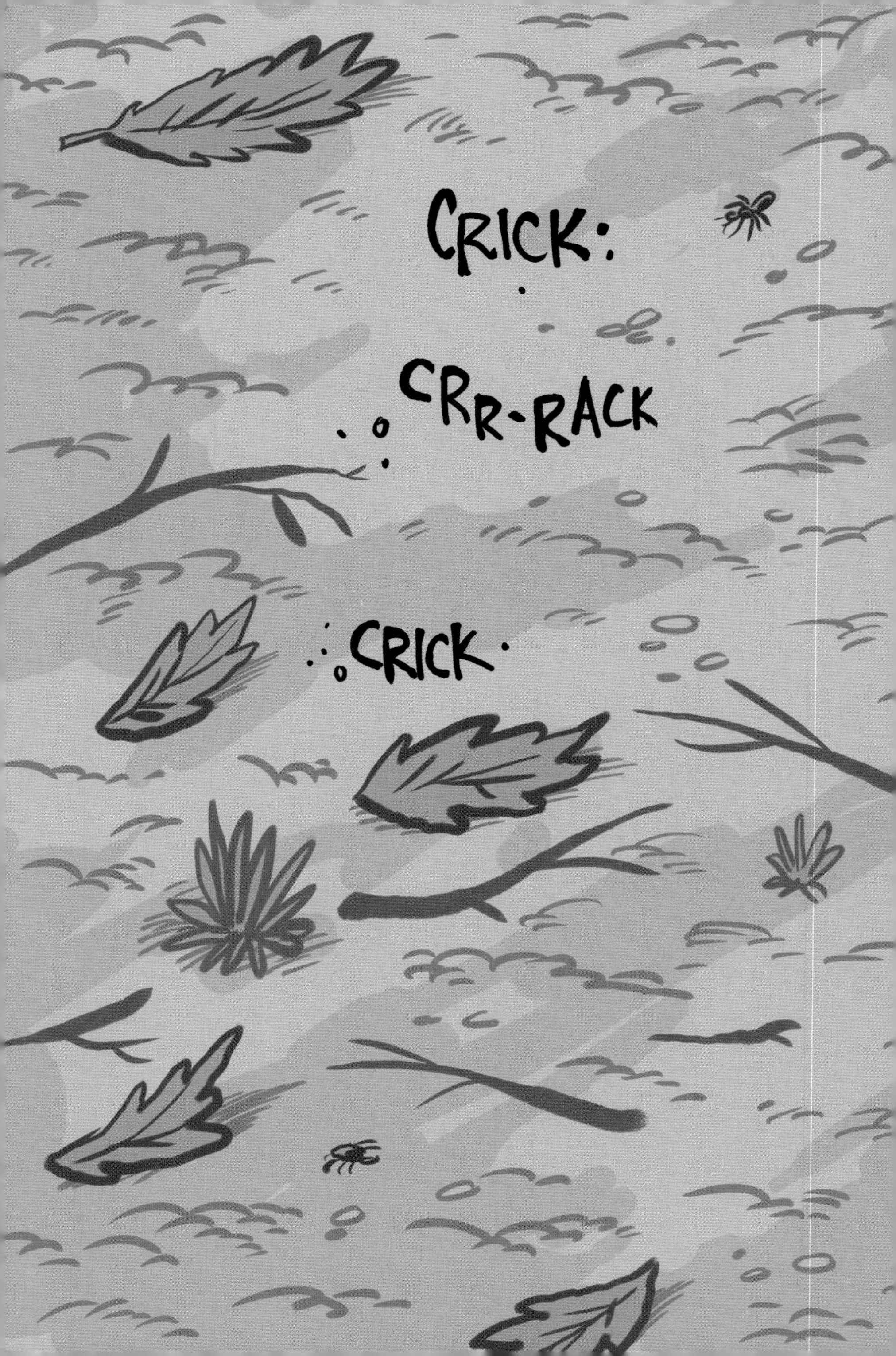
CRICK
CRR-RACK
CRICK

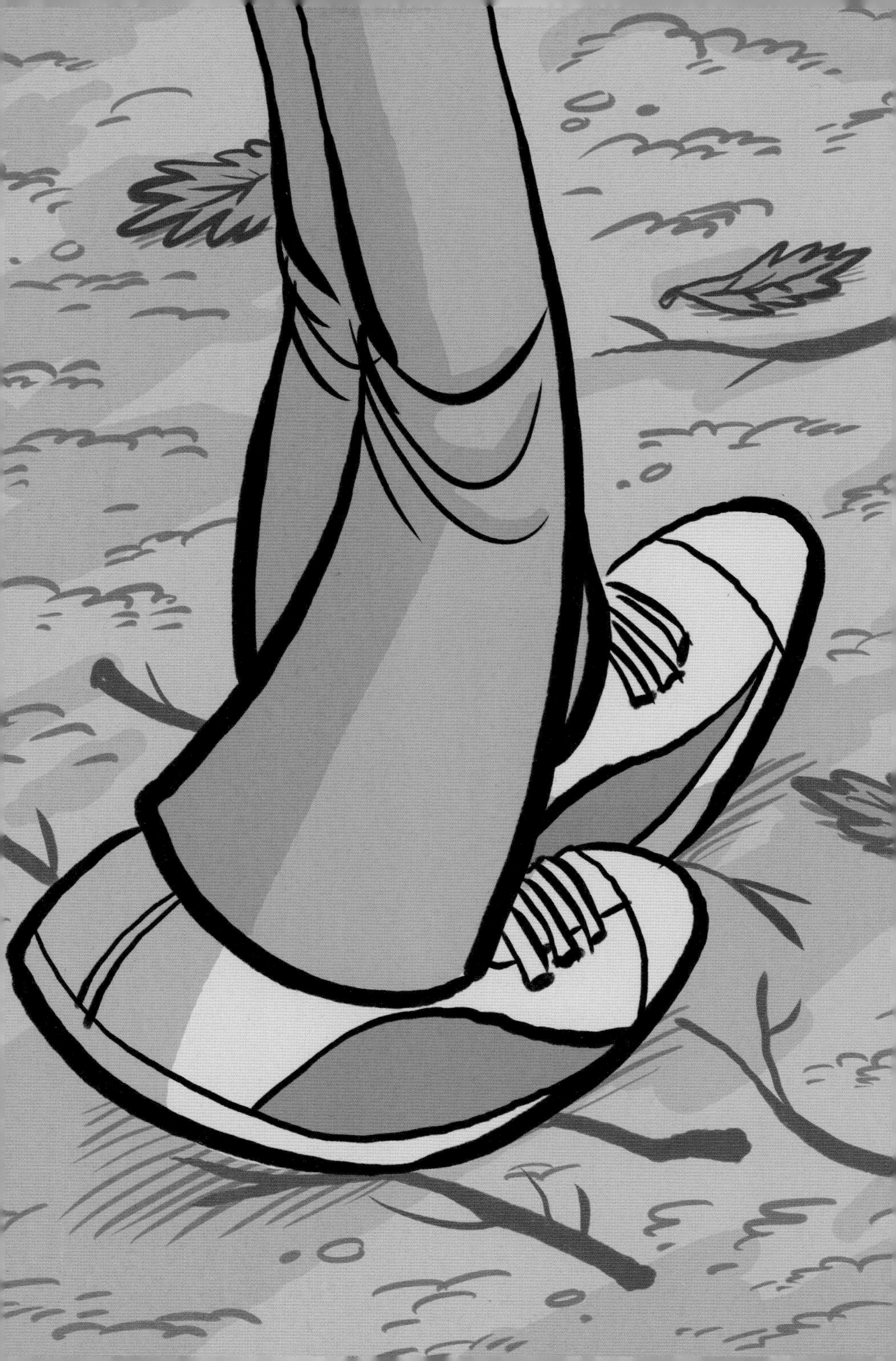

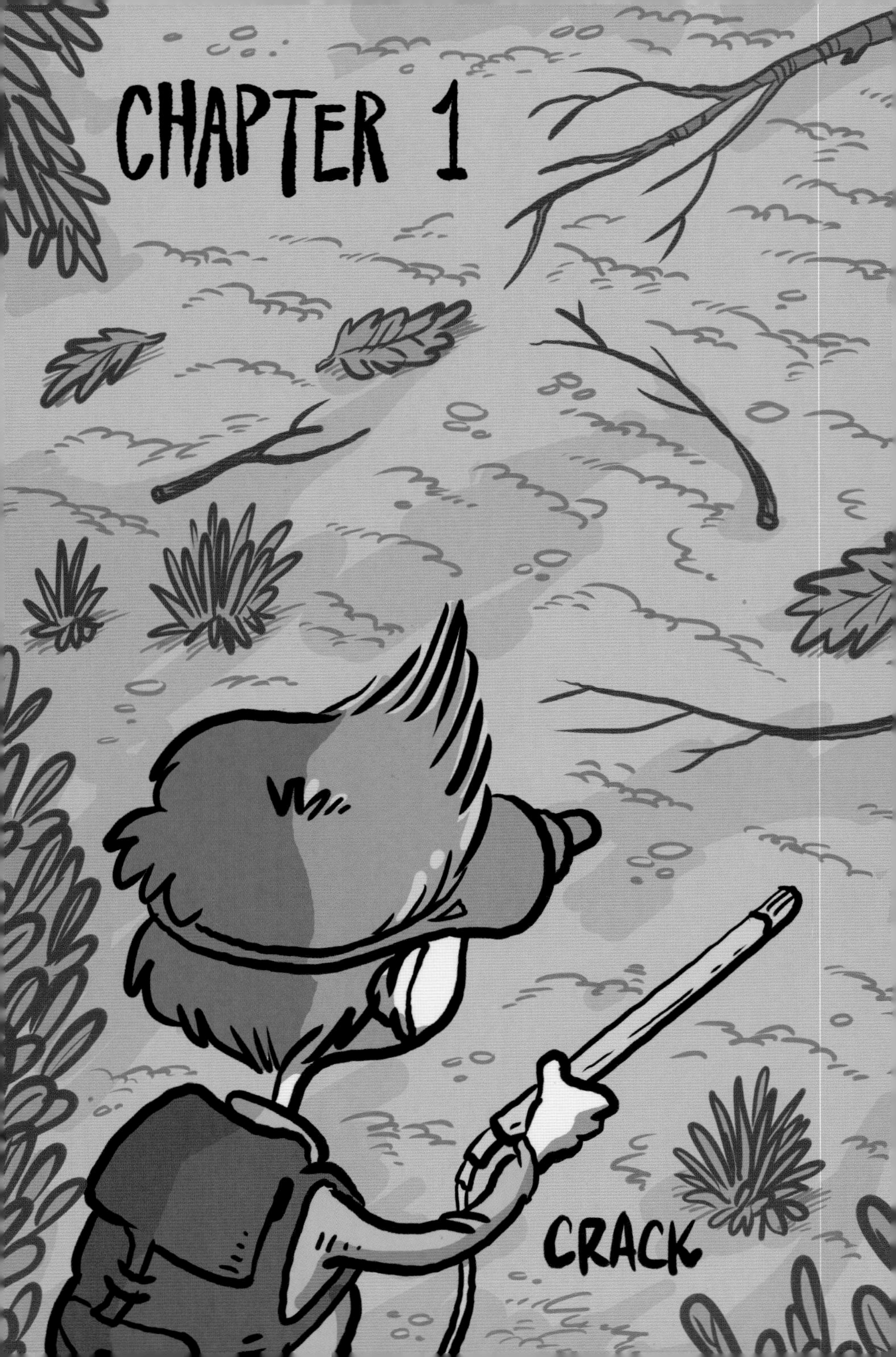
CHAPTER 1
CRACK

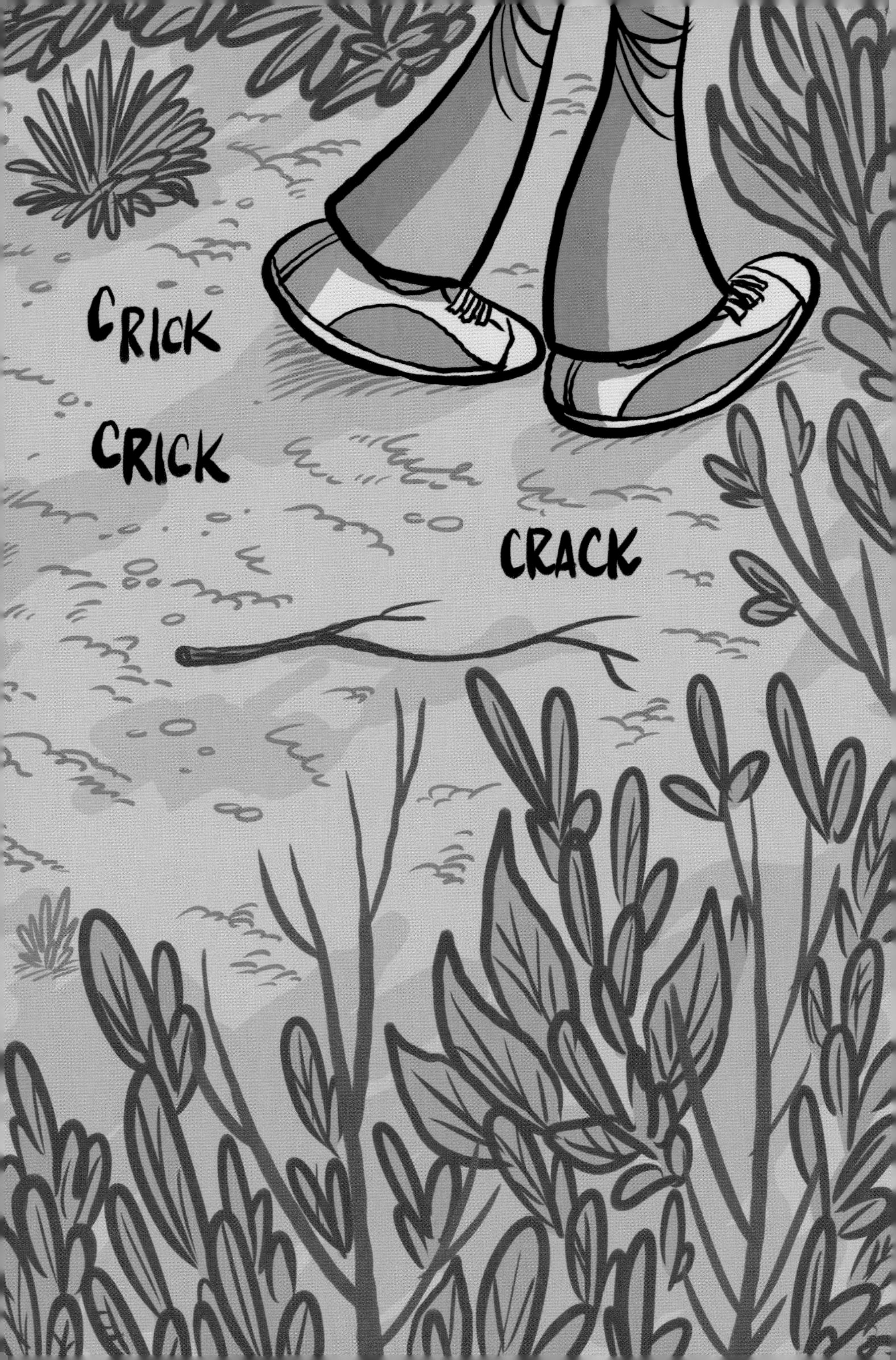
CRICK
CRICK
CRACK

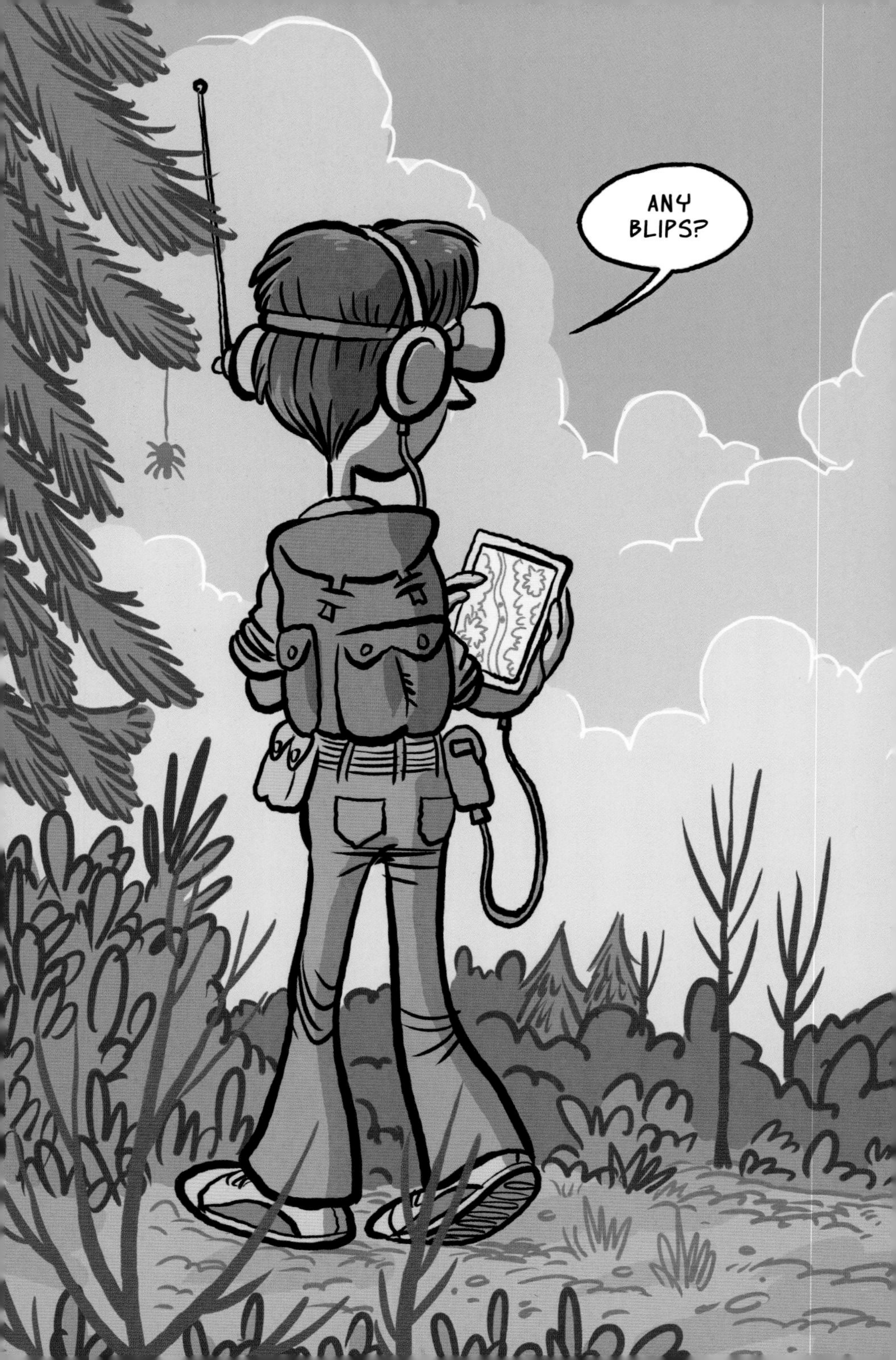
ANY BLIPS?

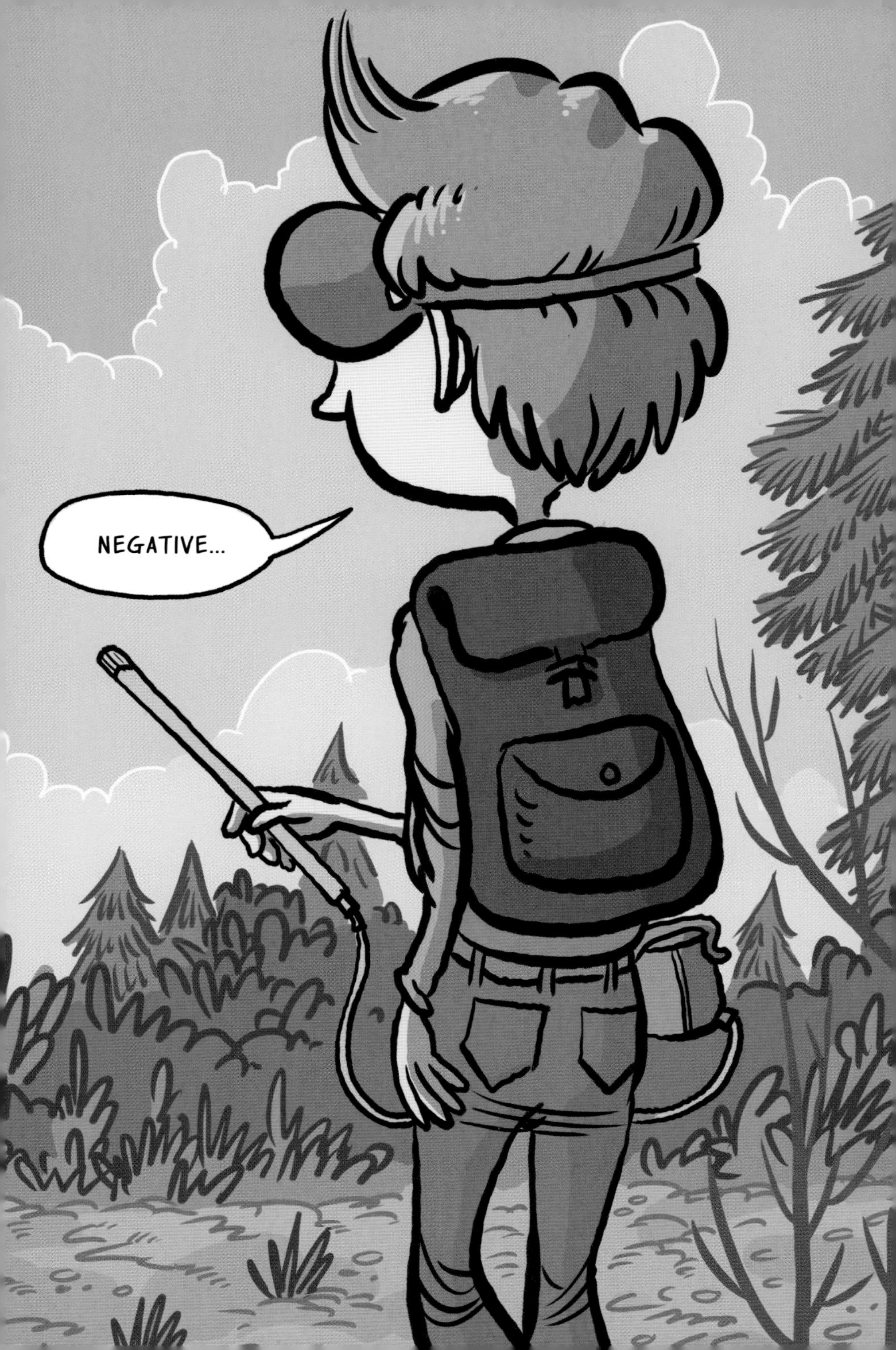
NEGATIVE...

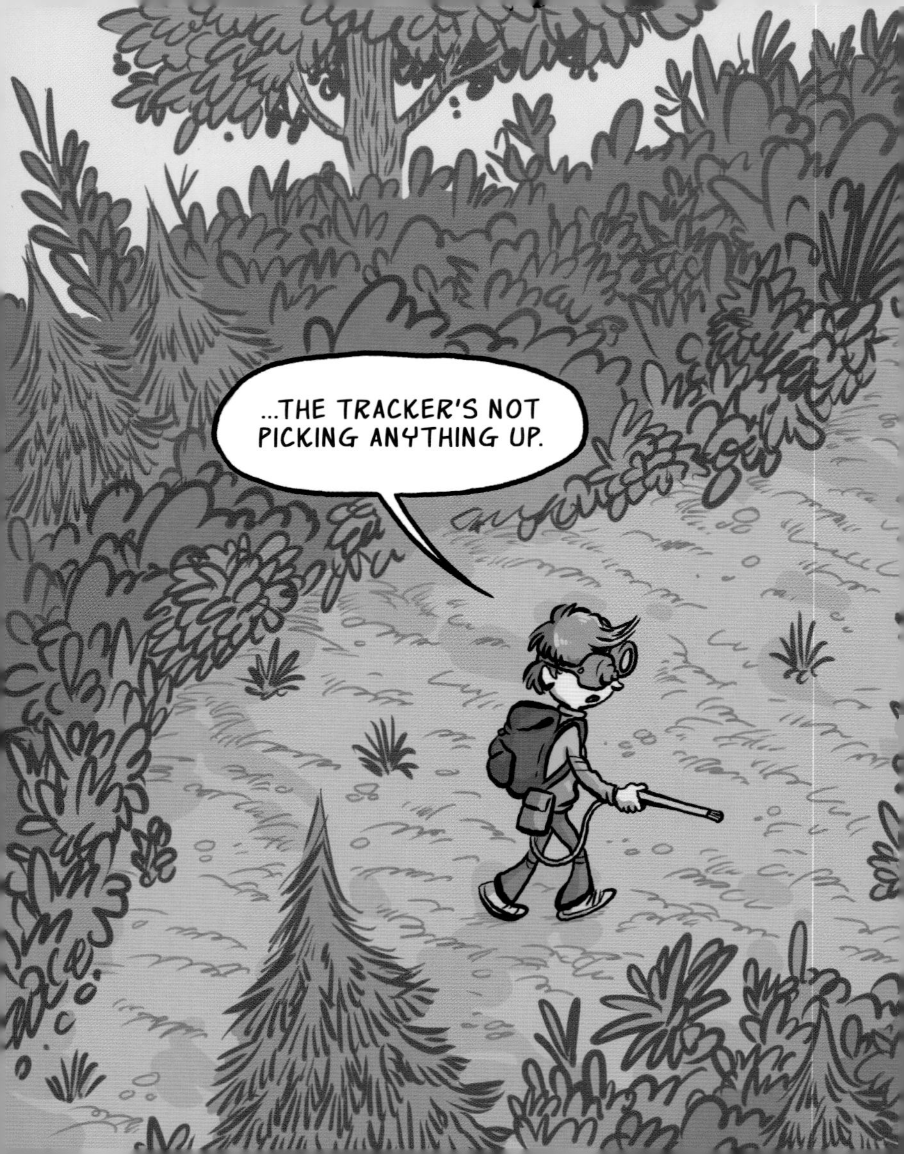
...THE TRACKER'S NOT PICKING ANYTHING UP.

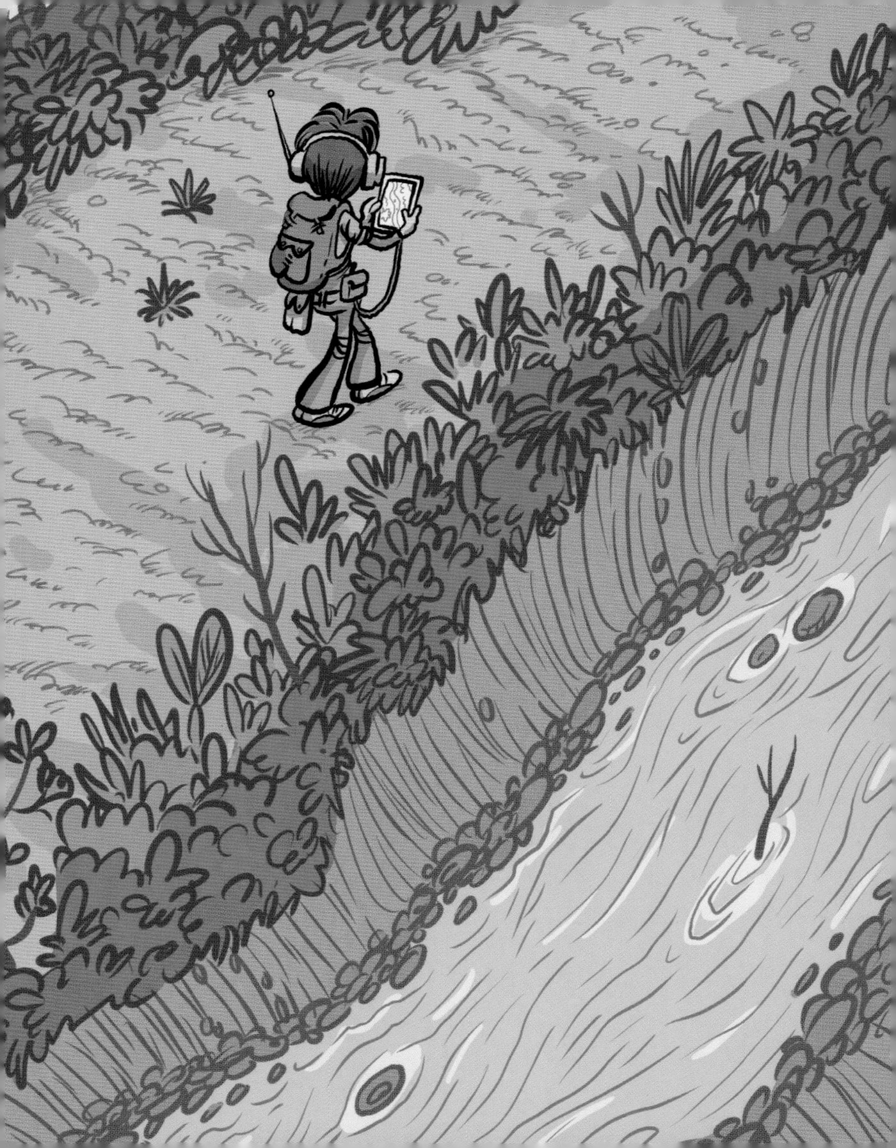

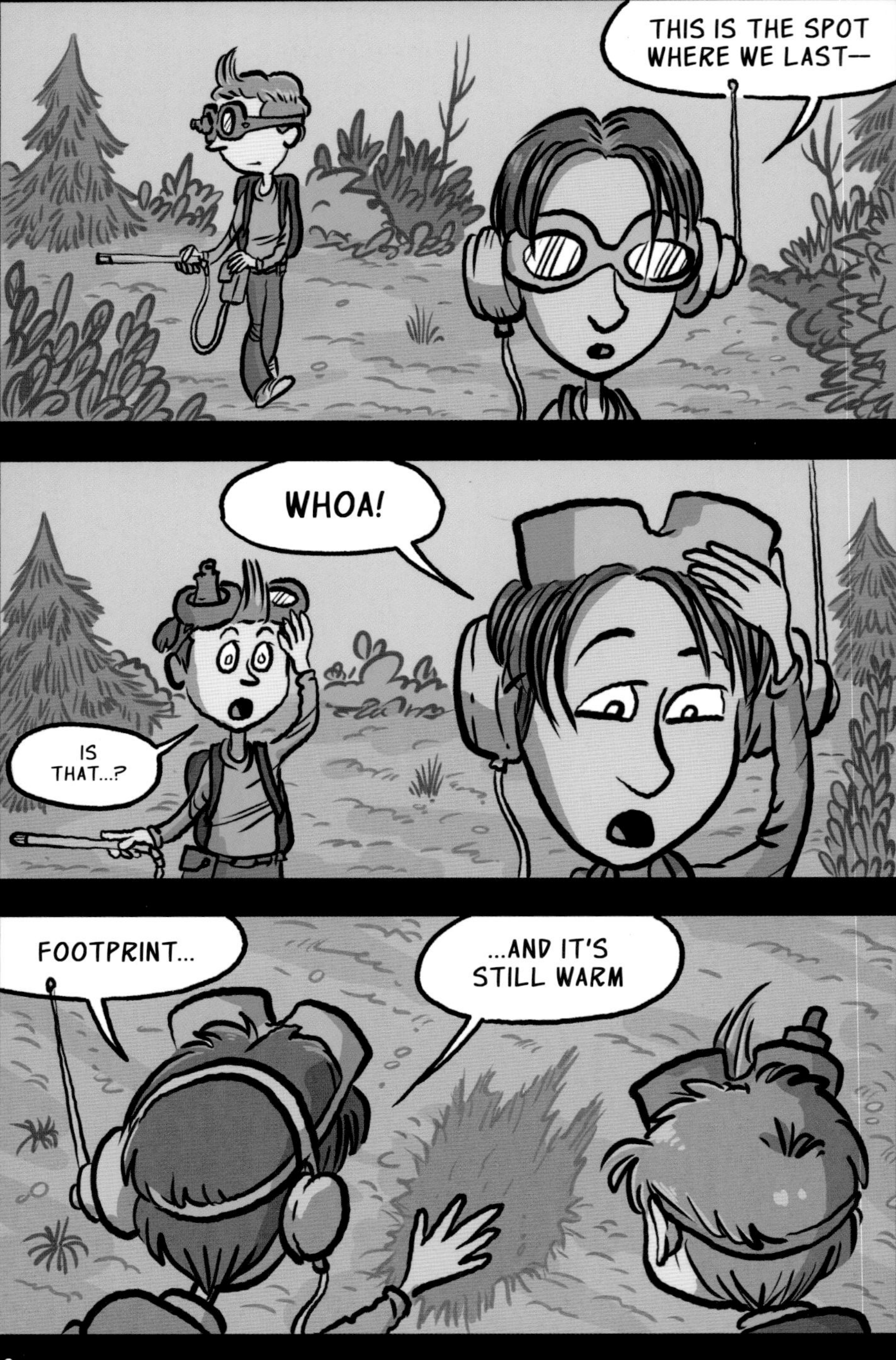
THIS IS THE SPOT WHERE WE LAST—
WHOA!
IS THAT...?
FOOTPRINT...
...AND IT'S STILL WARM

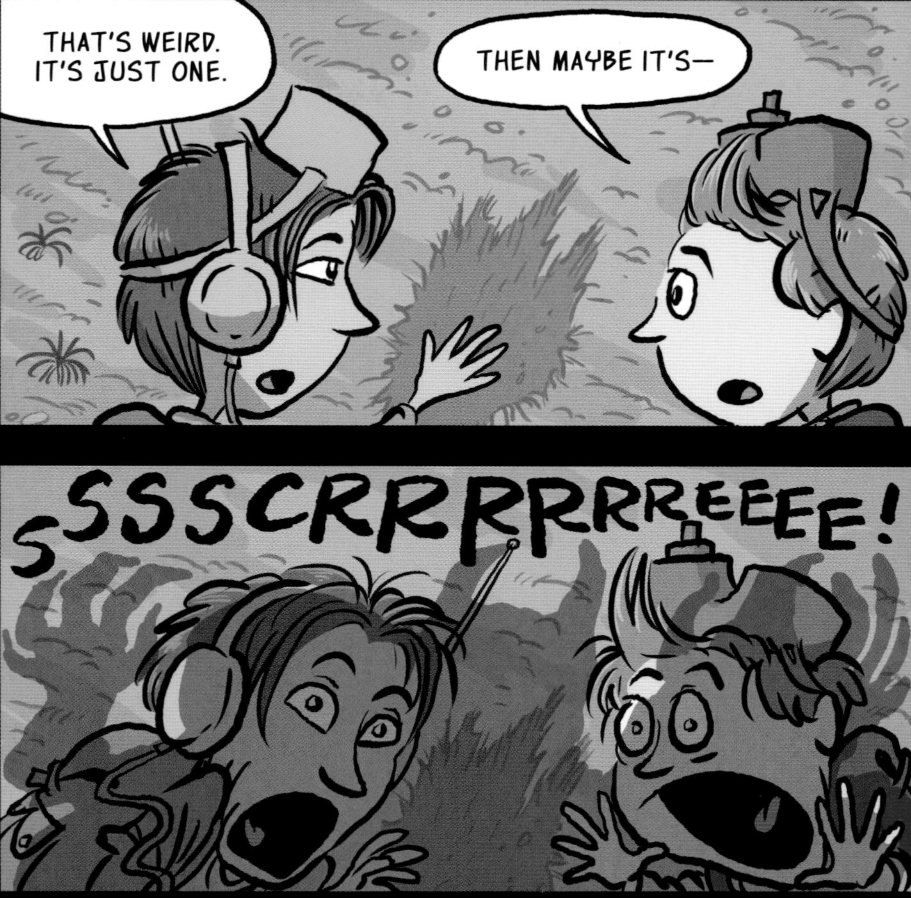
THAT'S WEIRD. IT'S JUST ONE.
THEN MAYBE IT'S—
SSSSCRRRRRREEEEE!

Scene #6 goes here—

Monster attack animation

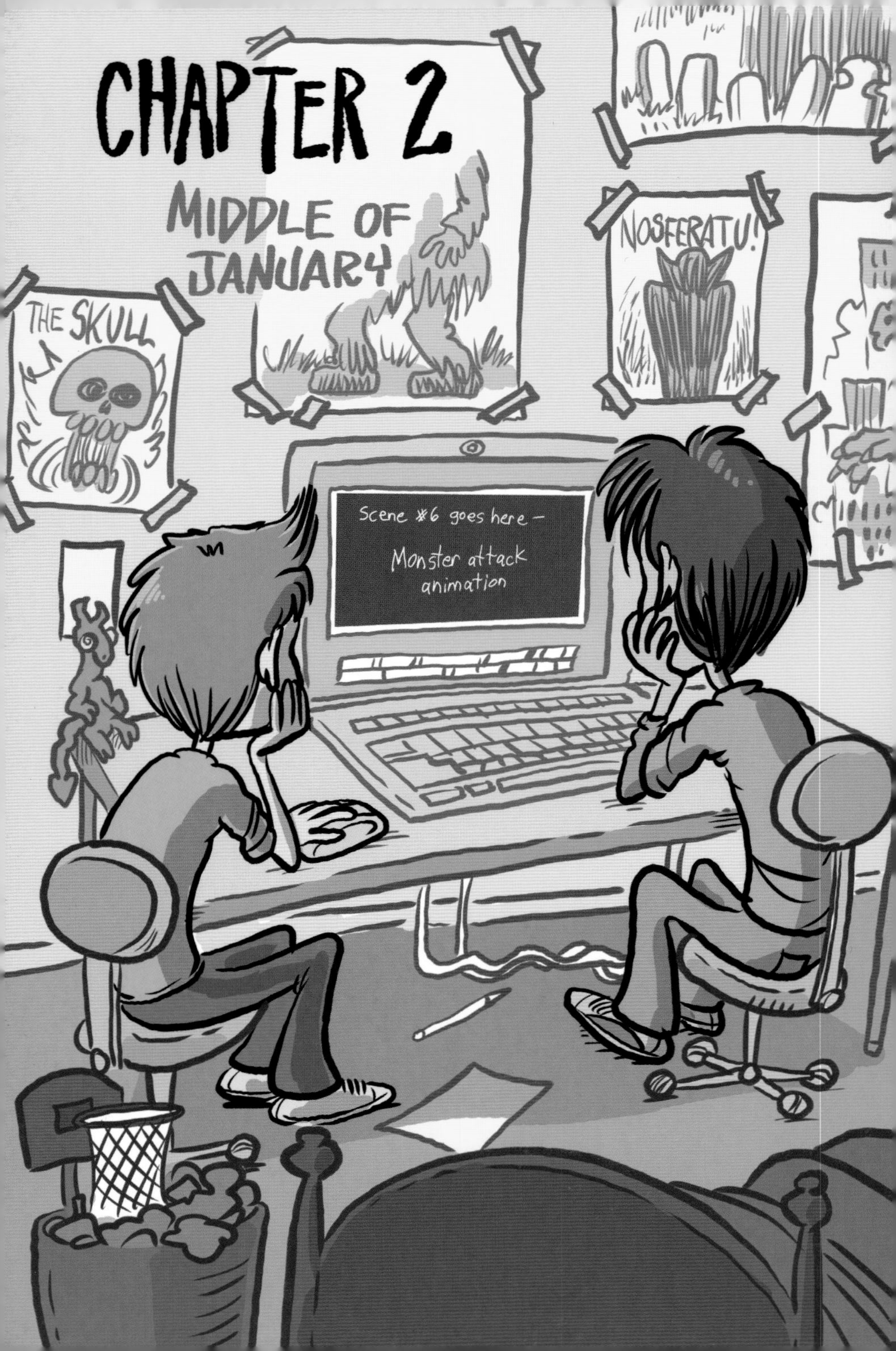
CHAPTER 2
MIDDLE OF JANUARY
THE SKULL
NOSFERATU!
Scene #6 goes here –
Monster attack animation

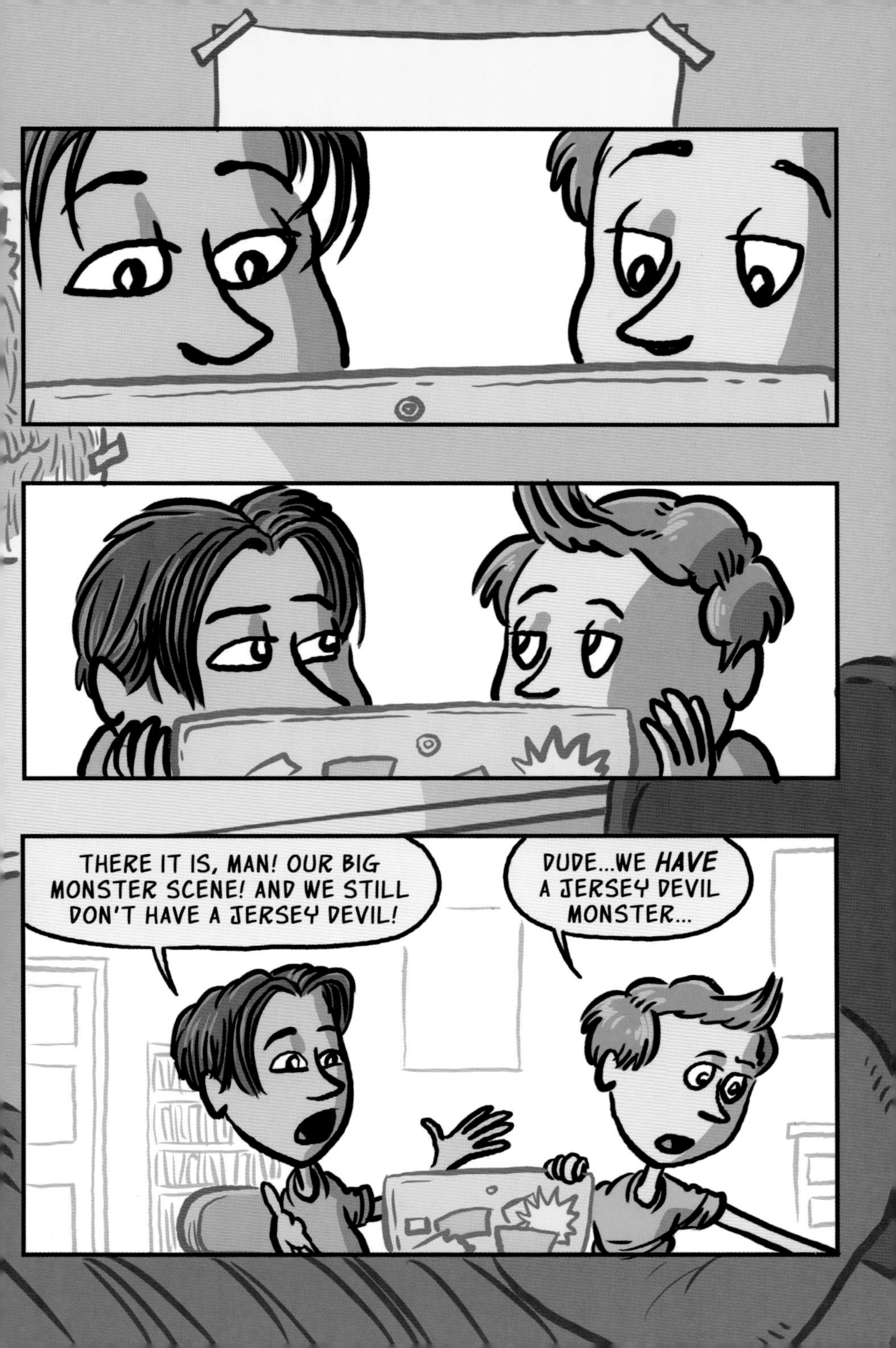
THERE IT IS, MAN! OUR BIG MONSTER SCENE! AND WE STILL DON'T HAVE A JERSEY DEVIL!
DUDE...WE *HAVE* A JERSEY DEVIL MONSTER...

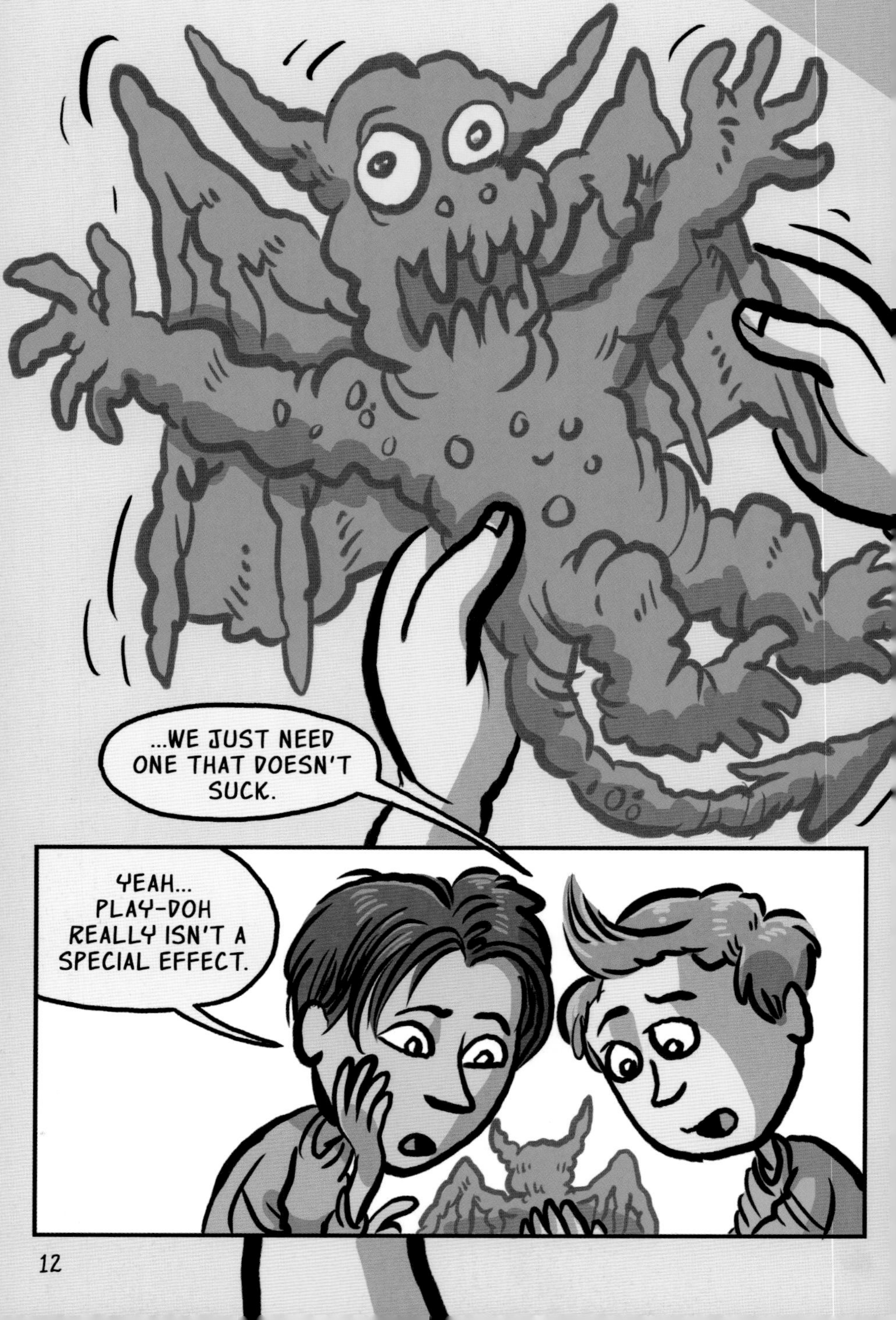
...WE JUST NEED ONE THAT DOESN'T SUCK.
YEAH... PLAY-DOH REALLY ISN'T A SPECIAL EFFECT.

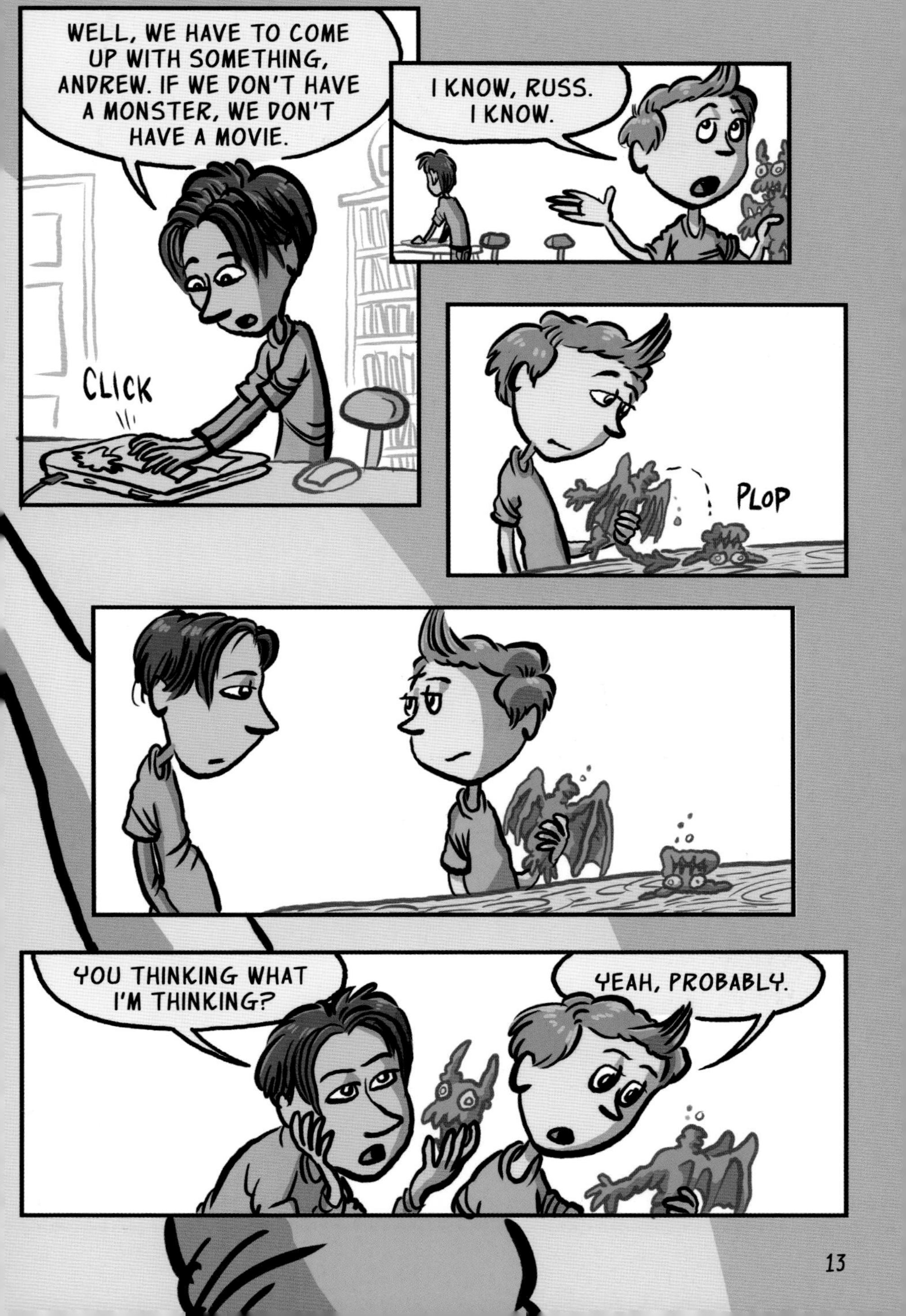
WELL, WE HAVE TO COME UP WITH SOMETHING, ANDREW. IF WE DON'T HAVE A MONSTER, WE DON'T HAVE A MOVIE.
CLICK
I KNOW, RUSS. I KNOW.
PLOP
YOU THINKING WHAT I'M THINKING?
YEAH, PROBABLY.

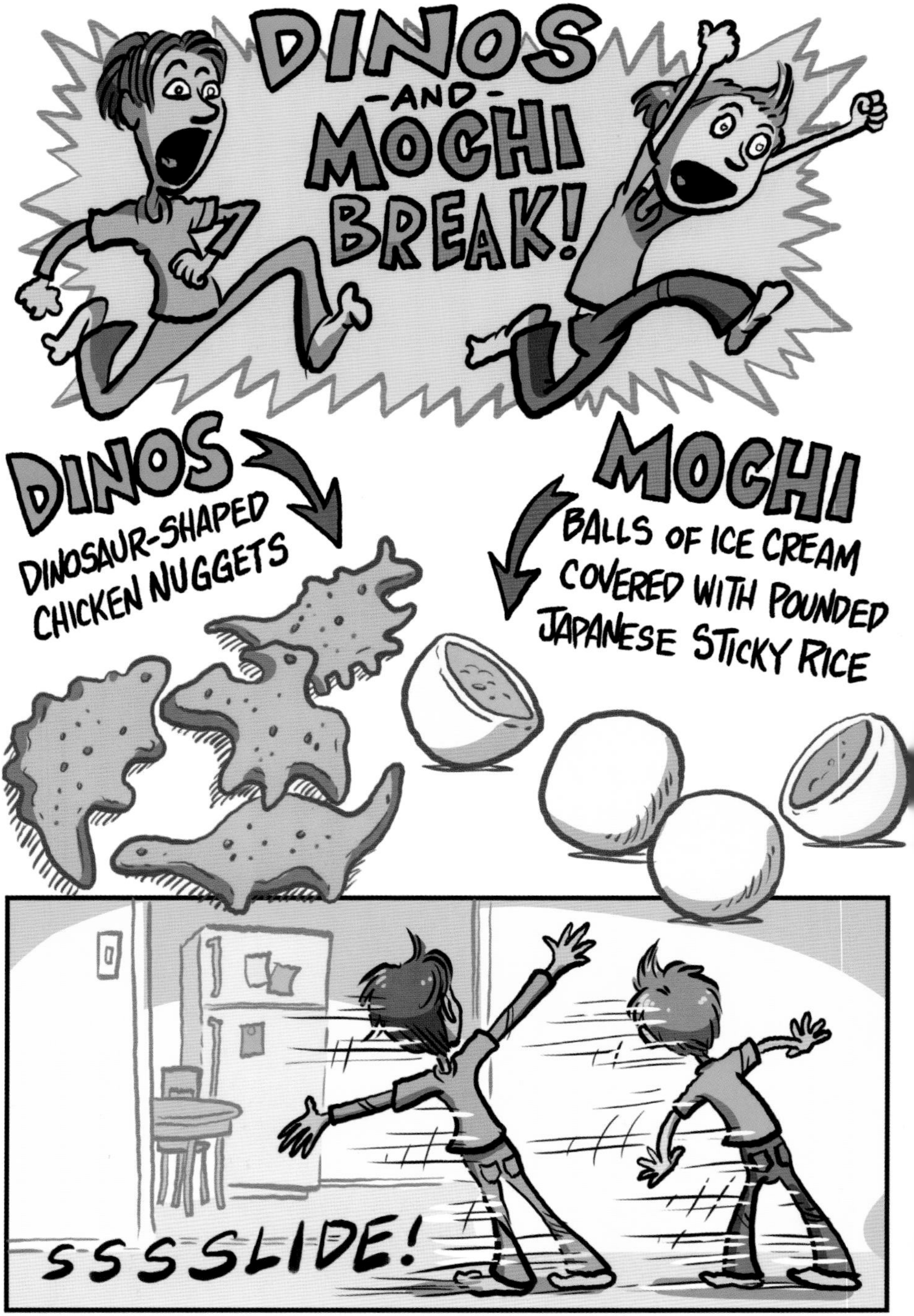
DINOS -AND- MOCHI BREAK!
DINOS
DINOSAUR-SHAPED CHICKEN NUGGETS
MOCHI
BALLS OF ICE CREAM COVERED WITH POUNDED JAPANESE STICKY RICE
SSSSLIDE!

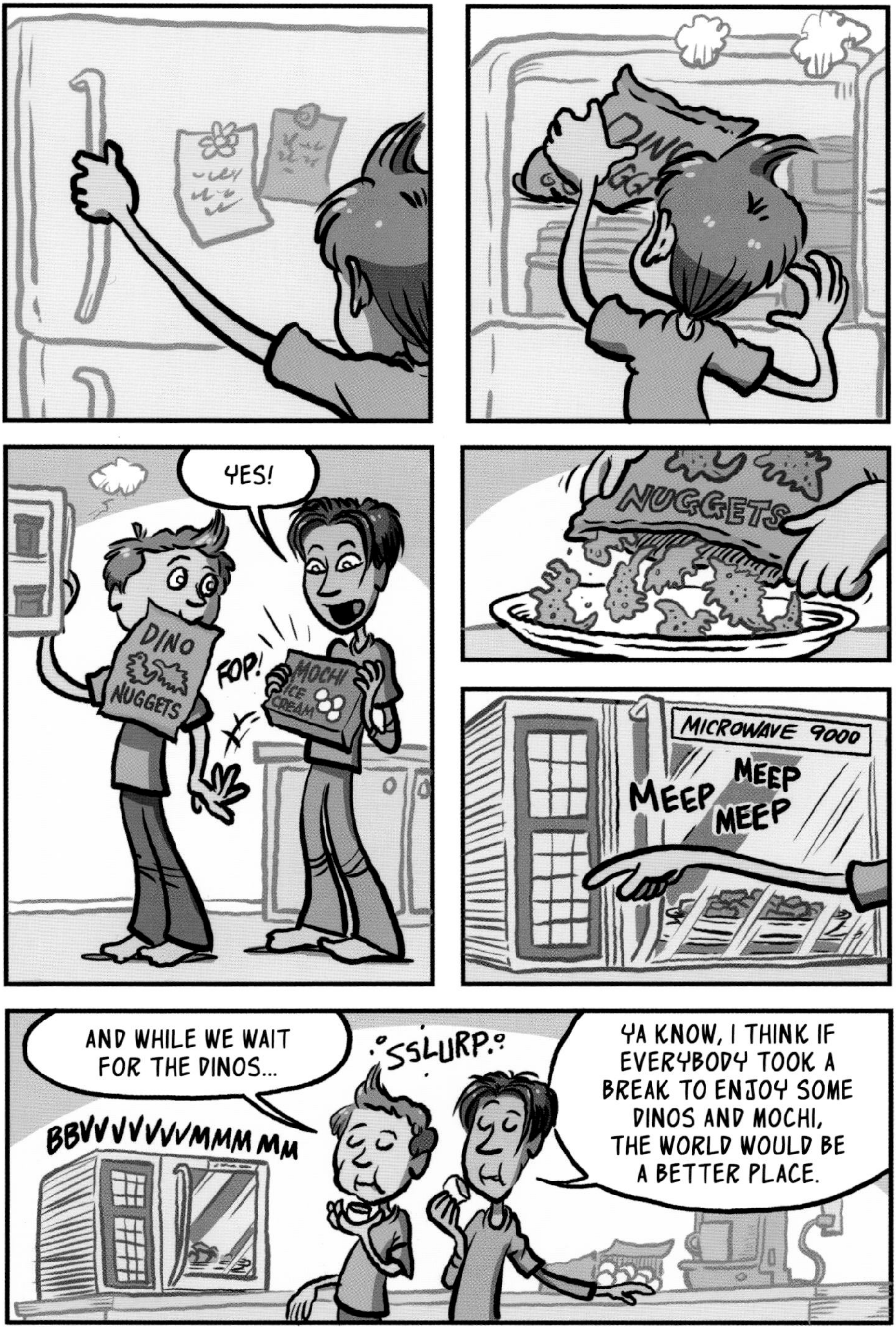
YES!
DINO NUGGETS
FOP!
MOCHI ICE CREAM
NUGGETS
MICROWAVE 9000
MEEP
MEEP
MEEP
AND WHILE WE WAIT FOR THE DINOS...
SSLURP.
BBVVVVVVVMMMMM
YA KNOW, I THINK IF EVERYBODY TOOK A BREAK TO ENJOY SOME DINOS AND MOCHI, THE WORLD WOULD BE A BETTER PLACE.

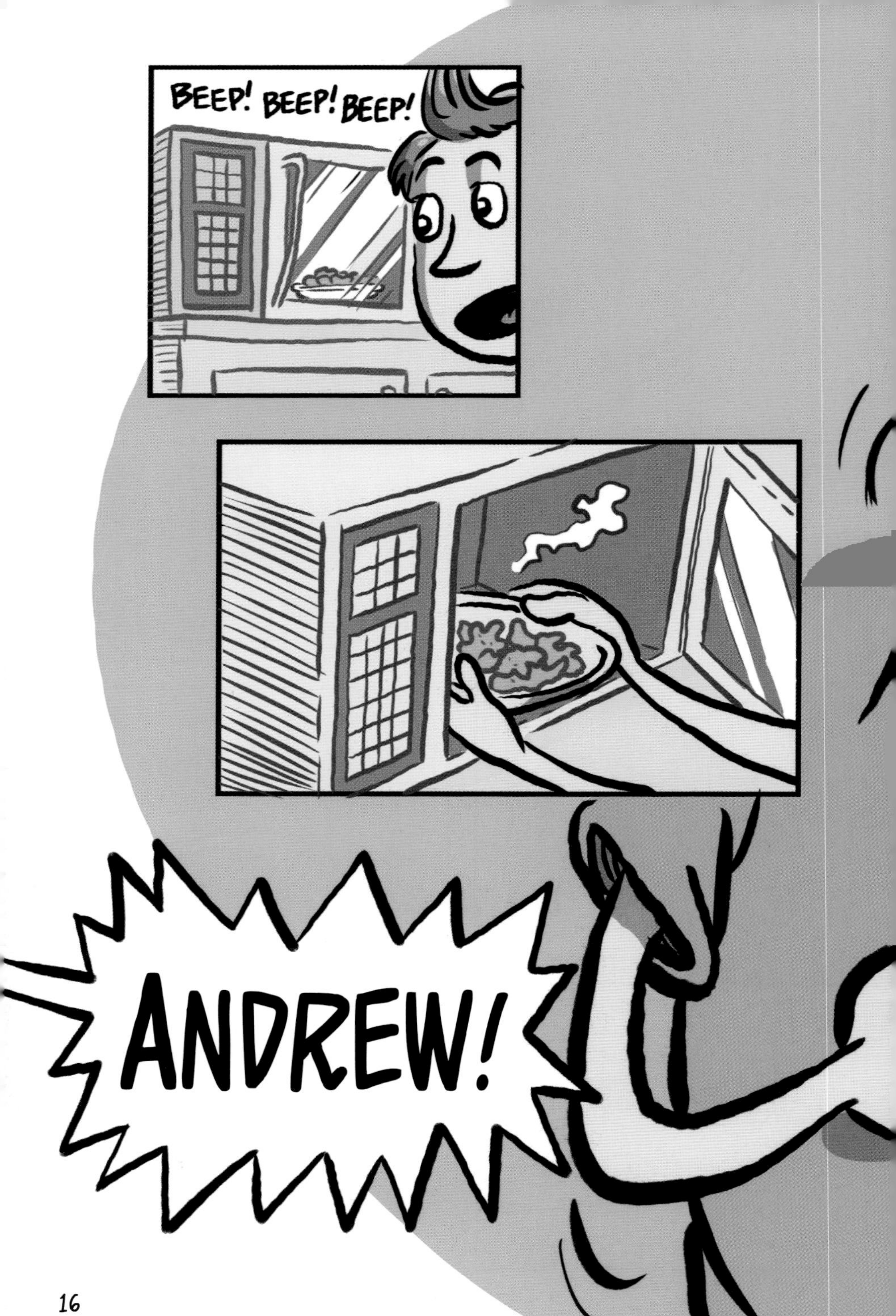
BEEP! BEEP! BEEP!
ANDREW!

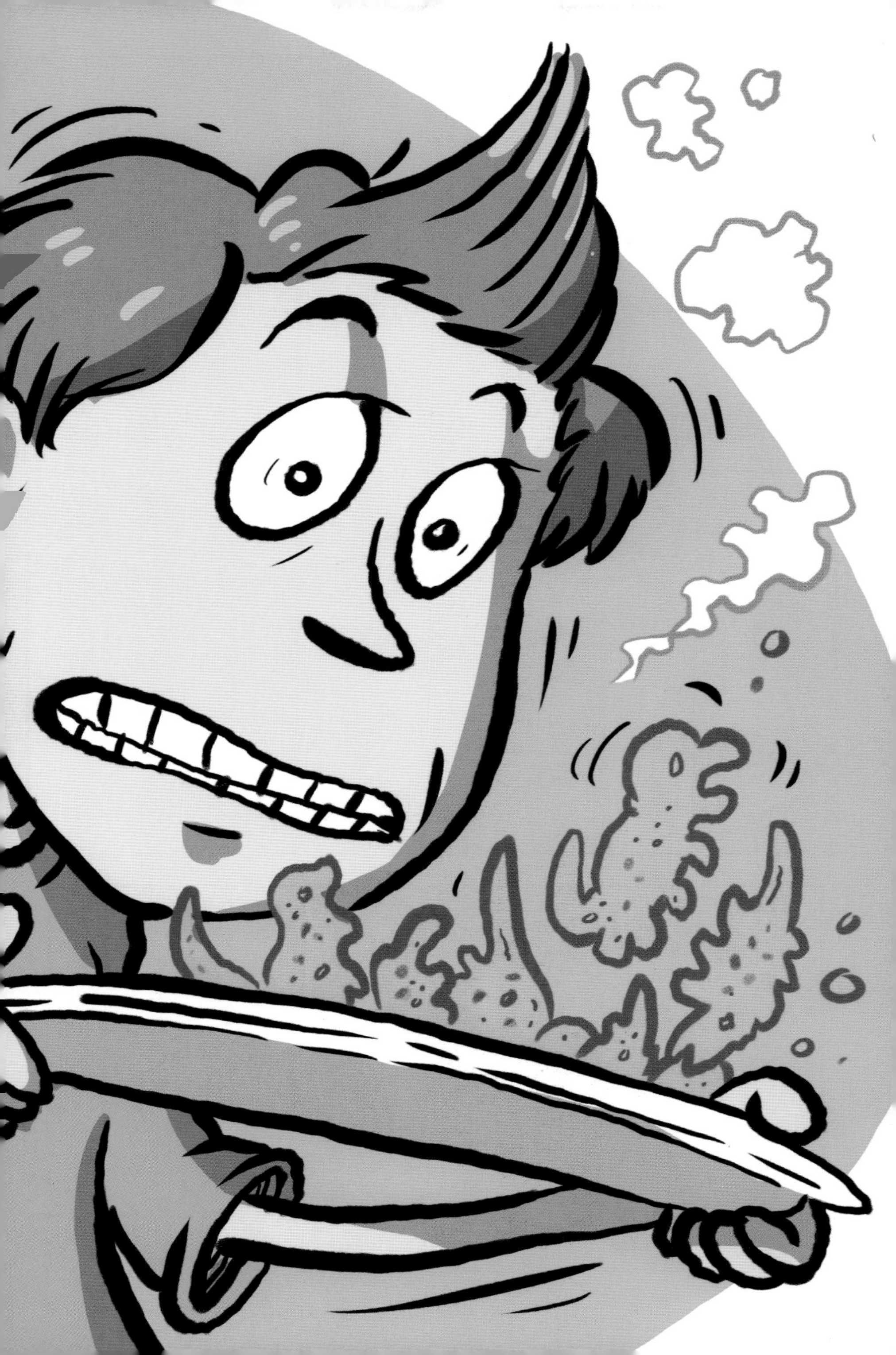

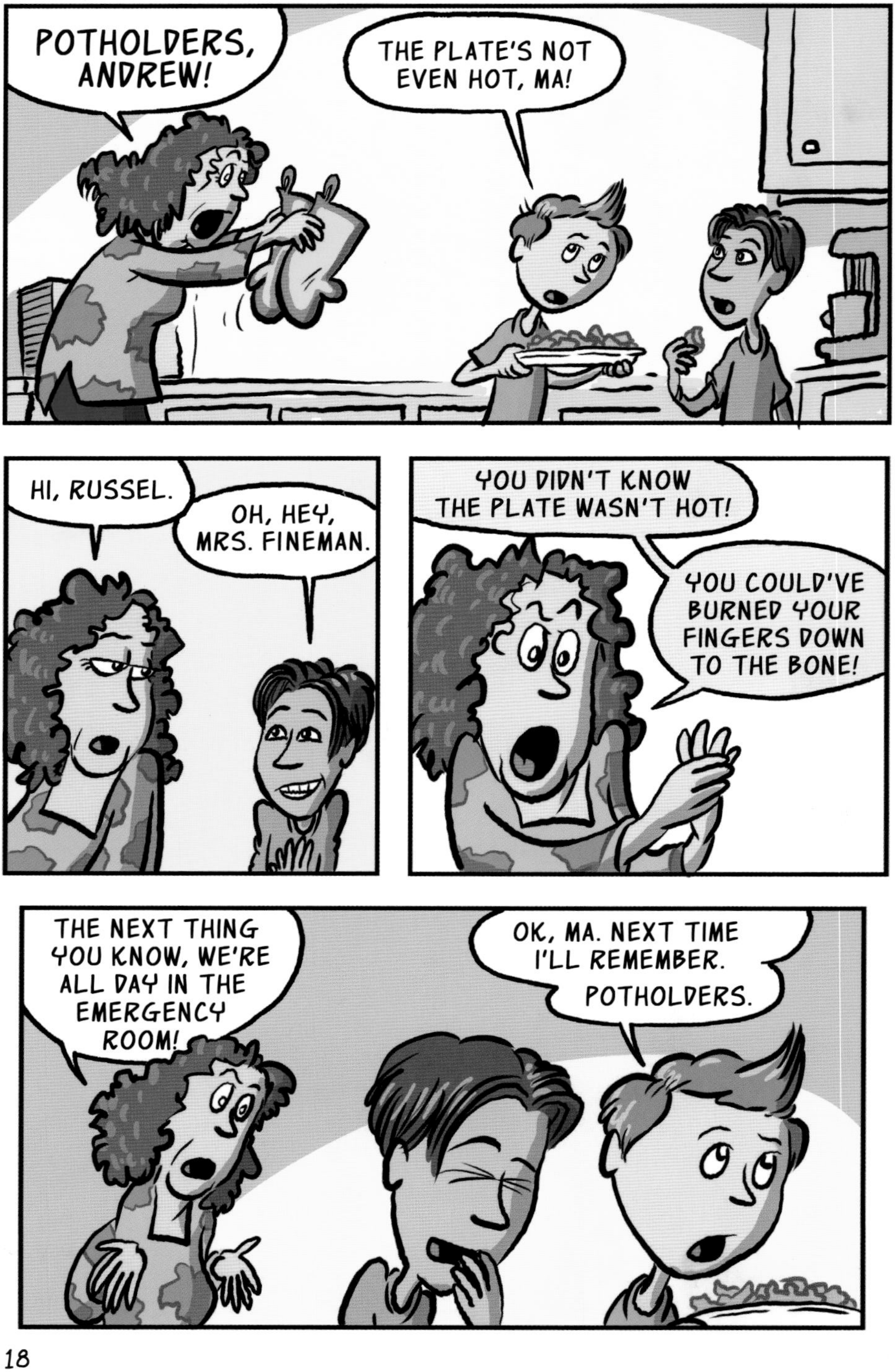
POTHOLDERS, ANDREW!
THE PLATE'S NOT EVEN HOT, MA!
HI, RUSSEL.
OH, HEY, MRS. FINEMAN.
YOU DIDN'T KNOW THE PLATE WASN'T HOT!
YOU COULD'VE BURNED YOUR FINGERS DOWN TO THE BONE!
THE NEXT THING YOU KNOW, WE'RE ALL DAY IN THE EMERGENCY ROOM!
OK, MA. NEXT TIME I'LL REMEMBER.
POTHOLDERS.

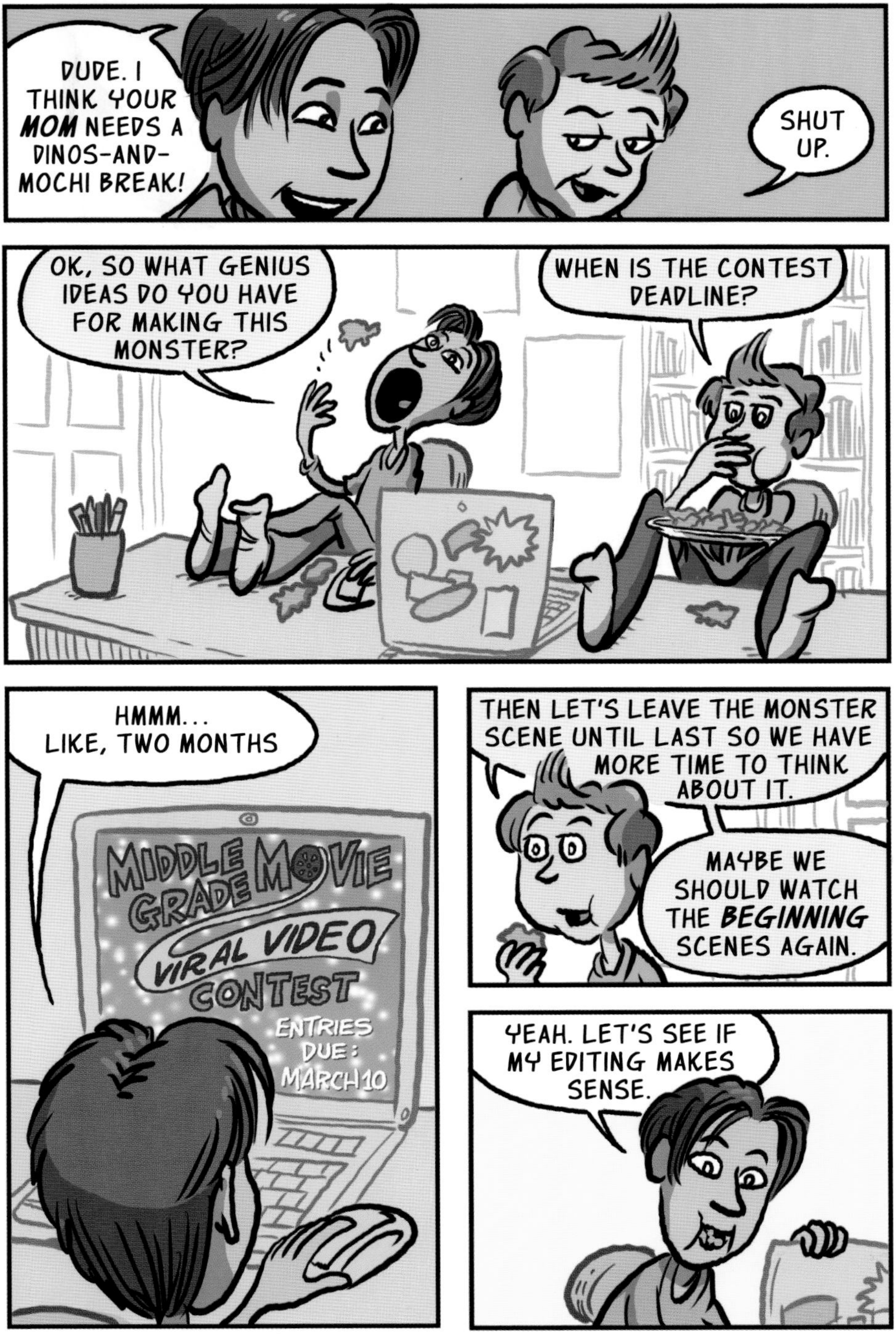
DUDE. I THINK YOUR MOM NEEDS A DINOS-AND-MOCHI BREAK!
SHUT UP.
OK, SO WHAT GENIUS IDEAS DO YOU HAVE FOR MAKING THIS MONSTER?
WHEN IS THE CONTEST DEADLINE?
HMMM... LIKE, TWO MONTHS
MIDDLE GRADE MOVIE
VIRAL VIDEO CONTEST
ENTRIES DUE: MARCH 10
THEN LET'S LEAVE THE MONSTER SCENE UNTIL LAST SO WE HAVE MORE TIME TO THINK ABOUT IT.
MAYBE WE SHOULD WATCH THE BEGINNING SCENES AGAIN.
YEAH. LET'S SEE IF MY EDITING MAKES SENSE.

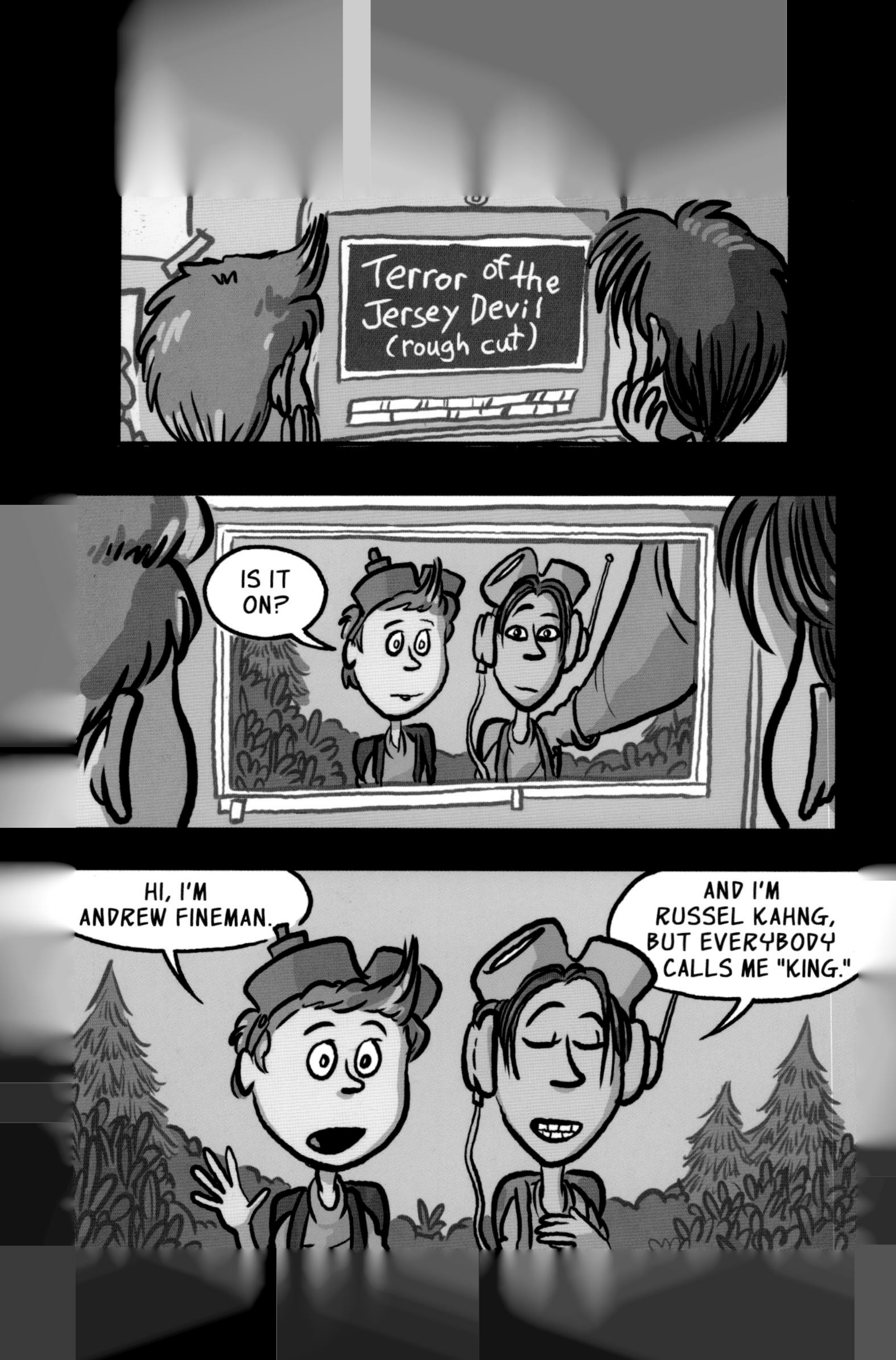
Terror of the Jersey Devil (rough cut)
IS IT ON?
HI, I'M ANDREW FINEMAN.
AND I'M RUSSEL KAHNG, BUT EVERYBODY CALLS ME "KING."

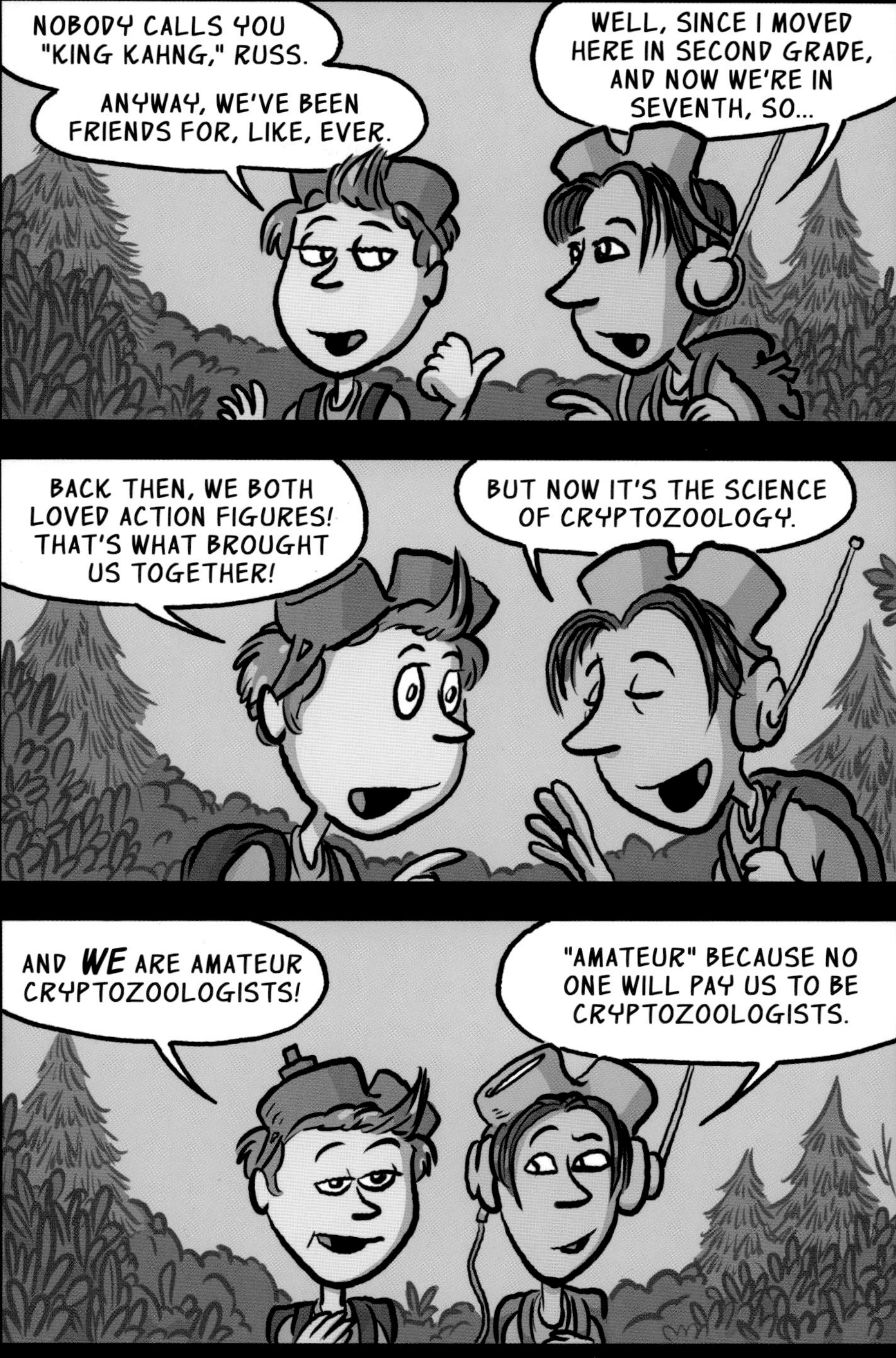
NOBODY CALLS YOU "KING KAHNG," RUSS.
ANYWAY, WE'VE BEEN FRIENDS FOR, LIKE, EVER.
WELL, SINCE I MOVED HERE IN SECOND GRADE, AND NOW WE'RE IN SEVENTH, SO...
BACK THEN, WE BOTH LOVED ACTION FIGURES! THAT'S WHAT BROUGHT US TOGETHER!
BUT NOW IT'S THE SCIENCE OF CRYPTOZOOLOGY.
AND **WE** ARE AMATEUR CRYPTOZOOLOGISTS!
"AMATEUR" BECAUSE NO ONE WILL PAY US TO BE CRYPTOZOOLOGISTS.

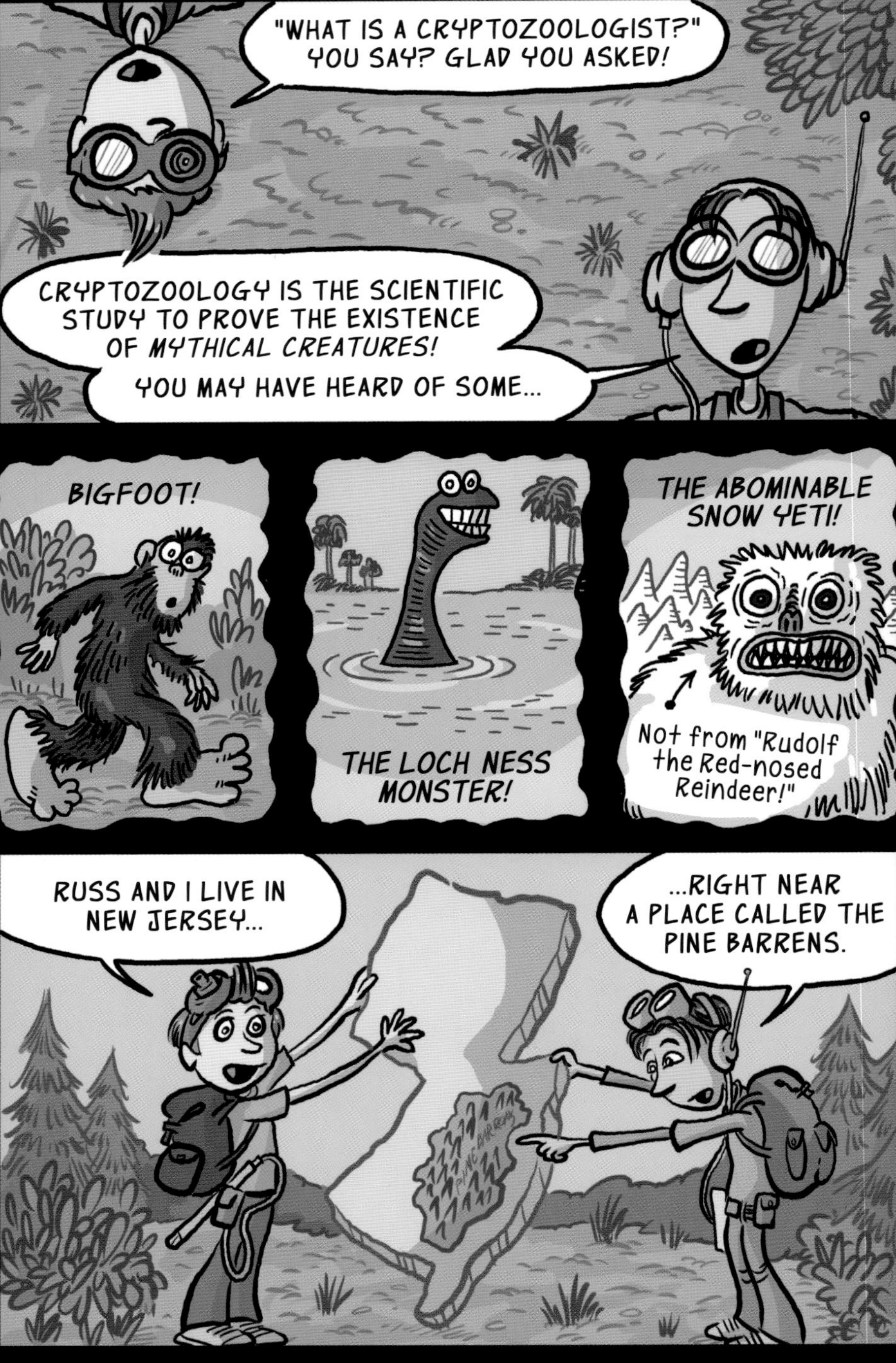
"WHAT IS A CRYPTOZOOLOGIST?" YOU SAY? GLAD YOU ASKED!
CRYPTOZOOLOGY IS THE SCIENTIFIC STUDY TO PROVE THE EXISTENCE OF *MYTHICAL CREATURES!*
YOU MAY HAVE HEARD OF SOME...
BIGFOOT!
THE LOCH NESS MONSTER!
THE ABOMINABLE SNOW YETI!
Not from "Rudolf the Red-nosed Reindeer!"
RUSS AND I LIVE IN NEW JERSEY...
...RIGHT NEAR A PLACE CALLED THE PINE BARRENS.

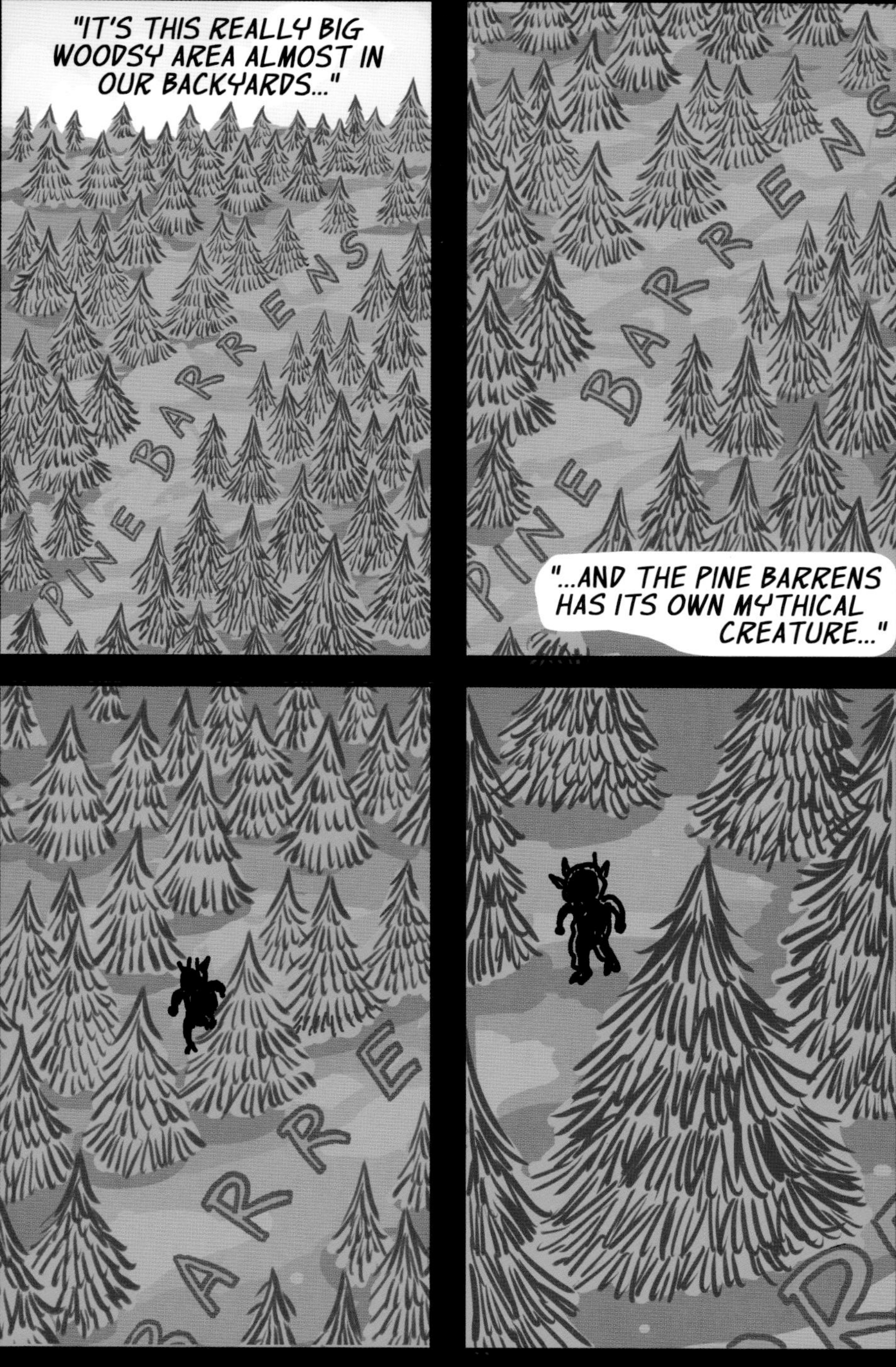

"IT'S THIS REALLY BIG WOODSY AREA ALMOST IN OUR BACKYARDS..."
PINE BARRENS
PINE BARRENS
"...AND THE PINE BARRENS HAS ITS OWN MYTHICAL CREATURE..."

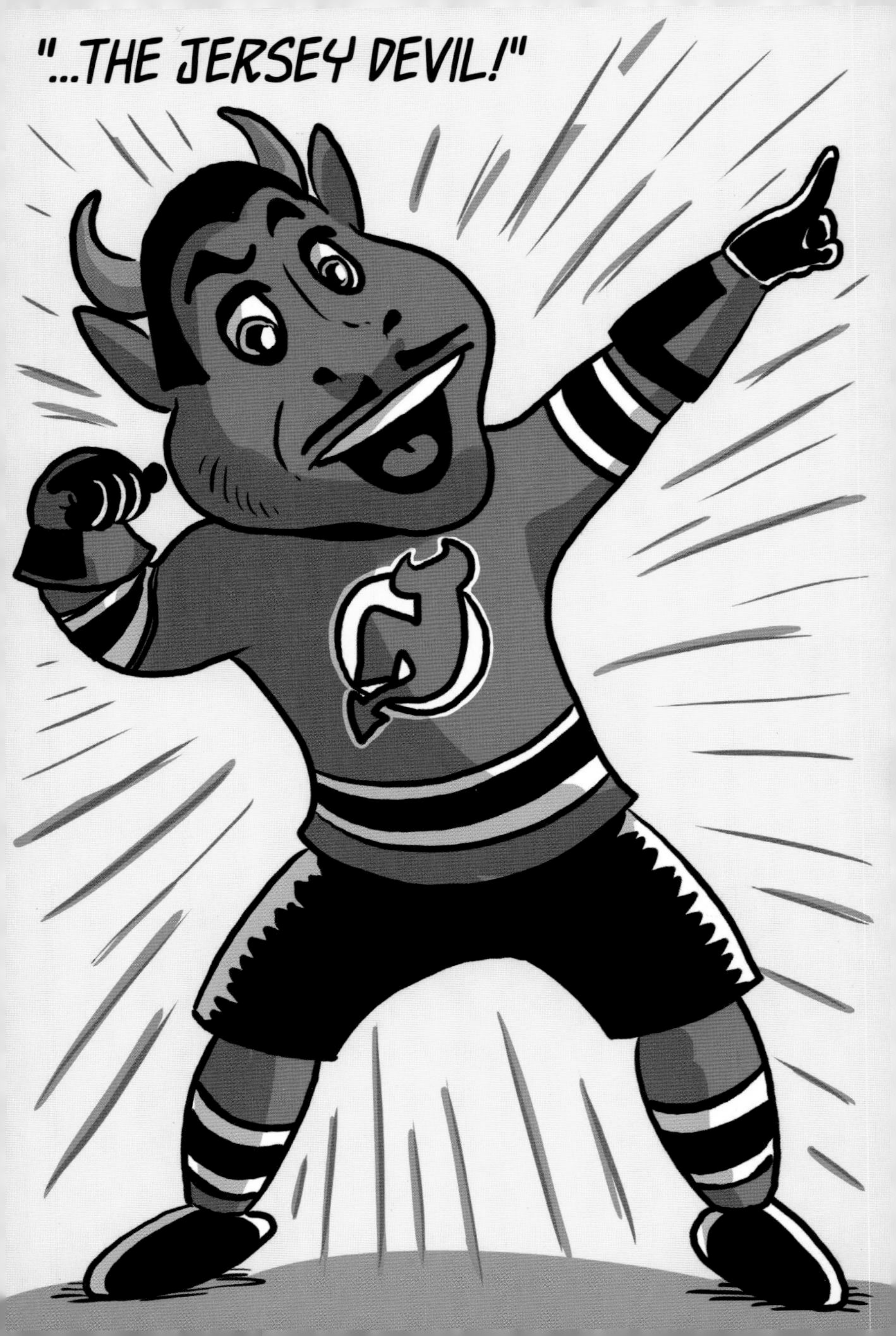
"...THE JERSEY DEVIL!"

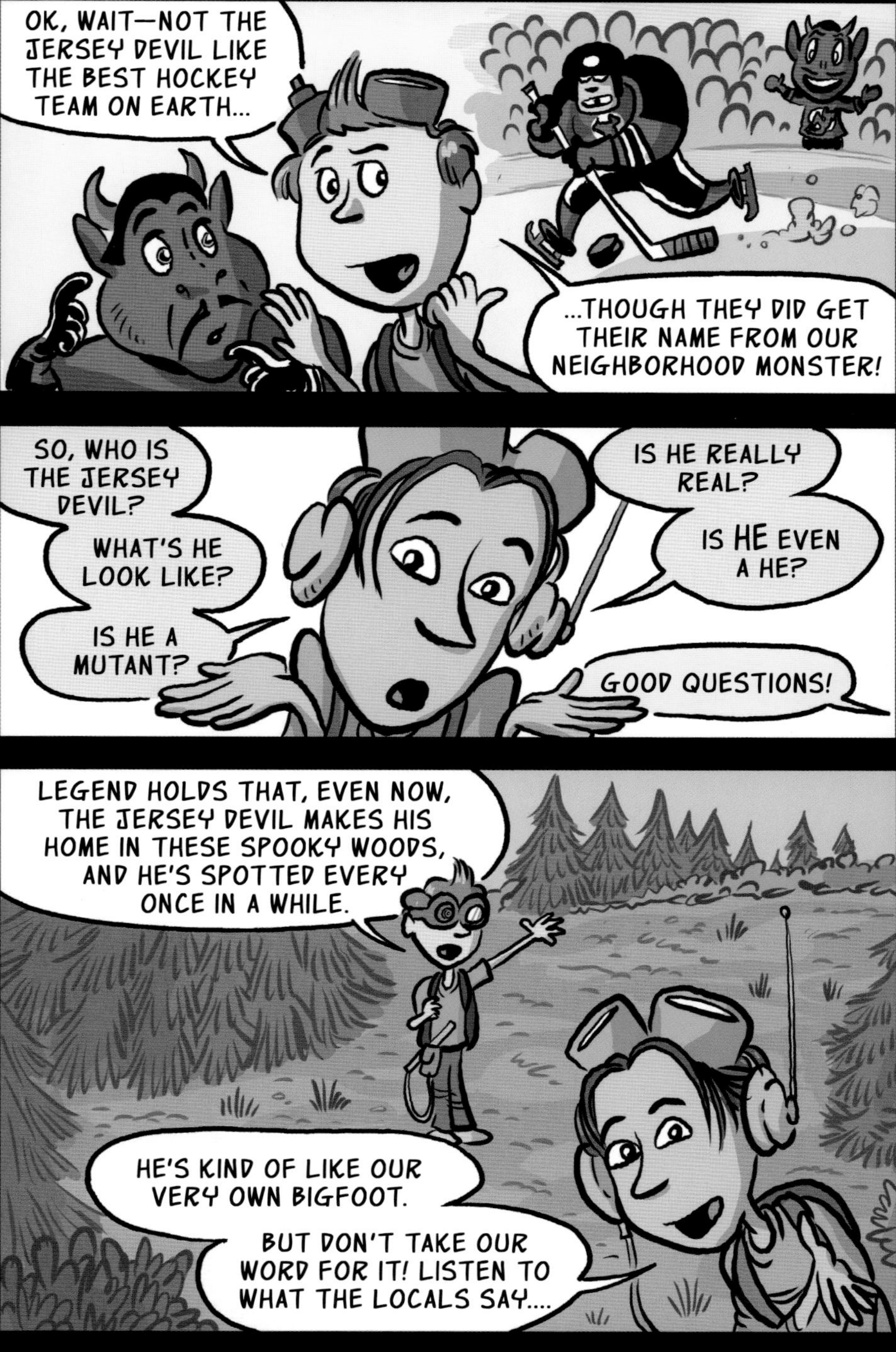
OK, WAIT—NOT THE JERSEY DEVIL LIKE THE BEST HOCKEY TEAM ON EARTH...
...THOUGH THEY DID GET THEIR NAME FROM OUR NEIGHBORHOOD MONSTER!
SO, WHO IS THE JERSEY DEVIL?
WHAT'S HE LOOK LIKE?
IS HE A MUTANT?
IS HE REALLY REAL?
IS HE EVEN A HE?
GOOD QUESTIONS!
LEGEND HOLDS THAT, EVEN NOW, THE JERSEY DEVIL MAKES HIS HOME IN THESE SPOOKY WOODS, AND HE'S SPOTTED EVERY ONCE IN A WHILE.
HE'S KIND OF LIKE OUR VERY OWN BIGFOOT.
BUT DON'T TAKE OUR WORD FOR IT! LISTEN TO WHAT THE LOCALS SAY....

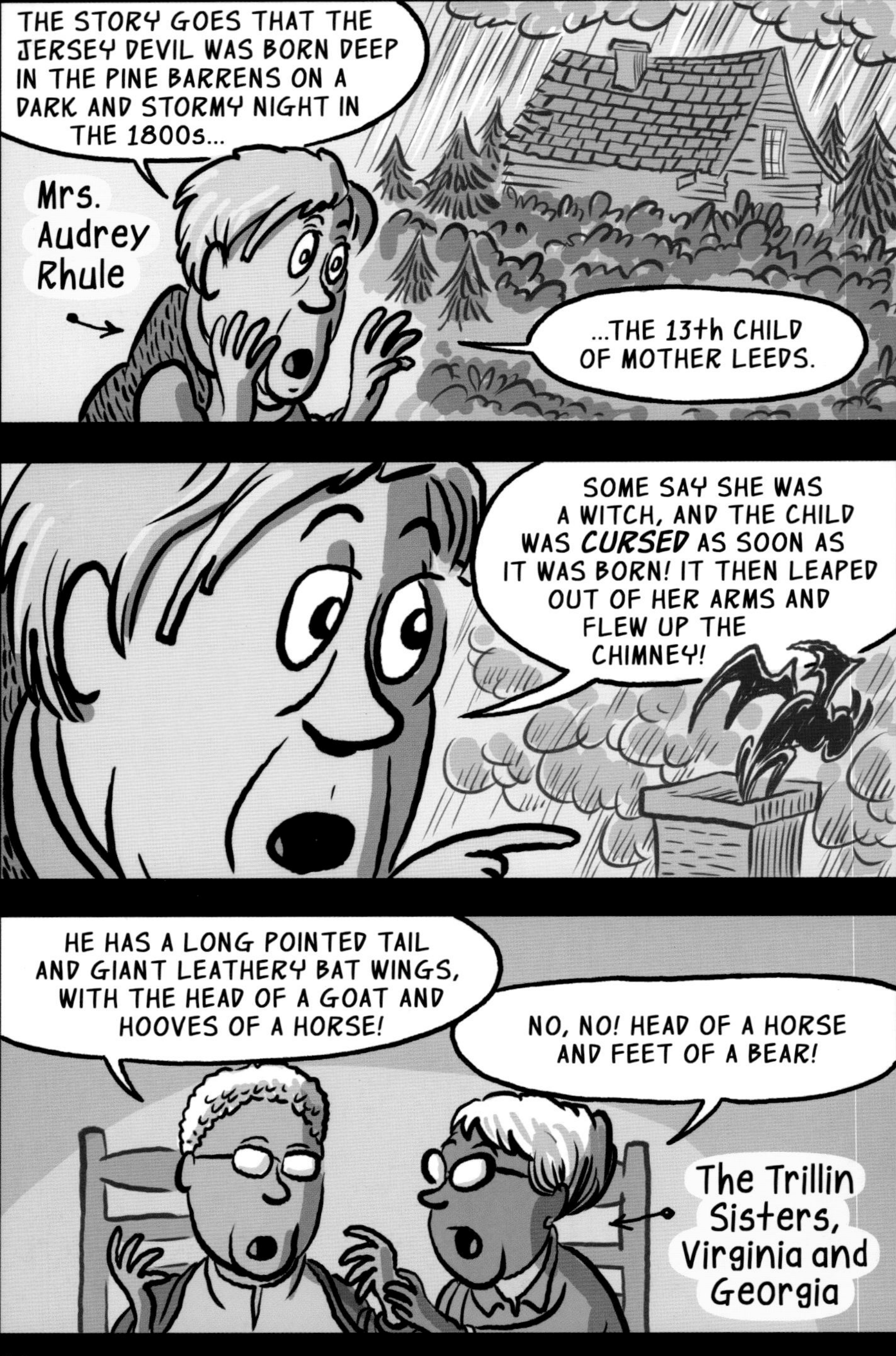
THE STORY GOES THAT THE JERSEY DEVIL WAS BORN DEEP IN THE PINE BARRENS ON A DARK AND STORMY NIGHT IN THE 1800s...
Mrs. Audrey Rhule
...THE 13th CHILD OF MOTHER LEEDS.
SOME SAY SHE WAS A WITCH, AND THE CHILD WAS *CURSED* AS SOON AS IT WAS BORN! IT THEN LEAPED OUT OF HER ARMS AND FLEW UP THE CHIMNEY!
HE HAS A LONG POINTED TAIL AND GIANT LEATHERY BAT WINGS, WITH THE HEAD OF A GOAT AND HOOVES OF A HORSE!
NO, NO! HEAD OF A HORSE AND FEET OF A BEAR!
The Trillin Sisters, Virginia and Georgia

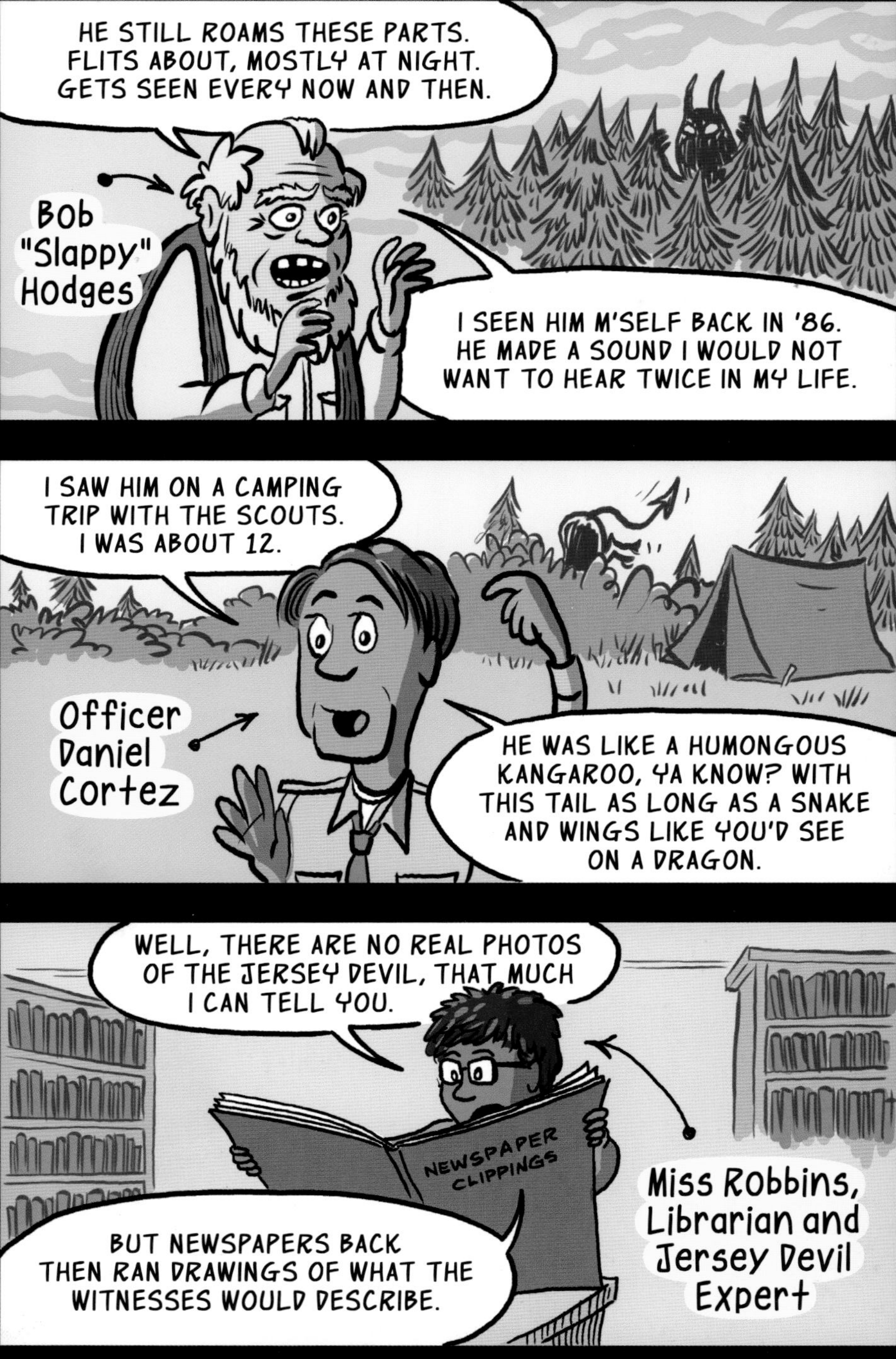
HE STILL ROAMS THESE PARTS. FLITS ABOUT, MOSTLY AT NIGHT. GETS SEEN EVERY NOW AND THEN.
Bob "Slappy" Hodges
I SEEN HIM M'SELF BACK IN '86. HE MADE A SOUND I WOULD NOT WANT TO HEAR TWICE IN MY LIFE.
I SAW HIM ON A CAMPING TRIP WITH THE SCOUTS. I WAS ABOUT 12.
Officer Daniel Cortez
HE WAS LIKE A HUMONGOUS KANGAROO, YA KNOW? WITH THIS TAIL AS LONG AS A SNAKE AND WINGS LIKE YOU'D SEE ON A DRAGON.
WELL, THERE ARE NO REAL PHOTOS OF THE JERSEY DEVIL, THAT MUCH I CAN TELL YOU.
NEWSPAPER CLIPPINGS
Miss Robbins, Librarian and Jersey Devil Expert
BUT NEWSPAPERS BACK THEN RAN DRAWINGS OF WHAT THE WITNESSES WOULD DESCRIBE.

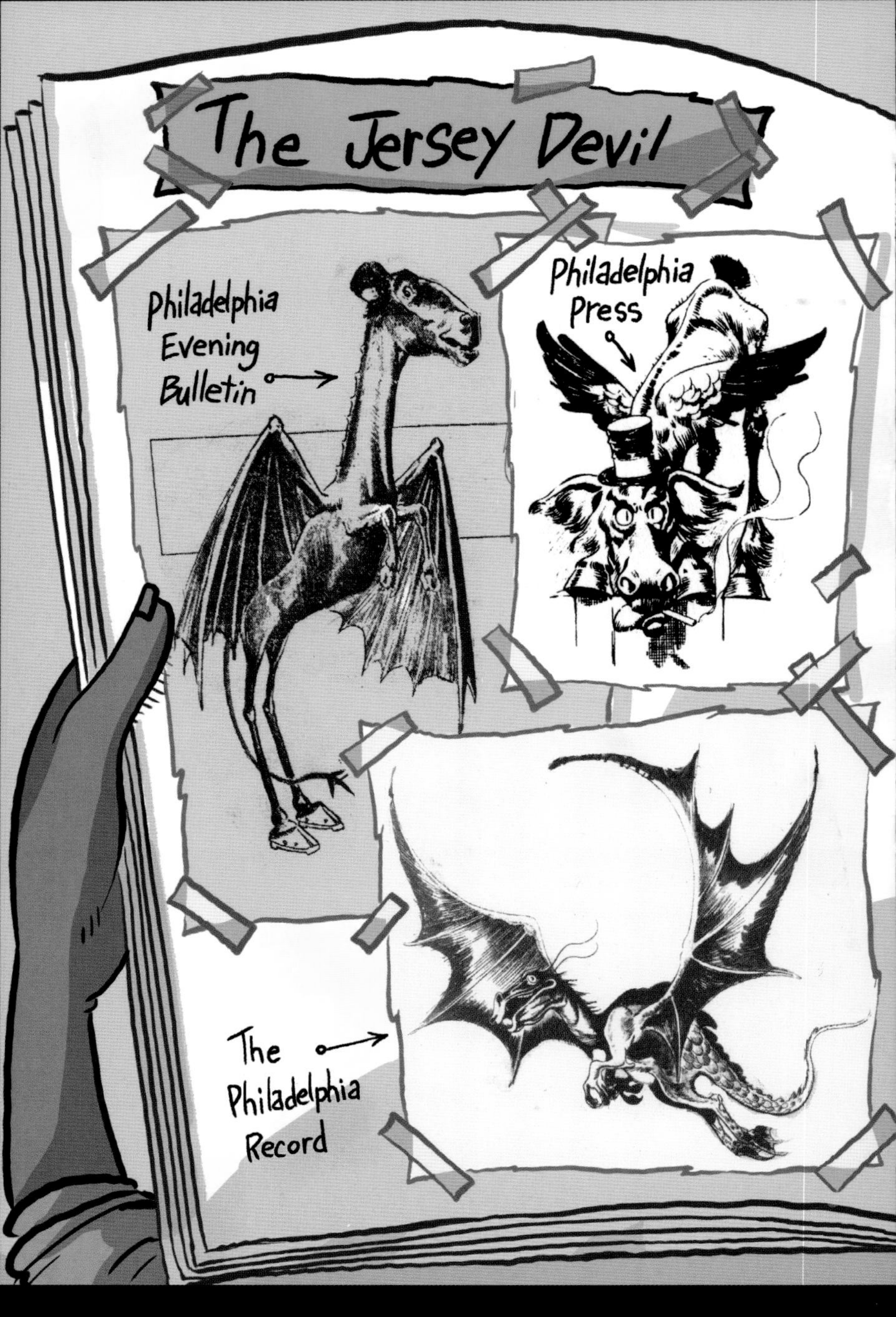
The Jersey Devil
Philadelphia Evening Bulletin
Philadelphia Press
The Philadelphia Record

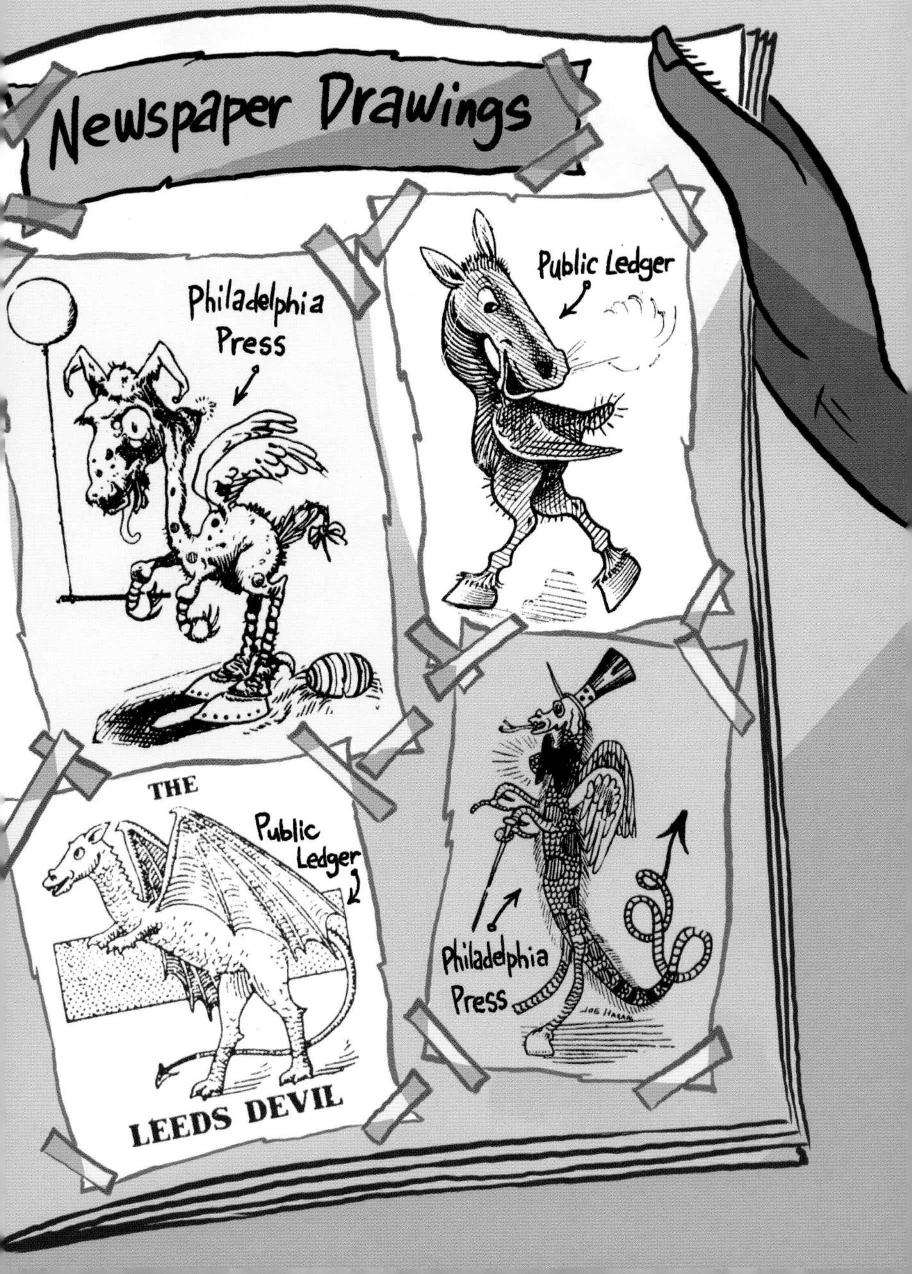

Newspaper Drawings
Philadelphia Press
Public Ledger
THE
Public Ledger
LEEDS DEVIL
Philadelphia Press

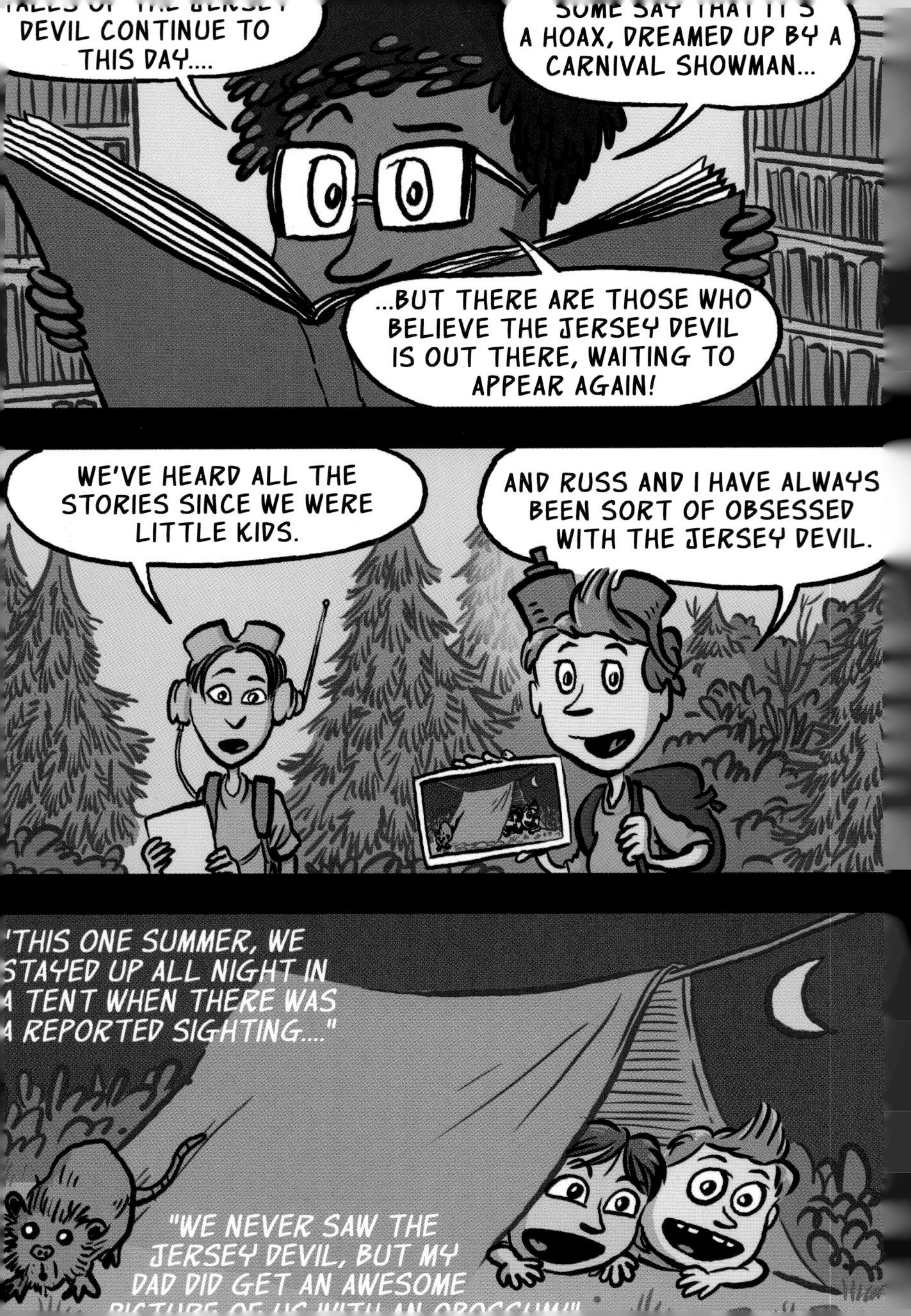
DEVIL CONTINUE TO THIS DAY....
SOME SAY THAT IT'S A HOAX, DREAMED UP BY A CARNIVAL SHOWMAN...
...BUT THERE ARE THOSE WHO BELIEVE THE JERSEY DEVIL IS OUT THERE, WAITING TO APPEAR AGAIN!
WE'VE HEARD ALL THE STORIES SINCE WE WERE LITTLE KIDS.
AND RUSS AND I HAVE ALWAYS BEEN SORT OF OBSESSED WITH THE JERSEY DEVIL.
"THIS ONE SUMMER, WE STAYED UP ALL NIGHT IN A TENT WHEN THERE WAS A REPORTED SIGHTING...."
"WE NEVER SAW THE JERSEY DEVIL, BUT MY DAD DID GET AN AWESOME

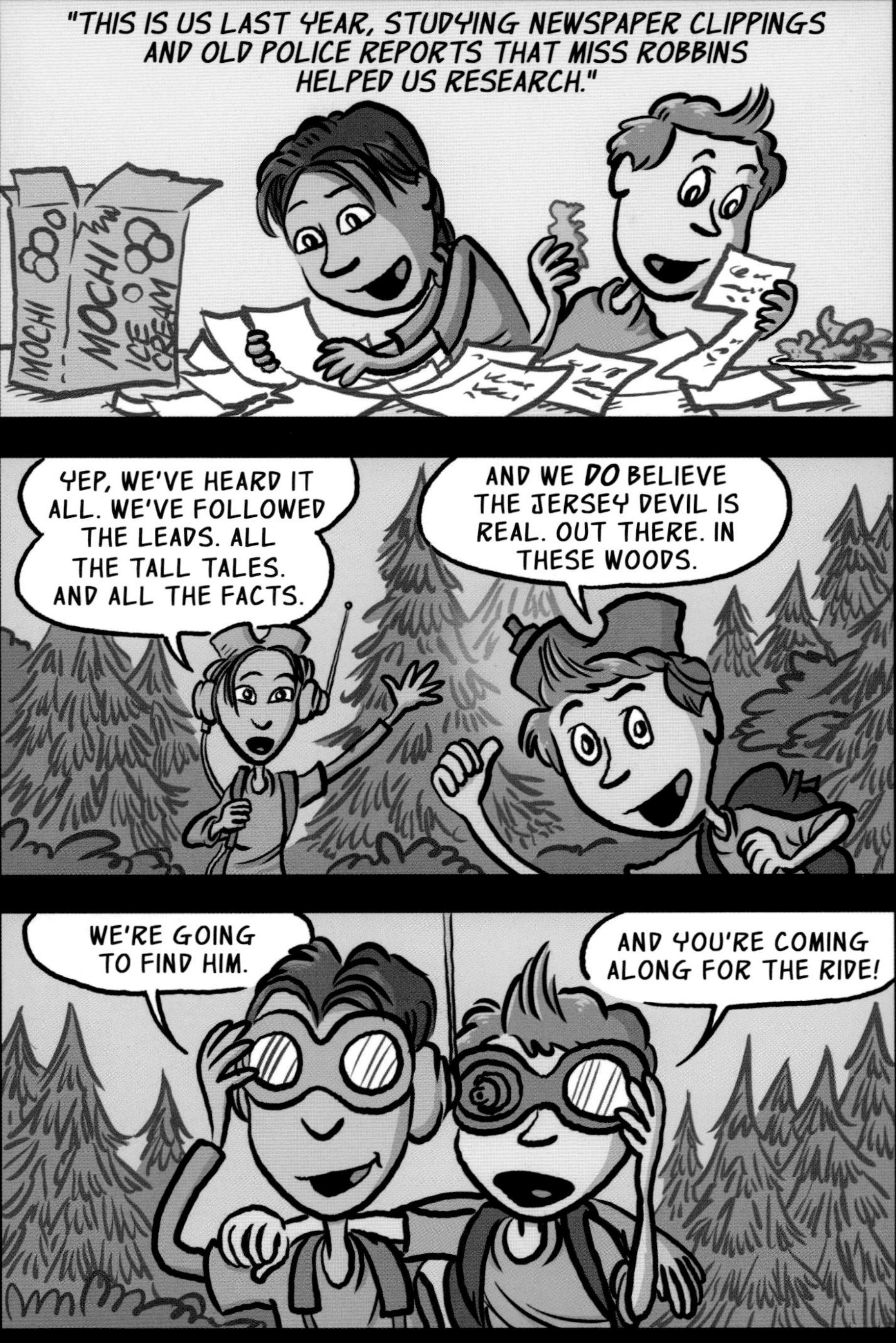
"THIS IS US LAST YEAR, STUDYING NEWSPAPER CLIPPINGS AND OLD POLICE REPORTS THAT MISS ROBBINS HELPED US RESEARCH."
MOCHI
MOCHI
ICE CREAM
YEP, WE'VE HEARD IT ALL. WE'VE FOLLOWED THE LEADS. ALL THE TALL TALES. AND ALL THE FACTS.
AND WE DO BELIEVE THE JERSEY DEVIL IS REAL. OUT THERE. IN THESE WOODS.
WE'RE GOING TO FIND HIM.
AND YOU'RE COMING ALONG FOR THE RIDE!

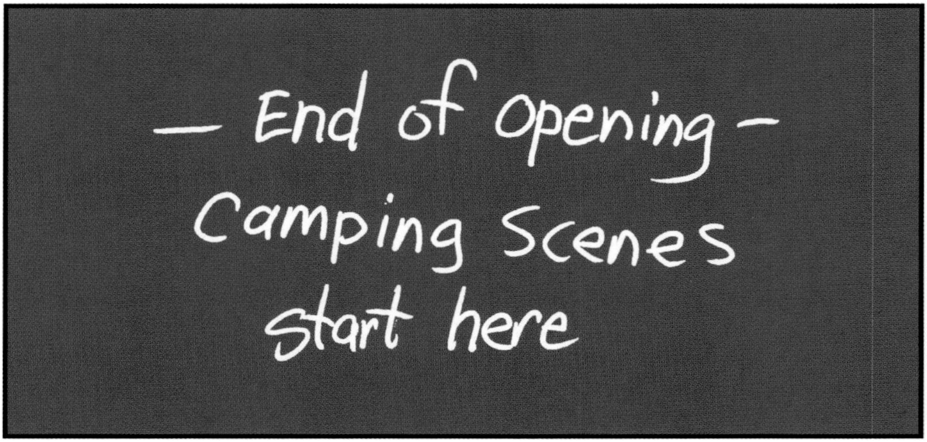
– End of opening –
Camping Scenes
start here

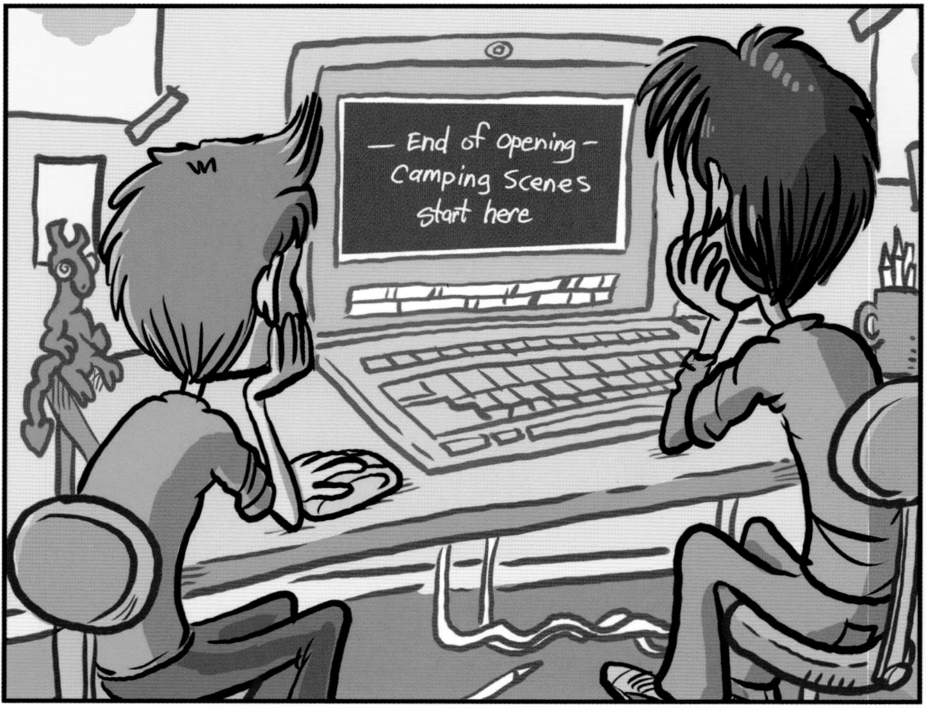
– End of opening –
Camping Scenes
start here

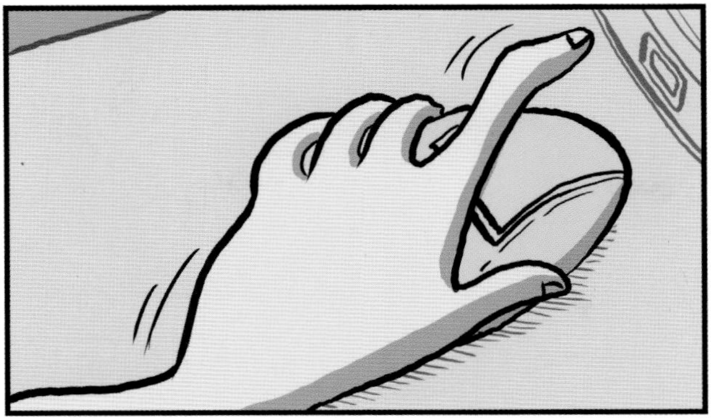

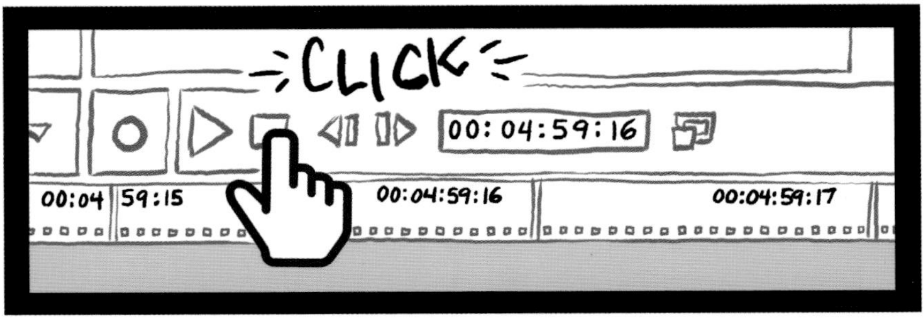
CLICK
00:04:59:16
00:04
59:15
00:04:59:16
00:04:59:17

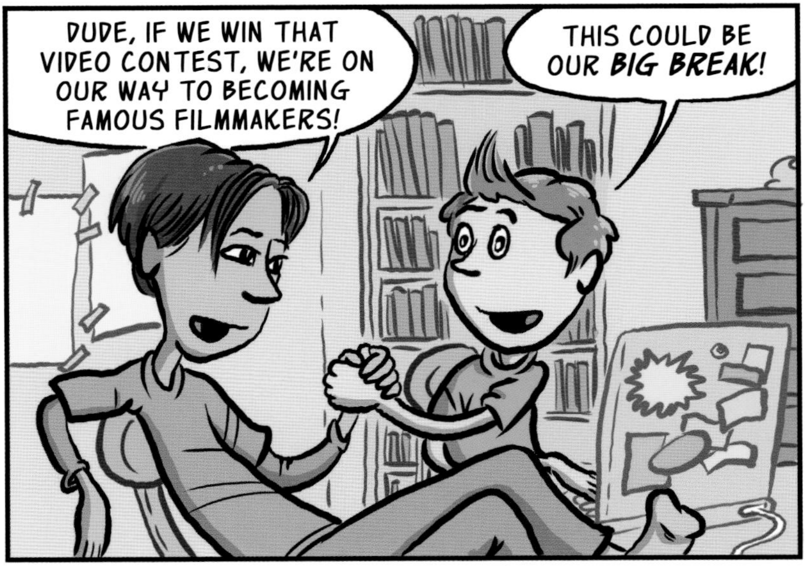
DUDE, IF WE WIN THAT VIDEO CONTEST, WE'RE ON OUR WAY TO BECOMING FAMOUS FILMMAKERS!
THIS COULD BE OUR ***BIG BREAK!***

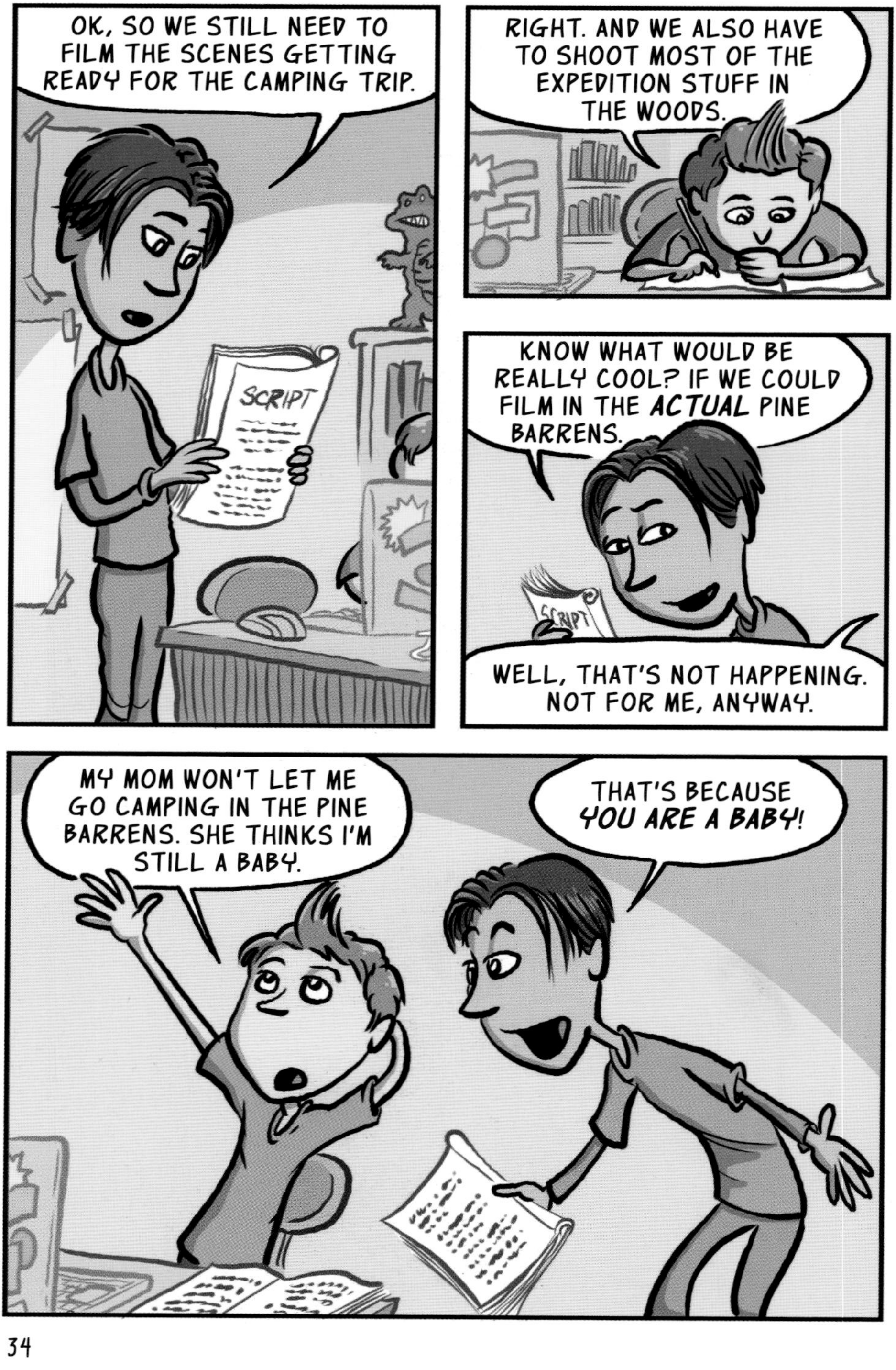
OK, SO WE STILL NEED TO FILM THE SCENES GETTING READY FOR THE CAMPING TRIP.
SCRIPT
RIGHT. AND WE ALSO HAVE TO SHOOT MOST OF THE EXPEDITION STUFF IN THE WOODS.
KNOW WHAT WOULD BE REALLY COOL? IF WE COULD FILM IN THE *ACTUAL* PINE BARRENS.
SCRIPT
WELL, THAT'S NOT HAPPENING. NOT FOR ME, ANYWAY.
MY MOM WON'T LET ME GO CAMPING IN THE PINE BARRENS. SHE THINKS I'M STILL A BABY.
THAT'S BECAUSE *YOU ARE A BABY*!

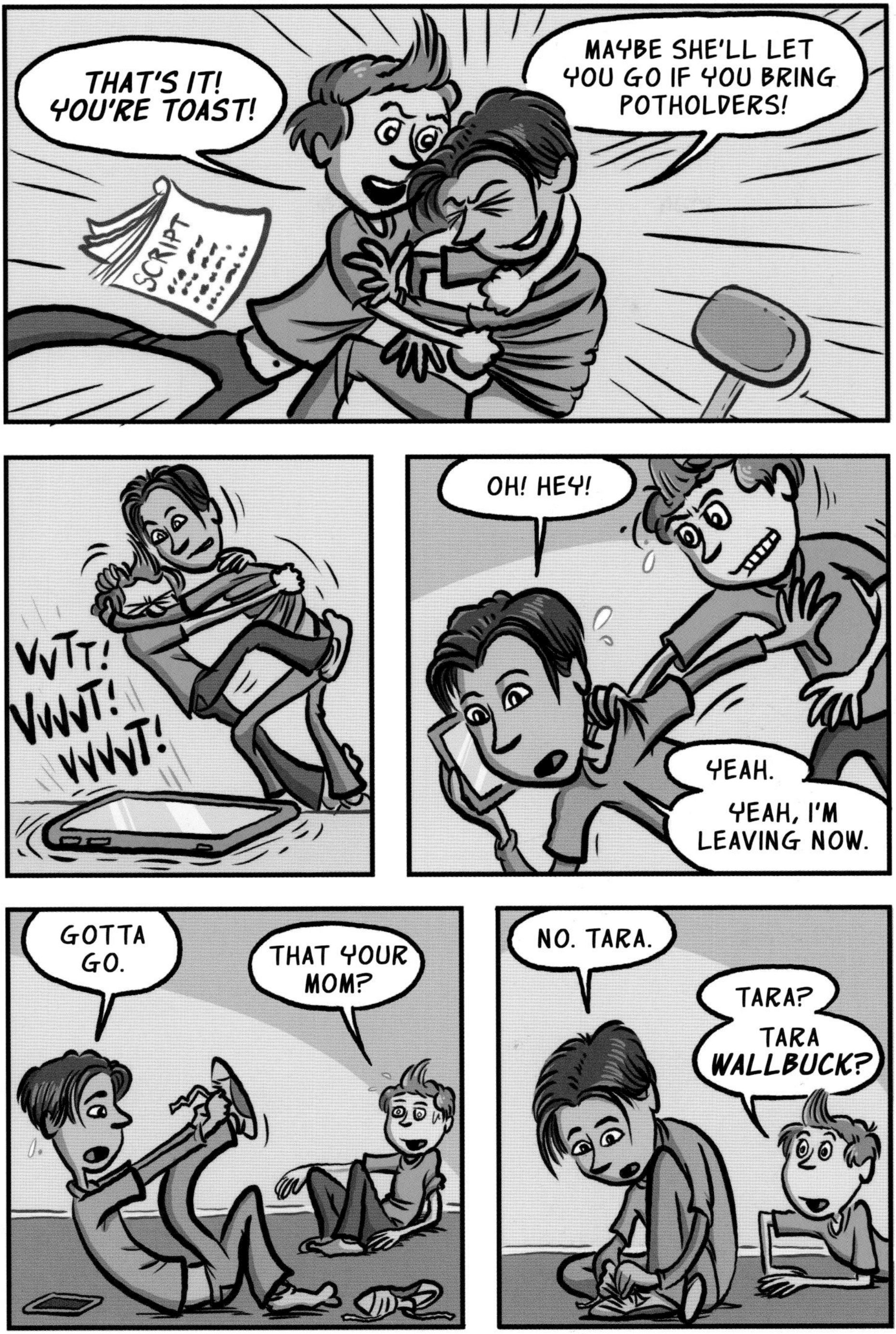
THAT'S IT! YOU'RE TOAST!
MAYBE SHE'LL LET YOU GO IF YOU BRING POTHOLDERS!
SCRIPT
VVTT! VVVVT! VVVVT!
OH! HEY!
YEAH.
YEAH, I'M LEAVING NOW.
GOTTA GO.
THAT YOUR MOM?
NO. TARA.
TARA?
TARA *WALLBUCK?*

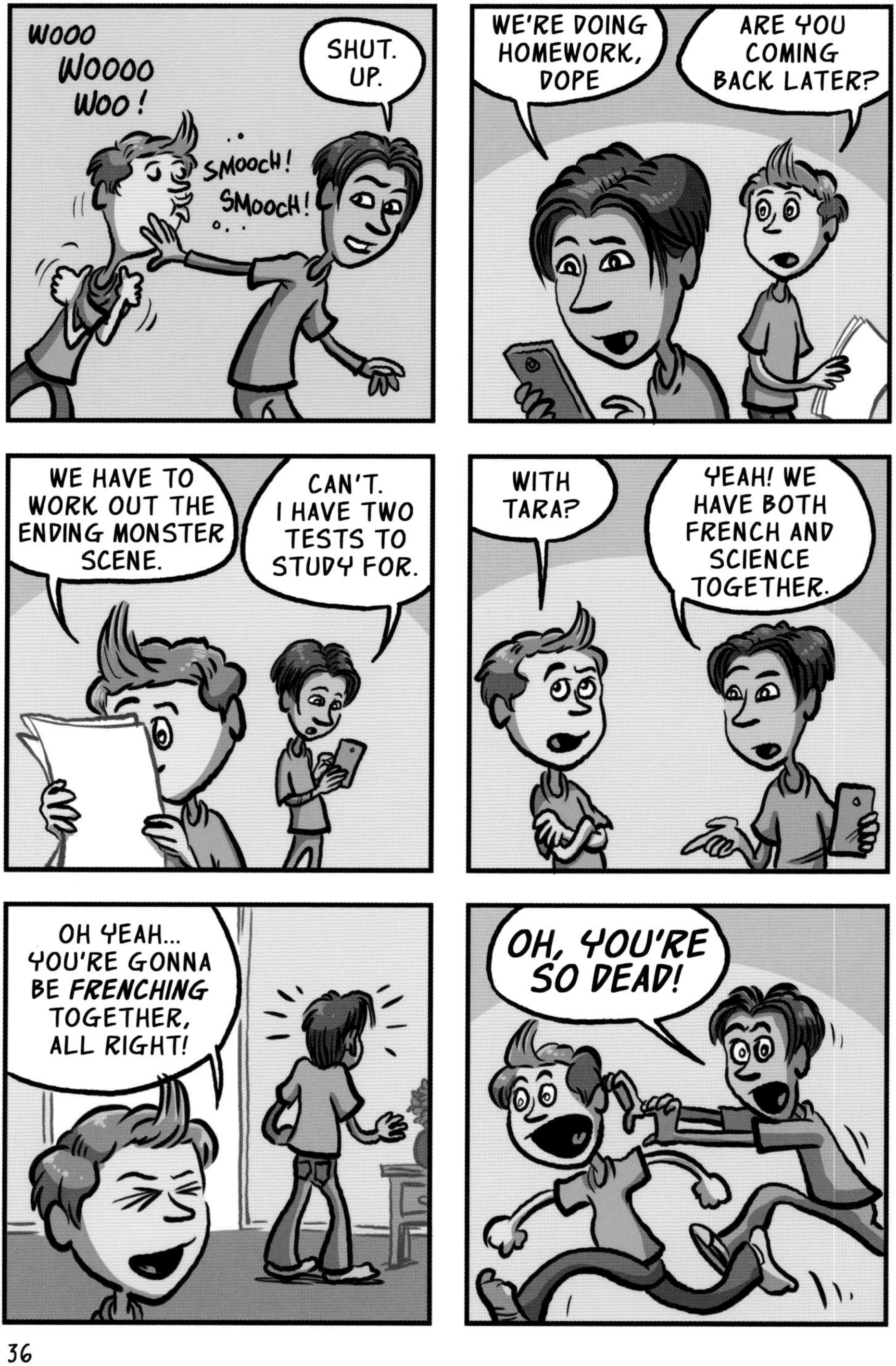
WOOO WOOOO WOO!
SHUT. UP.
SMOOCH! SMOOCH!
WE'RE DOING HOMEWORK, DOPE
ARE YOU COMING BACK LATER?
WE HAVE TO WORK OUT THE ENDING MONSTER SCENE.
CAN'T. I HAVE TWO TESTS TO STUDY FOR.
WITH TARA?
YEAH! WE HAVE BOTH FRENCH AND SCIENCE TOGETHER.
OH YEAH... YOU'RE GONNA BE *FRENCHING* TOGETHER, ALL RIGHT!
OH, YOU'RE SO DEAD!

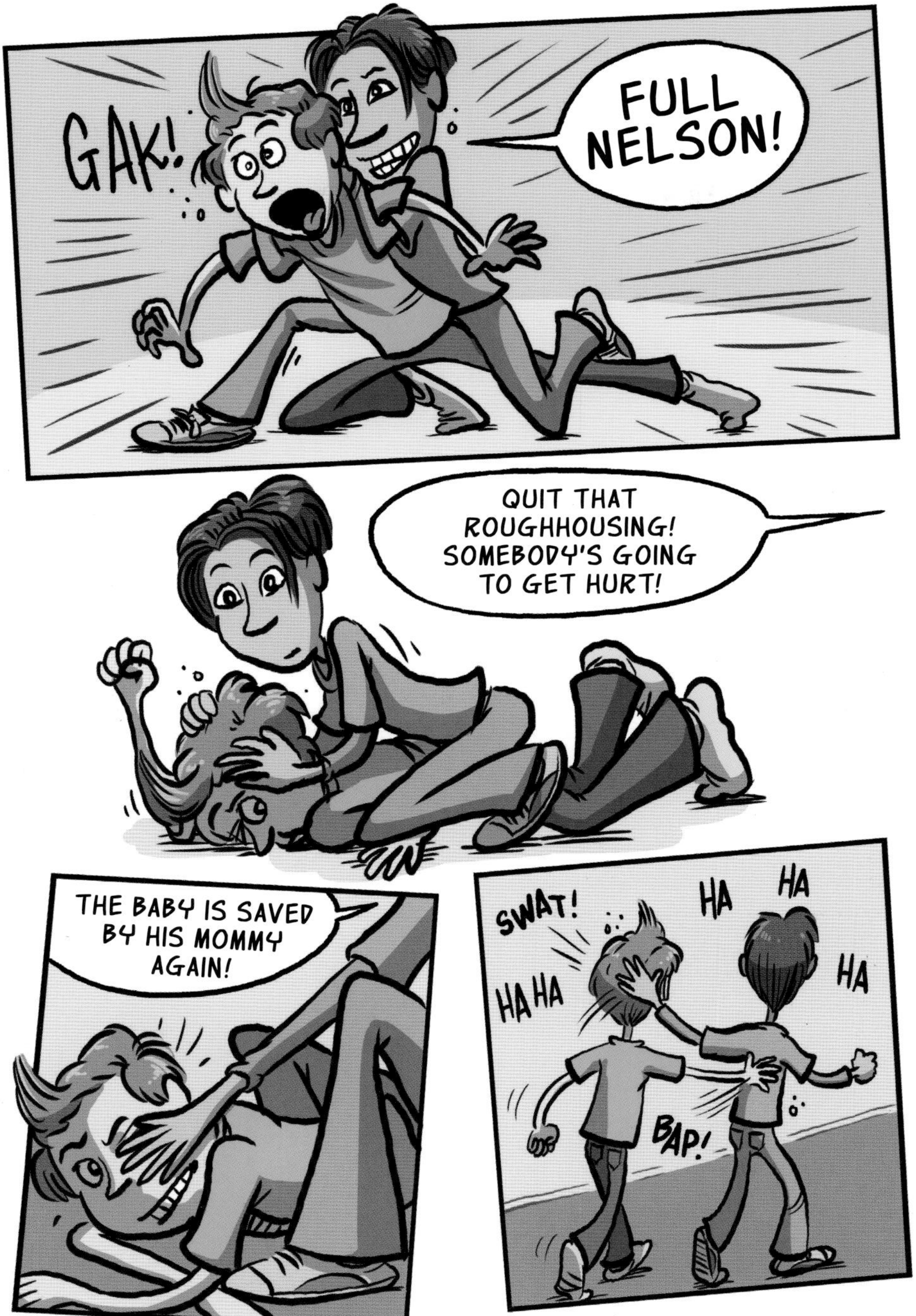
GAK!
FULL NELSON!
QUIT THAT ROUGHHOUSING! SOMEBODY'S GOING TO GET HURT!
THE BABY IS SAVED BY HIS MOMMY AGAIN!
SWAT!
HA
HA
HA
HA HA
BAP!

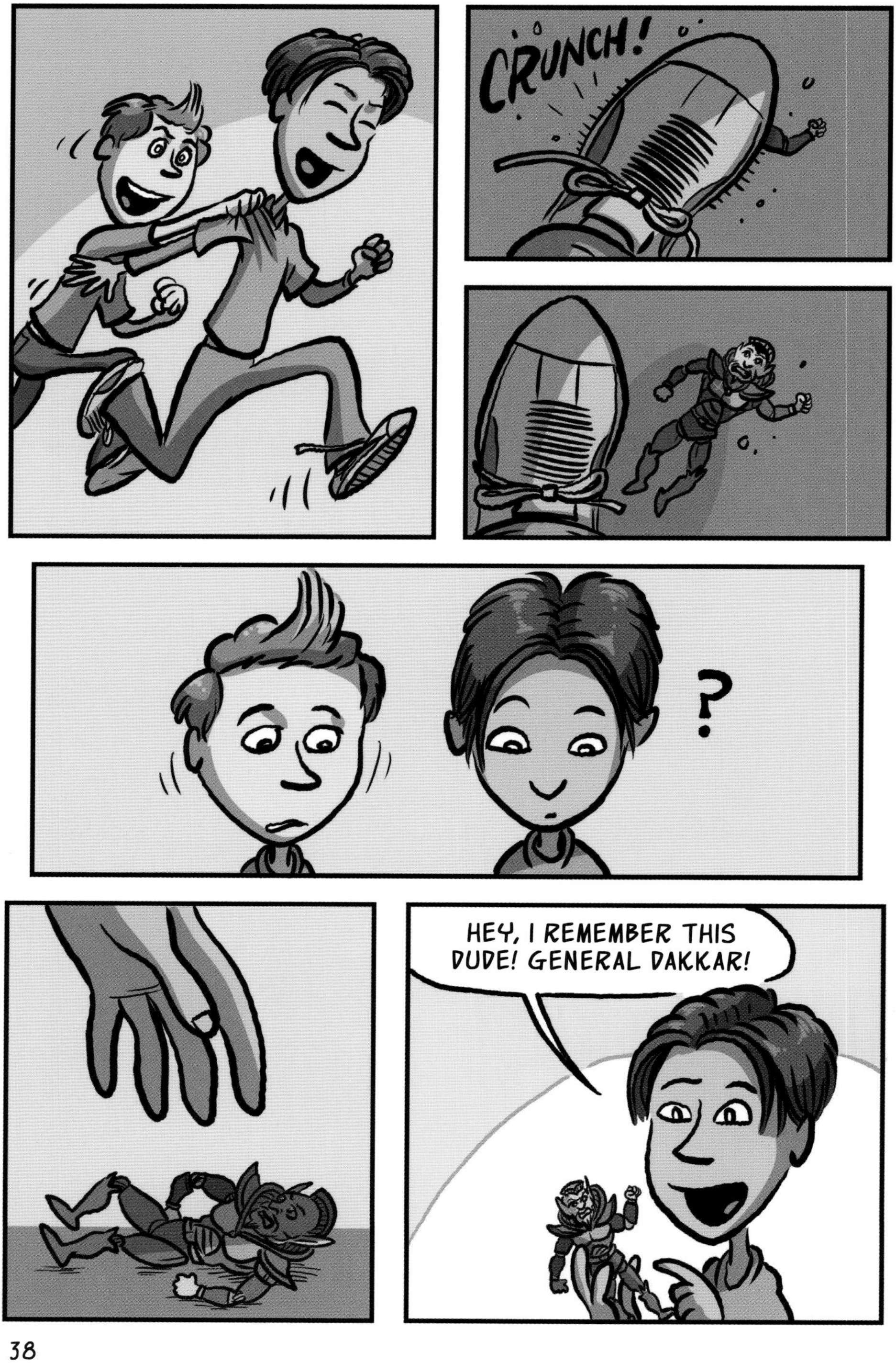
CRUNCH!
?
HEY, I REMEMBER THIS DUDE! GENERAL DAKKAR!

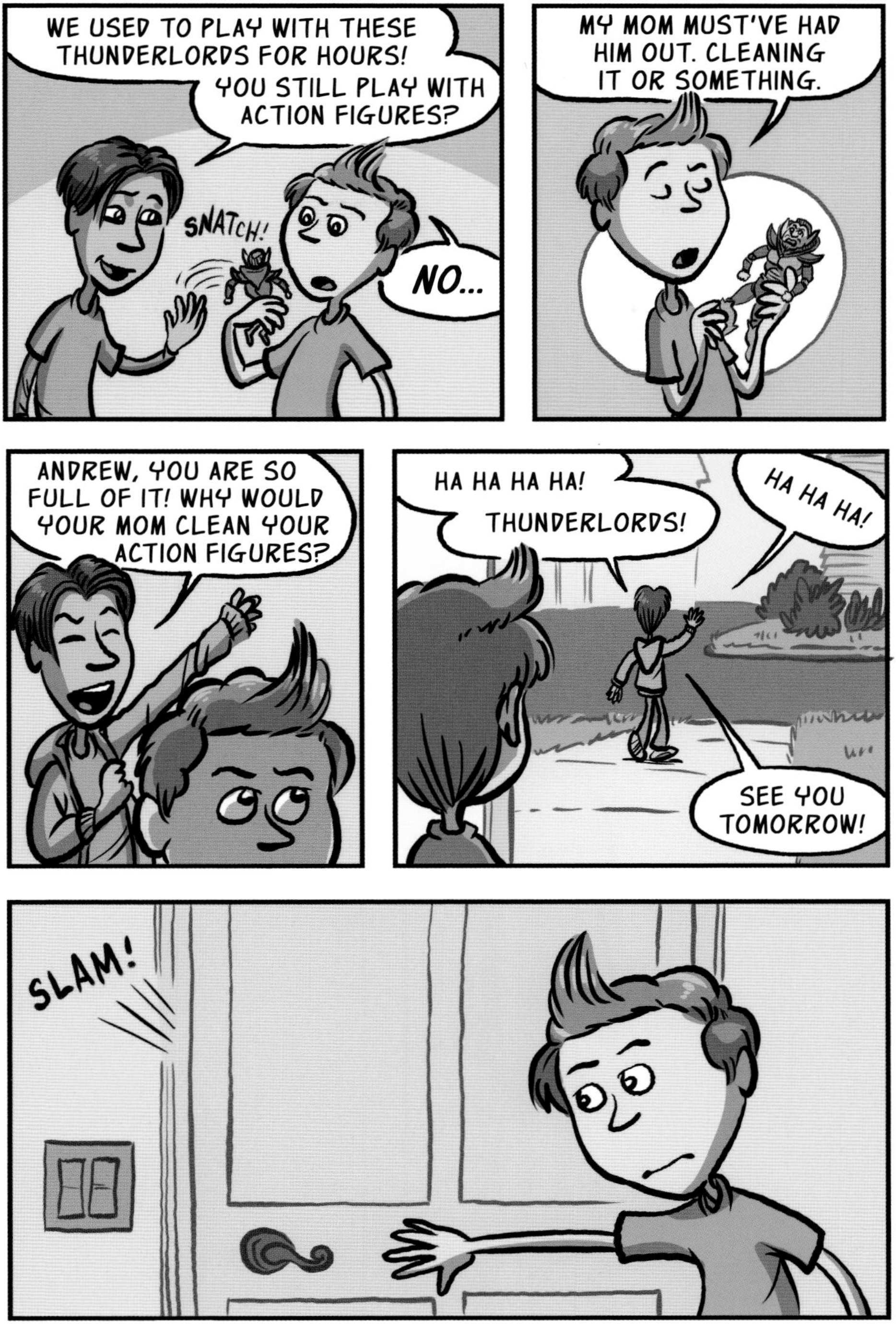
WE USED TO PLAY WITH THESE THUNDERLORDS FOR HOURS!
YOU STILL PLAY WITH ACTION FIGURES?
SNATCH!
NO...
MY MOM MUST'VE HAD HIM OUT. CLEANING IT OR SOMETHING.
ANDREW, YOU ARE SO FULL OF IT! WHY WOULD YOUR MOM CLEAN YOUR ACTION FIGURES?
HA HA HA HA!
THUNDERLORDS!
HA HA HA!
SEE YOU TOMORROW!
SLAM!

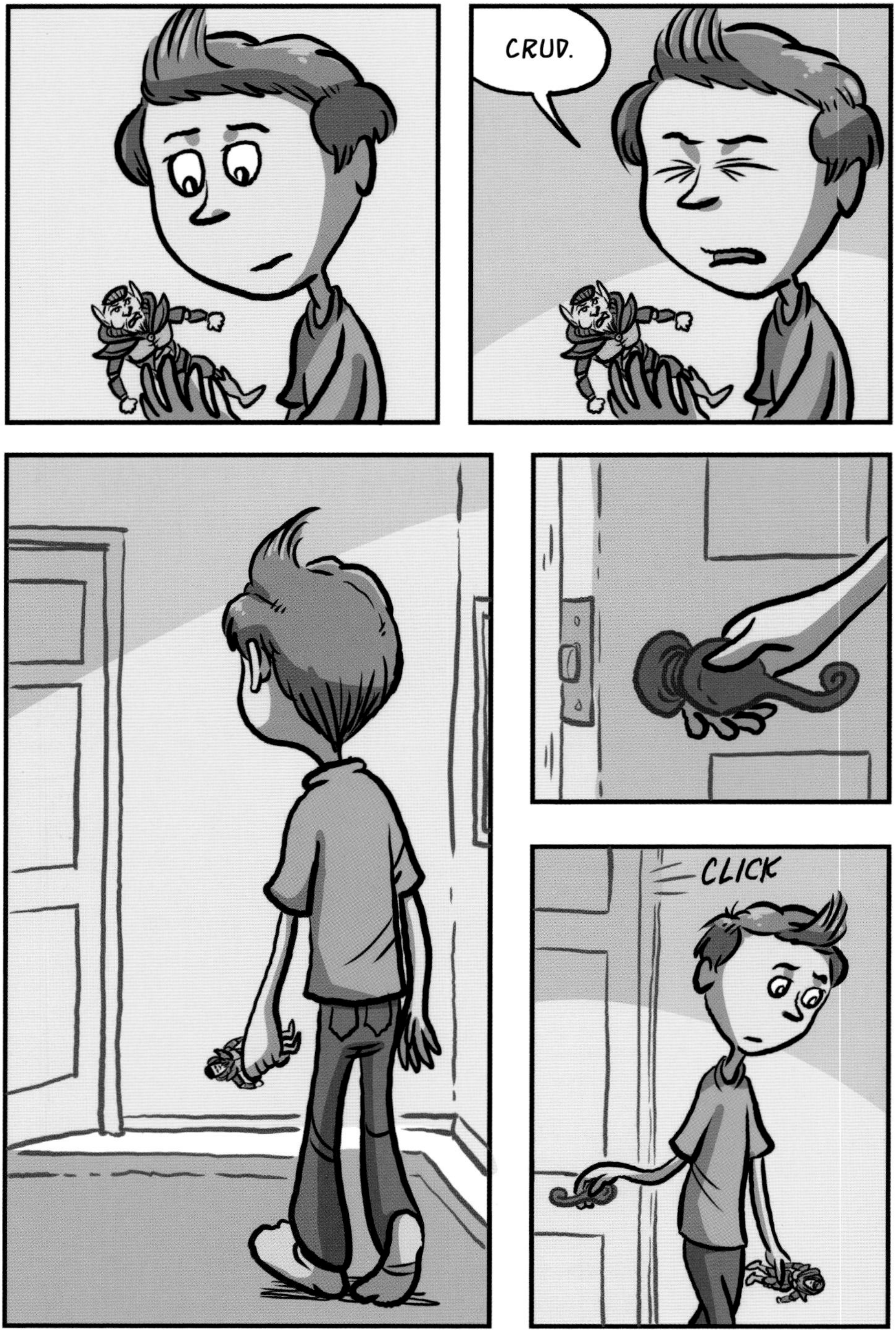
CRUD.
CLICK

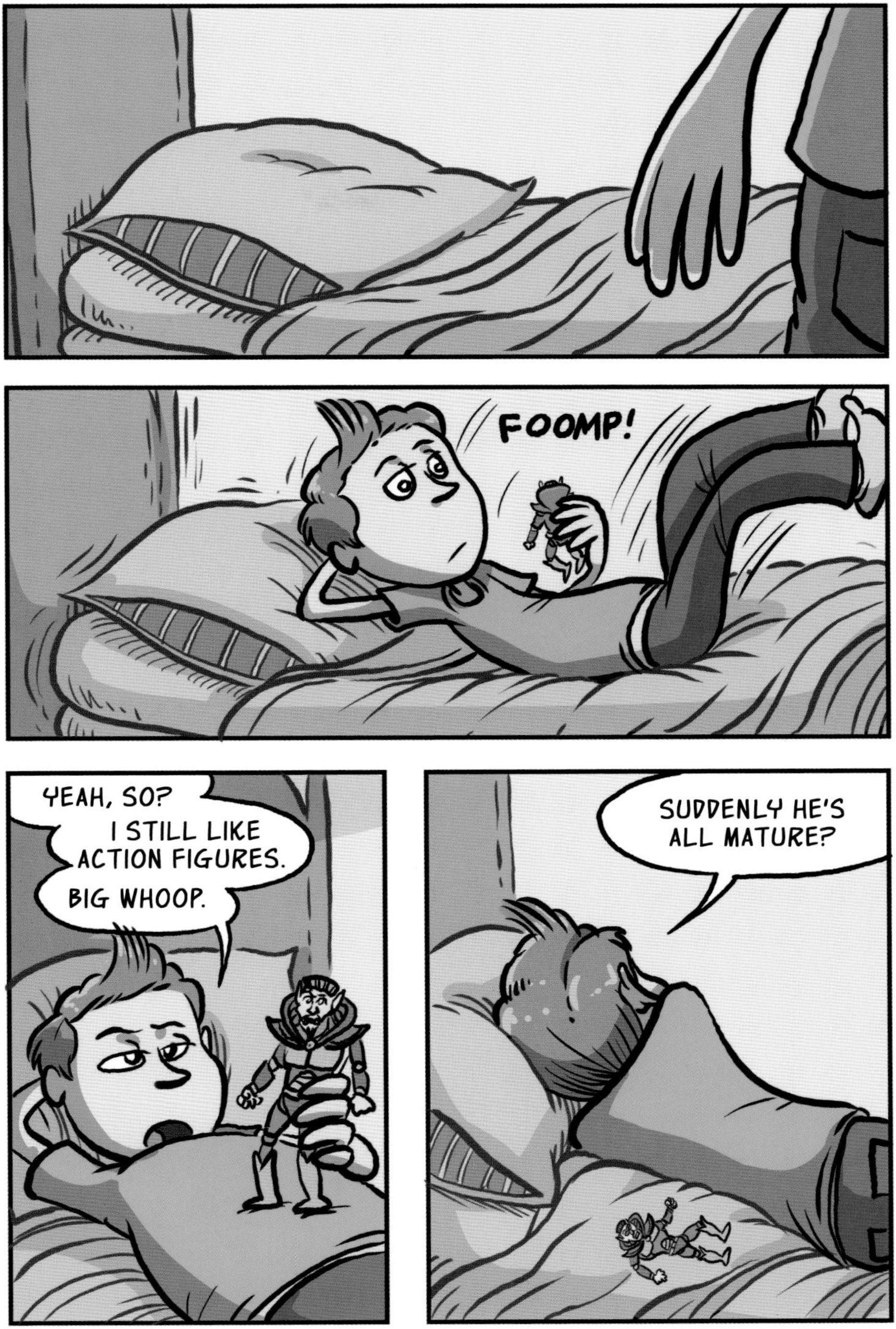
FOOMP!
YEAH, SO?
I STILL LIKE ACTION FIGURES.
BIG WHOOP.
SUDDENLY HE'S ALL MATURE?

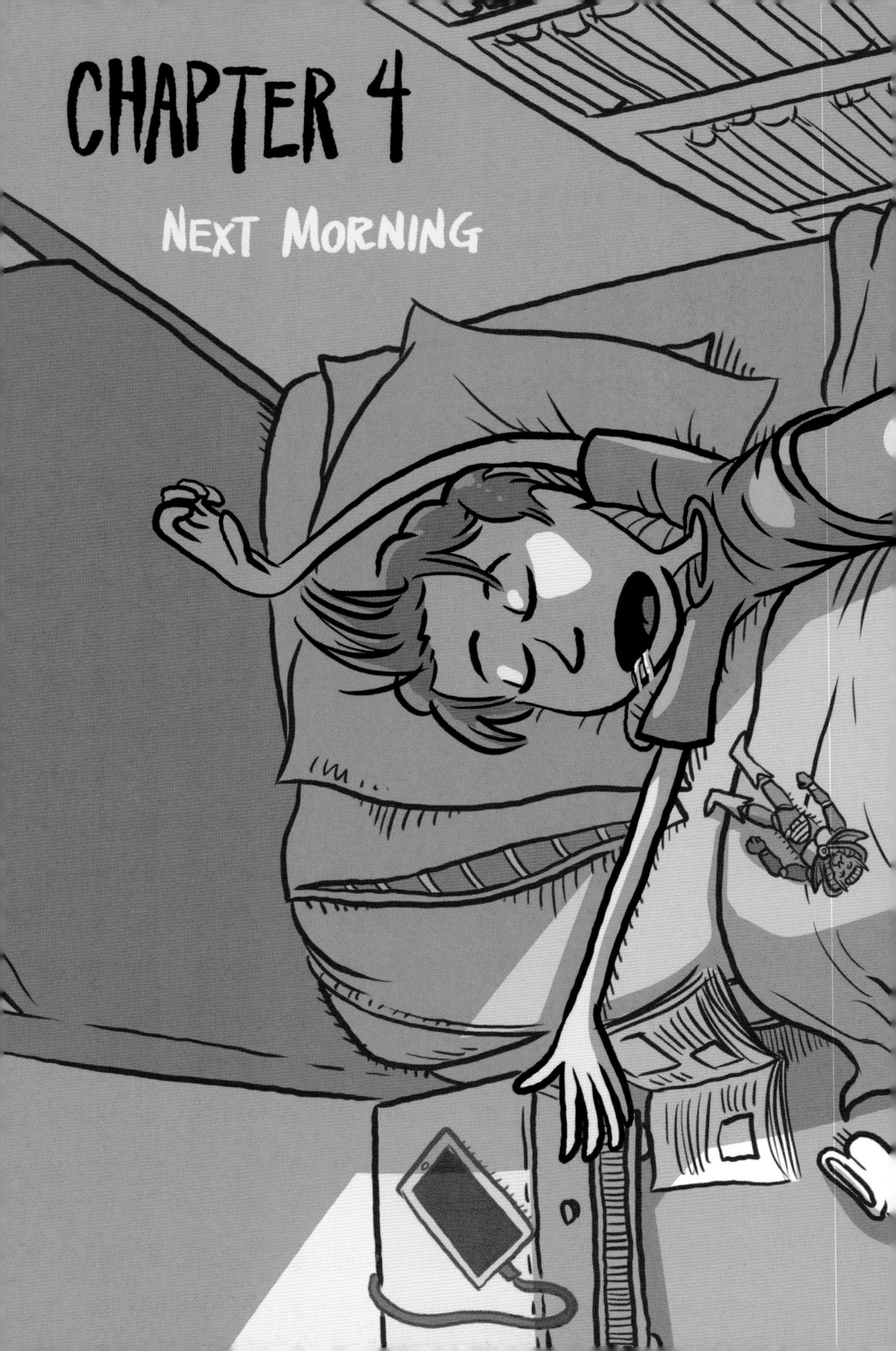
CHAPTER 4
NEXT MORNING

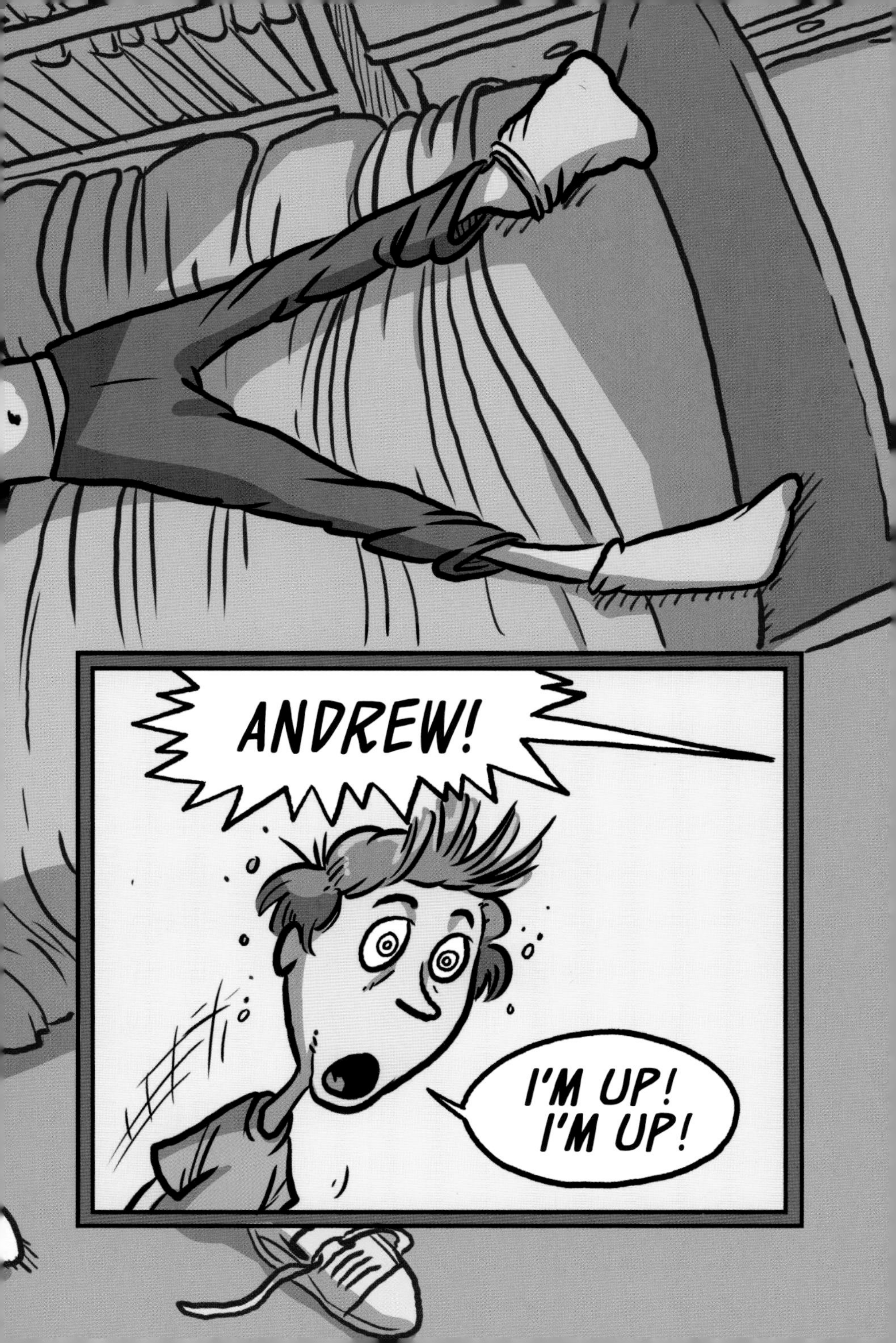
ANDREW!
I'M UP! I'M UP!

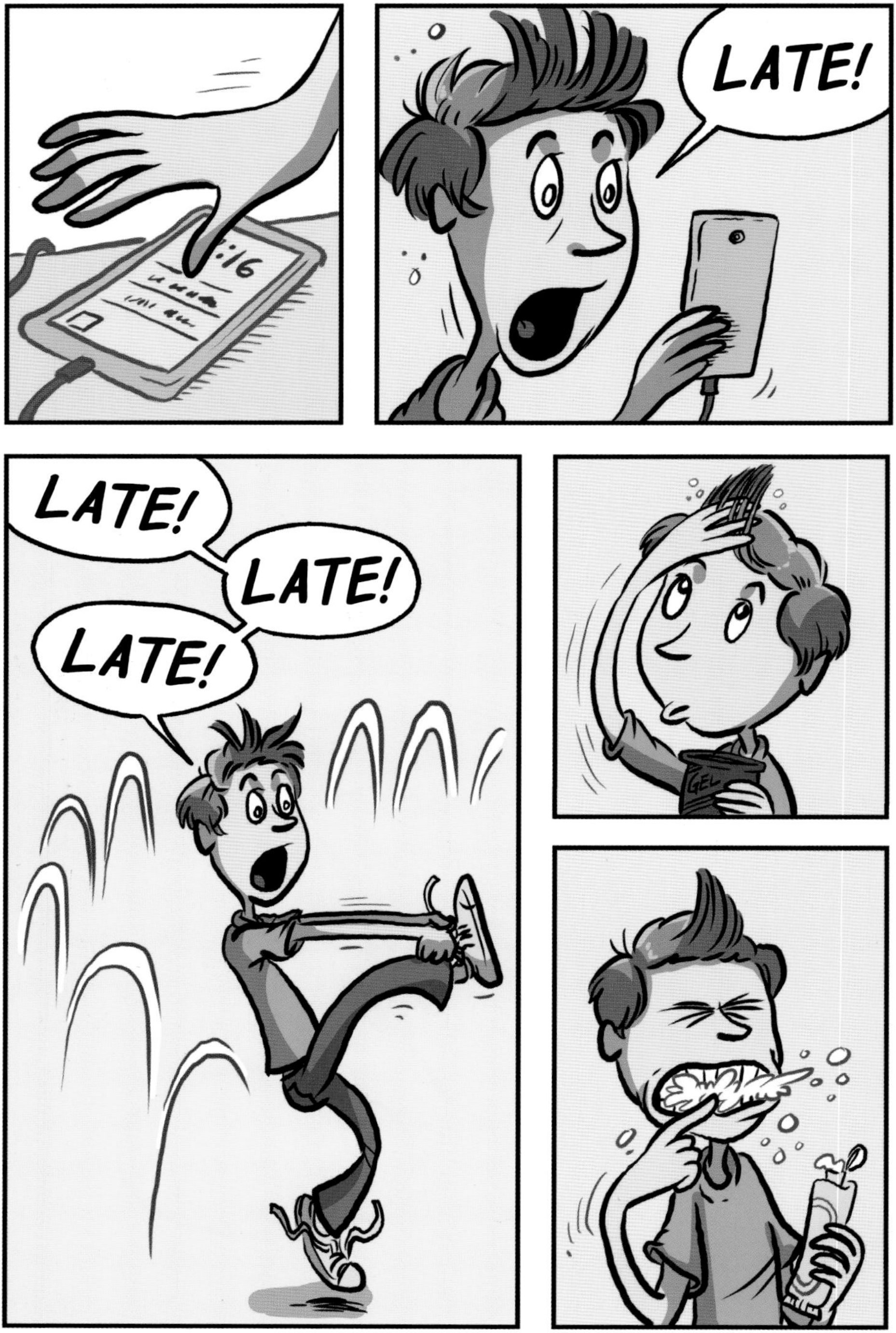
LATE!
LATE!
LATE!
LATE!
GEL

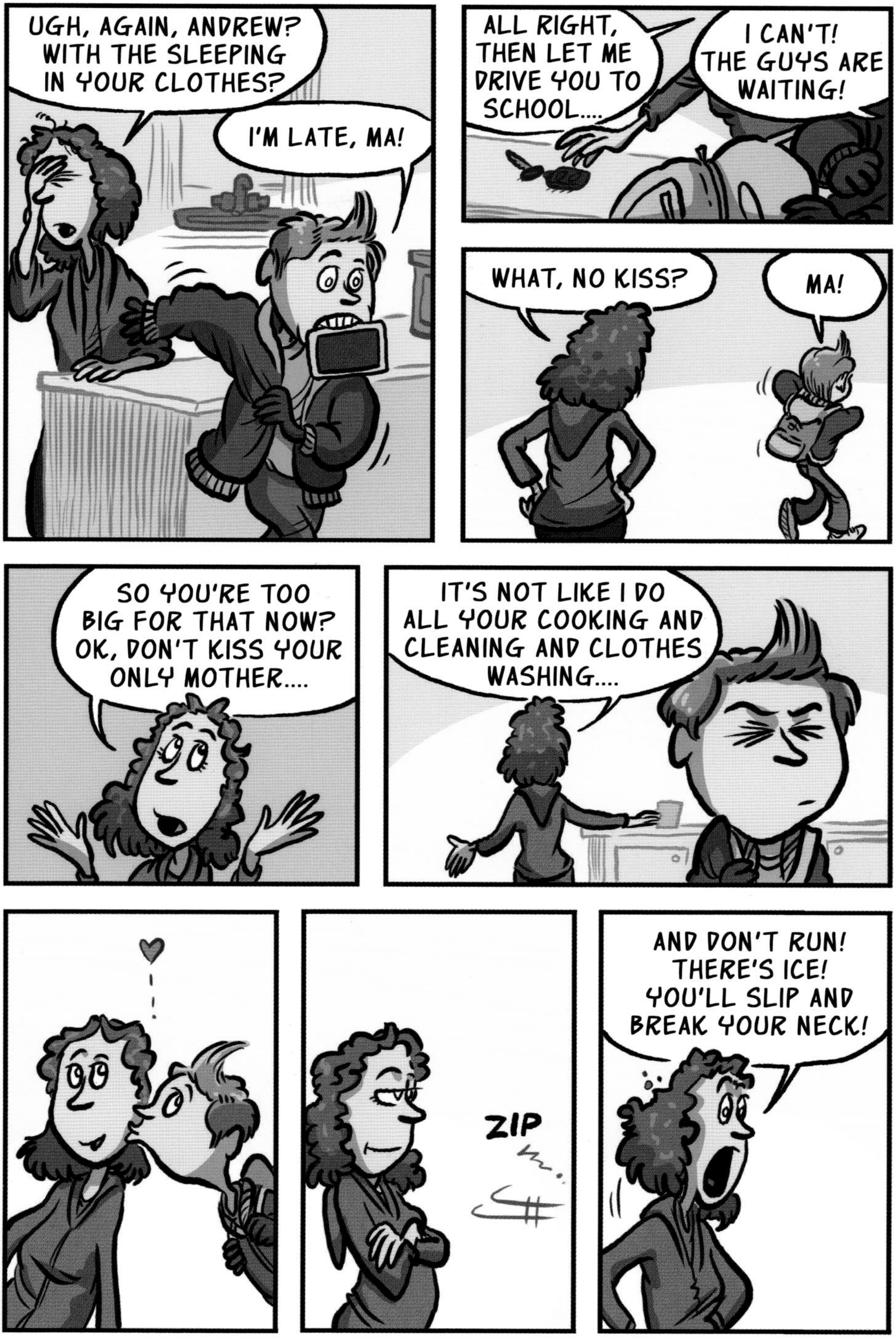
UGH, AGAIN, ANDREW? WITH THE SLEEPING IN YOUR CLOTHES?
I'M LATE, MA!
ALL RIGHT, THEN LET ME DRIVE YOU TO SCHOOL....
I CAN'T! THE GUYS ARE WAITING!
WHAT, NO KISS?
MA!
SO YOU'RE TOO BIG FOR THAT NOW? OK, DON'T KISS YOUR ONLY MOTHER....
IT'S NOT LIKE I DO ALL YOUR COOKING AND CLEANING AND CLOTHES WASHING....
ZIP
AND DON'T RUN! THERE'S ICE! YOU'LL SLIP AND BREAK YOUR NECK!

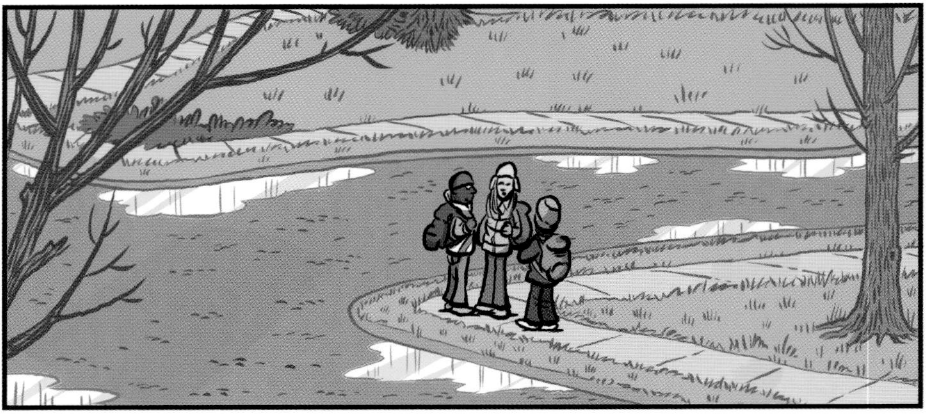

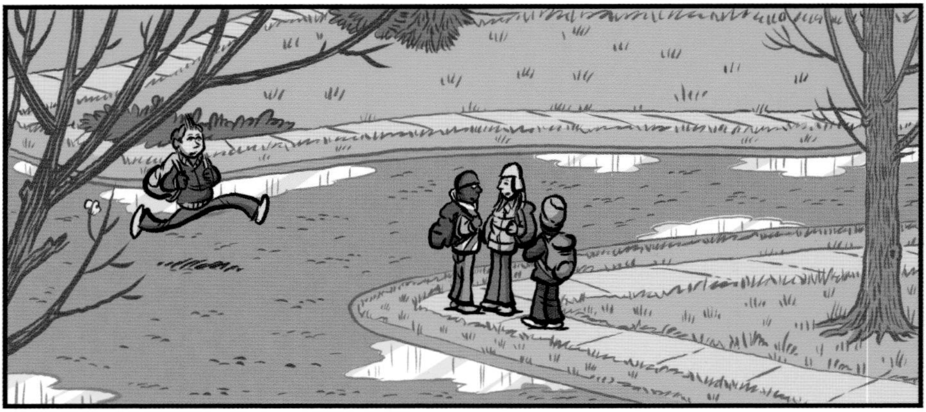

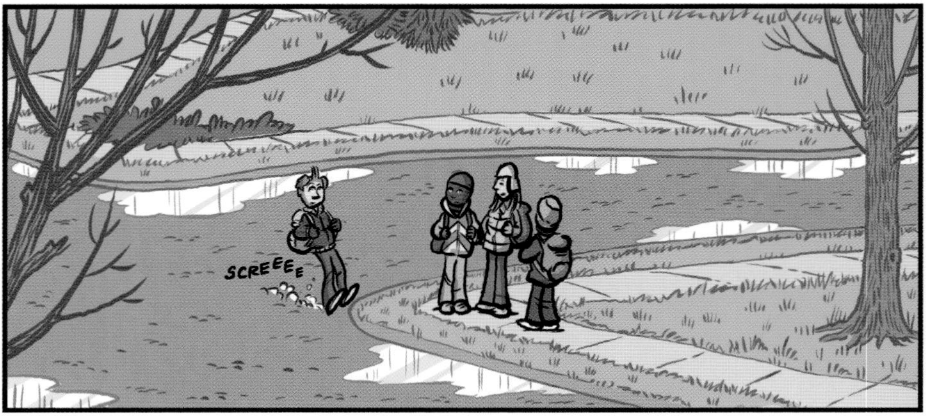
SCREEEEE

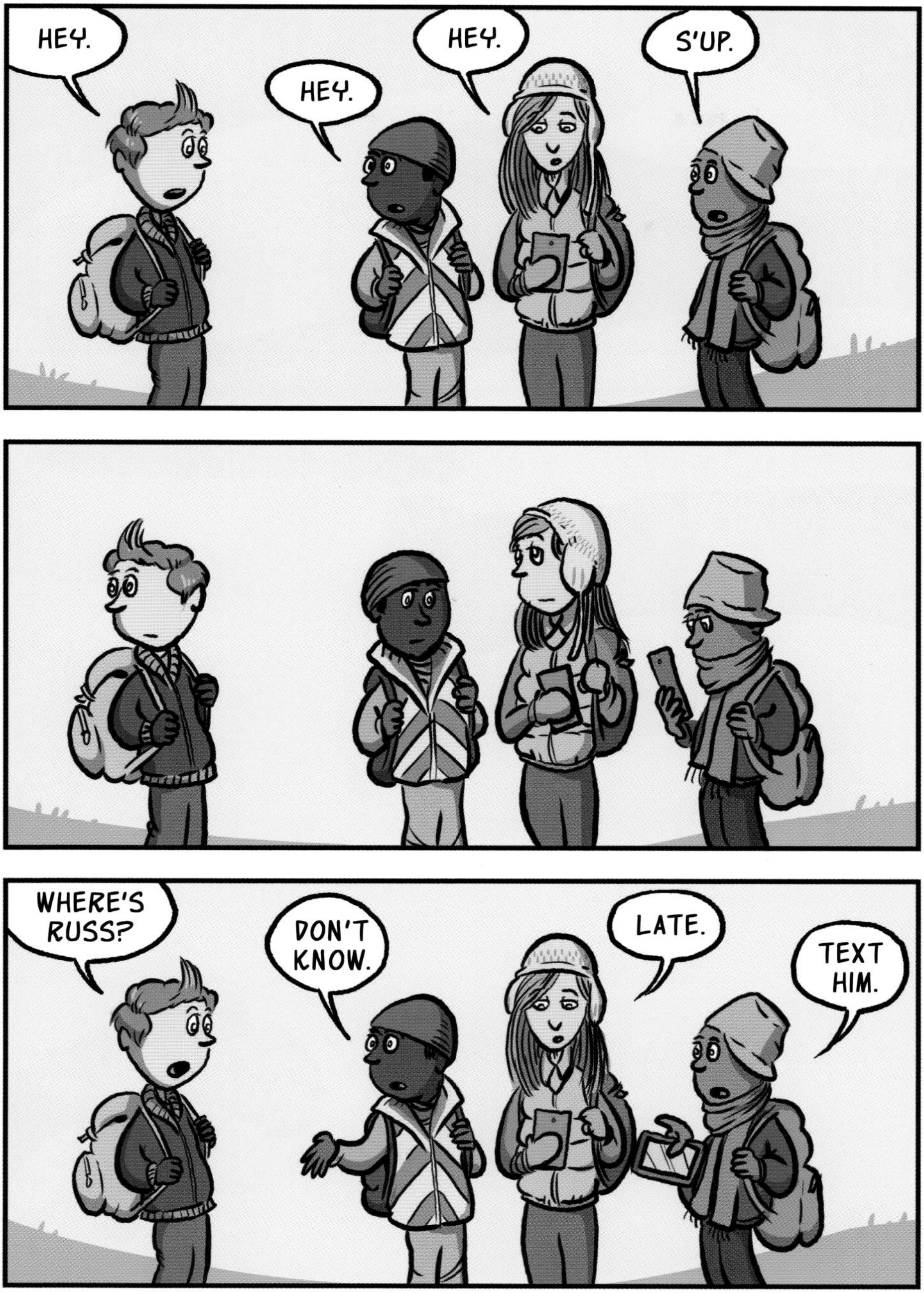
HEY.
HEY.
HEY.
S'UP.
WHERE'S RUSS?
DON'T KNOW.
LATE.
TEXT HIM.

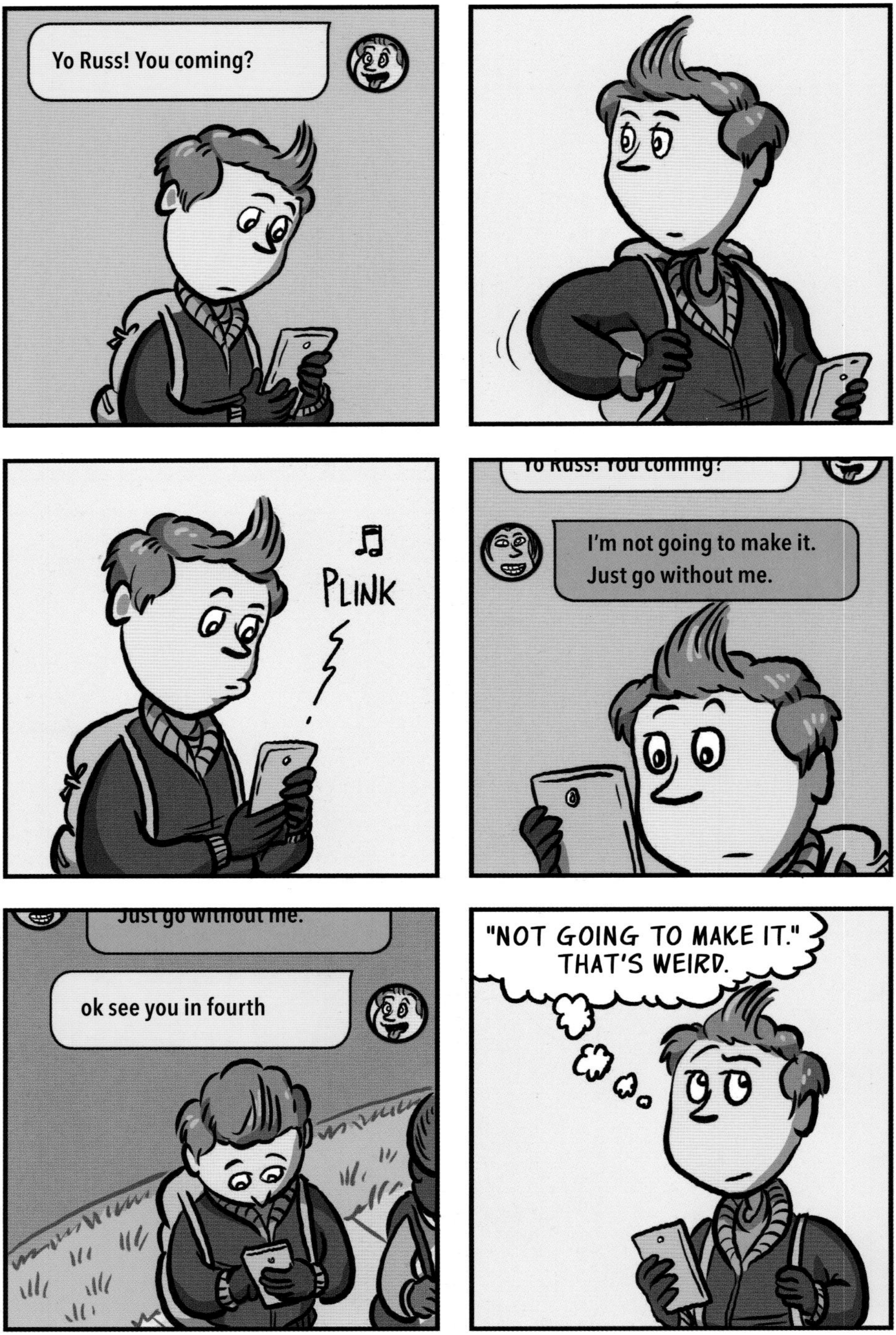
Yo Russ! You coming?
PLINK
I'm not going to make it.
Just go without me.
ok see you in fourth
"NOT GOING TO MAKE IT."
THAT'S WEIRD.

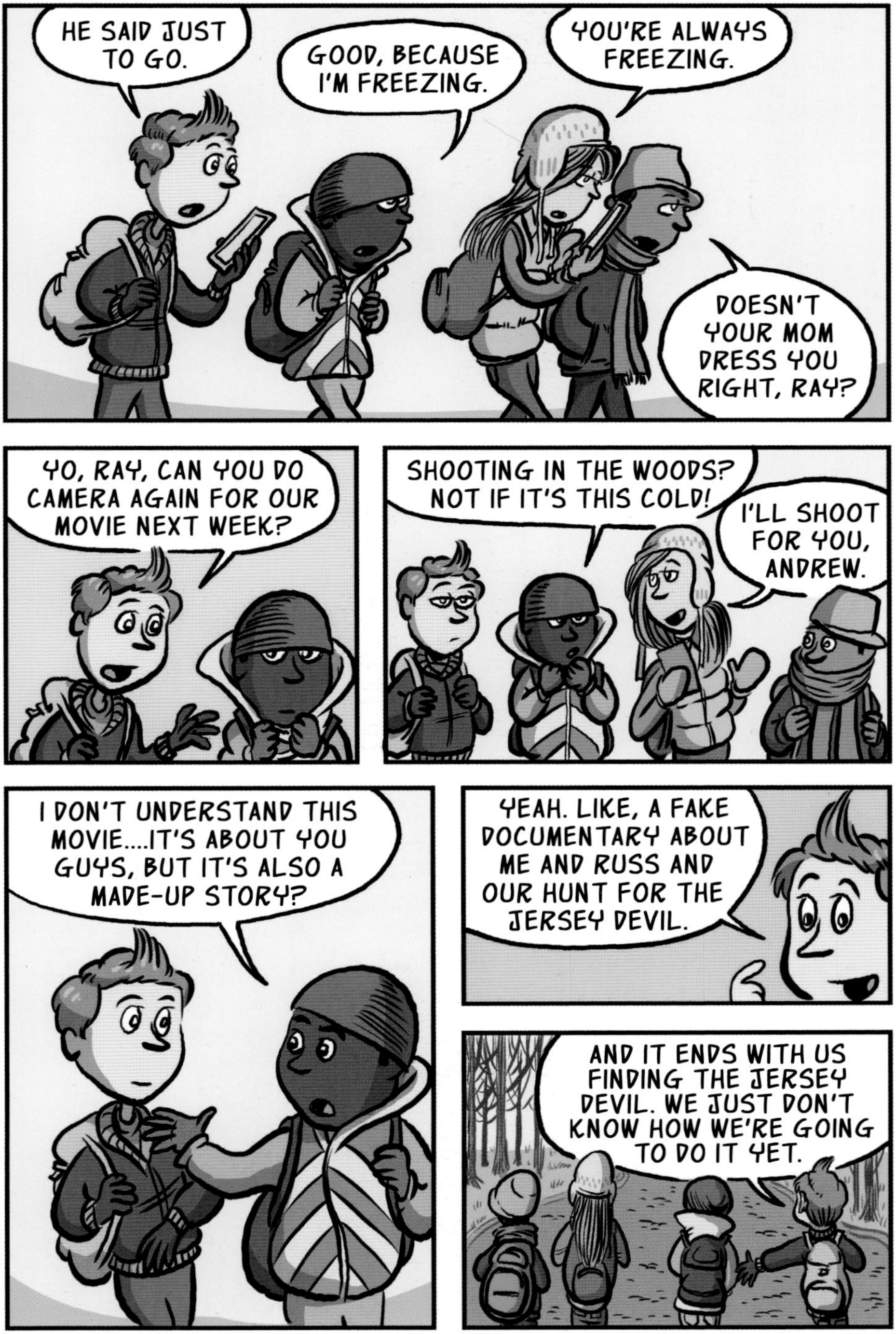
HE SAID JUST TO GO.
GOOD, BECAUSE I'M FREEZING.
YOU'RE ALWAYS FREEZING.
DOESN'T YOUR MOM DRESS YOU RIGHT, RAY?
YO, RAY, CAN YOU DO CAMERA AGAIN FOR OUR MOVIE NEXT WEEK?
SHOOTING IN THE WOODS? NOT IF IT'S THIS COLD!
I'LL SHOOT FOR YOU, ANDREW.
I DON'T UNDERSTAND THIS MOVIE....IT'S ABOUT YOU GUYS, BUT IT'S ALSO A MADE-UP STORY?
YEAH. LIKE, A FAKE DOCUMENTARY ABOUT ME AND RUSS AND OUR HUNT FOR THE JERSEY DEVIL.
AND IT ENDS WITH US FINDING THE JERSEY DEVIL. WE JUST DON'T KNOW HOW WE'RE GOING TO DO IT YET.

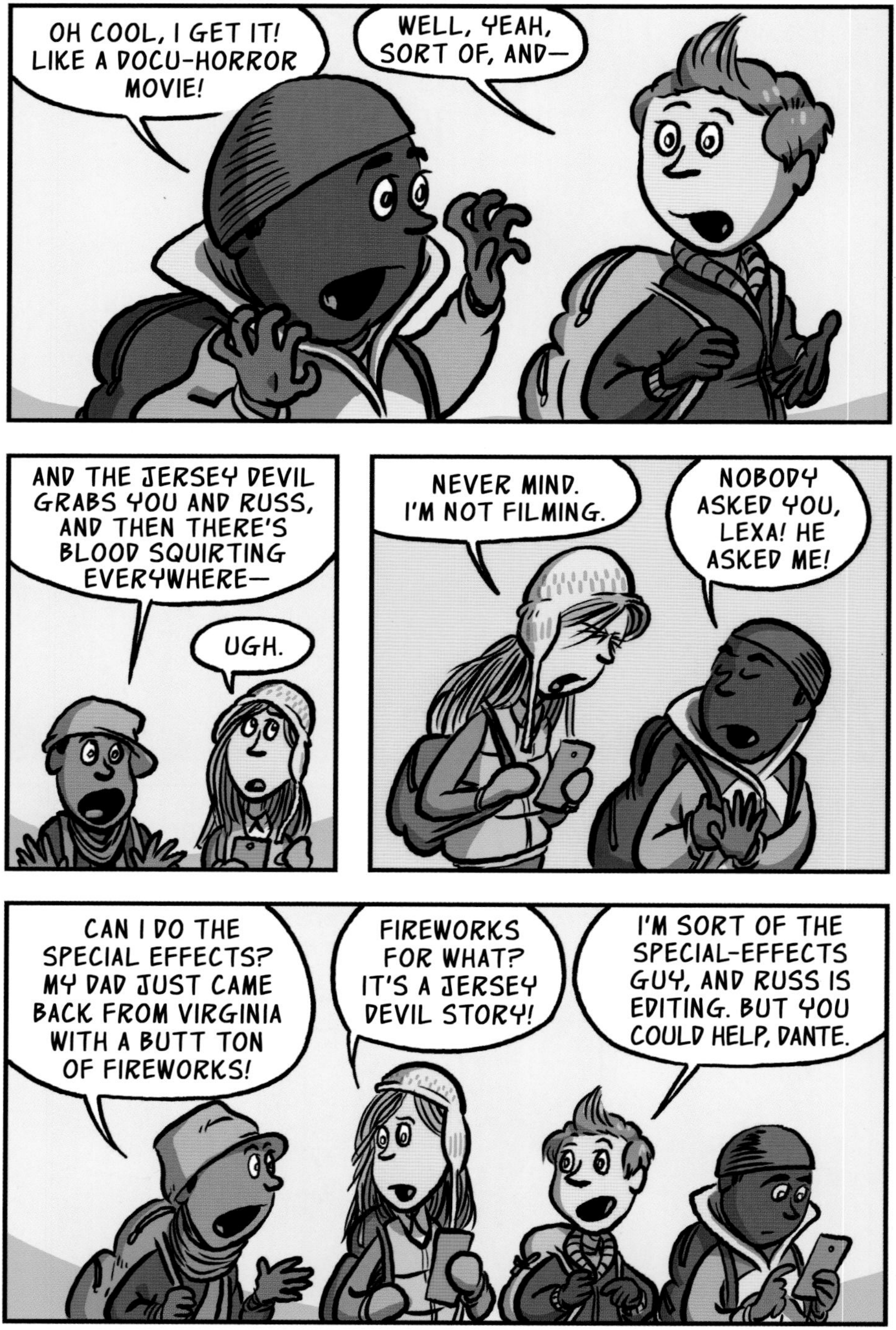
OH COOL, I GET IT! LIKE A DOCU-HORROR MOVIE!
WELL, YEAH, SORT OF, AND—
AND THE JERSEY DEVIL GRABS YOU AND RUSS, AND THEN THERE'S BLOOD SQUIRTING EVERYWHERE—
UGH.
NEVER MIND. I'M NOT FILMING.
NOBODY ASKED YOU, LEXA! HE ASKED ME!
CAN I DO THE SPECIAL EFFECTS? MY DAD JUST CAME BACK FROM VIRGINIA WITH A BUTT TON OF FIREWORKS!
FIREWORKS FOR WHAT? IT'S A JERSEY DEVIL STORY!
I'M SORT OF THE SPECIAL-EFFECTS GUY, AND RUSS IS EDITING. BUT YOU COULD HELP, DANTE.

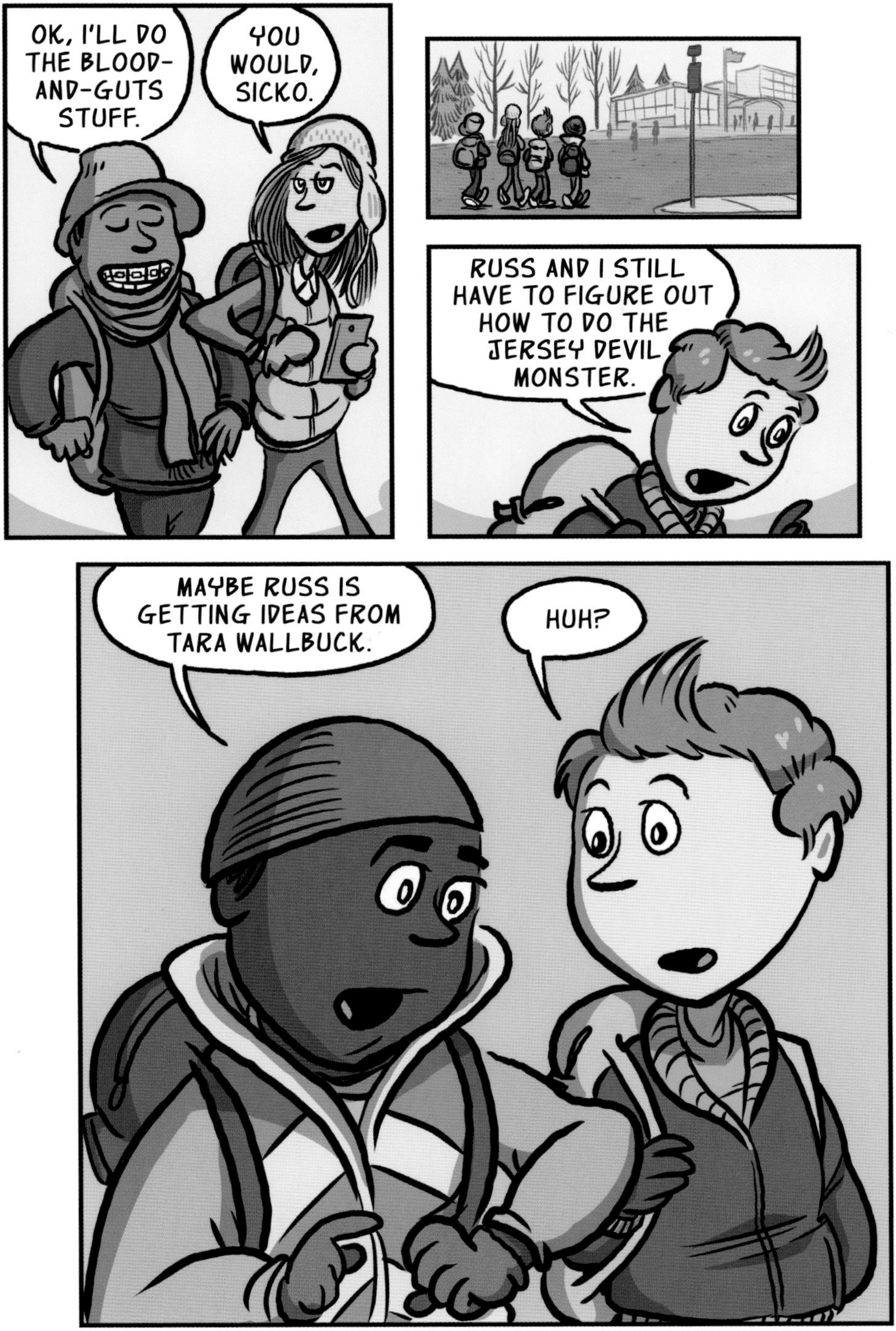
OK, I'LL DO THE BLOOD-AND-GUTS STUFF.
YOU WOULD, SICKO.
RUSS AND I STILL HAVE TO FIGURE OUT HOW TO DO THE JERSEY DEVIL MONSTER.
MAYBE RUSS IS GETTING IDEAS FROM TARA WALLBUCK.
HUH?

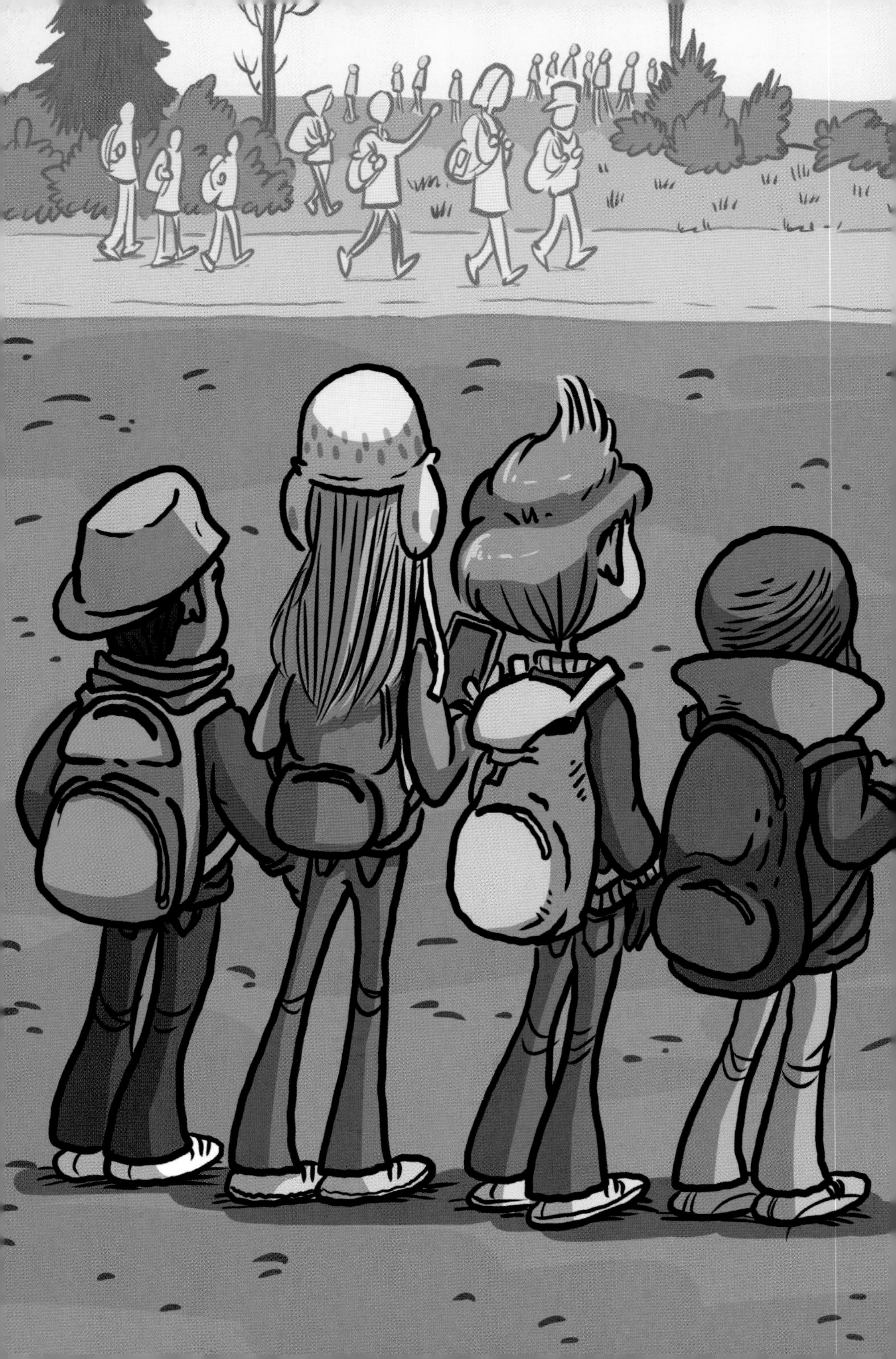

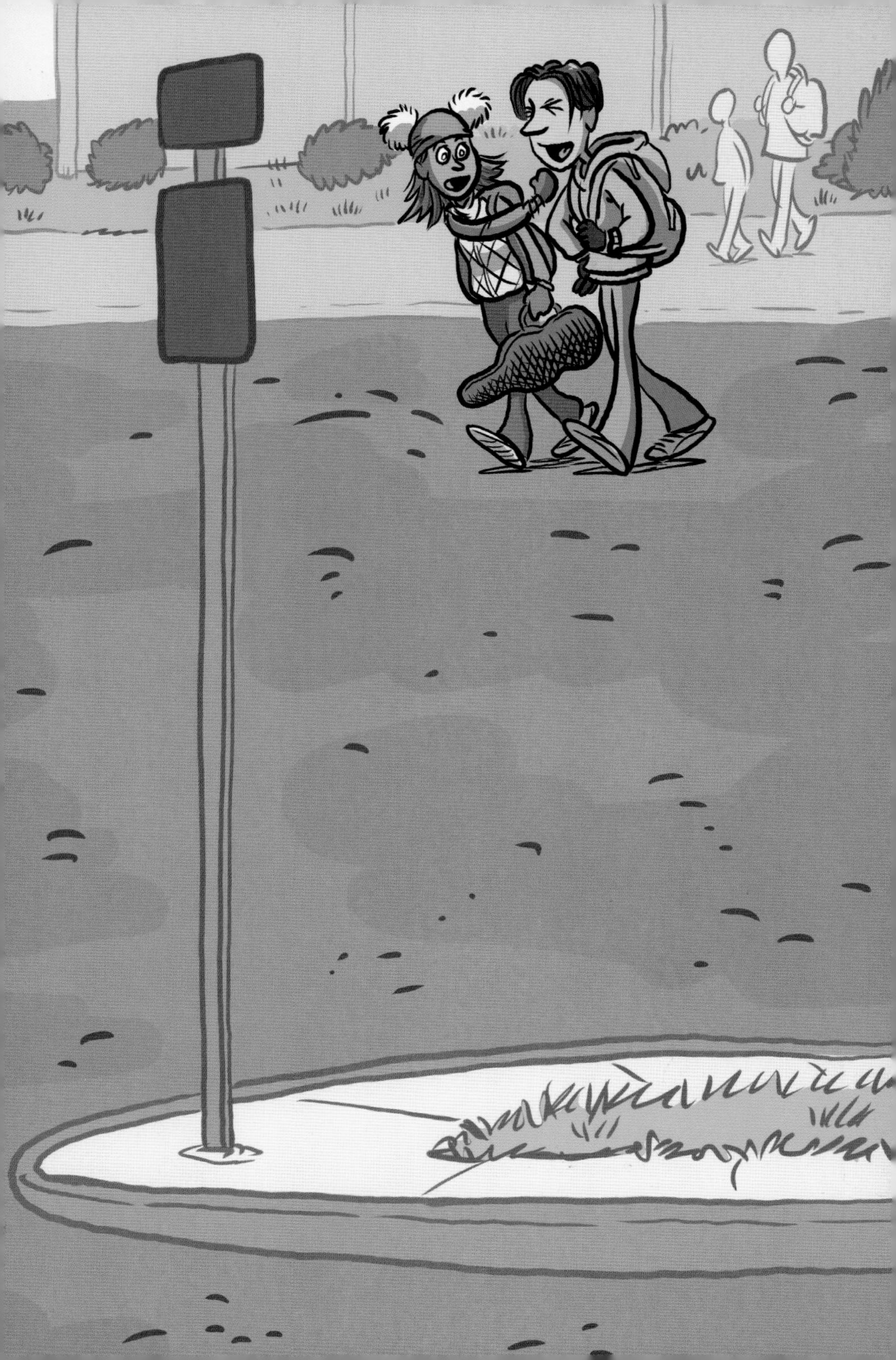

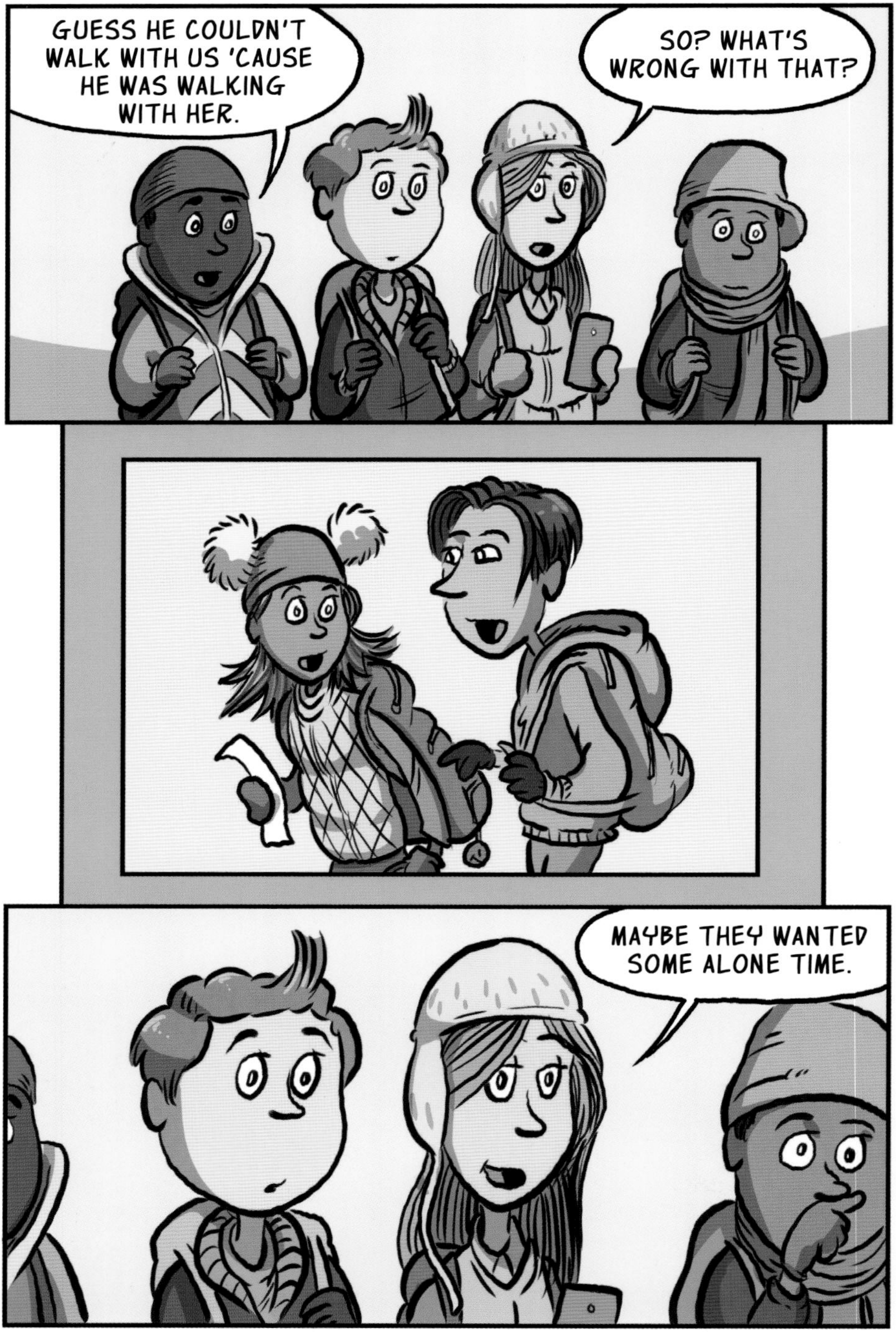
GUESS HE COULDN'T WALK WITH US 'CAUSE HE WAS WALKING WITH HER.
SO? WHAT'S WRONG WITH THAT?
MAYBE THEY WANTED SOME ALONE TIME.

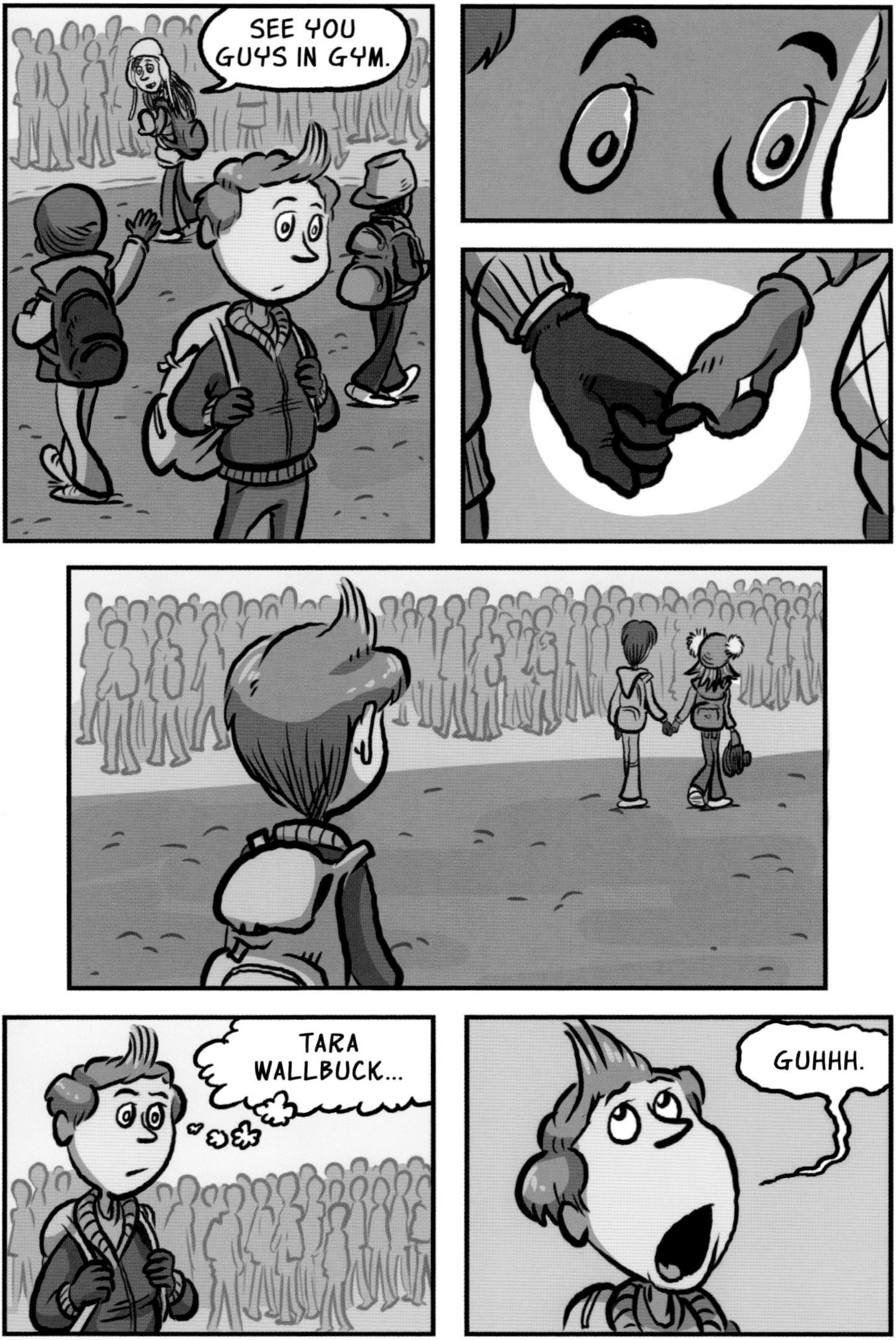
SEE YOU GUYS IN GYM.
TARA WALLBUCK...
GUHHH.

CHAPTER 5

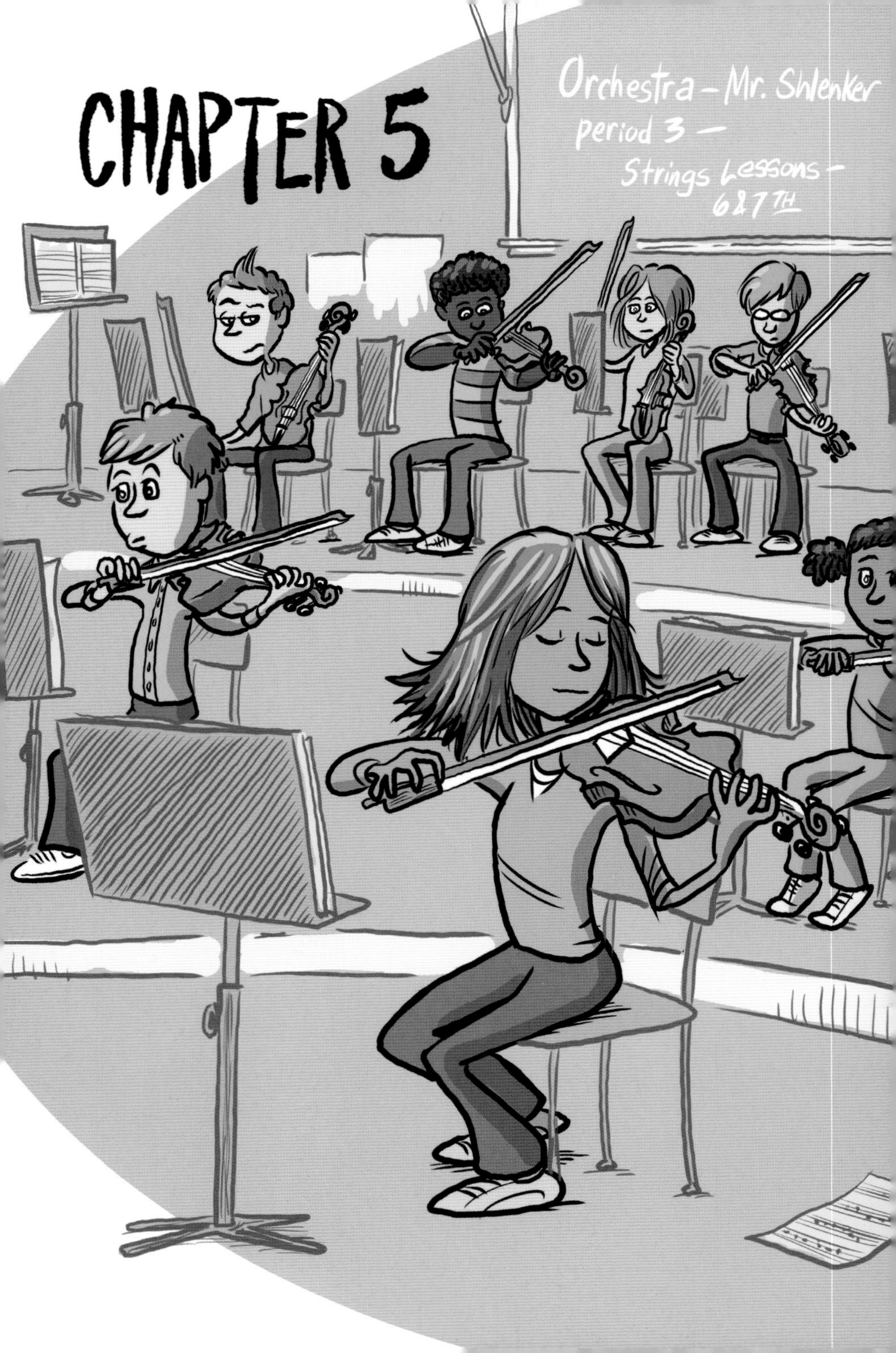
Orchestra - Mr. Shlenker
period 3 -
Strings Lessons -
6&7TH

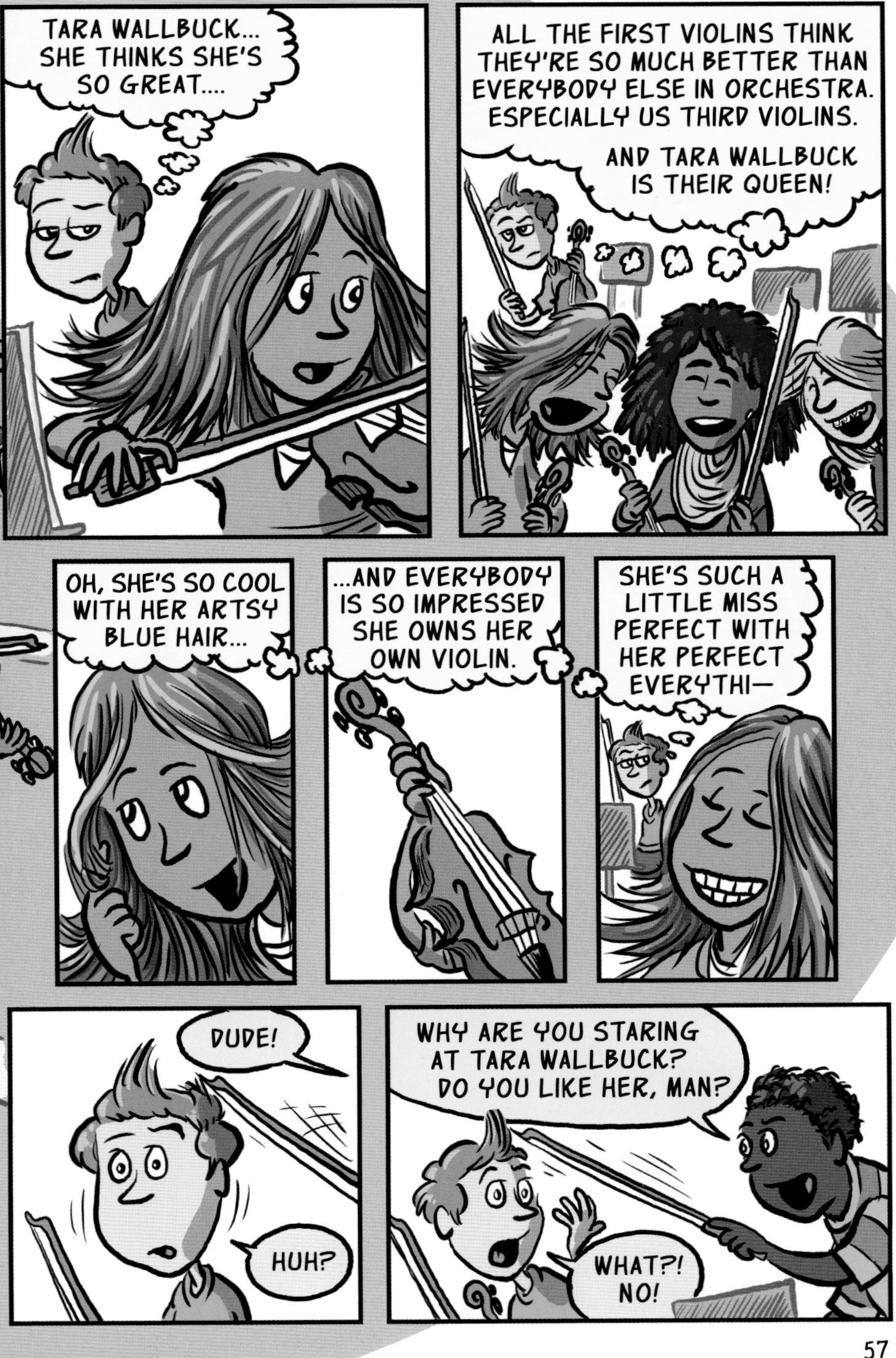
TARA WALLBUCK...
SHE THINKS SHE'S
SO GREAT....
ALL THE FIRST VIOLINS THINK THEY'RE SO MUCH BETTER THAN EVERYBODY ELSE IN ORCHESTRA. ESPECIALLY US THIRD VIOLINS.
AND TARA WALLBUCK IS THEIR QUEEN!
OH, SHE'S SO COOL WITH HER ARTSY BLUE HAIR...
...AND EVERYBODY IS SO IMPRESSED SHE OWNS HER OWN VIOLIN.
SHE'S SUCH A LITTLE MISS PERFECT WITH HER PERFECT EVERYTHI—
DUDE!
HUH?
WHY ARE YOU STARING AT TARA WALLBUCK? DO YOU LIKE HER, MAN?
WHAT?! NO!

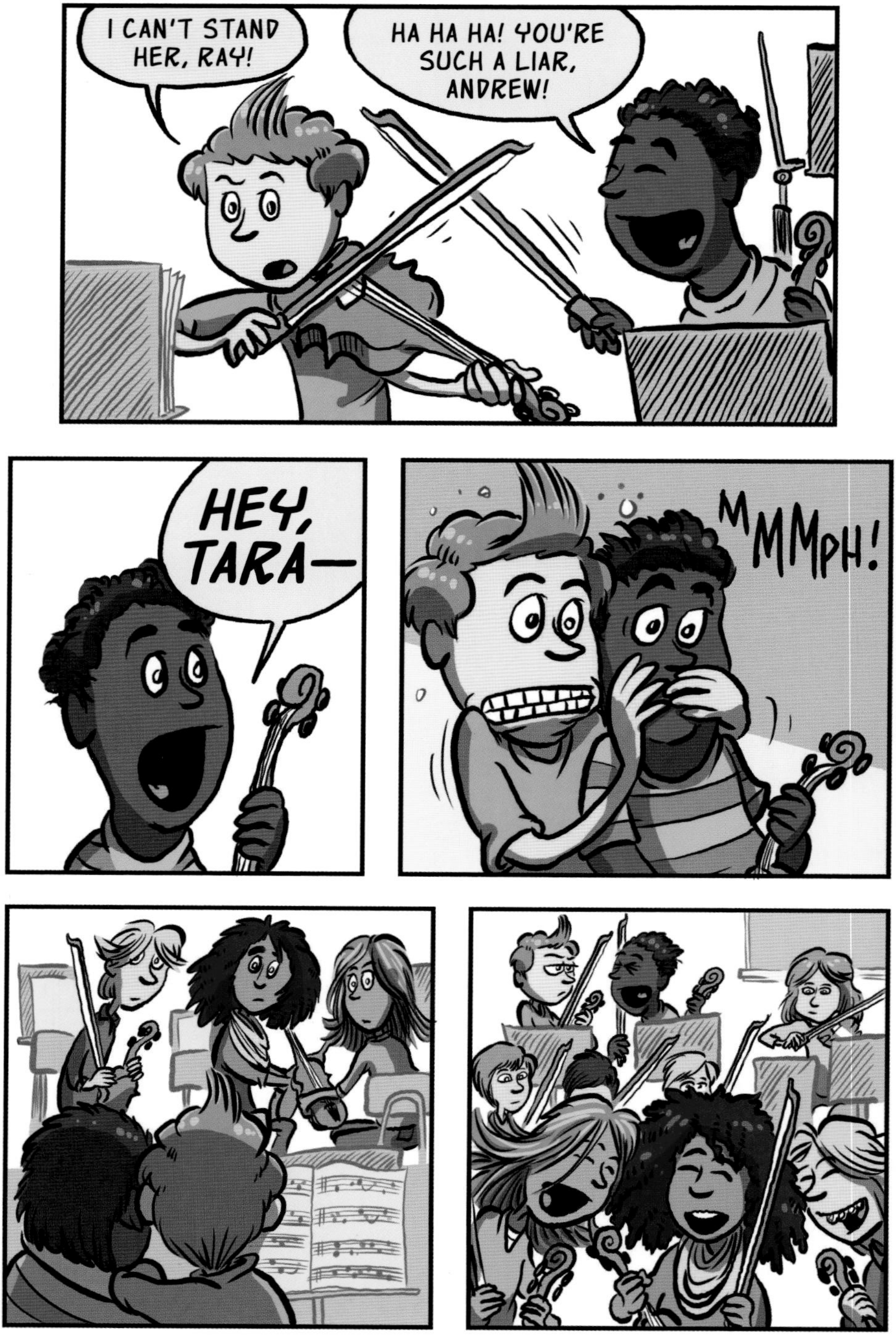
I CAN'T STAND HER, RAY!
HA HA HA! YOU'RE SUCH A LIAR, ANDREW!
HEY, TARA—
MMMPH!

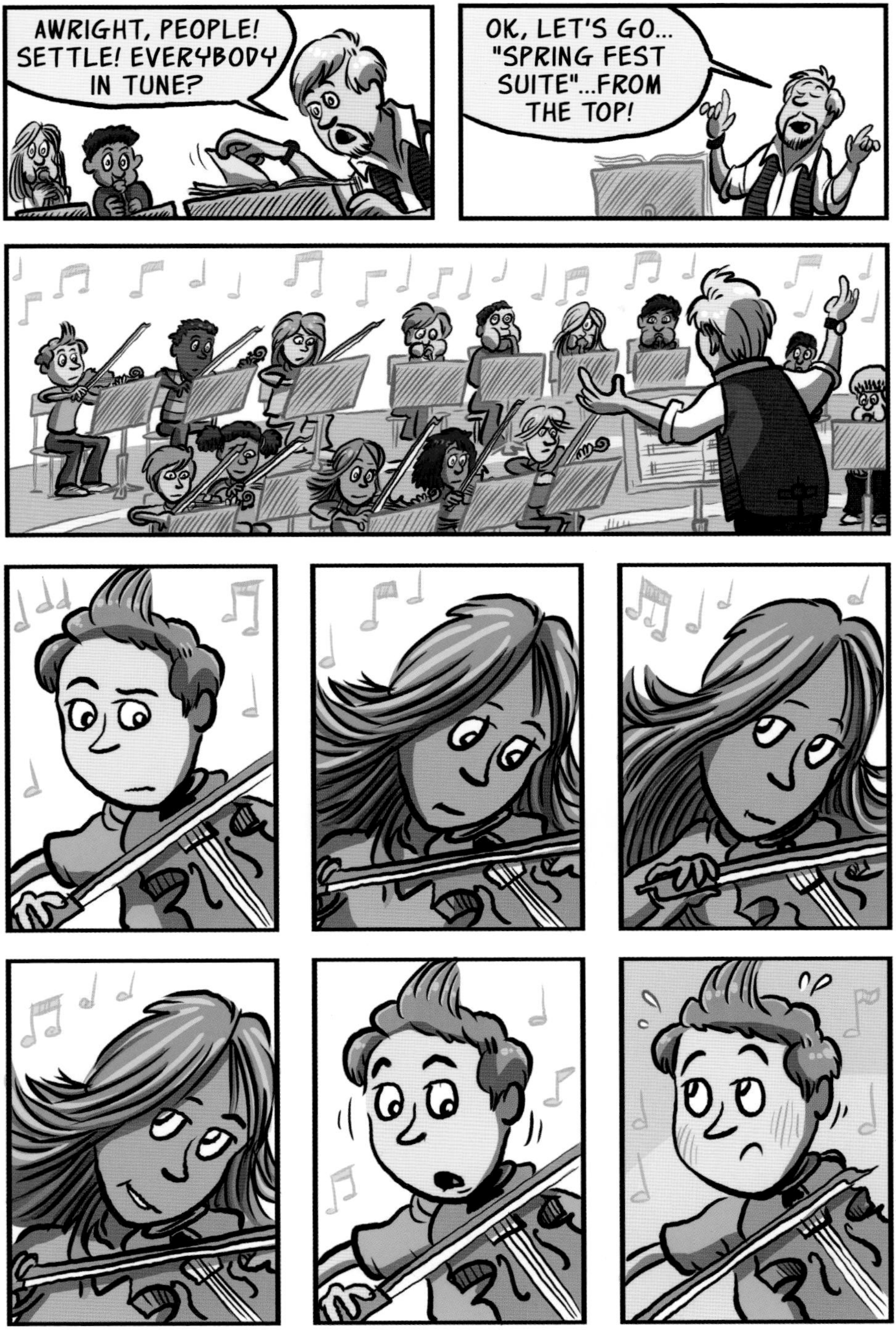
AWRIGHT, PEOPLE! SETTLE! EVERYBODY IN TUNE?
OK, LET'S GO... "SPRING FEST SUITE"...FROM THE TOP!

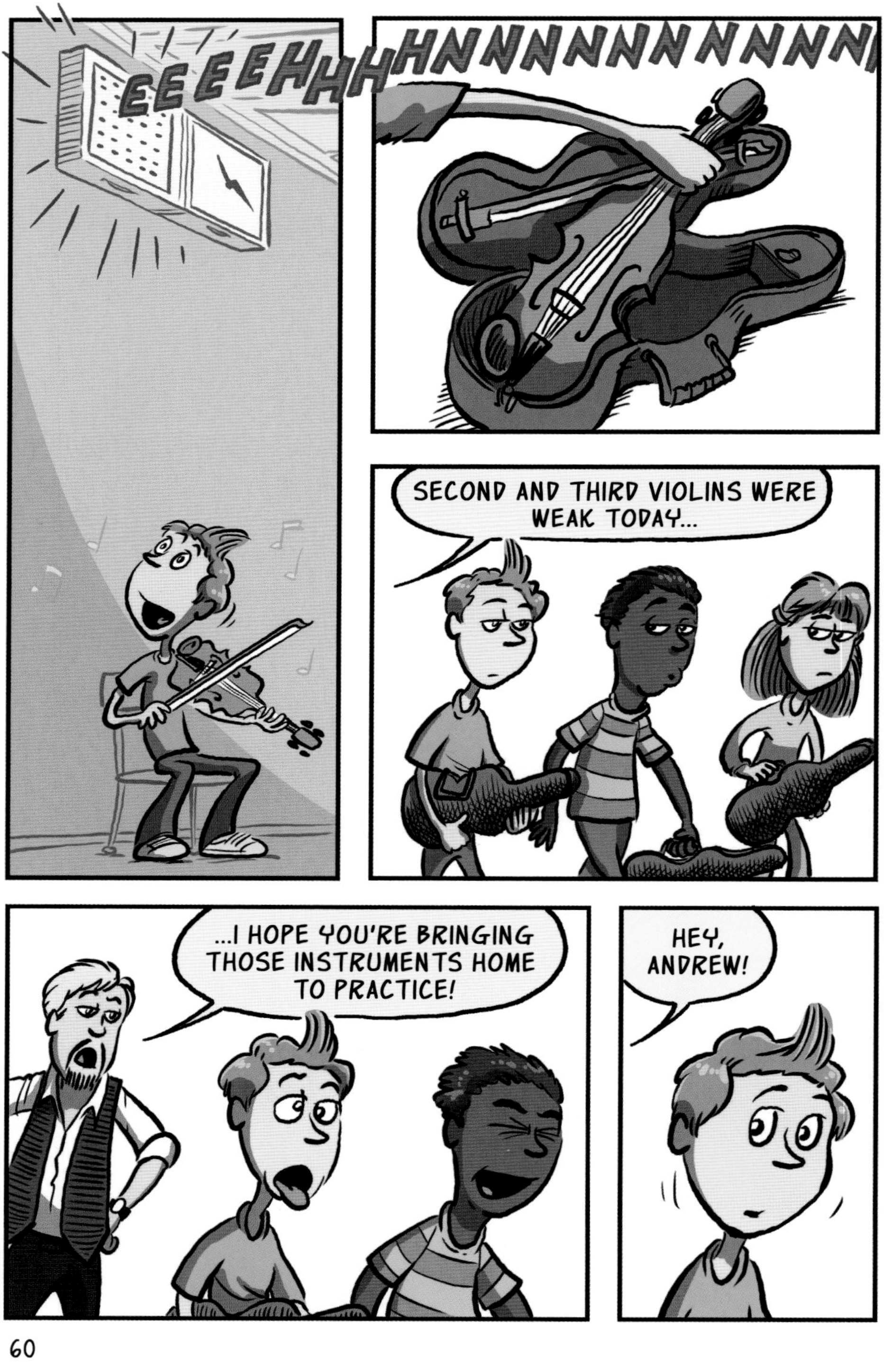
EEEEHHHHNNNNNNNNNNN
SECOND AND THIRD VIOLINS WERE WEAK TODAY...
...I HOPE YOU'RE BRINGING THOSE INSTRUMENTS HOME TO PRACTICE!
HEY, ANDREW!

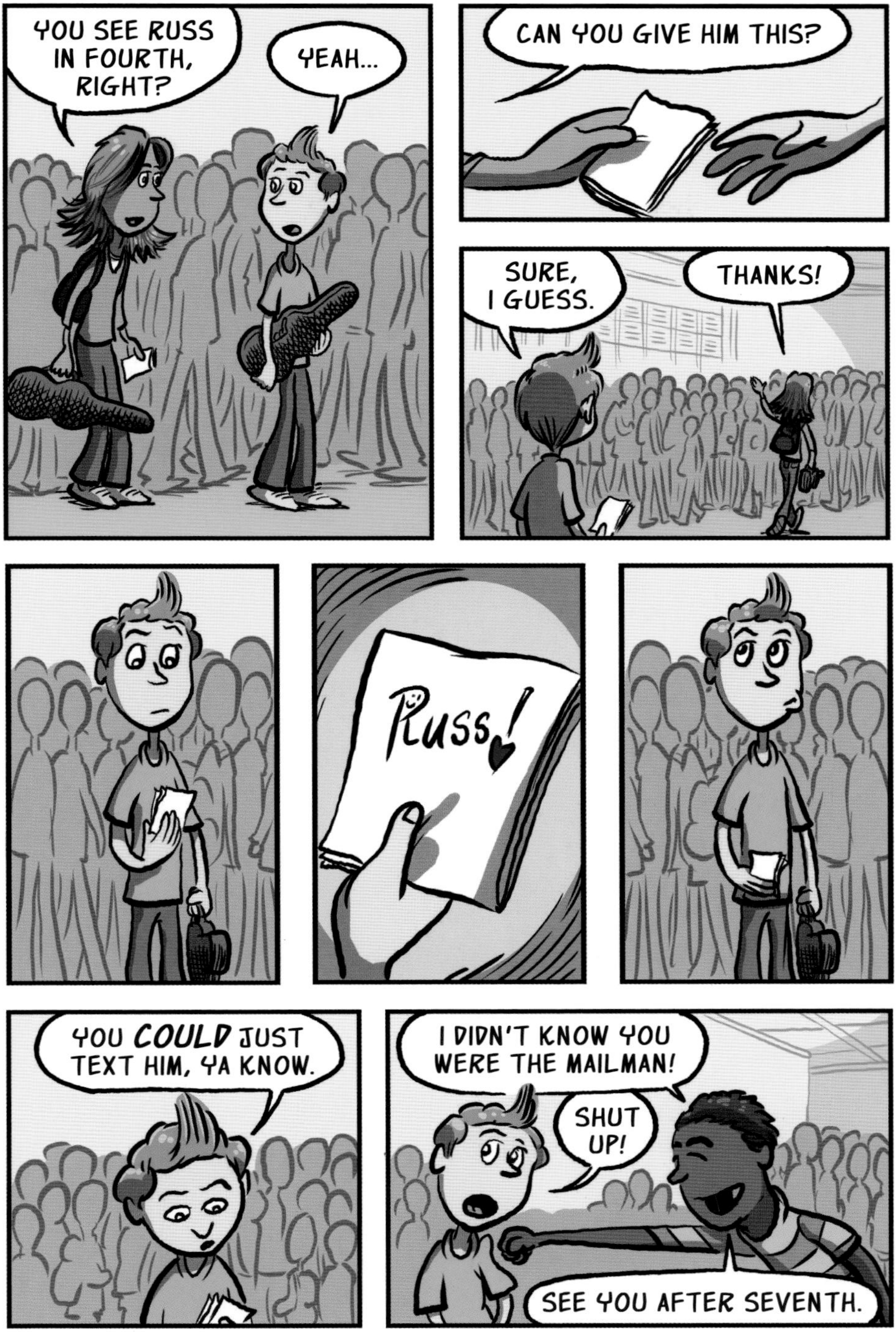
YOU SEE RUSS IN FOURTH, RIGHT?
YEAH...
CAN YOU GIVE HIM THIS?
SURE, I GUESS.
THANKS!
Russ!
YOU COULD JUST TEXT HIM, YA KNOW.
I DIDN'T KNOW YOU WERE THE MAILMAN!
SHUT UP!
SEE YOU AFTER SEVENTH.

CHAPTER 6

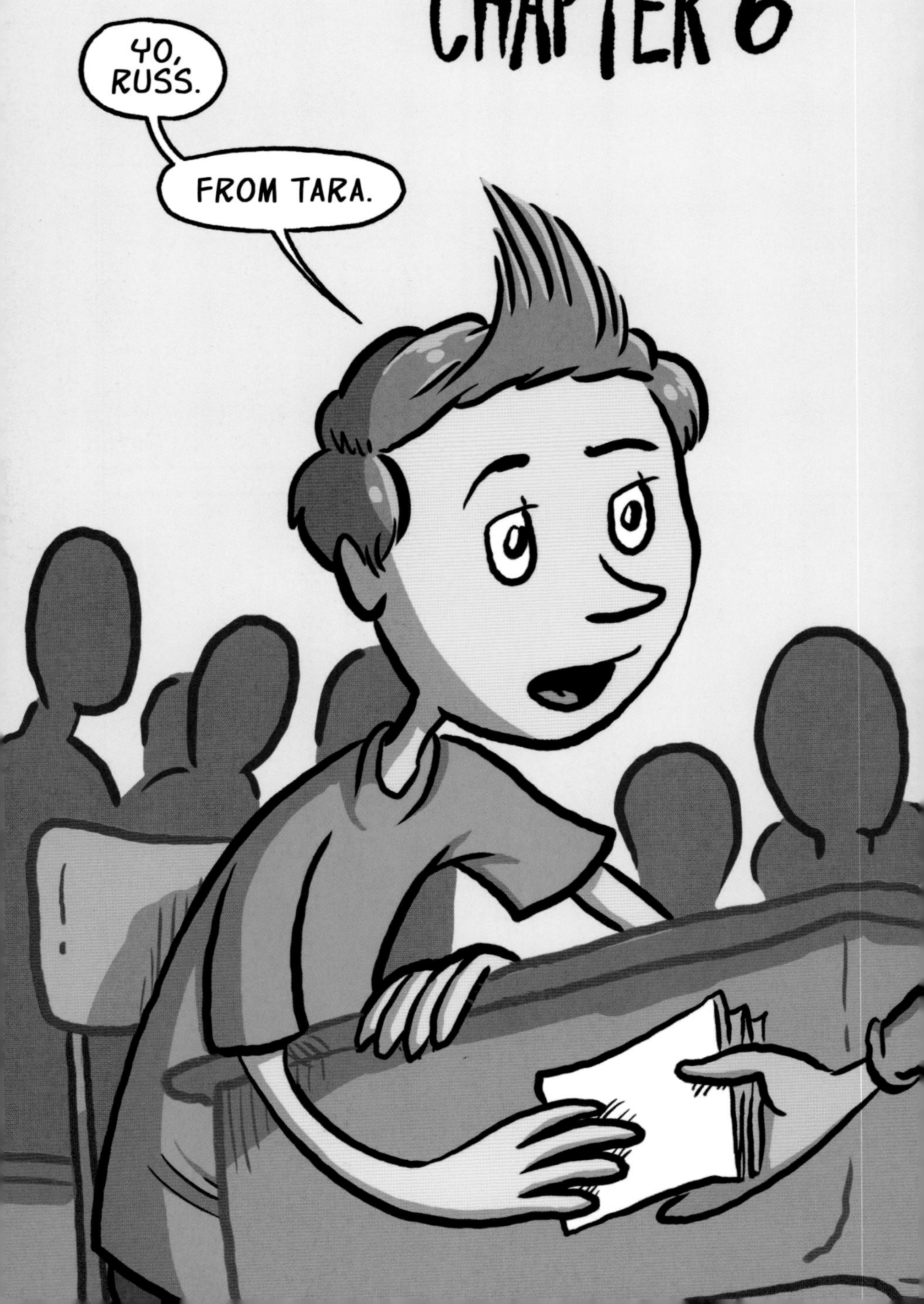
YO, RUSS.
FROM TARA.

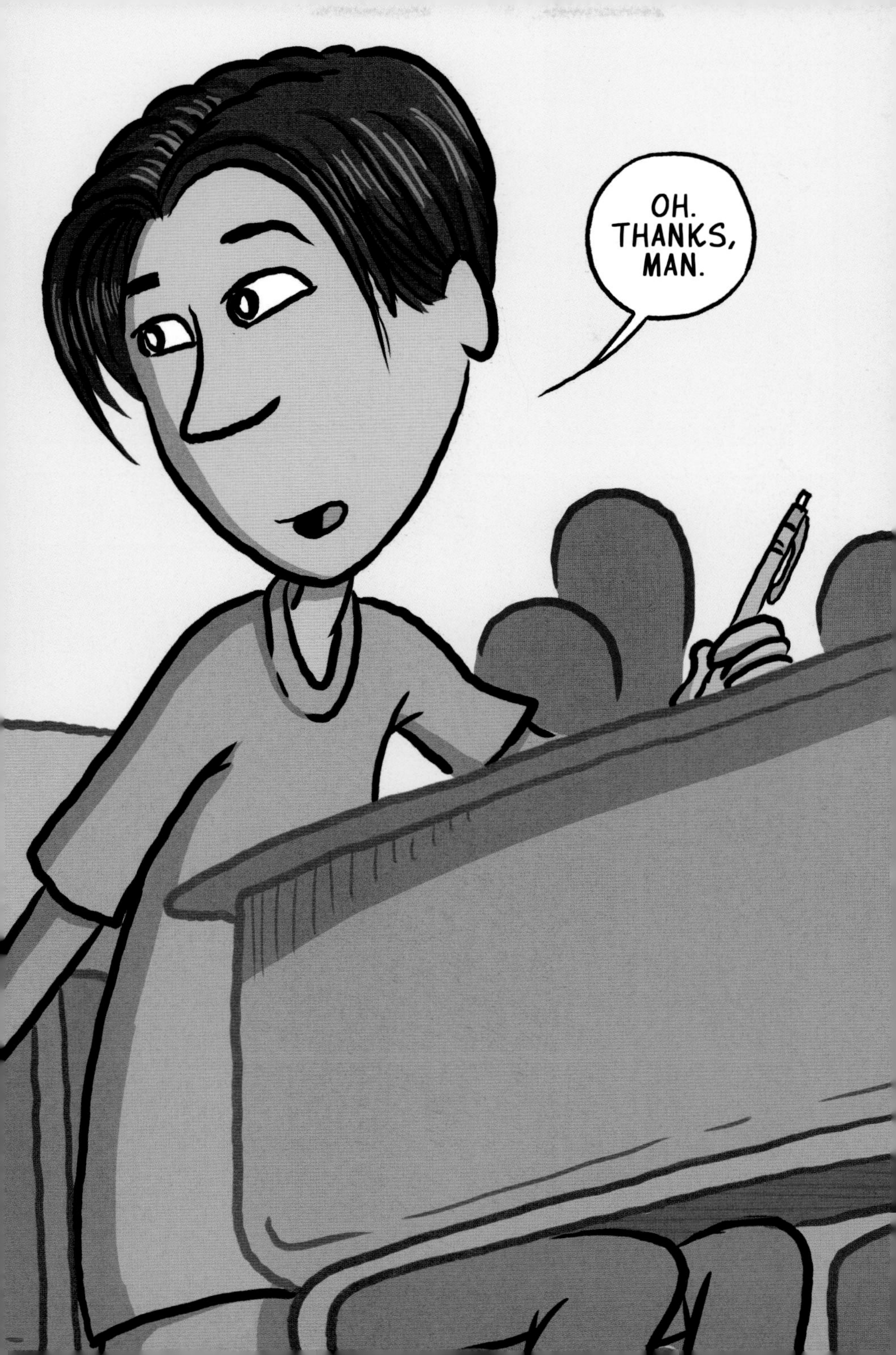
OH. THANKS, MAN.

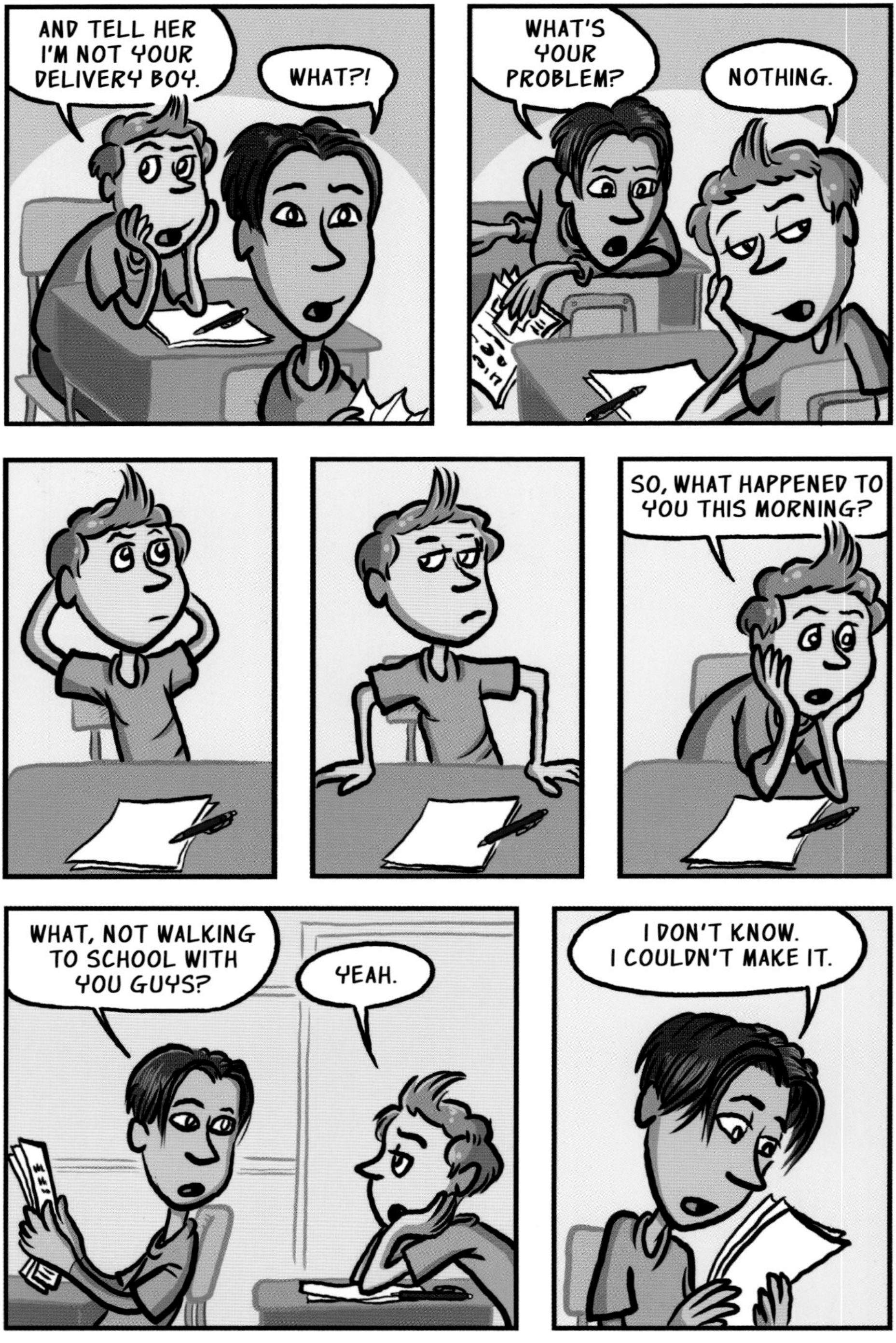
AND TELL HER I'M NOT YOUR DELIVERY BOY.
WHAT?!
WHAT'S YOUR PROBLEM?
NOTHING.
SO, WHAT HAPPENED TO YOU THIS MORNING?
WHAT, NOT WALKING TO SCHOOL WITH YOU GUYS?
YEAH.
I DON'T KNOW. I COULDN'T MAKE IT.

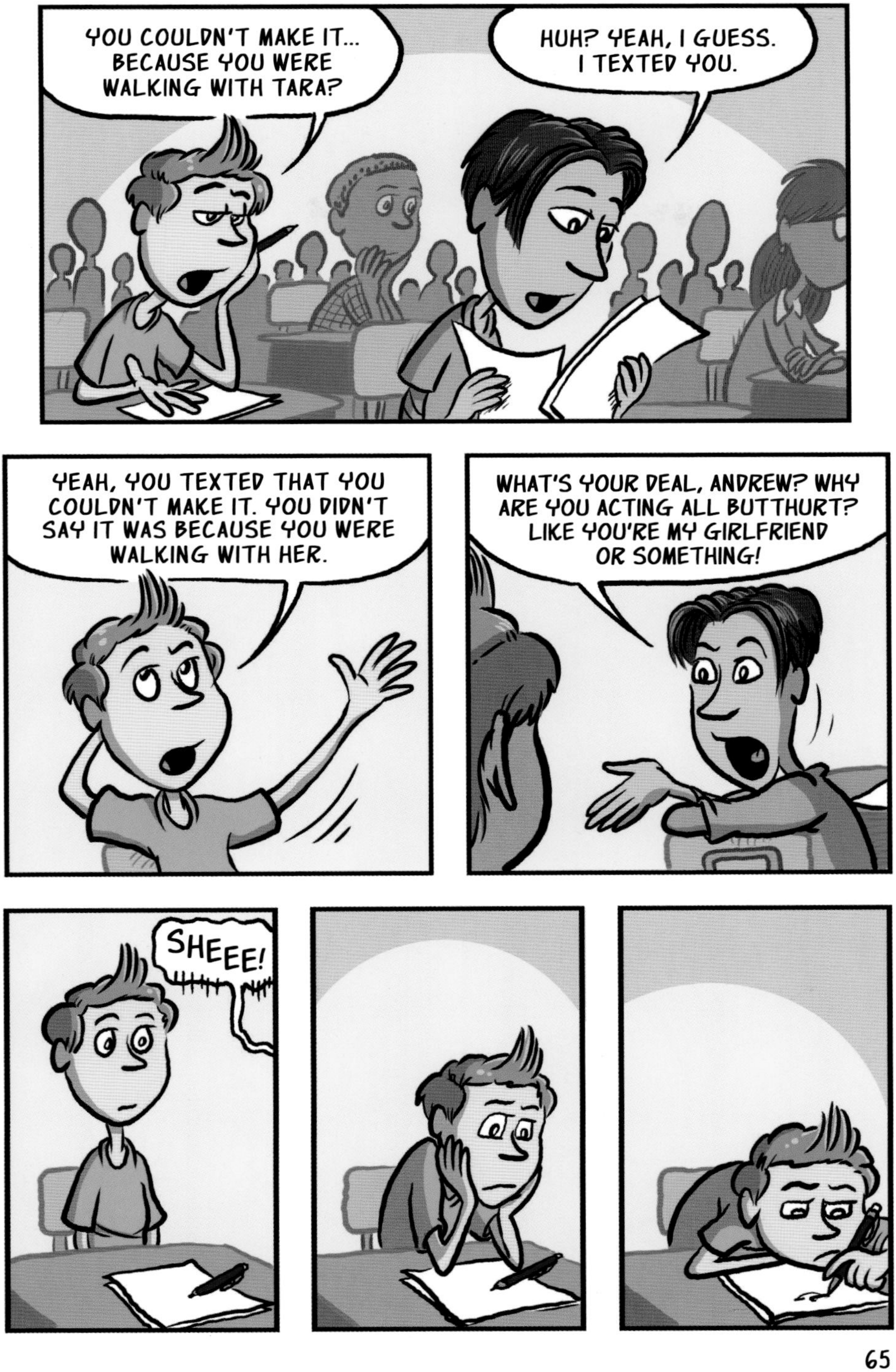
YOU COULDN'T MAKE IT... BECAUSE YOU WERE WALKING WITH TARA?
HUH? YEAH, I GUESS. I TEXTED YOU.
YEAH, YOU TEXTED THAT YOU COULDN'T MAKE IT. YOU DIDN'T SAY IT WAS BECAUSE YOU WERE WALKING WITH HER.
WHAT'S YOUR DEAL, ANDREW? WHY ARE YOU ACTING ALL BUTTHURT? LIKE YOU'RE MY GIRLFRIEND OR SOMETHING!
SHEEE!

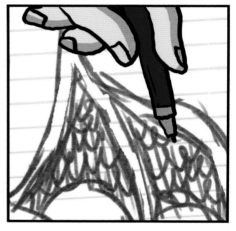

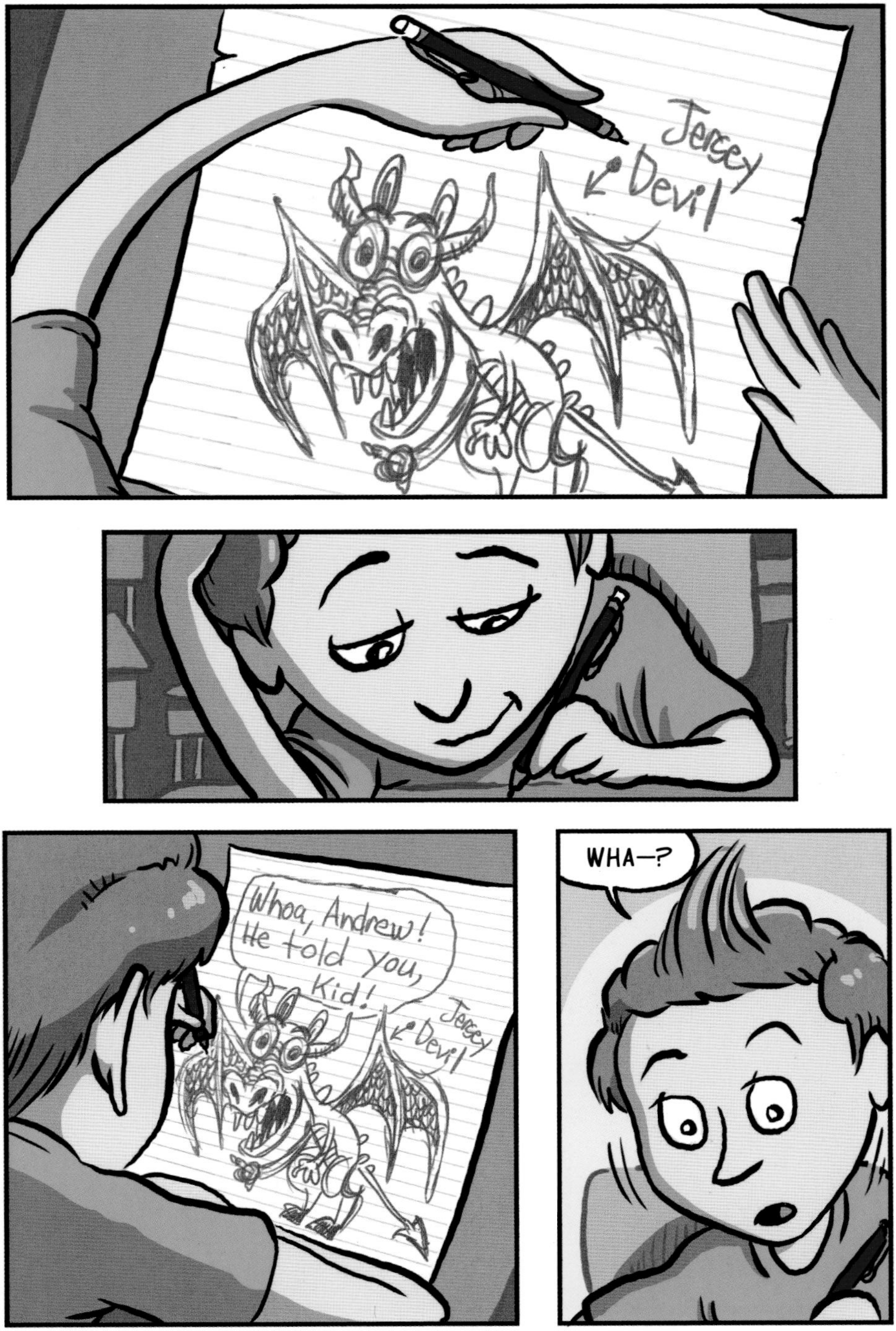
Jersey Devil
Whoa, Andrew! He told you, kid!
Jersey Devil
WHA—?

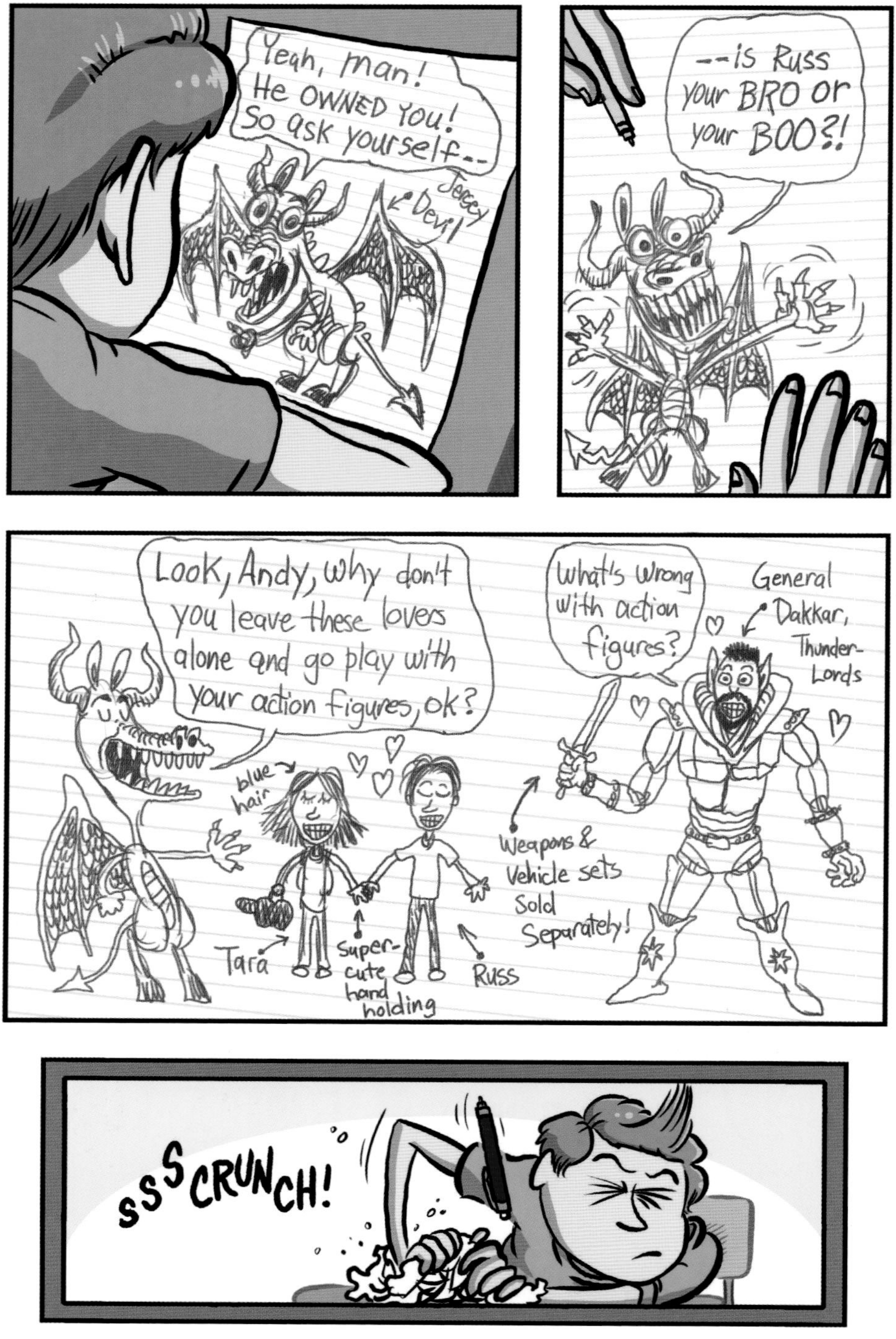
Yeah, man! He OWNED YOU! So ask yourself--
Jersey Devil
--is Russ your BRO or your BOO?!
Look, Andy, why don't you leave these lovers alone and go play with your action figures, ok?
What's wrong with action figures?
General Dakkar, Thunder-Lords
blue hair
Tara
super-cute hand holding
Russ
Weapons & Vehicle sets Sold Separately!
SSSCRUNCH!

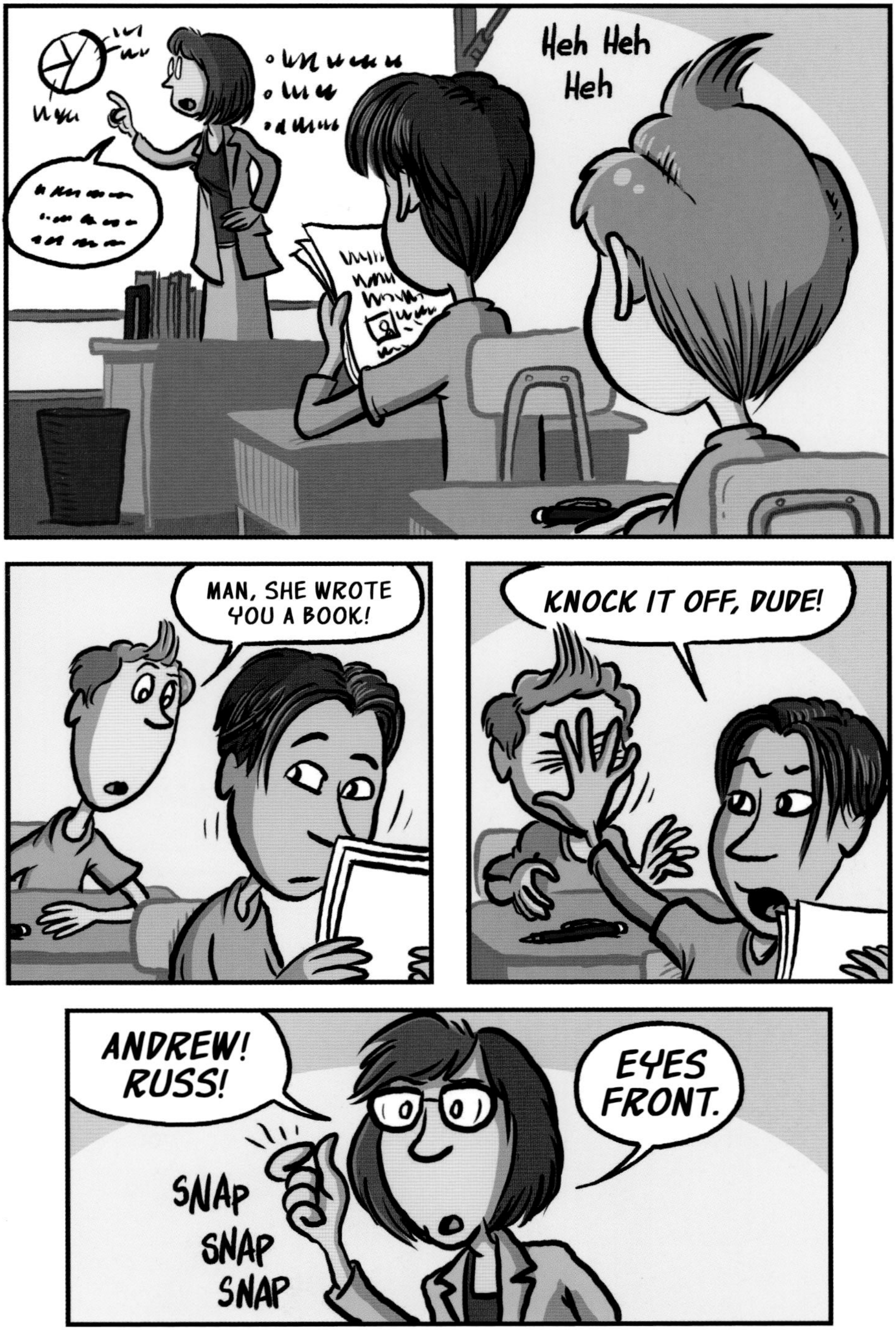
Heh Heh
Heh
MAN, SHE WROTE YOU A BOOK!
KNOCK IT OFF, DUDE!
ANDREW! RUSS!
EYES FRONT.
SNAP
SNAP
SNAP

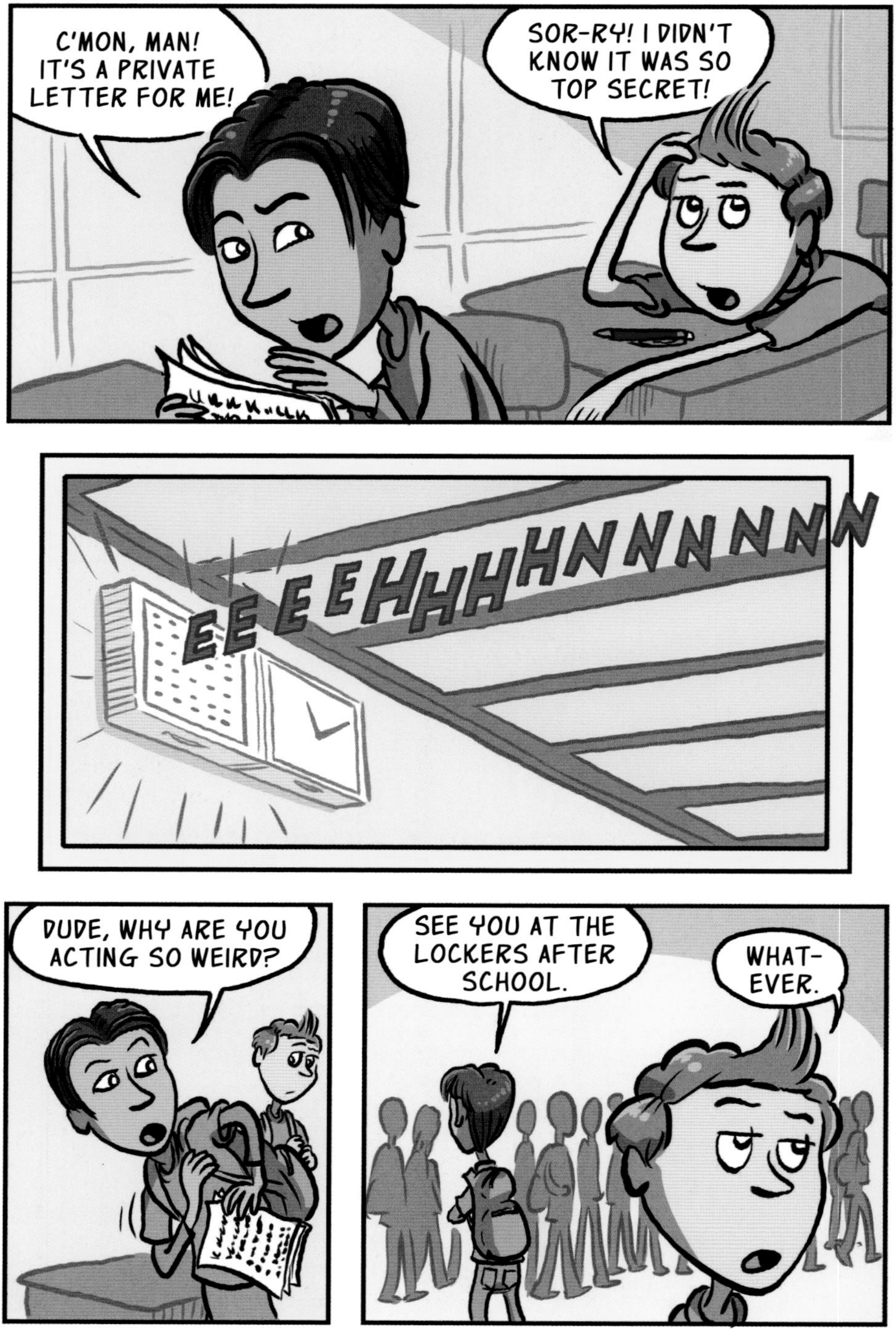
C'MON, MAN! IT'S A PRIVATE LETTER FOR ME!
SOR-RY! I DIDN'T KNOW IT WAS SO TOP SECRET!
EEEEHHHHNNNNNN
DUDE, WHY ARE YOU ACTING SO WEIRD?
SEE YOU AT THE LOCKERS AFTER SCHOOL.
WHAT-EVER.

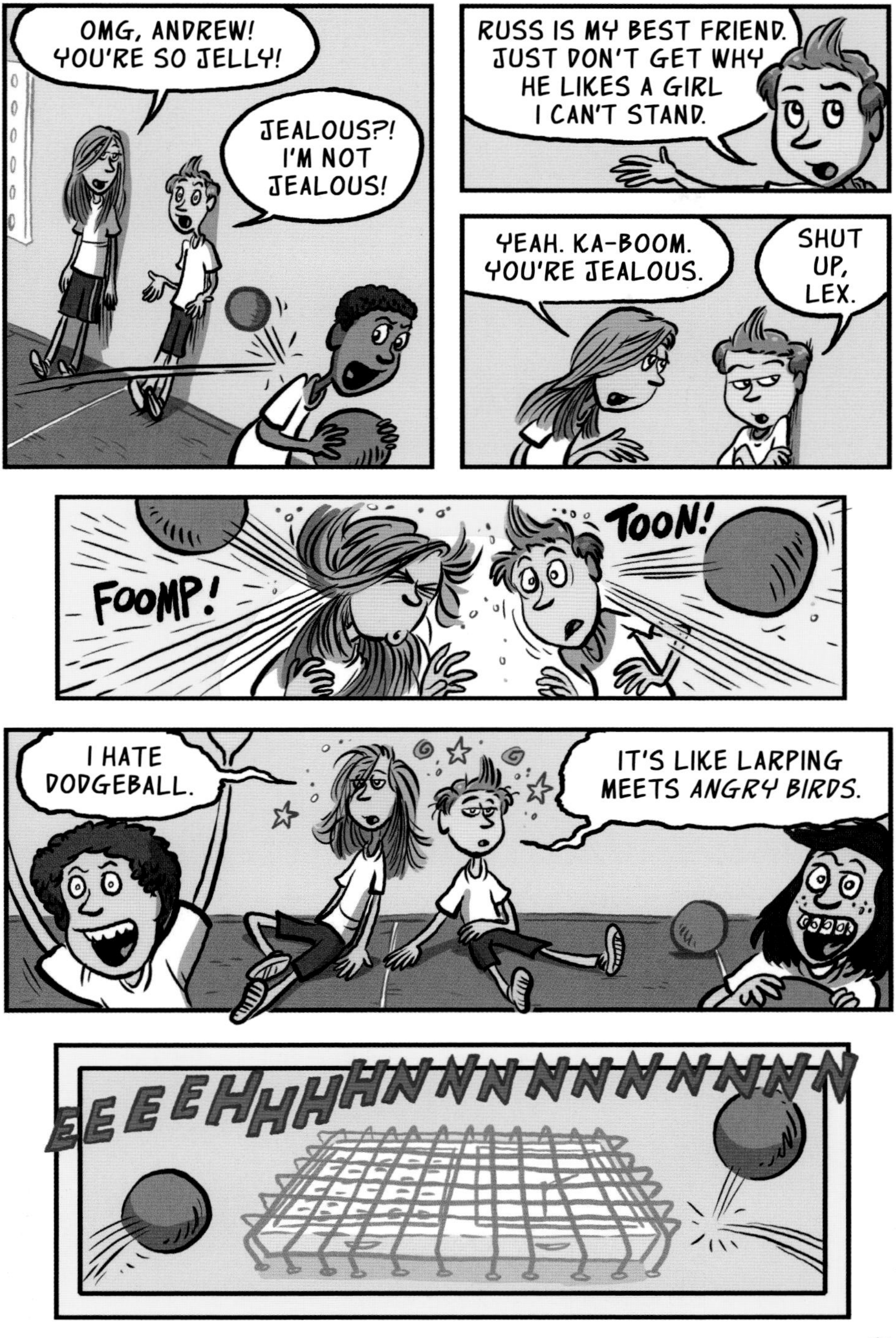
OMG, ANDREW! YOU'RE SO JELLY!
JEALOUS?! I'M NOT JEALOUS!
RUSS IS MY BEST FRIEND. JUST DON'T GET WHY HE LIKES A GIRL I CAN'T STAND.
YEAH. KA-BOOM. YOU'RE JEALOUS.
SHUT UP, LEX.
FOOMP!
TOON!
I HATE DODGEBALL.
IT'S LIKE LARPING MEETS *ANGRY BIRDS*.
EEEEHHHHHNNNNNNNNNNNN

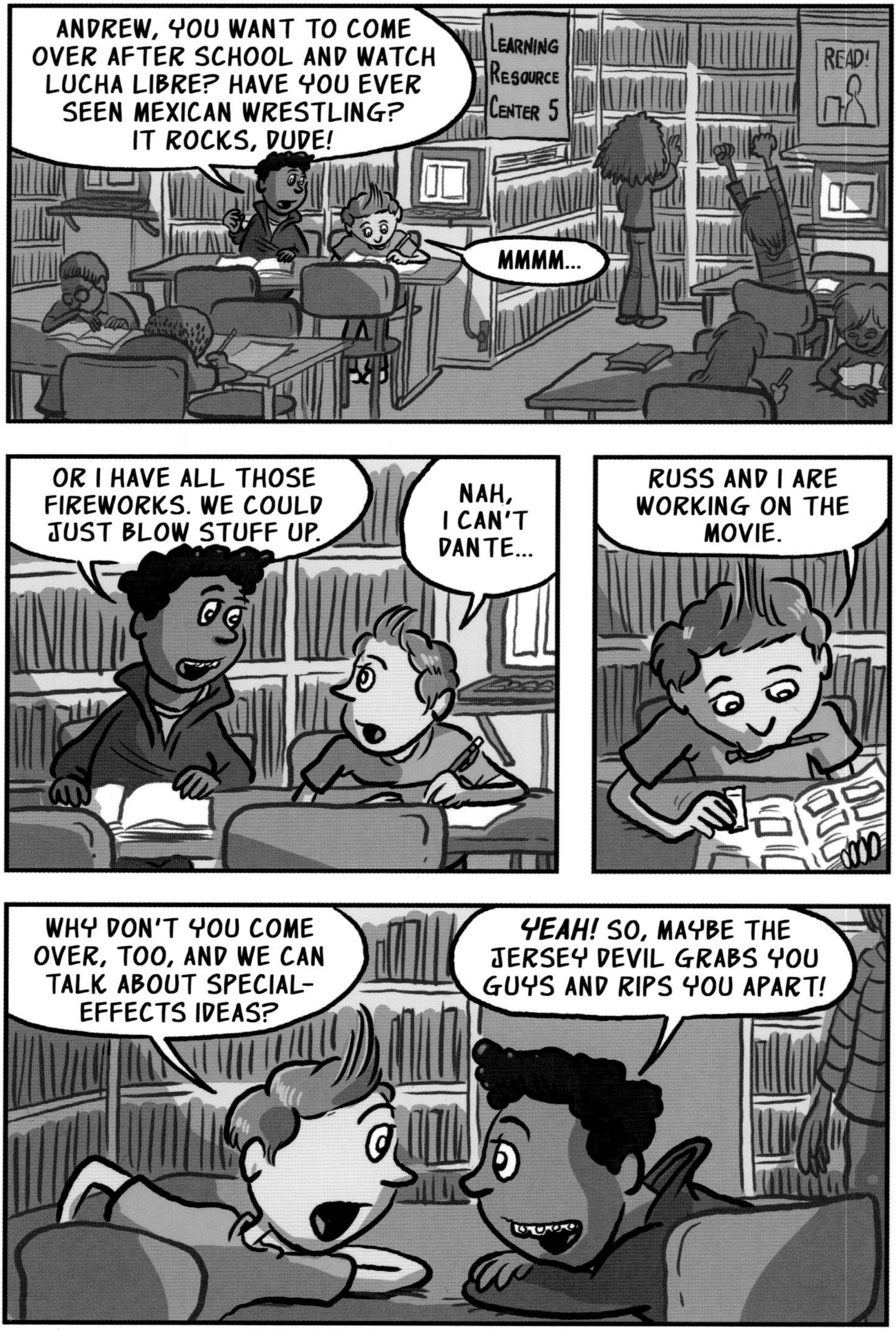

ANDREW, YOU WANT TO COME OVER AFTER SCHOOL AND WATCH LUCHA LIBRE? HAVE YOU EVER SEEN MEXICAN WRESTLING? IT ROCKS, DUDE!
LEARNING RESOURCE CENTER 5
READ!
MMMM...
OR I HAVE ALL THOSE FIREWORKS. WE COULD JUST BLOW STUFF UP.
NAH, I CAN'T DANTE...
RUSS AND I ARE WORKING ON THE MOVIE.
WHY DON'T YOU COME OVER, TOO, AND WE CAN TALK ABOUT SPECIAL-EFFECTS IDEAS?
YEAH! SO, MAYBE THE JERSEY DEVIL GRABS YOU GUYS AND RIPS YOU APART!

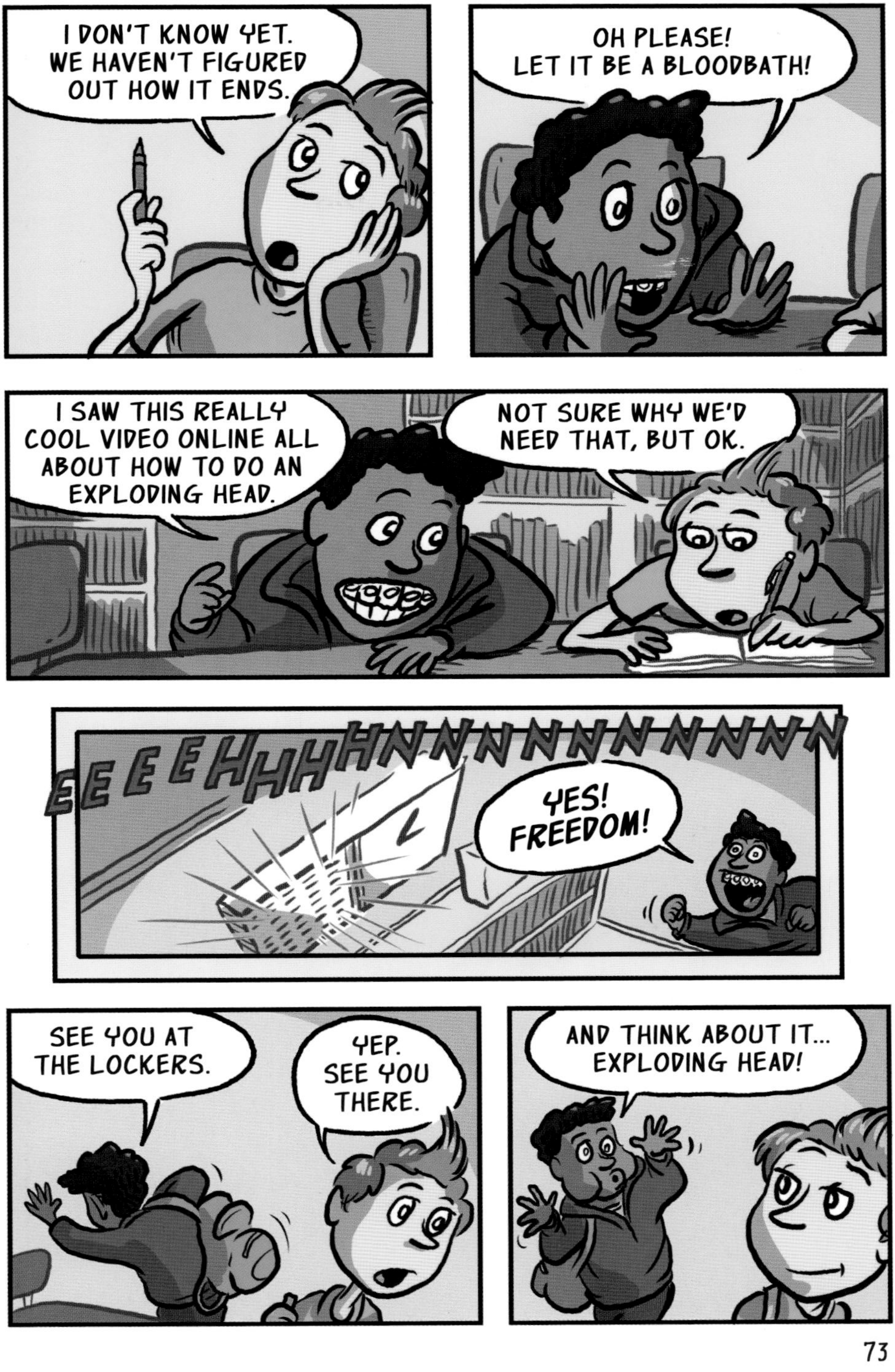
I DON'T KNOW YET. WE HAVEN'T FIGURED OUT HOW IT ENDS.
OH PLEASE! LET IT BE A BLOODBATH!
I SAW THIS REALLY COOL VIDEO ONLINE ALL ABOUT HOW TO DO AN EXPLODING HEAD.
NOT SURE WHY WE'D NEED THAT, BUT OK.
EEEEHHHHHNNNNNNNNNNN
YES! FREEDOM!
SEE YOU AT THE LOCKERS.
YEP. SEE YOU THERE.
AND THINK ABOUT IT... EXPLODING HEAD!

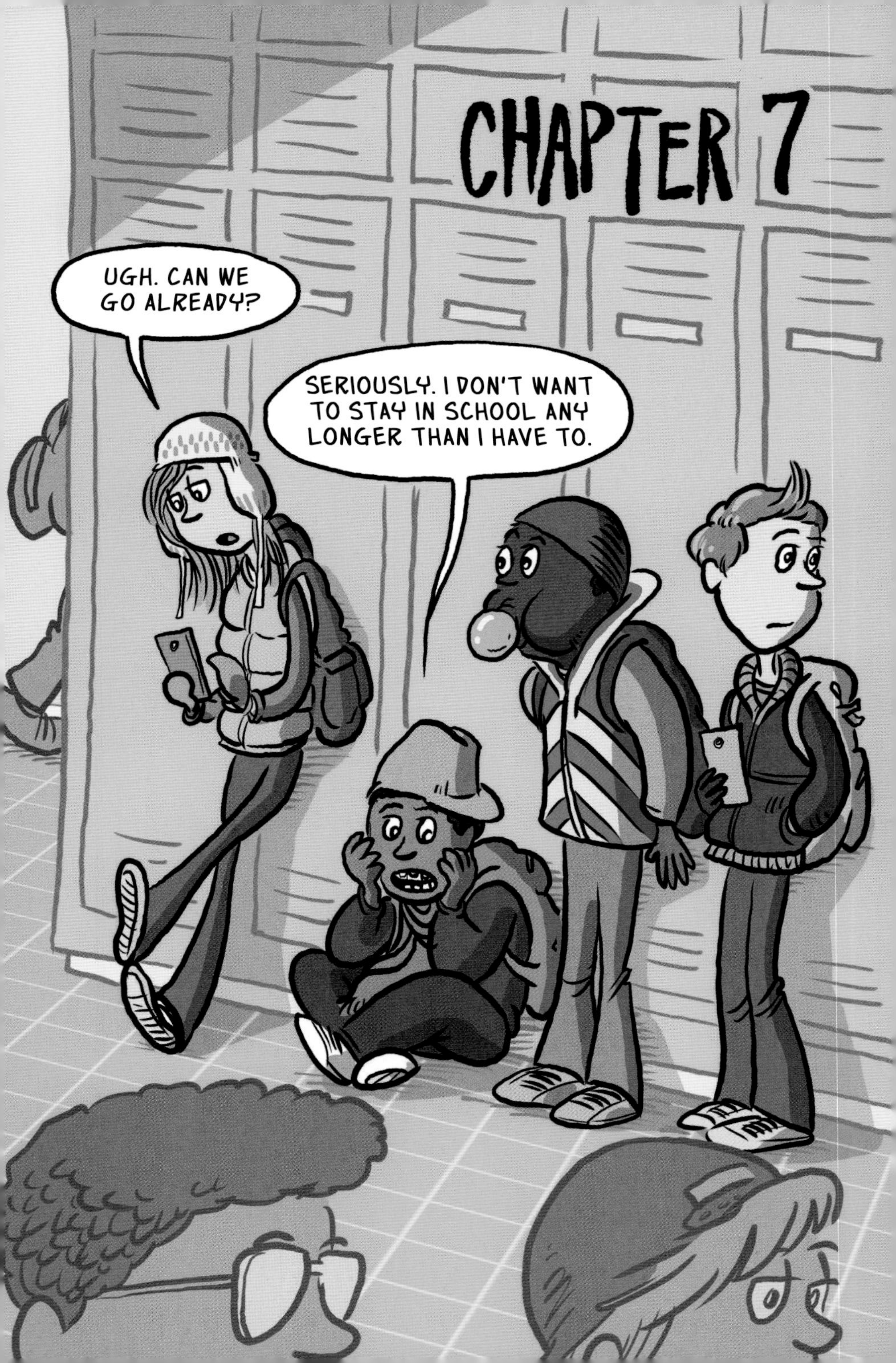
CHAPTER 7
UGH. CAN WE GO ALREADY?
SERIOUSLY. I DON'T WANT TO STAY IN SCHOOL ANY LONGER THAN I HAVE TO.

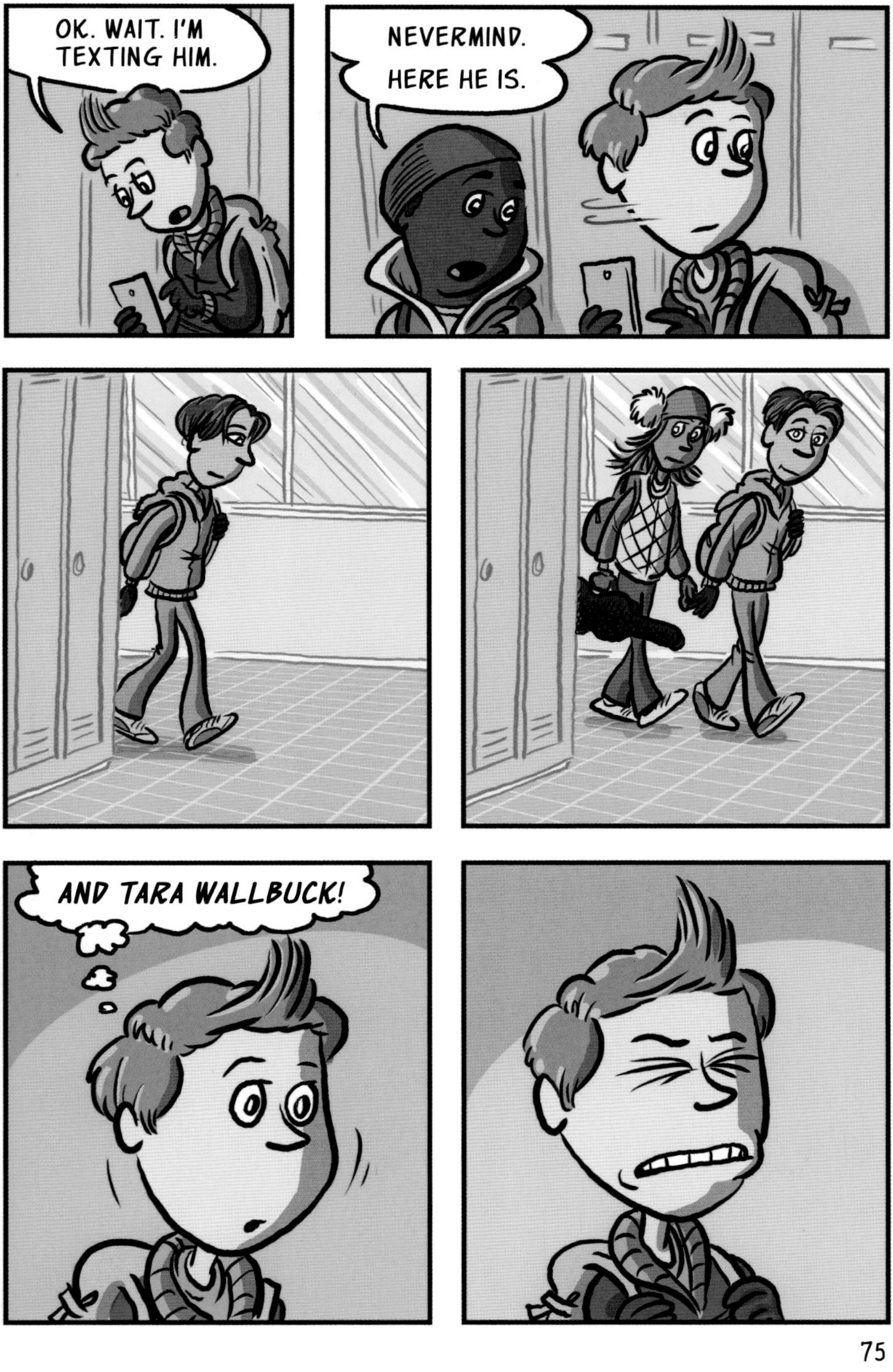
OK. WAIT. I'M TEXTING HIM.
NEVERMIND. HERE HE IS.
AND TARA WALLBUCK!

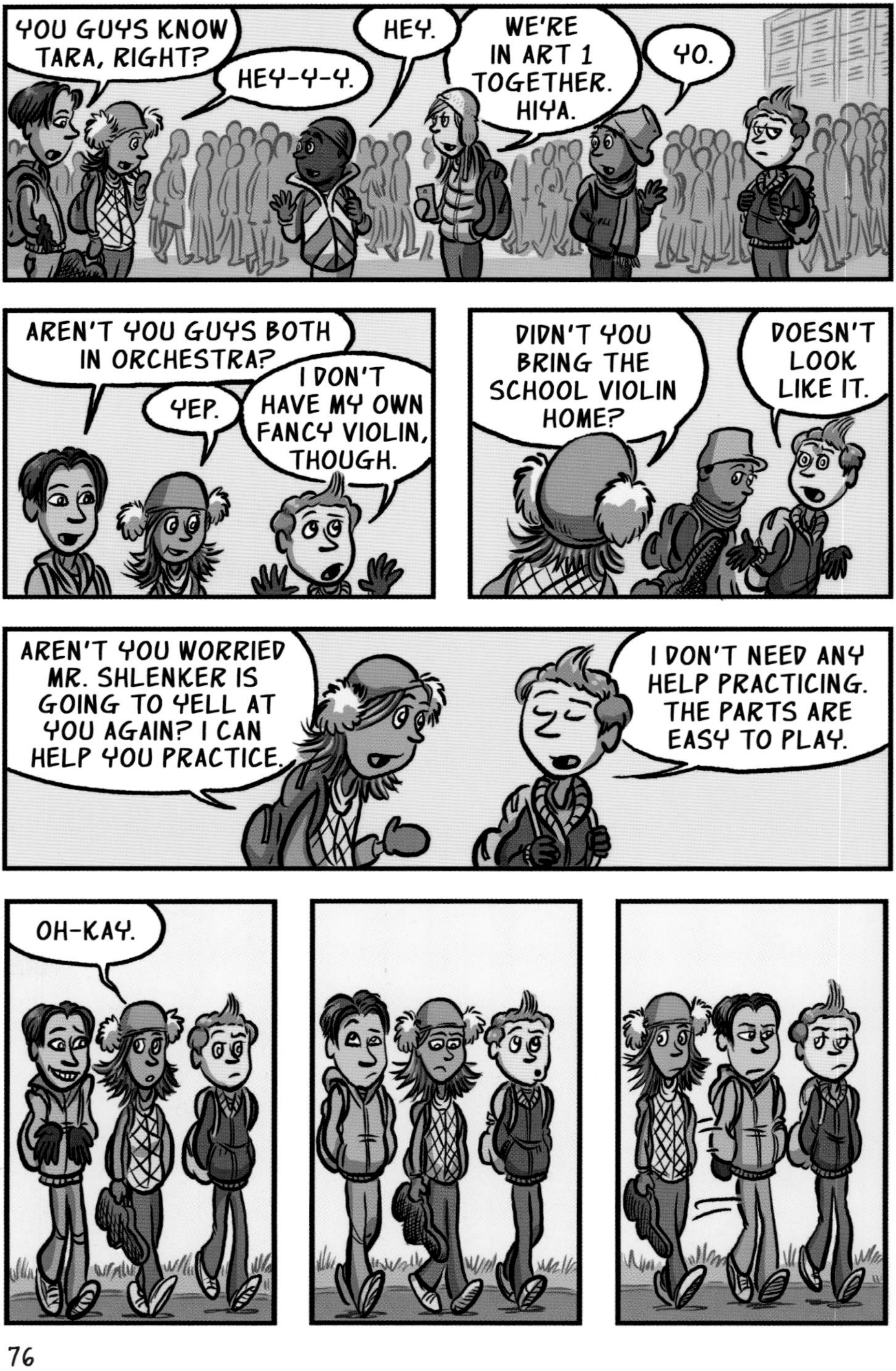
YOU GUYS KNOW TARA, RIGHT?
HEY-Y-Y.
HEY.
WE'RE IN ART 1 TOGETHER. HIYA.
YO.
AREN'T YOU GUYS BOTH IN ORCHESTRA?
YEP.
I DON'T HAVE MY OWN FANCY VIOLIN, THOUGH.
DIDN'T YOU BRING THE SCHOOL VIOLIN HOME?
DOESN'T LOOK LIKE IT.
AREN'T YOU WORRIED MR. SHLENKER IS GOING TO YELL AT YOU AGAIN? I CAN HELP YOU PRACTICE.
I DON'T NEED ANY HELP PRACTICING. THE PARTS ARE EASY TO PLAY.
OH-KAY.

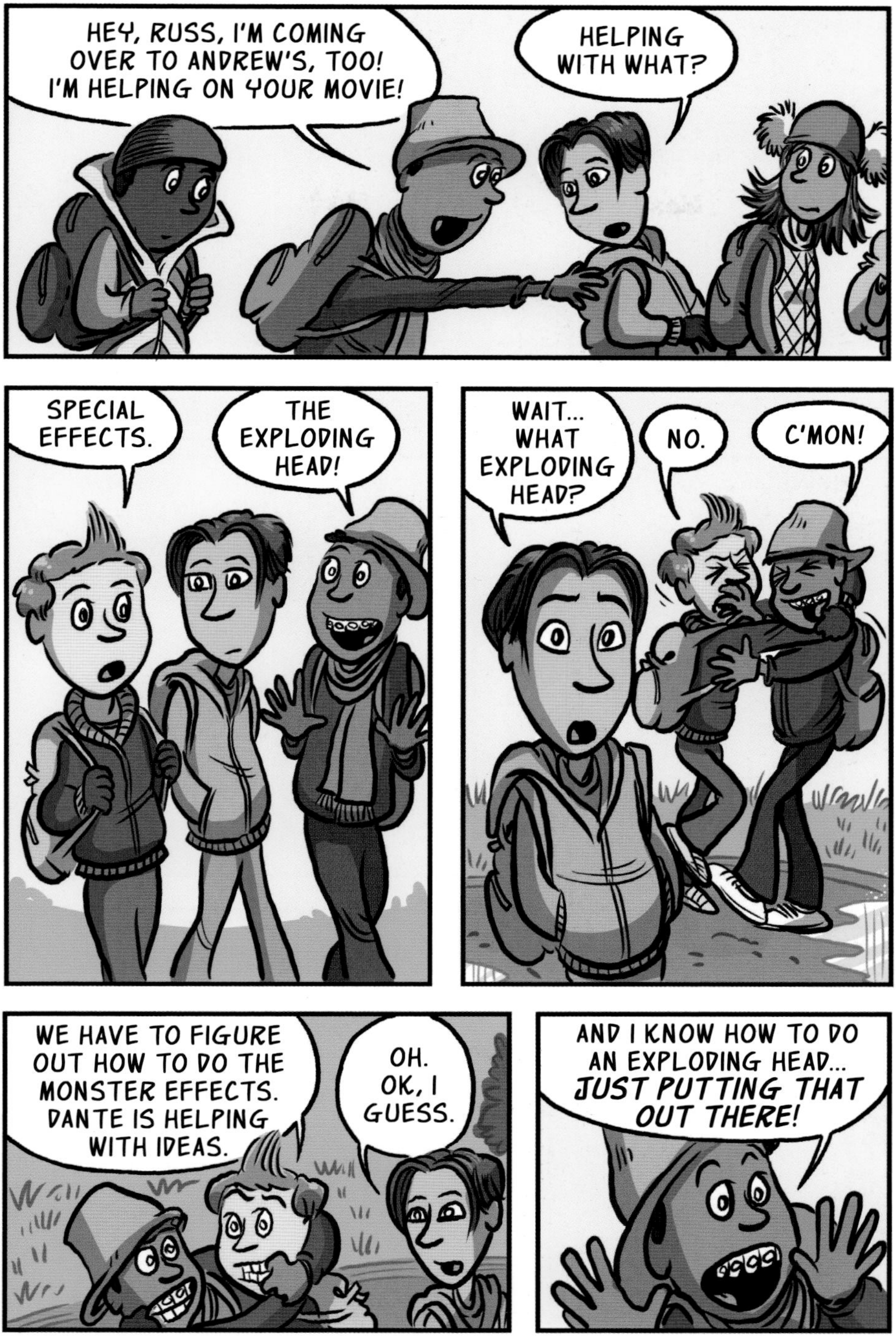

HEY, RUSS, I'M COMING OVER TO ANDREW'S, TOO! I'M HELPING ON YOUR MOVIE!
HELPING WITH WHAT?
SPECIAL EFFECTS.
THE EXPLODING HEAD!
WAIT... WHAT EXPLODING HEAD?
NO.
C'MON!
WE HAVE TO FIGURE OUT HOW TO DO THE MONSTER EFFECTS. DANTE IS HELPING WITH IDEAS.
OH. OK, I GUESS.
AND I KNOW HOW TO DO AN EXPLODING HEAD... *JUST PUTTING THAT OUT THERE!*

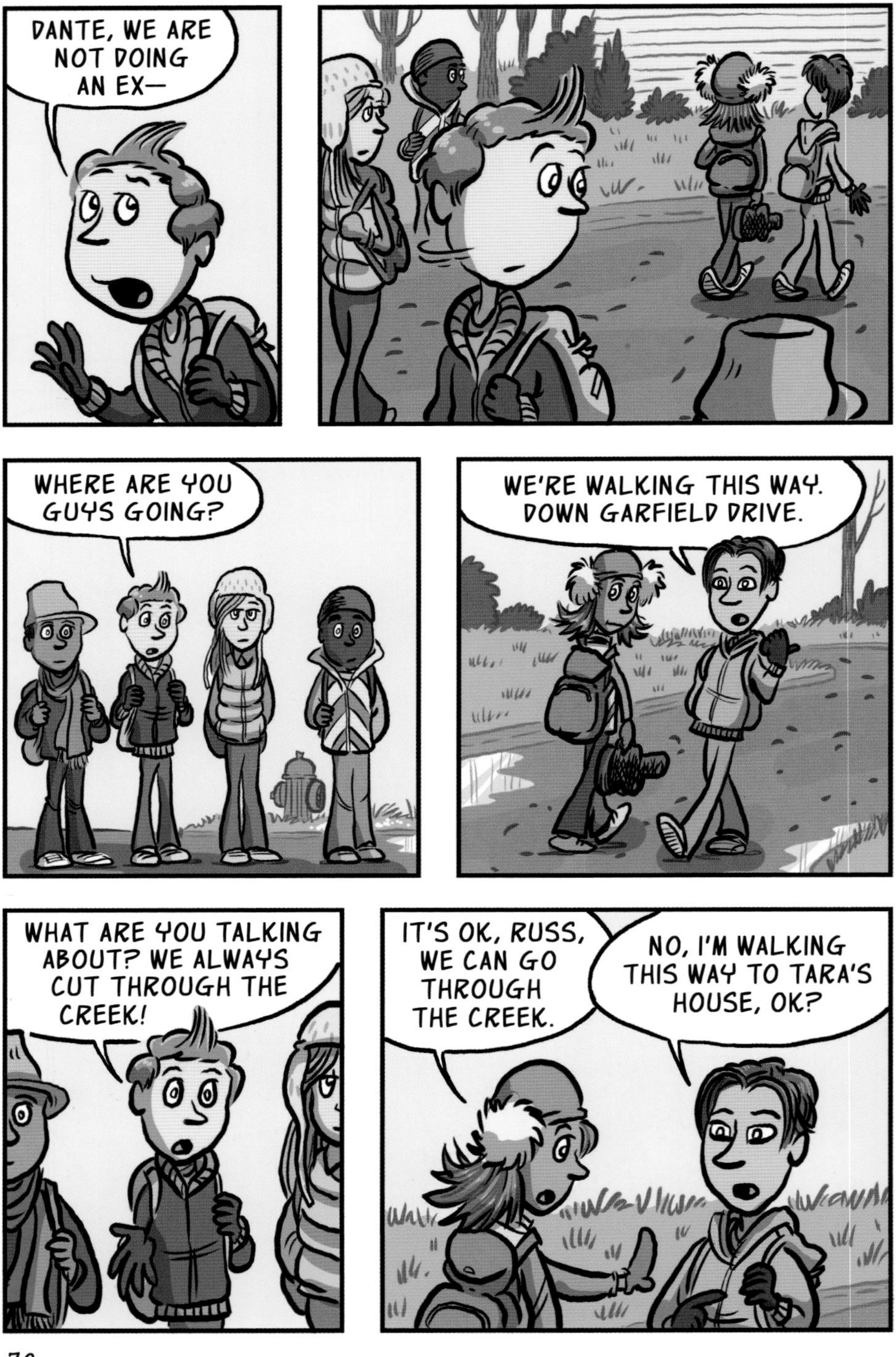
DANTE, WE ARE NOT DOING AN EX—
WHERE ARE YOU GUYS GOING?
WE'RE WALKING THIS WAY. DOWN GARFIELD DRIVE.
WHAT ARE YOU TALKING ABOUT? WE ALWAYS CUT THROUGH THE CREEK!
IT'S OK, RUSS, WE CAN GO THROUGH THE CREEK.
NO, I'M WALKING THIS WAY TO TARA'S HOUSE, OK?

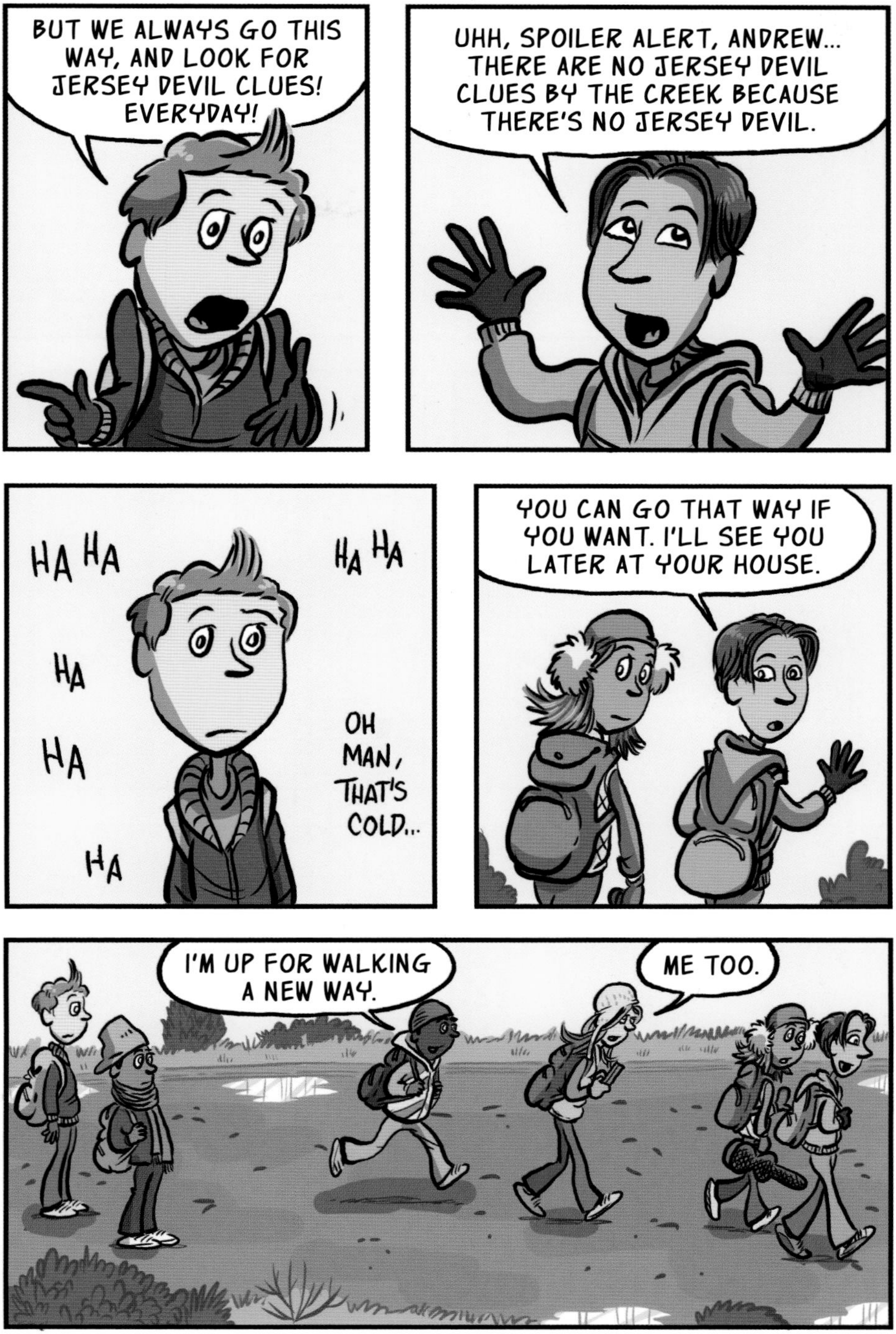
BUT WE ALWAYS GO THIS WAY, AND LOOK FOR JERSEY DEVIL CLUES! EVERYDAY!
UHH, SPOILER ALERT, ANDREW... THERE ARE NO JERSEY DEVIL CLUES BY THE CREEK BECAUSE THERE'S NO JERSEY DEVIL.
HA HA
HA HA
HA
HA
HA
OH MAN, THAT'S COLD...
YOU CAN GO THAT WAY IF YOU WANT. I'LL SEE YOU LATER AT YOUR HOUSE.
I'M UP FOR WALKING A NEW WAY.
ME TOO.

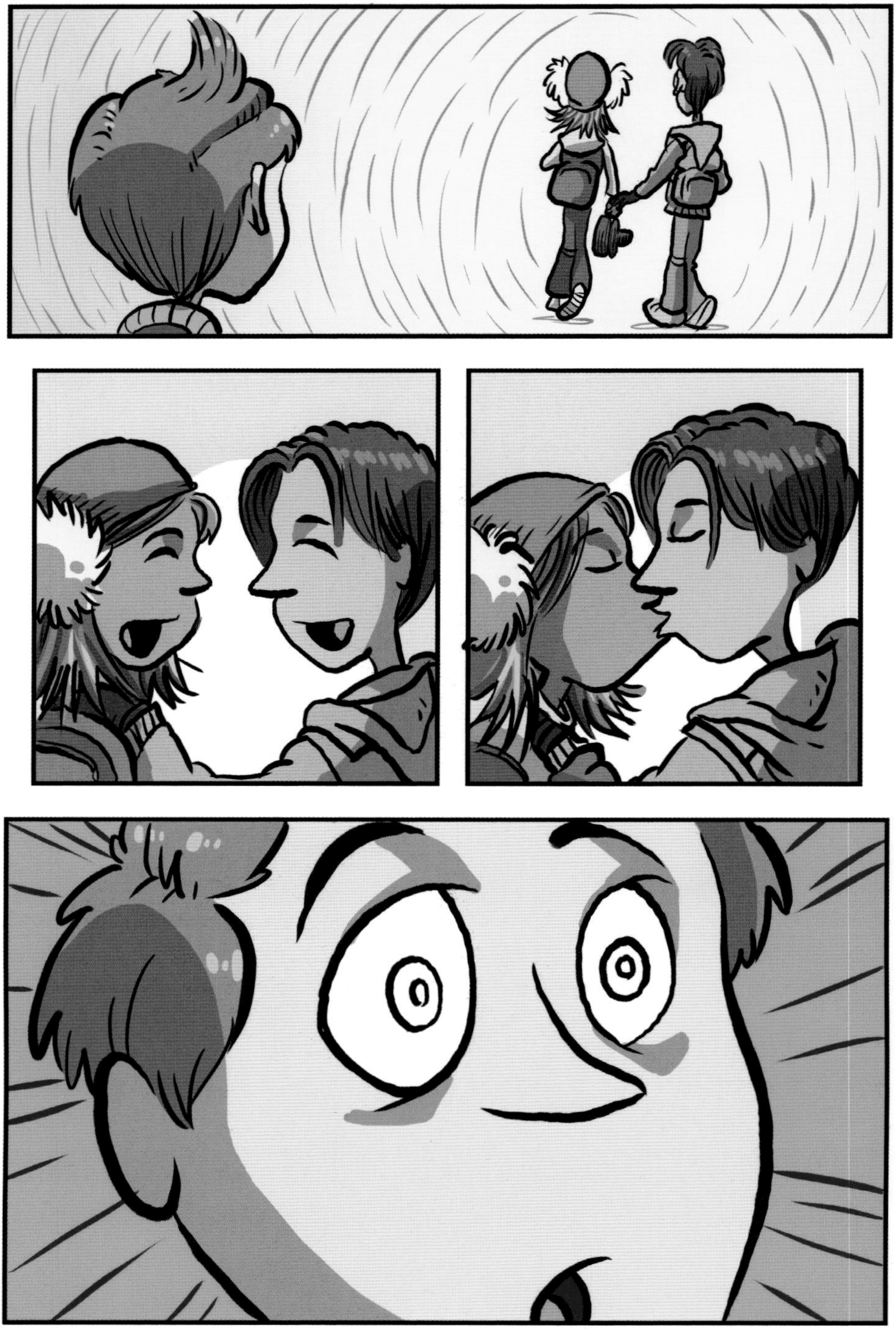

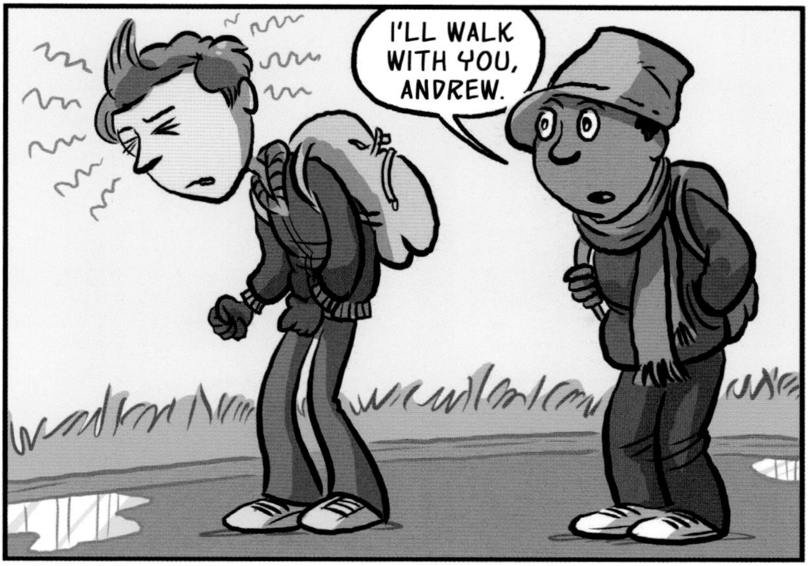
I'LL WALK WITH YOU, ANDREW.

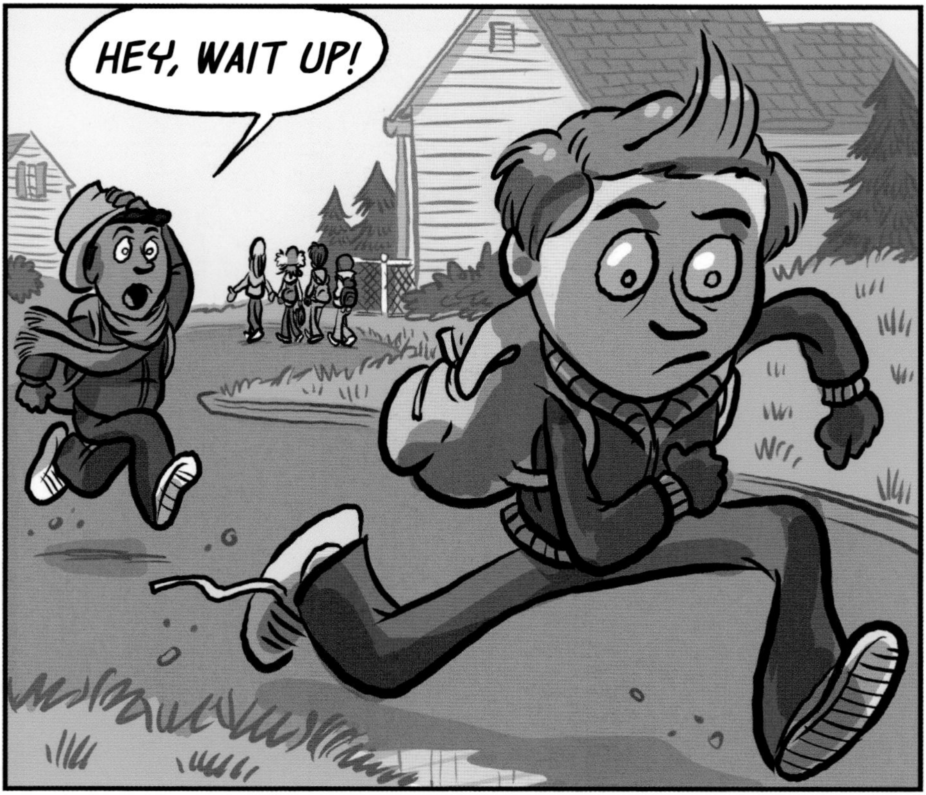
HEY, WAIT UP!

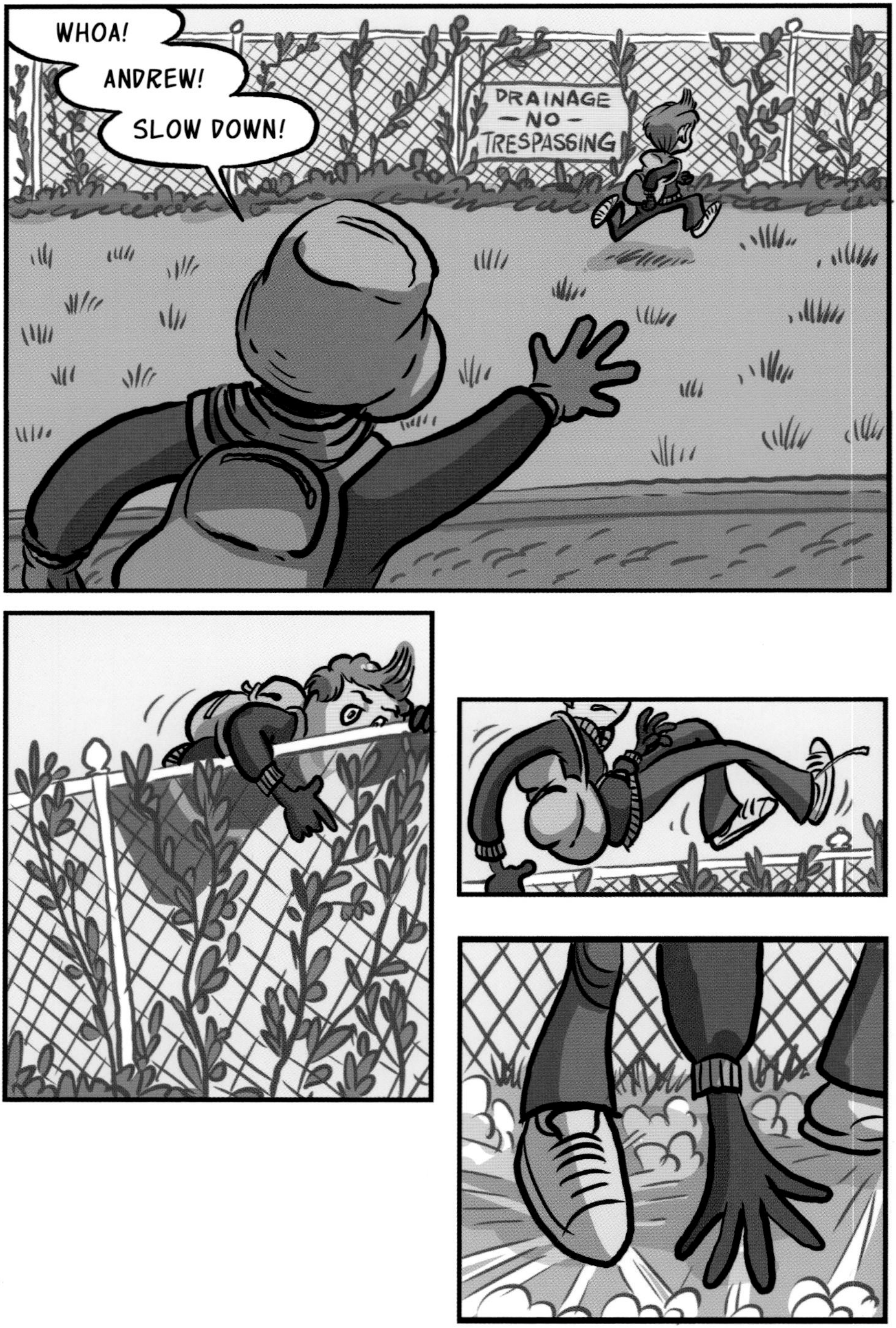
WHOA!
ANDREW!
SLOW DOWN!
DRAINAGE -NO- TRESPASSING

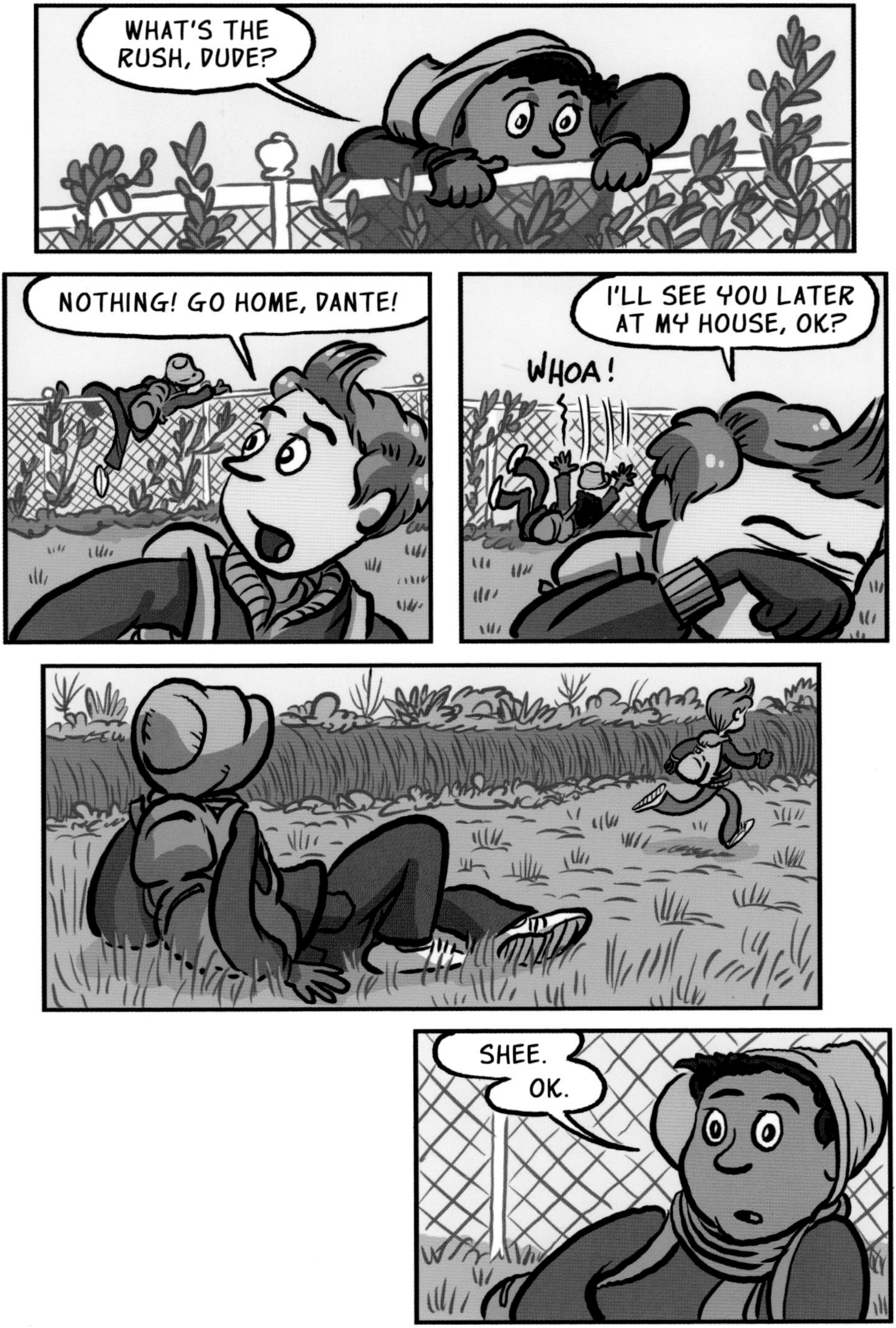
WHAT'S THE RUSH, DUDE?
NOTHING! GO HOME, DANTE!
I'LL SEE YOU LATER AT MY HOUSE, OK?
WHOA!
SHEE. OK.

CHAPTER 8

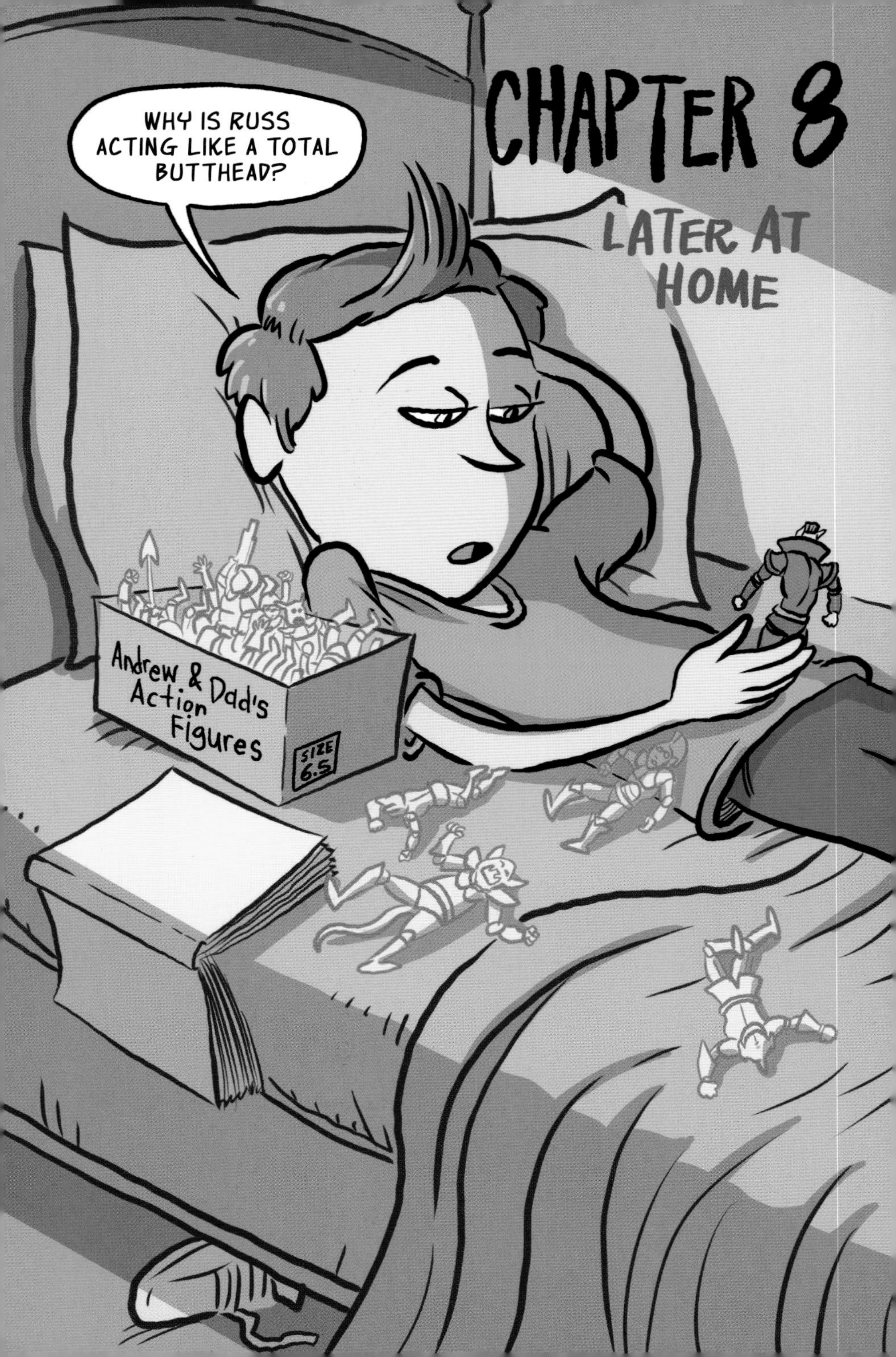
LATER AT HOME
WHY IS RUSS ACTING LIKE A TOTAL BUTTHEAD?
Andrew & Dad's Action Figures
SIZE 6.5

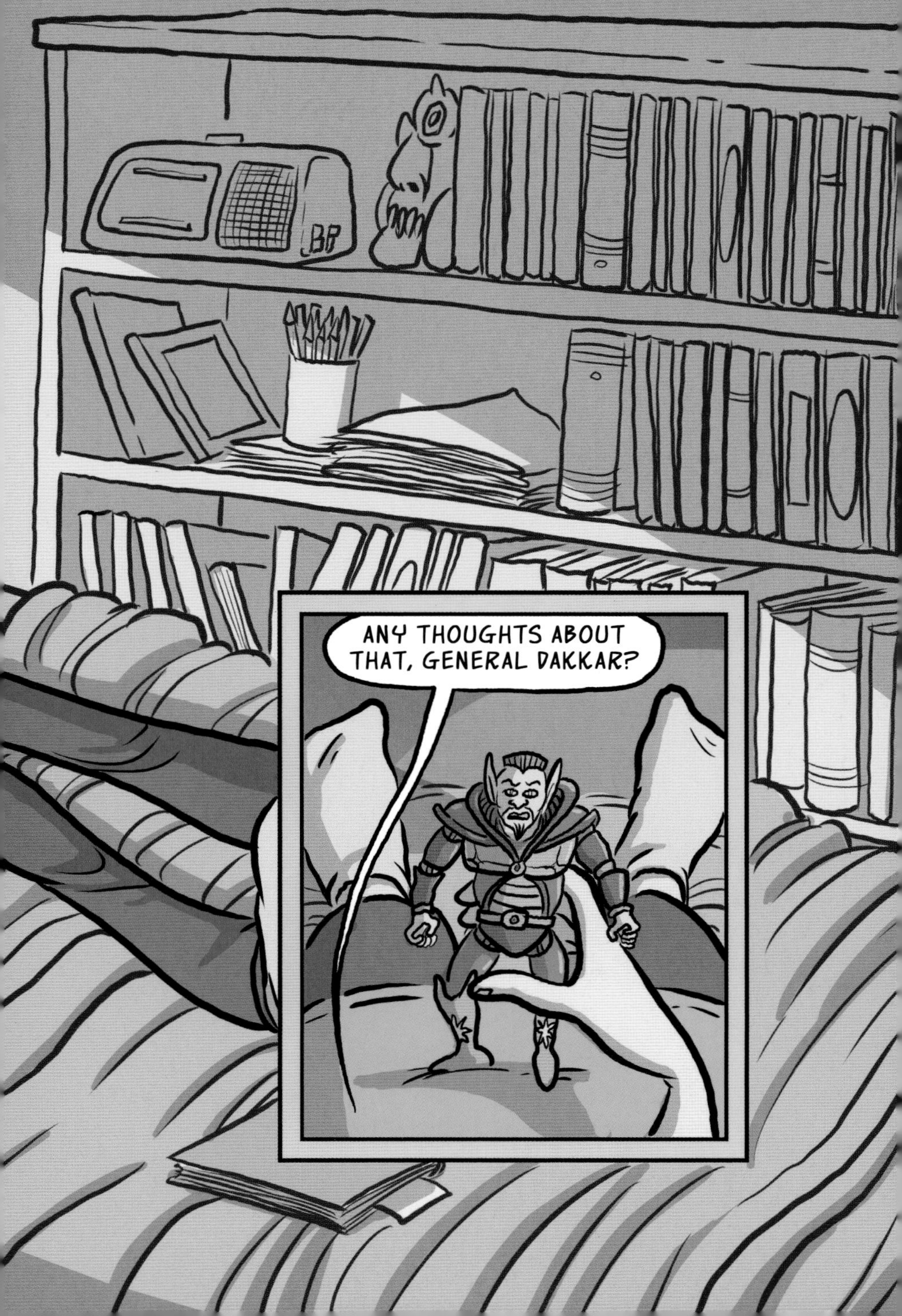
ANY THOUGHTS ABOUT THAT, GENERAL DAKKAR?

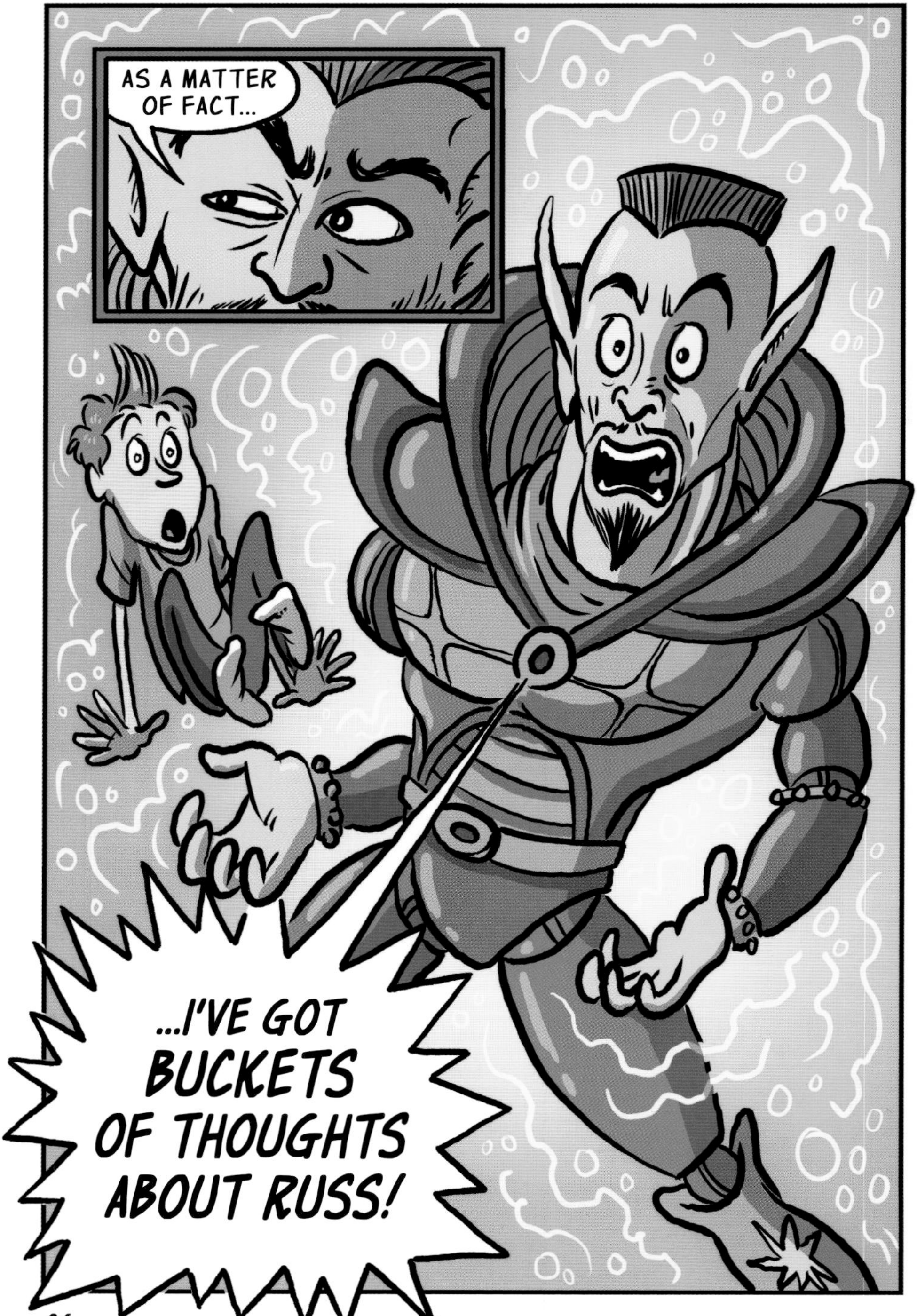
AS A MATTER OF FACT...
...I'VE GOT BUCKETS OF THOUGHTS ABOUT RUSS!

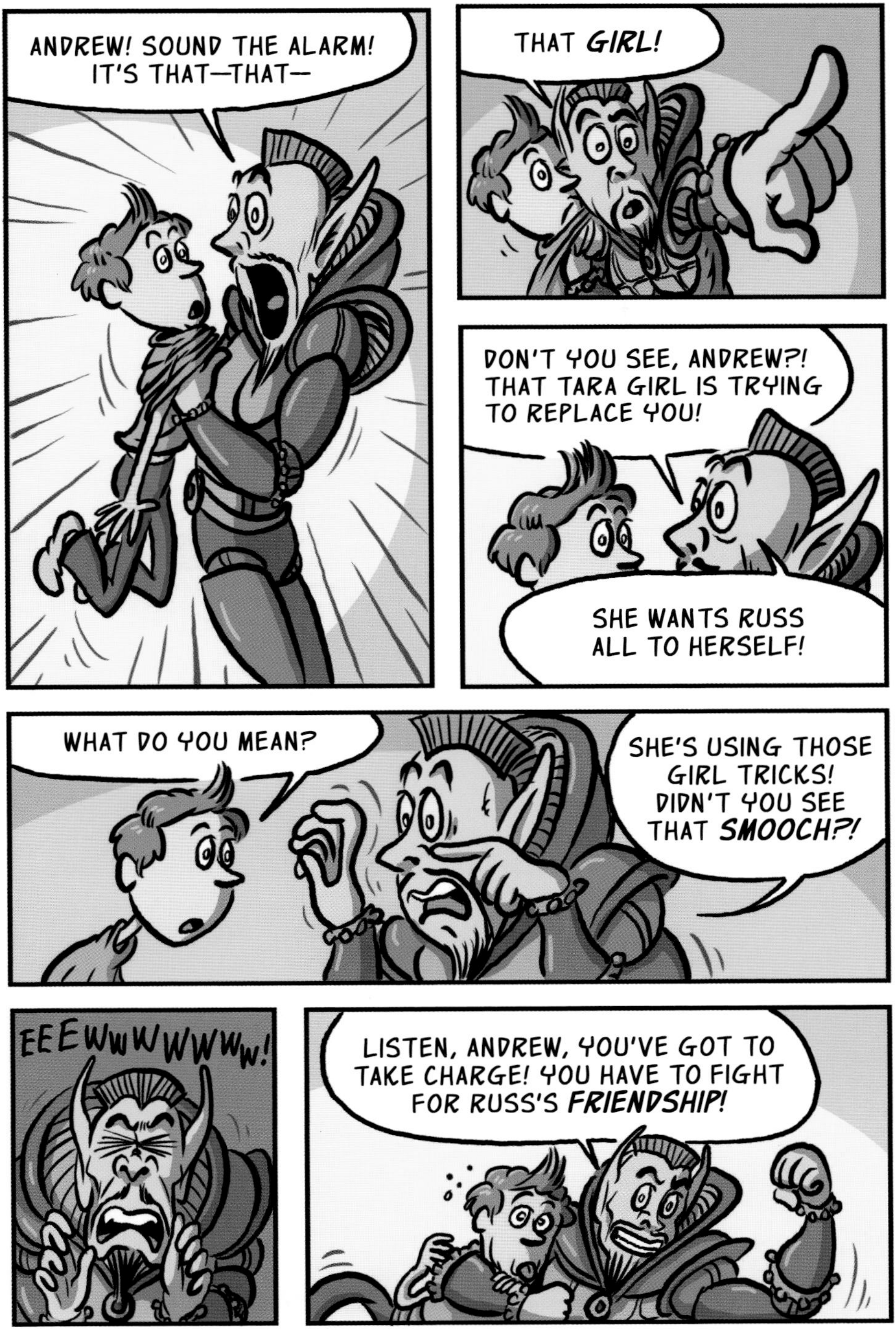
ANDREW! SOUND THE ALARM! IT'S THAT—THAT—
THAT GIRL!
DON'T YOU SEE, ANDREW?! THAT TARA GIRL IS TRYING TO REPLACE YOU!
SHE WANTS RUSS ALL TO HERSELF!
WHAT DO YOU MEAN?
SHE'S USING THOSE GIRL TRICKS! DIDN'T YOU SEE THAT SMOOCH?!
EEEWWWWWWWW!
LISTEN, ANDREW, YOU'VE GOT TO TAKE CHARGE! YOU HAVE TO FIGHT FOR RUSS'S FRIENDSHIP!

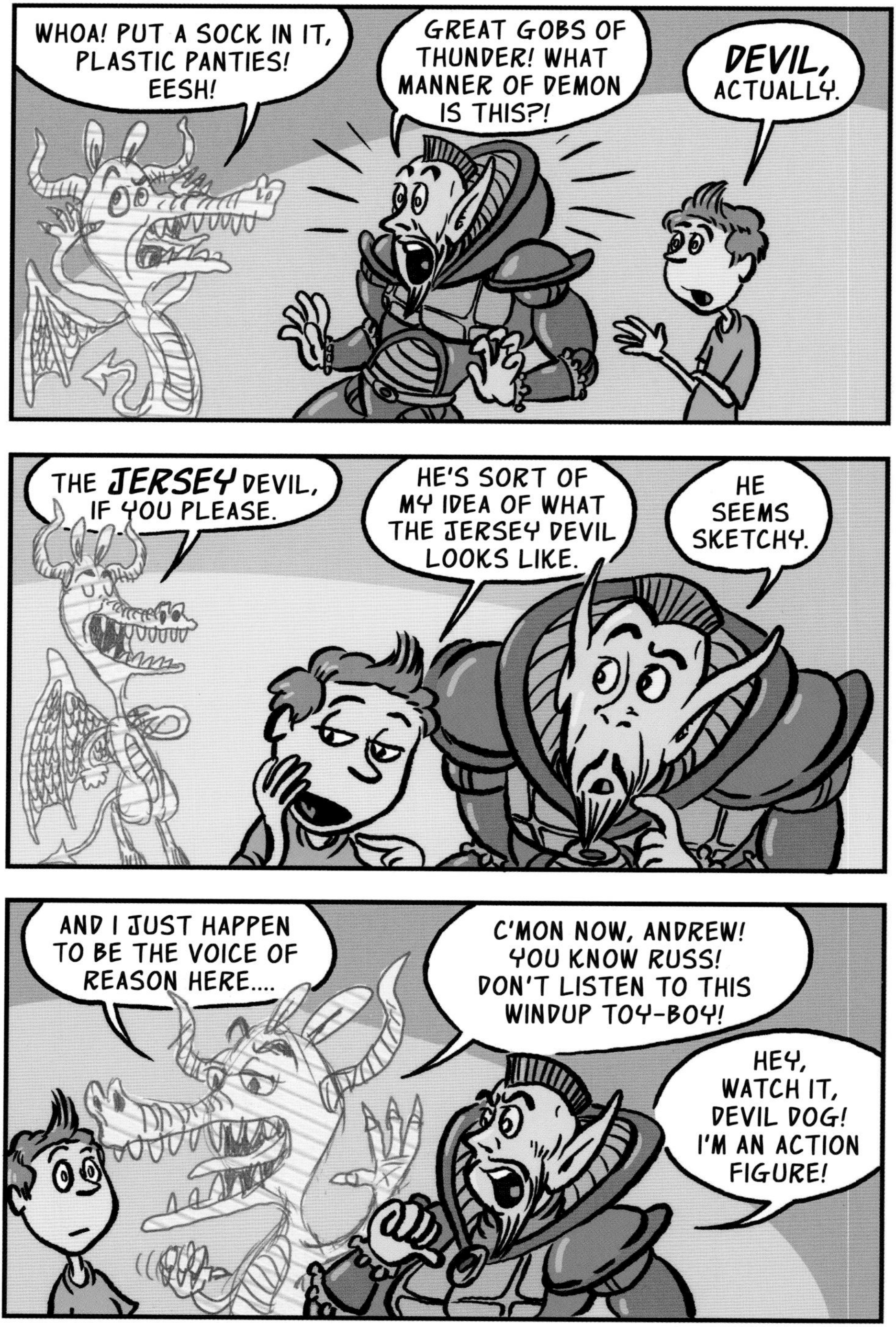
WHOA! PUT A SOCK IN IT, PLASTIC PANTIES! EESH!
GREAT GOBS OF THUNDER! WHAT MANNER OF DEMON IS THIS?!
DEVIL, ACTUALLY.
THE JERSEY DEVIL, IF YOU PLEASE.
HE'S SORT OF MY IDEA OF WHAT THE JERSEY DEVIL LOOKS LIKE.
HE SEEMS SKETCHY.
AND I JUST HAPPEN TO BE THE VOICE OF REASON HERE....
C'MON NOW, ANDREW! YOU KNOW RUSS! DON'T LISTEN TO THIS WINDUP TOY-BOY!
HEY, WATCH IT, DEVIL DOG! I'M AN ACTION FIGURE!

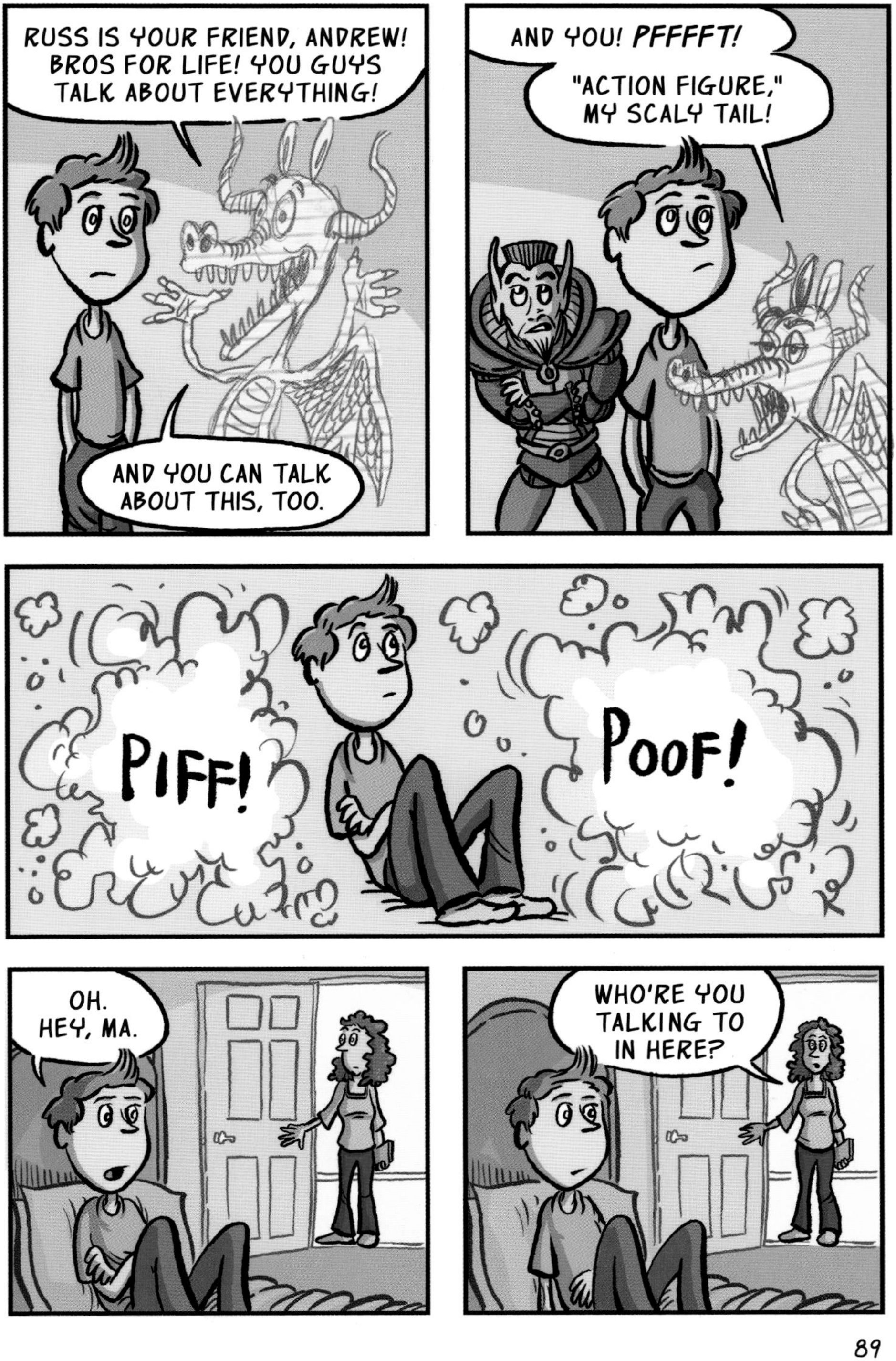
RUSS IS YOUR FRIEND, ANDREW! BROS FOR LIFE! YOU GUYS TALK ABOUT EVERYTHING!
AND YOU CAN TALK ABOUT THIS, TOO.
AND YOU! PFFFFT!
"ACTION FIGURE," MY SCALY TAIL!
PIFF!
POOF!
OH. HEY, MA.
WHO'RE YOU TALKING TO IN HERE?

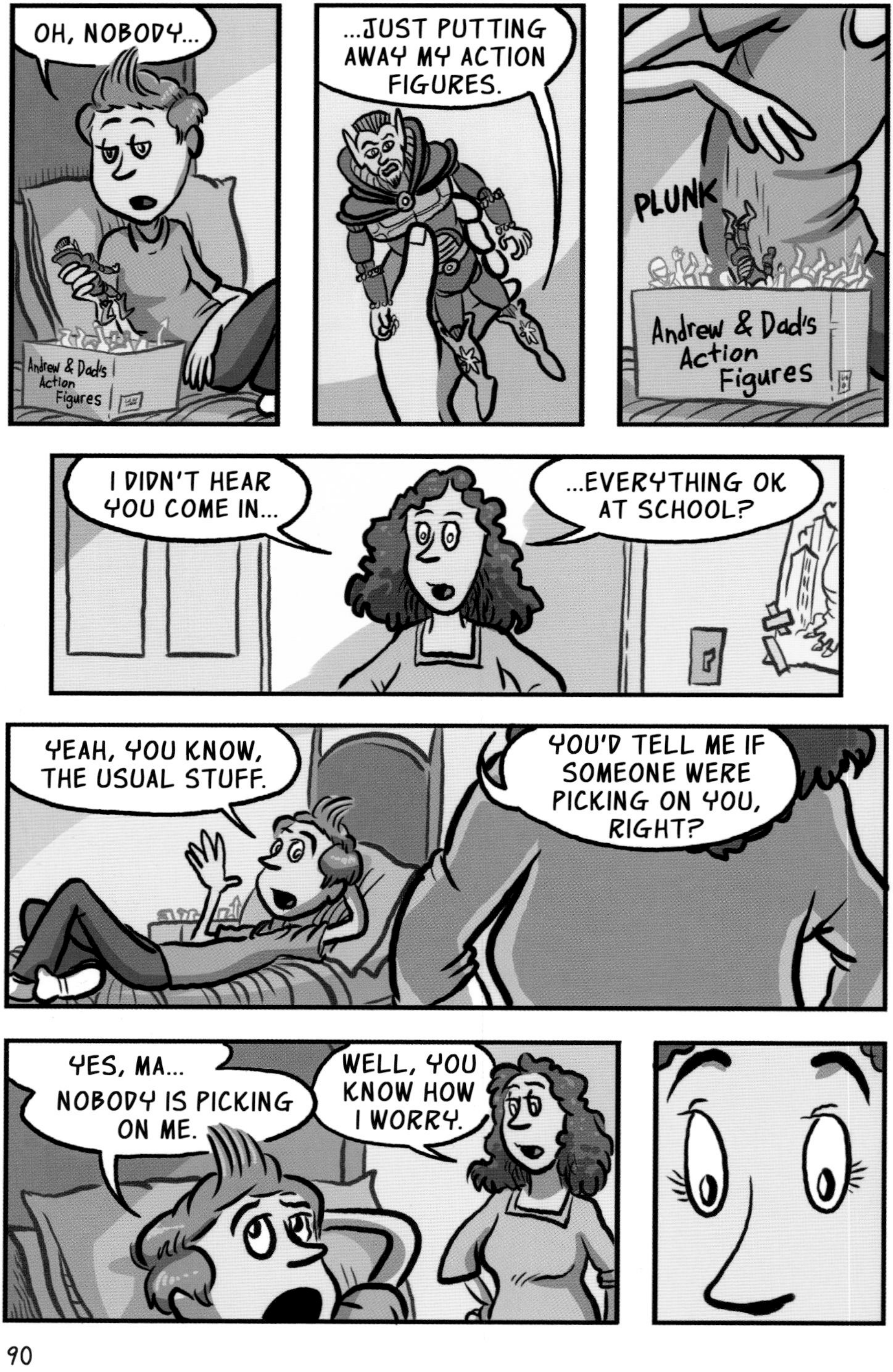
OH, NOBODY...
Andrew & Dad's Action Figures
...JUST PUTTING AWAY MY ACTION FIGURES.
PLUNK
Andrew & Dad's Action Figures
I DIDN'T HEAR YOU COME IN...
...EVERYTHING OK AT SCHOOL?
YEAH, YOU KNOW, THE USUAL STUFF.
YOU'D TELL ME IF SOMEONE WERE PICKING ON YOU, RIGHT?
YES, MA...
NOBODY IS PICKING ON ME.
WELL, YOU KNOW HOW I WORRY.

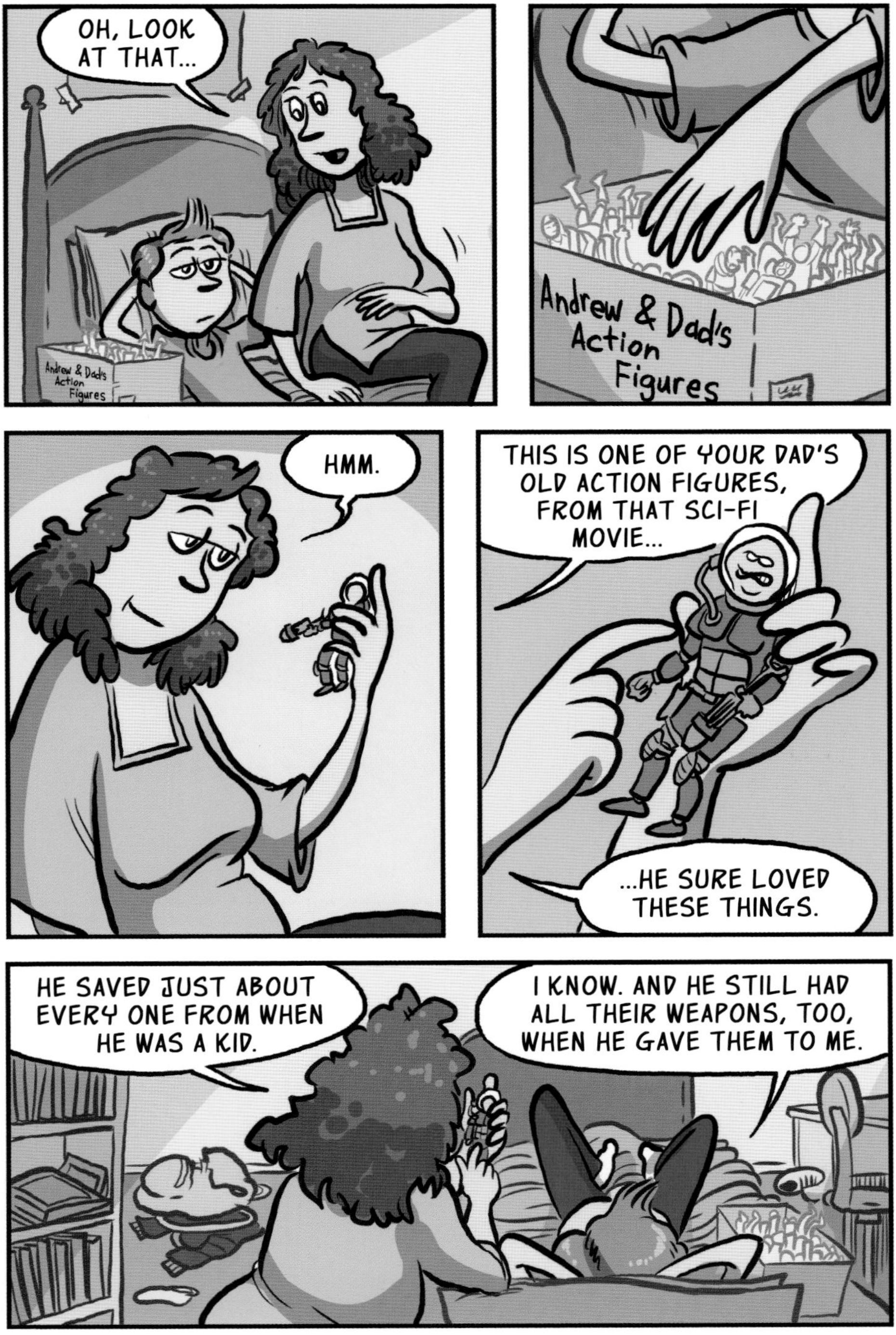
OH, LOOK AT THAT...
Andrew & Dad's Action Figures
Andrew & Dad's Action Figures
HMM.
THIS IS ONE OF YOUR DAD'S OLD ACTION FIGURES, FROM THAT SCI-FI MOVIE...
...HE SURE LOVED THESE THINGS.
HE SAVED JUST ABOUT EVERY ONE FROM WHEN HE WAS A KID.
I KNOW. AND HE STILL HAD ALL THEIR WEAPONS, TOO, WHEN HE GAVE THEM TO ME.

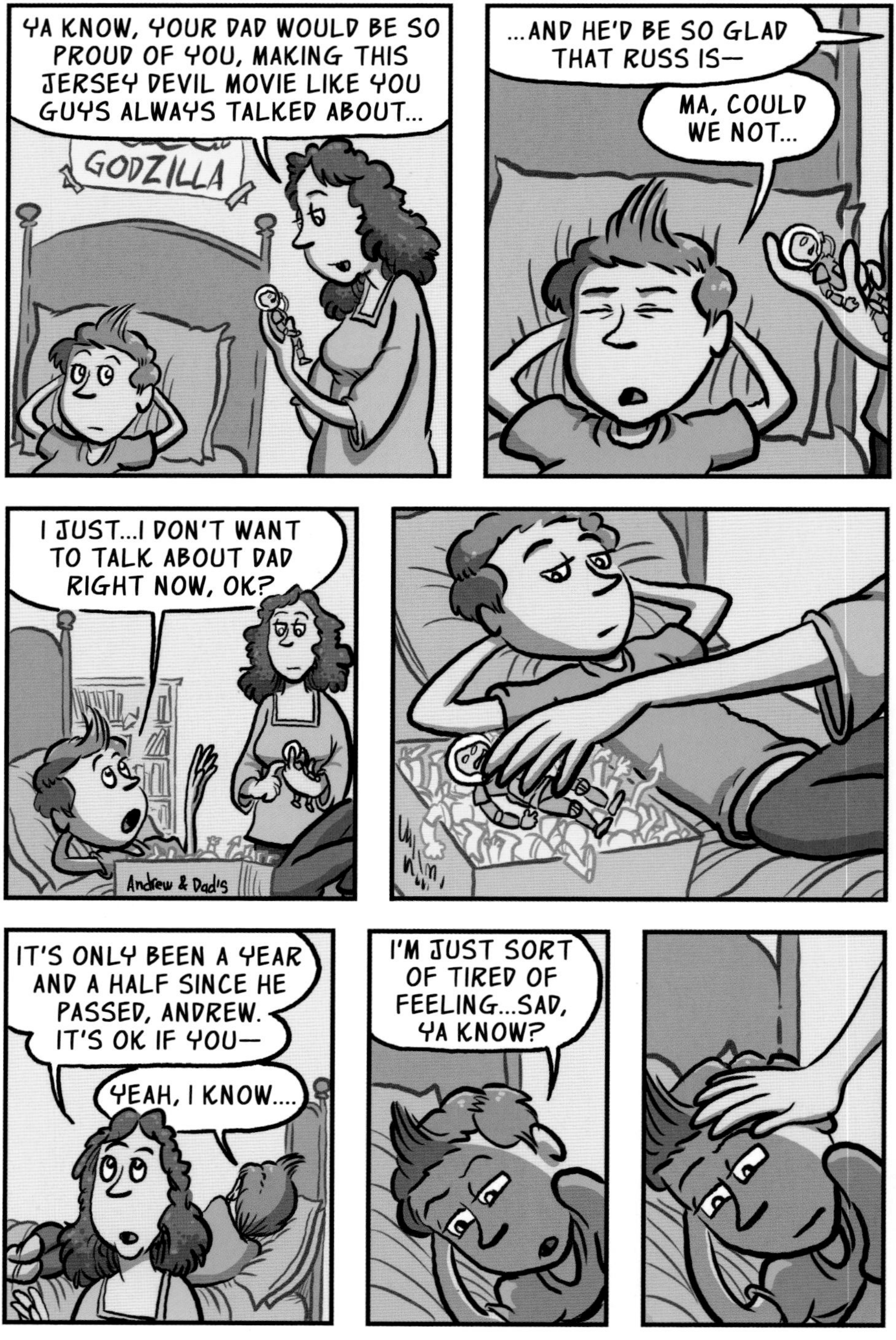
YA KNOW, YOUR DAD WOULD BE SO PROUD OF YOU, MAKING THIS JERSEY DEVIL MOVIE LIKE YOU GUYS ALWAYS TALKED ABOUT...
GODZILLA
...AND HE'D BE SO GLAD THAT RUSS IS—
MA, COULD WE NOT...
I JUST...I DON'T WANT TO TALK ABOUT DAD RIGHT NOW, OK?
Andrew & Dad's
IT'S ONLY BEEN A YEAR AND A HALF SINCE HE PASSED, ANDREW. IT'S OK IF YOU—
YEAH, I KNOW....
I'M JUST SORT OF TIRED OF FEELING...SAD, YA KNOW?

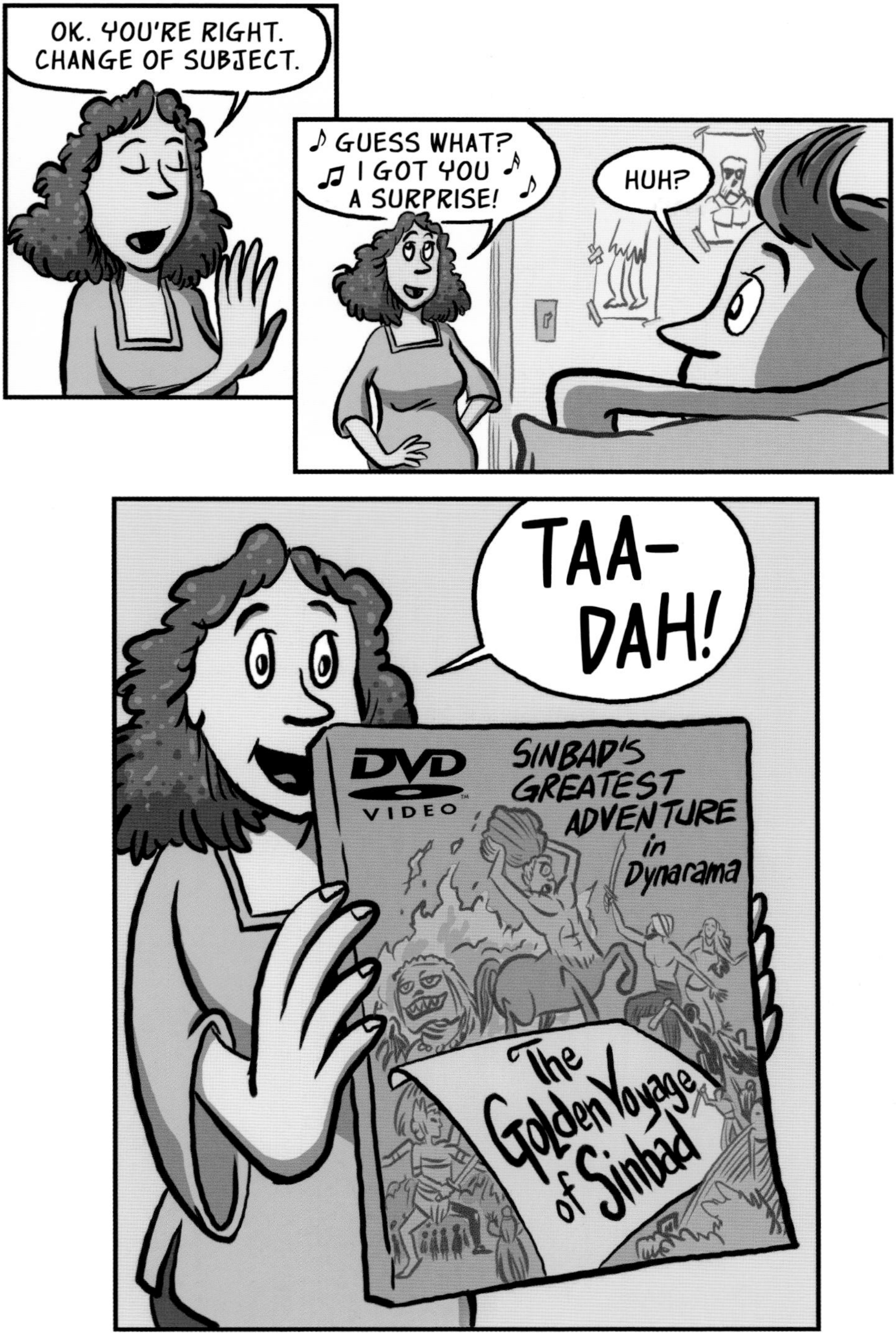
OK. YOU'RE RIGHT. CHANGE OF SUBJECT.
♪ GUESS WHAT? ♫ I GOT YOU ♪ A SURPRISE! ♪
HUH?
TAA- DAH!
DVD VIDEO
SINBAD'S GREATEST ADVENTURE in Dynarama
The Golden Voyage of Sinbad

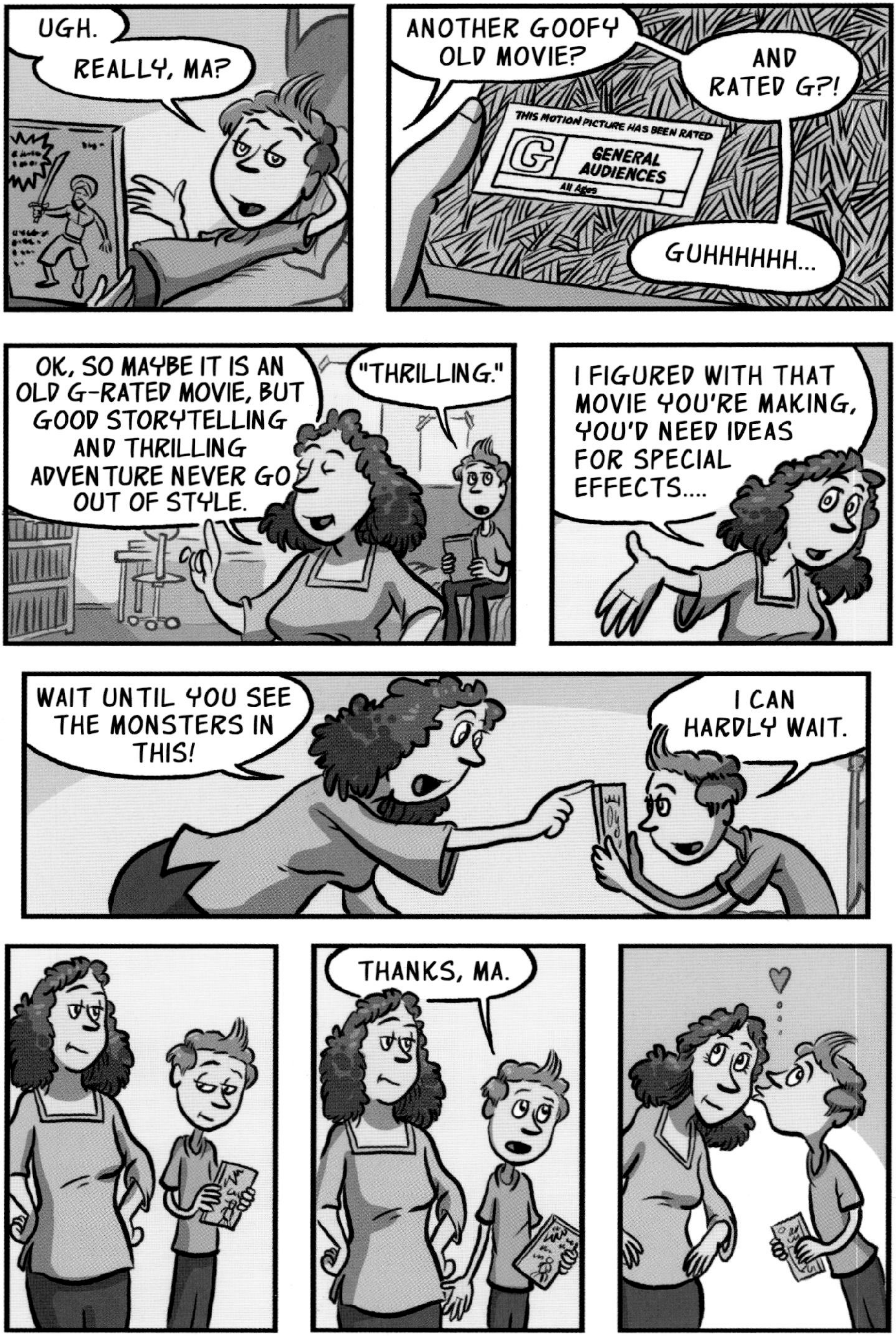
UGH.
REALLY, MA?
ANOTHER GOOFY OLD MOVIE?
AND RATED G?!
THIS MOTION PICTURE HAS BEEN RATED
G
GENERAL AUDIENCES
All Ages
GUHHHHHH...
OK, SO MAYBE IT IS AN OLD G-RATED MOVIE, BUT GOOD STORYTELLING AND THRILLING ADVENTURE NEVER GO OUT OF STYLE.
"THRILLING."
I FIGURED WITH THAT MOVIE YOU'RE MAKING, YOU'D NEED IDEAS FOR SPECIAL EFFECTS....
WAIT UNTIL YOU SEE THE MONSTERS IN THIS!
I CAN HARDLY WAIT.
THANKS, MA.

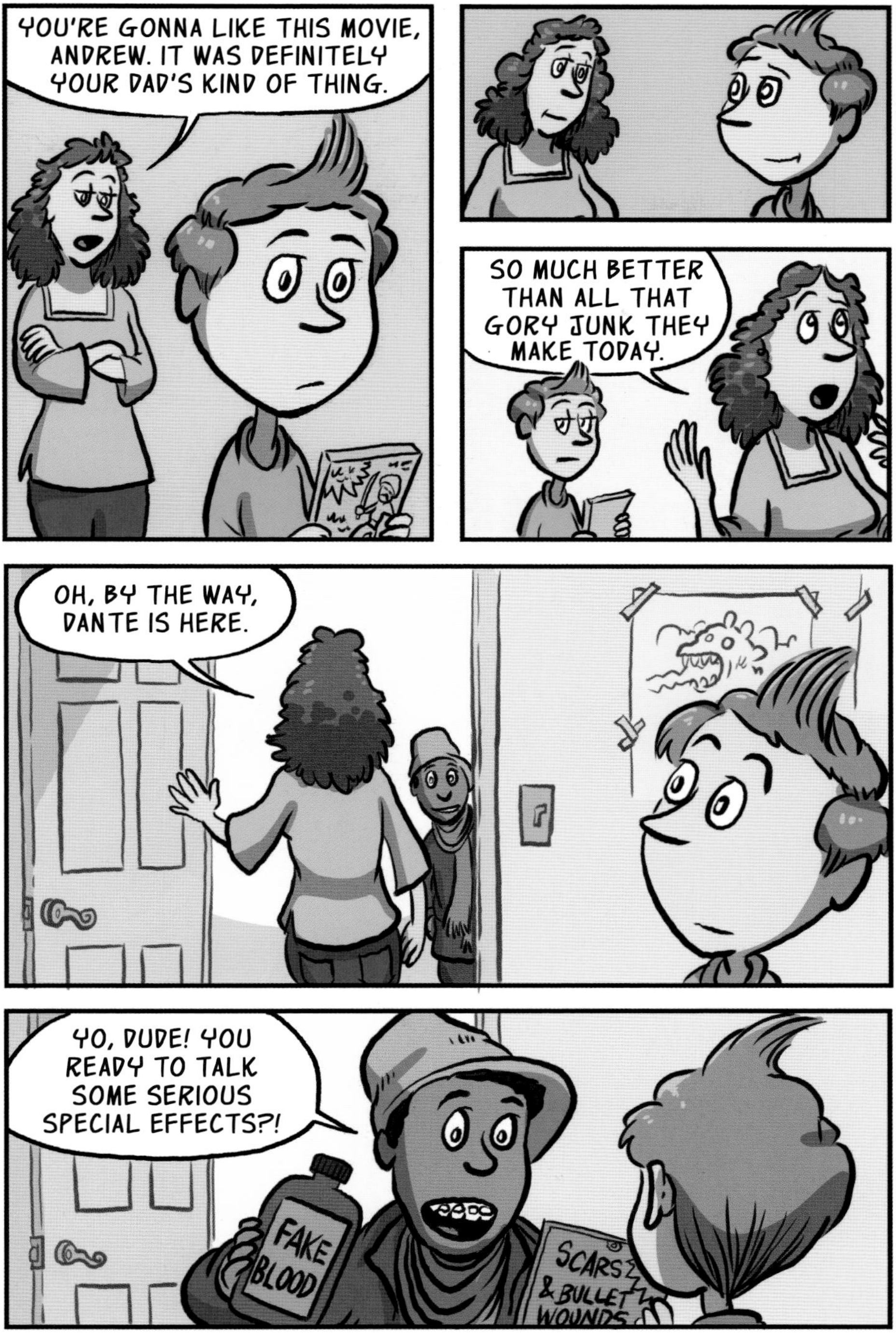
YOU'RE GONNA LIKE THIS MOVIE, ANDREW. IT WAS DEFINITELY YOUR DAD'S KIND OF THING.
SO MUCH BETTER THAN ALL THAT GORY JUNK THEY MAKE TODAY.
OH, BY THE WAY, DANTE IS HERE.
YO, DUDE! YOU READY TO TALK SOME SERIOUS SPECIAL EFFECTS?!
FAKE BLOOD
SCARS & BULLET WOUNDS

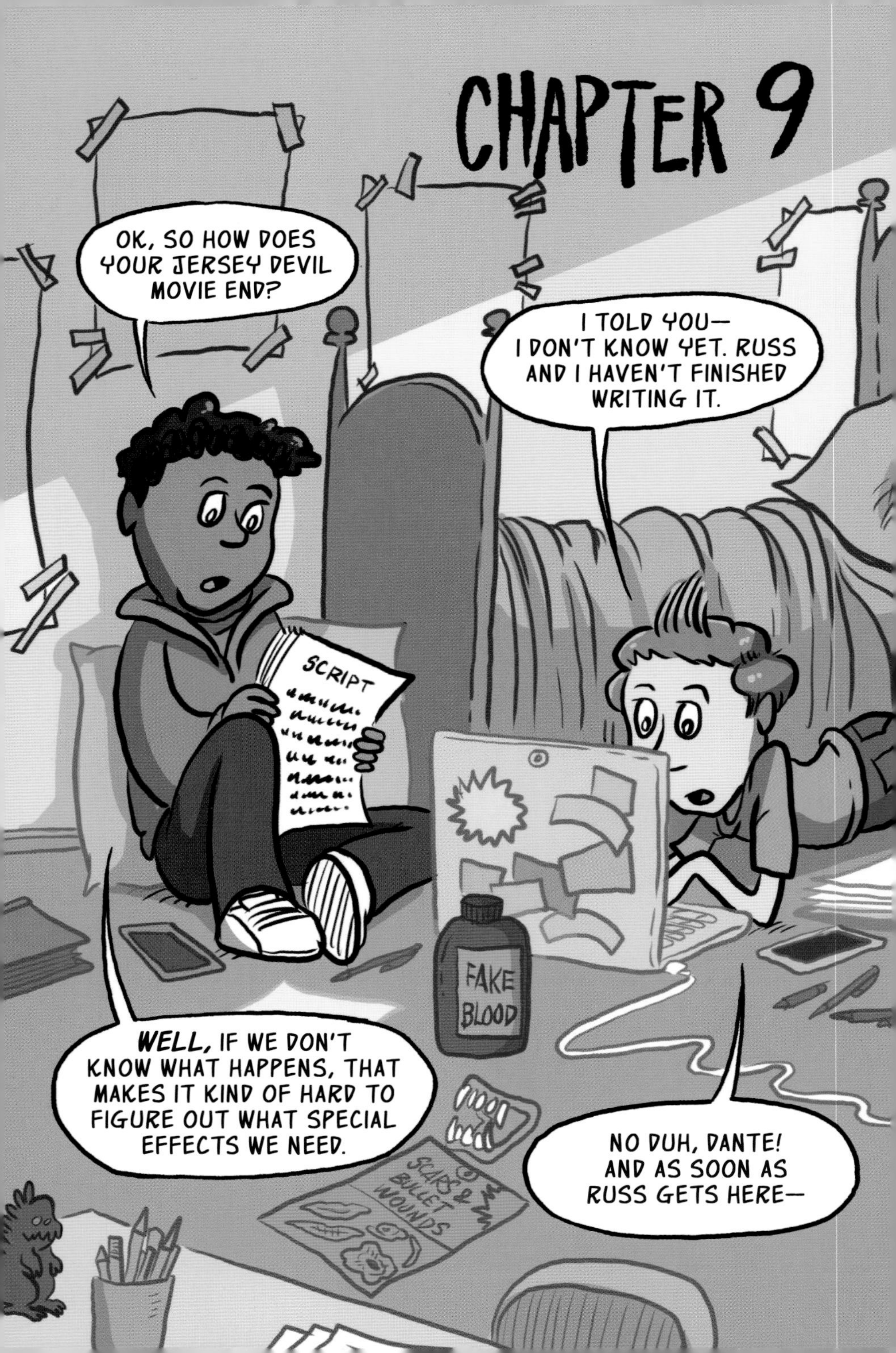
CHAPTER 9
OK, SO HOW DOES YOUR JERSEY DEVIL MOVIE END?
I TOLD YOU— I DON'T KNOW YET. RUSS AND I HAVEN'T FINISHED WRITING IT.
SCRIPT
FAKE BLOOD
WELL, IF WE DON'T KNOW WHAT HAPPENS, THAT MAKES IT KIND OF HARD TO FIGURE OUT WHAT SPECIAL EFFECTS WE NEED.
NO DUH, DANTE! AND AS SOON AS RUSS GETS HERE—
SCARS & BULLET WOUNDS

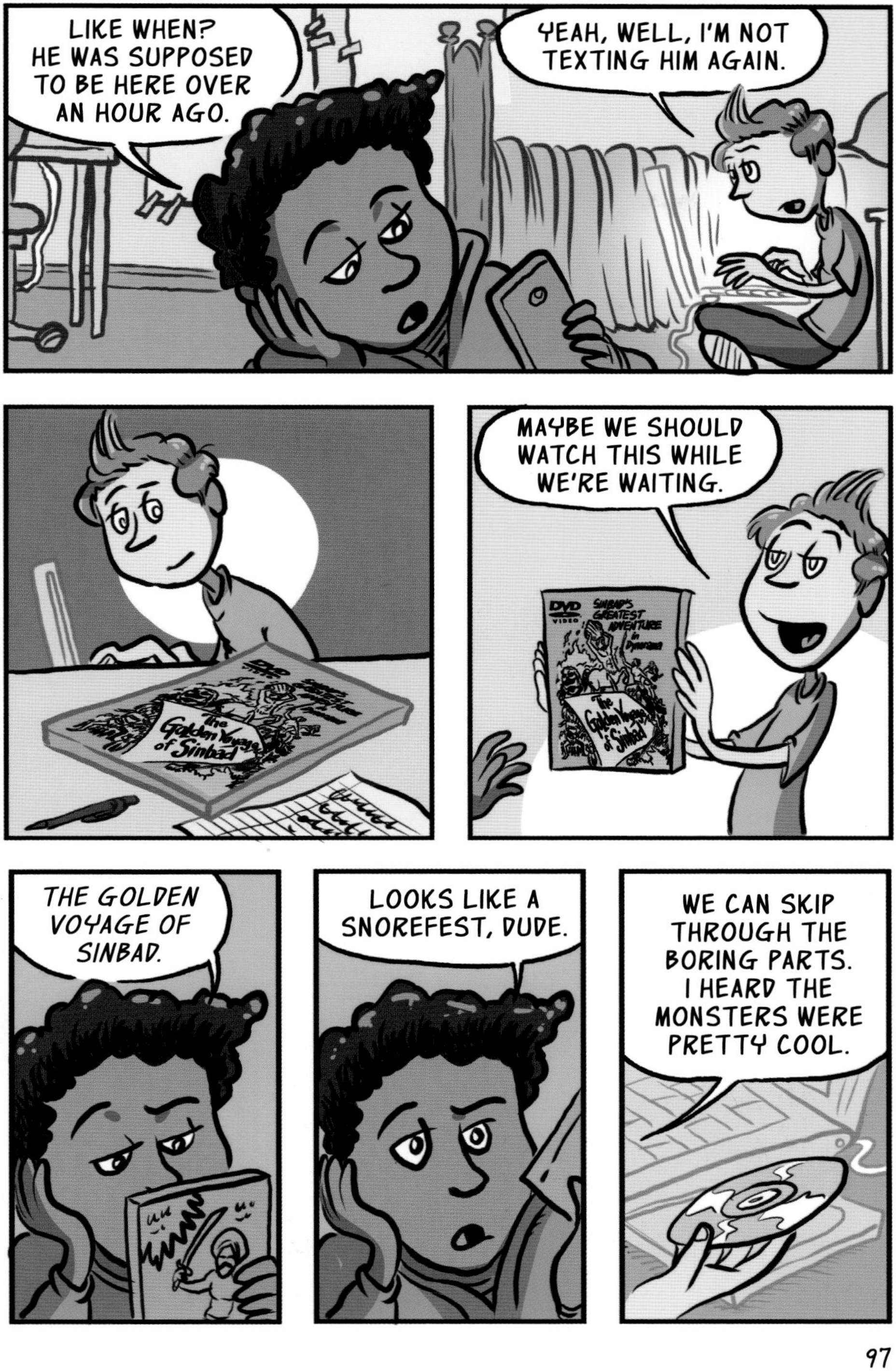
LIKE WHEN? HE WAS SUPPOSED TO BE HERE OVER AN HOUR AGO.
YEAH, WELL, I'M NOT TEXTING HIM AGAIN.
MAYBE WE SHOULD WATCH THIS WHILE WE'RE WAITING.
THE GOLDEN VOYAGE OF SINBAD.
LOOKS LIKE A SNOREFEST, DUDE.
WE CAN SKIP THROUGH THE BORING PARTS. I HEARD THE MONSTERS WERE PRETTY COOL.

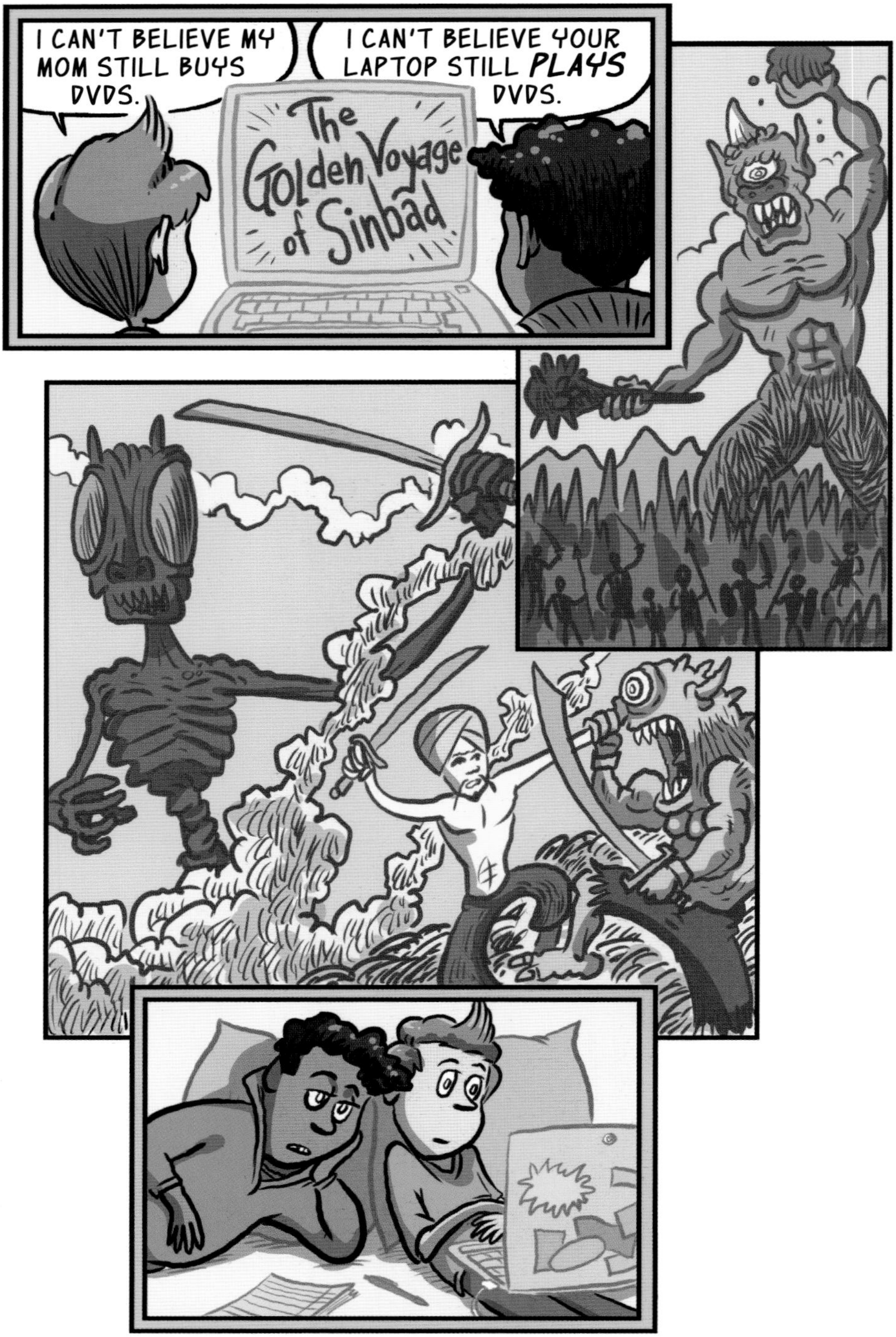
I CAN'T BELIEVE MY MOM STILL BUYS DVDS.
I CAN'T BELIEVE YOUR LAPTOP STILL PLAYS DVDS.
The Golden Voyage of Sinbad

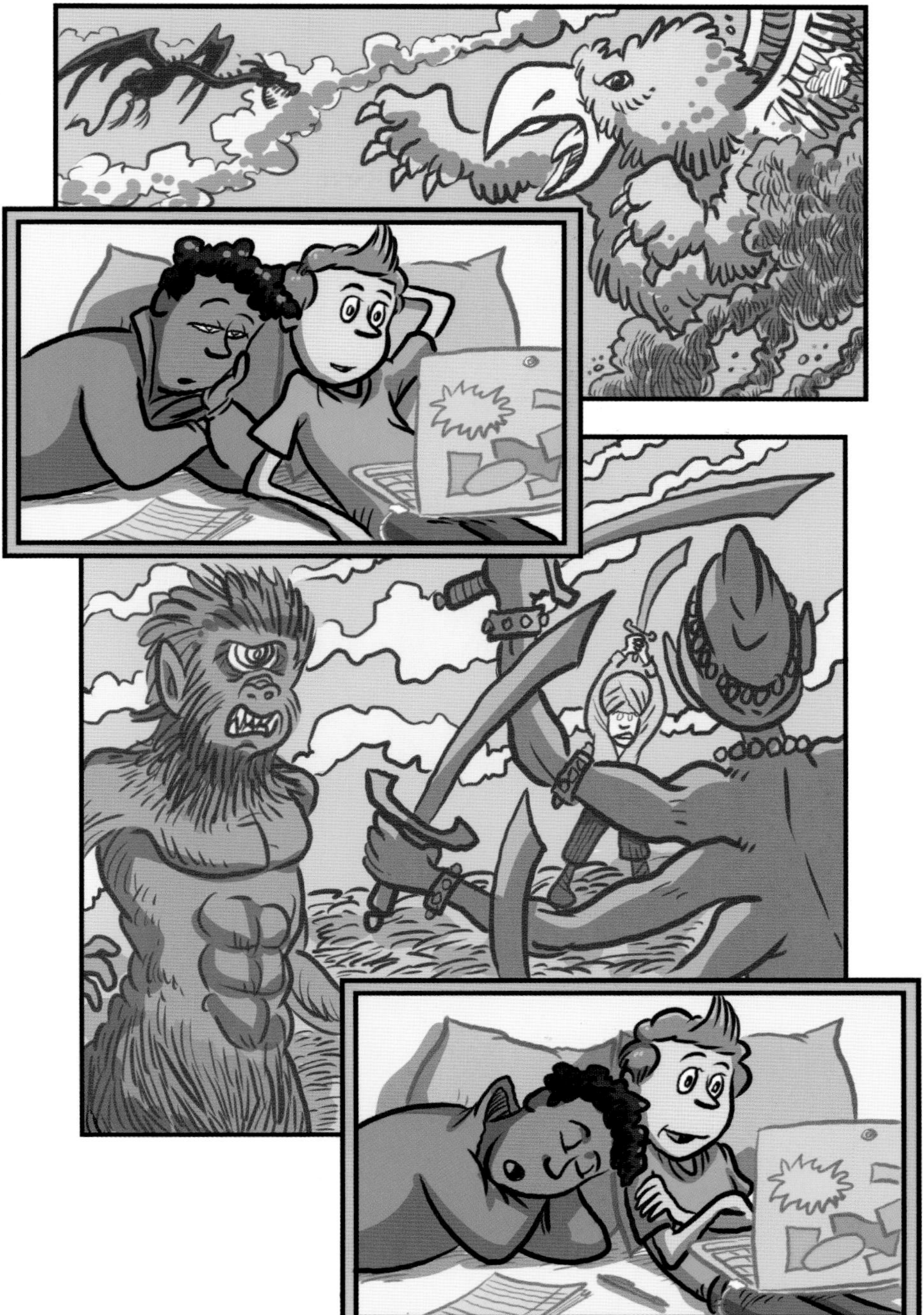

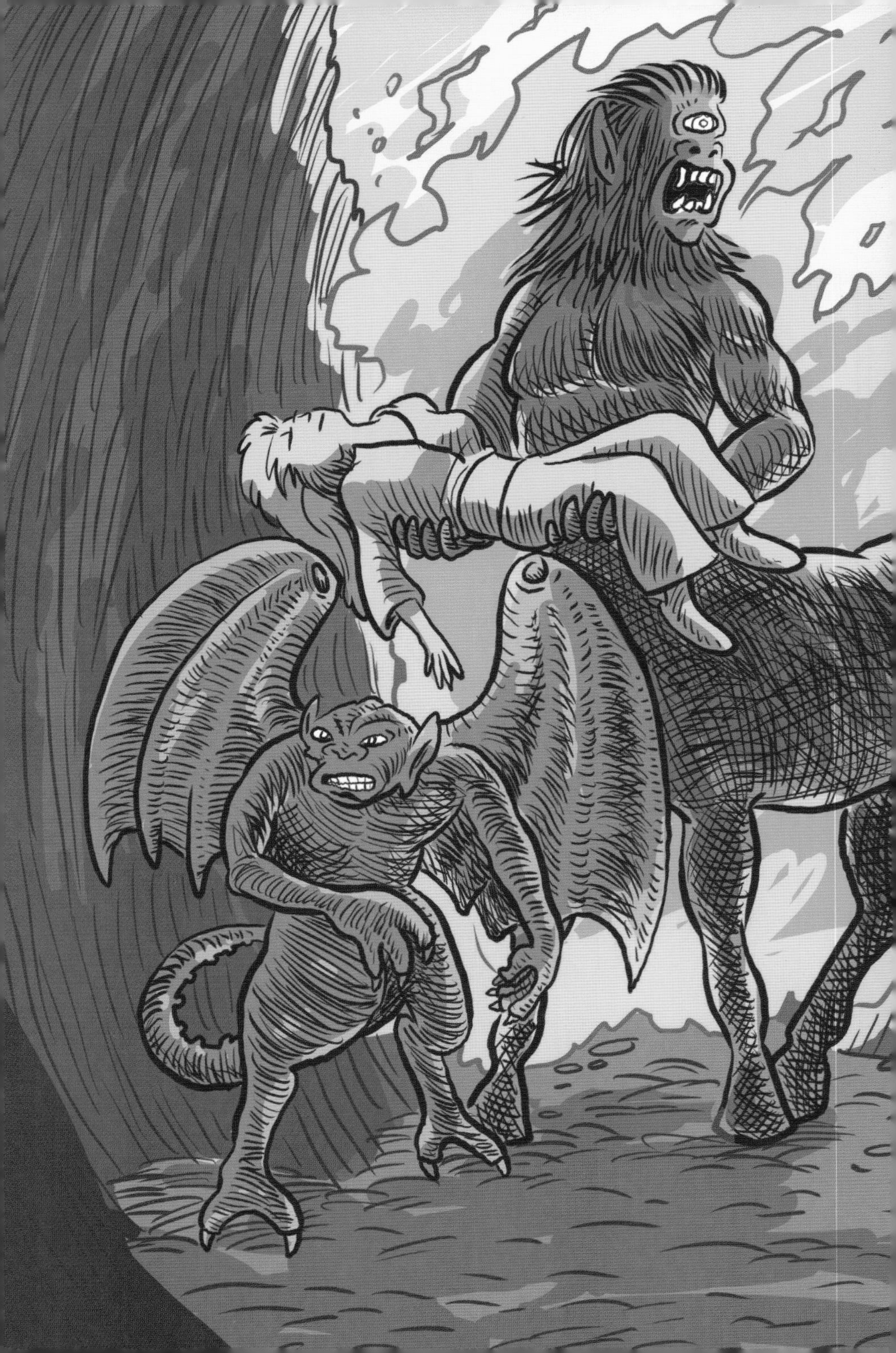

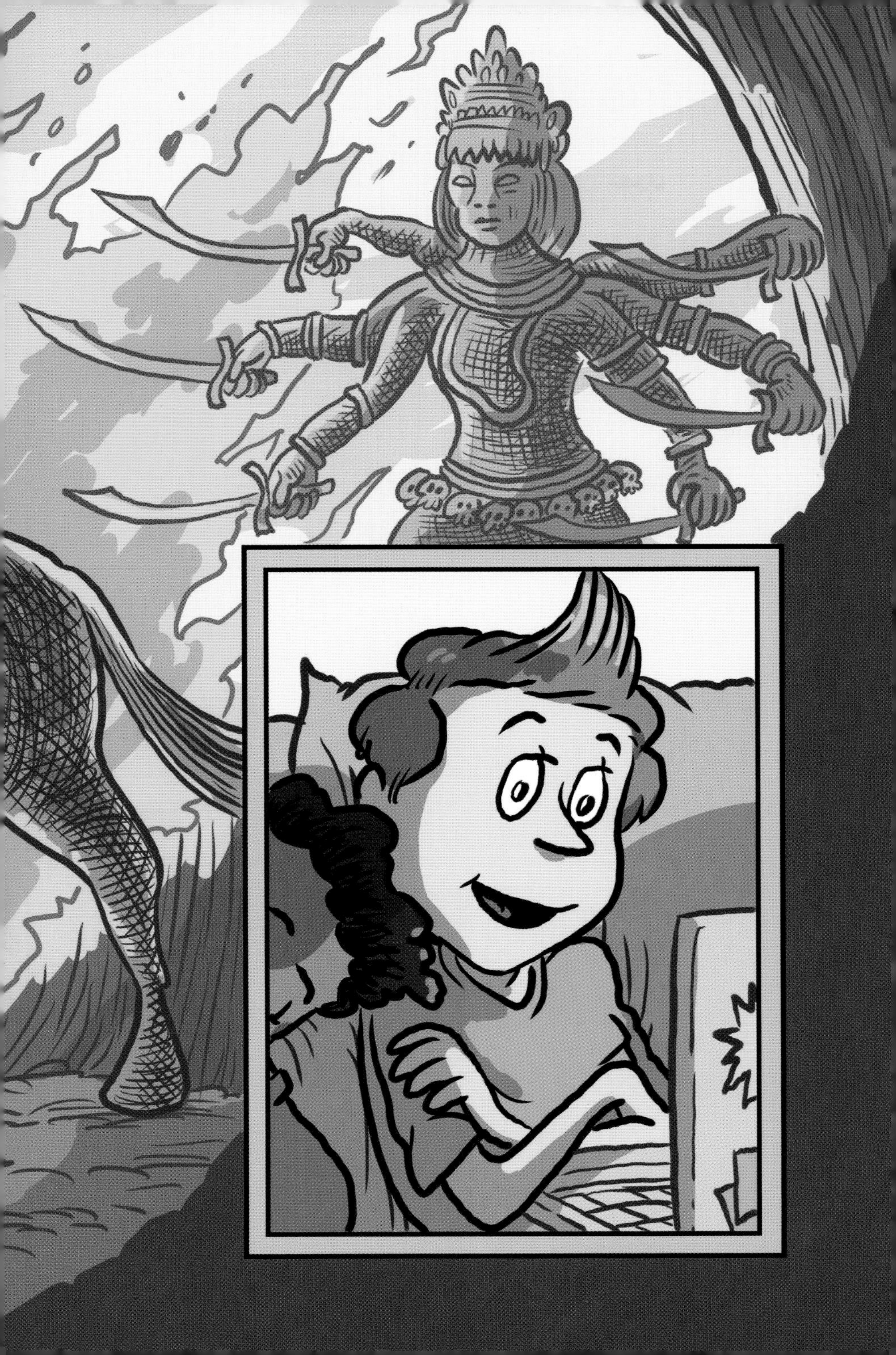

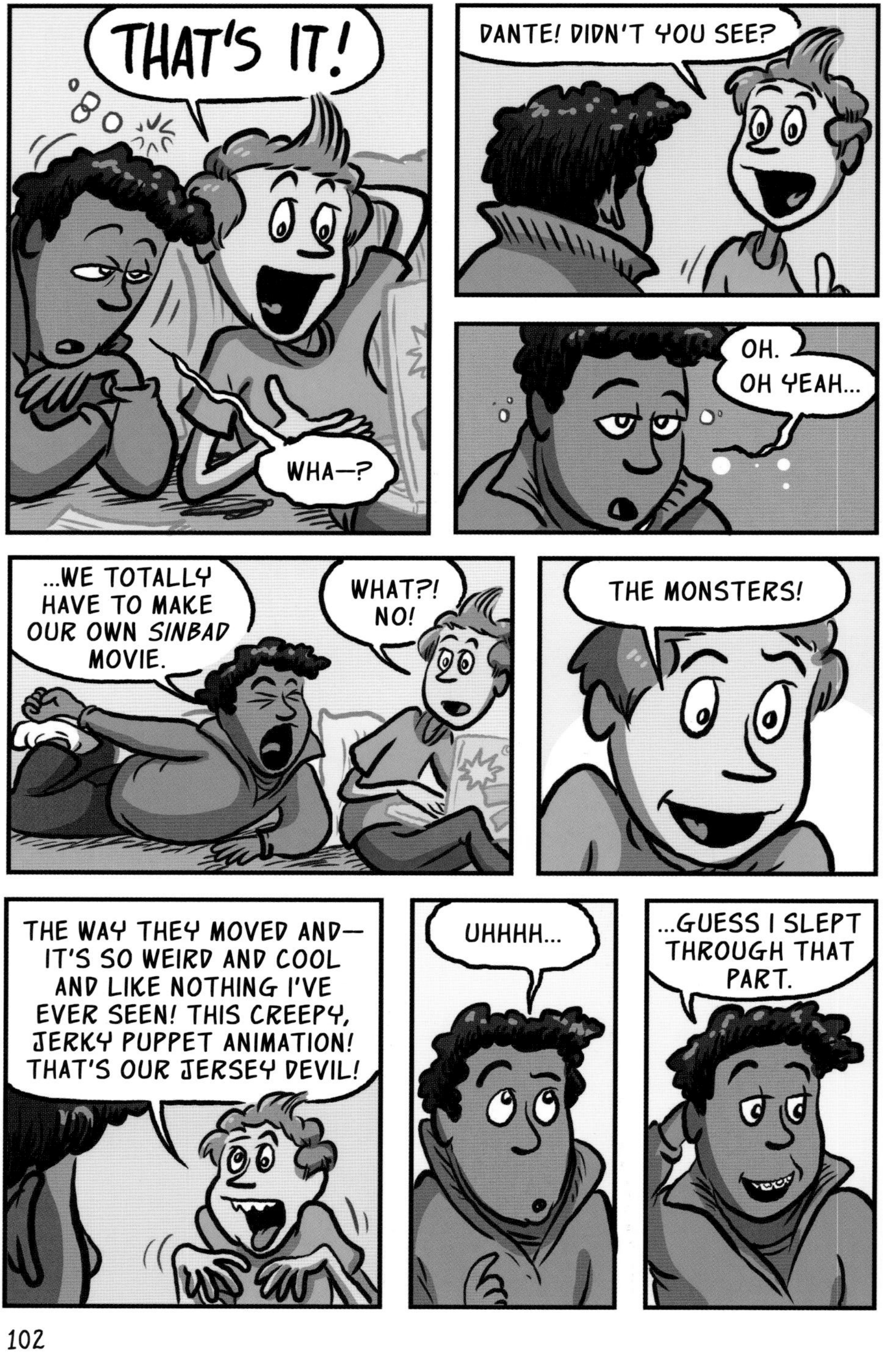
THAT'S IT!
WHA—?
DANTE! DIDN'T YOU SEE?
OH.
OH YEAH...
...WE TOTALLY HAVE TO MAKE OUR OWN *SINBAD* MOVIE.
WHAT?! NO!
THE MONSTERS!
THE WAY THEY MOVED AND— IT'S SO WEIRD AND COOL AND LIKE NOTHING I'VE EVER SEEN! THIS CREEPY, JERKY PUPPET ANIMATION! THAT'S OUR JERSEY DEVIL!
UHHHH...
...GUESS I SLEPT THROUGH THAT PART.

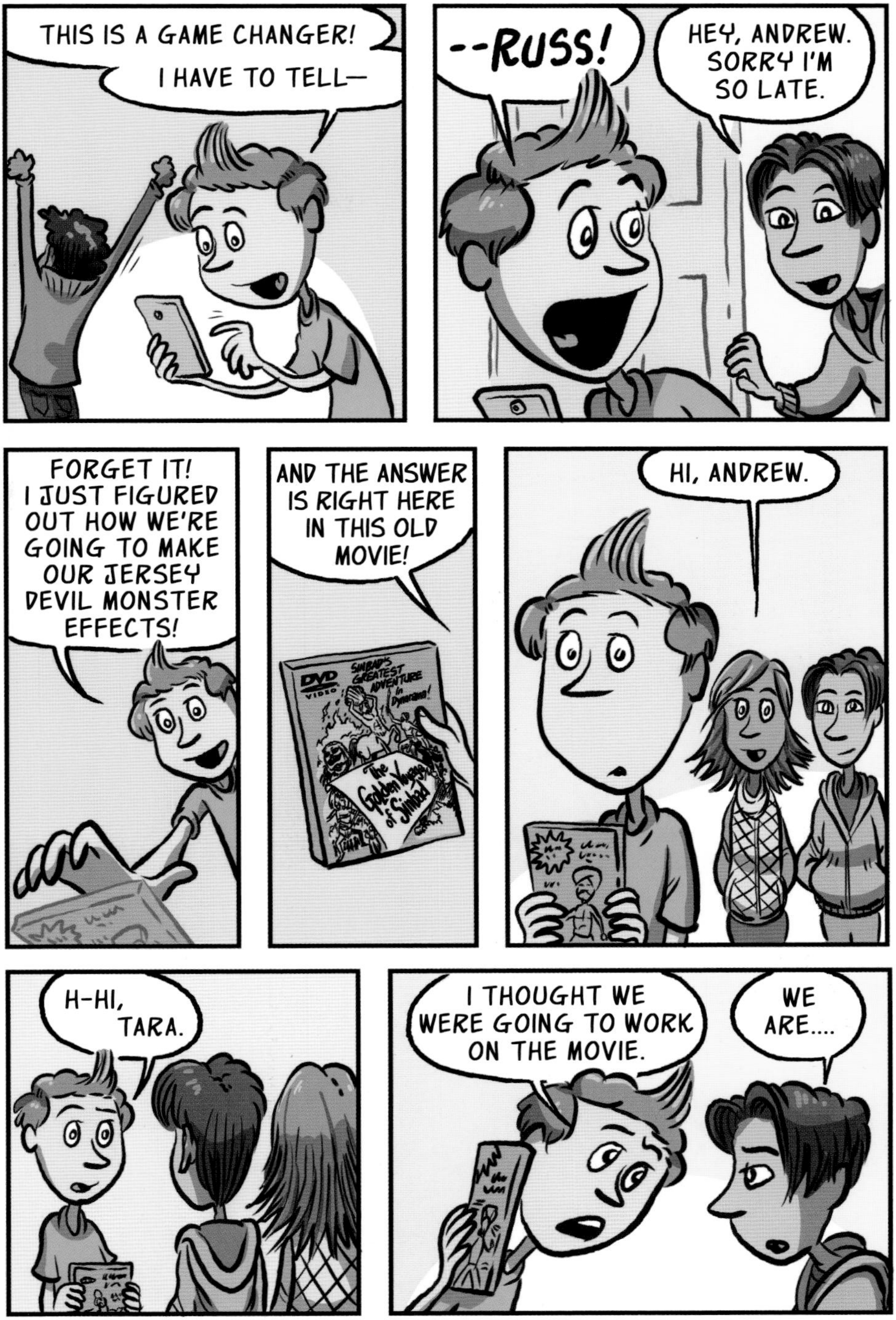
THIS IS A GAME CHANGER!
I HAVE TO TELL—
--RUSS!
HEY, ANDREW. SORRY I'M SO LATE.
FORGET IT! I JUST FIGURED OUT HOW WE'RE GOING TO MAKE OUR JERSEY DEVIL MONSTER EFFECTS!
AND THE ANSWER IS RIGHT HERE IN THIS OLD MOVIE!
DVD VIDEO
SINBAD'S GREATEST ADVENTURE in Dynarama!
The Golden Voyage of Sinbad
HI, ANDREW.
H-HI, TARA.
I THOUGHT WE WERE GOING TO WORK ON THE MOVIE.
WE ARE....

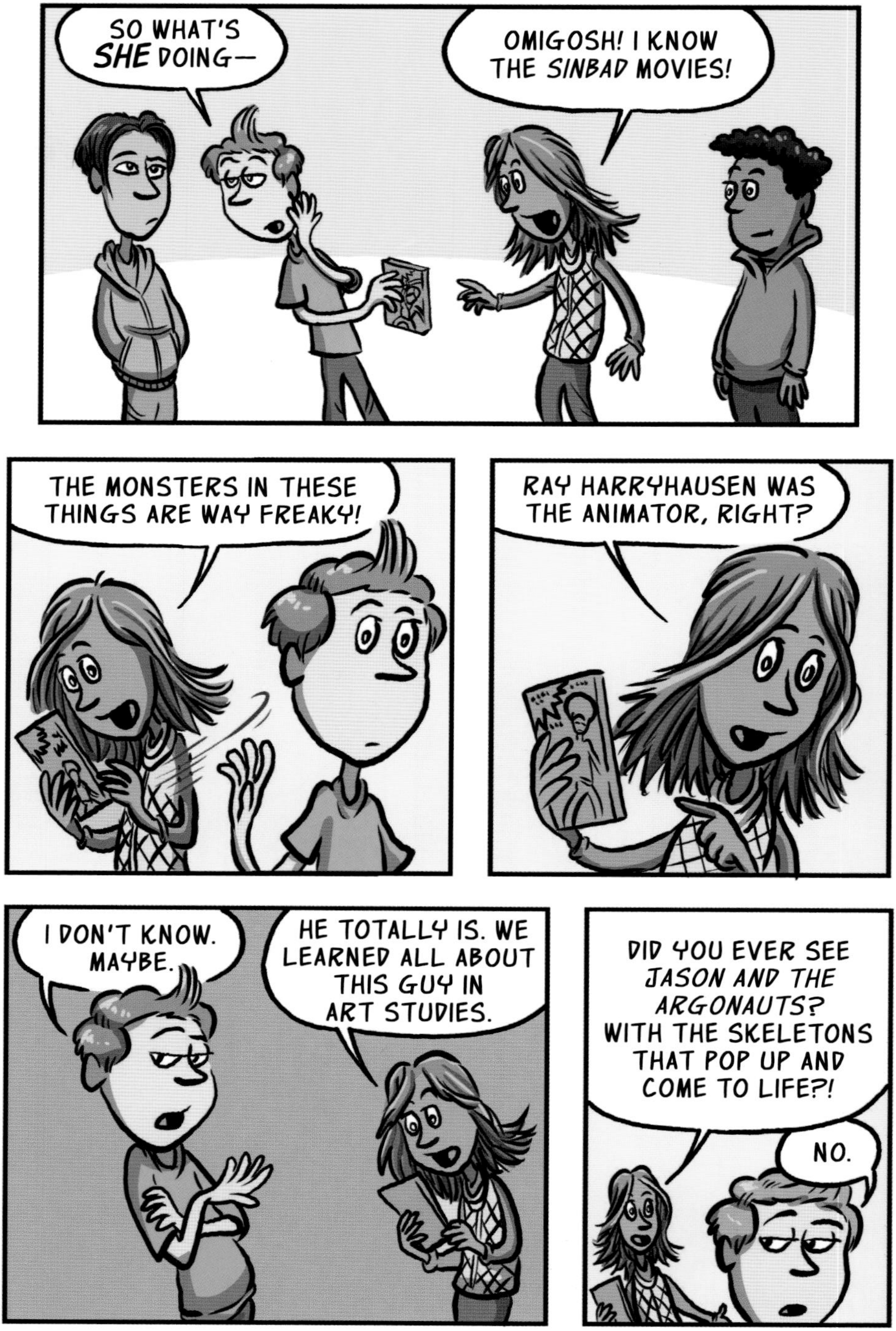
SO WHAT'S *SHE* DOING—
OMIGOSH! I KNOW THE *SINBAD* MOVIES!
THE MONSTERS IN THESE THINGS ARE WAY FREAKY!
RAY HARRYHAUSEN WAS THE ANIMATOR, RIGHT?
I DON'T KNOW. MAYBE.
HE TOTALLY IS. WE LEARNED ALL ABOUT THIS GUY IN ART STUDIES.
DID YOU EVER SEE *JASON AND THE ARGONAUTS*? WITH THE SKELETONS THAT POP UP AND COME TO LIFE?!
NO.

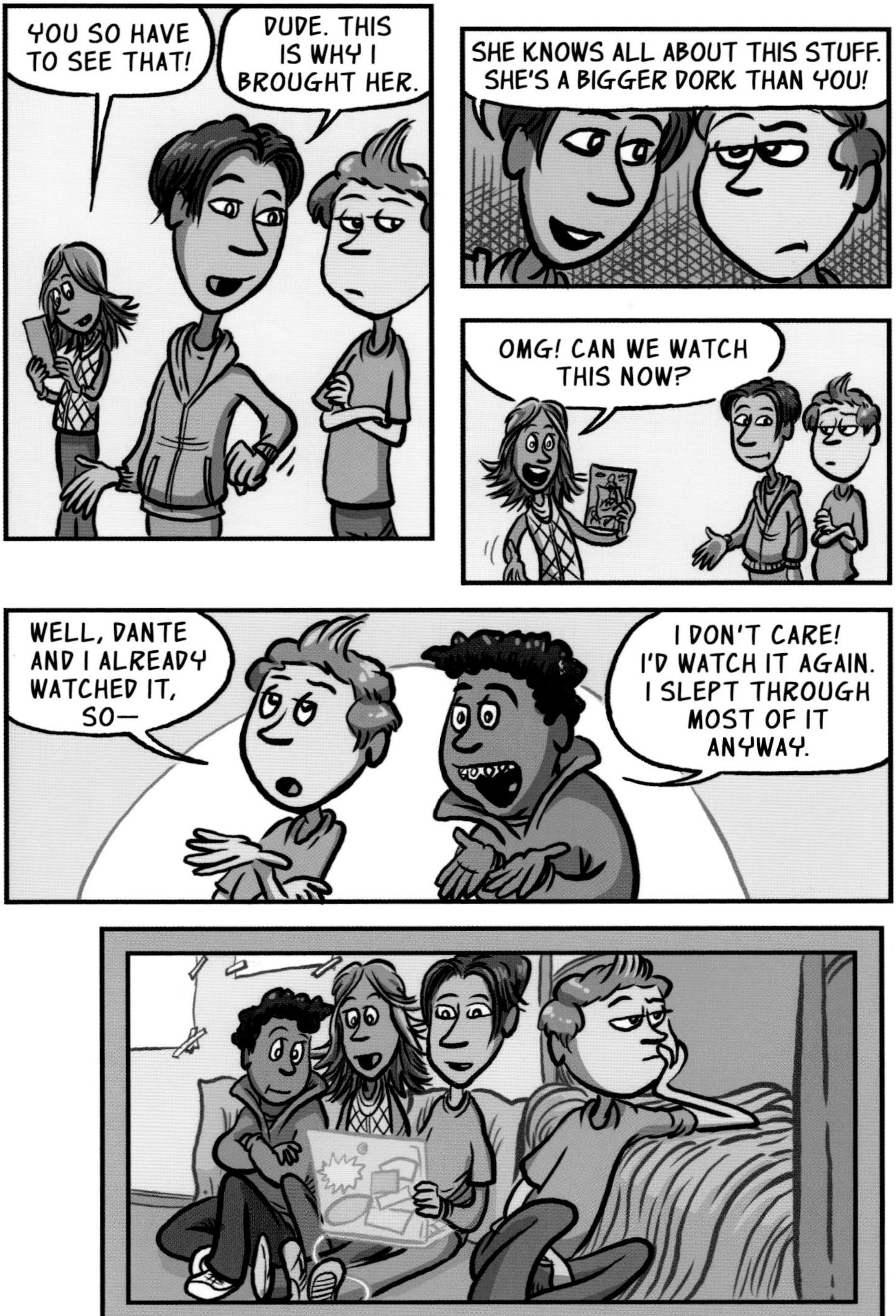
YOU SO HAVE TO SEE THAT!
DUDE. THIS IS WHY I BROUGHT HER.
SHE KNOWS ALL ABOUT THIS STUFF. SHE'S A BIGGER DORK THAN YOU!
OMG! CAN WE WATCH THIS NOW?
WELL, DANTE AND I ALREADY WATCHED IT, SO—
I DON'T CARE! I'D WATCH IT AGAIN. I SLEPT THROUGH MOST OF IT ANYWAY.

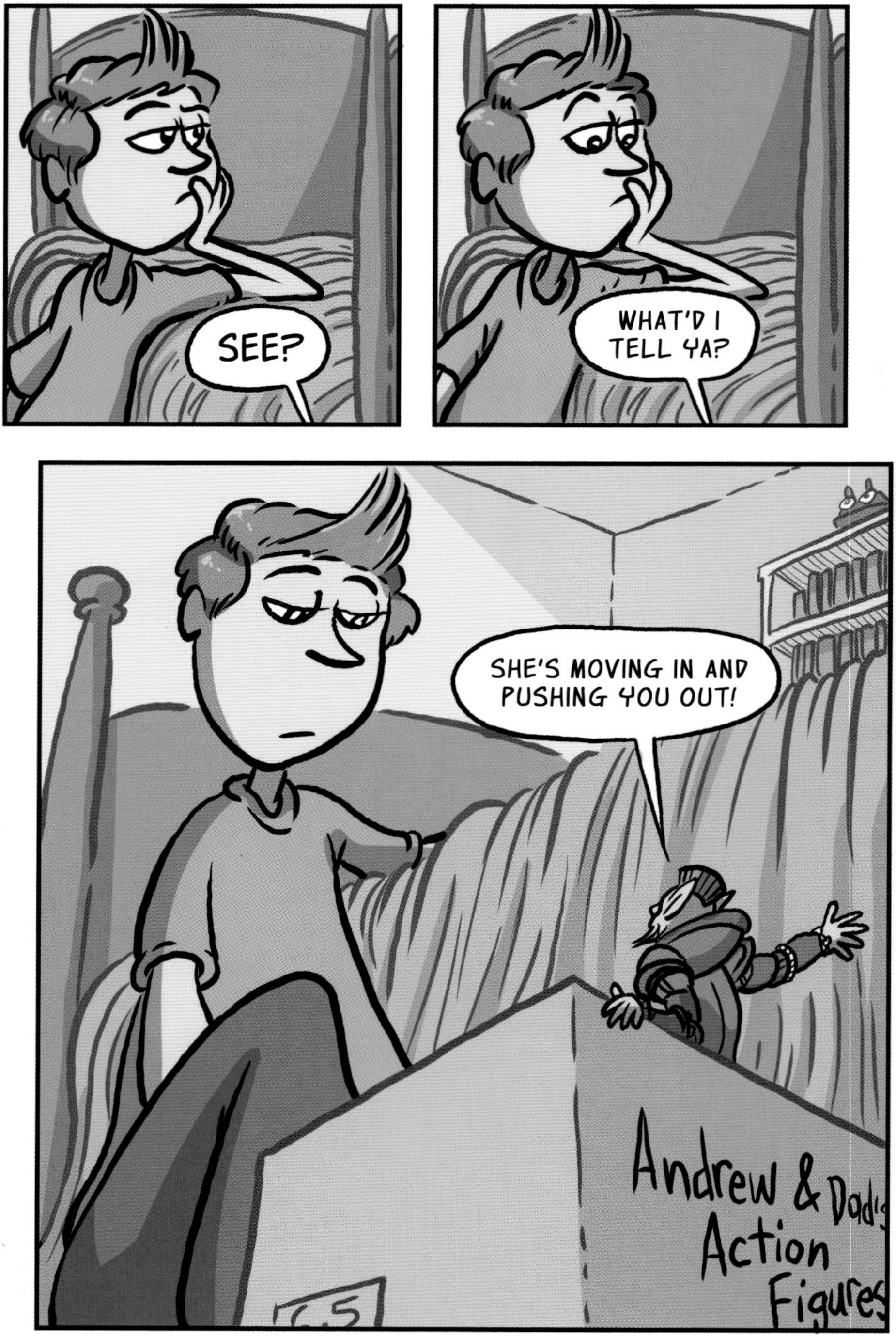
SEE?
WHAT'D I TELL YA?
SHE'S MOVING IN AND PUSHING YOU OUT!
Andrew & Dad's Action Figures

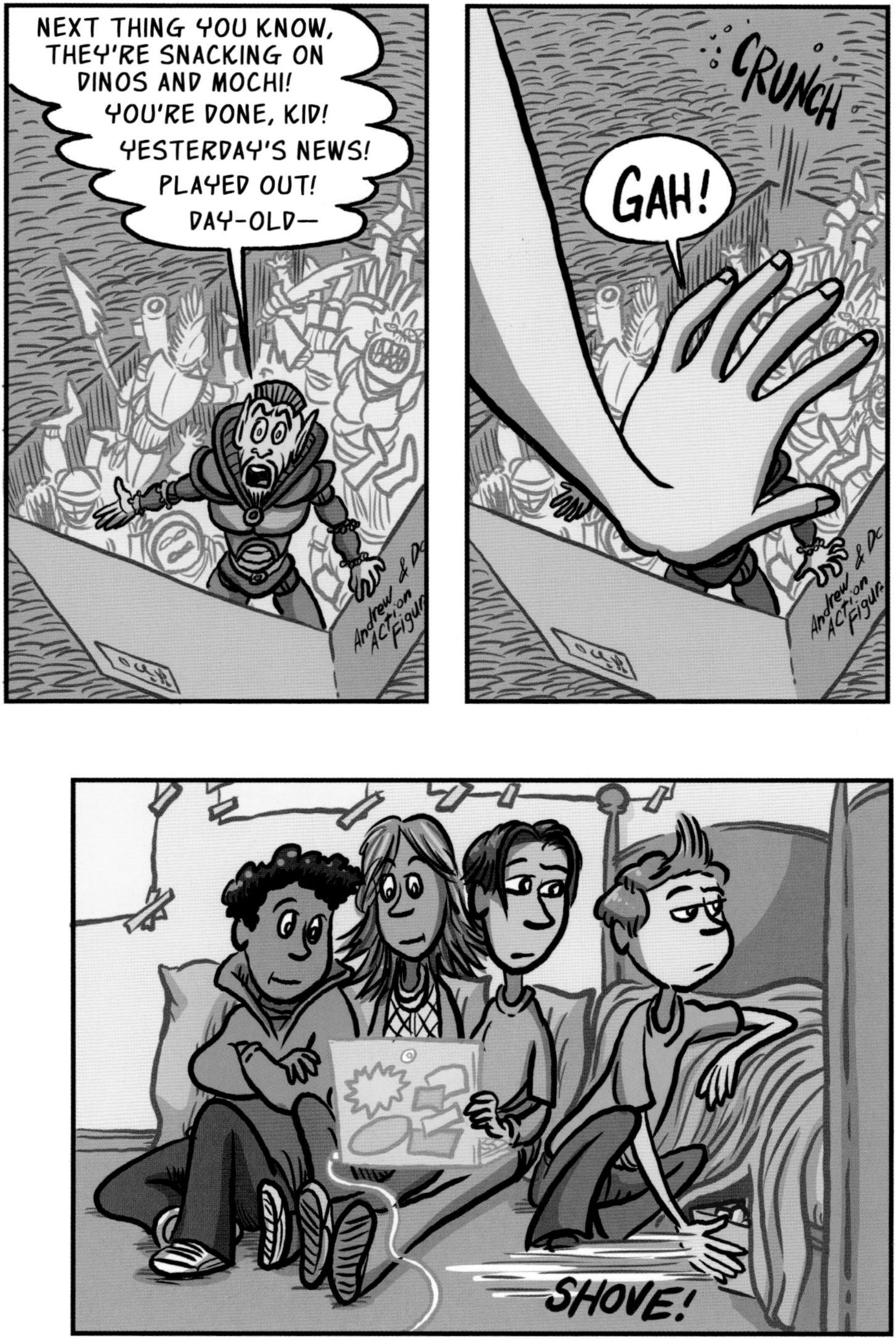
NEXT THING YOU KNOW, THEY'RE SNACKING ON DINOS AND MOCHI!
YOU'RE DONE, KID!
YESTERDAY'S NEWS!
PLAYED OUT!
DAY-OLD—
CRUNCH
GAH!
SHOVE!

CHAPTER 10

A FEW DAYS LATER

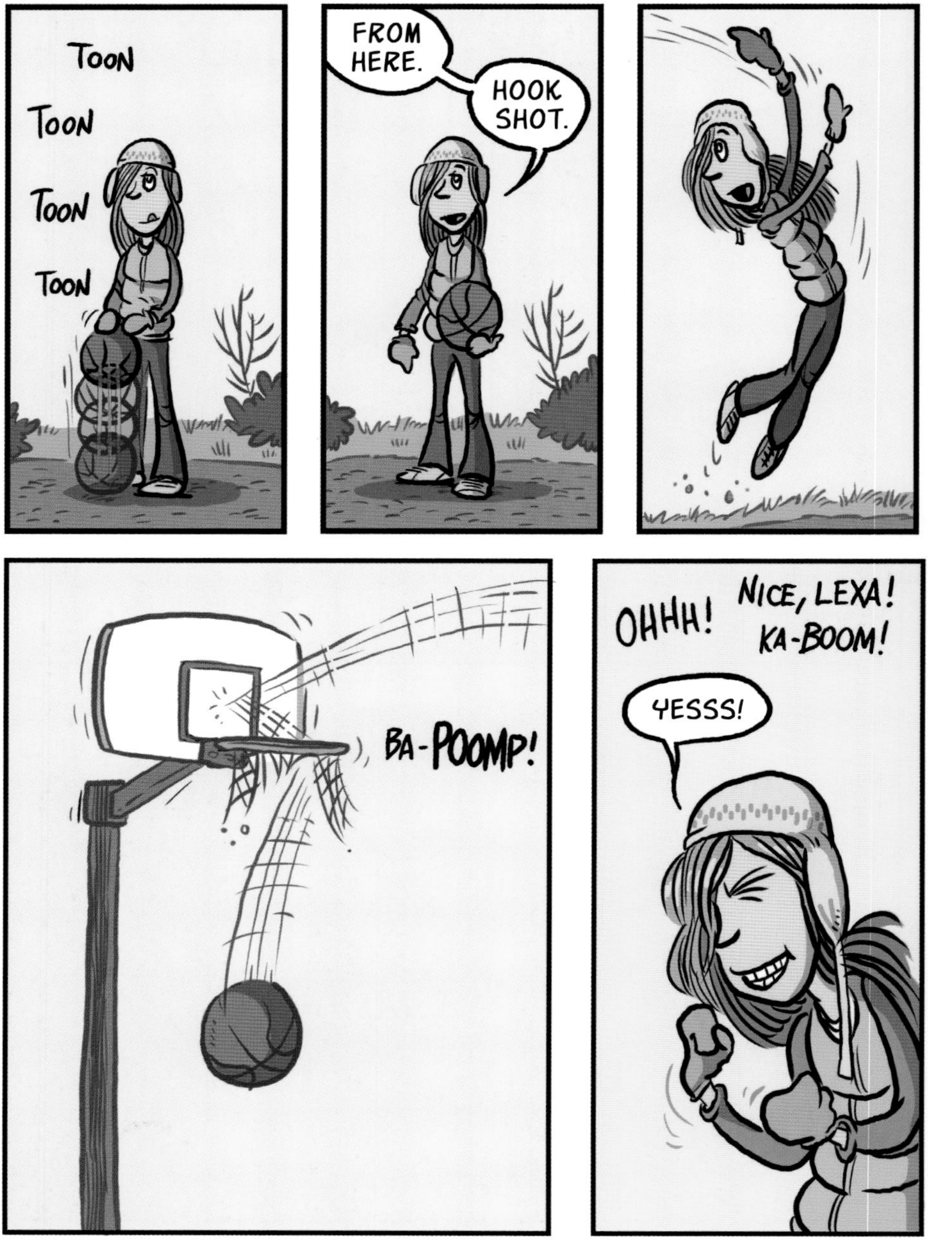
TOON
TOON
TOON
TOON
FROM HERE.
HOOK SHOT.
BA-POOMP!
OHHH!
NICE, LEXA!
KA-BOOM!
YESSS!

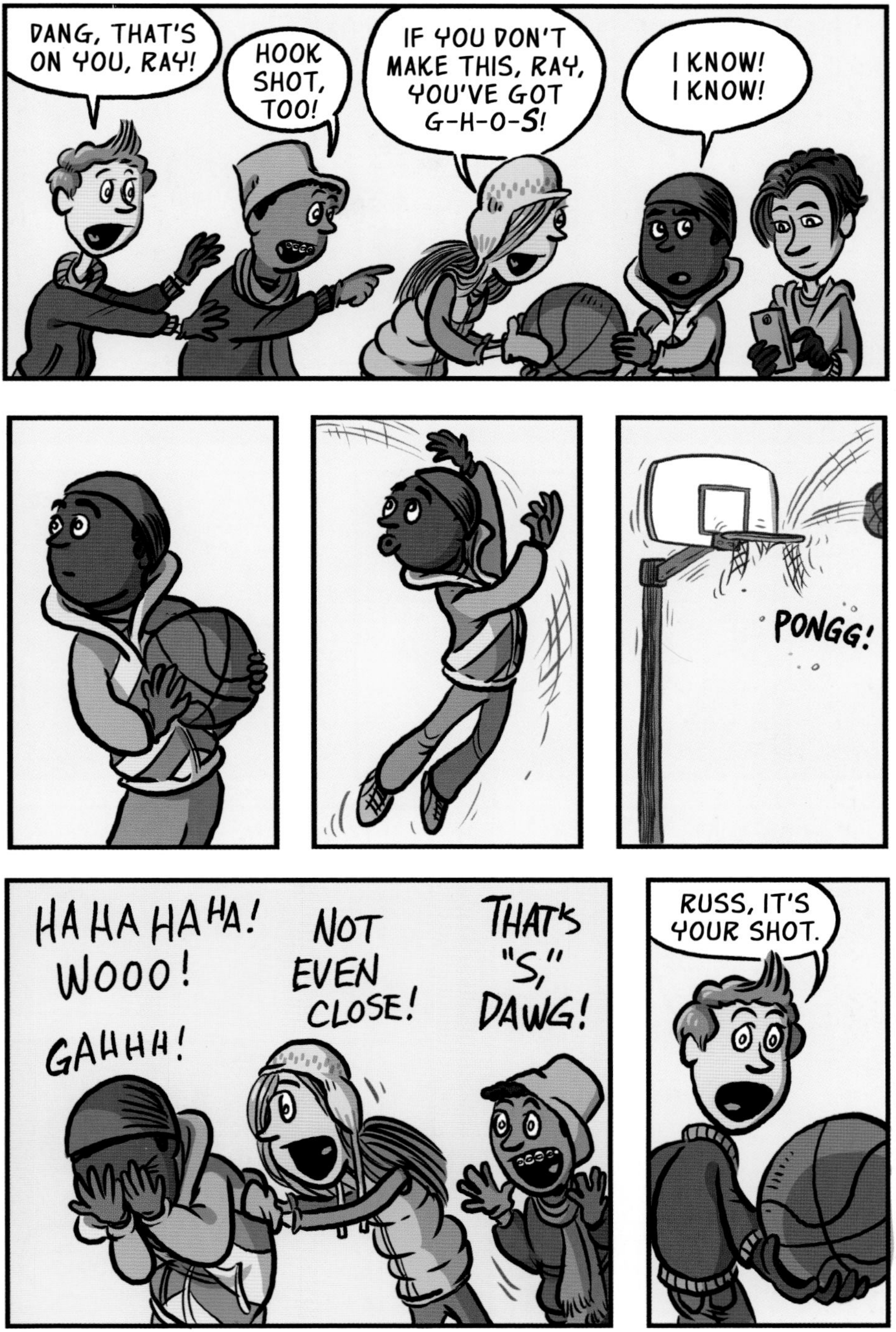
DANG, THAT'S ON YOU, RAY!
HOOK SHOT, TOO!
IF YOU DON'T MAKE THIS, RAY, YOU'VE GOT G-H-O-S!
I KNOW! I KNOW!
PONGG!
HA HA HA HA HA!
WOOO!
GAHHH!
NOT EVEN CLOSE!
THAT'S "S," DAWG!
RUSS, IT'S YOUR SHOT.

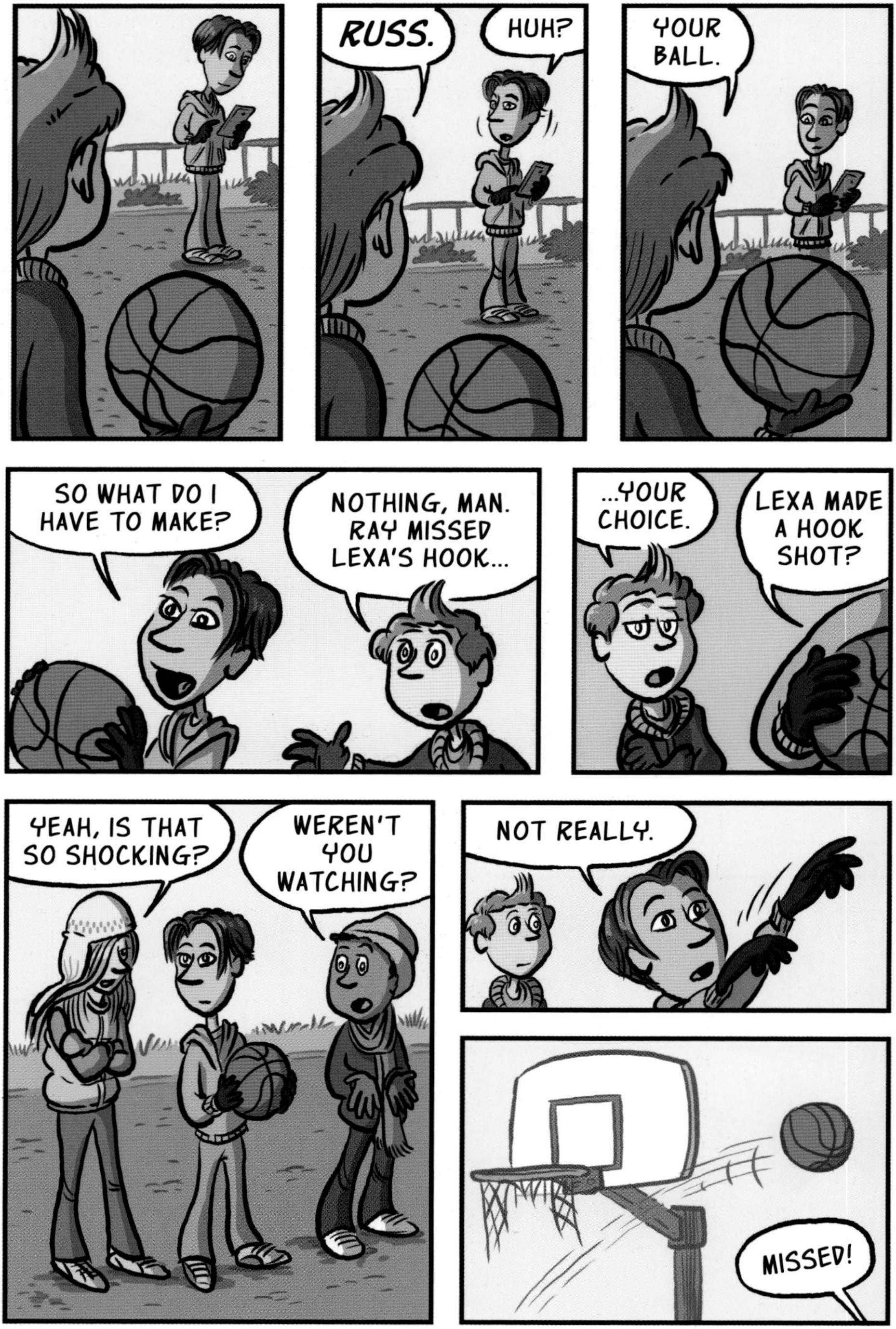
RUSS.
HUH?
YOUR BALL.
SO WHAT DO I HAVE TO MAKE?
NOTHING, MAN. RAY MISSED LEXA'S HOOK...
...YOUR CHOICE.
LEXA MADE A HOOK SHOT?
YEAH, IS THAT SO SHOCKING?
WEREN'T YOU WATCHING?
NOT REALLY.
MISSED!

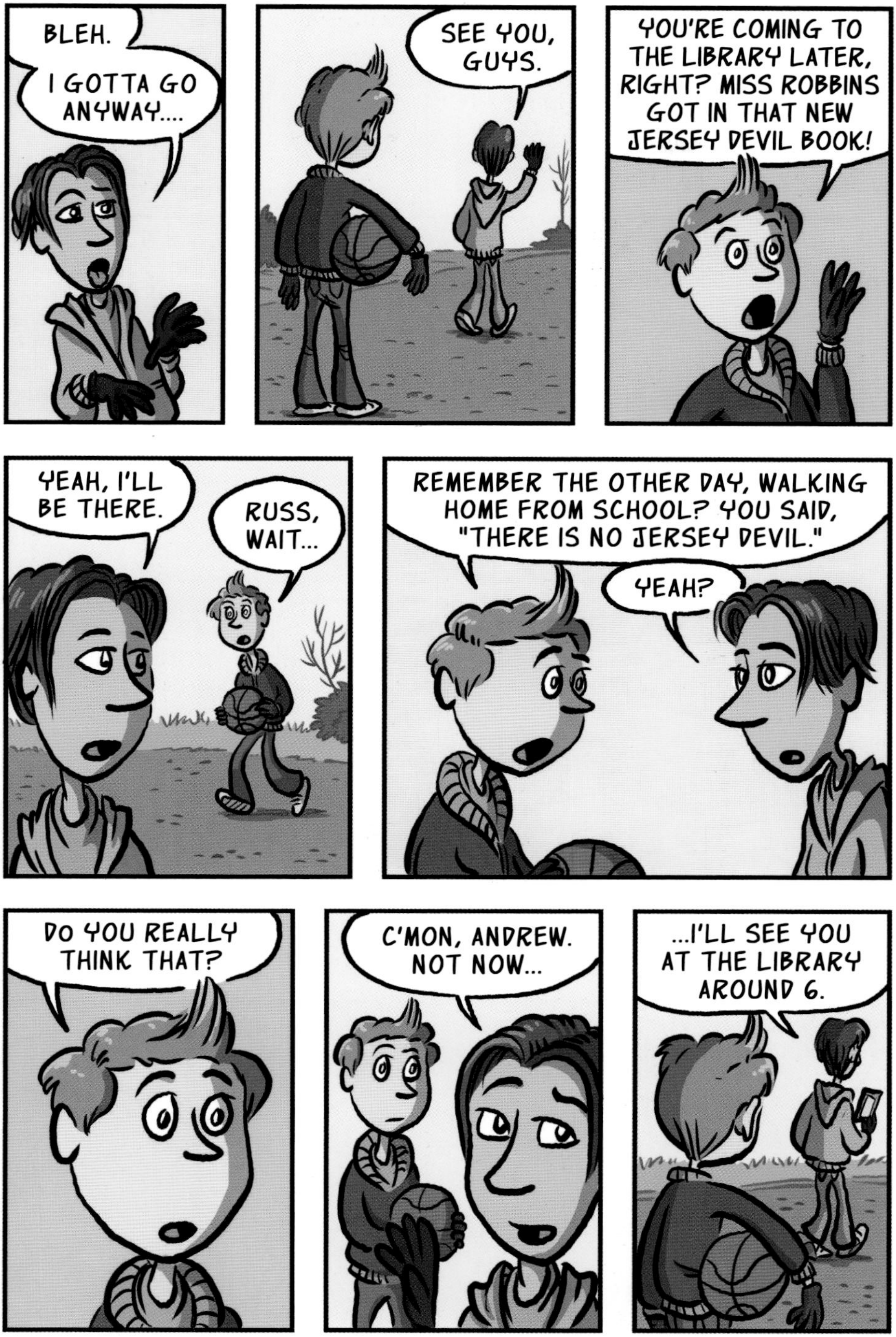
BLEH.
I GOTTA GO ANYWAY....
SEE YOU, GUYS.
YOU'RE COMING TO THE LIBRARY LATER, RIGHT? MISS ROBBINS GOT IN THAT NEW JERSEY DEVIL BOOK!
YEAH, I'LL BE THERE.
RUSS, WAIT...
REMEMBER THE OTHER DAY, WALKING HOME FROM SCHOOL? YOU SAID, "THERE IS NO JERSEY DEVIL."
YEAH?
DO YOU REALLY THINK THAT?
C'MON, ANDREW. NOT NOW...
...I'LL SEE YOU AT THE LIBRARY AROUND 6.

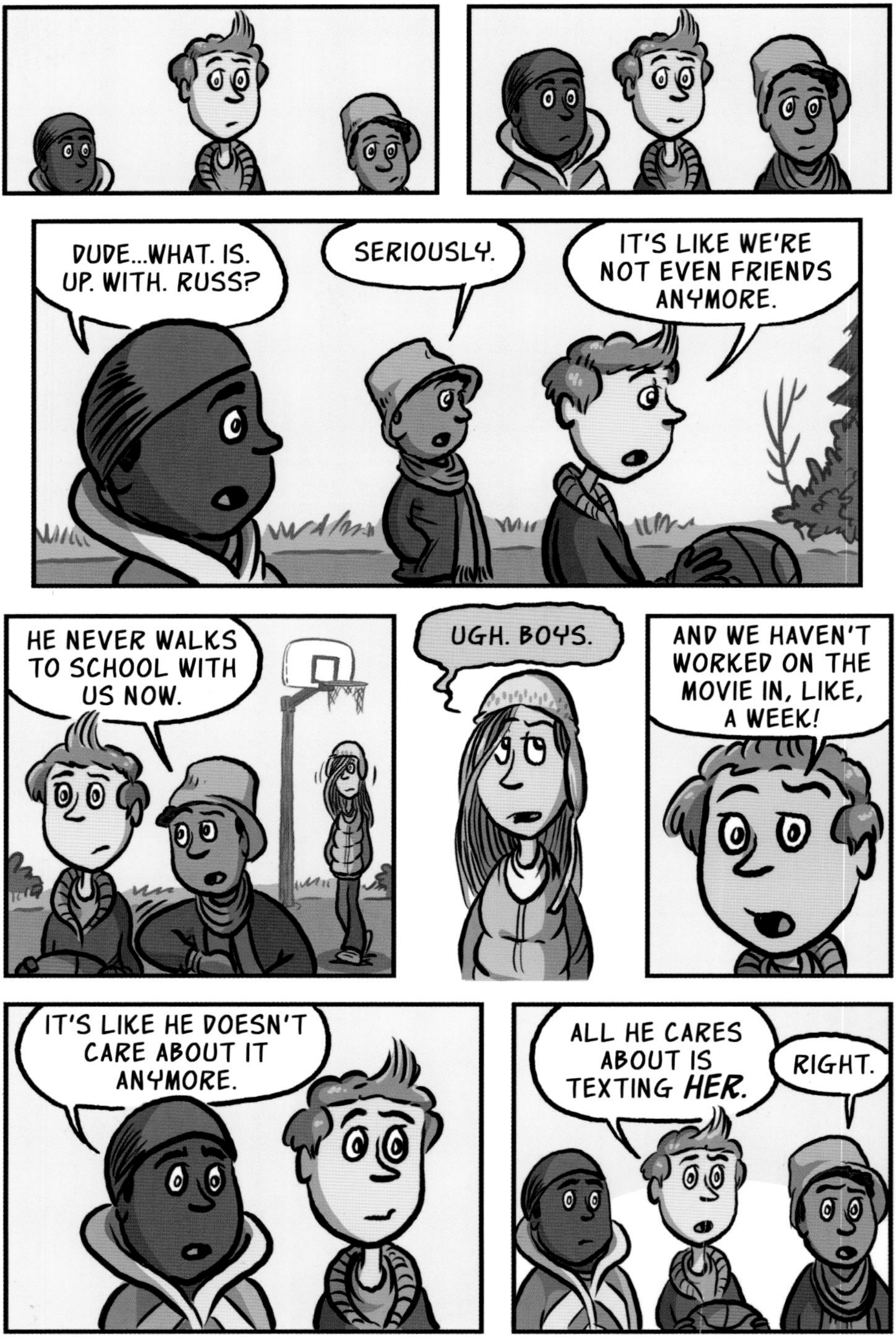
DUDE...WHAT. IS. UP. WITH. RUSS?
SERIOUSLY.
IT'S LIKE WE'RE NOT EVEN FRIENDS ANYMORE.
HE NEVER WALKS TO SCHOOL WITH US NOW.
UGH. BOYS.
AND WE HAVEN'T WORKED ON THE MOVIE IN, LIKE, A WEEK!
IT'S LIKE HE DOESN'T CARE ABOUT IT ANYMORE.
ALL HE CARES ABOUT IS TEXTING ***HER***.
RIGHT.

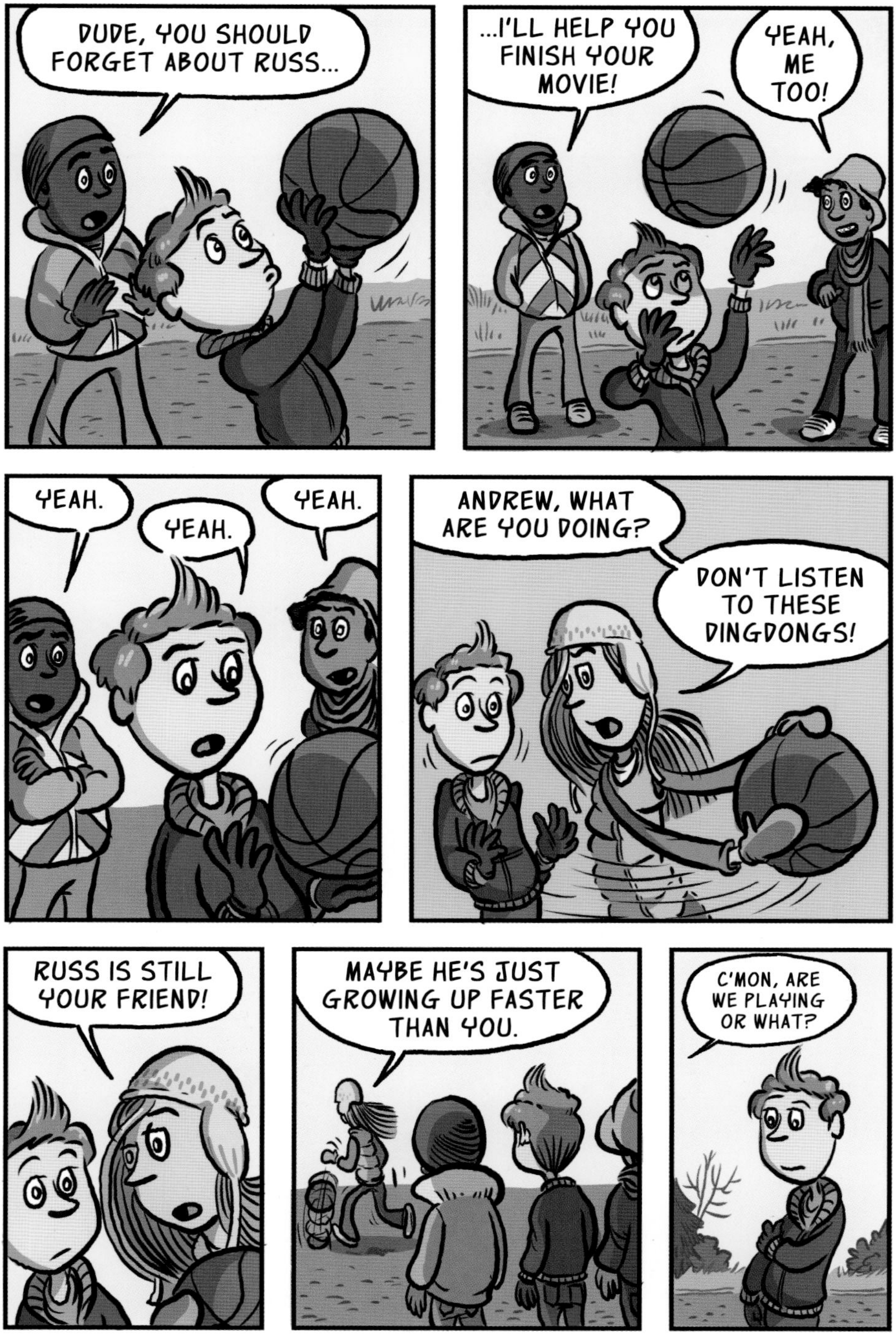
DUDE, YOU SHOULD FORGET ABOUT RUSS...
...I'LL HELP YOU FINISH YOUR MOVIE!
YEAH, ME TOO!
YEAH.
YEAH.
YEAH.
ANDREW, WHAT ARE YOU DOING?
DON'T LISTEN TO THESE DINGDONGS!
RUSS IS STILL YOUR FRIEND!
MAYBE HE'S JUST GROWING UP FASTER THAN YOU.
C'MON, ARE WE PLAYING OR WHAT?

CHAPTER 11

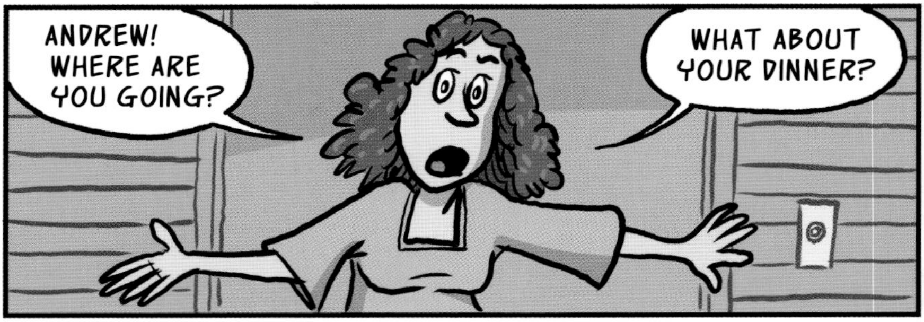
ANDREW! WHERE ARE YOU GOING?
WHAT ABOUT YOUR DINNER?

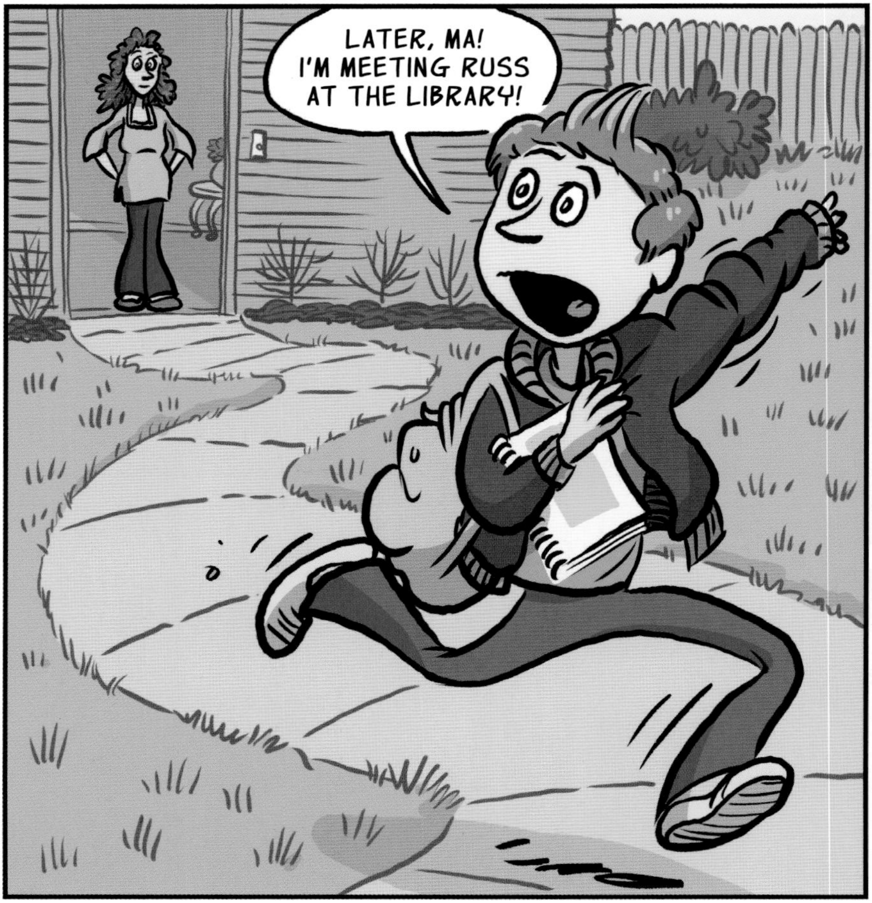
LATER, MA! I'M MEETING RUSS AT THE LIBRARY!

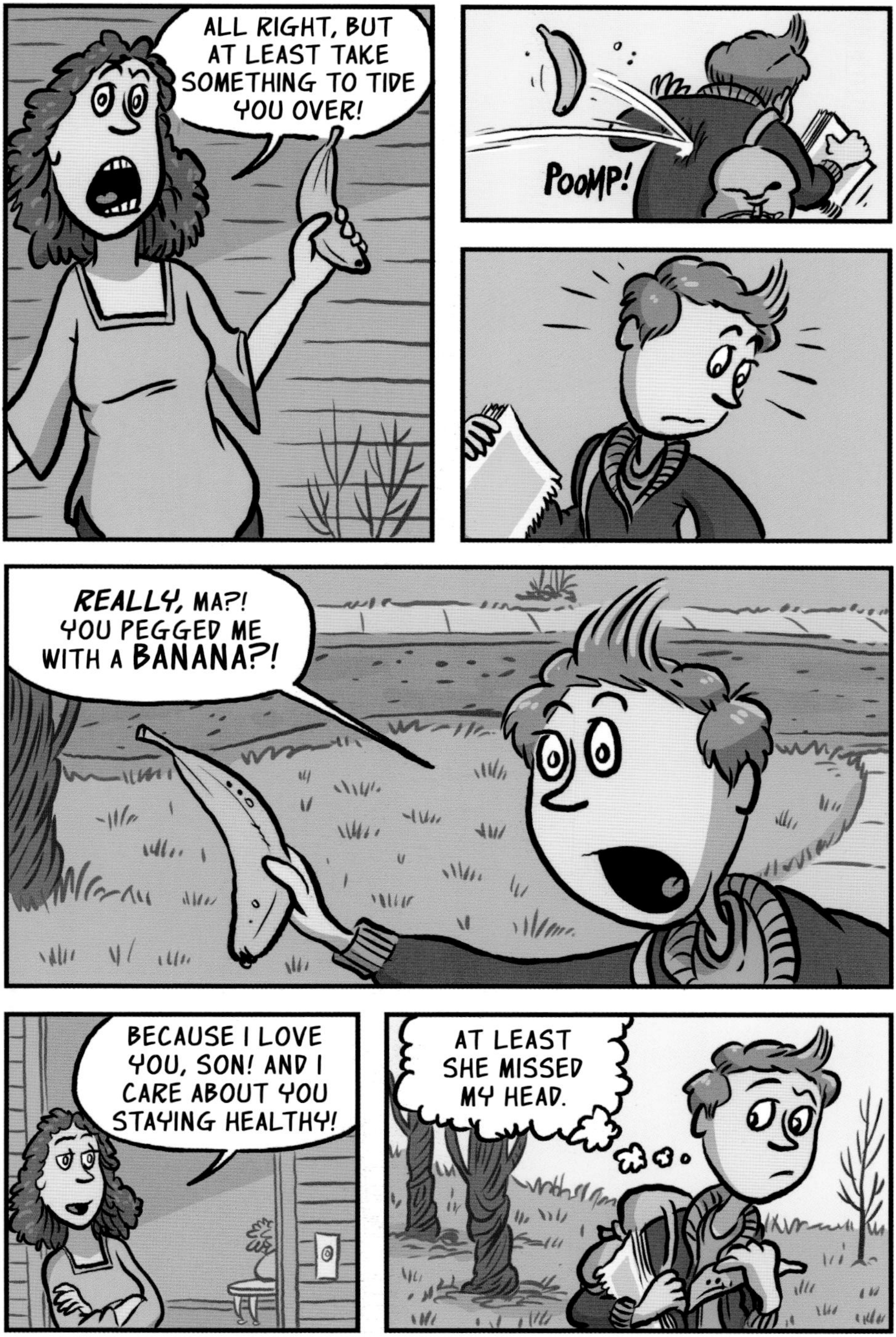
ALL RIGHT, BUT AT LEAST TAKE SOMETHING TO TIDE YOU OVER!
POOMP!
REALLY, MA?! YOU PEGGED ME WITH A BANANA?!
BECAUSE I LOVE YOU, SON! AND I CARE ABOUT YOU STAYING HEALTHY!
AT LEAST SHE MISSED MY HEAD.

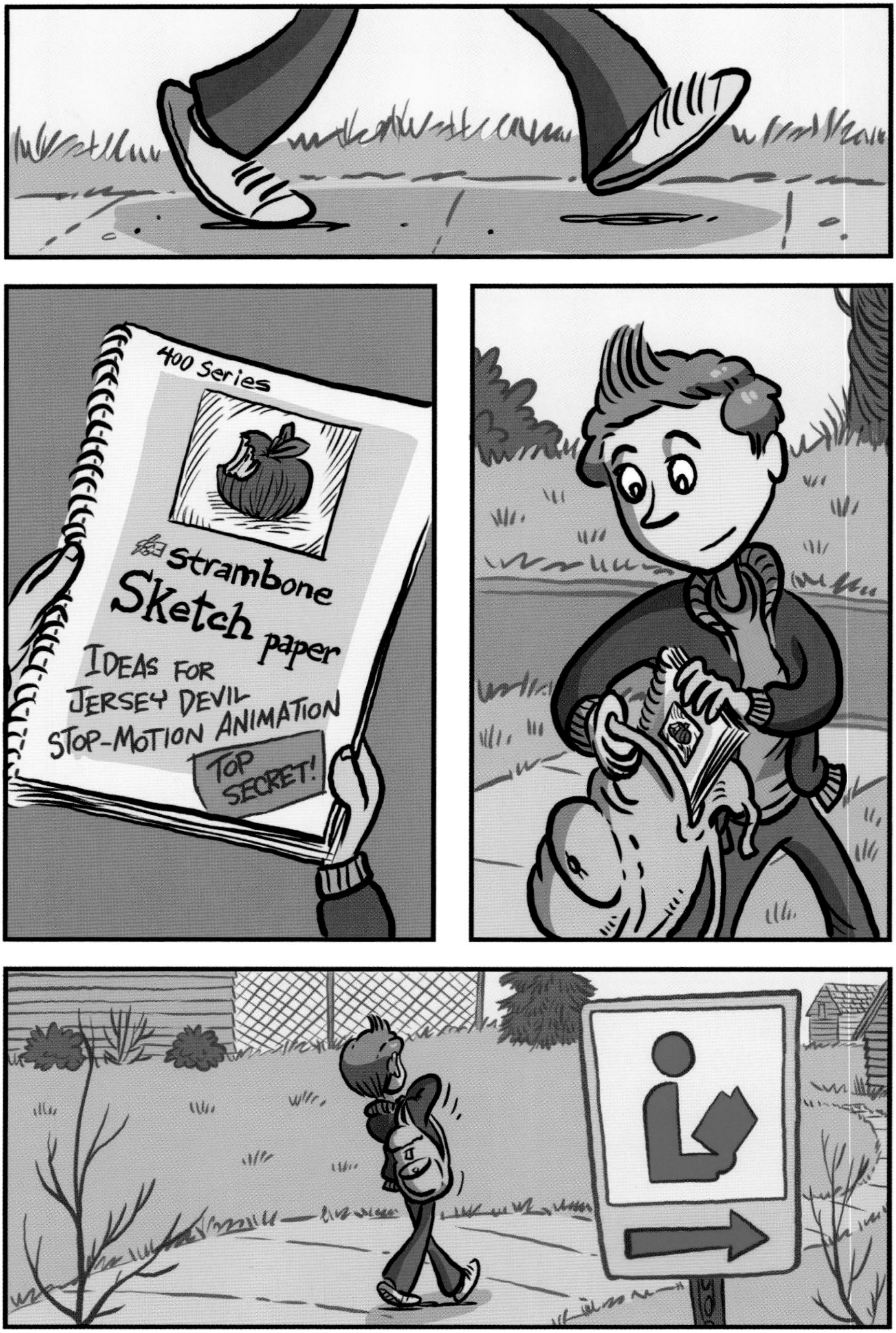
400 Series
strambone
Sketch paper
IDEAS FOR
JERSEY DEVIL
STOP-MOTION ANIMATION
TOP SECRET!

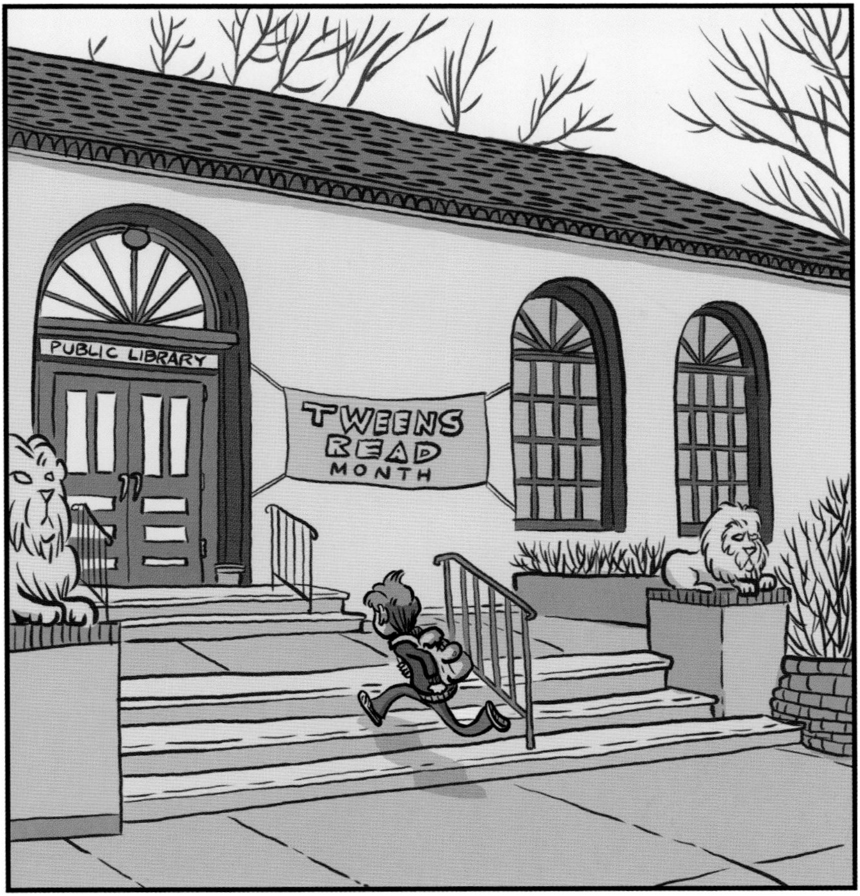
PUBLIC LIBRARY
TWEENS READ MONTH

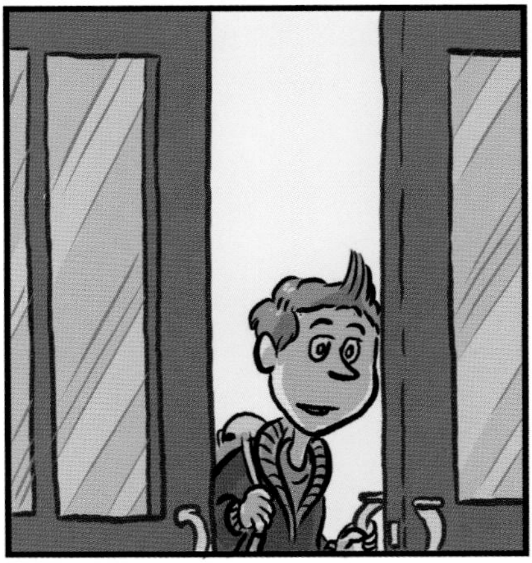

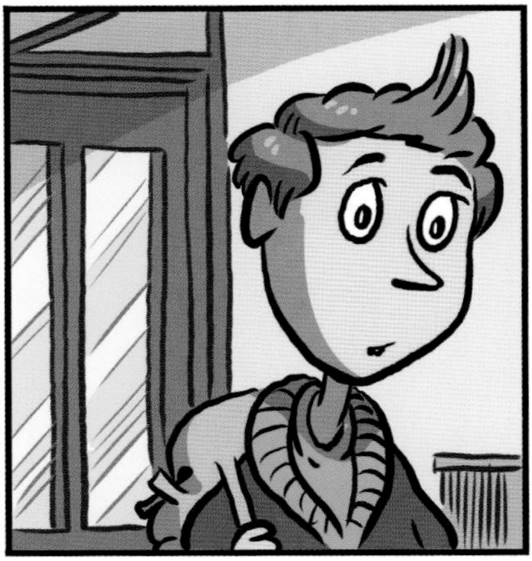

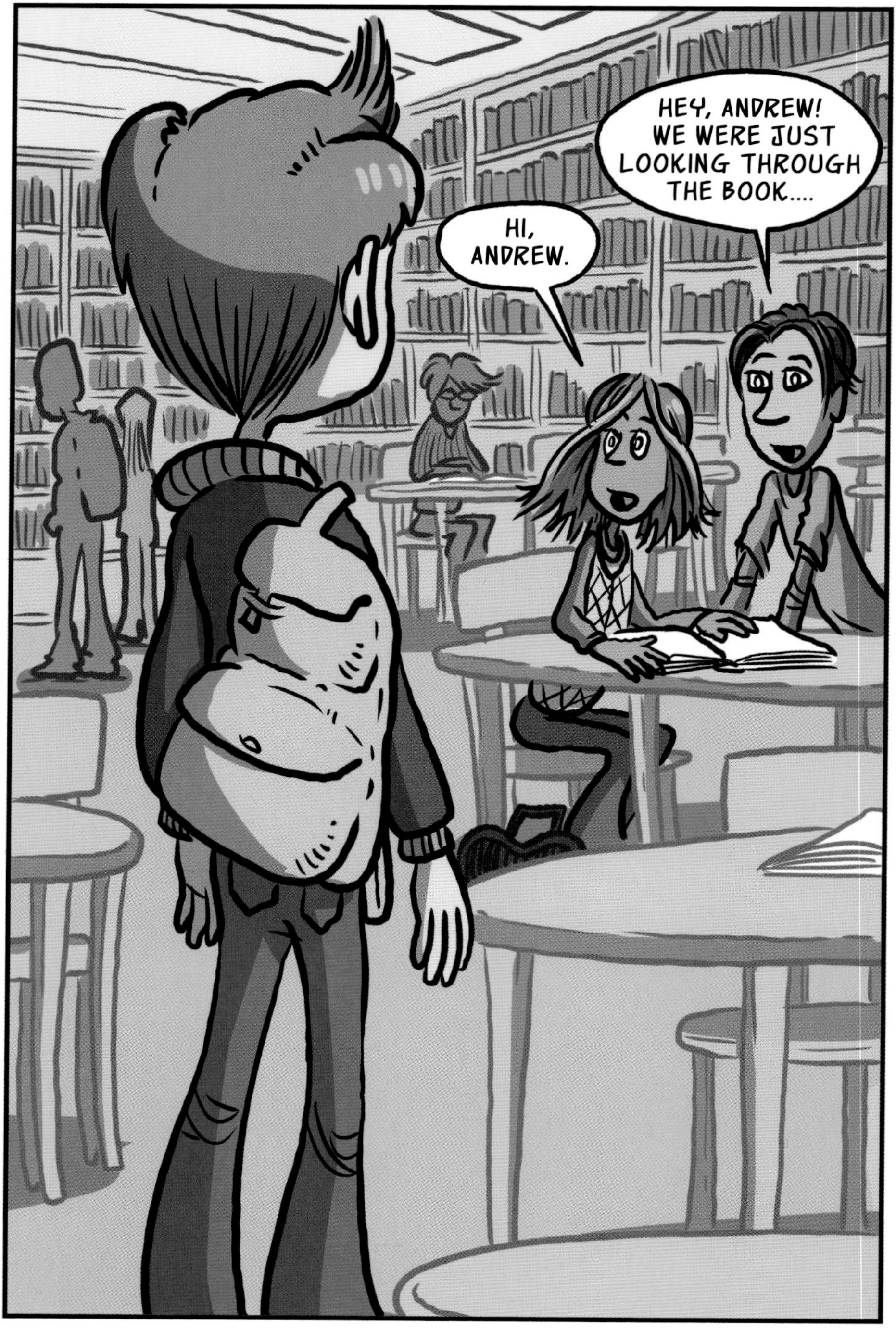
HI, ANDREW.
HEY, ANDREW! WE WERE JUST LOOKING THROUGH THE BOOK....

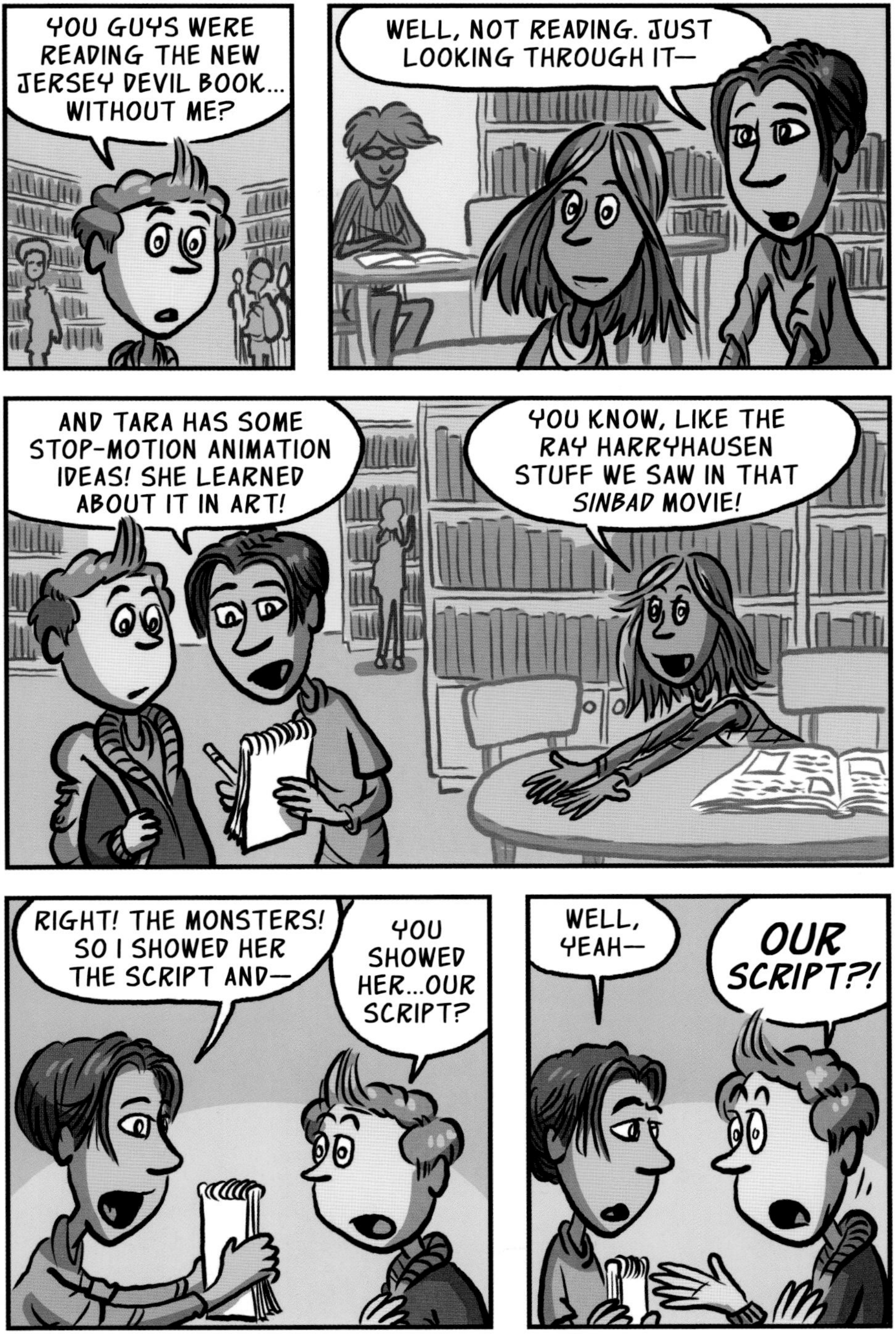
YOU GUYS WERE READING THE NEW JERSEY DEVIL BOOK... WITHOUT ME?
WELL, NOT READING. JUST LOOKING THROUGH IT—
AND TARA HAS SOME STOP-MOTION ANIMATION IDEAS! SHE LEARNED ABOUT IT IN ART!
YOU KNOW, LIKE THE RAY HARRYHAUSEN STUFF WE SAW IN THAT *SINBAD* MOVIE!
RIGHT! THE MONSTERS! SO I SHOWED HER THE SCRIPT AND—
YOU SHOWED HER...OUR SCRIPT?
WELL, YEAH—
OUR SCRIPT?!

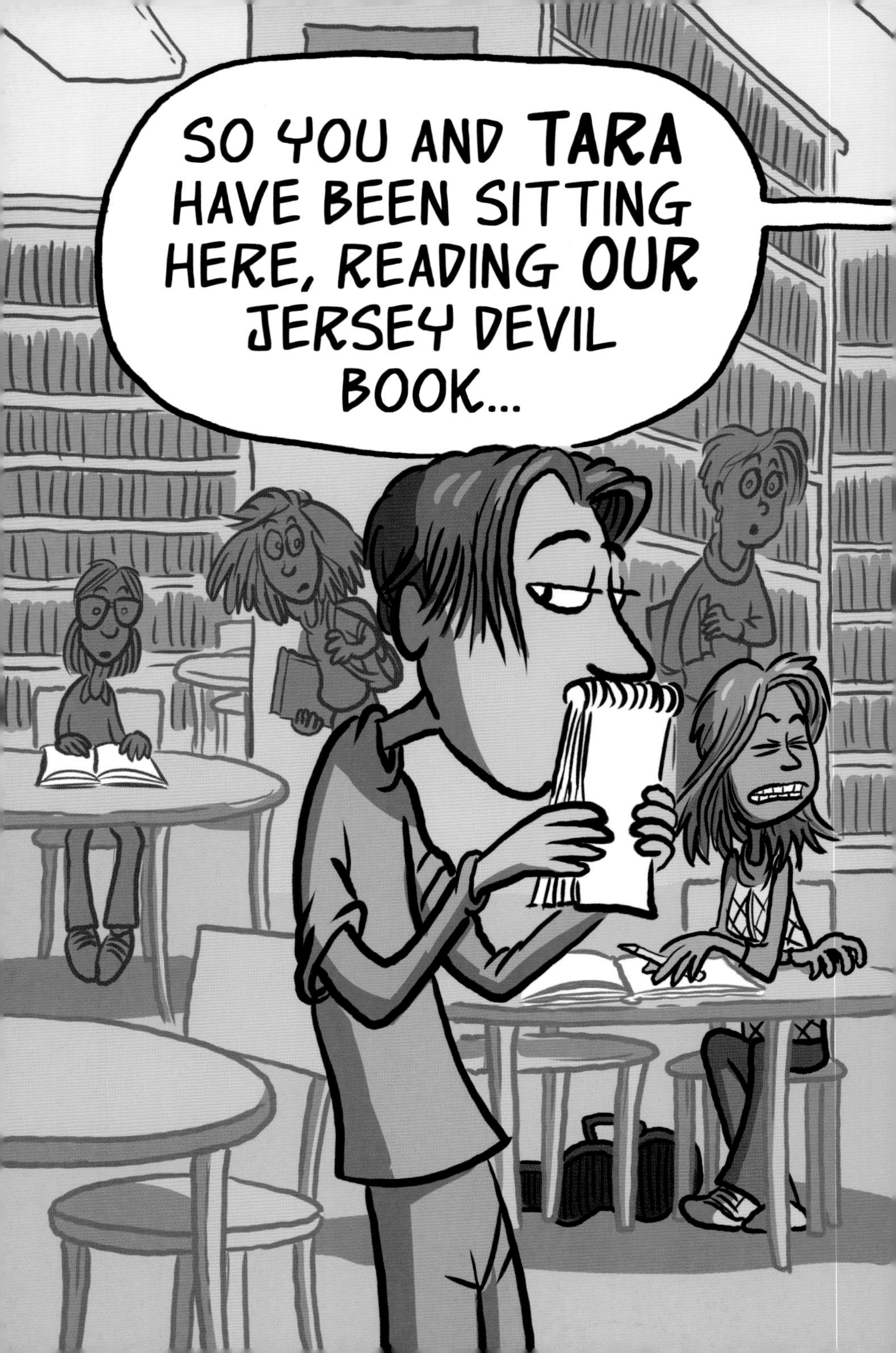
SO YOU AND TARA HAVE BEEN SITTING HERE, READING OUR JERSEY DEVIL BOOK...

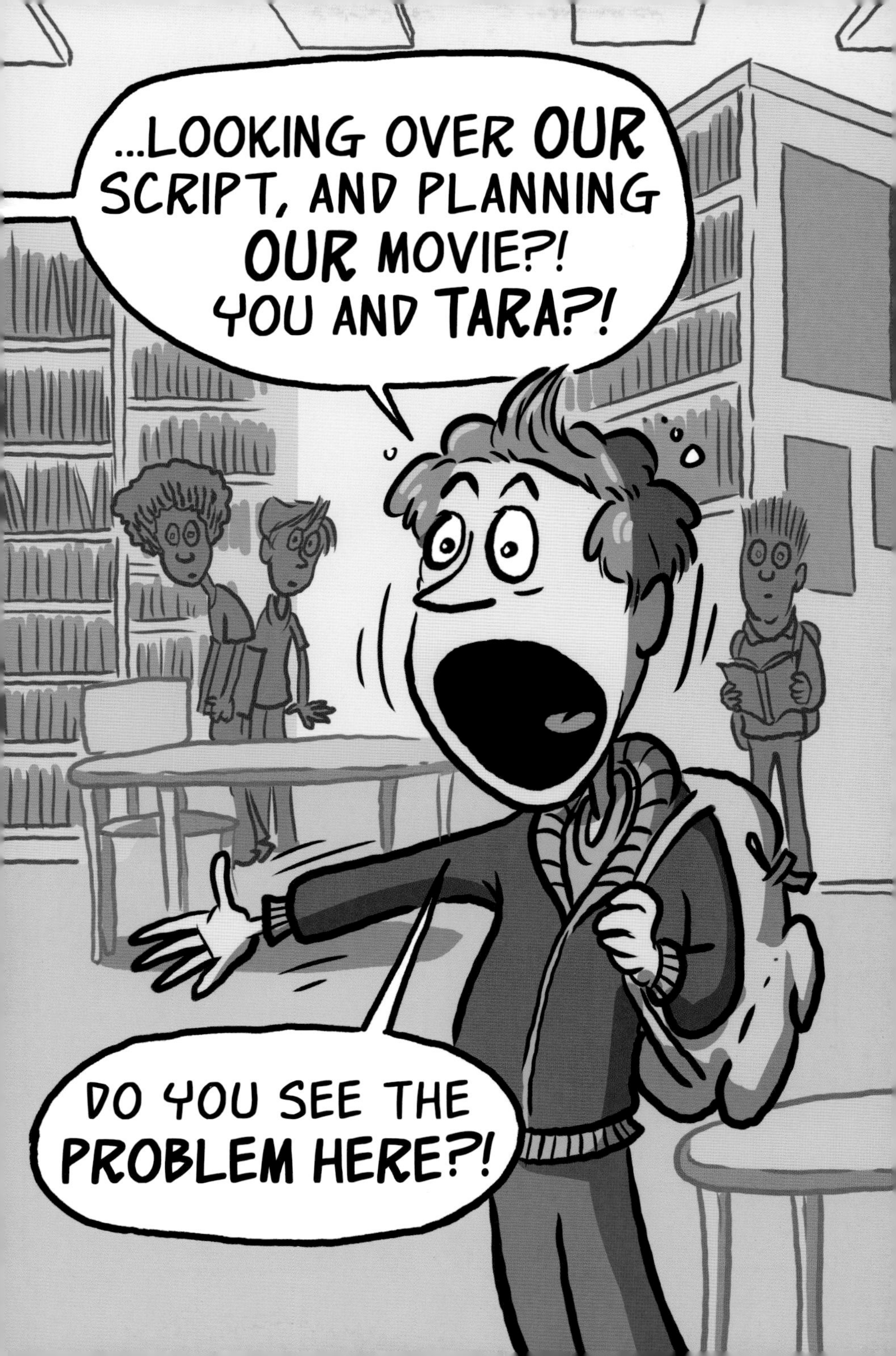
...LOOKING OVER OUR SCRIPT, AND PLANNING OUR MOVIE?! YOU AND TARA?!
DO YOU SEE THE PROBLEM HERE?!

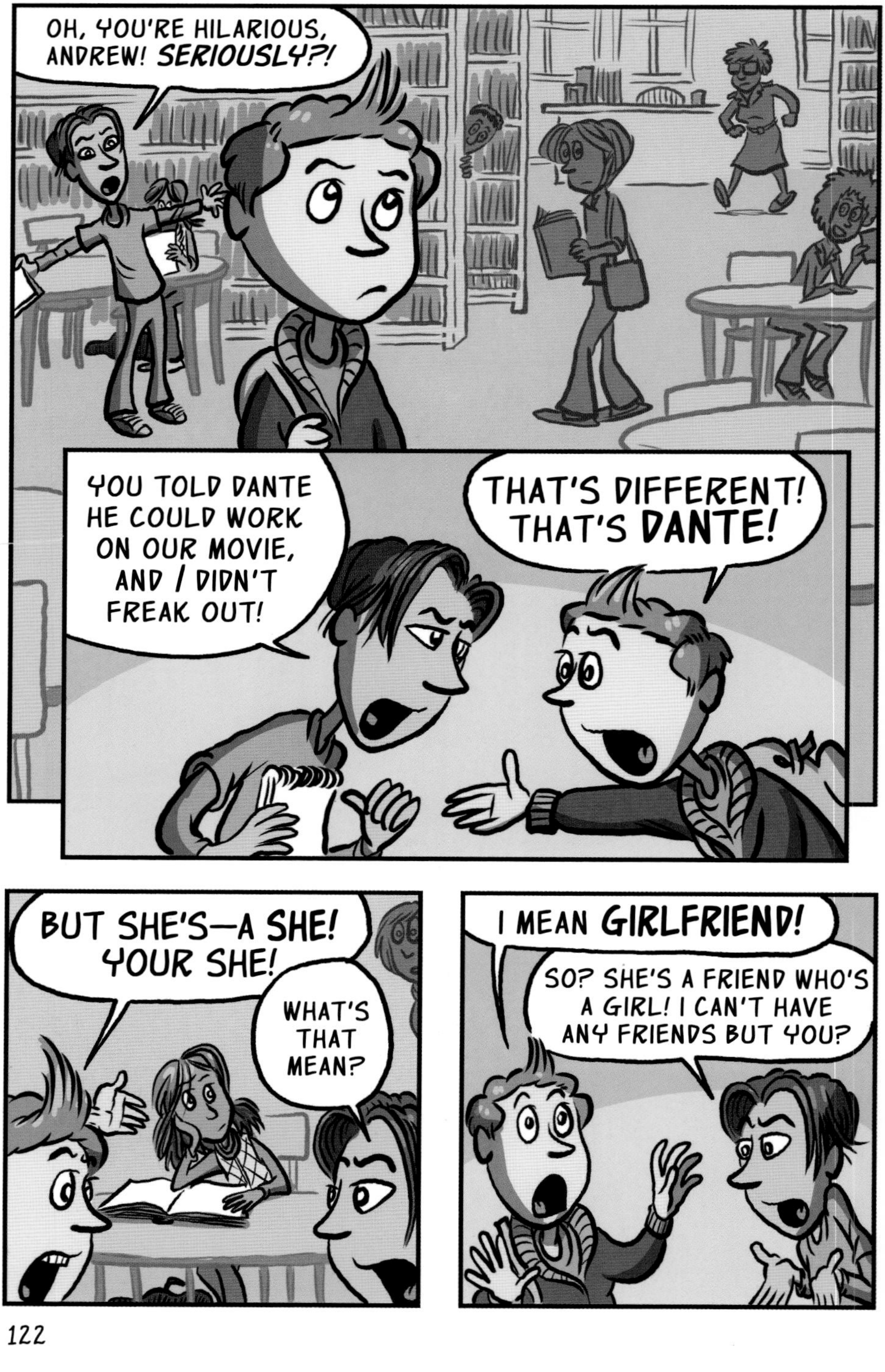

OH, YOU'RE HILARIOUS, ANDREW! SERIOUSLY?!
YOU TOLD DANTE HE COULD WORK ON OUR MOVIE, AND I DIDN'T FREAK OUT!
THAT'S DIFFERENT! THAT'S DANTE!
BUT SHE'S—A SHE! YOUR SHE!
WHAT'S THAT MEAN?
I MEAN GIRLFRIEND!
SO? SHE'S A FRIEND WHO'S A GIRL! I CAN'T HAVE ANY FRIENDS BUT YOU?

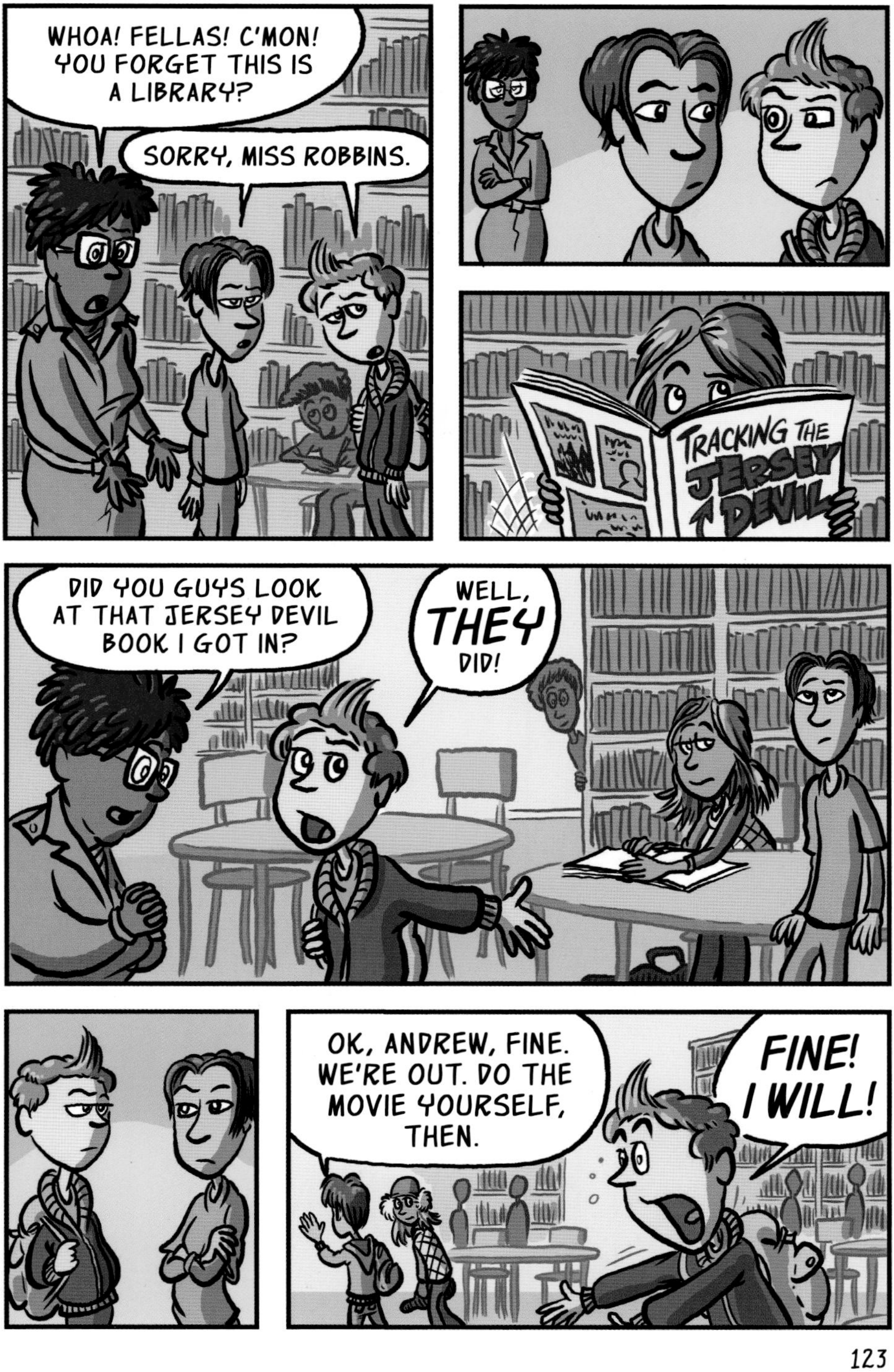
WHOA! FELLAS! C'MON! YOU FORGET THIS IS A LIBRARY?
SORRY, MISS ROBBINS.
TRACKING THE JERSEY DEVIL
DID YOU GUYS LOOK AT THAT JERSEY DEVIL BOOK I GOT IN?
WELL, THEY DID!
OK, ANDREW, FINE. WE'RE OUT. DO THE MOVIE YOURSELF, THEN.
FINE! I WILL!

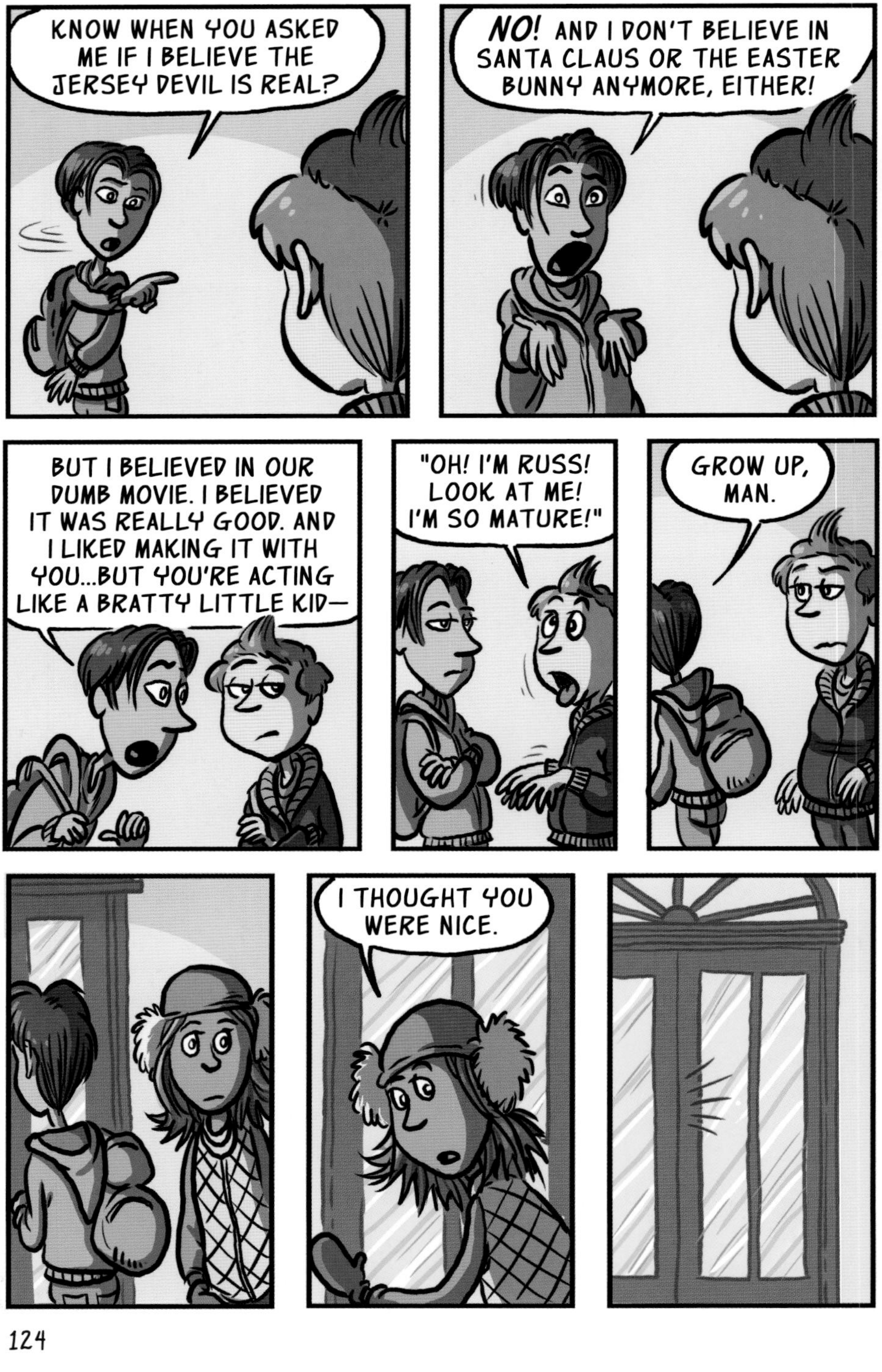
KNOW WHEN YOU ASKED ME IF I BELIEVE THE JERSEY DEVIL IS REAL?
NO! AND I DON'T BELIEVE IN SANTA CLAUS OR THE EASTER BUNNY ANYMORE, EITHER!
BUT I BELIEVED IN OUR DUMB MOVIE. I BELIEVED IT WAS REALLY GOOD. AND I LIKED MAKING IT WITH YOU...BUT YOU'RE ACTING LIKE A BRATTY LITTLE KID—
"OH! I'M RUSS! LOOK AT ME! I'M SO MATURE!"
GROW UP, MAN.
I THOUGHT YOU WERE NICE.

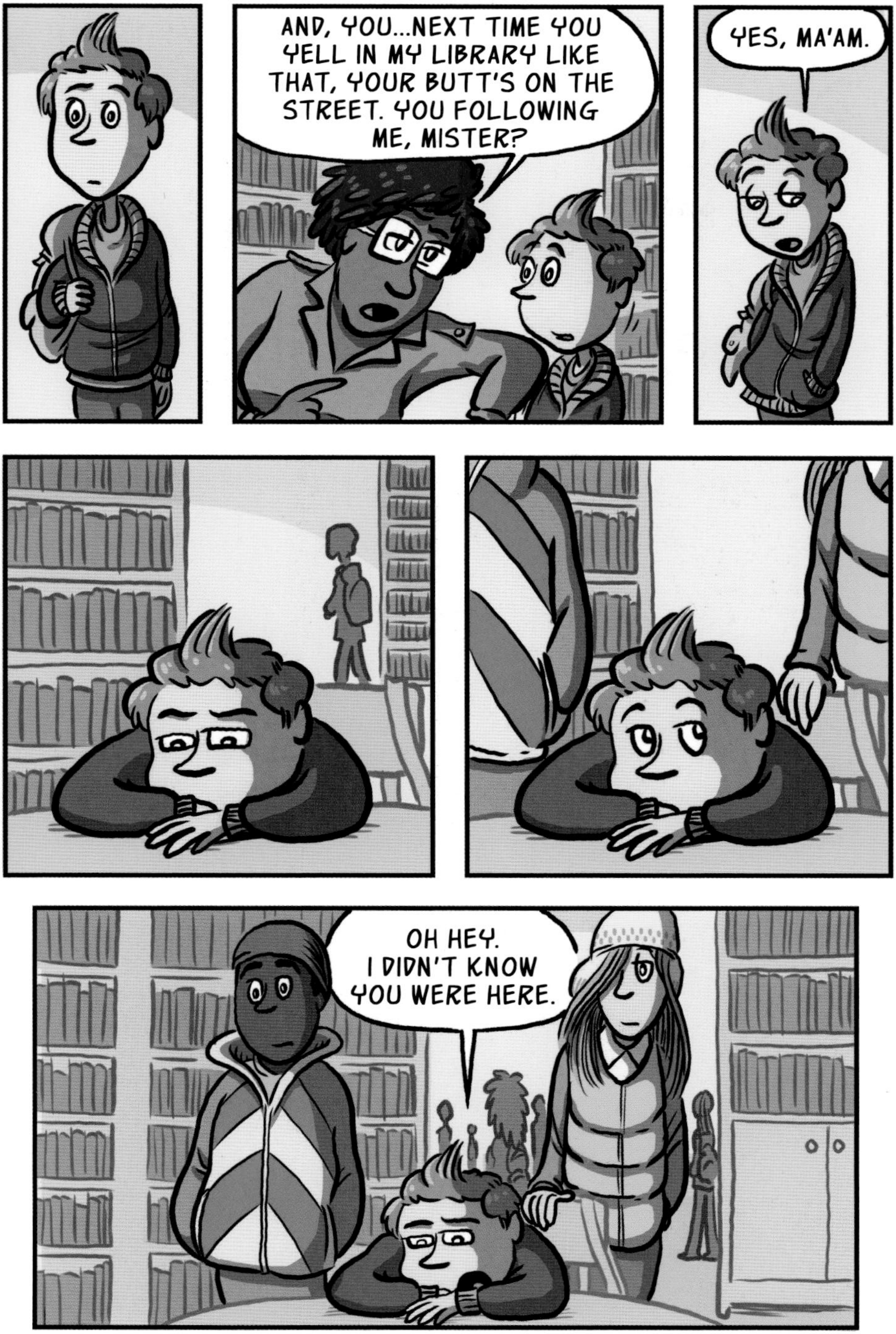

AND, YOU...NEXT TIME YOU YELL IN MY LIBRARY LIKE THAT, YOUR BUTT'S ON THE STREET. YOU FOLLOWING ME, MISTER?
YES, MA'AM.
OH HEY. I DIDN'T KNOW YOU WERE HERE.

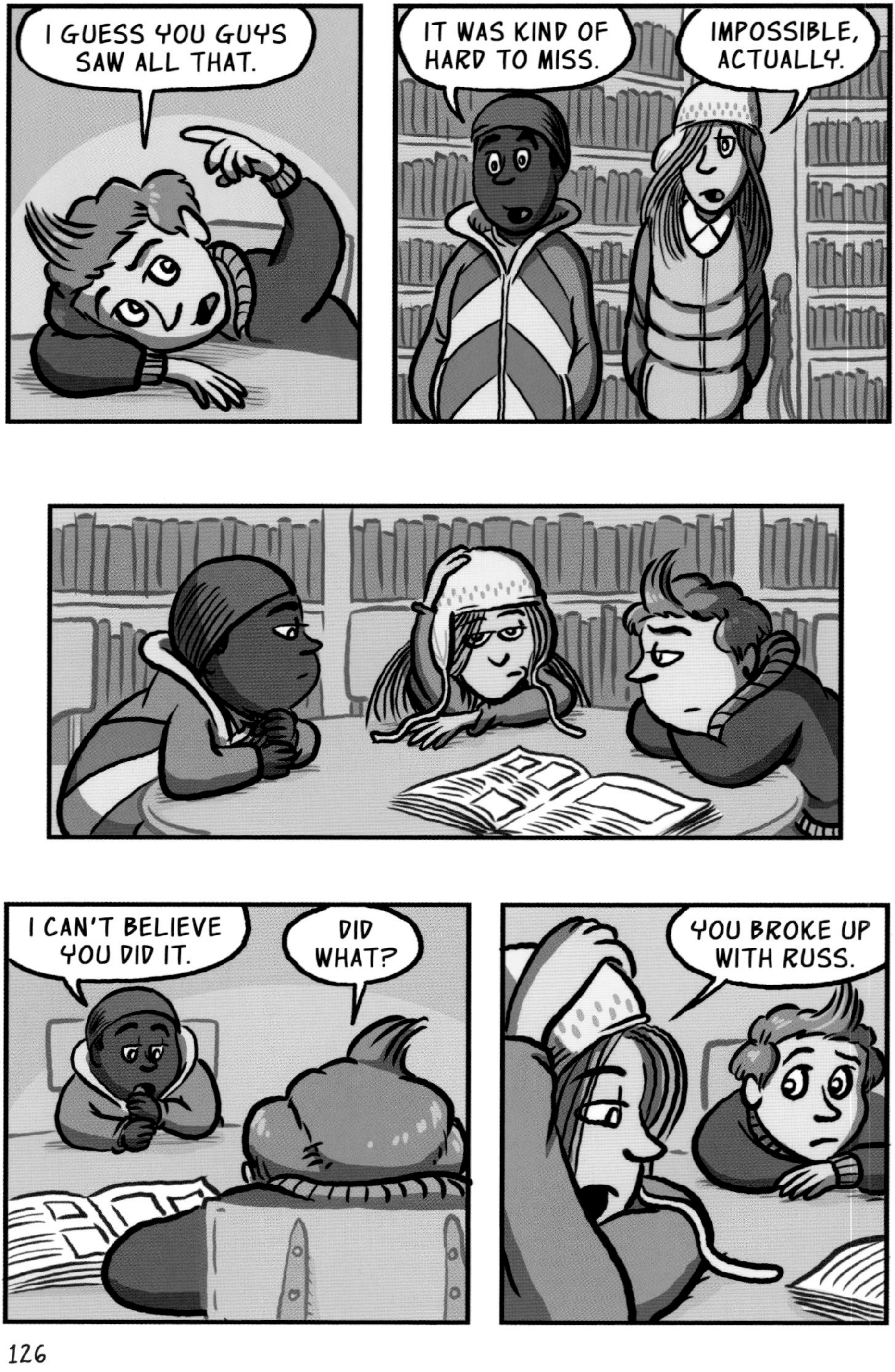
I GUESS YOU GUYS SAW ALL THAT.
IT WAS KIND OF HARD TO MISS.
IMPOSSIBLE, ACTUALLY.
I CAN'T BELIEVE YOU DID IT.
DID WHAT?
YOU BROKE UP WITH RUSS.

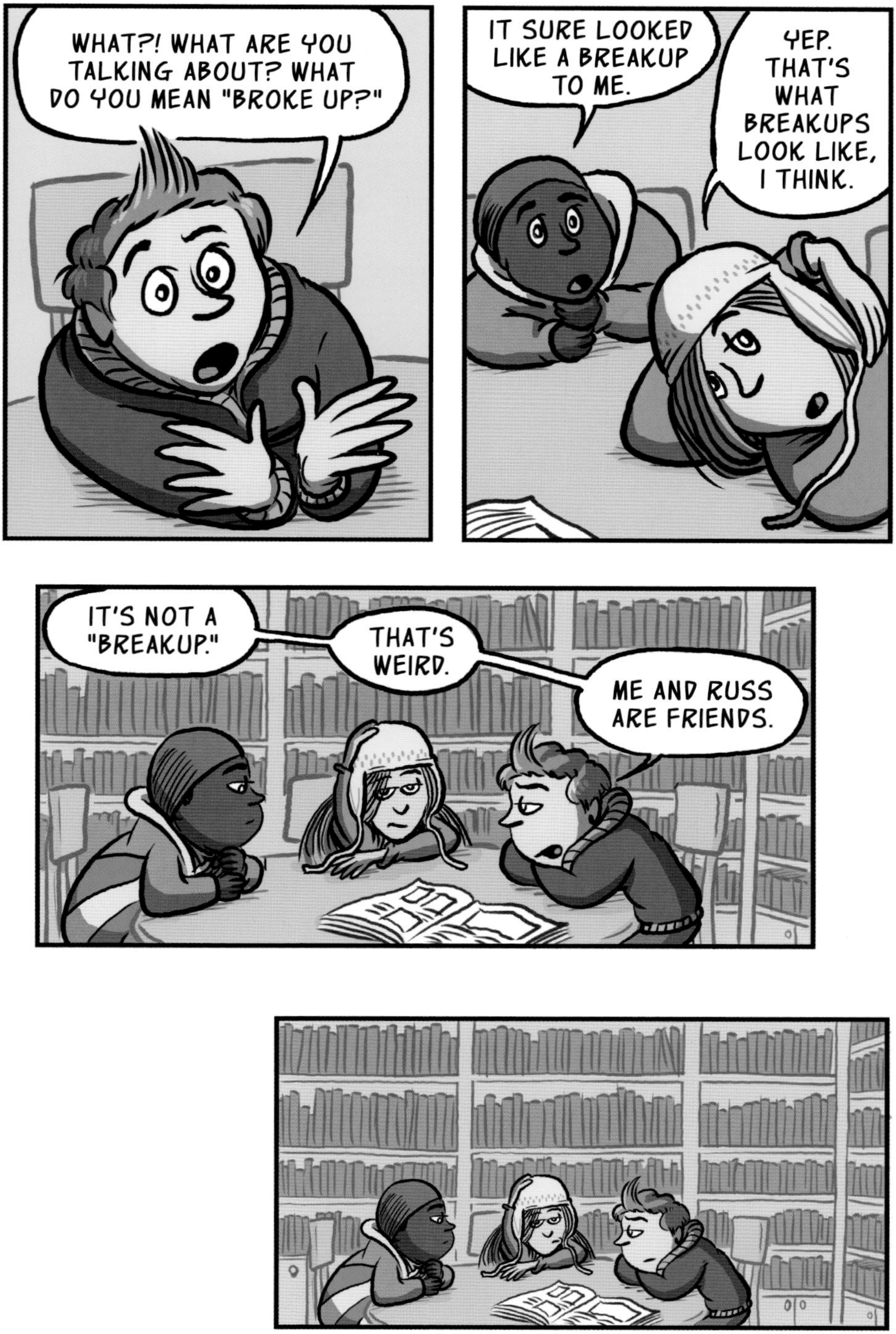
WHAT?! WHAT ARE YOU TALKING ABOUT? WHAT DO YOU MEAN "BROKE UP?"
IT SURE LOOKED LIKE A BREAKUP TO ME.
YEP. THAT'S WHAT BREAKUPS LOOK LIKE, I THINK.
IT'S NOT A "BREAKUP."
THAT'S WEIRD.
ME AND RUSS ARE FRIENDS.

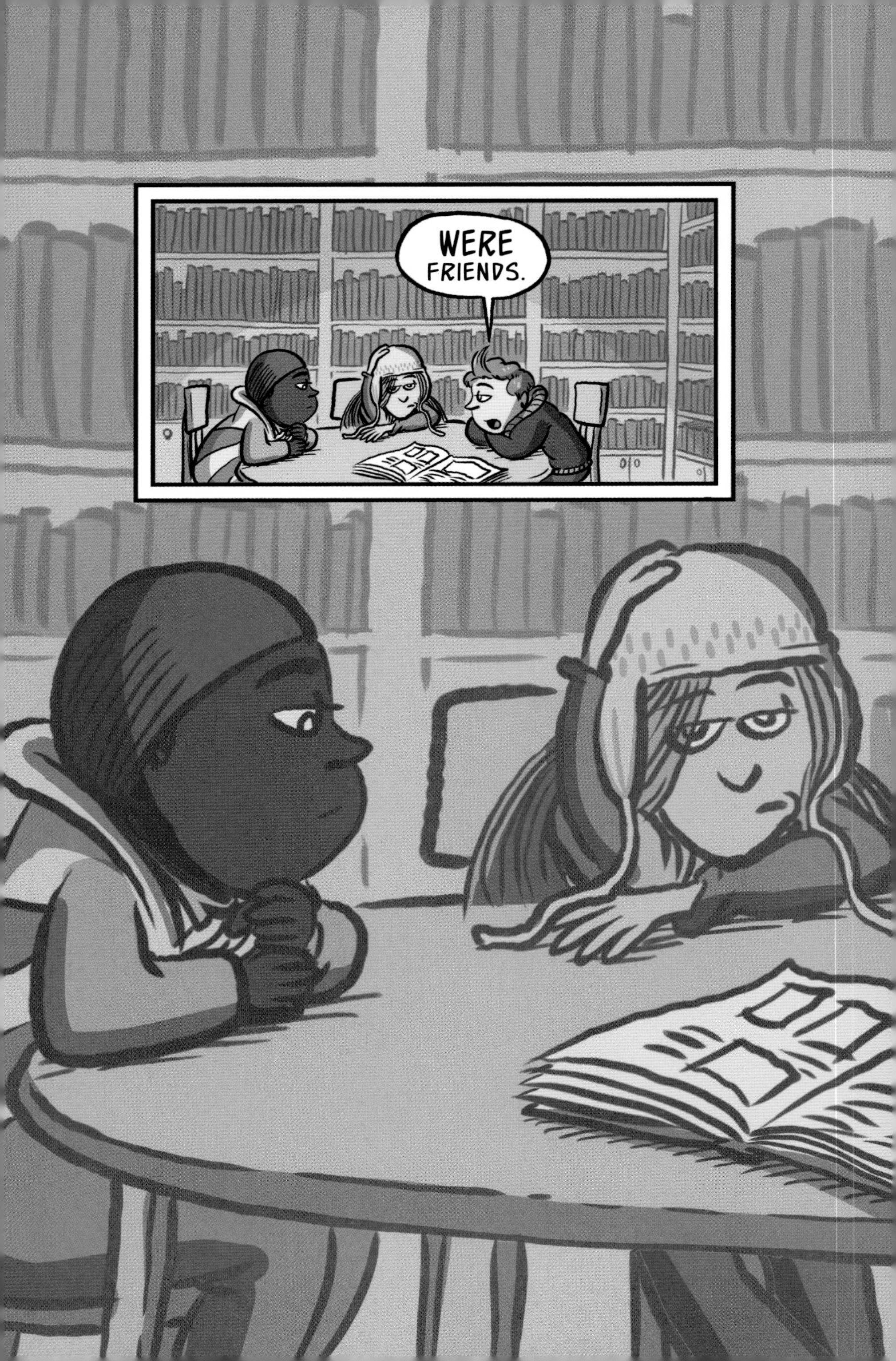
WERE
FRIENDS.

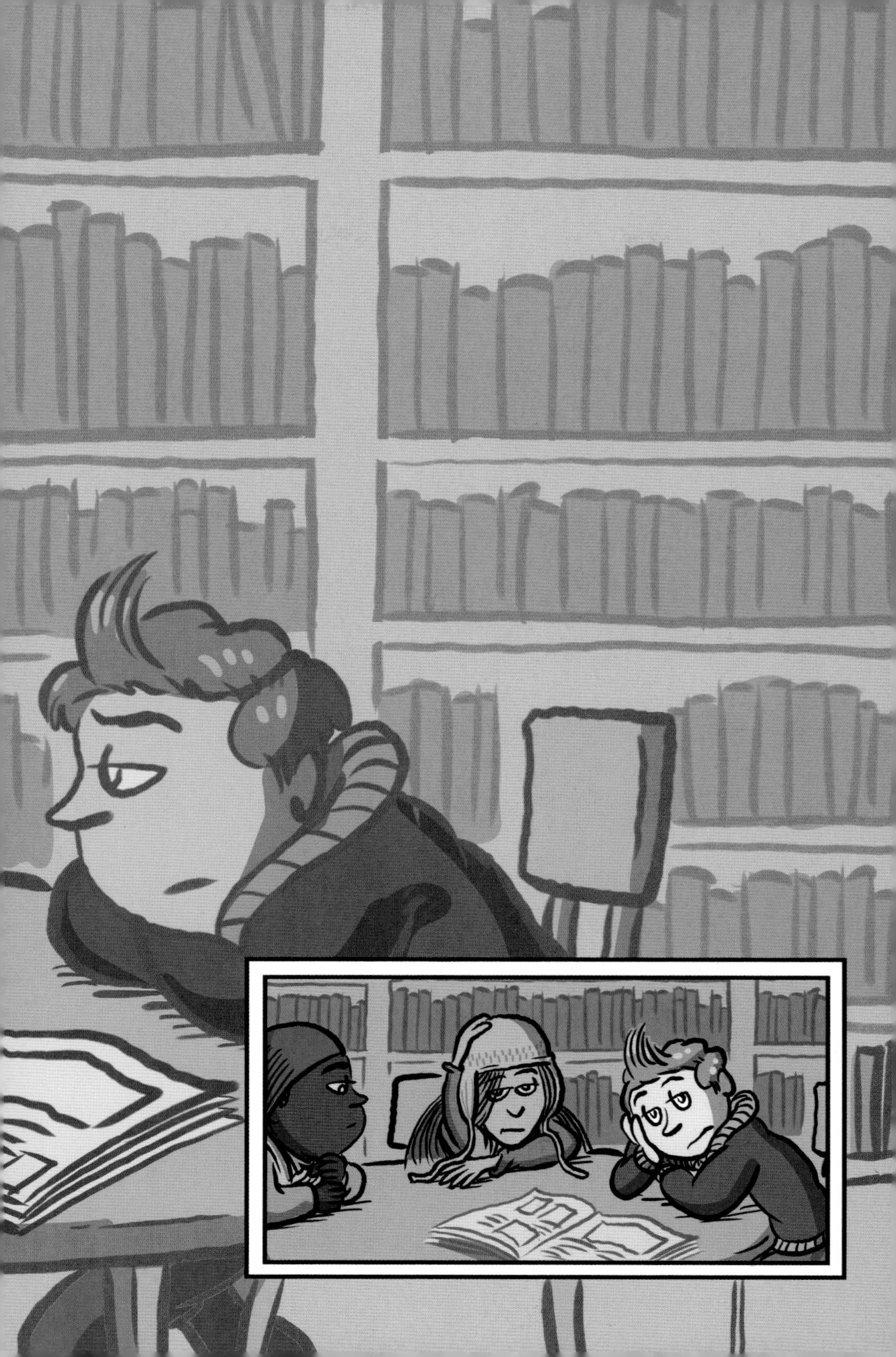

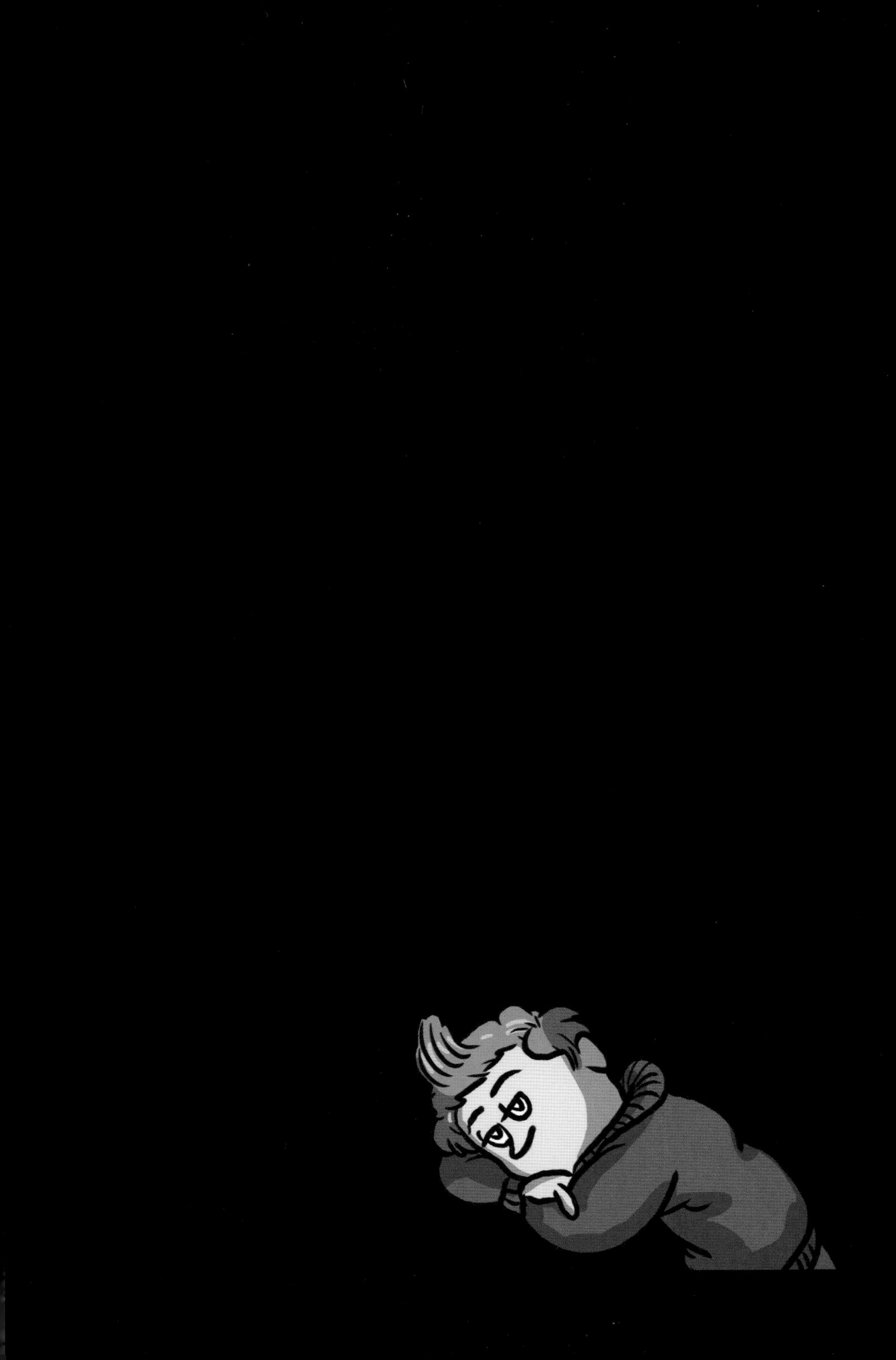

CHAPTER 12

A WEEK LATER

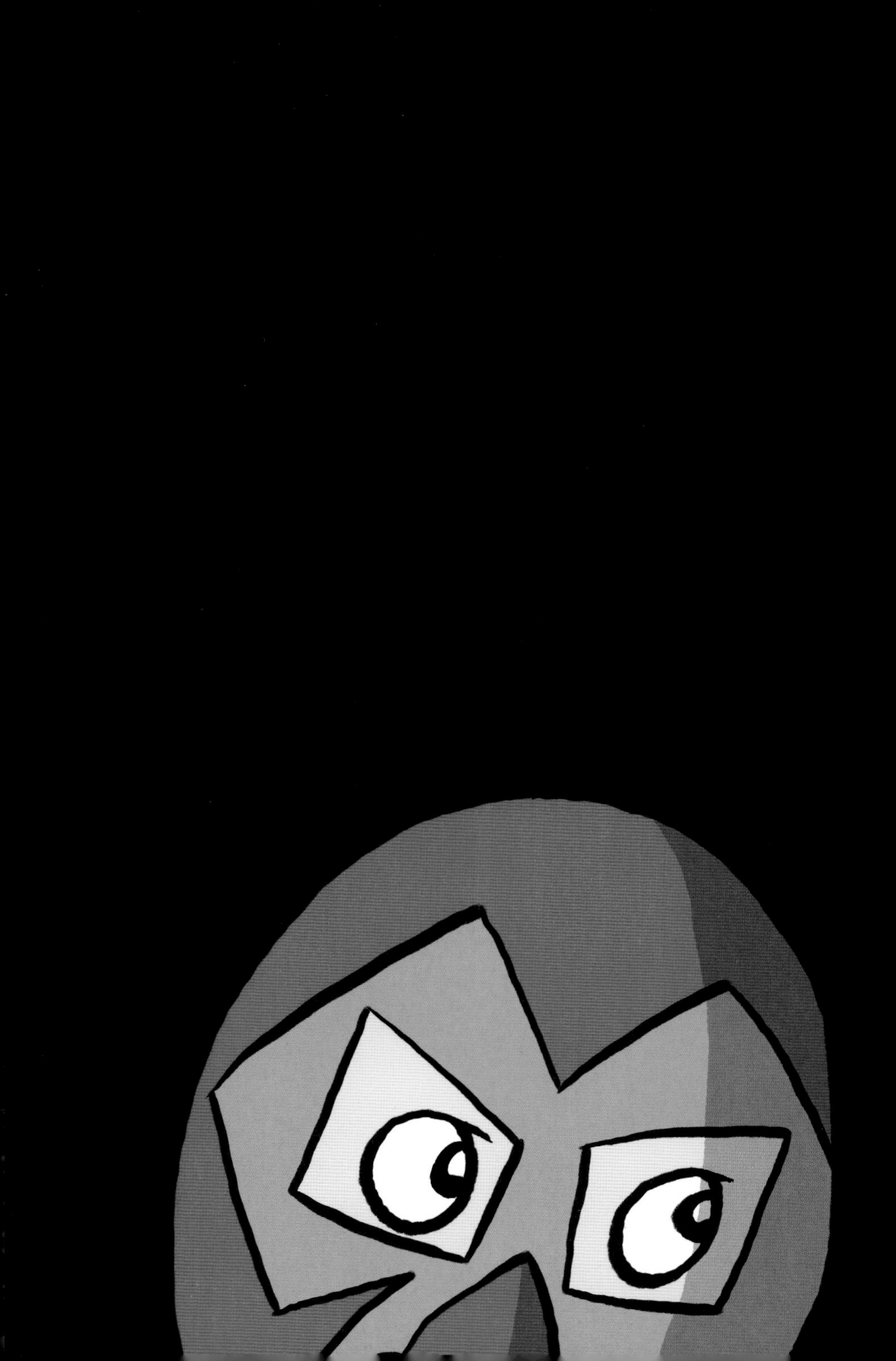

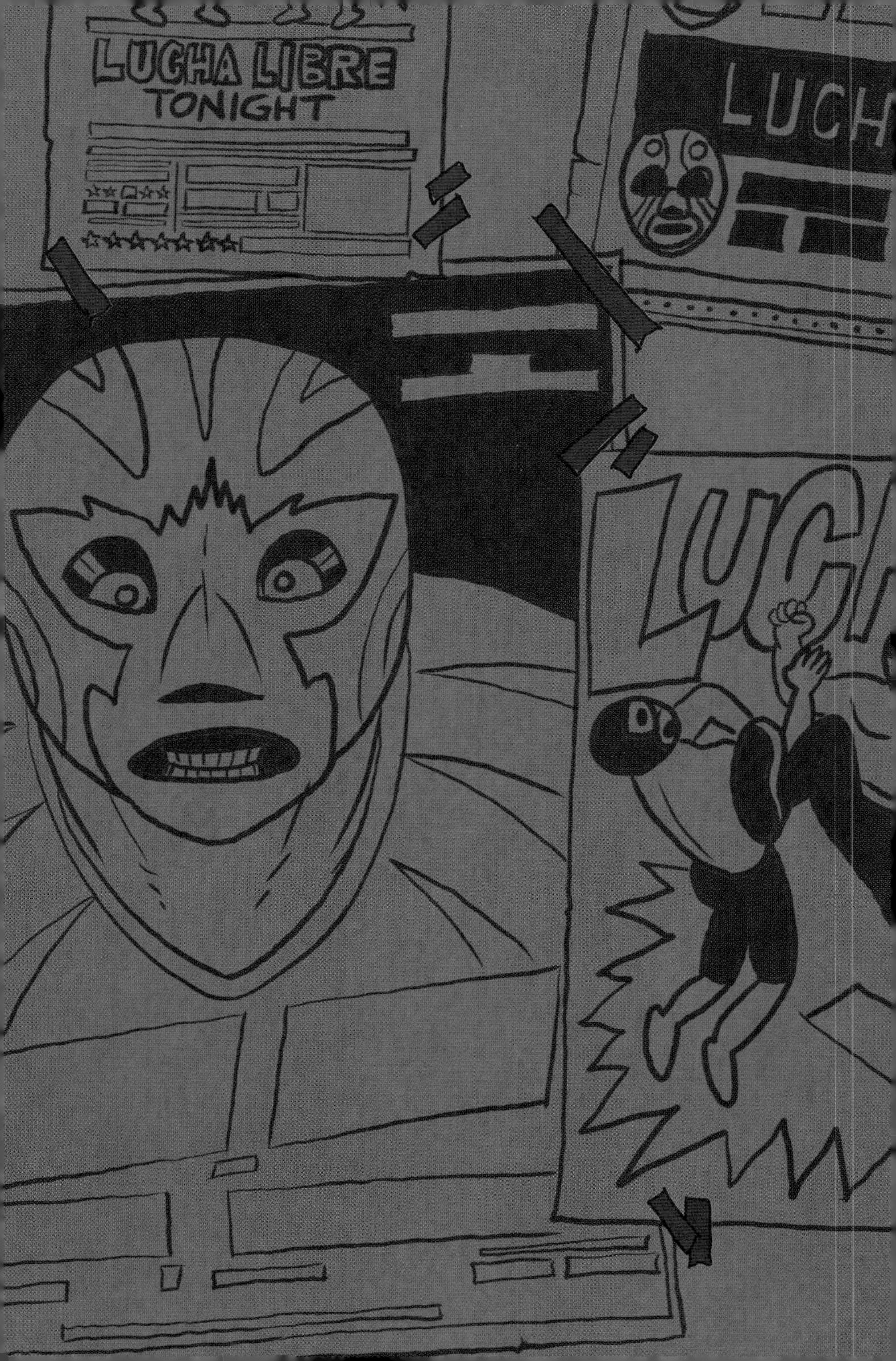
LUCHA LIBRE
TONIGHT
LUCH

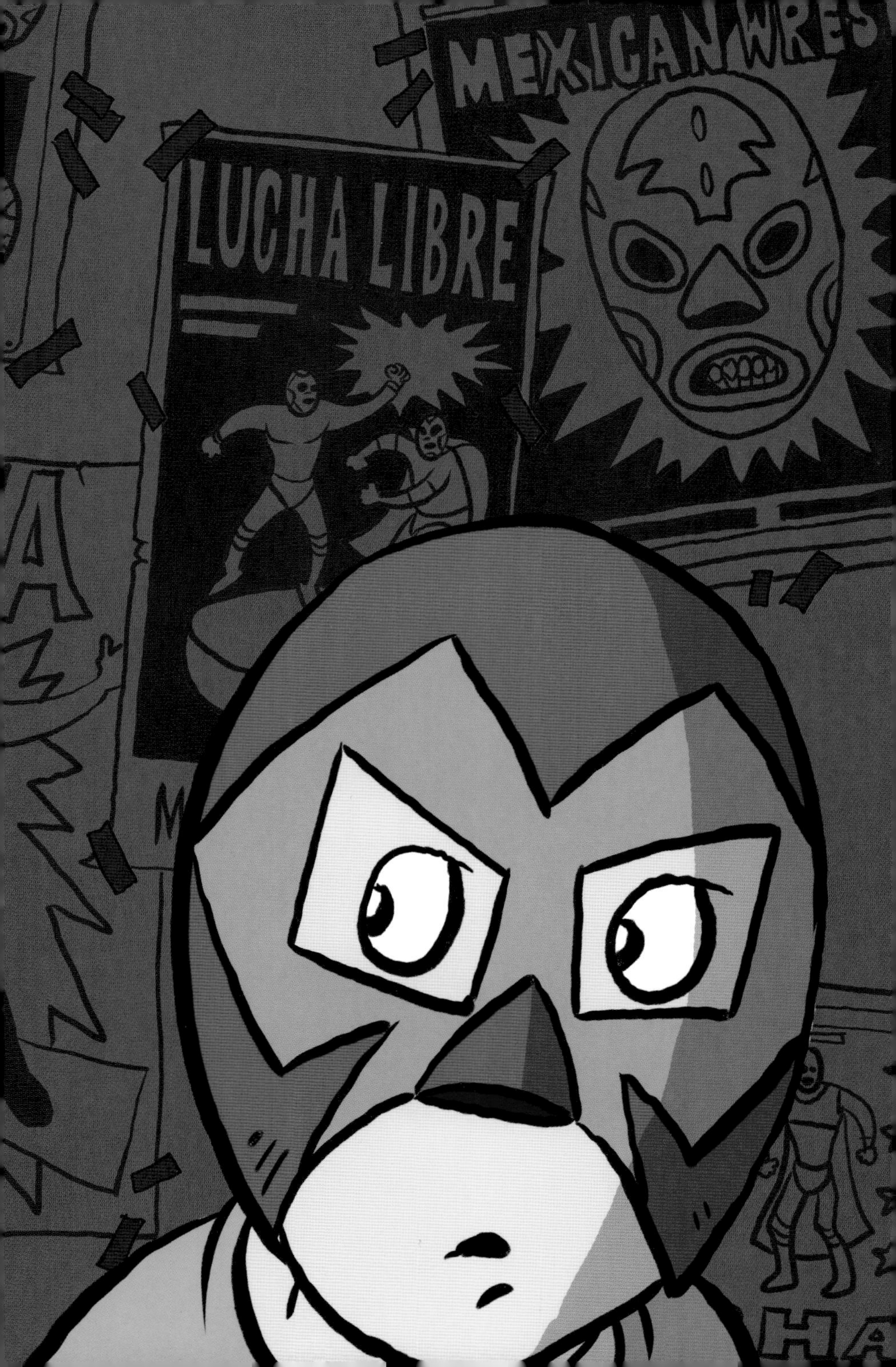
LUCHA LIBRE
MEXICAN

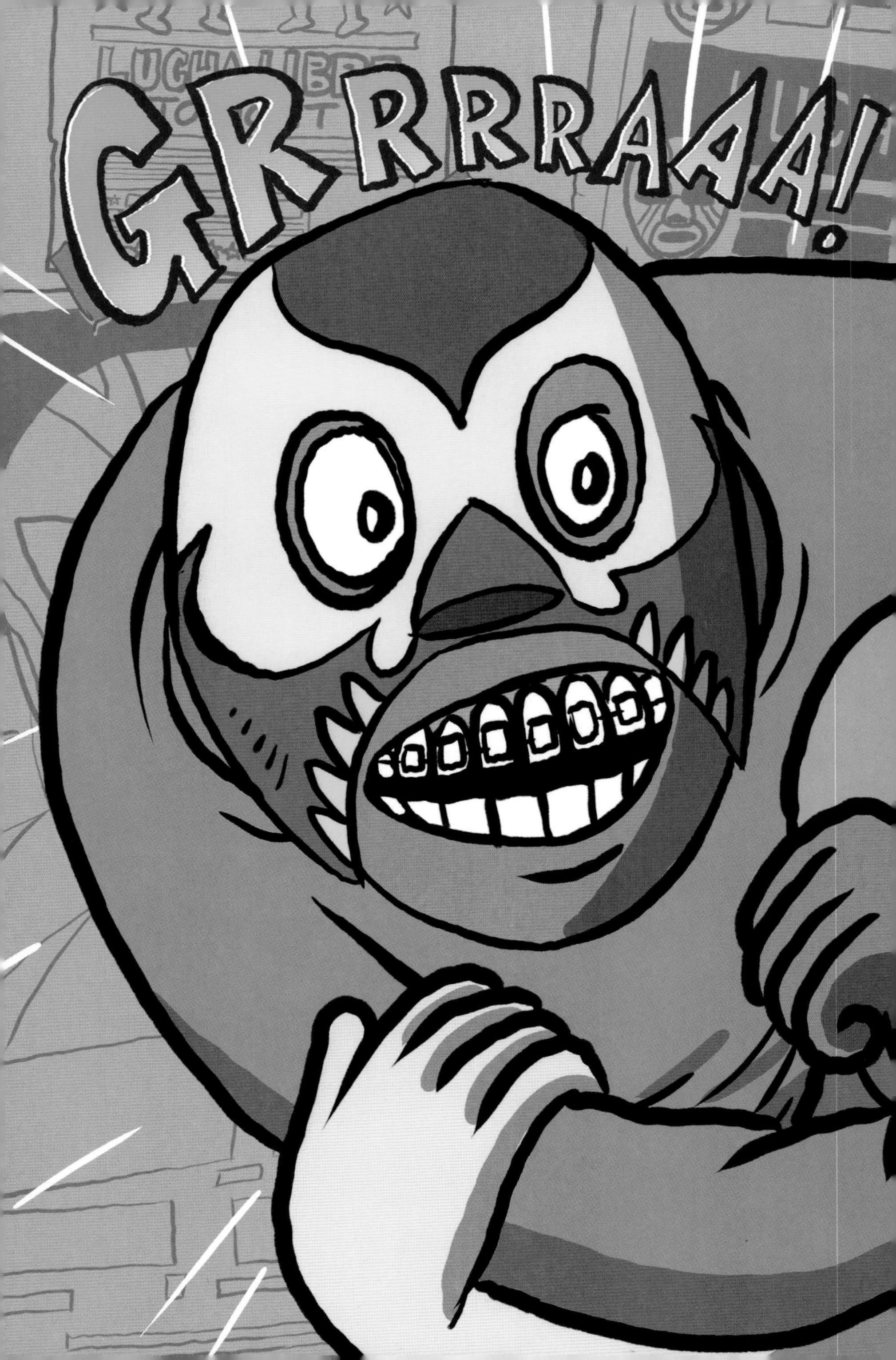
GRRRRAAA!

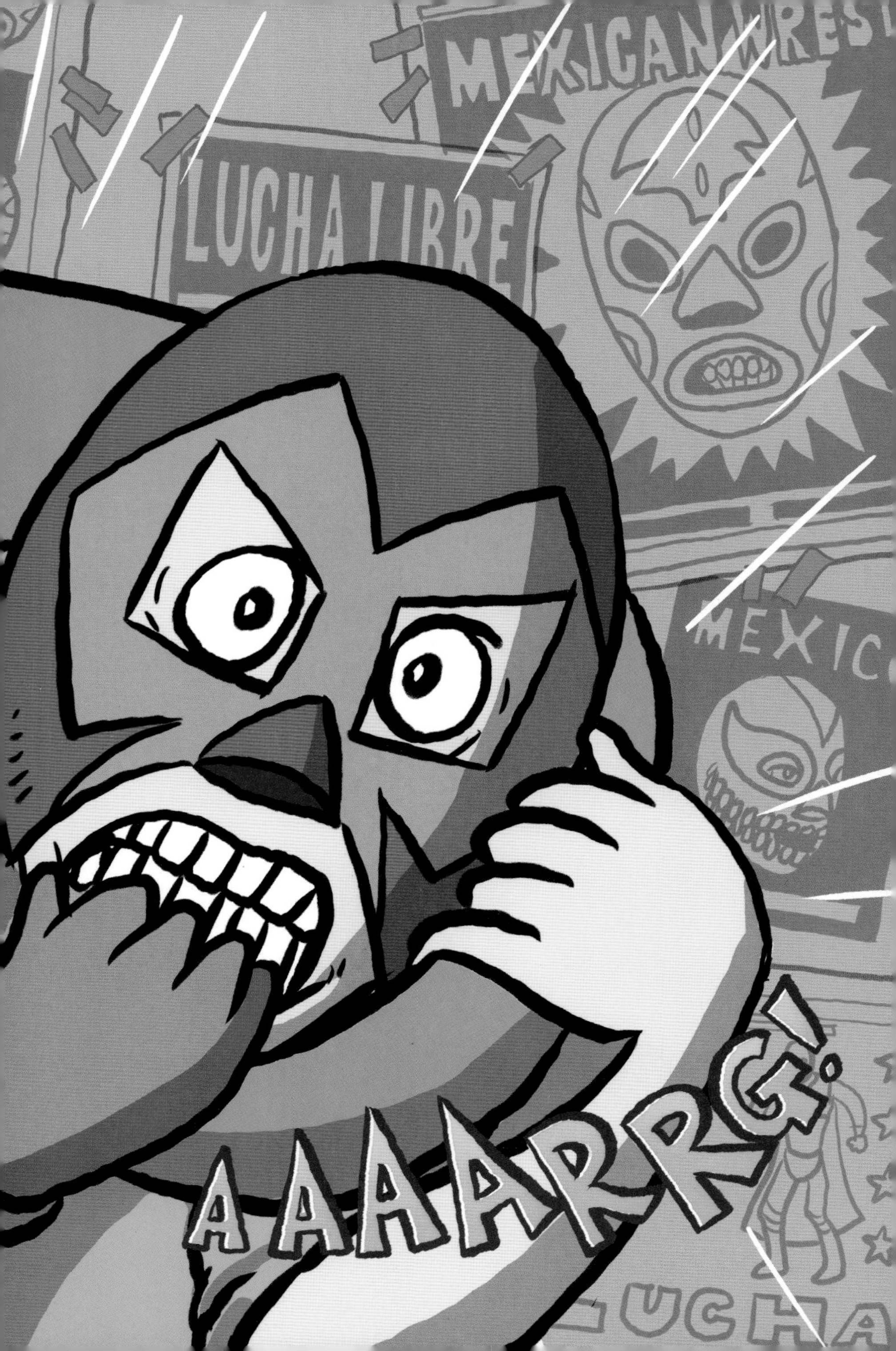
MEXICAN WREST
LUCHA LIBRE
MEXIC
LUCHA
AAAARRG!

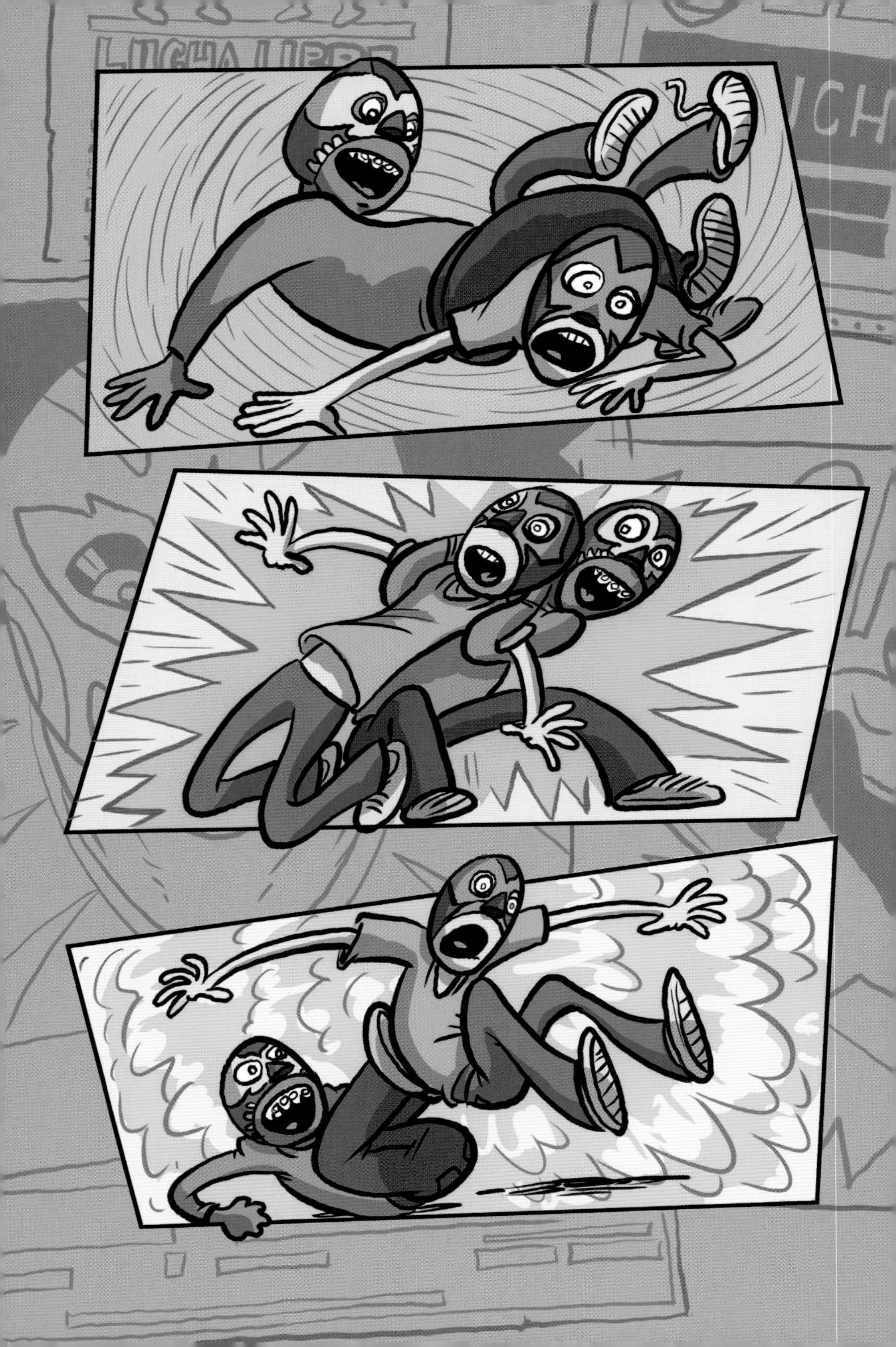

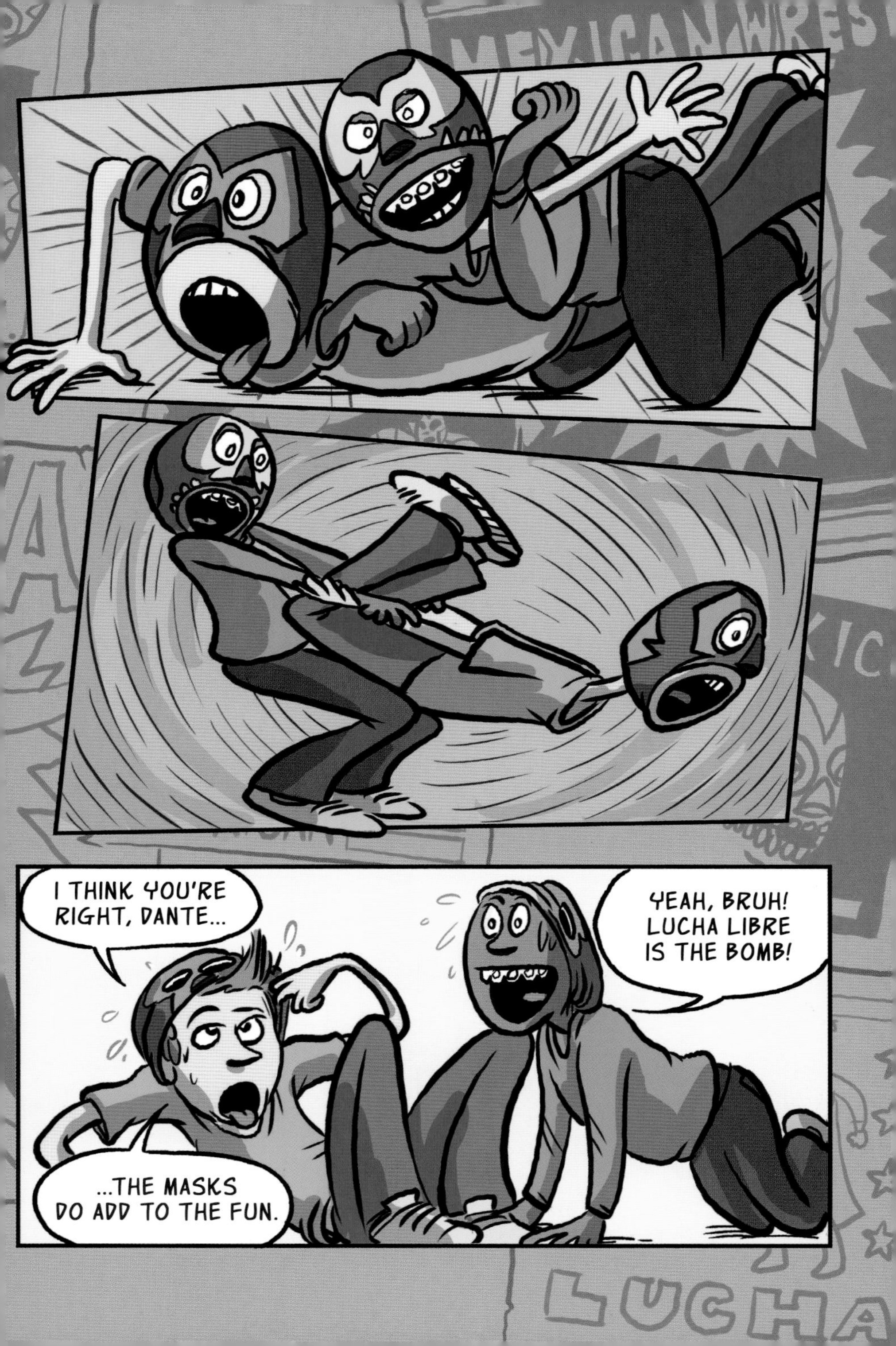
I THINK YOU'RE RIGHT, DANTE...
...THE MASKS DO ADD TO THE FUN.
YEAH, BRUH! LUCHA LIBRE IS THE BOMB!
LUCHA

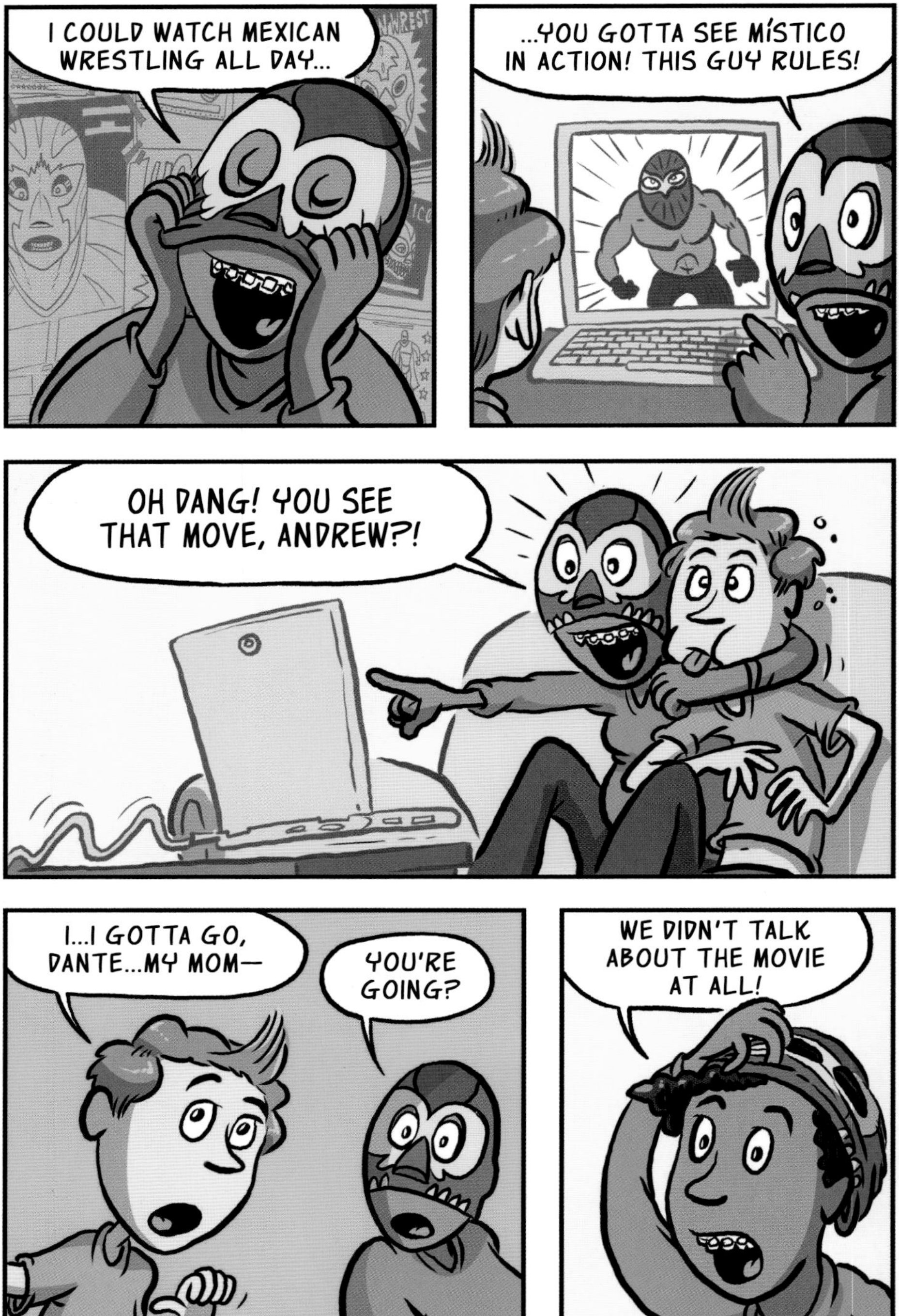
I COULD WATCH MEXICAN WRESTLING ALL DAY...
...YOU GOTTA SEE MÍSTICO IN ACTION! THIS GUY RULES!
OH DANG! YOU SEE THAT MOVE, ANDREW?!
I...I GOTTA GO, DANTE...MY MOM—
YOU'RE GOING?
WE DIDN'T TALK ABOUT THE MOVIE AT ALL!

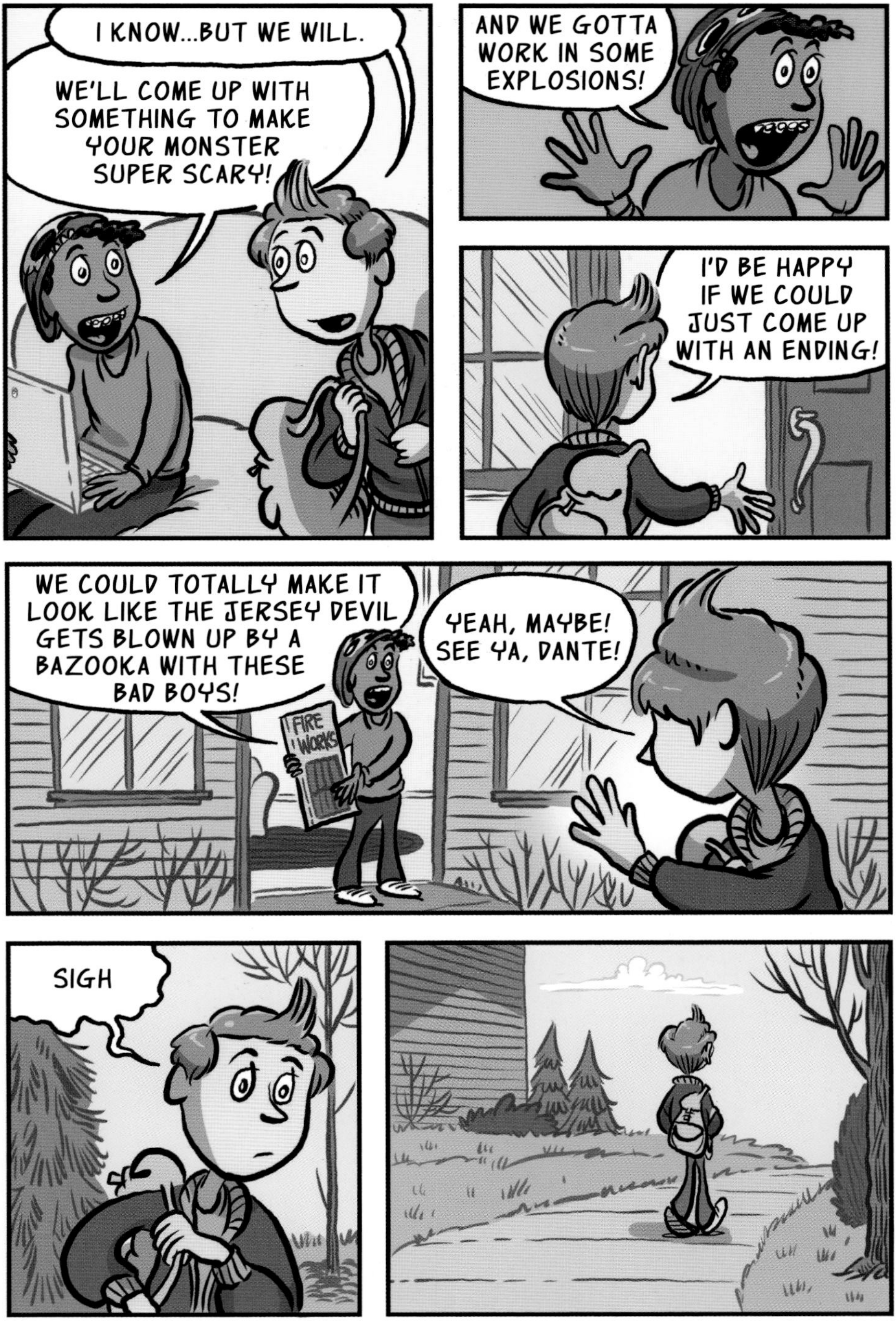
I KNOW...BUT WE WILL.
WE'LL COME UP WITH SOMETHING TO MAKE YOUR MONSTER SUPER SCARY!
AND WE GOTTA WORK IN SOME EXPLOSIONS!
I'D BE HAPPY IF WE COULD JUST COME UP WITH AN ENDING!
WE COULD TOTALLY MAKE IT LOOK LIKE THE JERSEY DEVIL GETS BLOWN UP BY A BAZOOKA WITH THESE BAD BOYS!
FIRE WORKS
YEAH, MAYBE! SEE YA, DANTE!
SIGH

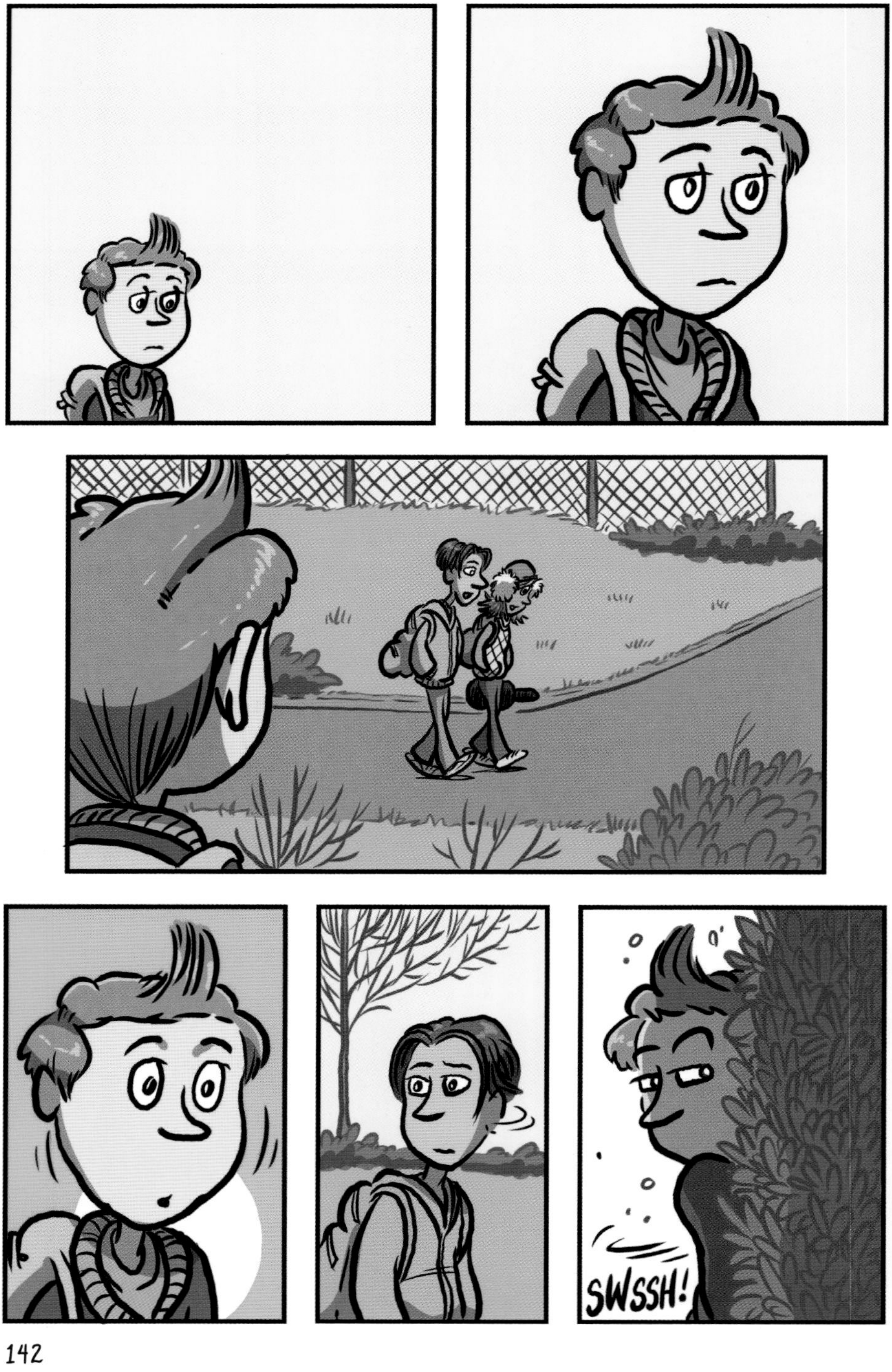
SWSSH!

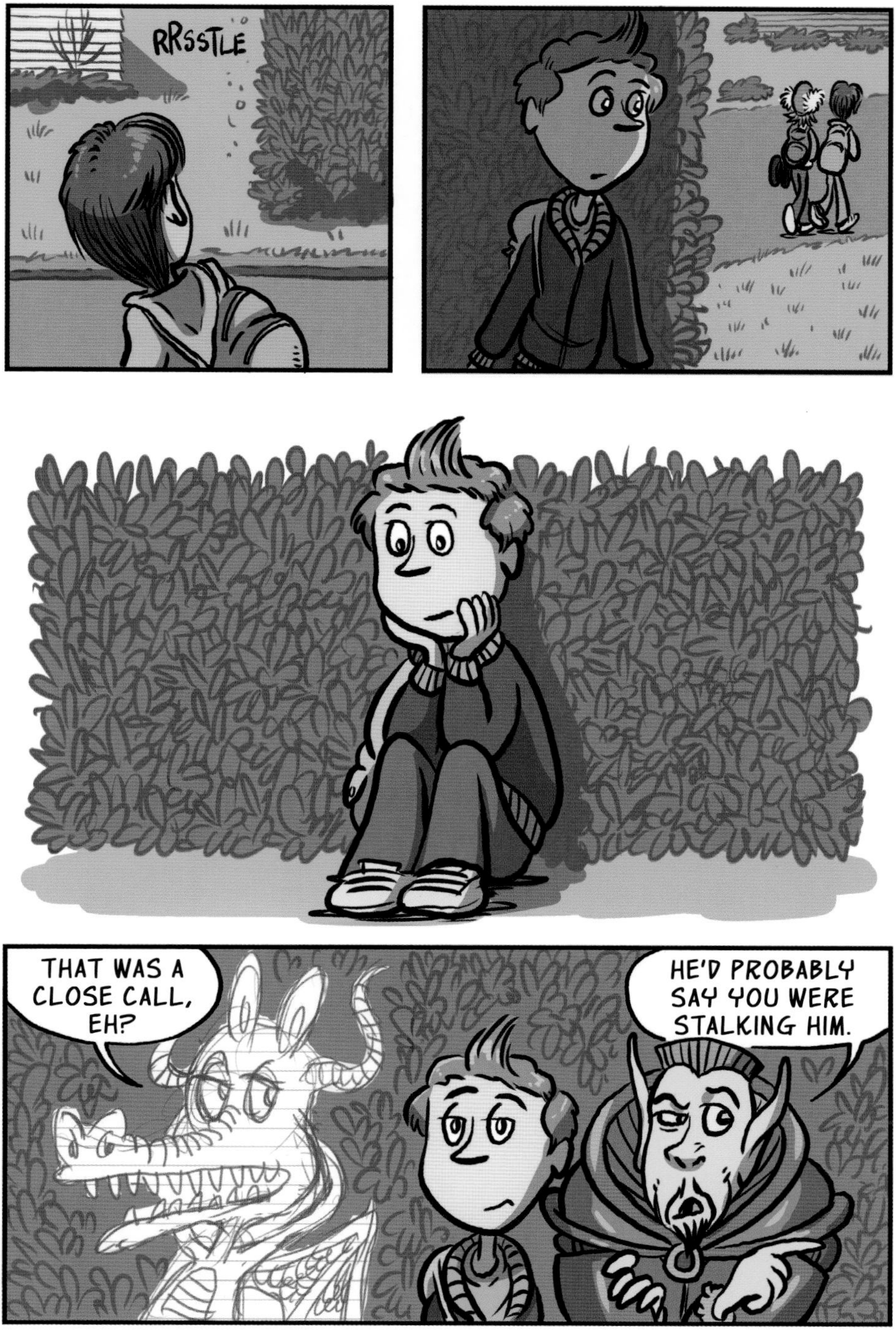
RRSSTLE
THAT WAS A CLOSE CALL, EH?
HE'D PROBABLY SAY YOU WERE STALKING HIM.

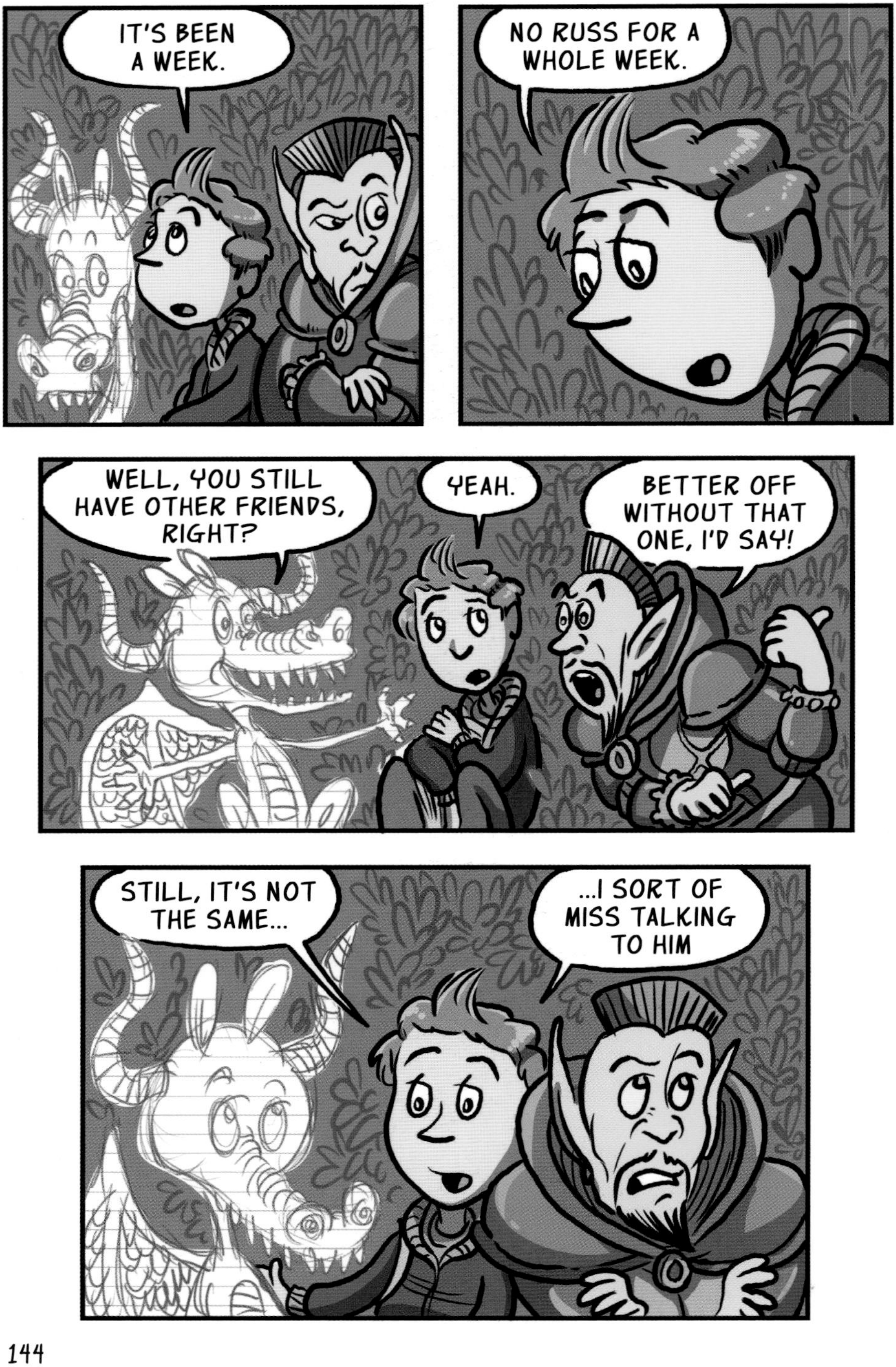
IT'S BEEN A WEEK.
NO RUSS FOR A WHOLE WEEK.
WELL, YOU STILL HAVE OTHER FRIENDS, RIGHT?
YEAH.
BETTER OFF WITHOUT THAT ONE, I'D SAY!
STILL, IT'S NOT THE SAME...
...I SORT OF MISS TALKING TO HIM

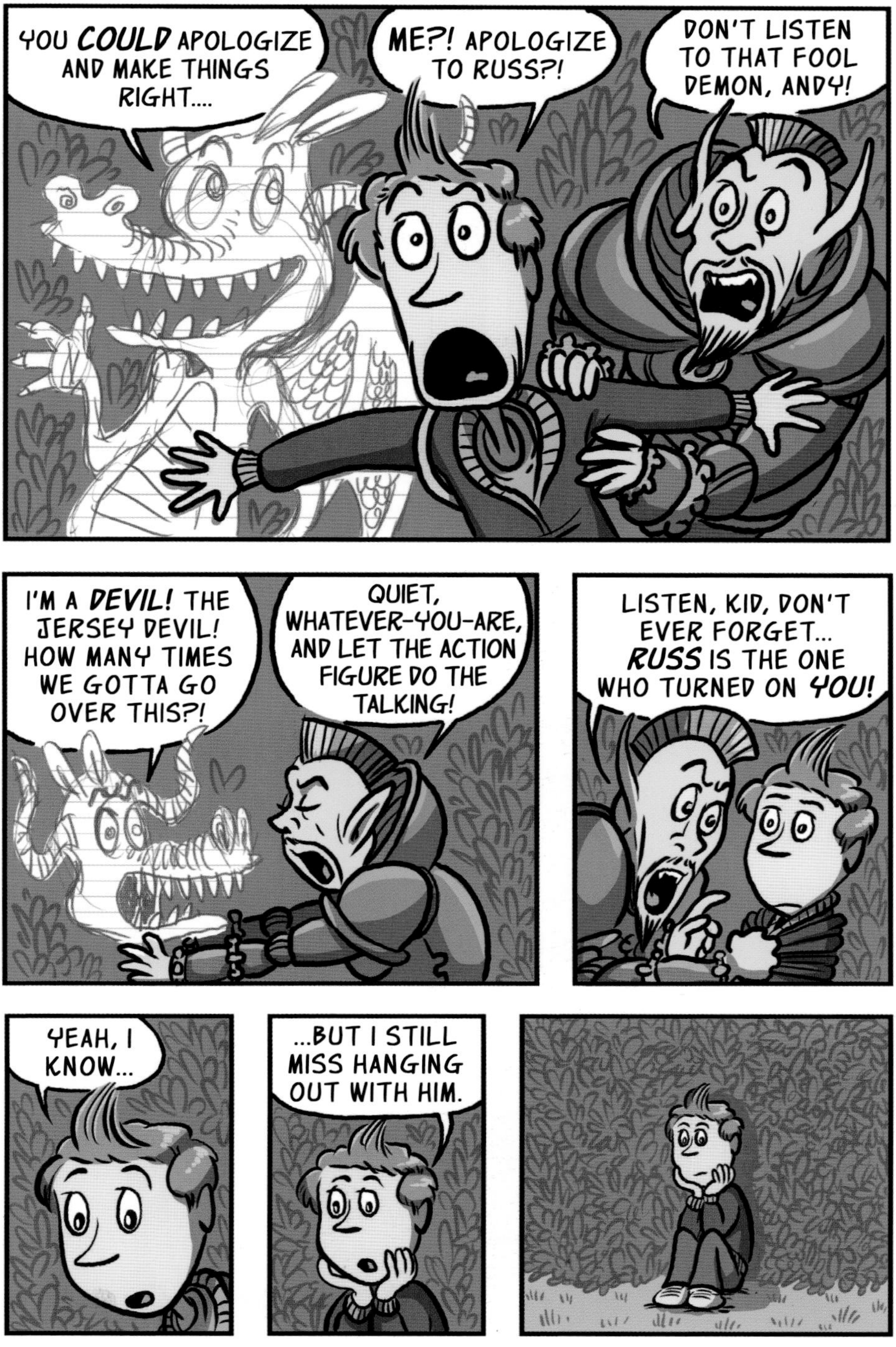
YOU COULD APOLOGIZE AND MAKE THINGS RIGHT....
ME?! APOLOGIZE TO RUSS?!
DON'T LISTEN TO THAT FOOL DEMON, ANDY!
I'M A DEVIL! THE JERSEY DEVIL! HOW MANY TIMES WE GOTTA GO OVER THIS?!
QUIET, WHATEVER-YOU-ARE, AND LET THE ACTION FIGURE DO THE TALKING!
LISTEN, KID, DON'T EVER FORGET... RUSS IS THE ONE WHO TURNED ON YOU!
YEAH, I KNOW...
...BUT I STILL MISS HANGING OUT WITH HIM.

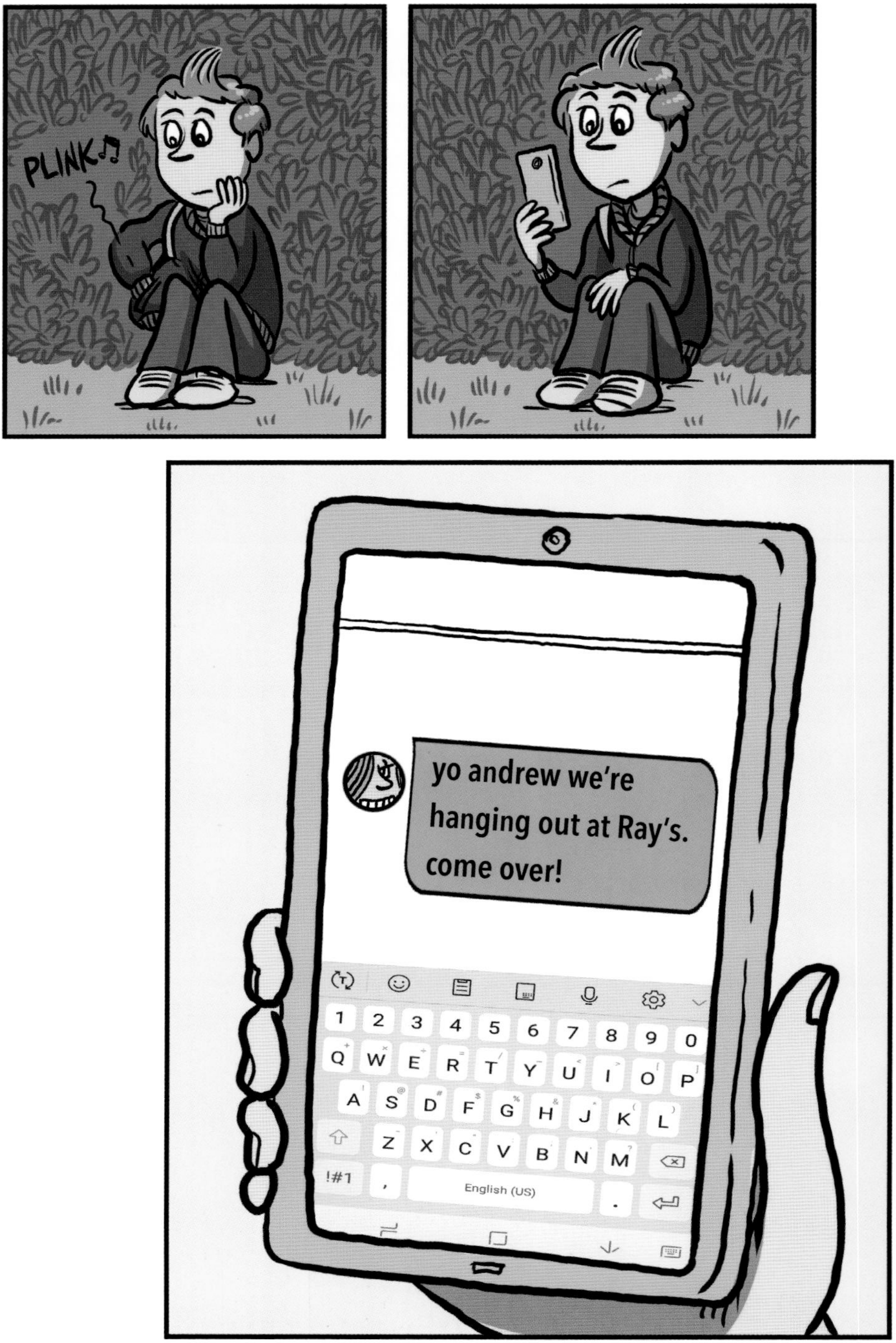
PLINK
yo andrew we're hanging out at Ray's. come over!

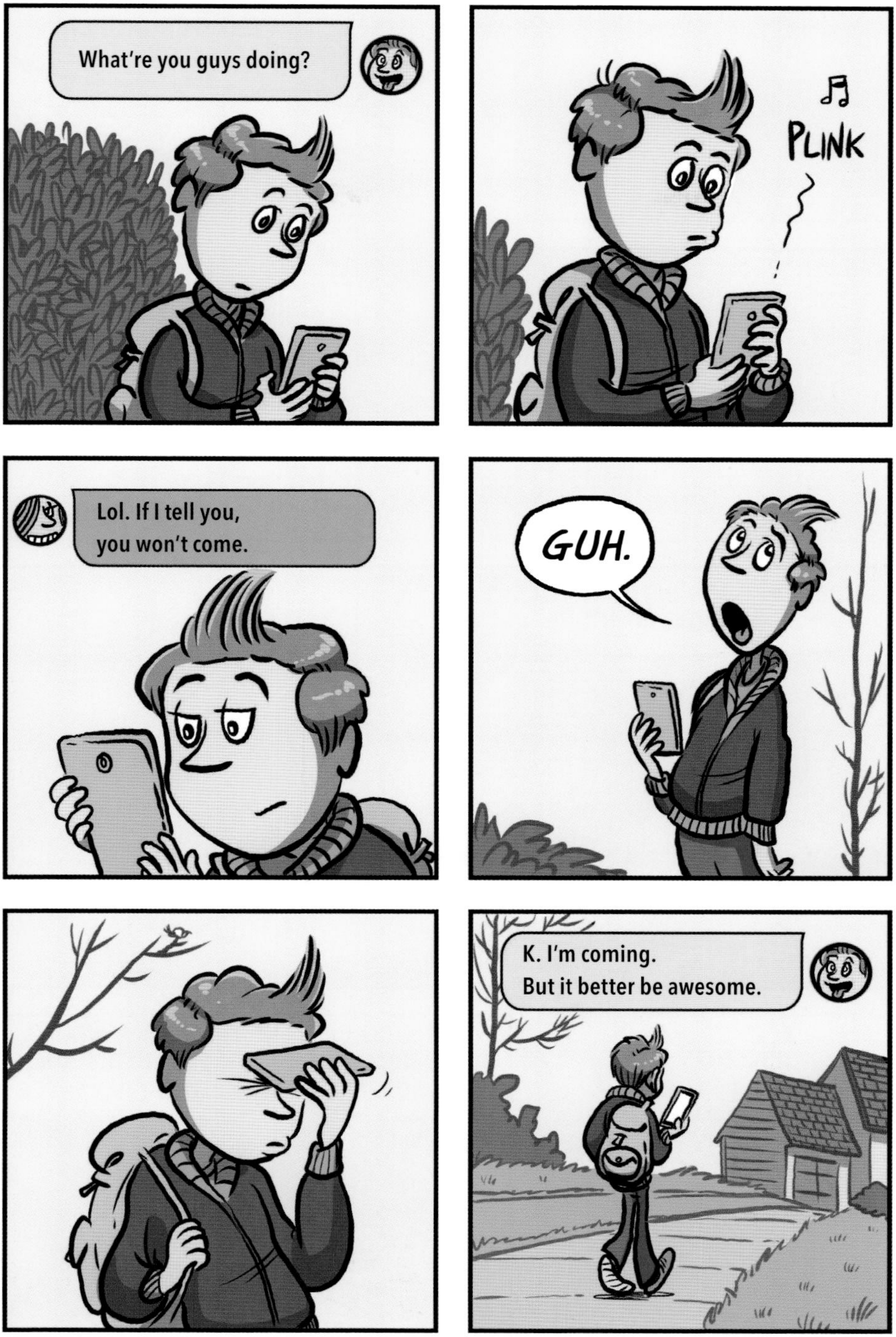
What're you guys doing?
♫
PLINK
Lol. If I tell you,
you won't come.
GUH.
K. I'm coming.
But it better be awesome.

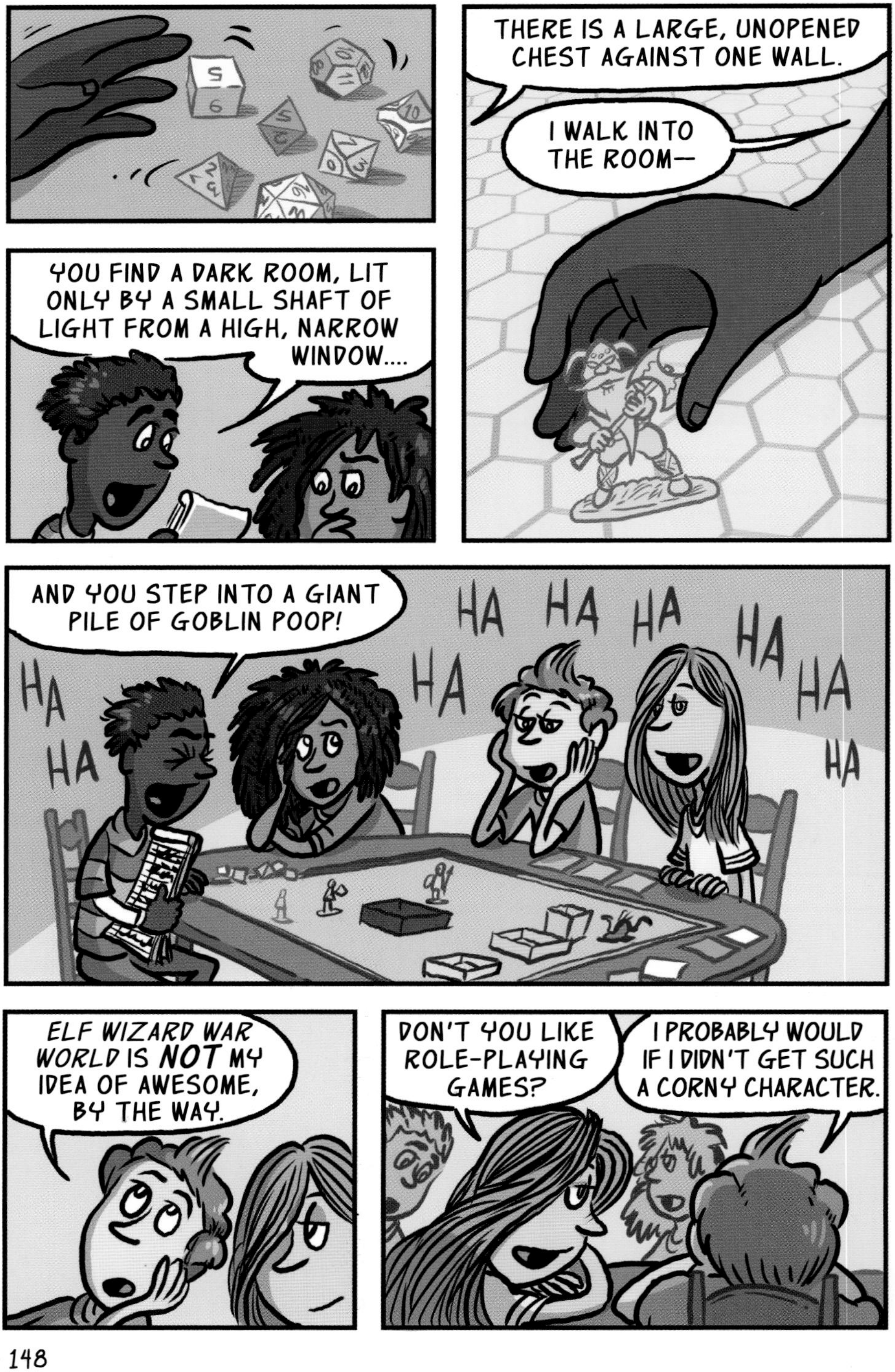
THERE IS A LARGE, UNOPENED CHEST AGAINST ONE WALL.
I WALK INTO THE ROOM—
YOU FIND A DARK ROOM, LIT ONLY BY A SMALL SHAFT OF LIGHT FROM A HIGH, NARROW WINDOW....
AND YOU STEP INTO A GIANT PILE OF GOBLIN POOP!
HA HA HA HA HA HA HA HA HA HA
ELF WIZARD WAR WORLD IS **NOT** MY IDEA OF AWESOME, BY THE WAY.
DON'T YOU LIKE ROLE-PLAYING GAMES?
I PROBABLY WOULD IF I DIDN'T GET SUCH A CORNY CHARACTER.

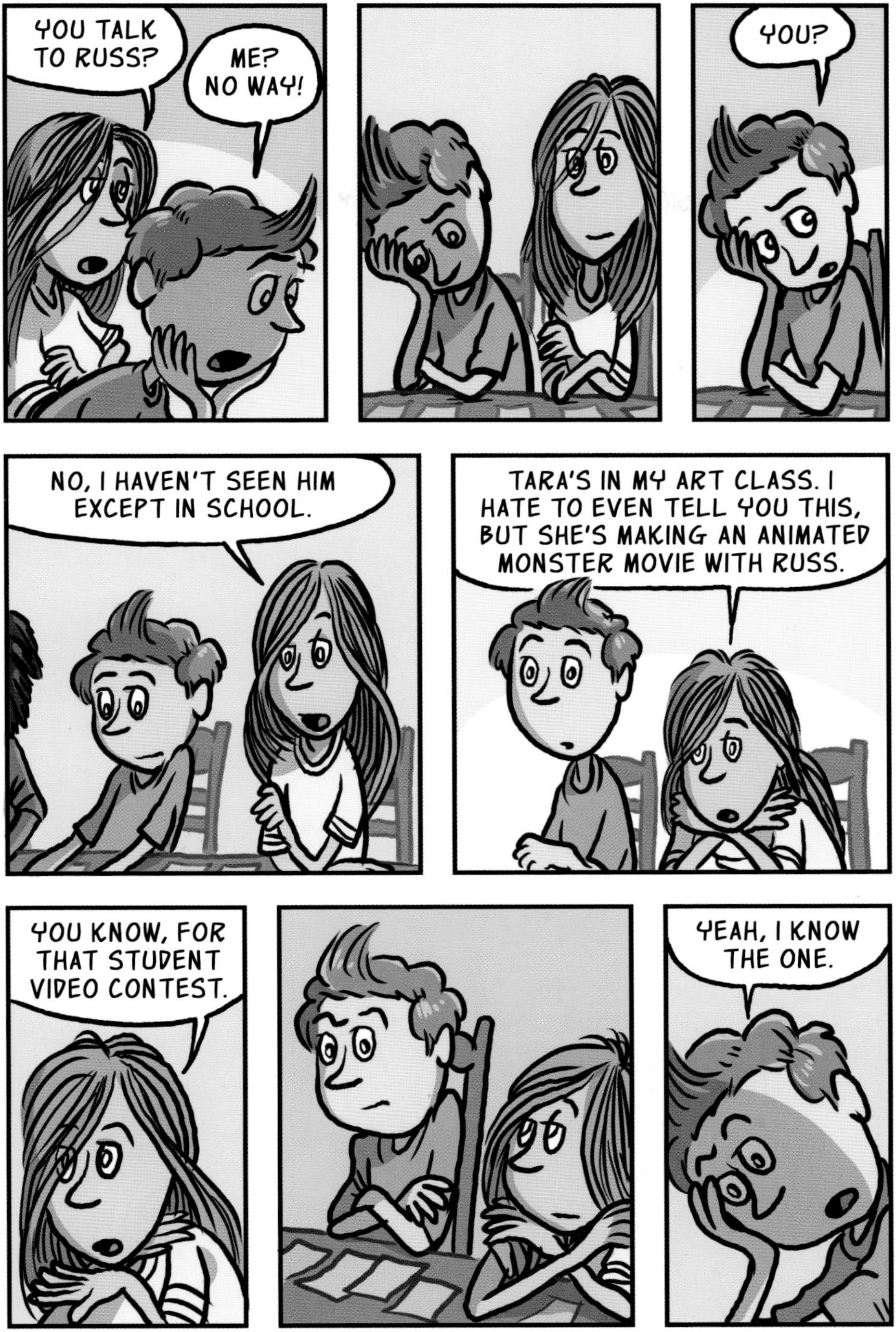
YOU TALK TO RUSS?
ME? NO WAY!
YOU?
NO, I HAVEN'T SEEN HIM EXCEPT IN SCHOOL.
TARA'S IN MY ART CLASS. I HATE TO EVEN TELL YOU THIS, BUT SHE'S MAKING AN ANIMATED MONSTER MOVIE WITH RUSS.
YOU KNOW, FOR THAT STUDENT VIDEO CONTEST.
YEAH, I KNOW THE ONE.

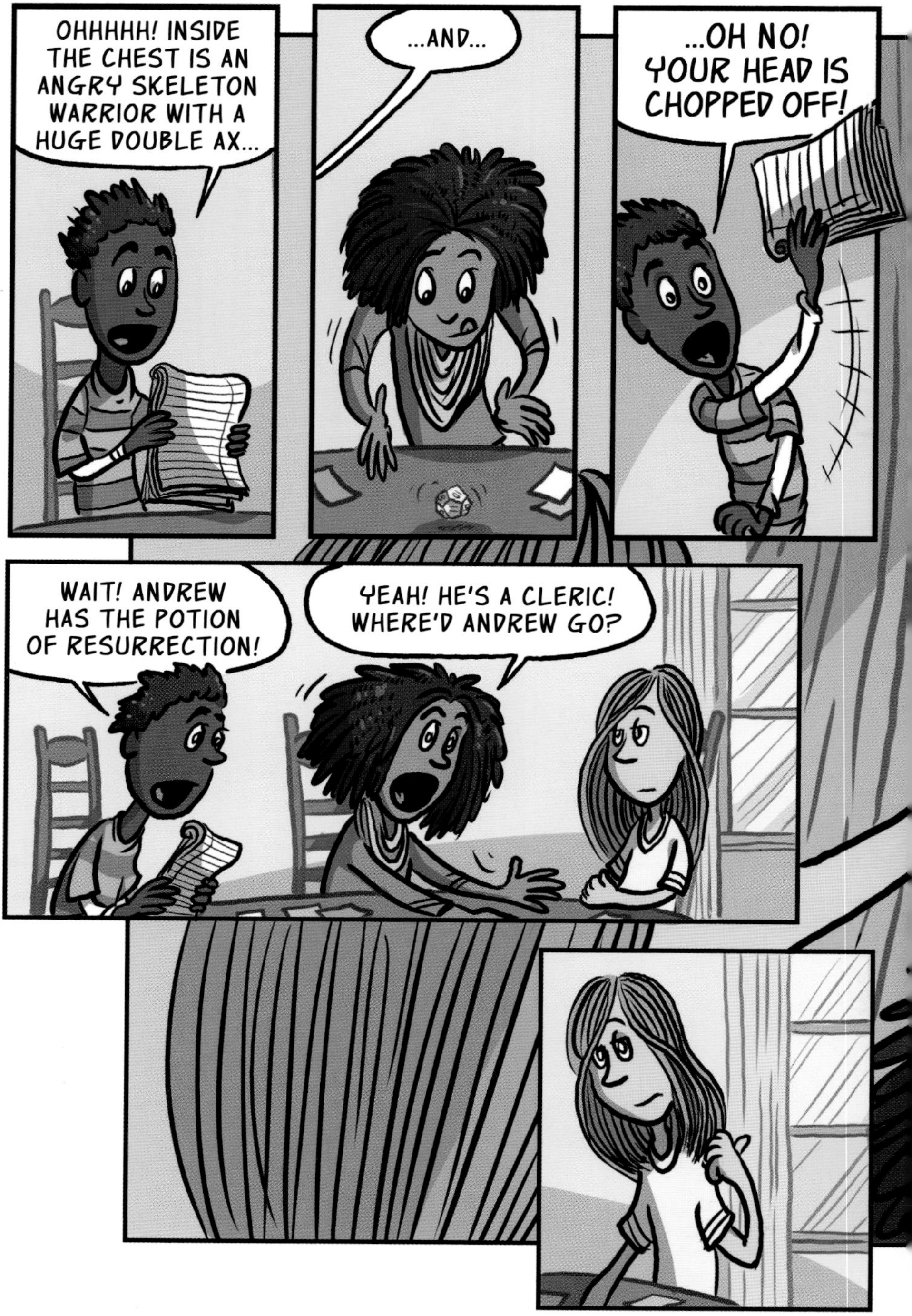
OHHHHH! INSIDE THE CHEST IS AN ANGRY SKELETON WARRIOR WITH A HUGE DOUBLE AX...
...AND...
...OH NO! YOUR HEAD IS CHOPPED OFF!
WAIT! ANDREW HAS THE POTION OF RESURRECTION!
YEAH! HE'S A CLERIC! WHERE'D ANDREW GO?

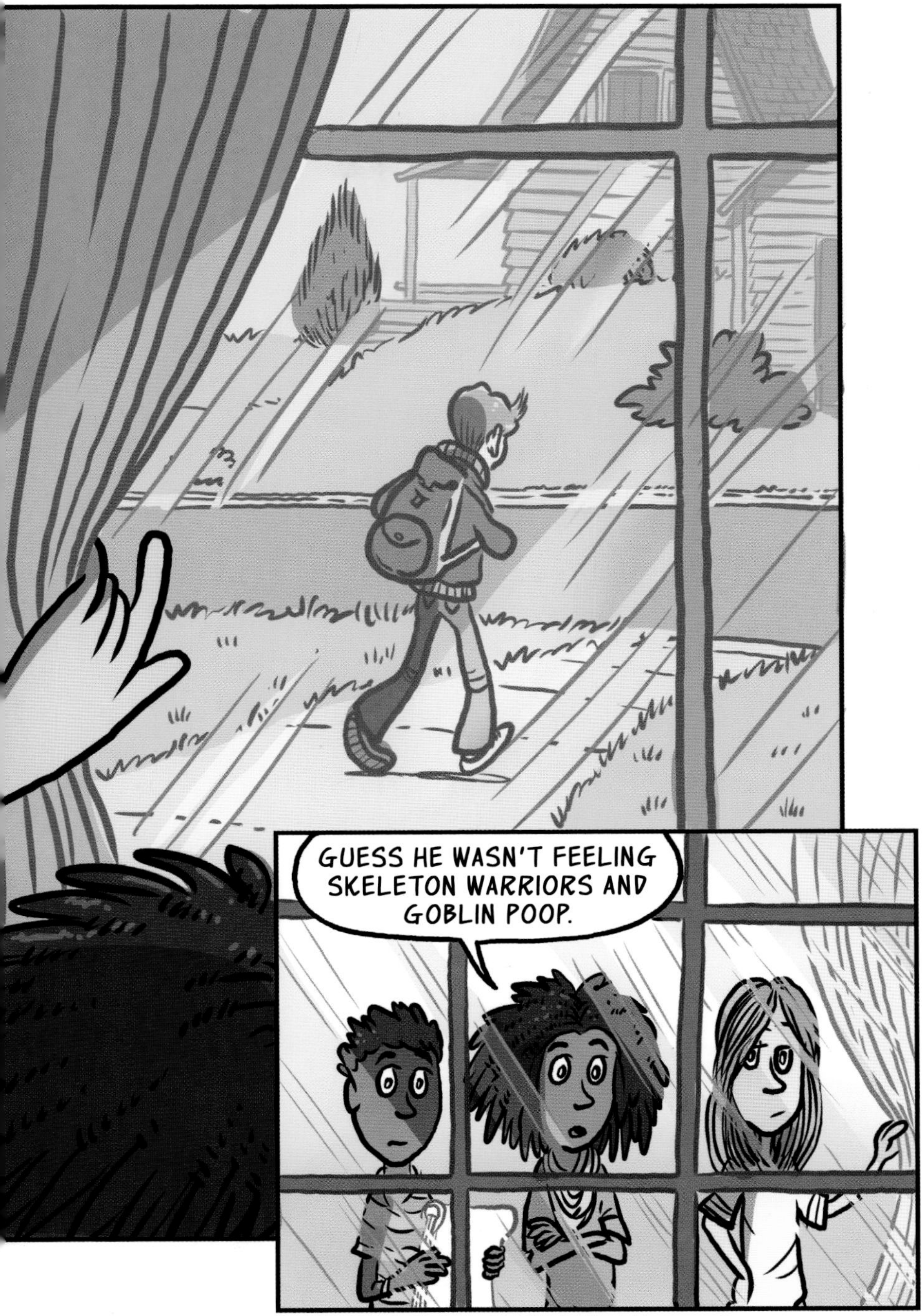
GUESS HE WASN'T FEELING SKELETON WARRIORS AND GOBLIN POOP.

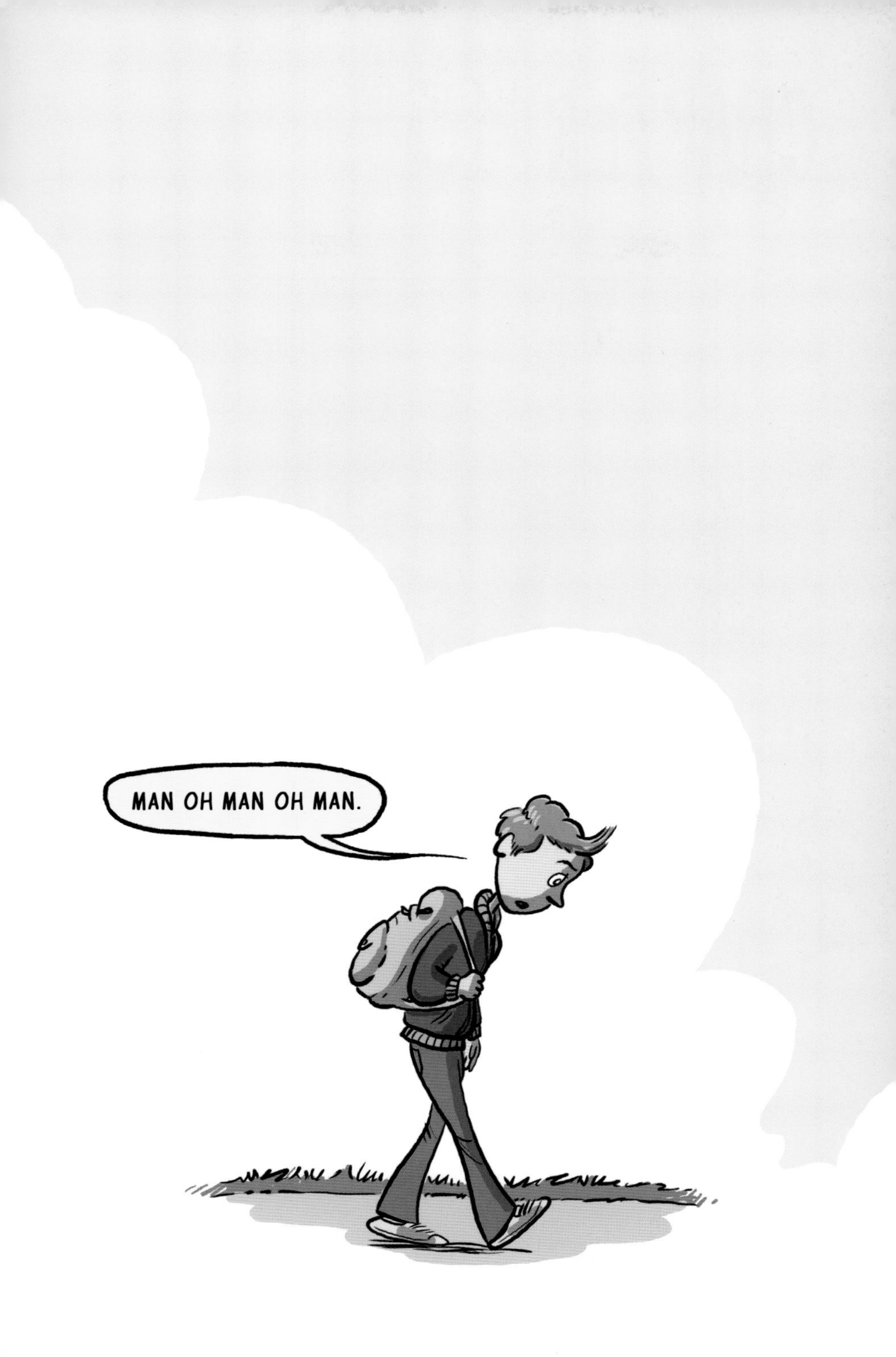
MAN OH MAN OH MAN.

CHAPTER 13

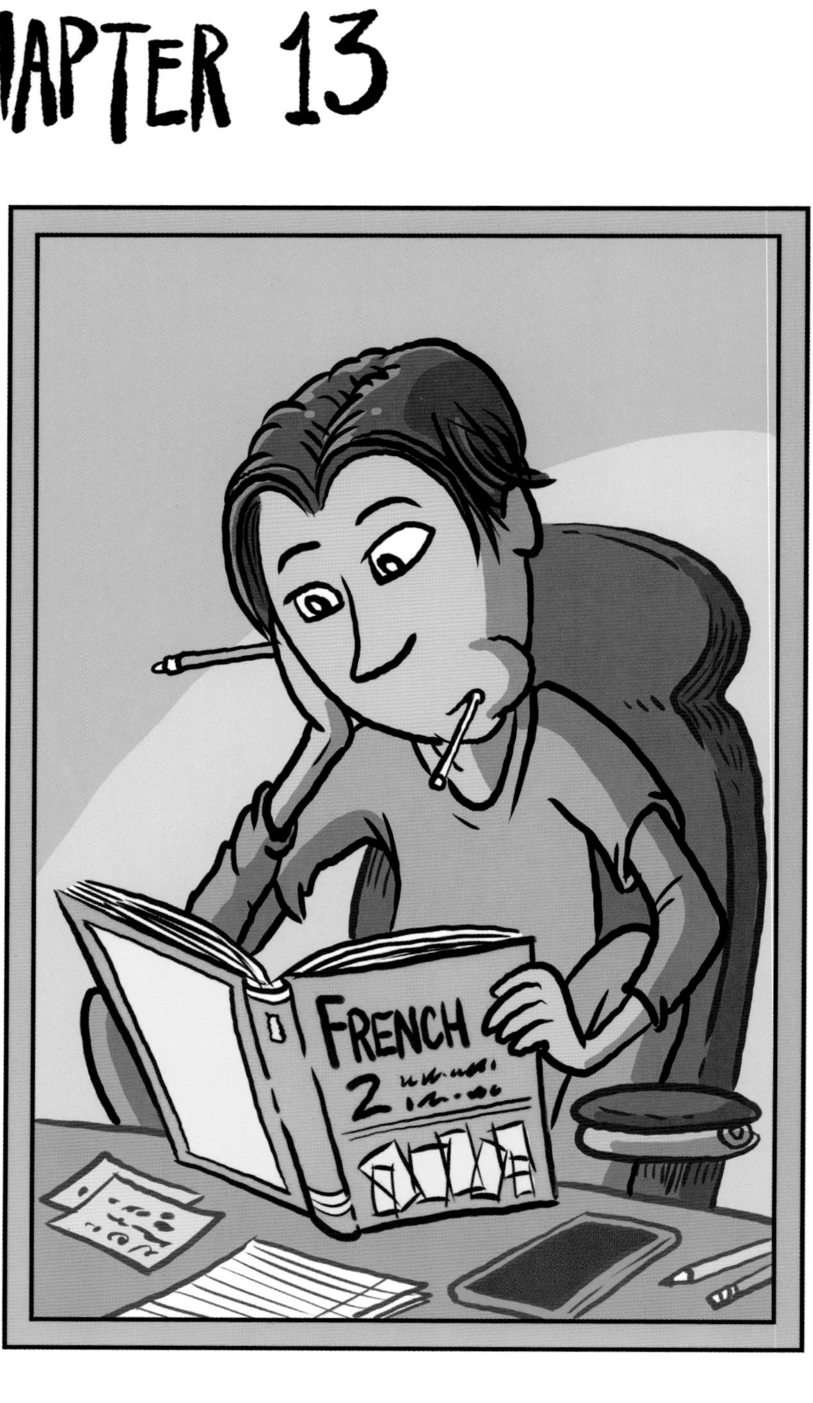
FRENCH
2

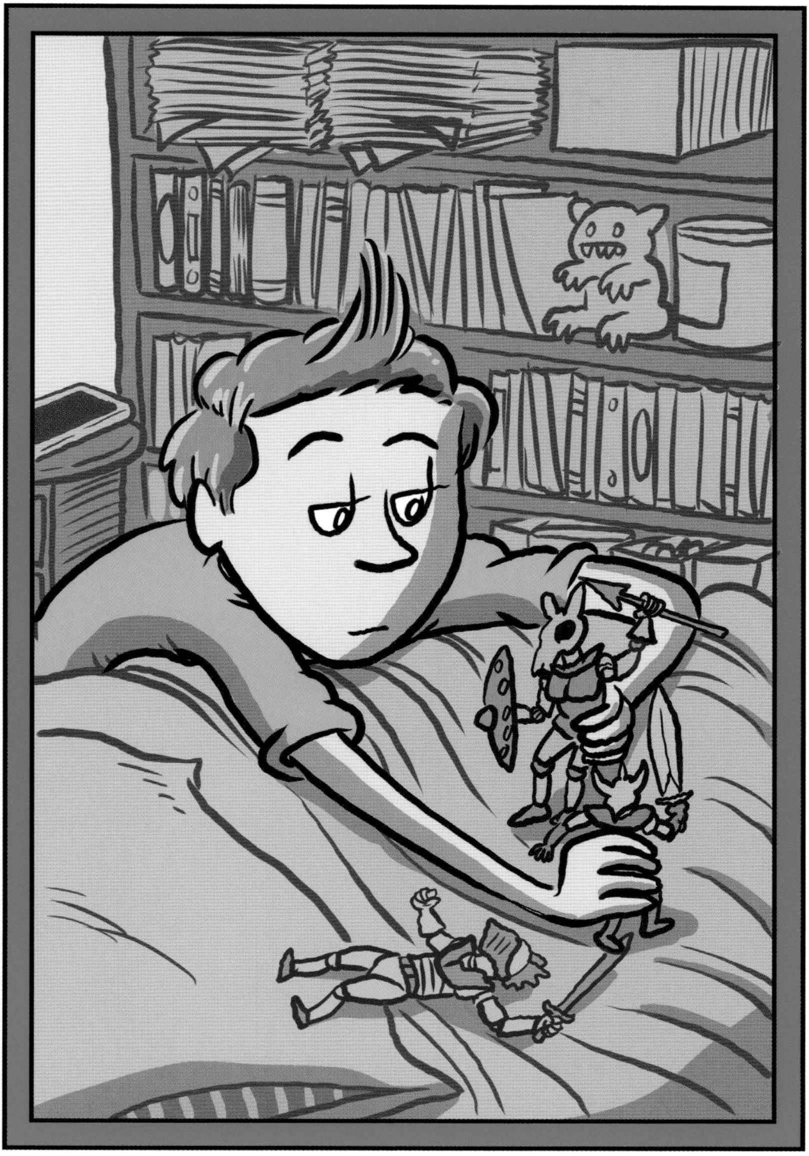

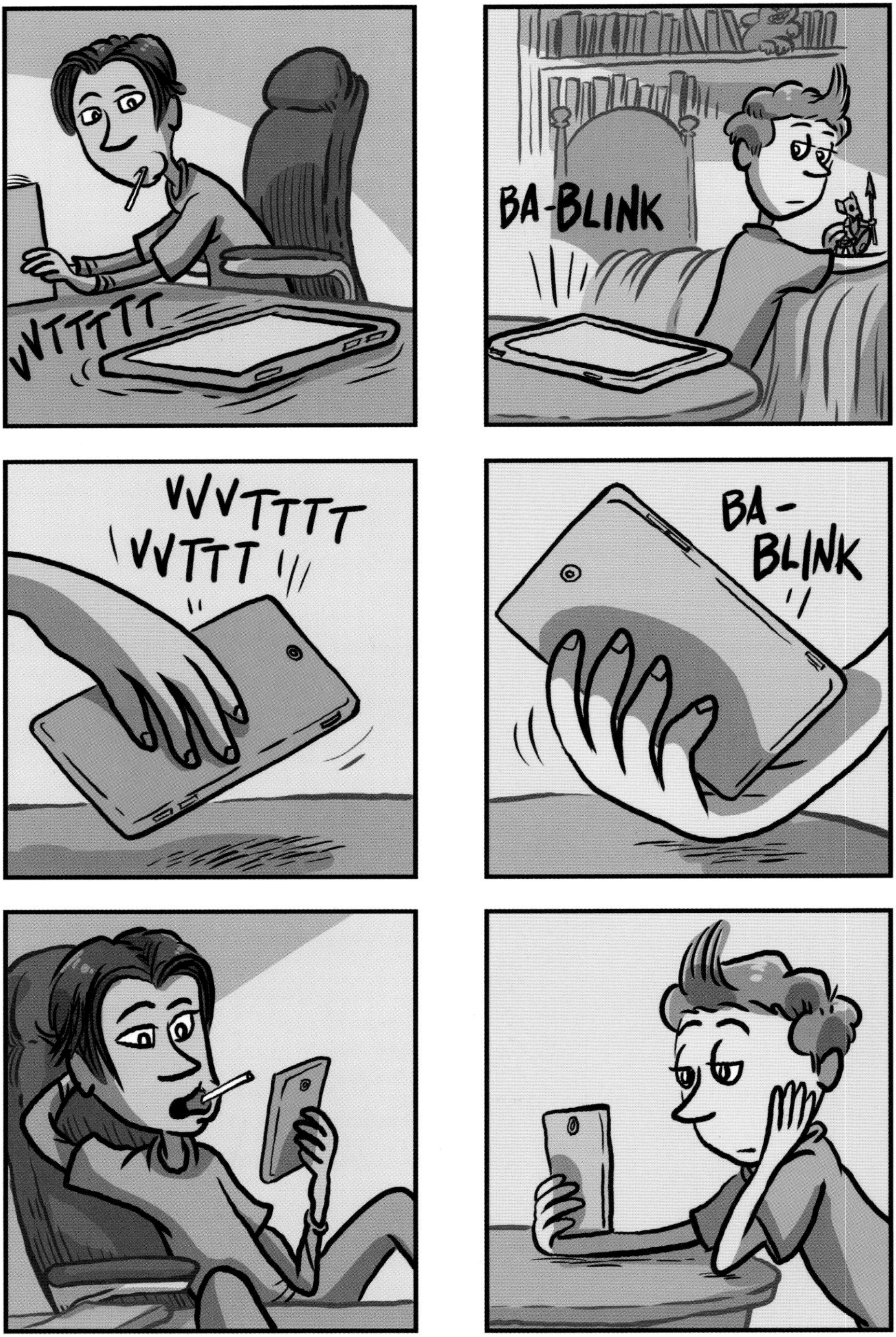
VVTTTTT
BA-BLINK
VVVTTTT
VVTTT
BA-
BLINK

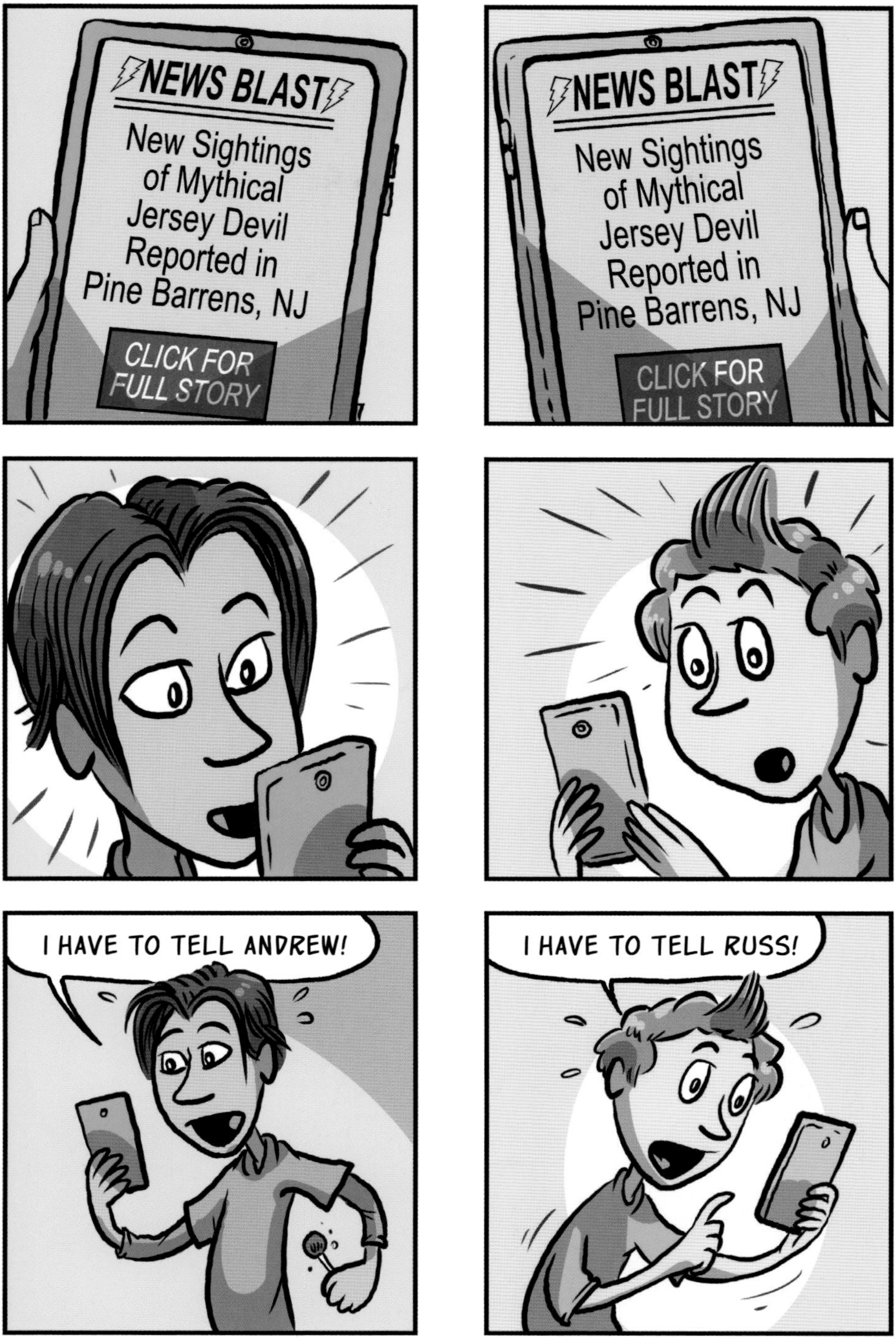
NEWS BLAST
New Sightings of Mythical Jersey Devil Reported in Pine Barrens, NJ
CLICK FOR FULL STORY
NEWS BLAST
New Sightings of Mythical Jersey Devil Reported in Pine Barrens, NJ
CLICK FOR FULL STORY
I HAVE TO TELL ANDREW!
I HAVE TO TELL RUSS!

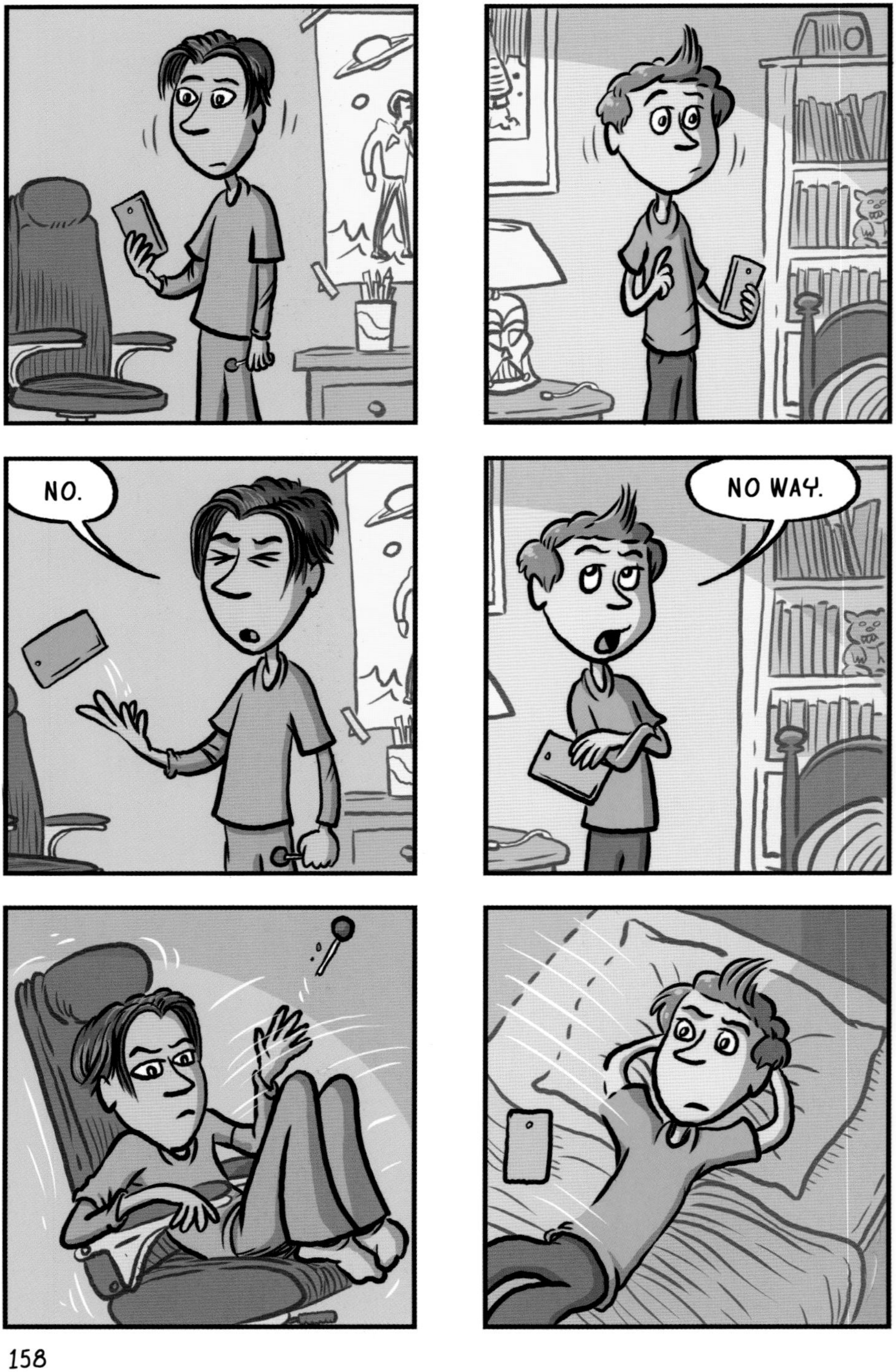
NO.
NO WAY.

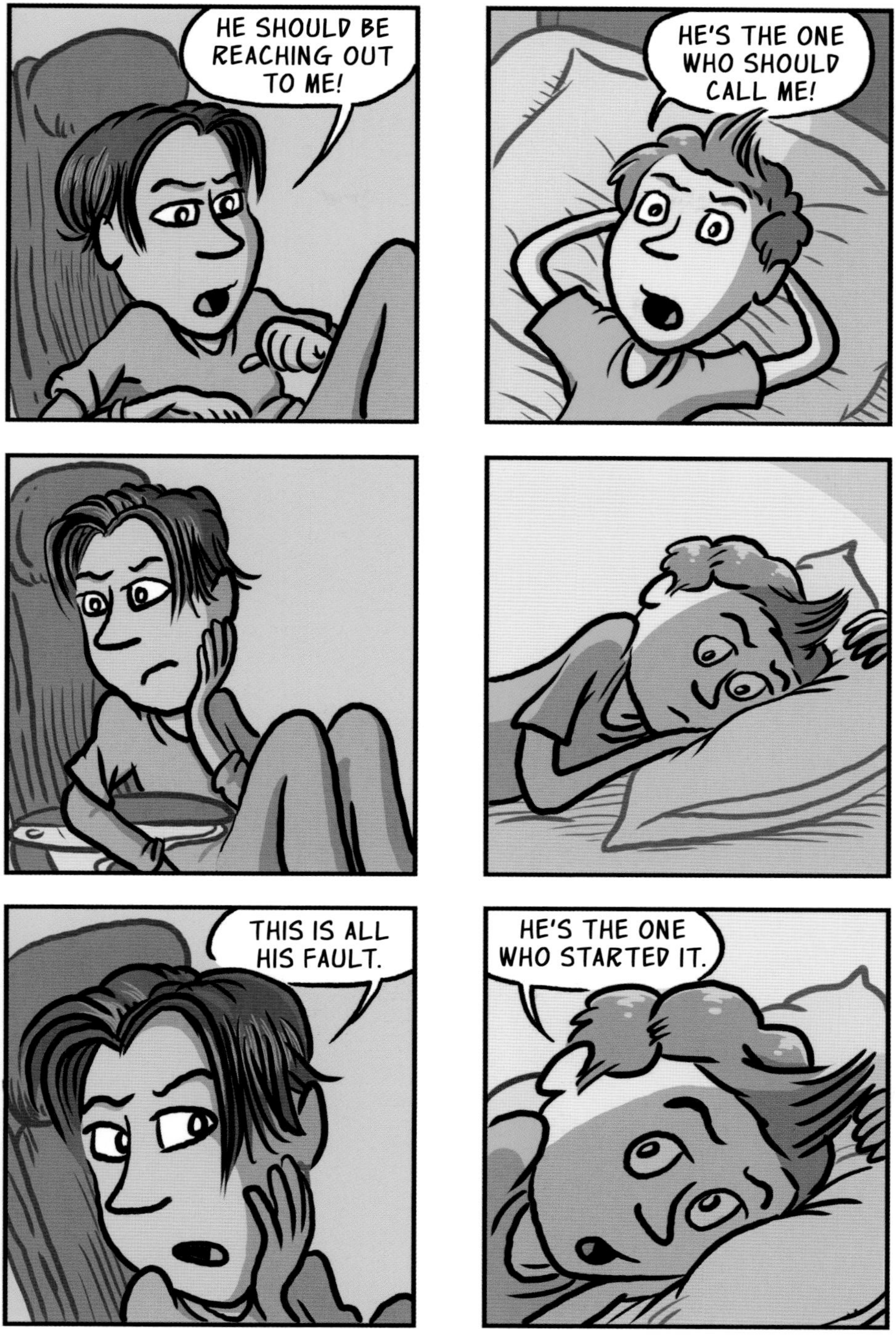
HE SHOULD BE REACHING OUT TO ME!
HE'S THE ONE WHO SHOULD CALL ME!
THIS IS ALL HIS FAULT.
HE'S THE ONE WHO STARTED IT.

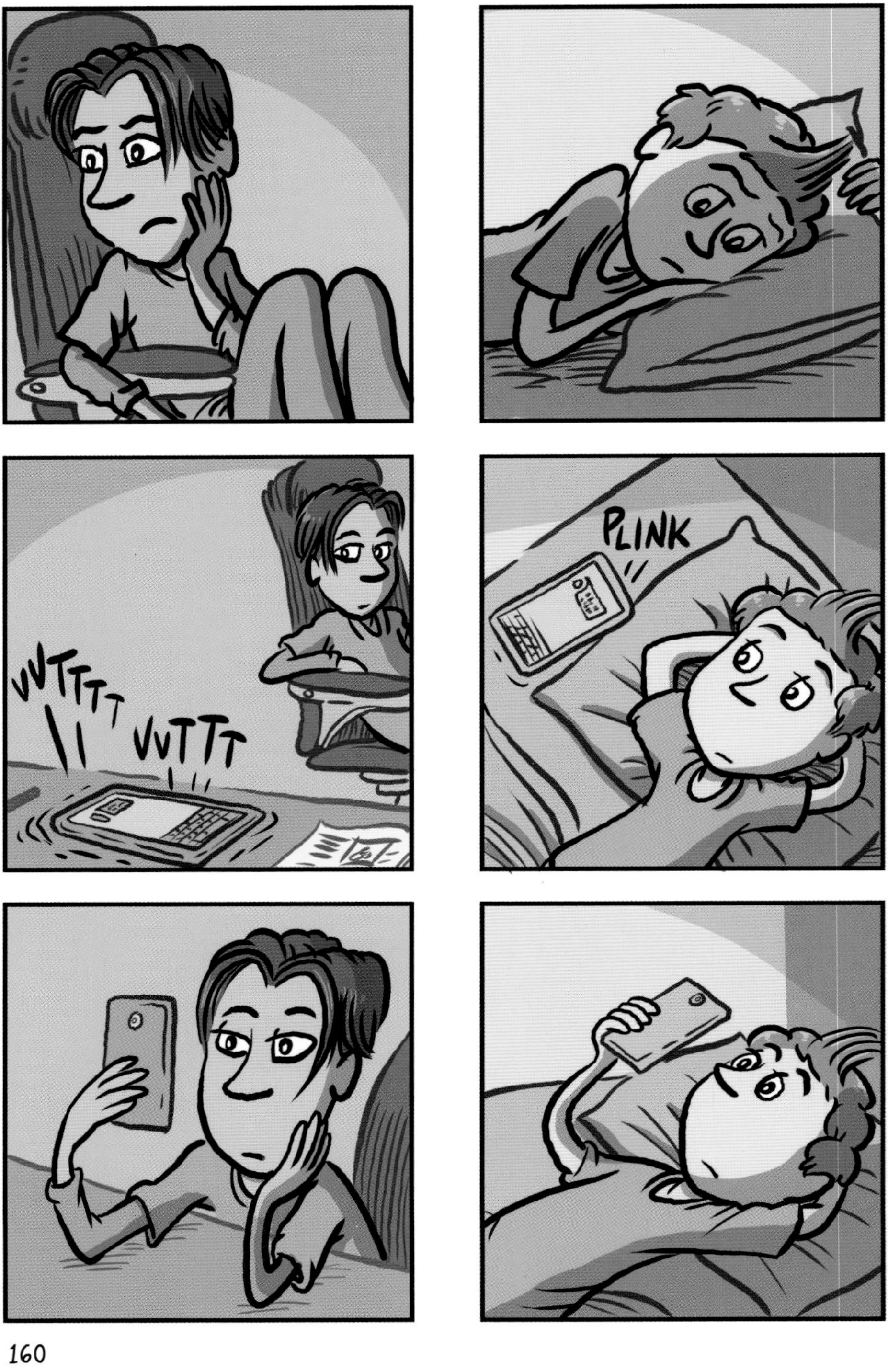
VVTTTTT
VVTTT
PLINK

Russ! Emergency meeting! At the library in 15 min!
Enter message
Andrew you have to come to the library! Like pronto!
Enter message

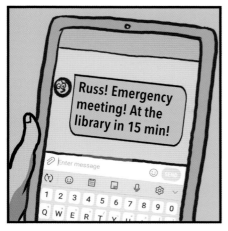

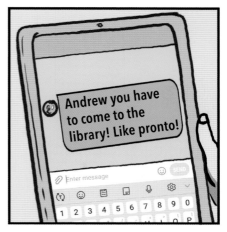

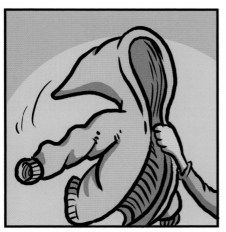

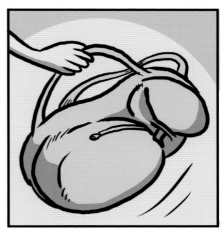

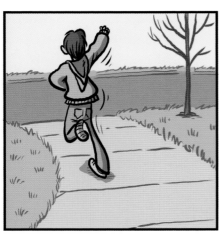

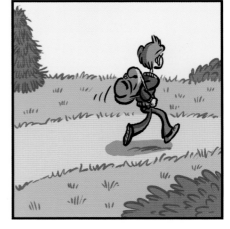

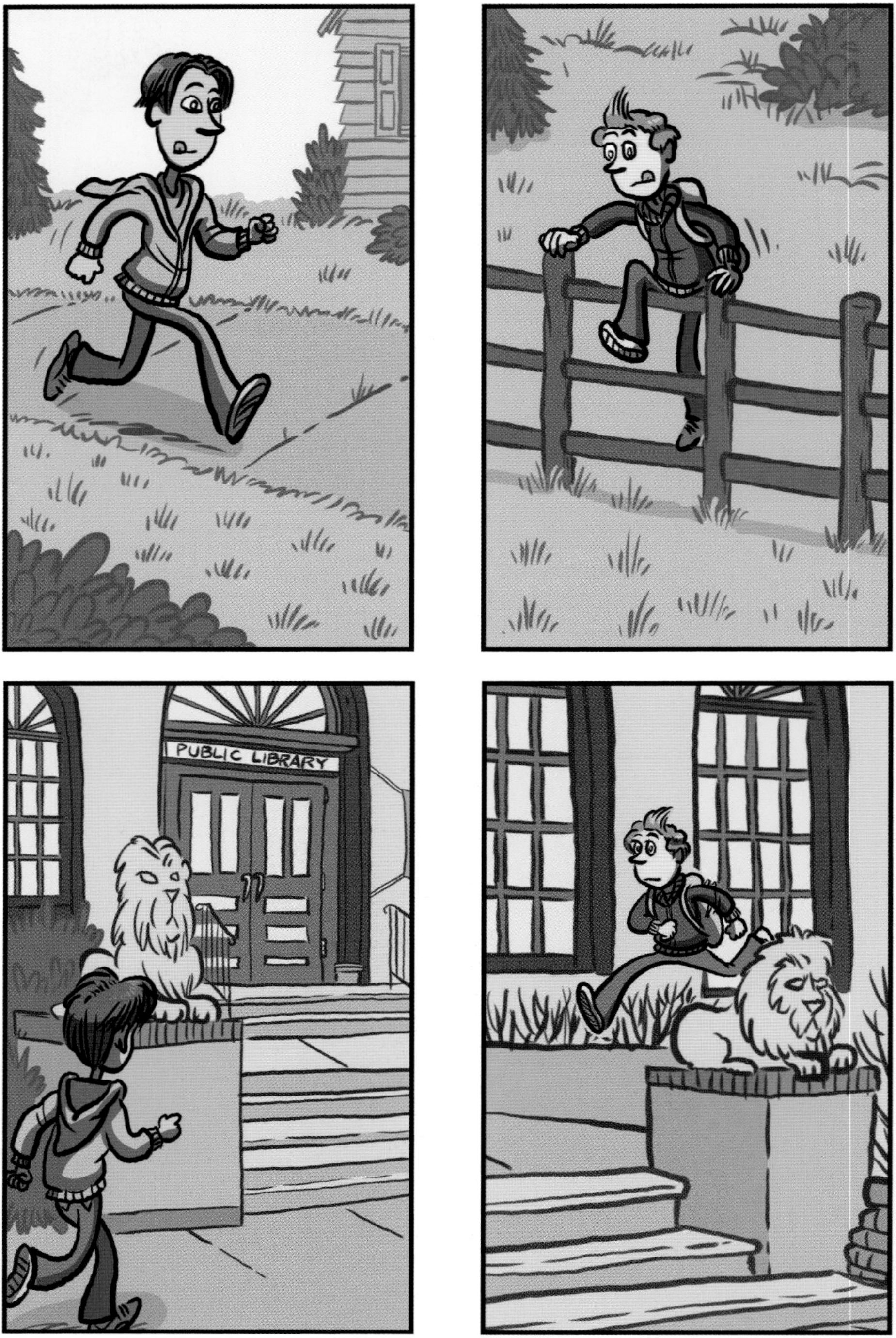
PUBLIC LIBRARY

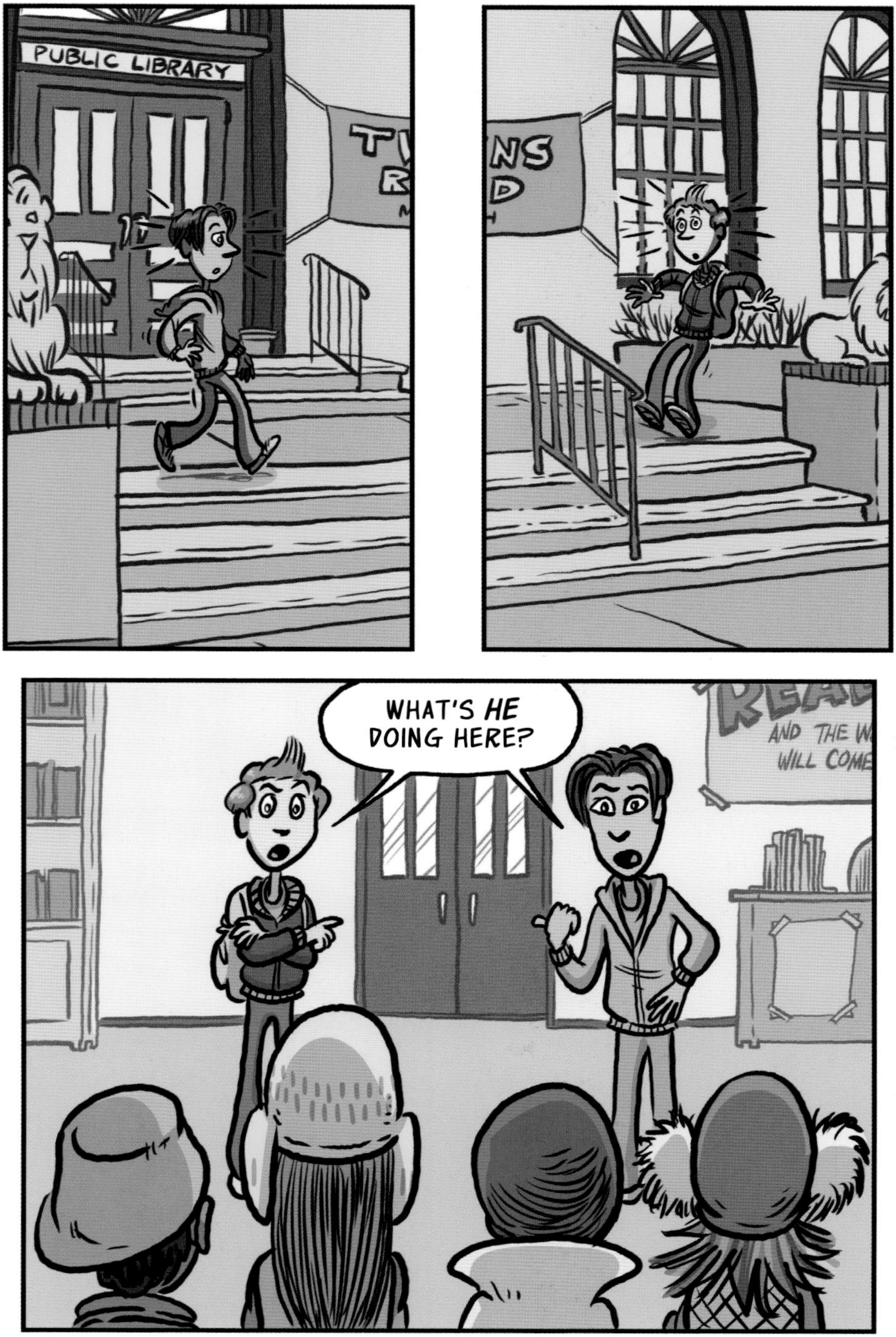
PUBLIC LIBRARY
WHAT'S *HE* DOING HERE?

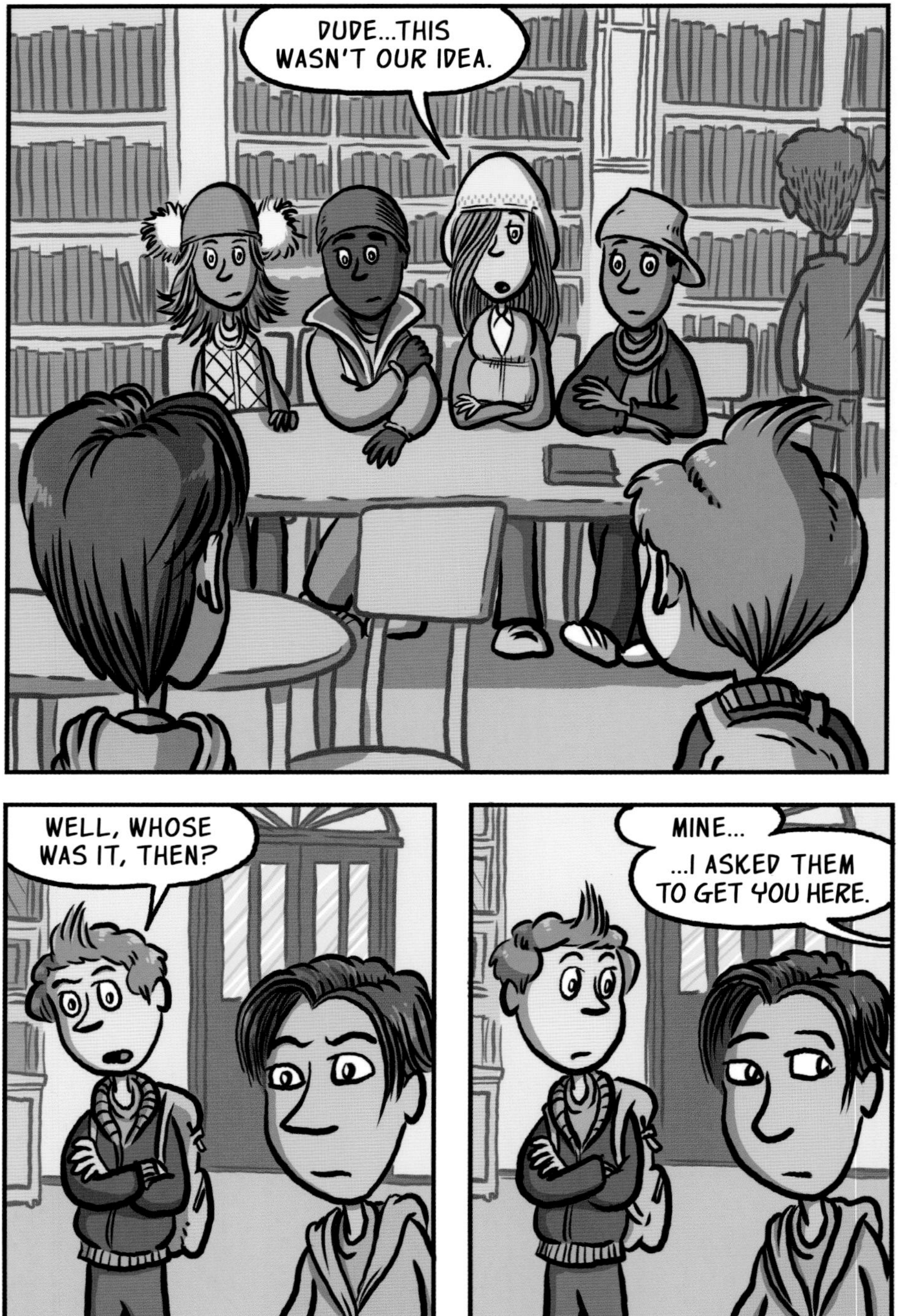
DUDE...THIS WASN'T OUR IDEA.
WELL, WHOSE WAS IT, THEN?
MINE...
...I ASKED THEM TO GET YOU HERE.

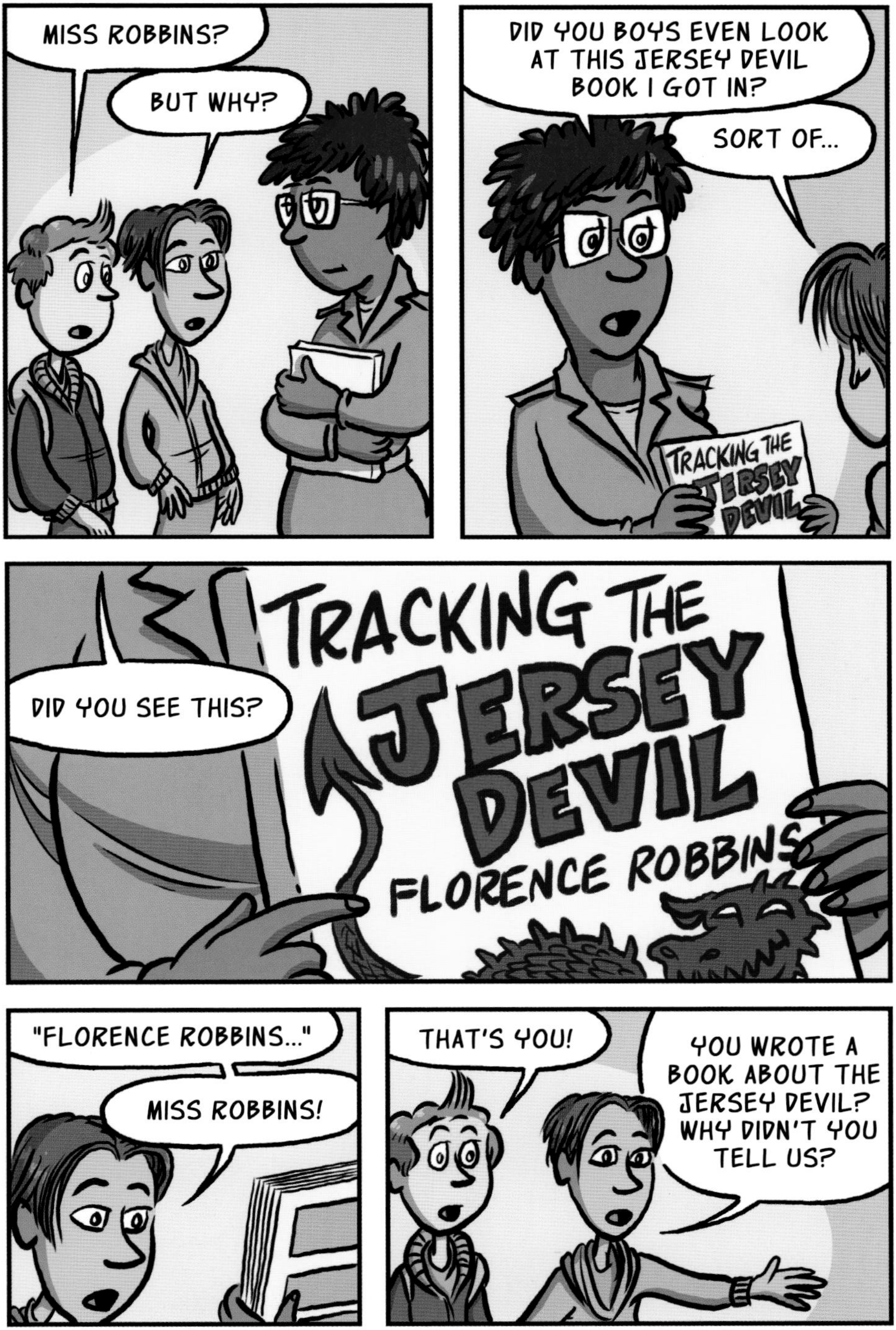

MISS ROBBINS?
BUT WHY?
DID YOU BOYS EVEN LOOK AT THIS JERSEY DEVIL BOOK I GOT IN?
SORT OF...
TRACKING THE JERSEY DEVIL
DID YOU SEE THIS?
TRACKING THE JERSEY DEVIL
FLORENCE ROBBINS
"FLORENCE ROBBINS..."
MISS ROBBINS!
THAT'S YOU!
YOU WROTE A BOOK ABOUT THE JERSEY DEVIL? WHY DIDN'T YOU TELL US?

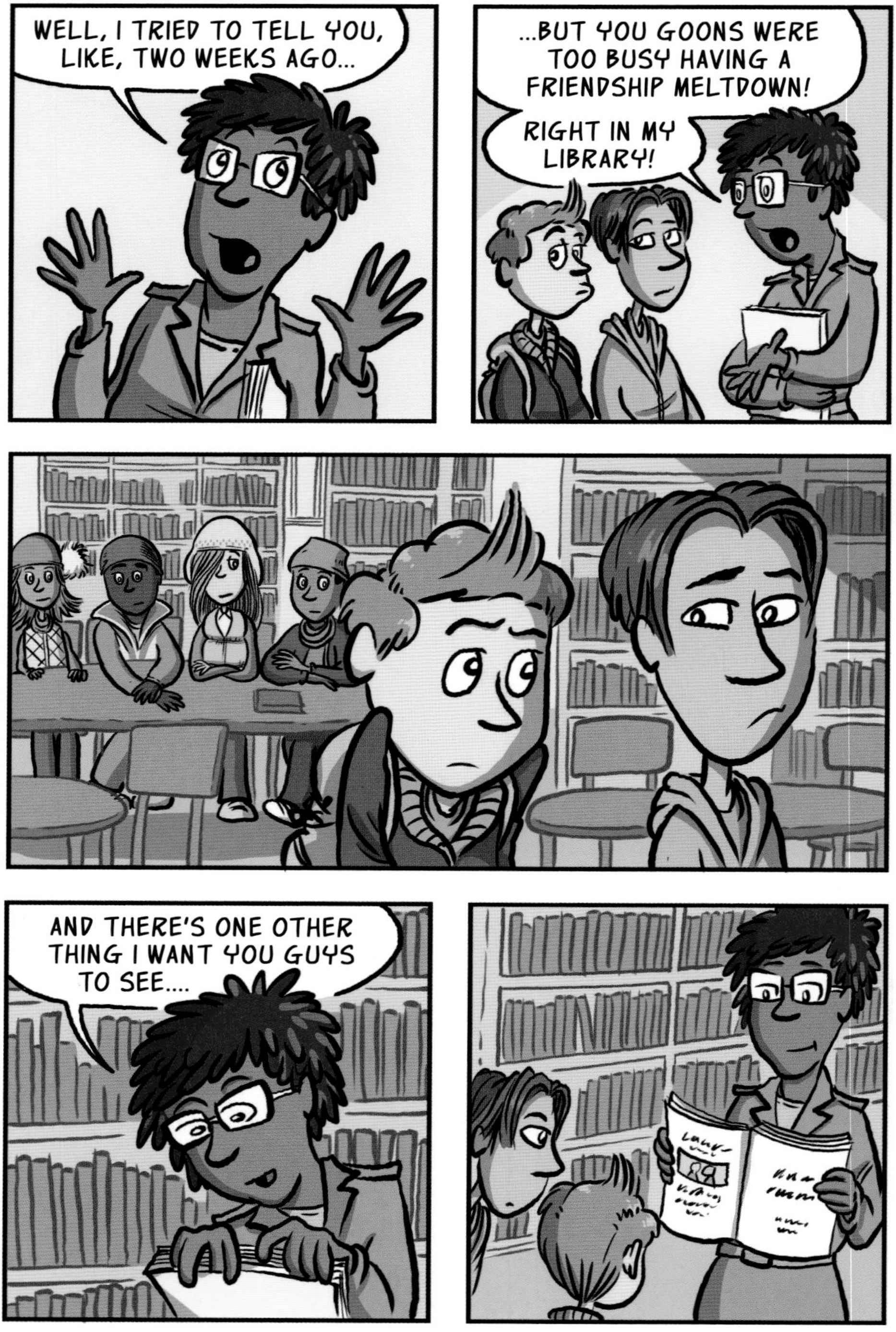
WELL, I TRIED TO TELL YOU, LIKE, TWO WEEKS AGO...
...BUT YOU GOONS WERE TOO BUSY HAVING A FRIENDSHIP MELTDOWN!
RIGHT IN MY LIBRARY!
AND THERE'S ONE OTHER THING I WANT YOU GUYS TO SEE....

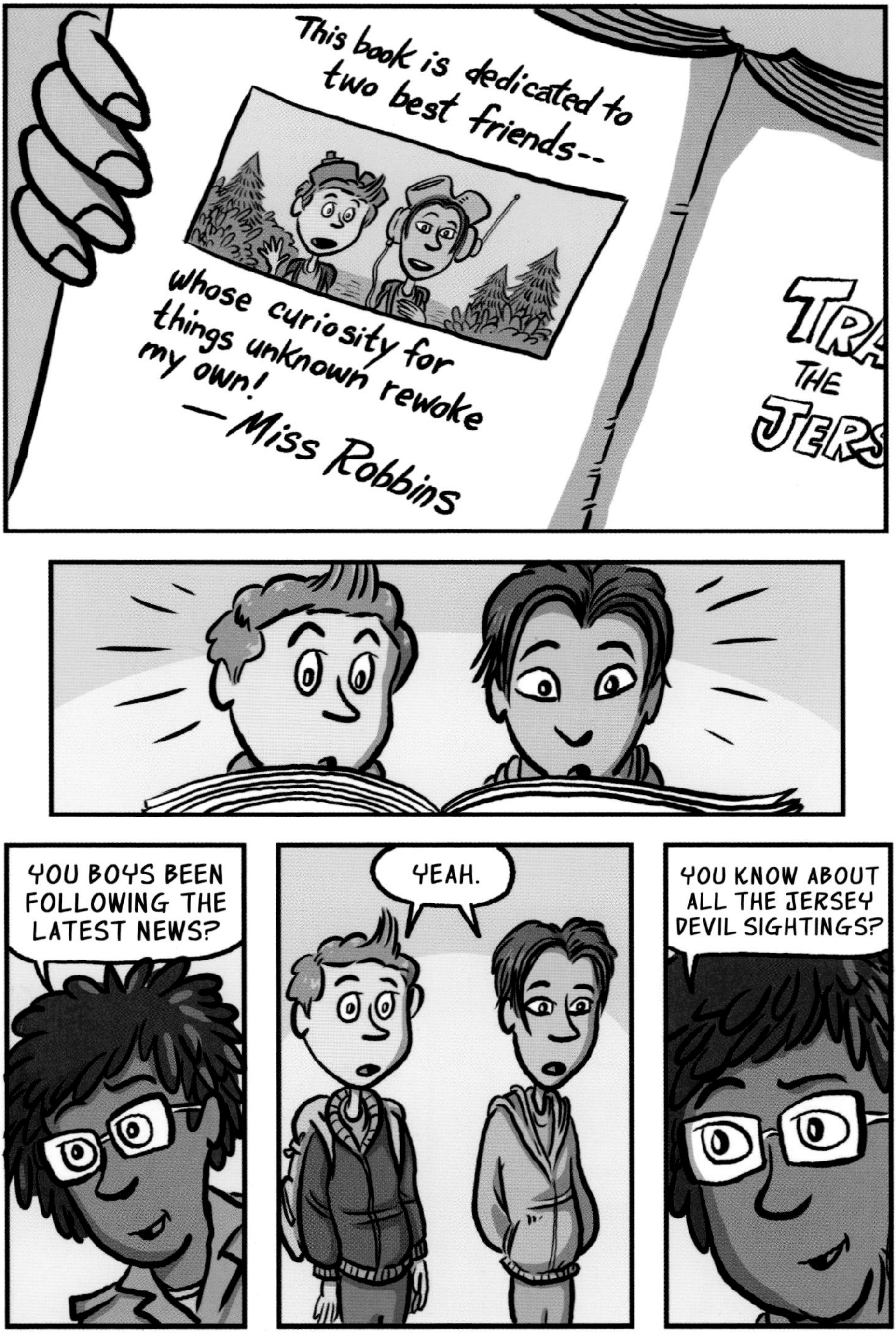
This book is dedicated to two best friends--
whose curiosity for things unknown rewoke my own!
—Miss Robbins
THE
YOU BOYS BEEN FOLLOWING THE LATEST NEWS?
YEAH.
YOU KNOW ABOUT ALL THE JERSEY DEVIL SIGHTINGS?

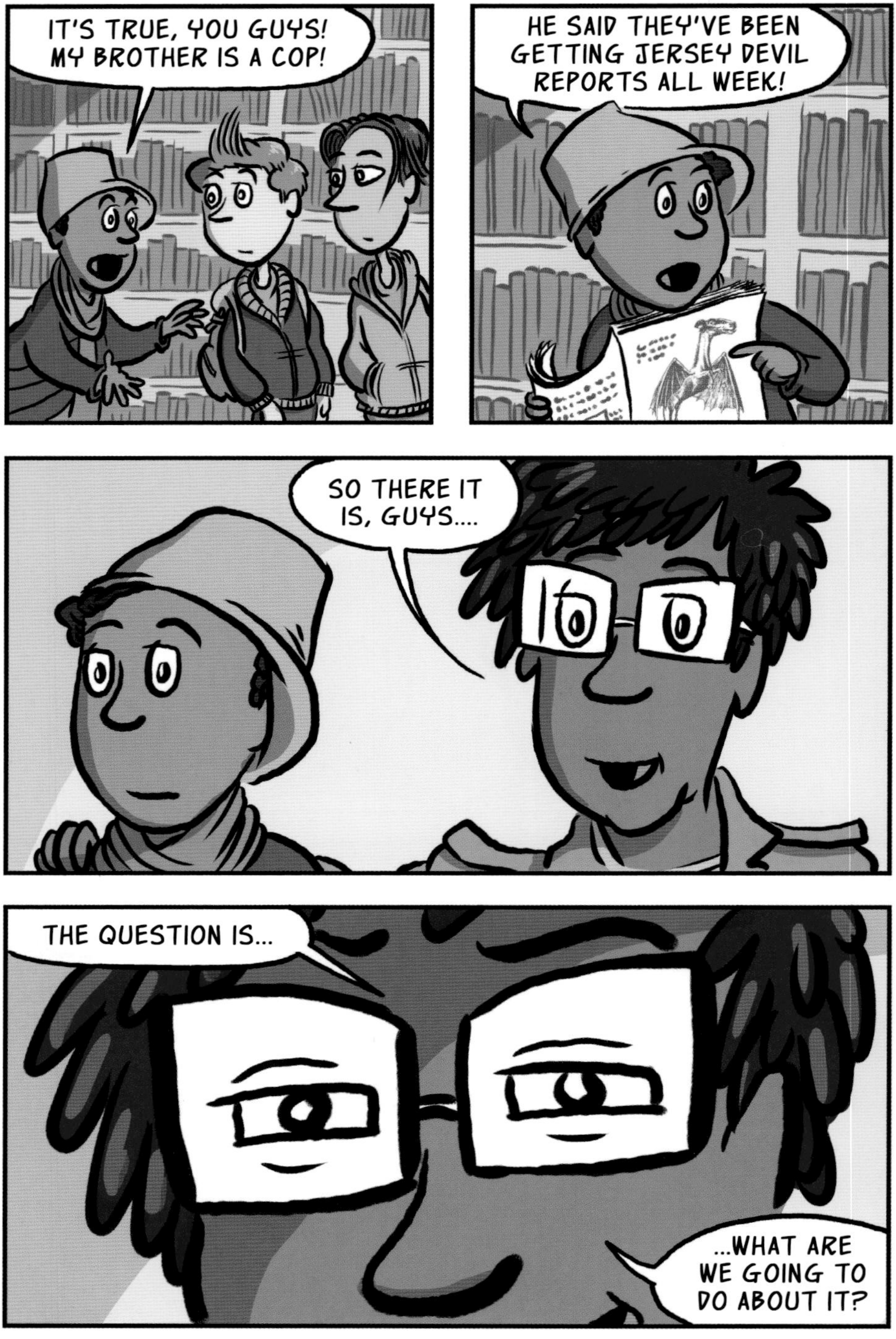
IT'S TRUE, YOU GUYS! MY BROTHER IS A COP!
HE SAID THEY'VE BEEN GETTING JERSEY DEVIL REPORTS ALL WEEK!
SO THERE IT IS, GUYS....
THE QUESTION IS...
...WHAT ARE WE GOING TO DO ABOUT IT?

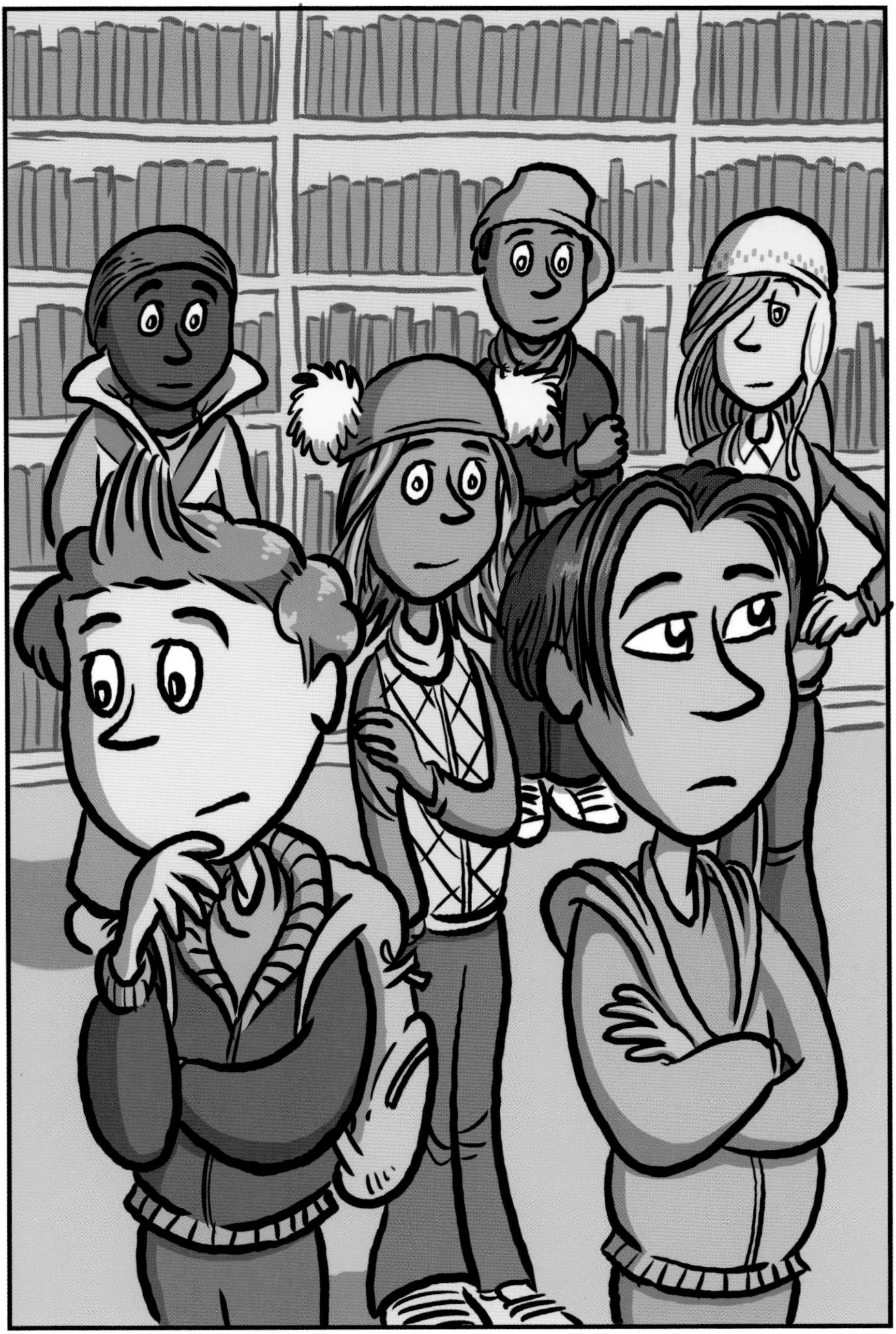

CHAPTER 14

THAT NIGHT

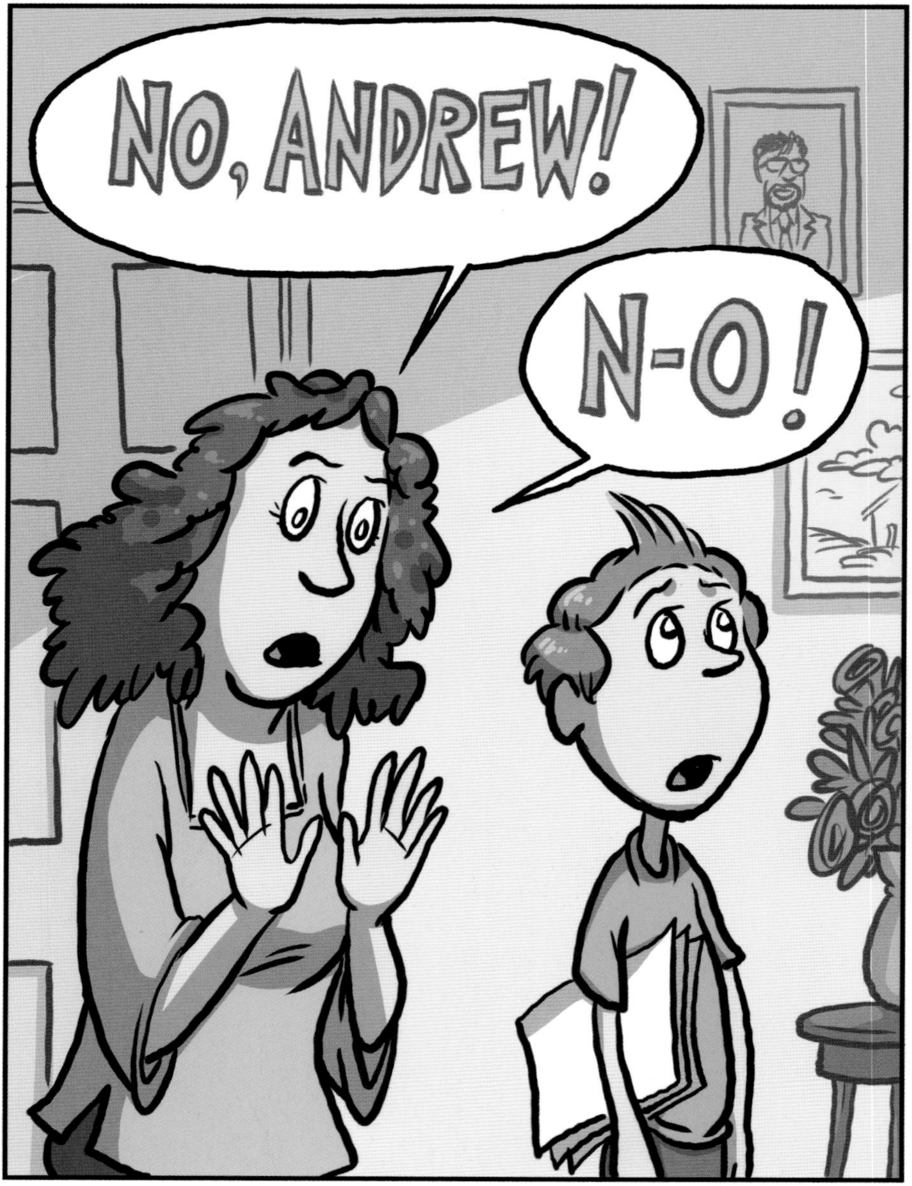

NO, ANDREW!
N-O!

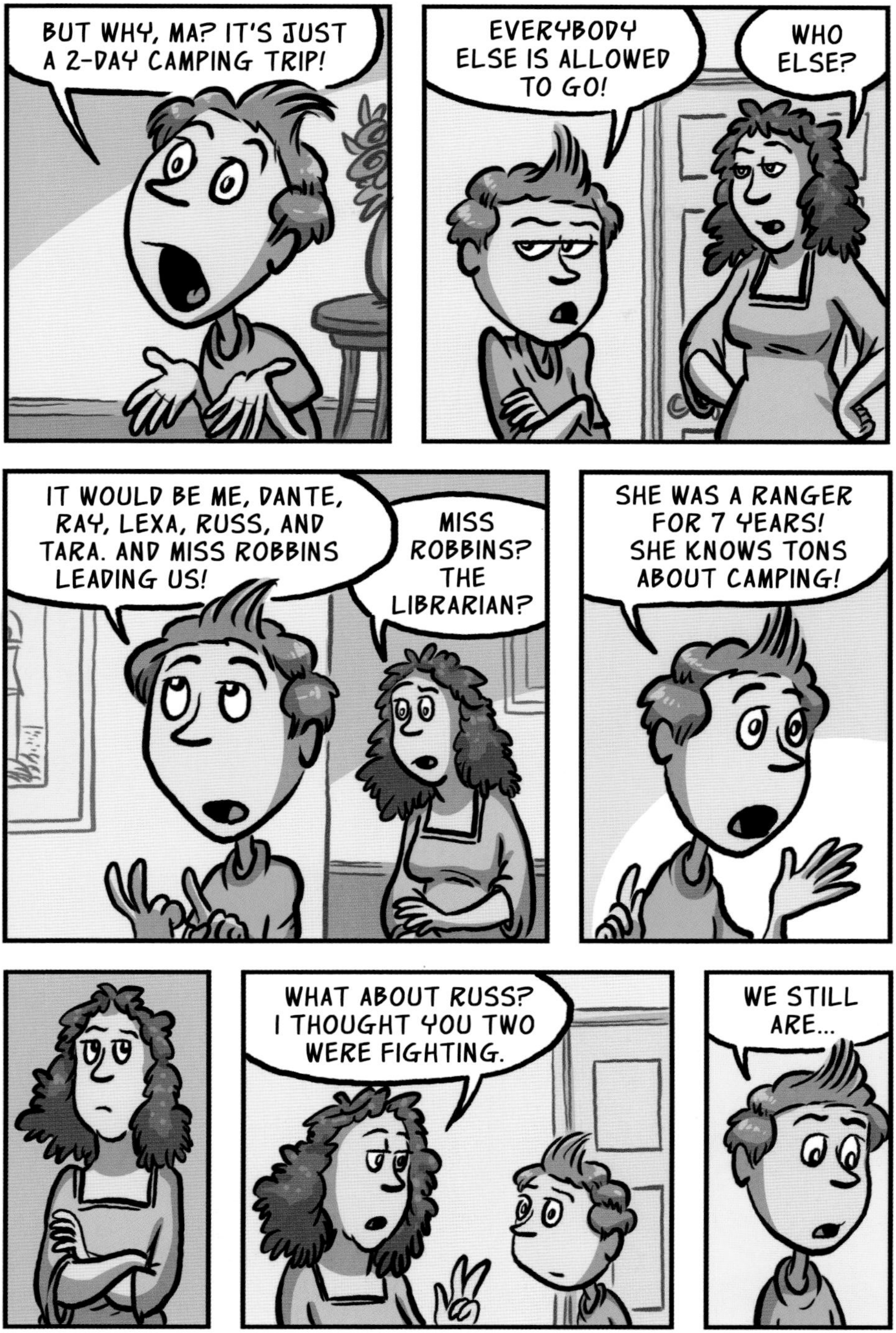
BUT WHY, MA? IT'S JUST A 2-DAY CAMPING TRIP!
EVERYBODY ELSE IS ALLOWED TO GO!
WHO ELSE?
IT WOULD BE ME, DANTE, RAY, LEXA, RUSS, AND TARA. AND MISS ROBBINS LEADING US!
MISS ROBBINS? THE LIBRARIAN?
SHE WAS A RANGER FOR 7 YEARS! SHE KNOWS TONS ABOUT CAMPING!
WHAT ABOUT RUSS? I THOUGHT YOU TWO WERE FIGHTING.
WE STILL ARE...

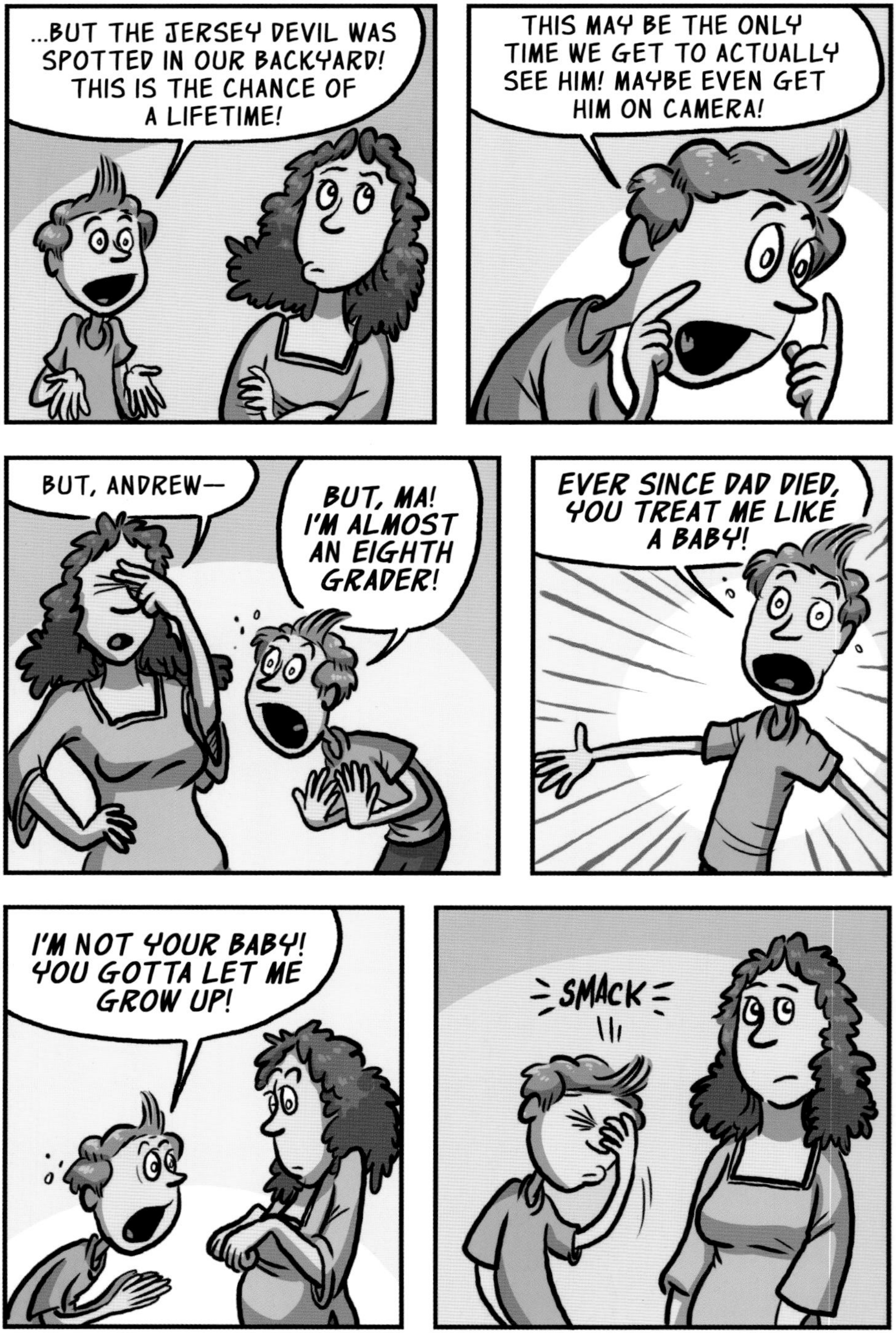
...BUT THE JERSEY DEVIL WAS SPOTTED IN OUR BACKYARD! THIS IS THE CHANCE OF A LIFETIME!
THIS MAY BE THE ONLY TIME WE GET TO ACTUALLY SEE HIM! MAYBE EVEN GET HIM ON CAMERA!
BUT, ANDREW—
BUT, MA! I'M ALMOST AN EIGHTH GRADER!
EVER SINCE DAD DIED, YOU TREAT ME LIKE A BABY!
I'M NOT YOUR BABY! YOU GOTTA LET ME GROW UP!
SMACK

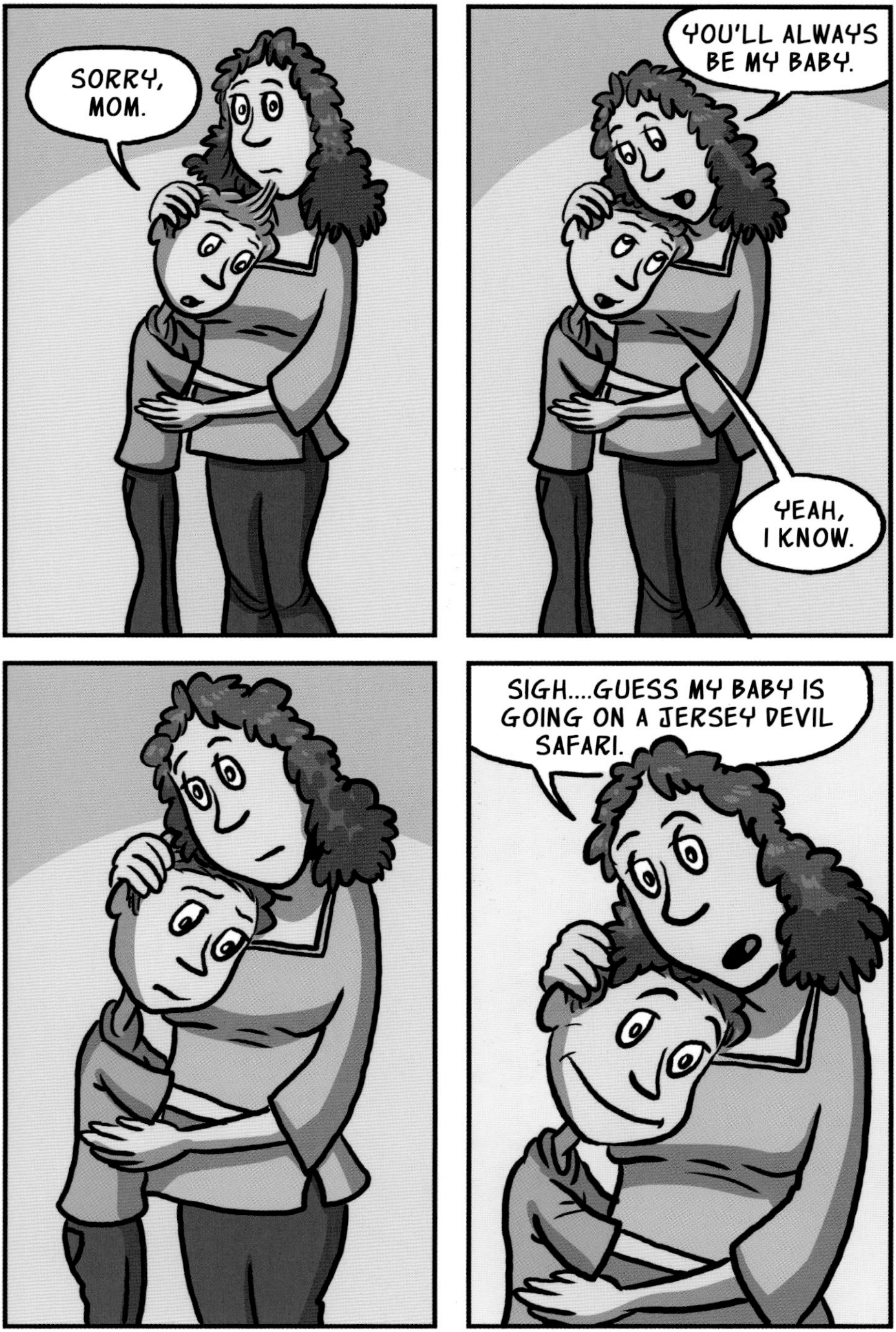
SORRY, MOM.
YOU'LL ALWAYS BE MY BABY.
YEAH, I KNOW.
SIGH....GUESS MY BABY IS GOING ON A JERSEY DEVIL SAFARI.

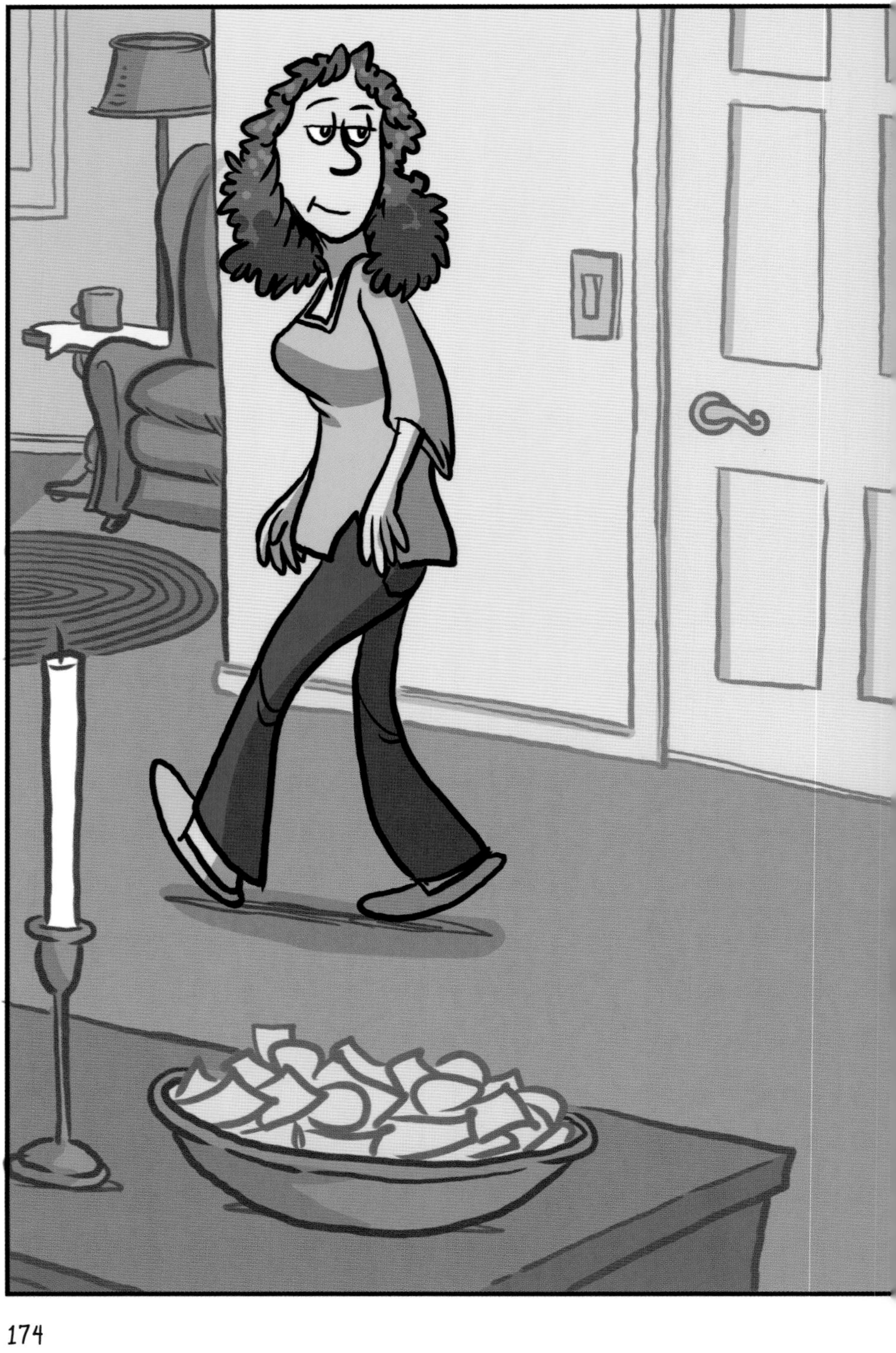

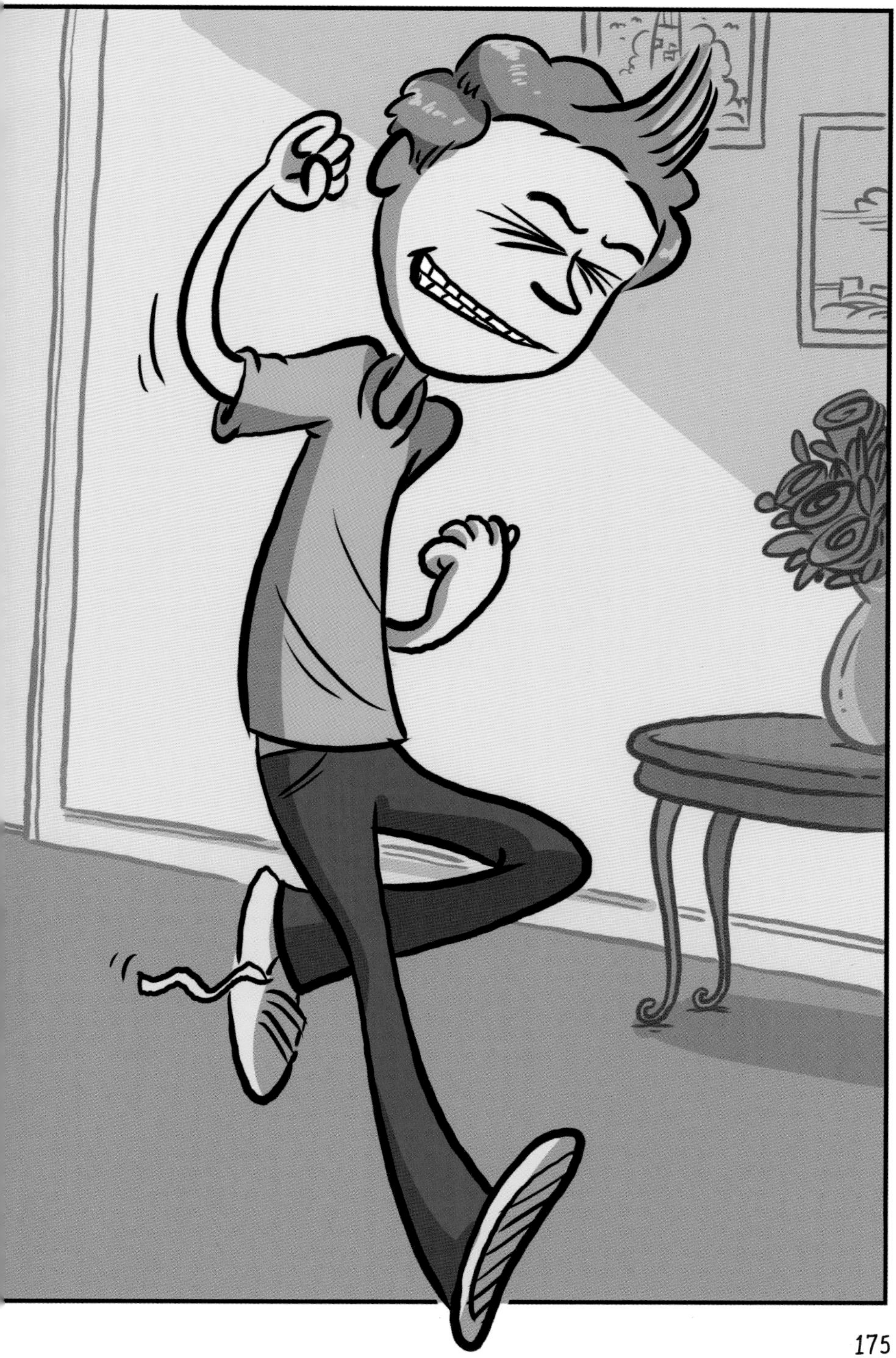

CHAPTER 15 THAT WEEKEND

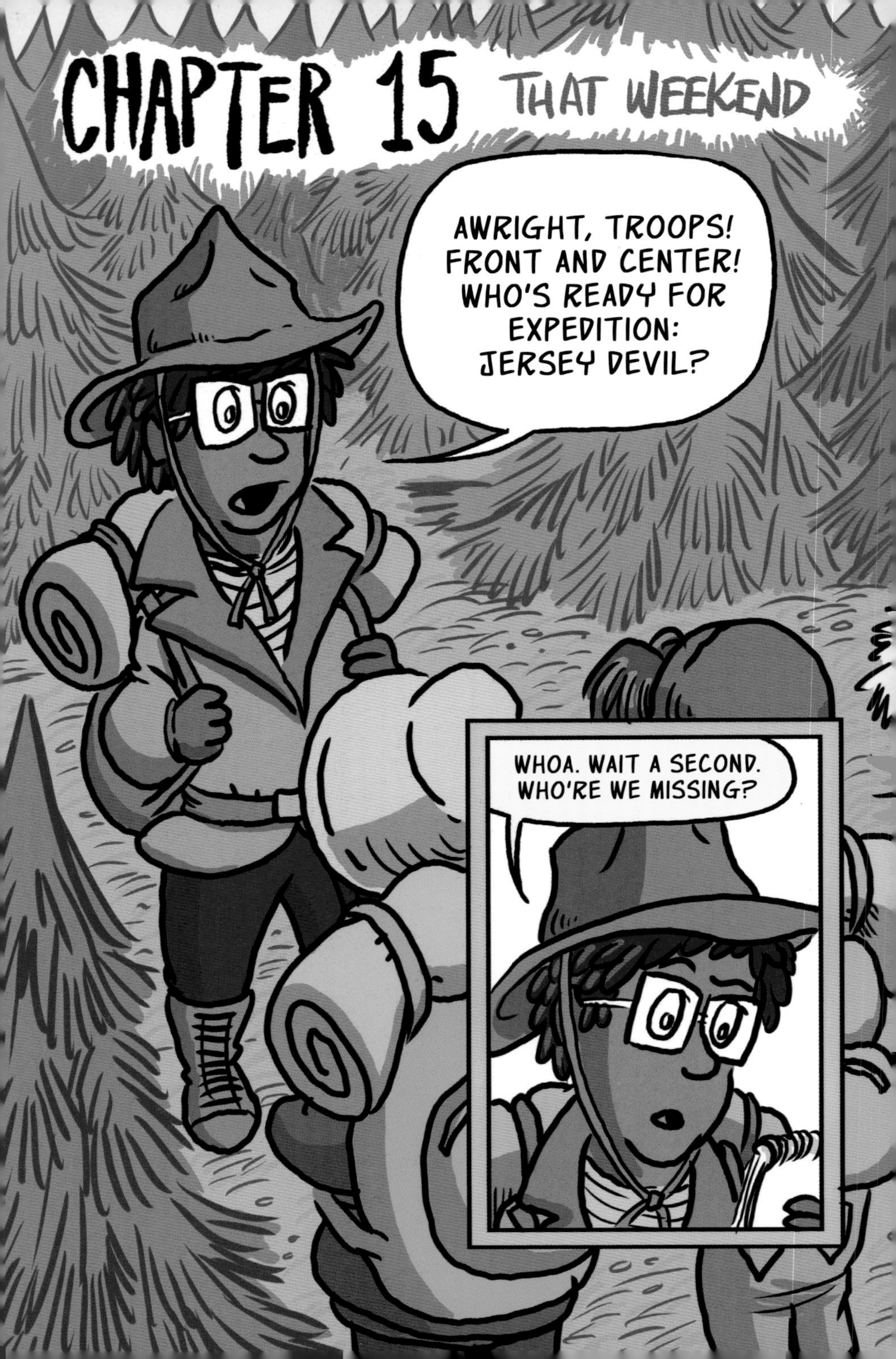
AWRIGHT, TROOPS! FRONT AND CENTER! WHO'S READY FOR EXPEDITION: JERSEY DEVIL?
WHOA. WAIT A SECOND. WHO'RE WE MISSING?

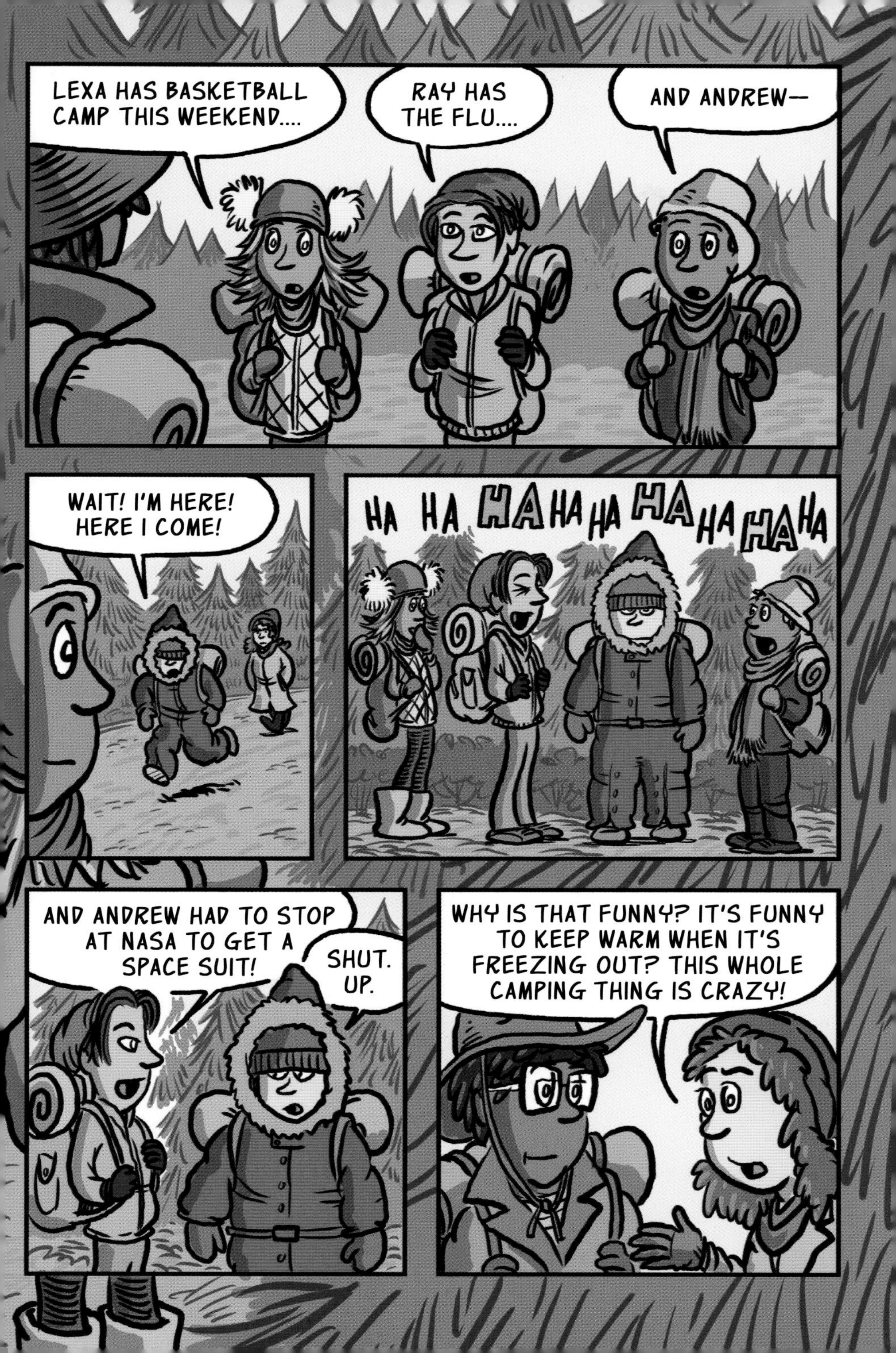
LEXA HAS BASKETBALL CAMP THIS WEEKEND....
RAY HAS THE FLU....
AND ANDREW—
WAIT! I'M HERE! HERE I COME!
HA HA HA HA HA HA HA HA HA HA
AND ANDREW HAD TO STOP AT NASA TO GET A SPACE SUIT!
SHUT. UP.
WHY IS THAT FUNNY? IT'S FUNNY TO KEEP WARM WHEN IT'S FREEZING OUT? THIS WHOLE CAMPING THING IS CRAZY!

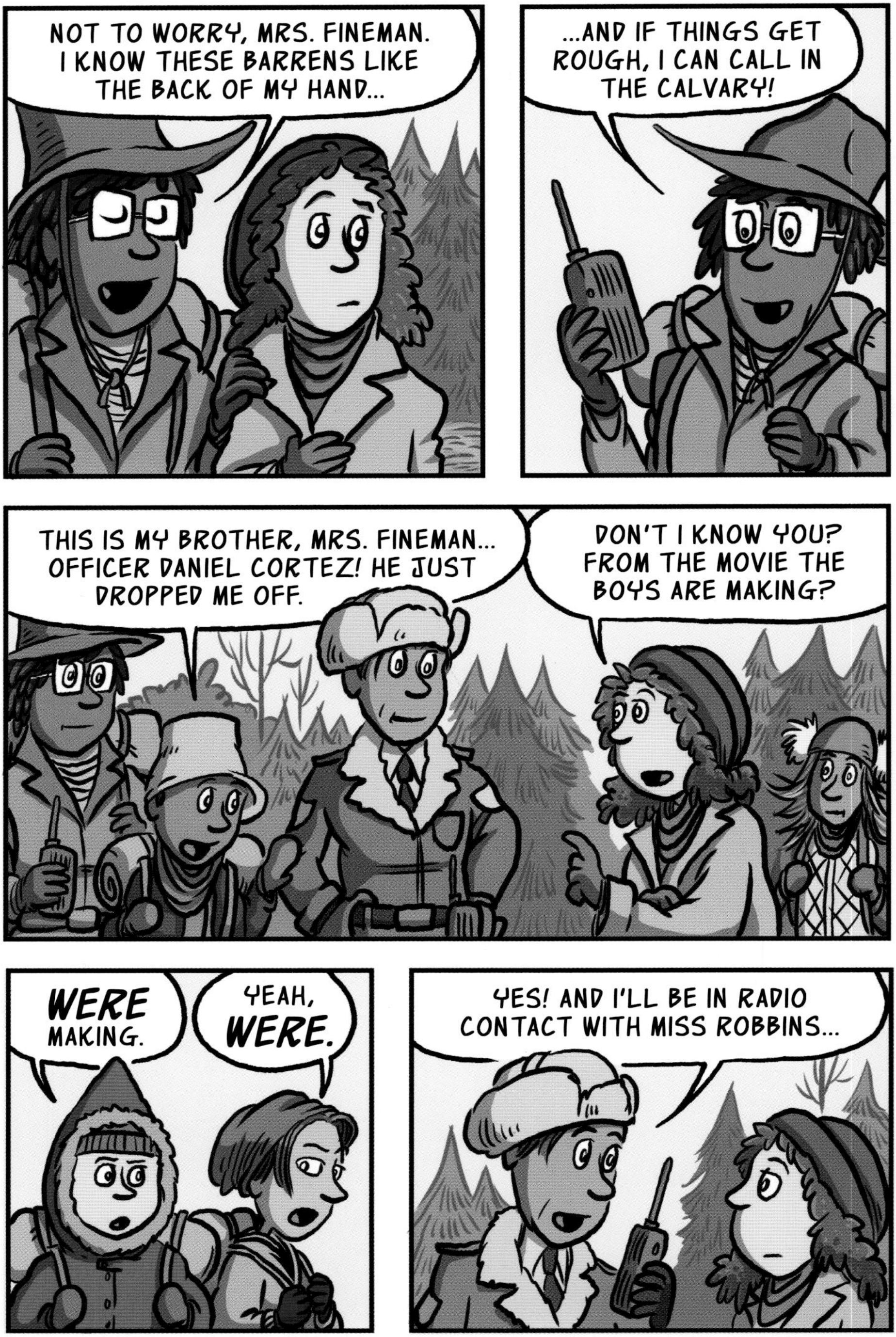
NOT TO WORRY, MRS. FINEMAN. I KNOW THESE BARRENS LIKE THE BACK OF MY HAND...
...AND IF THINGS GET ROUGH, I CAN CALL IN THE CALVARY!
THIS IS MY BROTHER, MRS. FINEMAN... OFFICER DANIEL CORTEZ! HE JUST DROPPED ME OFF.
DON'T I KNOW YOU? FROM THE MOVIE THE BOYS ARE MAKING?
WERE MAKING.
YEAH, WERE.
YES! AND I'LL BE IN RADIO CONTACT WITH MISS ROBBINS...

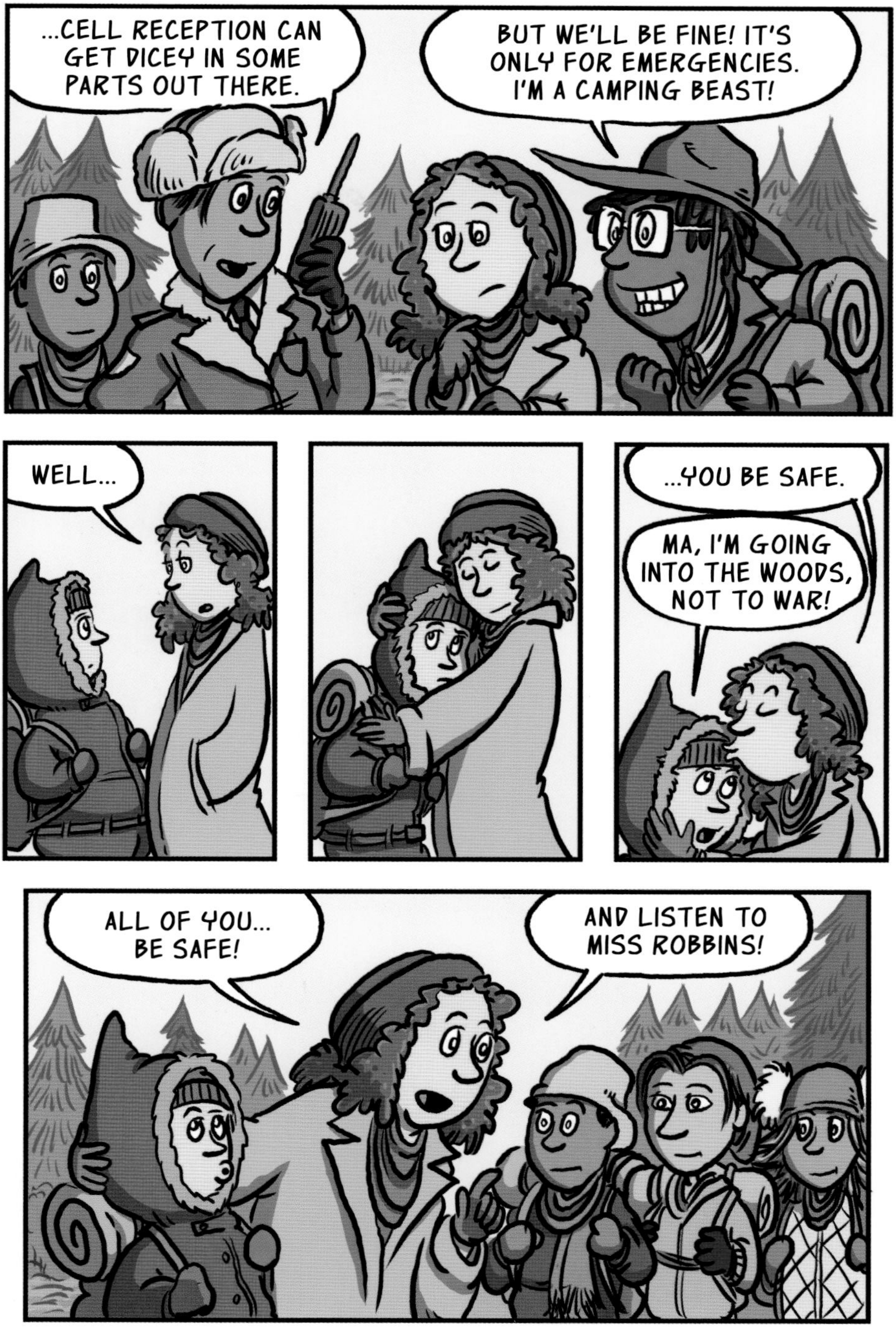
...CELL RECEPTION CAN GET DICEY IN SOME PARTS OUT THERE.
BUT WE'LL BE FINE! IT'S ONLY FOR EMERGENCIES. I'M A CAMPING BEAST!
WELL...
...YOU BE SAFE.
MA, I'M GOING INTO THE WOODS, NOT TO WAR!
ALL OF YOU... BE SAFE!
AND LISTEN TO MISS ROBBINS!

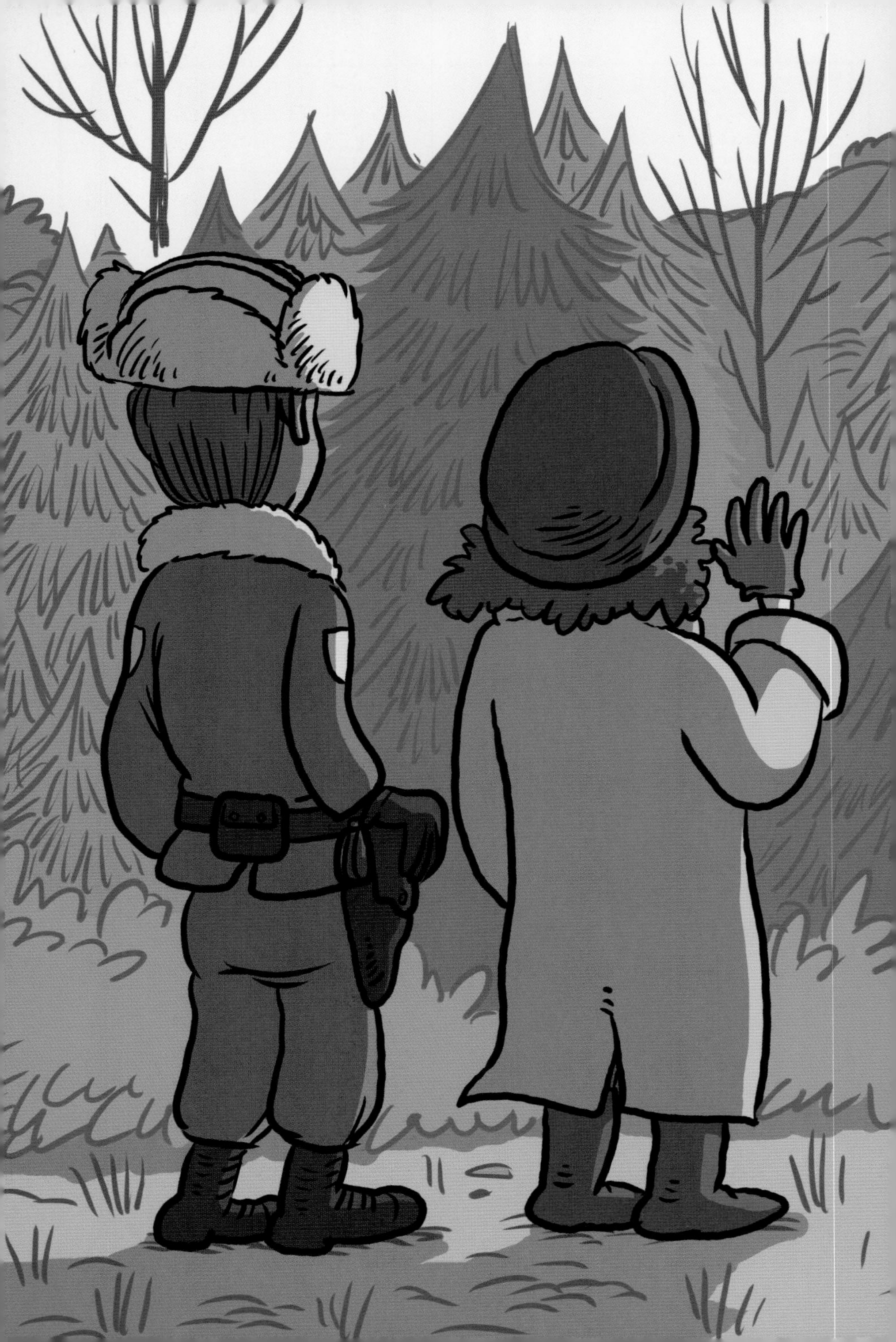

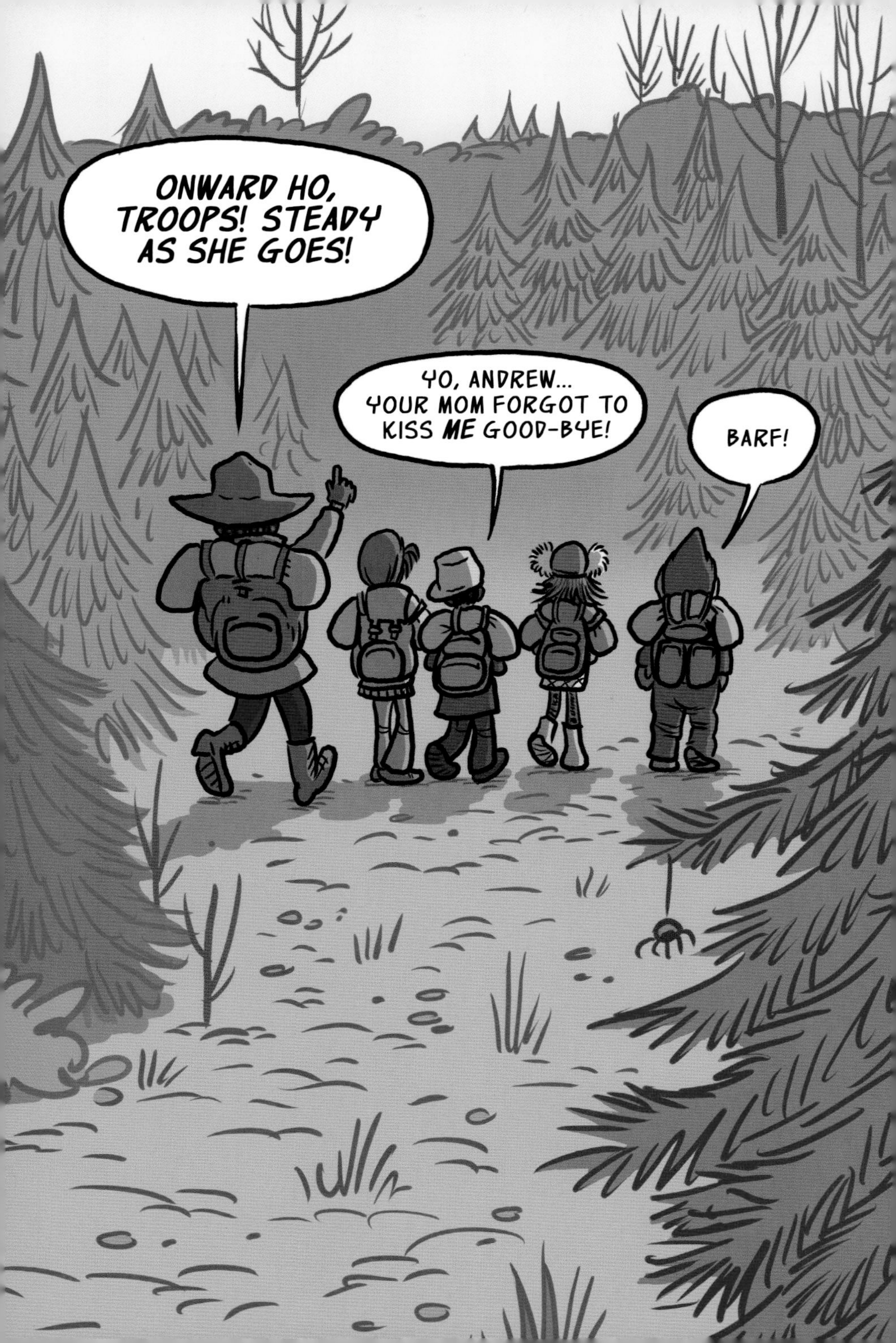
ONWARD HO, TROOPS! STEADY AS SHE GOES!
YO, ANDREW... YOUR MOM FORGOT TO KISS **ME** GOOD-BYE!
BARF!

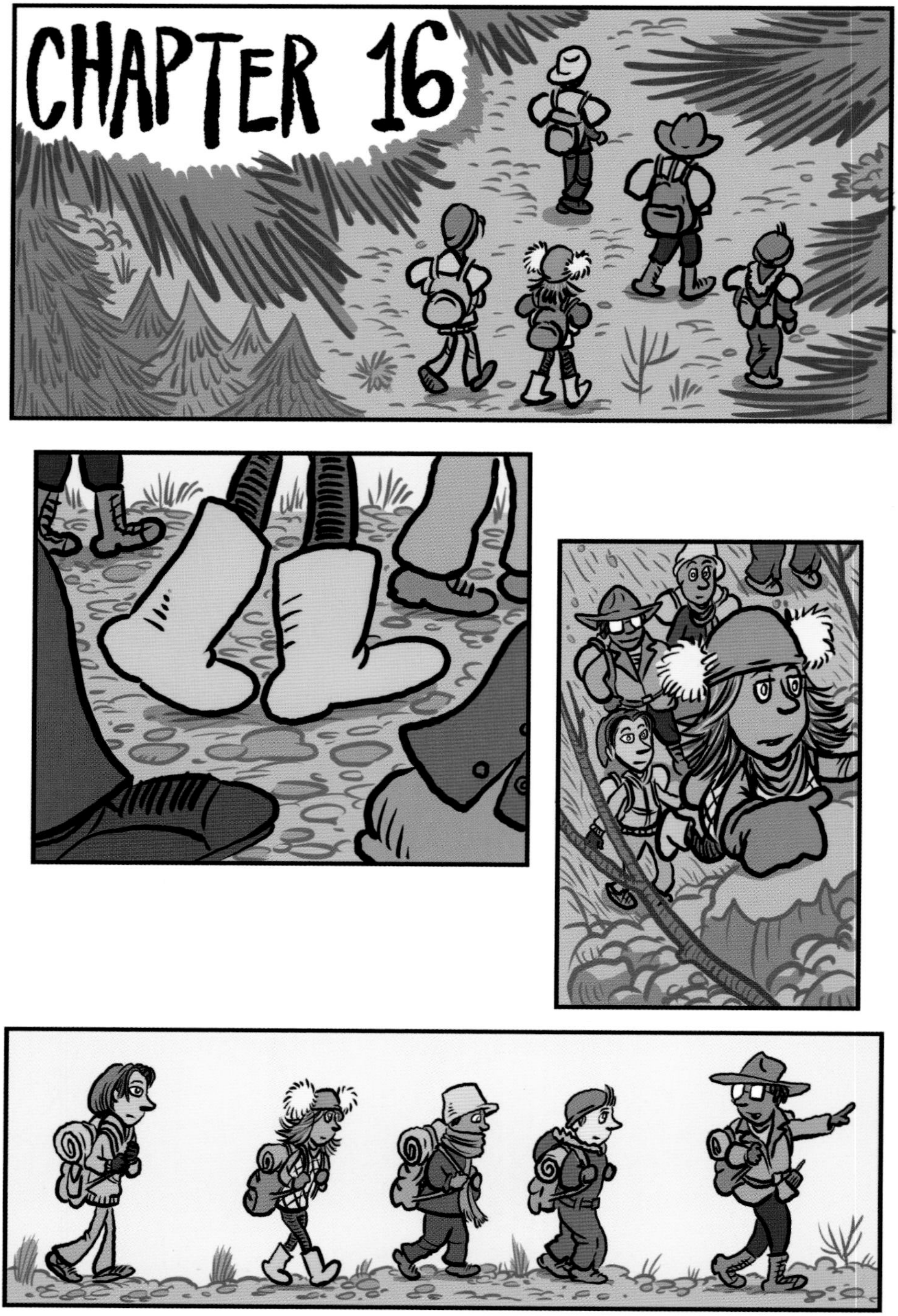
CHAPTER 16

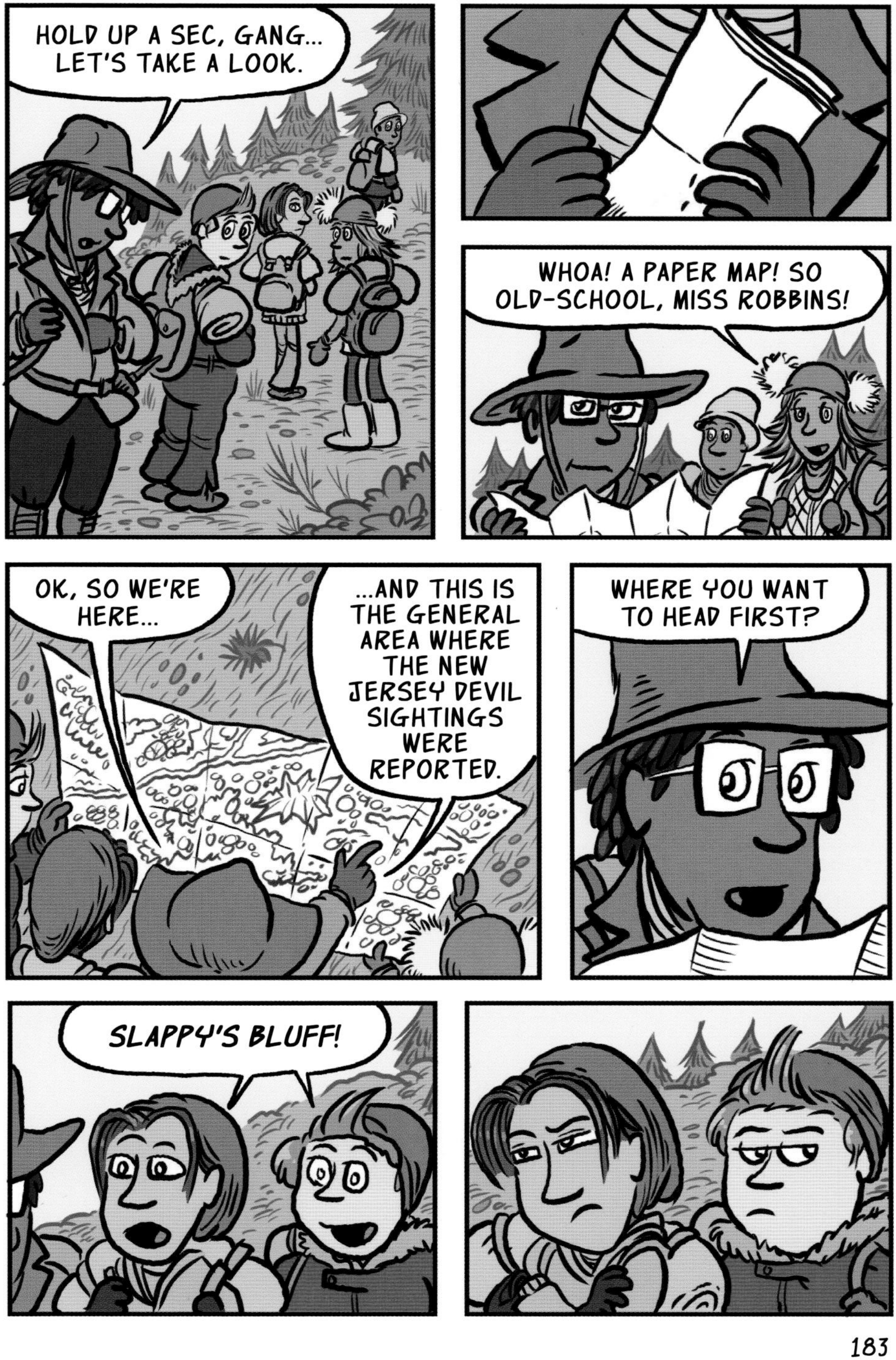
HOLD UP A SEC, GANG... LET'S TAKE A LOOK.
WHOA! A PAPER MAP! SO OLD-SCHOOL, MISS ROBBINS!
OK, SO WE'RE HERE...
...AND THIS IS THE GENERAL AREA WHERE THE NEW JERSEY DEVIL SIGHTINGS WERE REPORTED.
WHERE YOU WANT TO HEAD FIRST?
SLAPPY'S BLUFF!

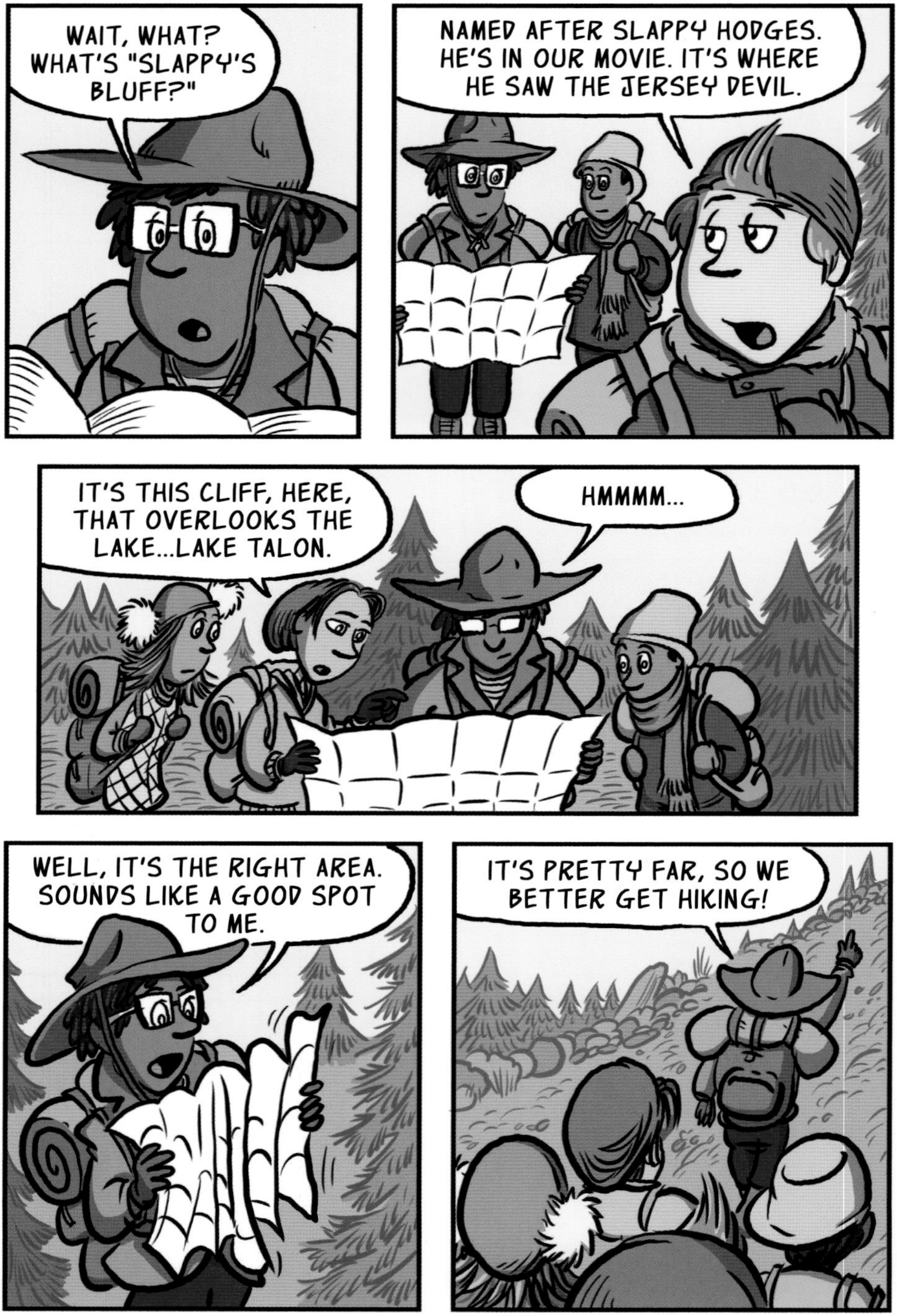
WAIT, WHAT? WHAT'S "SLAPPY'S BLUFF?"
NAMED AFTER SLAPPY HODGES. HE'S IN OUR MOVIE. IT'S WHERE HE SAW THE JERSEY DEVIL.
IT'S THIS CLIFF, HERE, THAT OVERLOOKS THE LAKE...LAKE TALON.
HMMMM...
WELL, IT'S THE RIGHT AREA. SOUNDS LIKE A GOOD SPOT TO ME.
IT'S PRETTY FAR, SO WE BETTER GET HIKING!

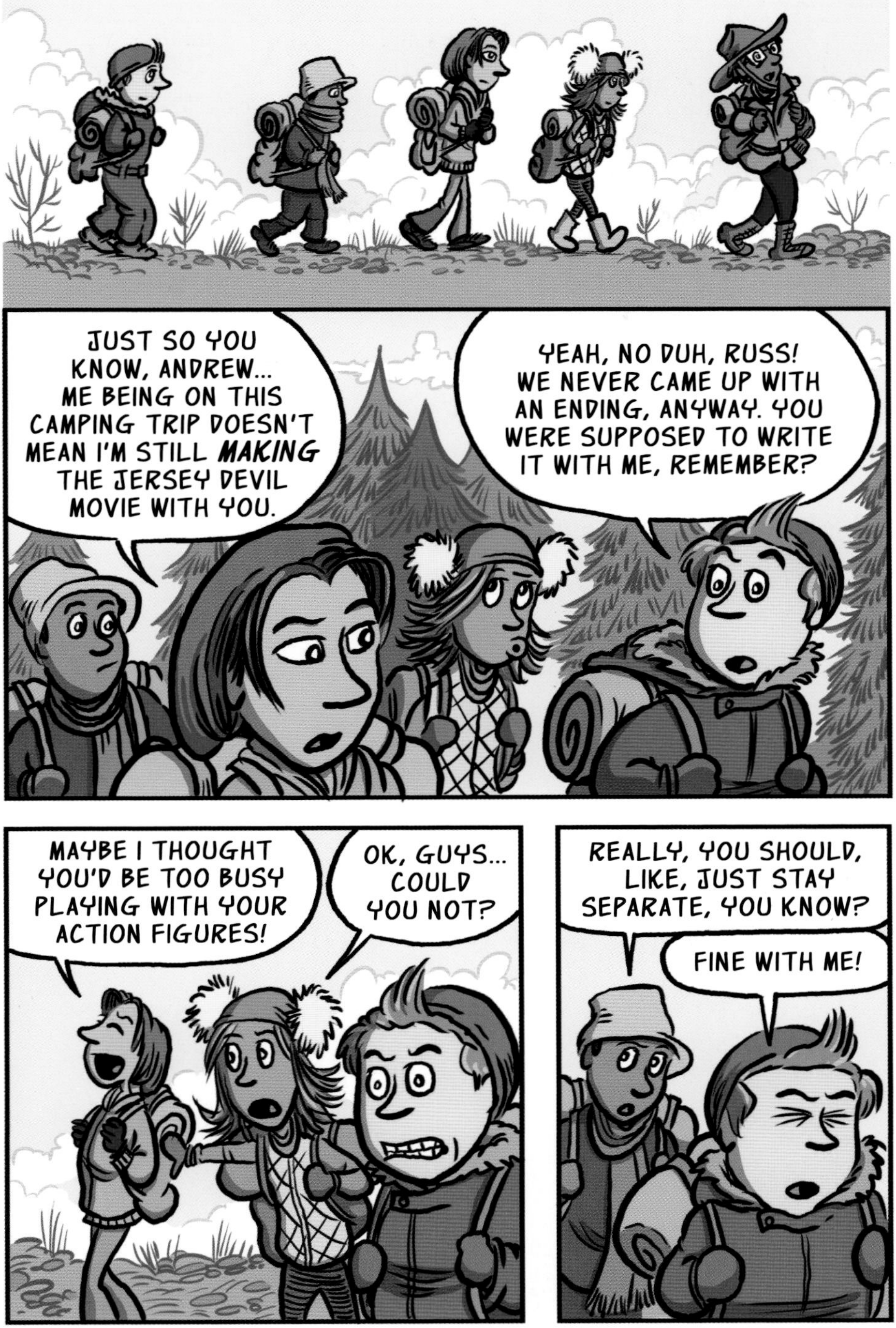
JUST SO YOU KNOW, ANDREW... ME BEING ON THIS CAMPING TRIP DOESN'T MEAN I'M STILL *MAKING* THE JERSEY DEVIL MOVIE WITH YOU.
YEAH, NO DUH, RUSS! WE NEVER CAME UP WITH AN ENDING, ANYWAY. YOU WERE SUPPOSED TO WRITE IT WITH ME, REMEMBER?
MAYBE I THOUGHT YOU'D BE TOO BUSY PLAYING WITH YOUR ACTION FIGURES!
OK, GUYS... COULD YOU NOT?
REALLY, YOU SHOULD, LIKE, JUST STAY SEPARATE, YOU KNOW?
FINE WITH ME!

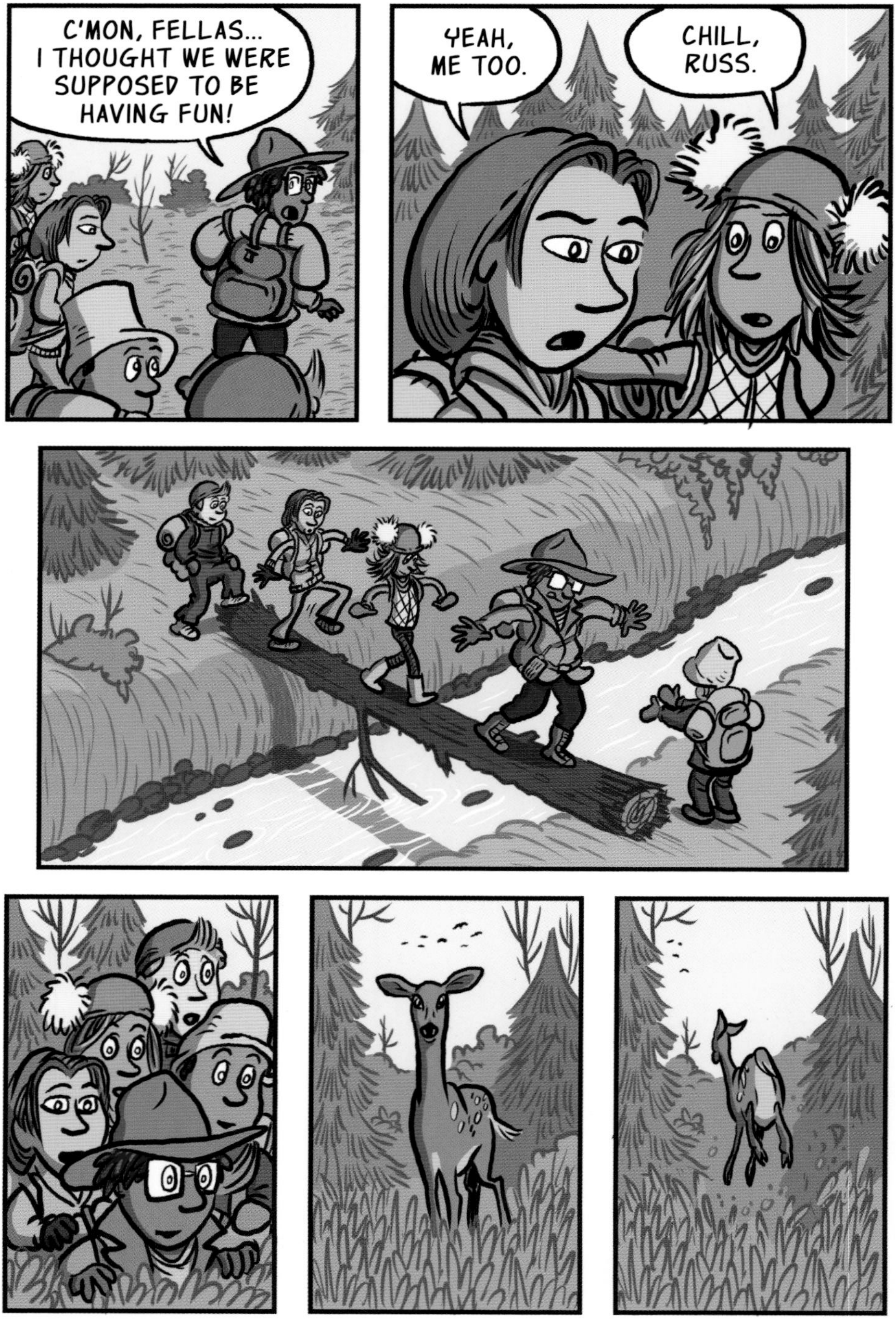
C'MON, FELLAS... I THOUGHT WE WERE SUPPOSED TO BE HAVING FUN!
YEAH, ME TOO.
CHILL, RUSS.

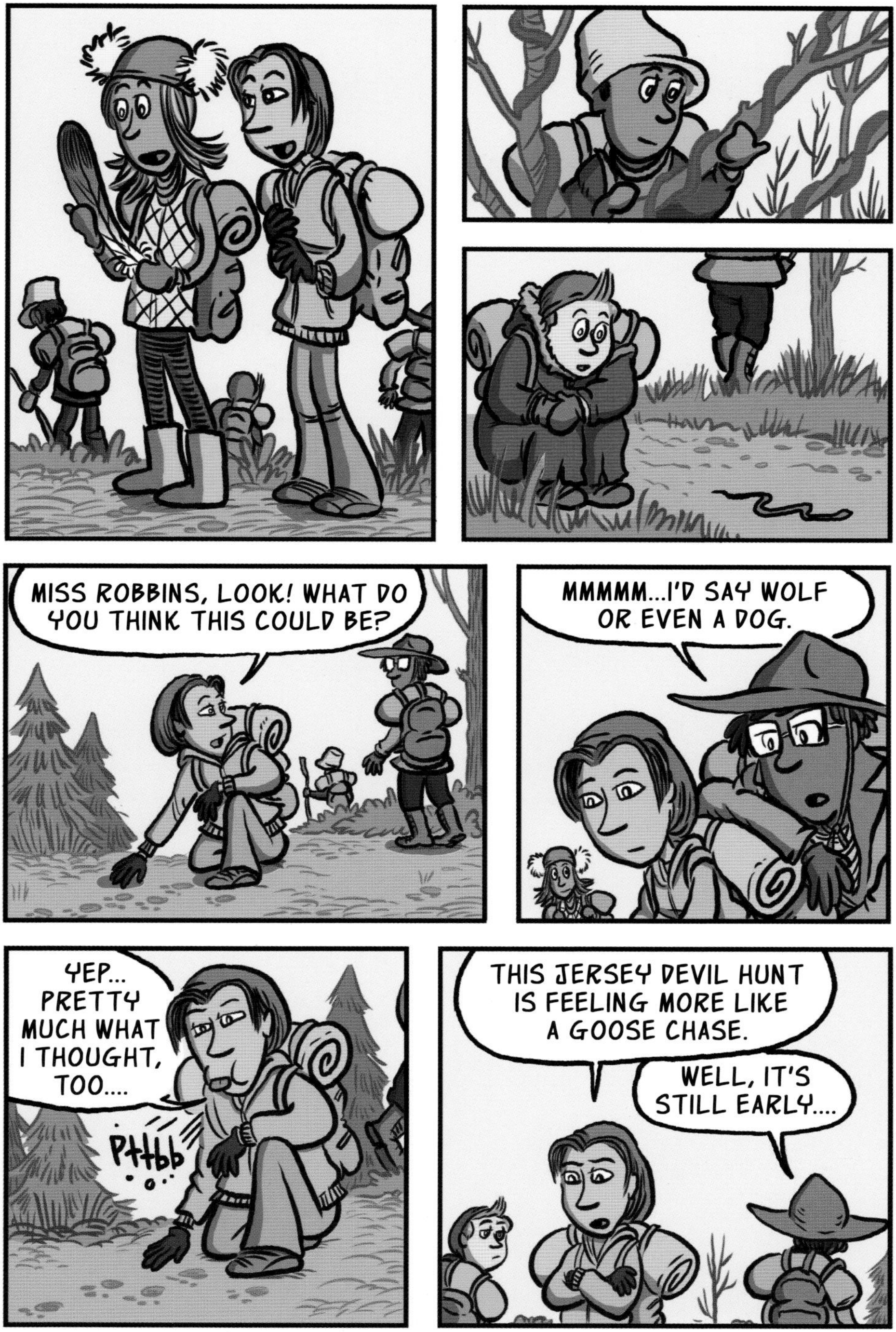
MISS ROBBINS, LOOK! WHAT DO YOU THINK THIS COULD BE?
MMMMM...I'D SAY WOLF OR EVEN A DOG.
YEP... PRETTY MUCH WHAT I THOUGHT, TOO....
PTTBB
THIS JERSEY DEVIL HUNT IS FEELING MORE LIKE A GOOSE CHASE.
WELL, IT'S STILL EARLY....

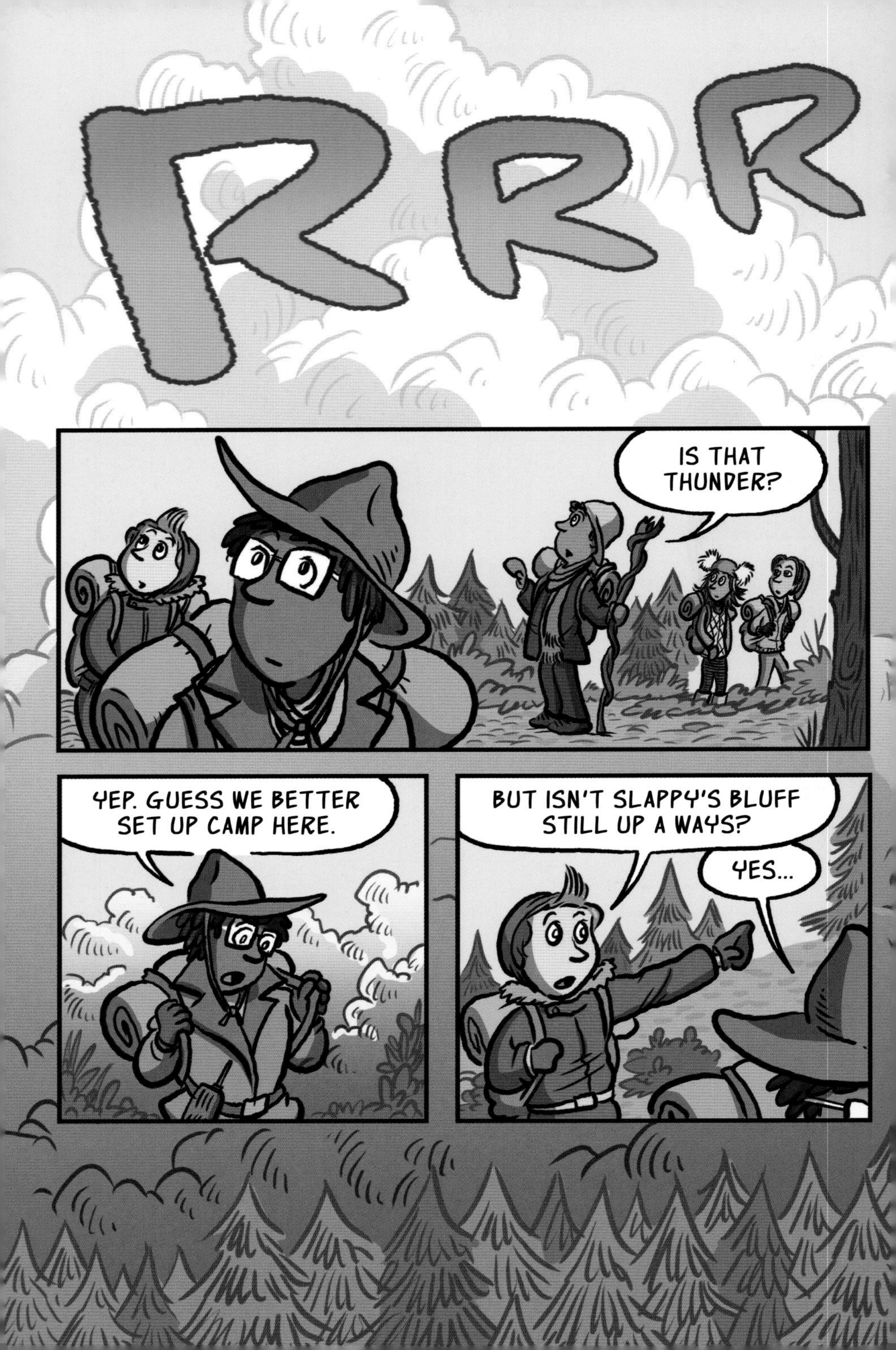
RRR
IS THAT THUNDER?
YEP. GUESS WE BETTER SET UP CAMP HERE.
BUT ISN'T SLAPPY'S BLUFF STILL UP A WAYS?
YES...

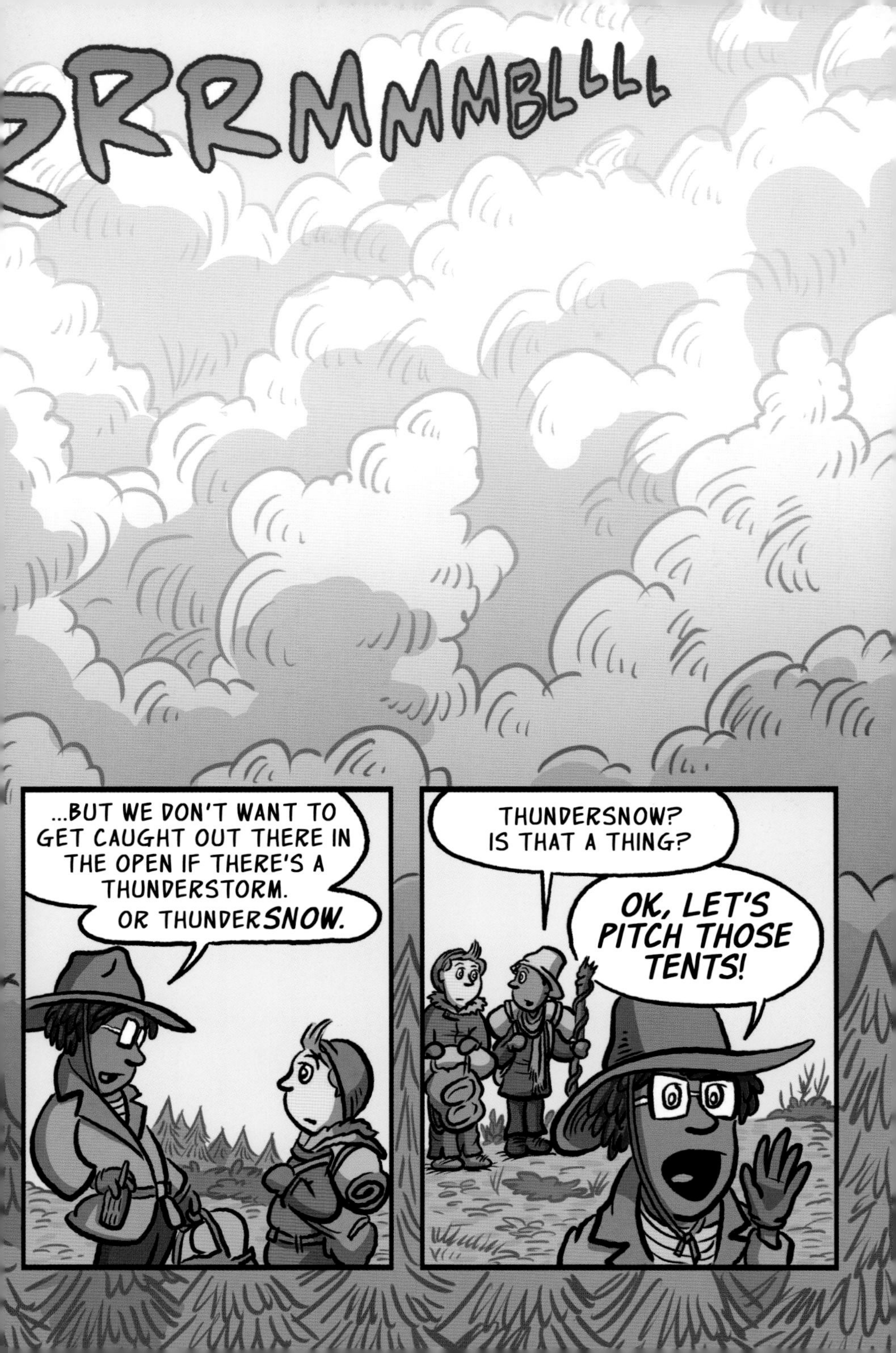
RRRMMMBLLL
...BUT WE DON'T WANT TO GET CAUGHT OUT THERE IN THE OPEN IF THERE'S A THUNDERSTORM. OR THUNDER*SNOW*.
THUNDERSNOW? IS THAT A THING?
OK, LET'S PITCH THOSE TENTS!

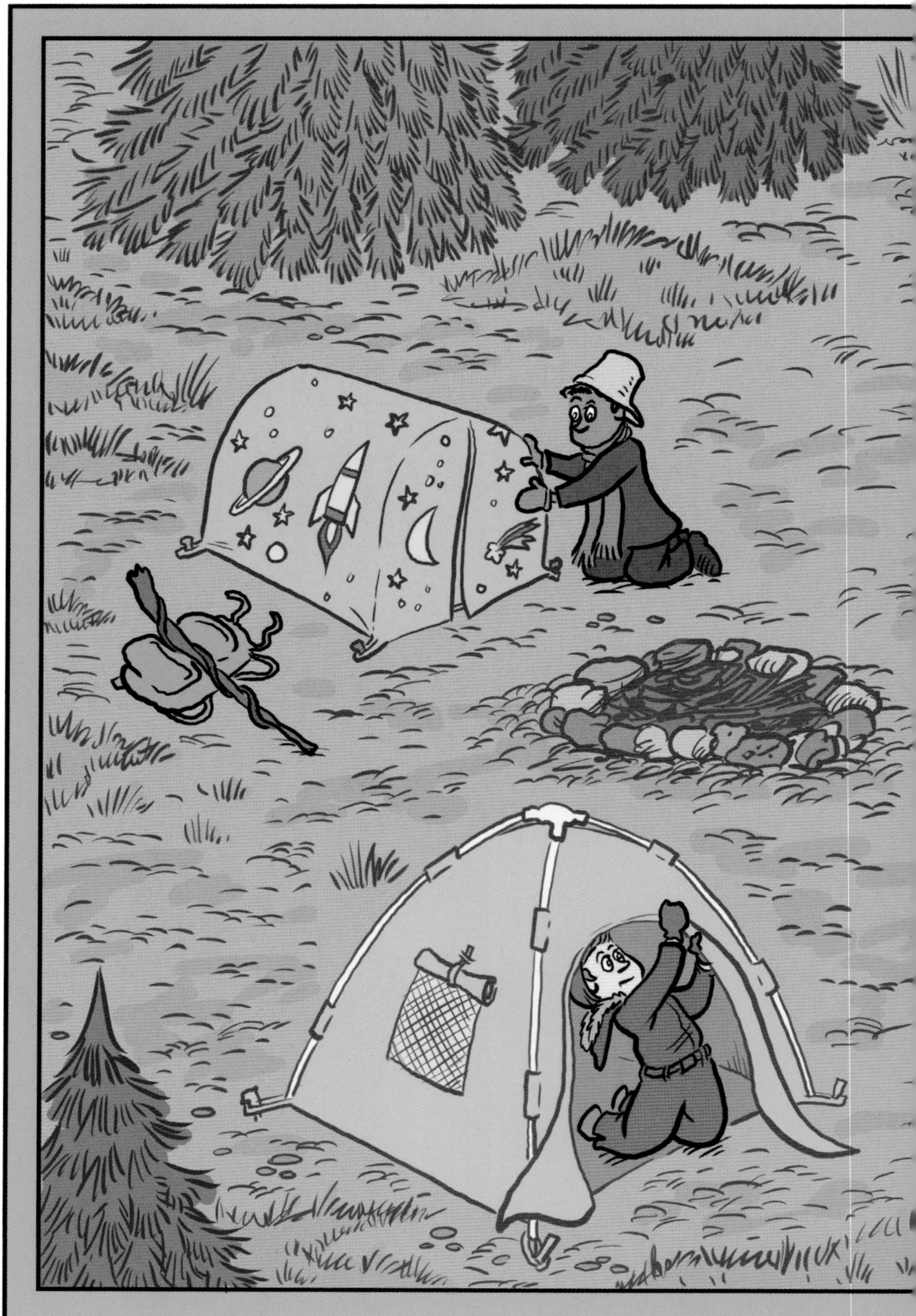

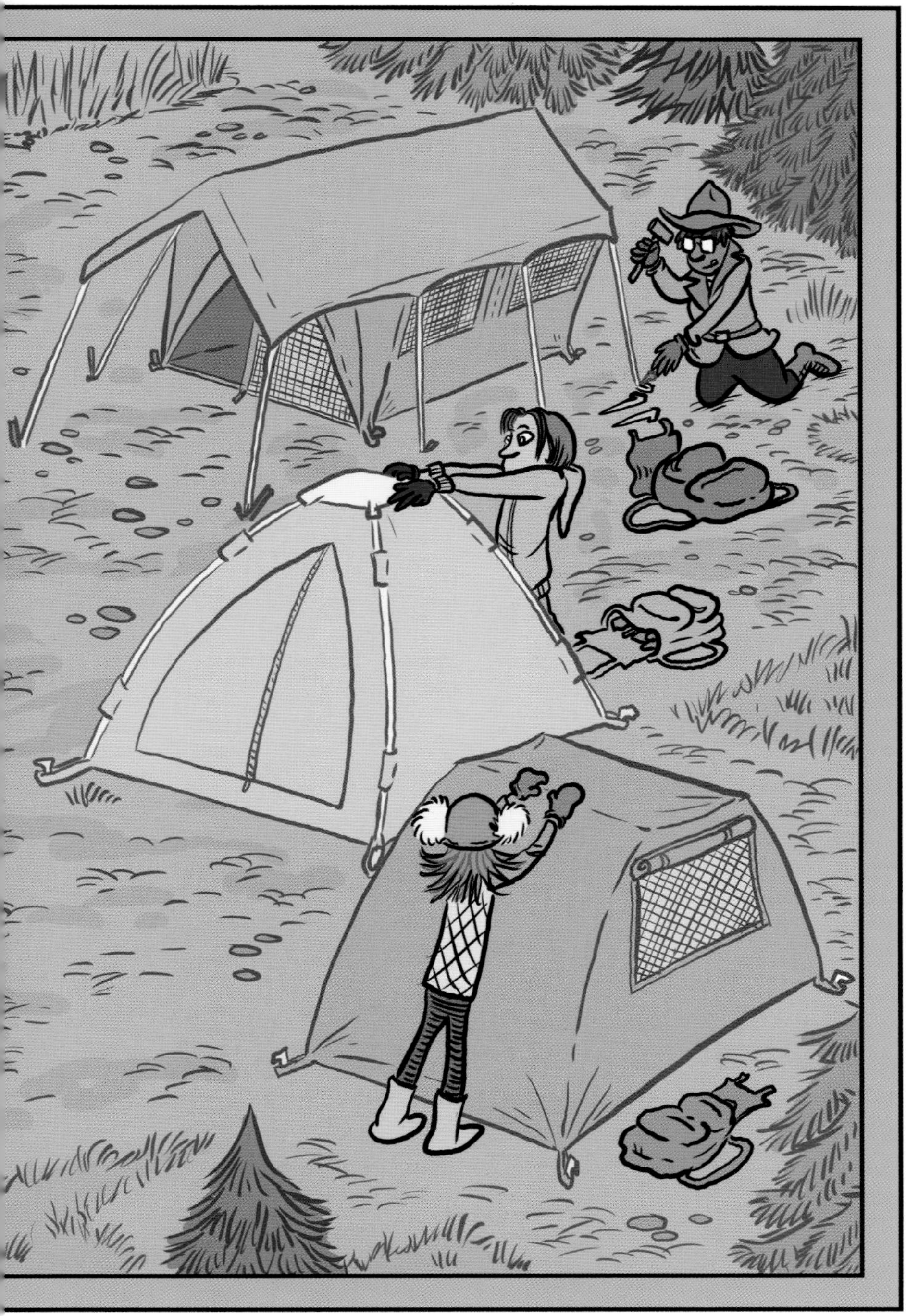

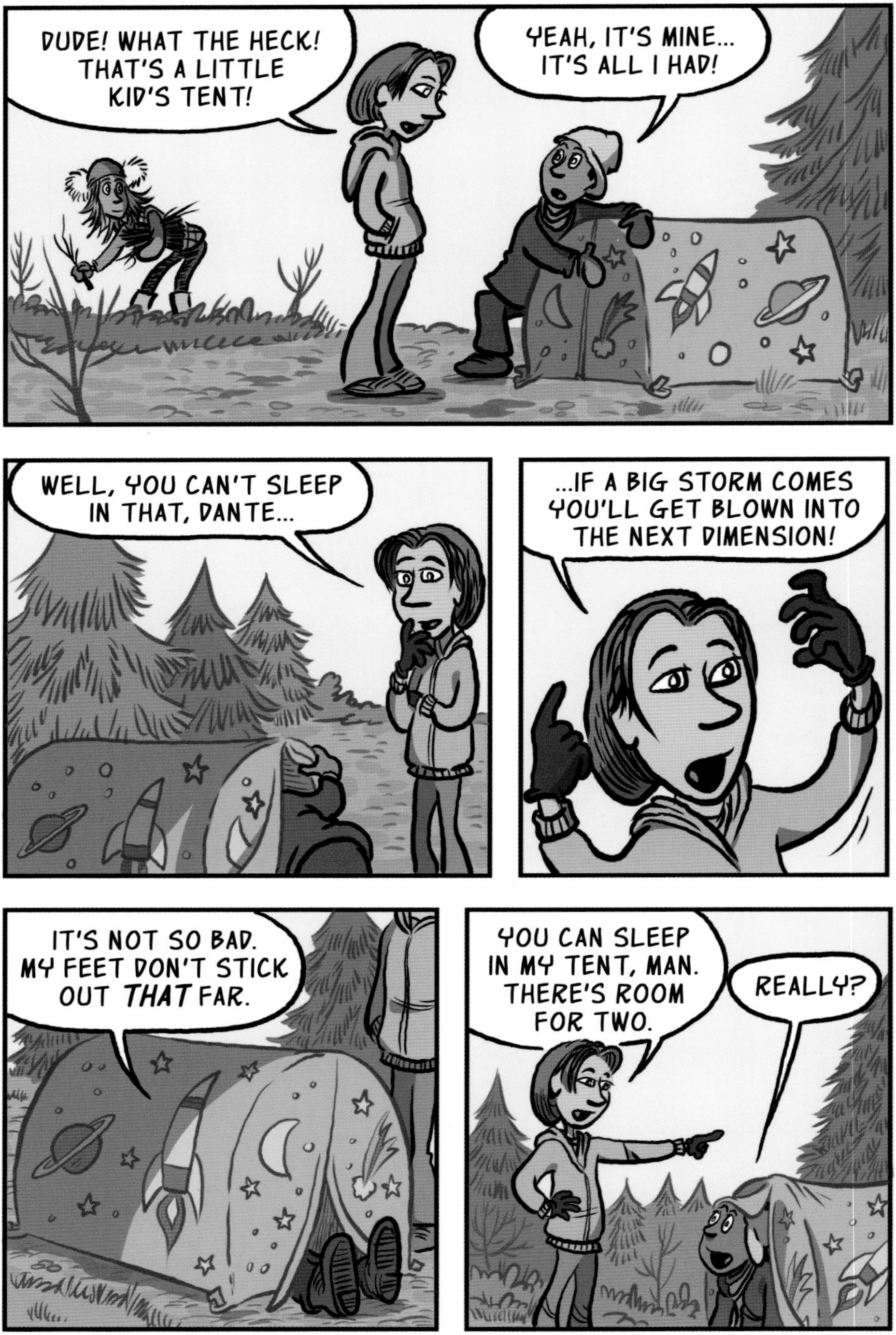
DUDE! WHAT THE HECK! THAT'S A LITTLE KID'S TENT!
YEAH, IT'S MINE... IT'S ALL I HAD!
WELL, YOU CAN'T SLEEP IN THAT, DANTE...
...IF A BIG STORM COMES YOU'LL GET BLOWN INTO THE NEXT DIMENSION!
IT'S NOT SO BAD. MY FEET DON'T STICK OUT *THAT* FAR.
YOU CAN SLEEP IN MY TENT, MAN. THERE'S ROOM FOR TWO.
REALLY?

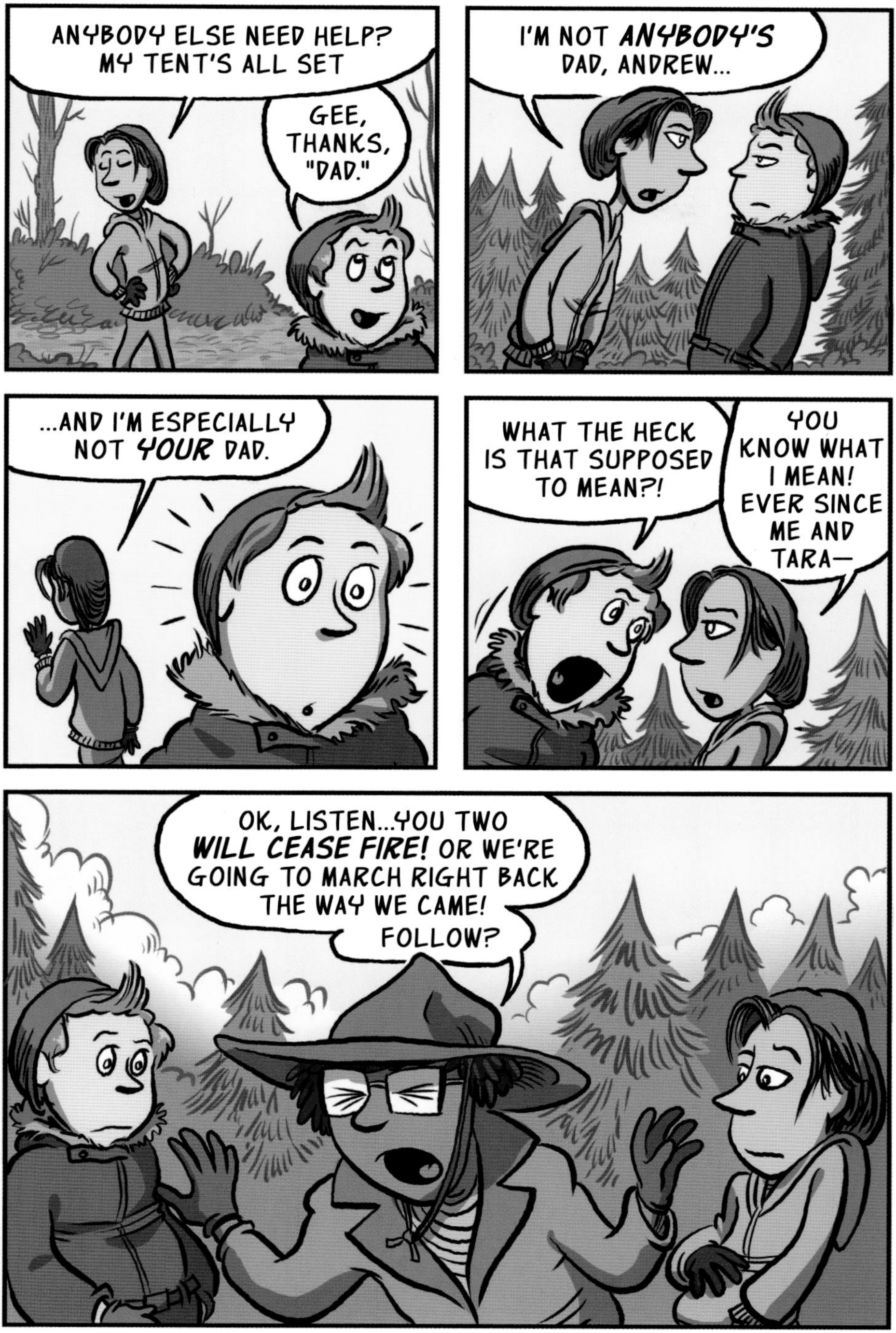
ANYBODY ELSE NEED HELP? MY TENT'S ALL SET
GEE, THANKS, "DAD."
I'M NOT ANYBODY'S DAD, ANDREW...
...AND I'M ESPECIALLY NOT YOUR DAD.
WHAT THE HECK IS THAT SUPPOSED TO MEAN?!
YOU KNOW WHAT I MEAN! EVER SINCE ME AND TARA—
OK, LISTEN...YOU TWO WILL CEASE FIRE! OR WE'RE GOING TO MARCH RIGHT BACK THE WAY WE CAME!
FOLLOW?

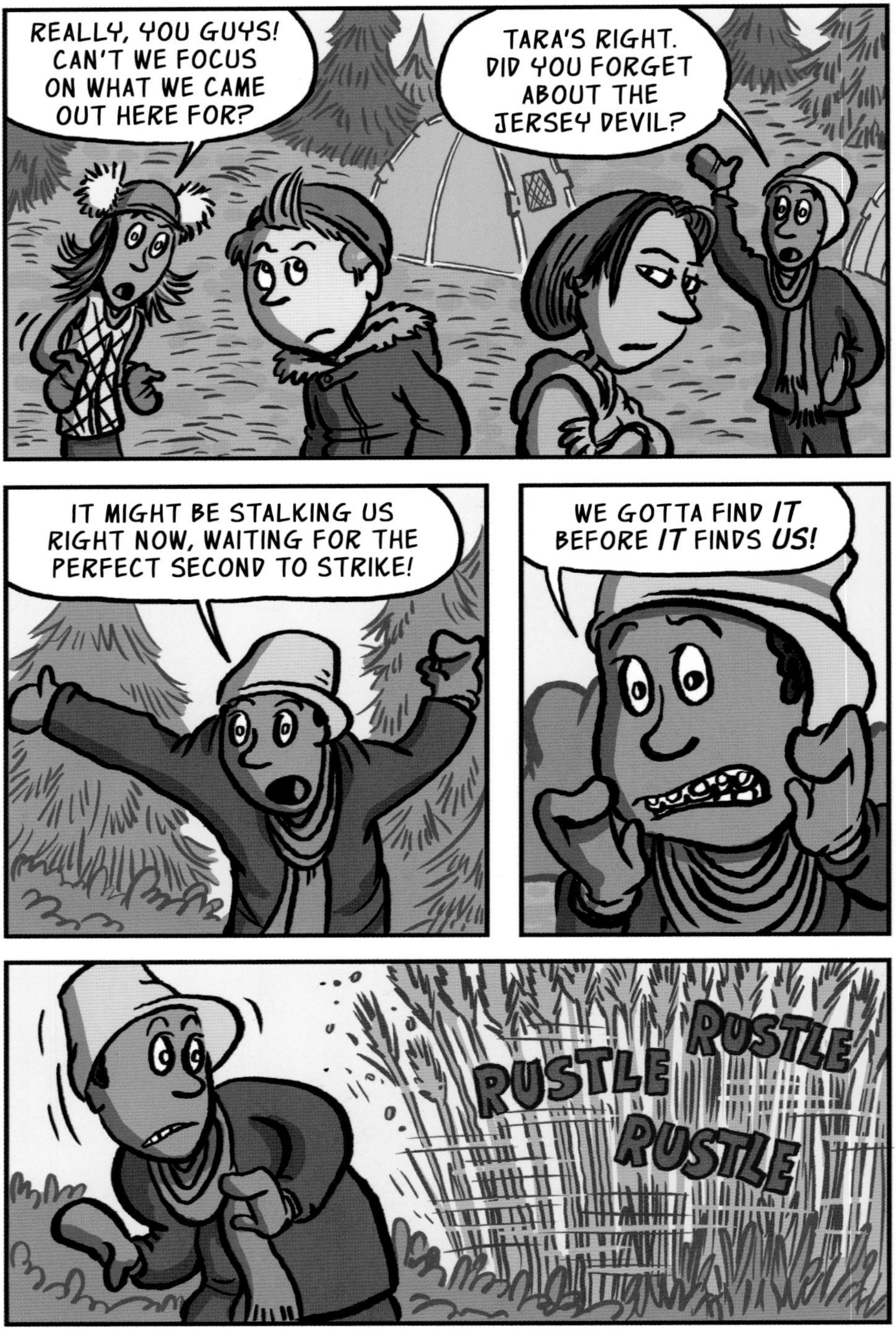
REALLY, YOU GUYS! CAN'T WE FOCUS ON WHAT WE CAME OUT HERE FOR?
TARA'S RIGHT. DID YOU FORGET ABOUT THE JERSEY DEVIL?
IT MIGHT BE STALKING US RIGHT NOW, WAITING FOR THE PERFECT SECOND TO STRIKE!
WE GOTTA FIND *IT* BEFORE *IT* FINDS *US*!
RUSTLE
RUSTLE
RUSTLE

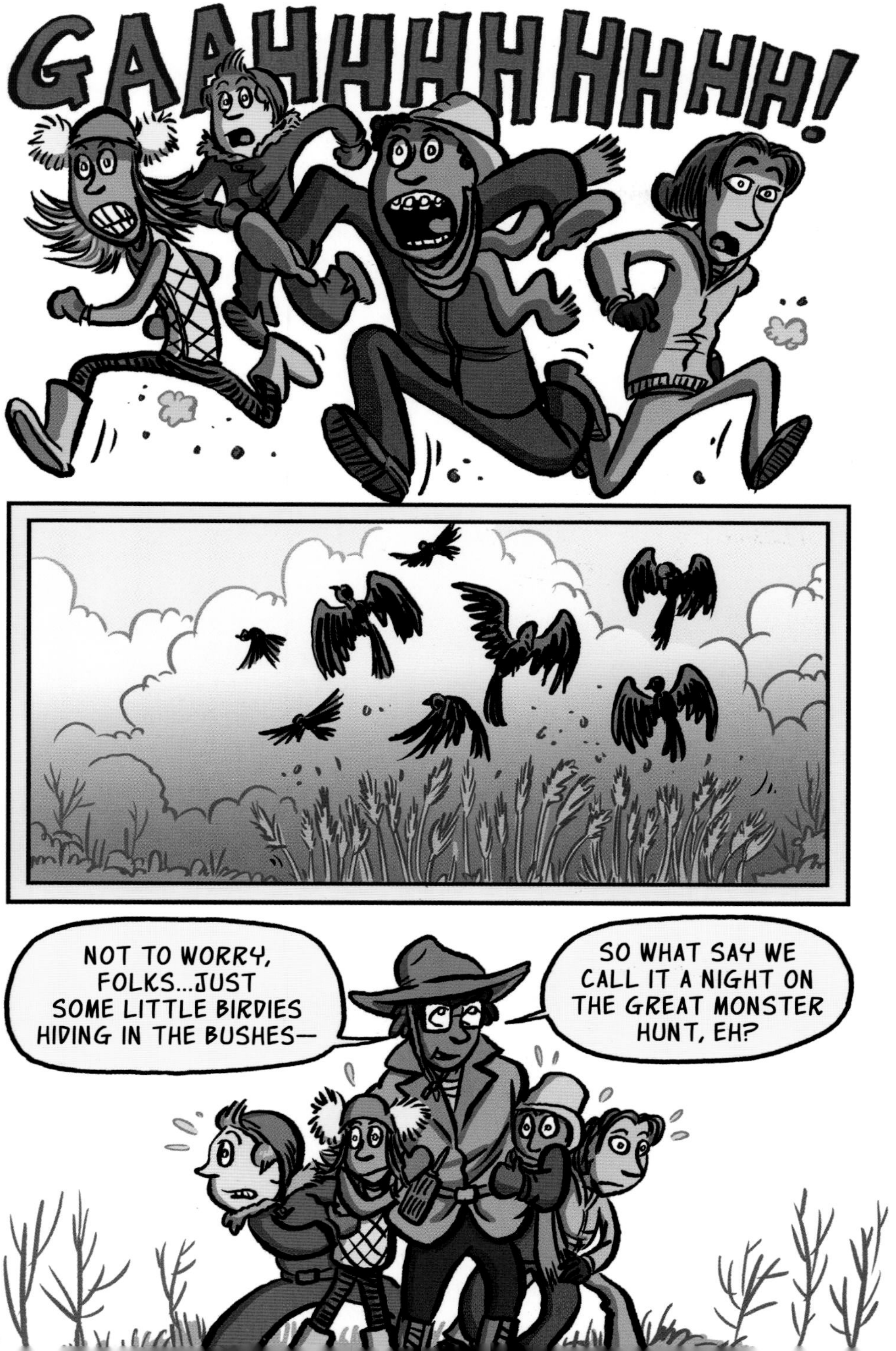
GAAHHHHHHHHH!
NOT TO WORRY, FOLKS...JUST SOME LITTLE BIRDIES HIDING IN THE BUSHES—
SO WHAT SAY WE CALL IT A NIGHT ON THE GREAT MONSTER HUNT, EH?

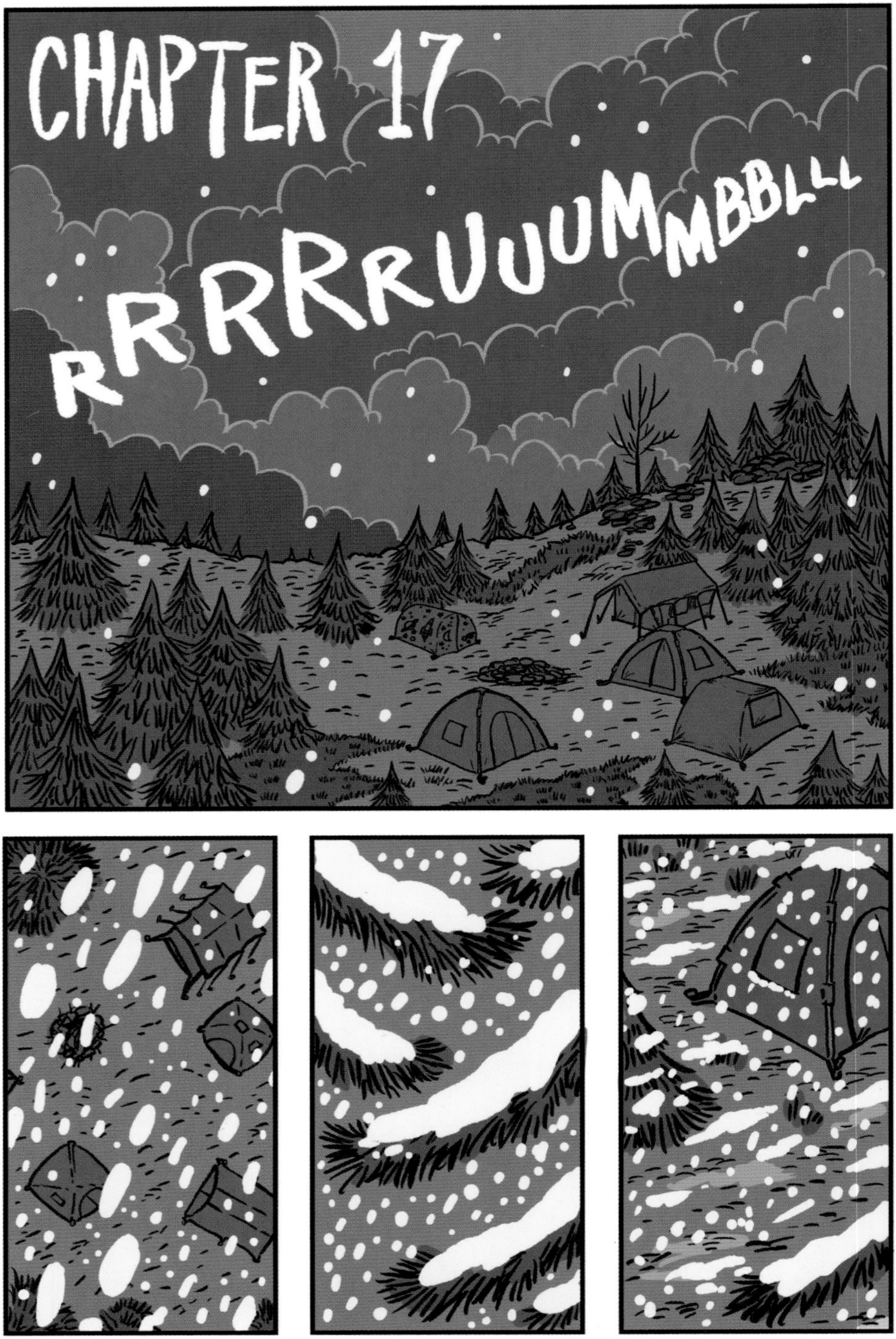
CHAPTER 17
RRRRRRUUUUMMBBLLL

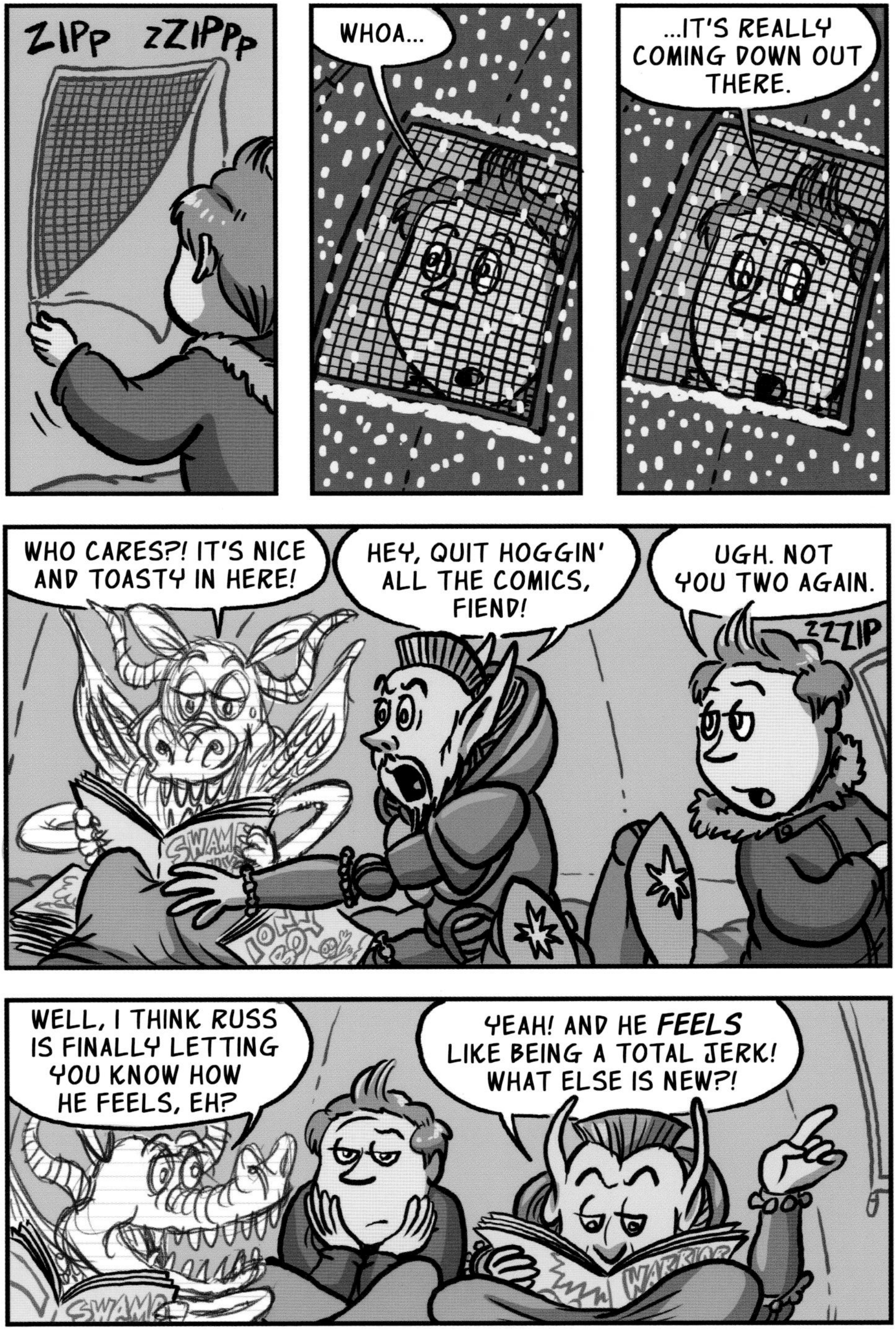
ZIPP ZZIPPP
WHOA...
...IT'S REALLY COMING DOWN OUT THERE.
WHO CARES?! IT'S NICE AND TOASTY IN HERE!
HEY, QUIT HOGGIN' ALL THE COMICS, FIEND!
UGH. NOT YOU TWO AGAIN.
ZZZIP
WELL, I THINK RUSS IS FINALLY LETTING YOU KNOW HOW HE FEELS, EH?
YEAH! AND HE *FEELS* LIKE BEING A TOTAL JERK! WHAT ELSE IS NEW?!

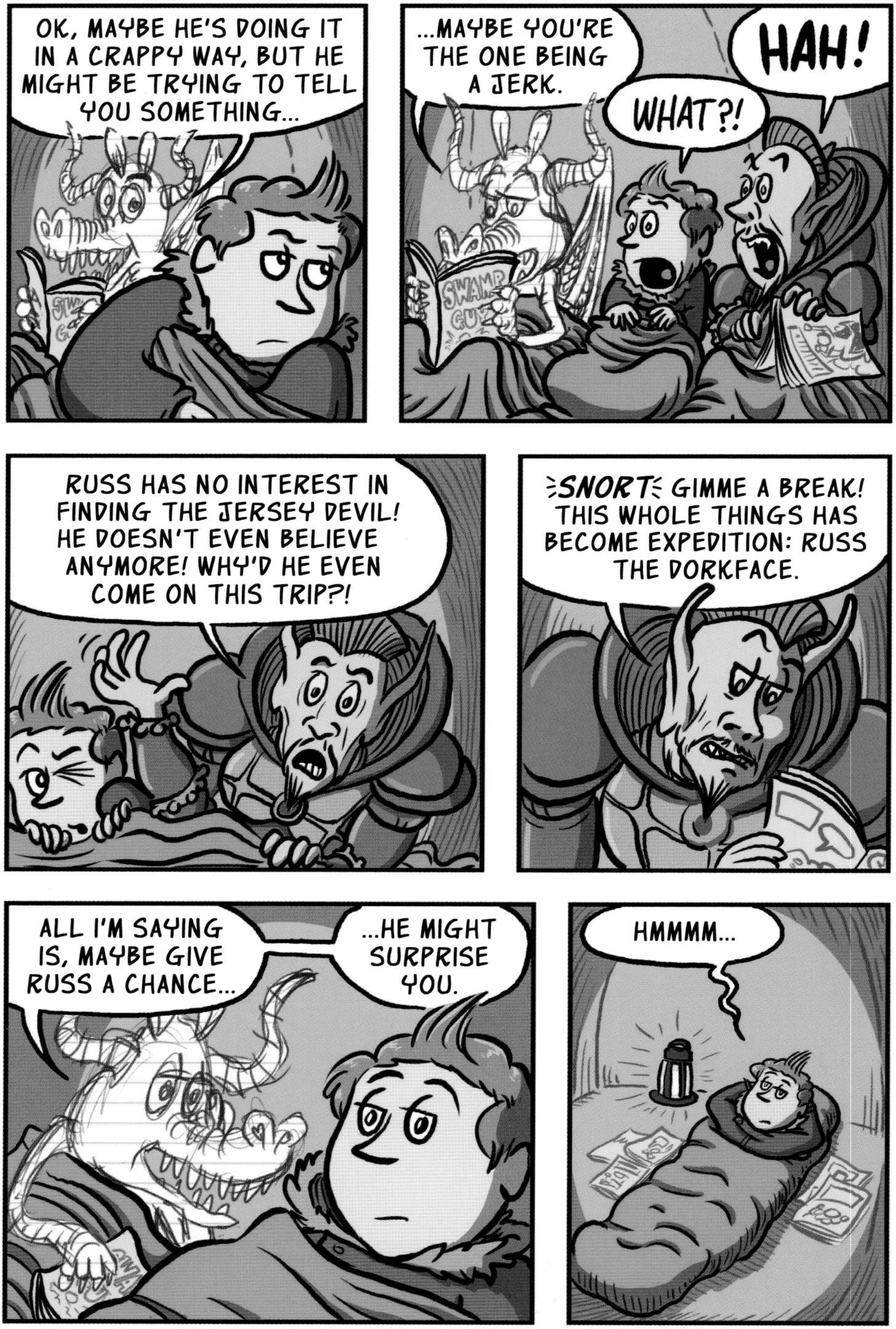
OK, MAYBE HE'S DOING IT IN A CRAPPY WAY, BUT HE MIGHT BE TRYING TO TELL YOU SOMETHING...
...MAYBE YOU'RE THE ONE BEING A JERK.
HAH!
WHAT?!
RUSS HAS NO INTEREST IN FINDING THE JERSEY DEVIL! HE DOESN'T EVEN BELIEVE ANYMORE! WHY'D HE EVEN COME ON THIS TRIP?!
SNORT GIMME A BREAK! THIS WHOLE THINGS HAS BECOME EXPEDITION: RUSS THE DORKFACE.
ALL I'M SAYING IS, MAYBE GIVE RUSS A CHANCE...
...HE MIGHT SURPRISE YOU.
HMMMM...

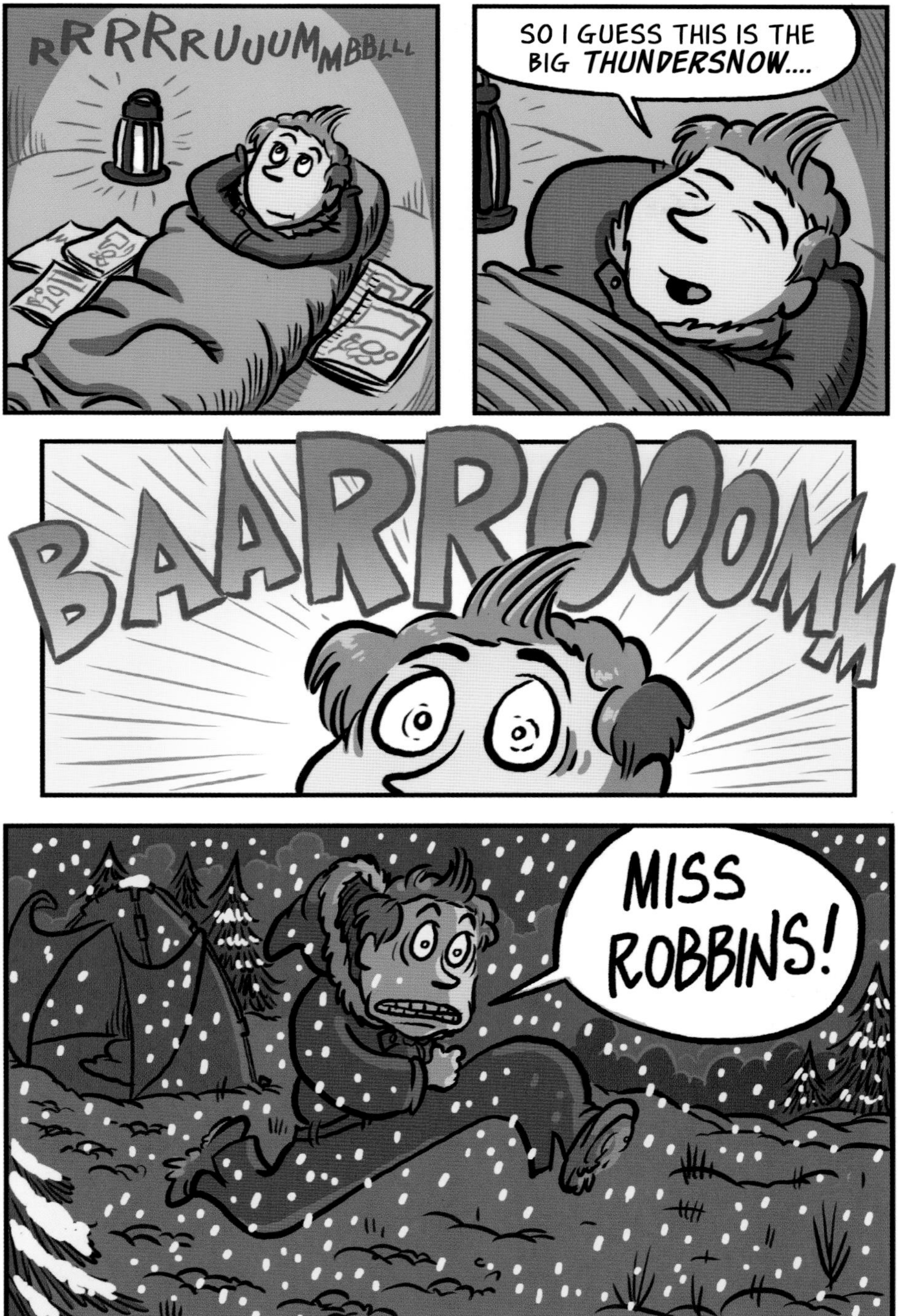
RRRRRUUUMMBBLLL
SO I GUESS THIS IS THE BIG THUNDERSNOW....
BAARROOOMM
MISS ROBBINS!

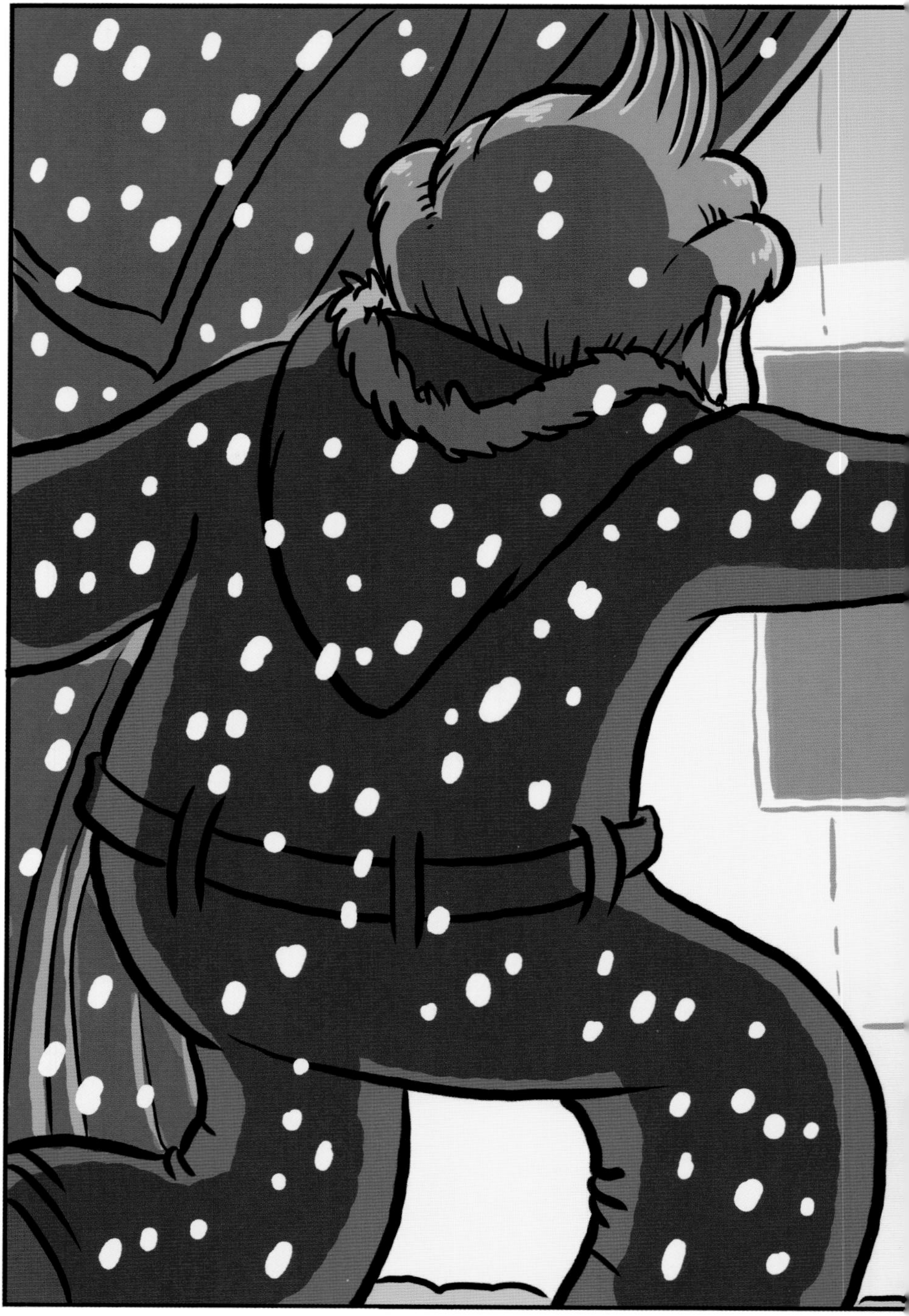

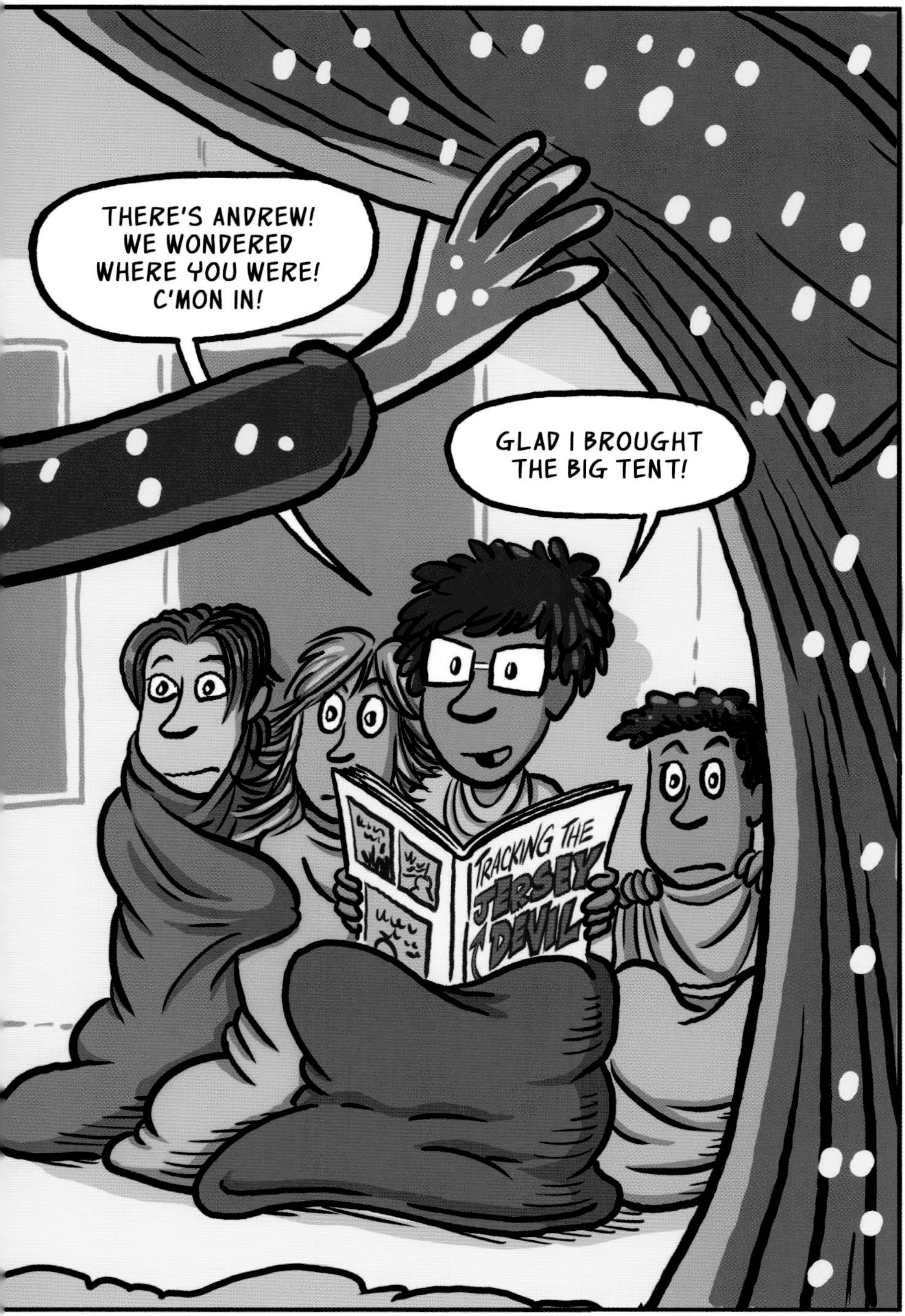
THERE'S ANDREW! WE WONDERED WHERE YOU WERE! C'MON IN!
GLAD I BROUGHT THE BIG TENT!
TRACKING THE JERSEY DEVIL

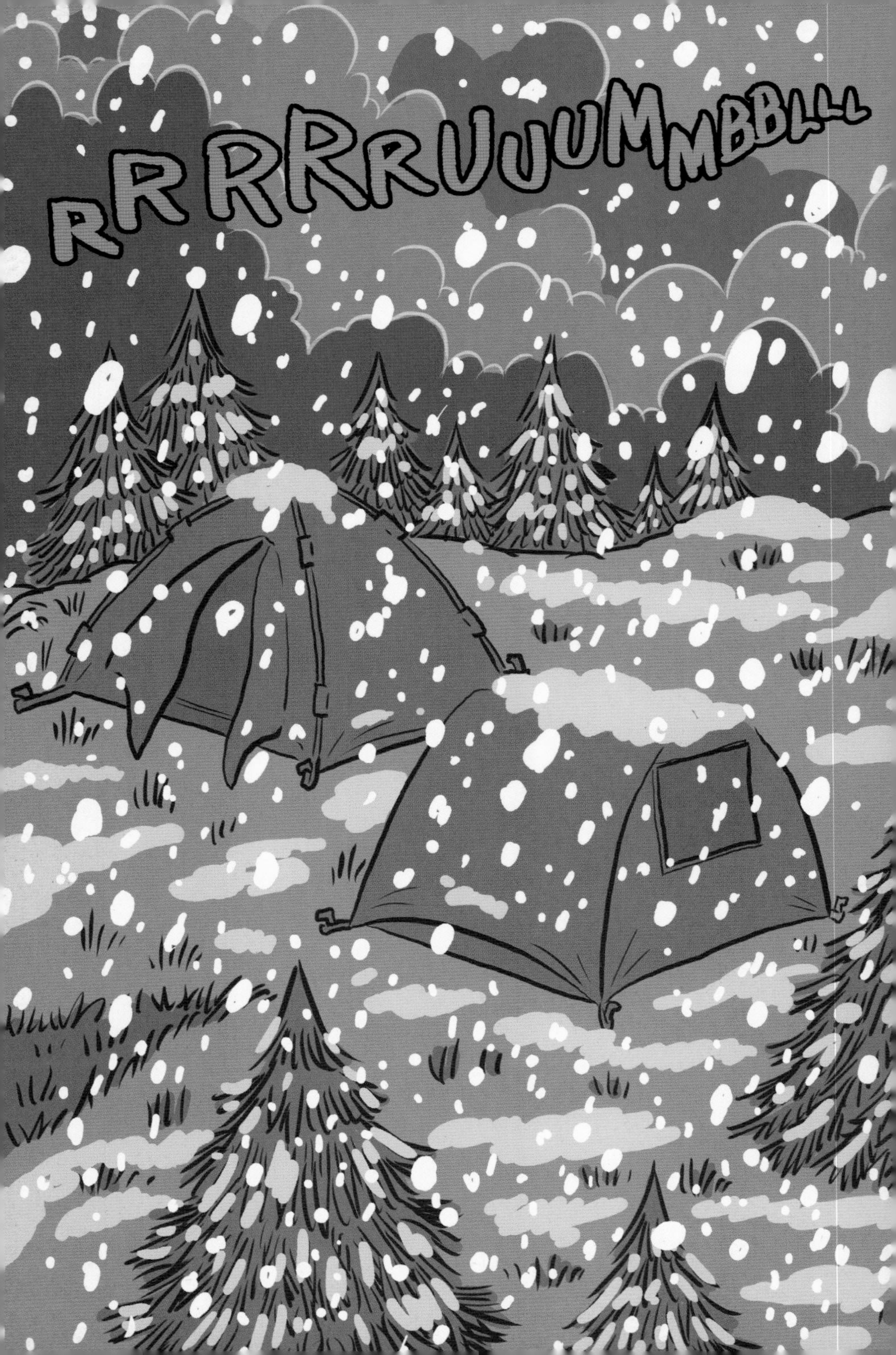
RRRRRRUUUMMMBBLLL

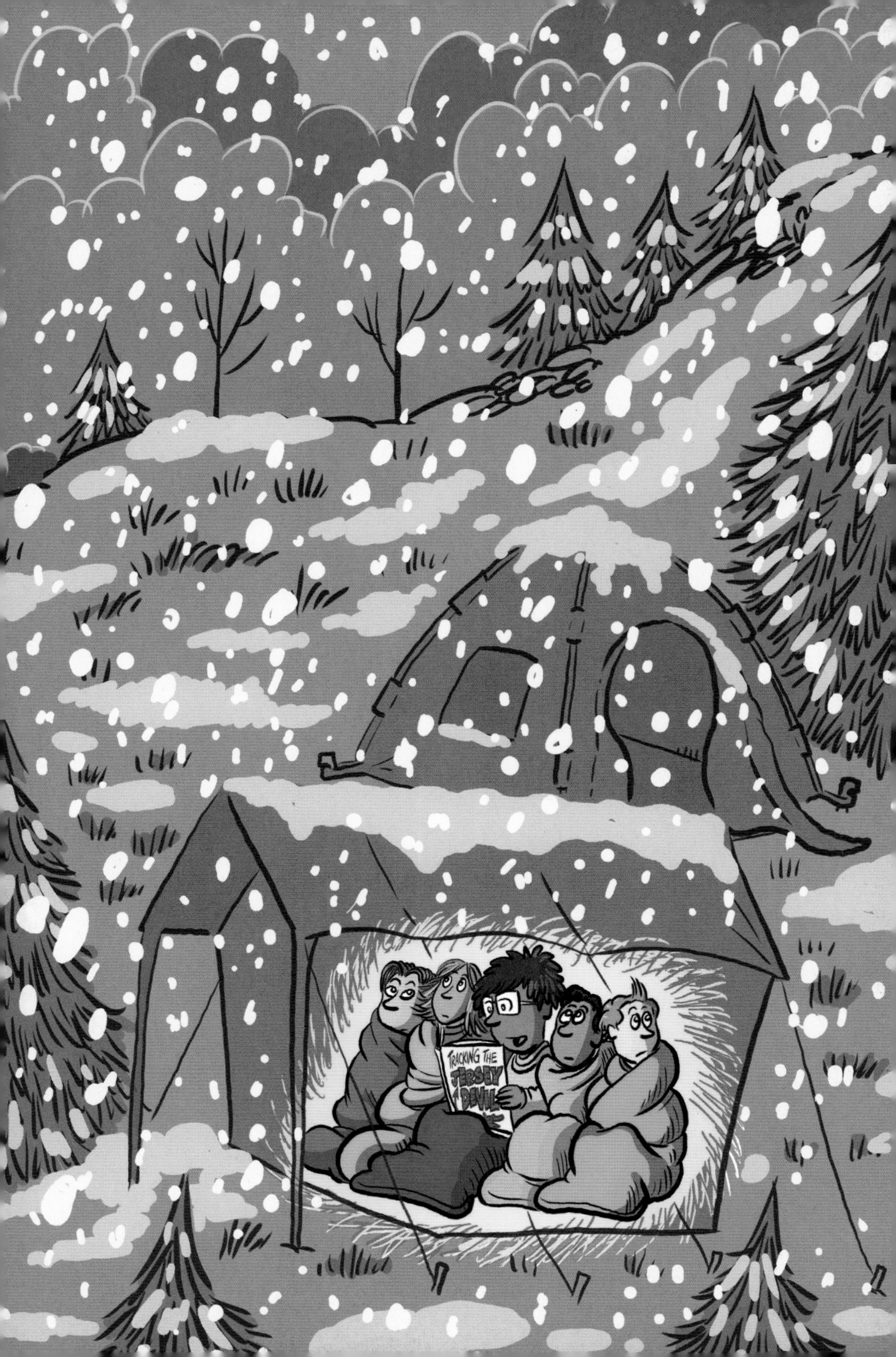
TRACKING THE
JERSEY
DEVIL

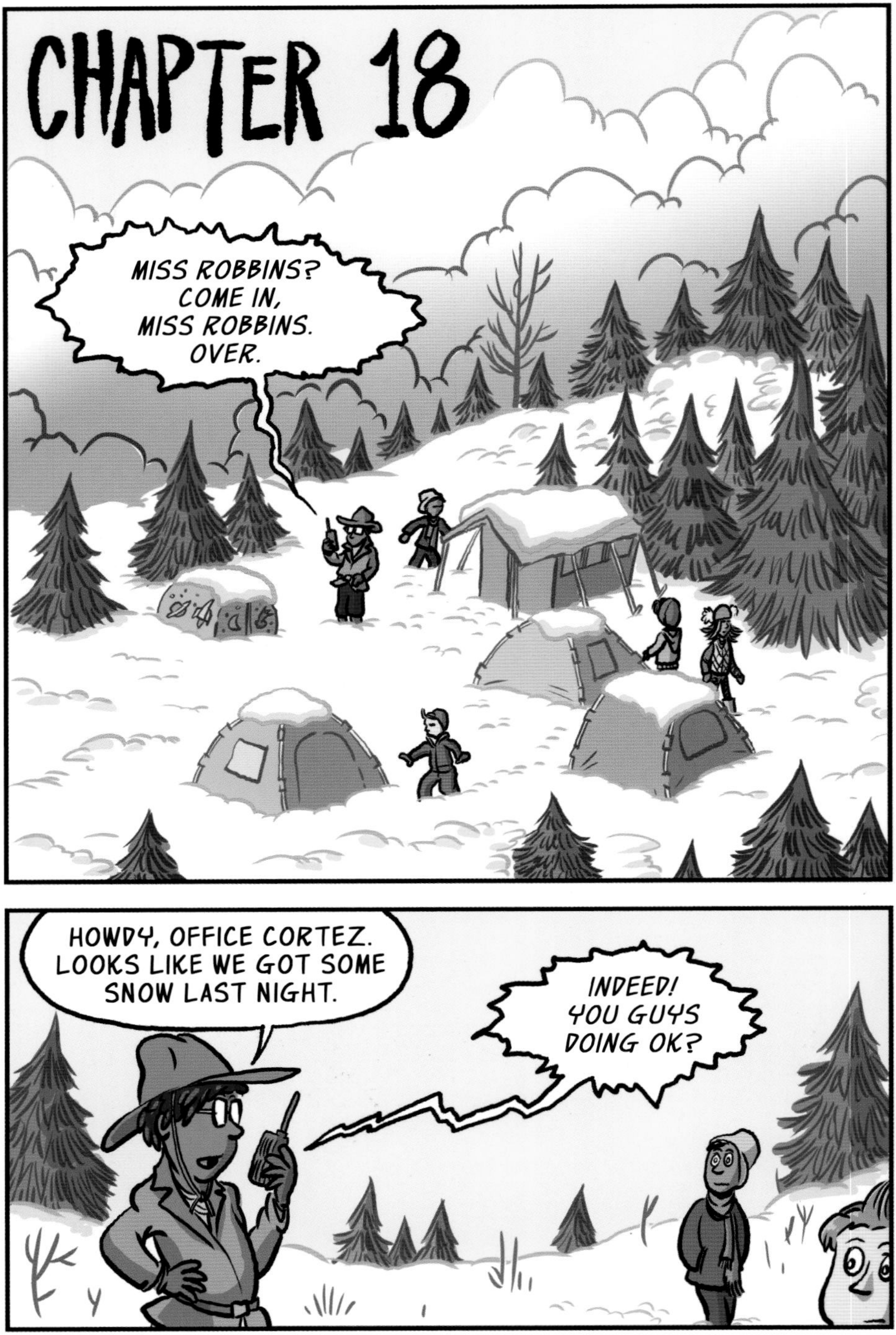
CHAPTER 18
MISS ROBBINS? COME IN, MISS ROBBINS. OVER.
HOWDY, OFFICE CORTEZ. LOOKS LIKE WE GOT SOME SNOW LAST NIGHT.
INDEED! YOU GUYS DOING OK?

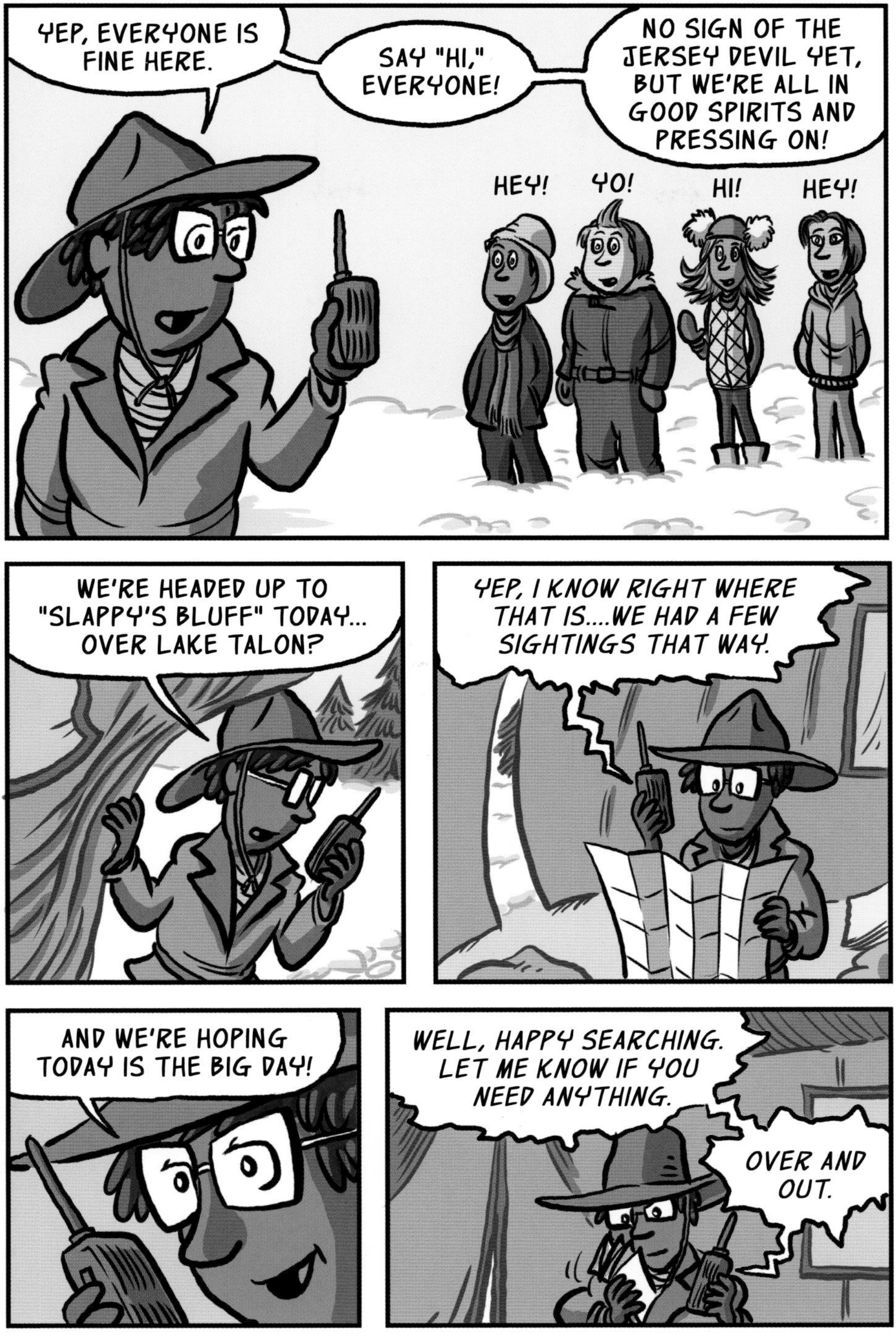
YEP, EVERYONE IS FINE HERE.
SAY "HI," EVERYONE!
NO SIGN OF THE JERSEY DEVIL YET, BUT WE'RE ALL IN GOOD SPIRITS AND PRESSING ON!
HEY!
YO!
HI!
HEY!
WE'RE HEADED UP TO "SLAPPY'S BLUFF" TODAY... OVER LAKE TALON?
YEP, I KNOW RIGHT WHERE THAT IS....WE HAD A FEW SIGHTINGS THAT WAY.
AND WE'RE HOPING TODAY IS THE BIG DAY!
WELL, HAPPY SEARCHING. LET ME KNOW IF YOU NEED ANYTHING.
OVER AND OUT.

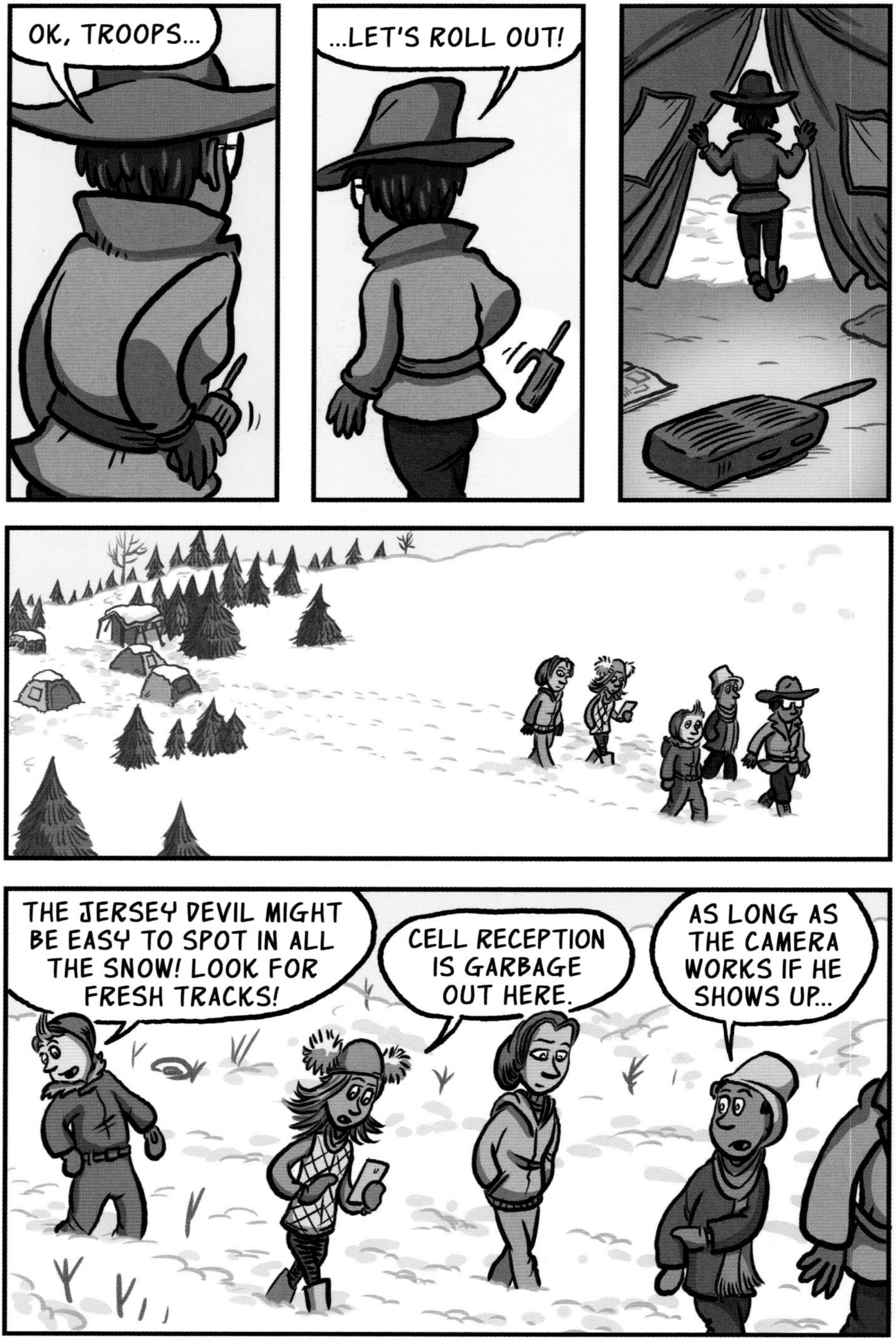
OK, TROOPS...
...LET'S ROLL OUT!
THE JERSEY DEVIL MIGHT BE EASY TO SPOT IN ALL THE SNOW! LOOK FOR FRESH TRACKS!
CELL RECEPTION IS GARBAGE OUT HERE.
AS LONG AS THE CAMERA WORKS IF HE SHOWS UP...

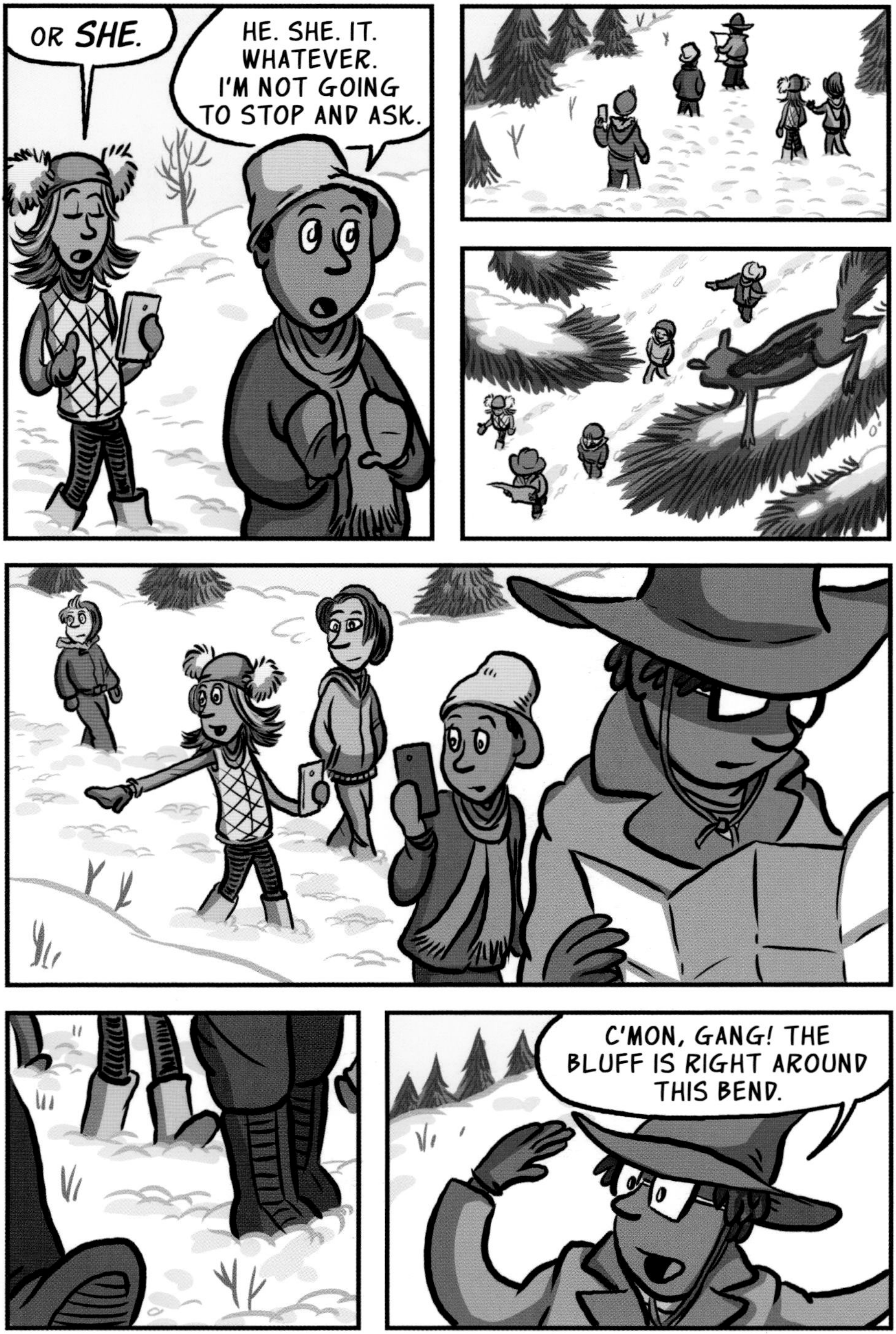
OR SHE.
HE. SHE. IT. WHATEVER. I'M NOT GOING TO STOP AND ASK.
C'MON, GANG! THE BLUFF IS RIGHT AROUND THIS BEND.

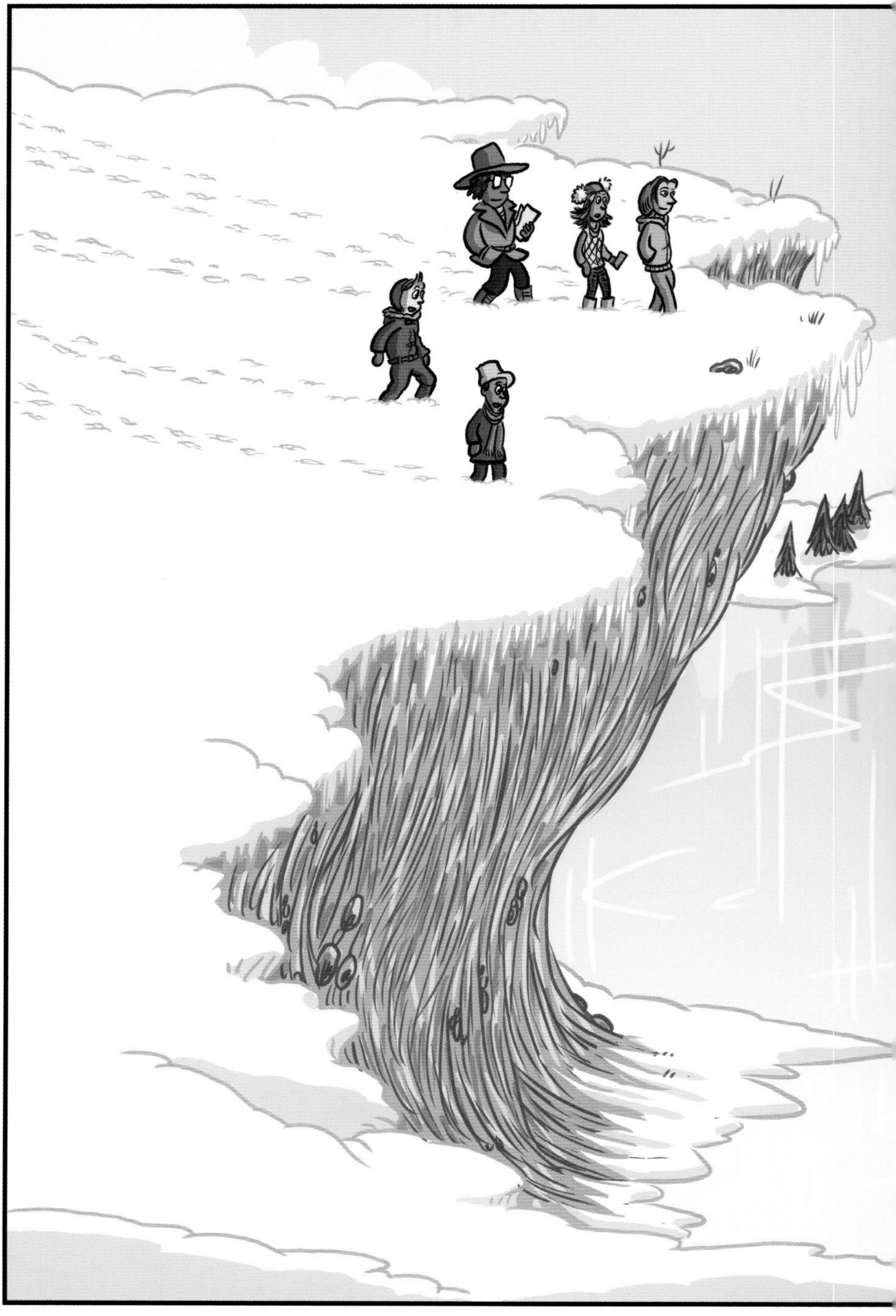

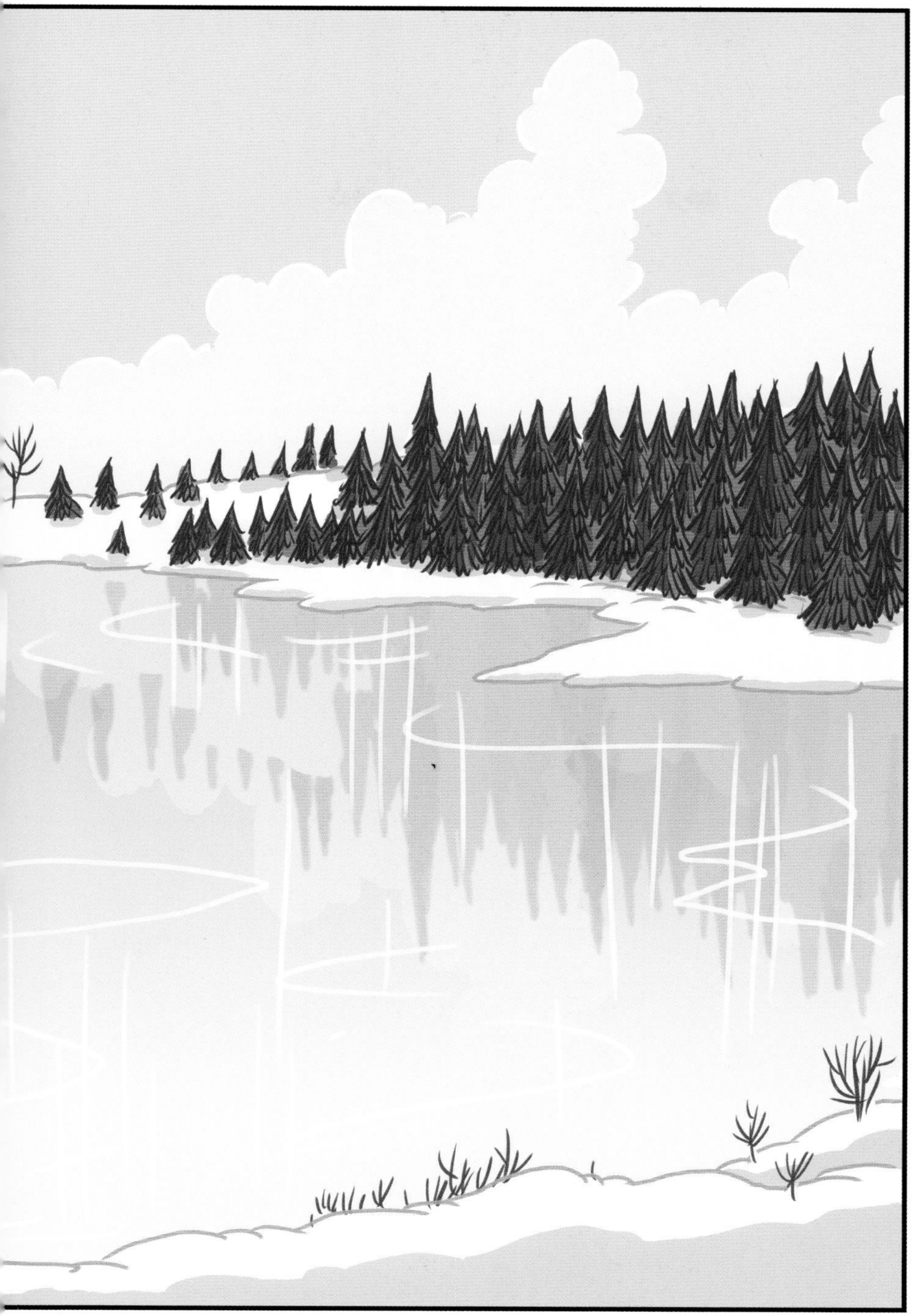

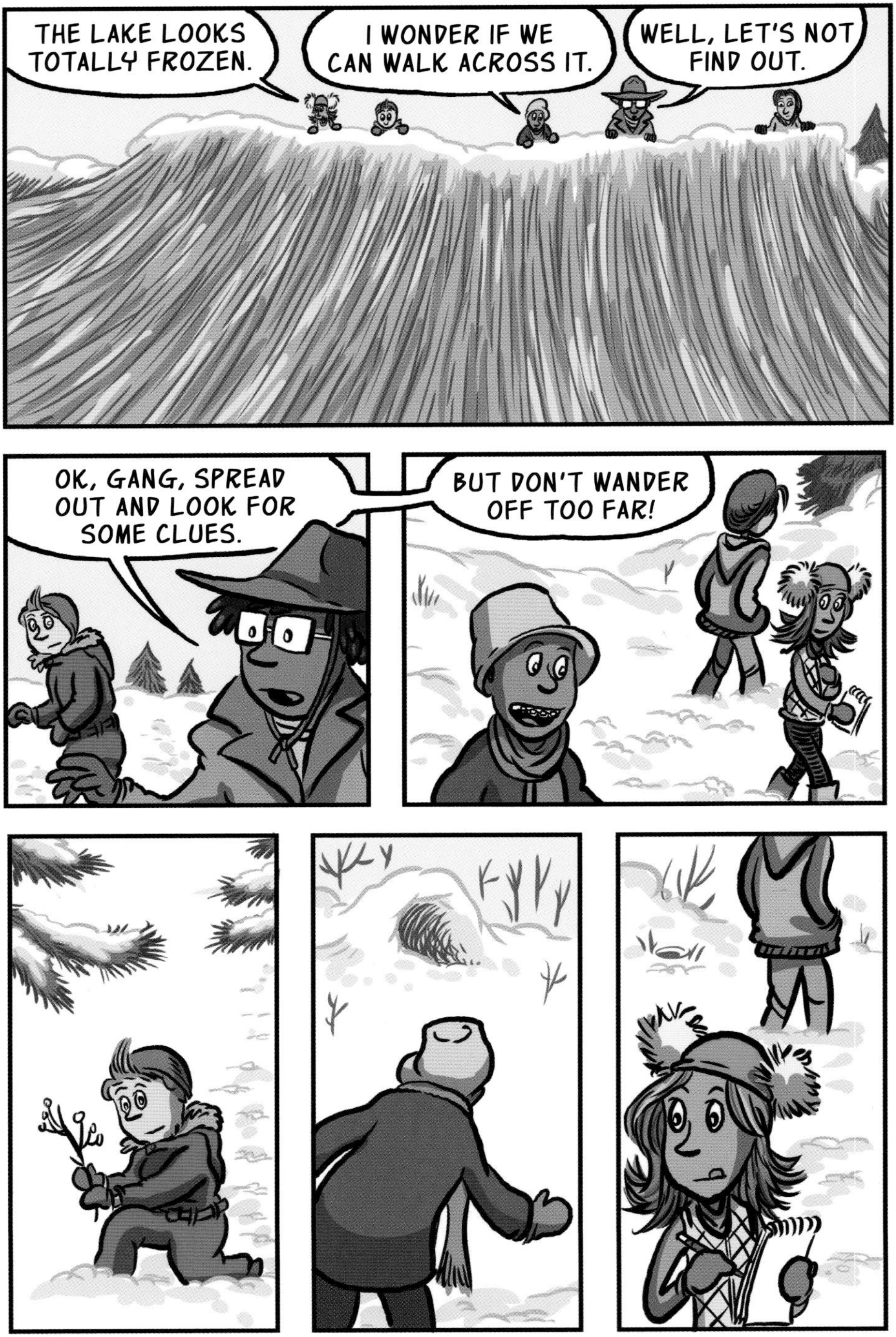

THE LAKE LOOKS TOTALLY FROZEN.
I WONDER IF WE CAN WALK ACROSS IT.
WELL, LET'S NOT FIND OUT.
OK, GANG, SPREAD OUT AND LOOK FOR SOME CLUES.
BUT DON'T WANDER OFF TOO FAR!

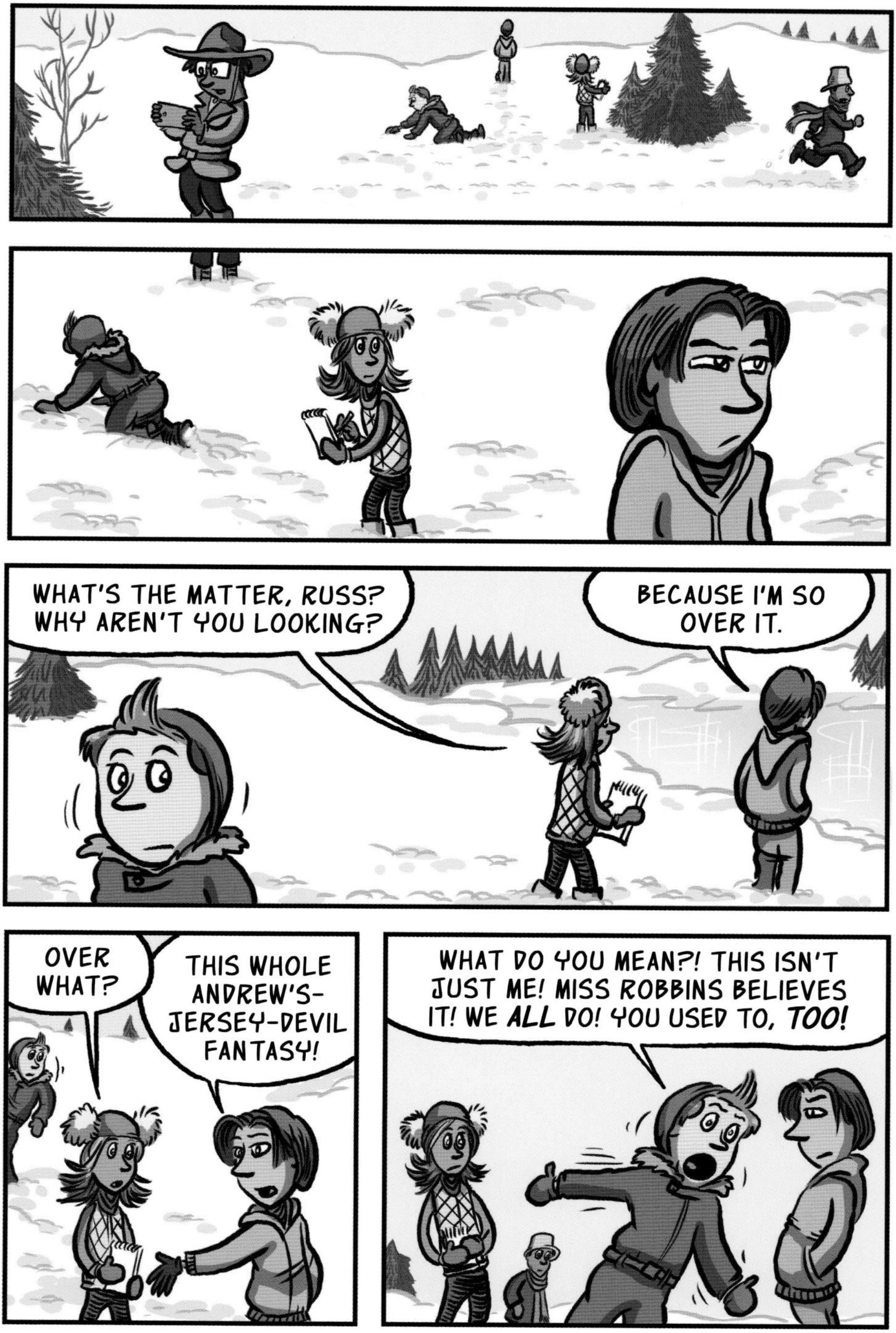
WHAT'S THE MATTER, RUSS? WHY AREN'T YOU LOOKING?
BECAUSE I'M SO OVER IT.
OVER WHAT?
THIS WHOLE ANDREW'S-JERSEY-DEVIL FANTASY!
WHAT DO YOU MEAN?! THIS ISN'T JUST ME! MISS ROBBINS BELIEVES IT! WE *ALL* DO! YOU USED TO, *TOO!*

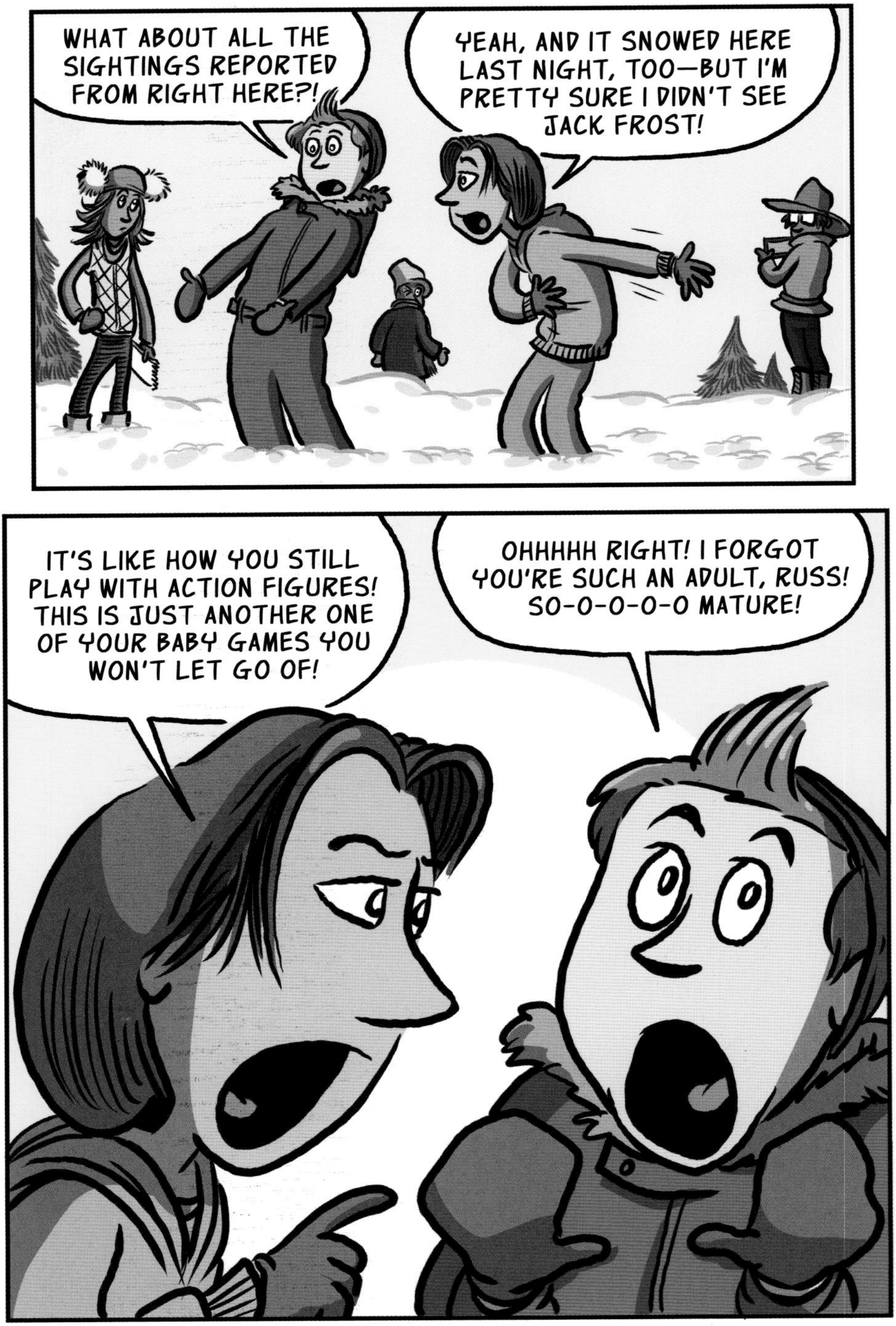
WHAT ABOUT ALL THE SIGHTINGS REPORTED FROM RIGHT HERE?!
YEAH, AND IT SNOWED HERE LAST NIGHT, TOO—BUT I'M PRETTY SURE I DIDN'T SEE JACK FROST!
IT'S LIKE HOW YOU STILL PLAY WITH ACTION FIGURES! THIS IS JUST ANOTHER ONE OF YOUR BABY GAMES YOU WON'T LET GO OF!
OHHHHH RIGHT! I FORGOT YOU'RE SUCH AN ADULT, RUSS! SO-O-O-O-O MATURE!

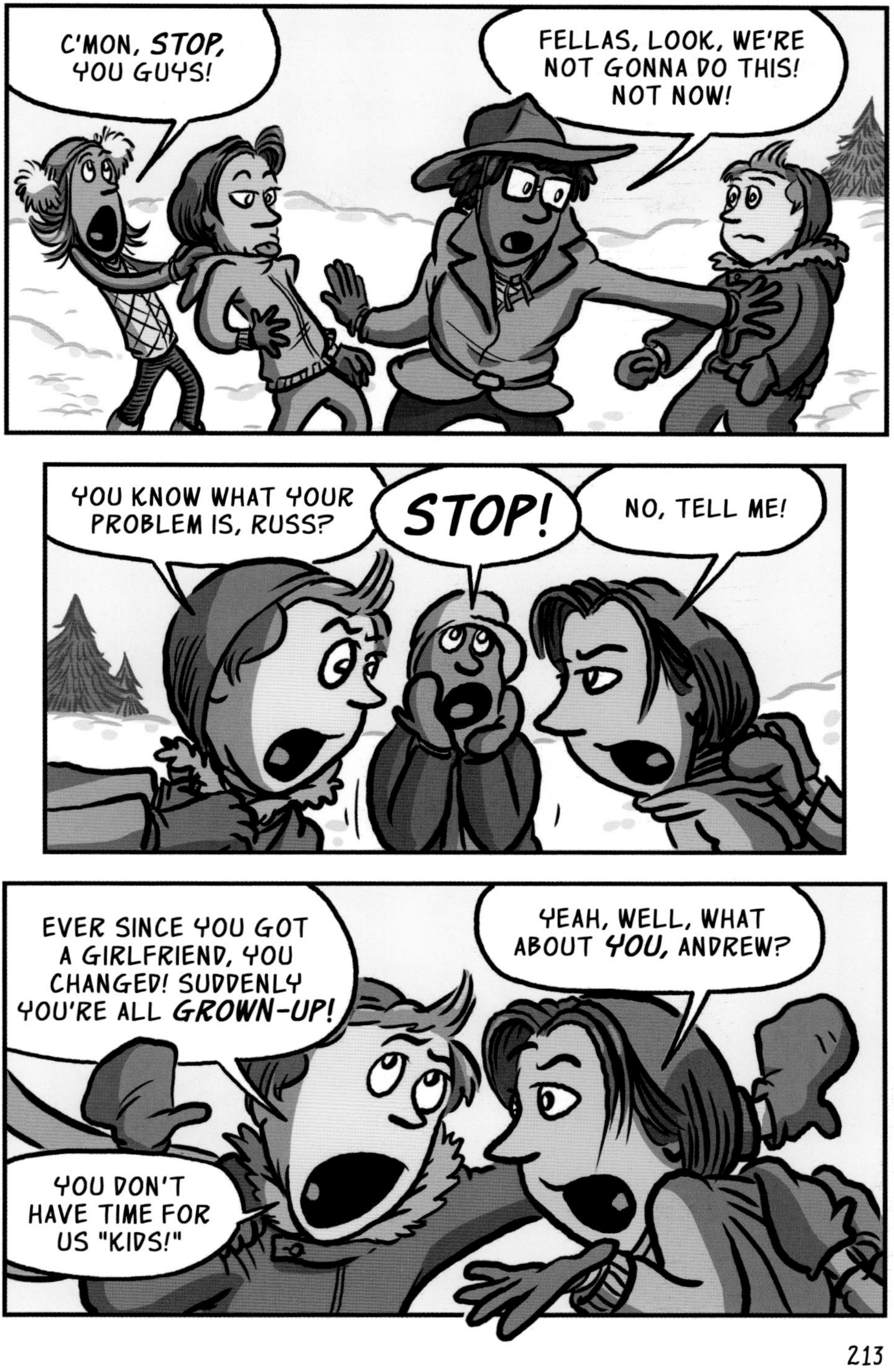
C'MON, STOP, YOU GUYS!
FELLAS, LOOK, WE'RE NOT GONNA DO THIS! NOT NOW!
YOU KNOW WHAT YOUR PROBLEM IS, RUSS?
STOP!
NO, TELL ME!
EVER SINCE YOU GOT A GIRLFRIEND, YOU CHANGED! SUDDENLY YOU'RE ALL GROWN-UP!
YEAH, WELL, WHAT ABOUT YOU, ANDREW?
YOU DON'T HAVE TIME FOR US "KIDS!"

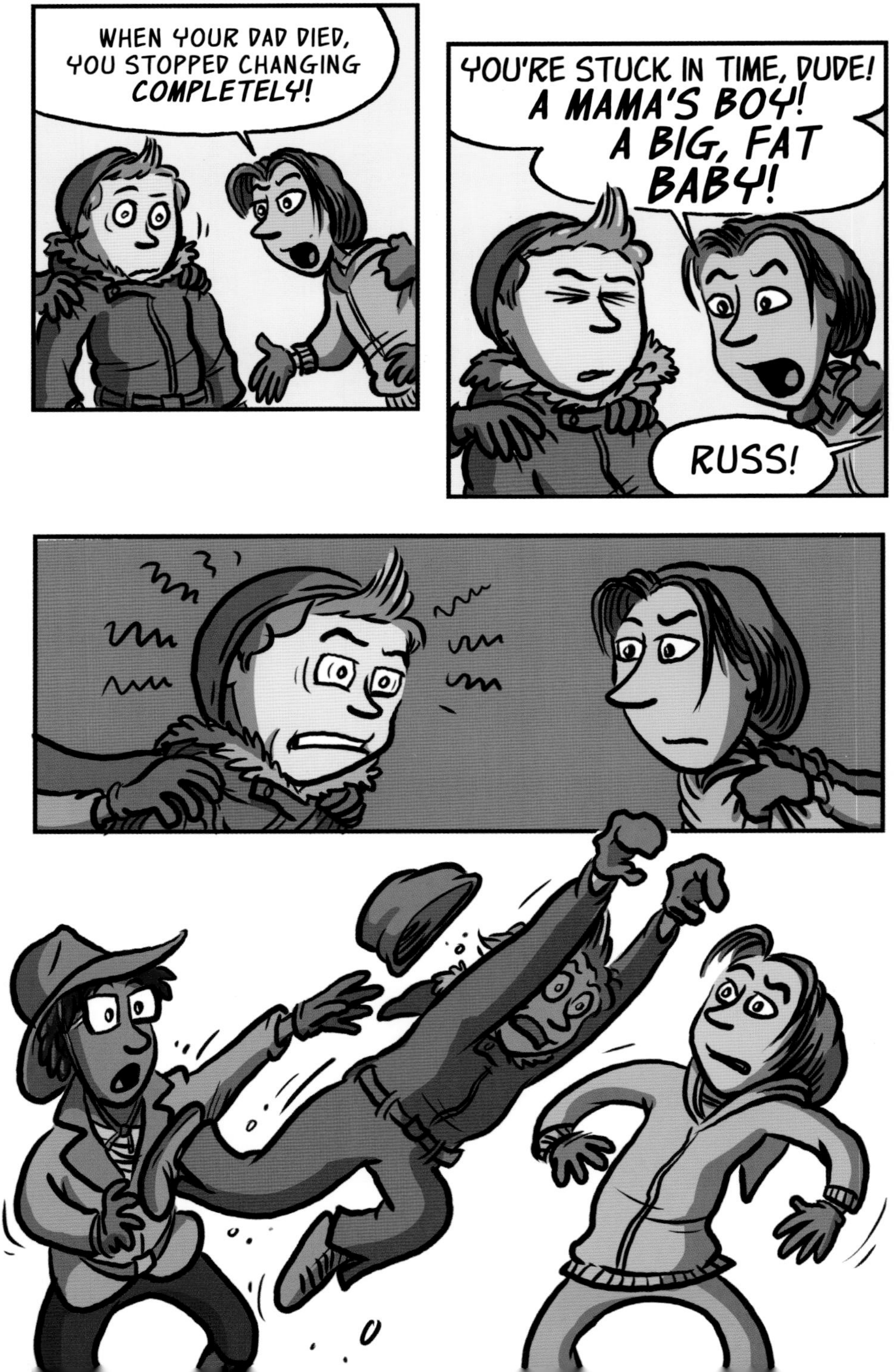
WHEN YOUR DAD DIED, YOU STOPPED CHANGING COMPLETELY!
YOU'RE STUCK IN TIME, DUDE! A MAMA'S BOY! A BIG, FAT BABY!
RUSS!

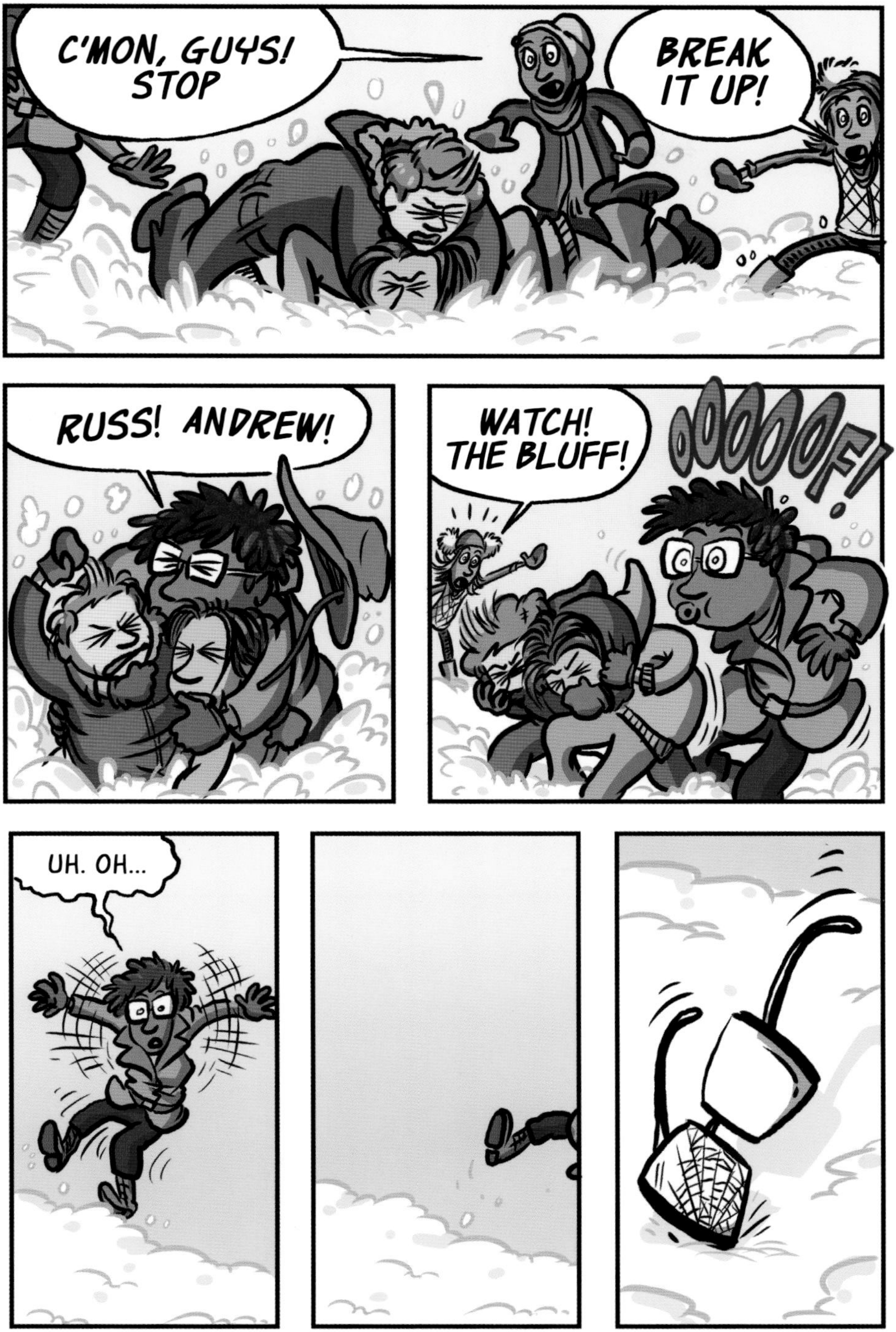
C'MON, GUYS! STOP
BREAK IT UP!
RUSS! ANDREW!
WATCH! THE BLUFF!
OOOOOOF!
UH. OH...

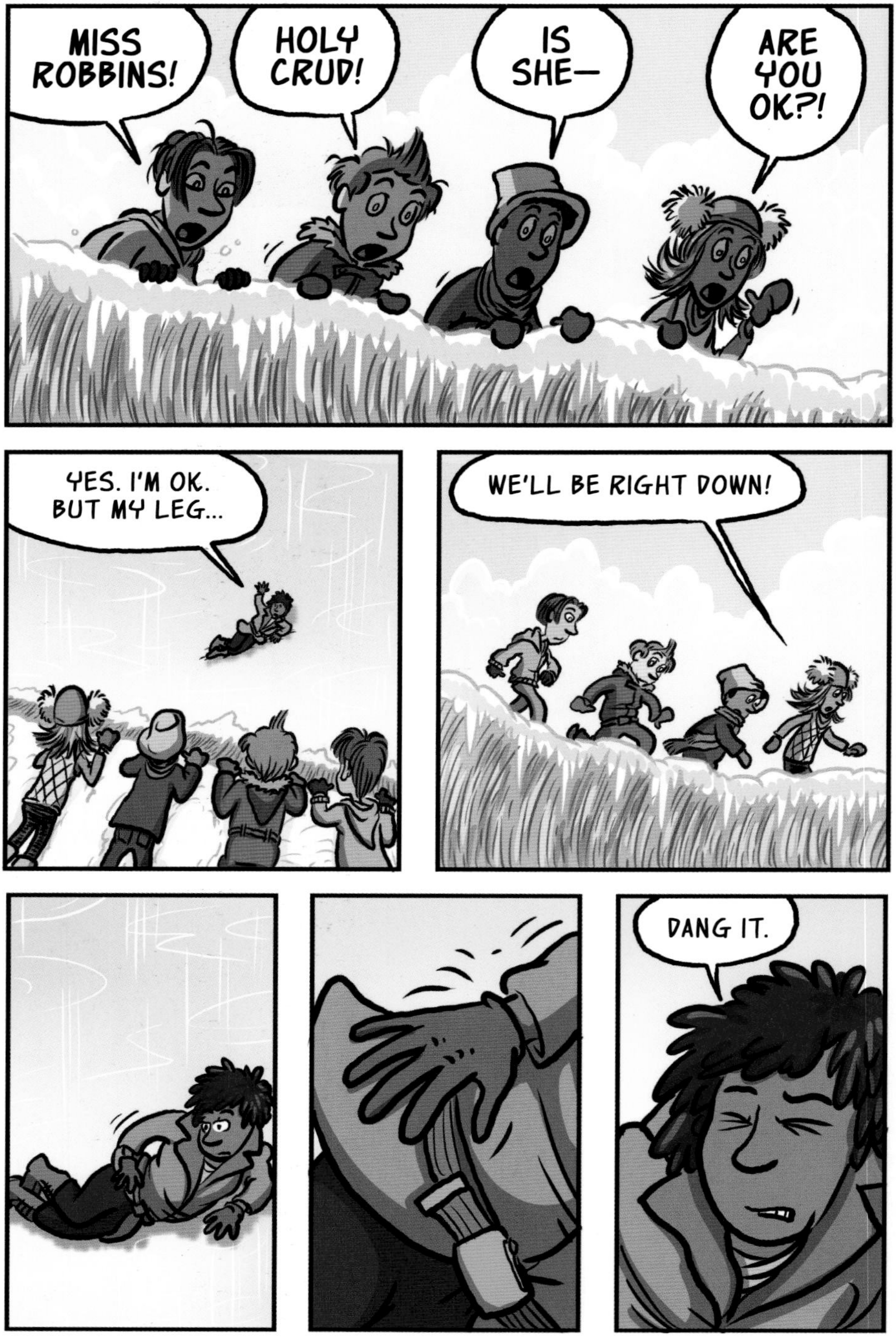
MISS ROBBINS!
HOLY CRUD!
IS SHE—
ARE YOU OK?!
YES. I'M OK. BUT MY LEG...
WE'LL BE RIGHT DOWN!
DANG IT.

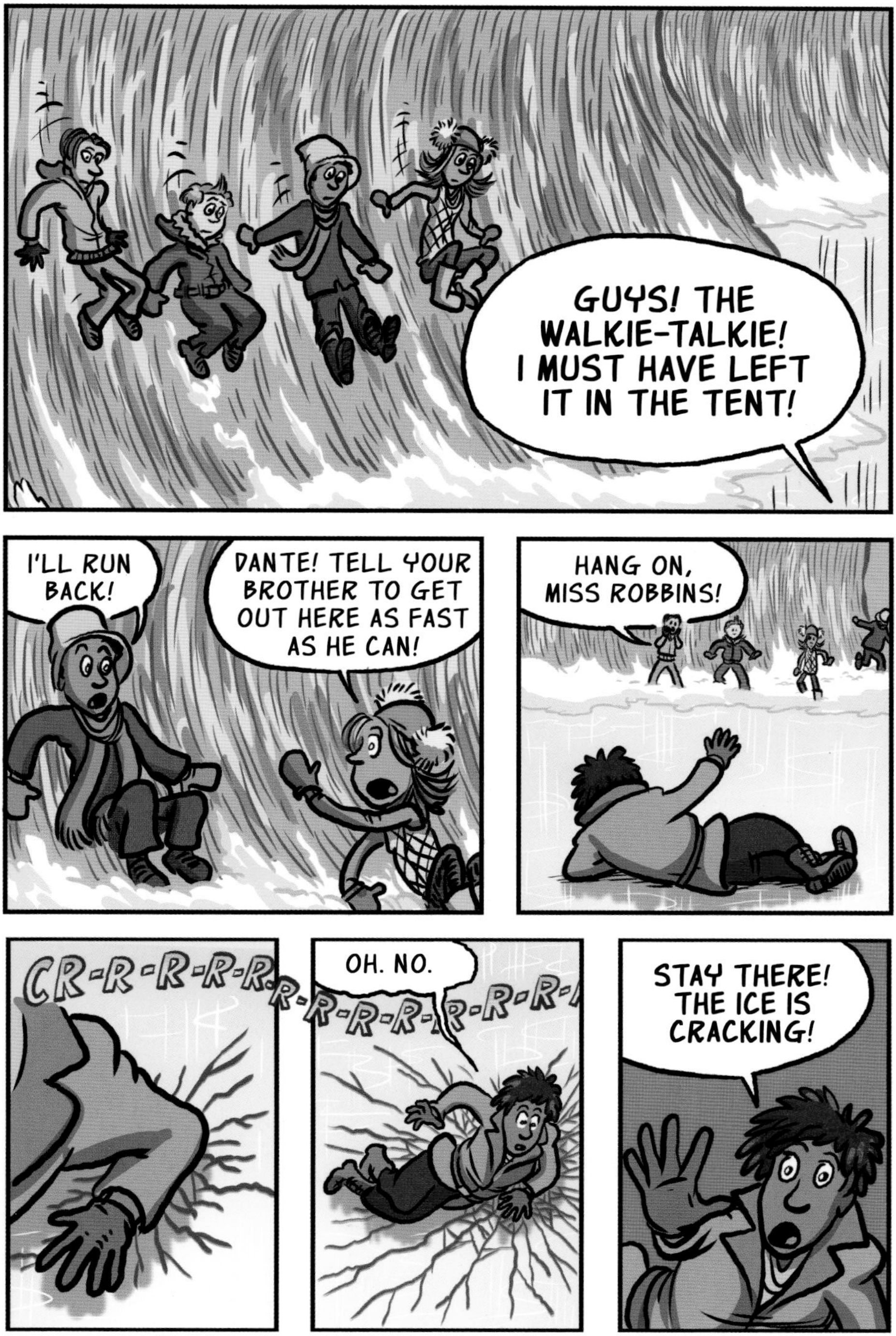
GUYS! THE WALKIE-TALKIE! I MUST HAVE LEFT IT IN THE TENT!
I'LL RUN BACK!
DANTE! TELL YOUR BROTHER TO GET OUT HERE AS FAST AS HE CAN!
HANG ON, MISS ROBBINS!
CR-R-R-R-R-R-R-R-R-R-R-R-R-R
OH. NO.
STAY THERE! THE ICE IS CRACKING!

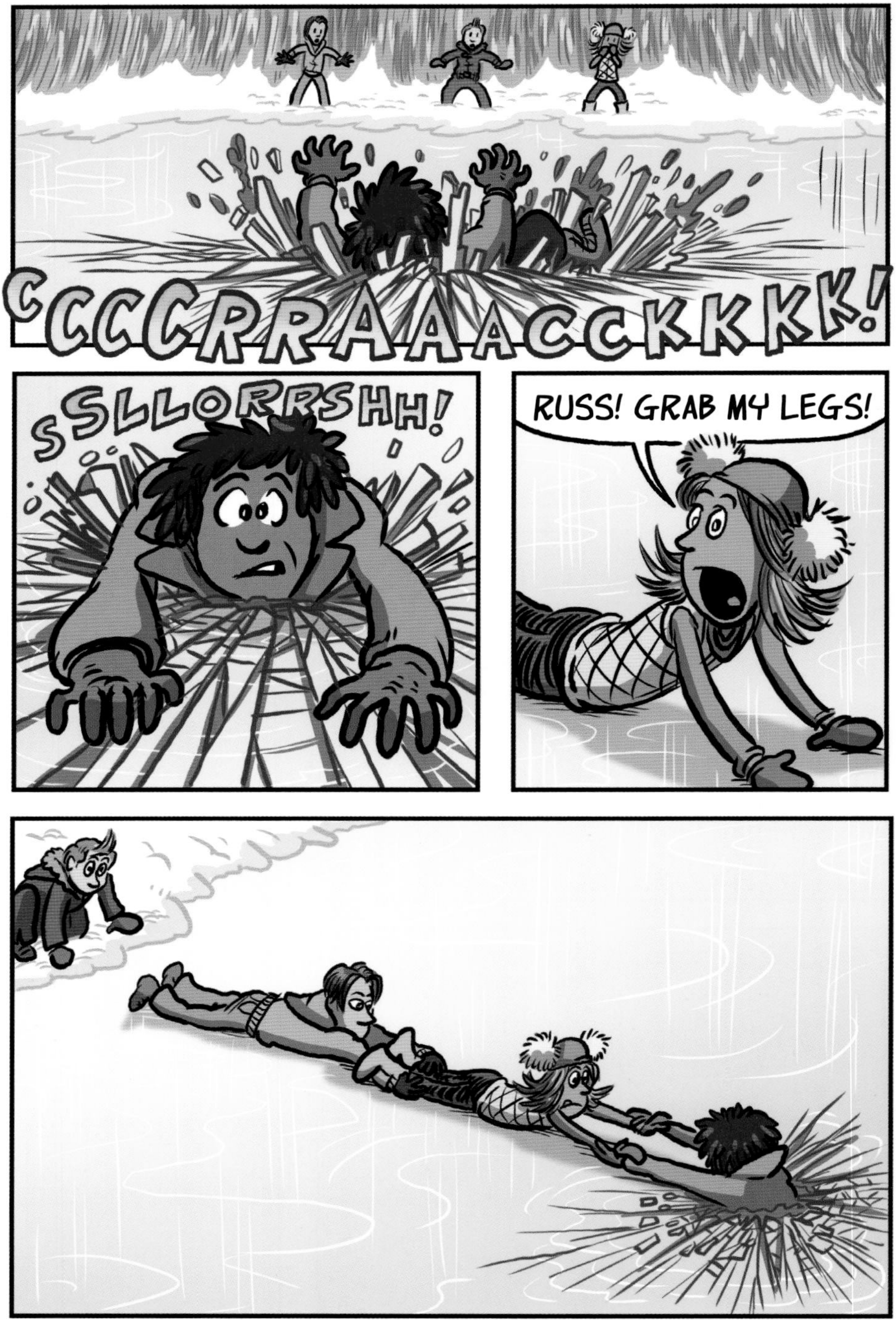
CCCCRRAAACCKKKK!
sSLLORRSHH!
RUSS! GRAB MY LEGS!

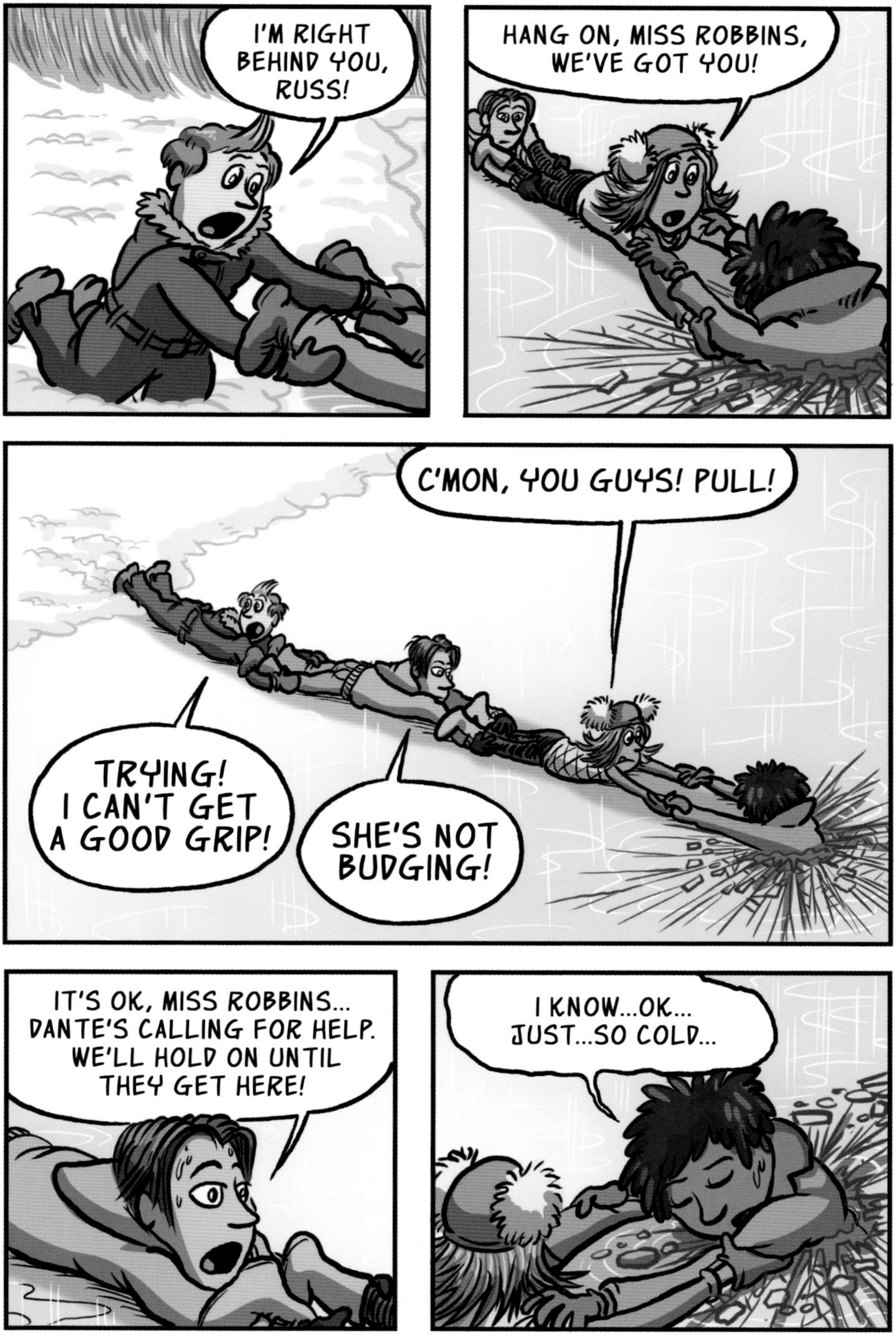
I'M RIGHT BEHIND YOU, RUSS!
HANG ON, MISS ROBBINS, WE'VE GOT YOU!
C'MON, YOU GUYS! PULL!
TRYING! I CAN'T GET A GOOD GRIP!
SHE'S NOT BUDGING!
IT'S OK, MISS ROBBINS... DANTE'S CALLING FOR HELP. WE'LL HOLD ON UNTIL THEY GET HERE!
I KNOW...OK... JUST...SO COLD...

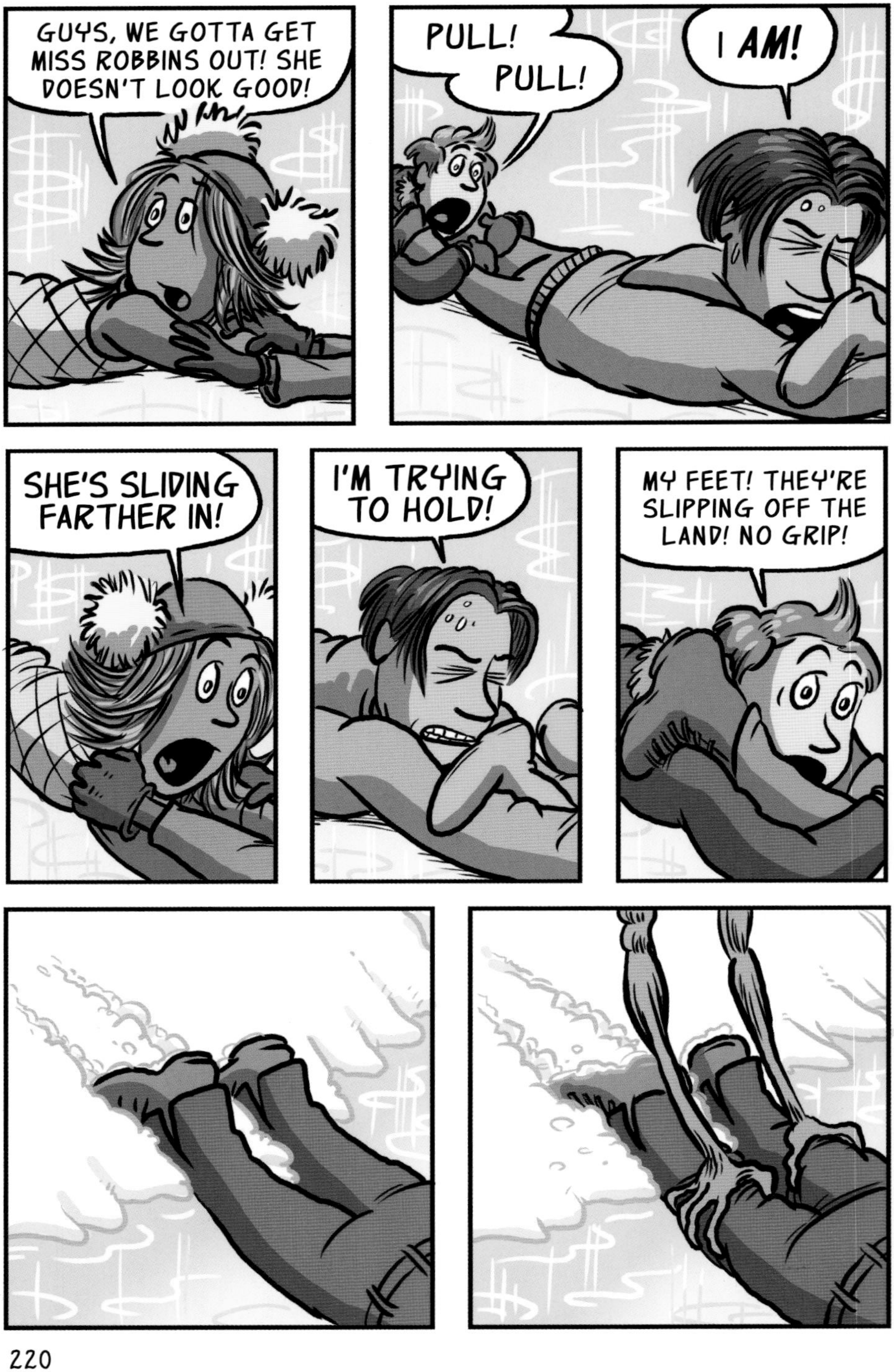
GUYS, WE GOTTA GET MISS ROBBINS OUT! SHE DOESN'T LOOK GOOD!
PULL! PULL!
I AM!
SHE'S SLIDING FARTHER IN!
I'M TRYING TO HOLD!
MY FEET! THEY'RE SLIPPING OFF THE LAND! NO GRIP!

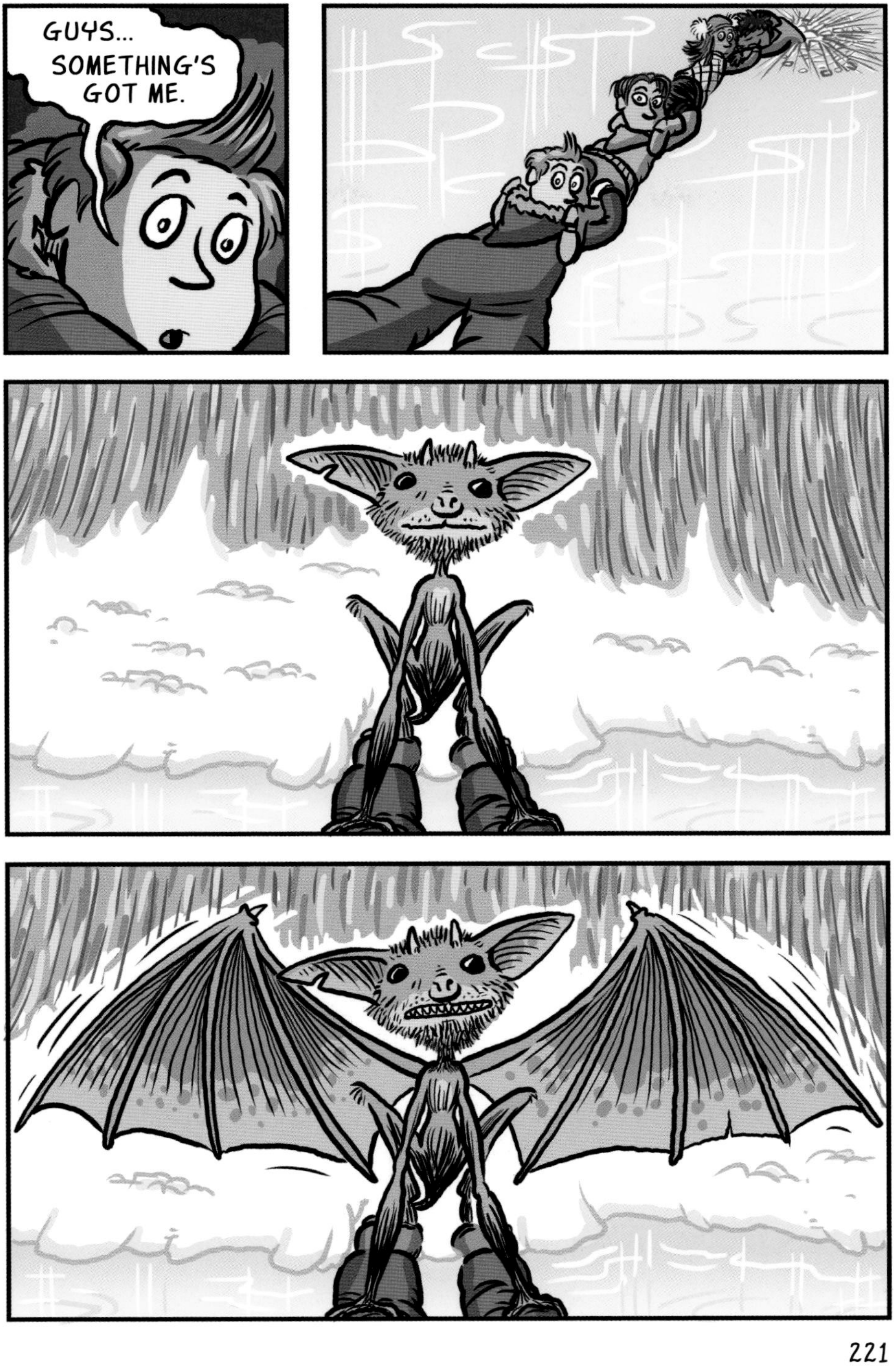
GUYS...
SOMETHING'S GOT ME.

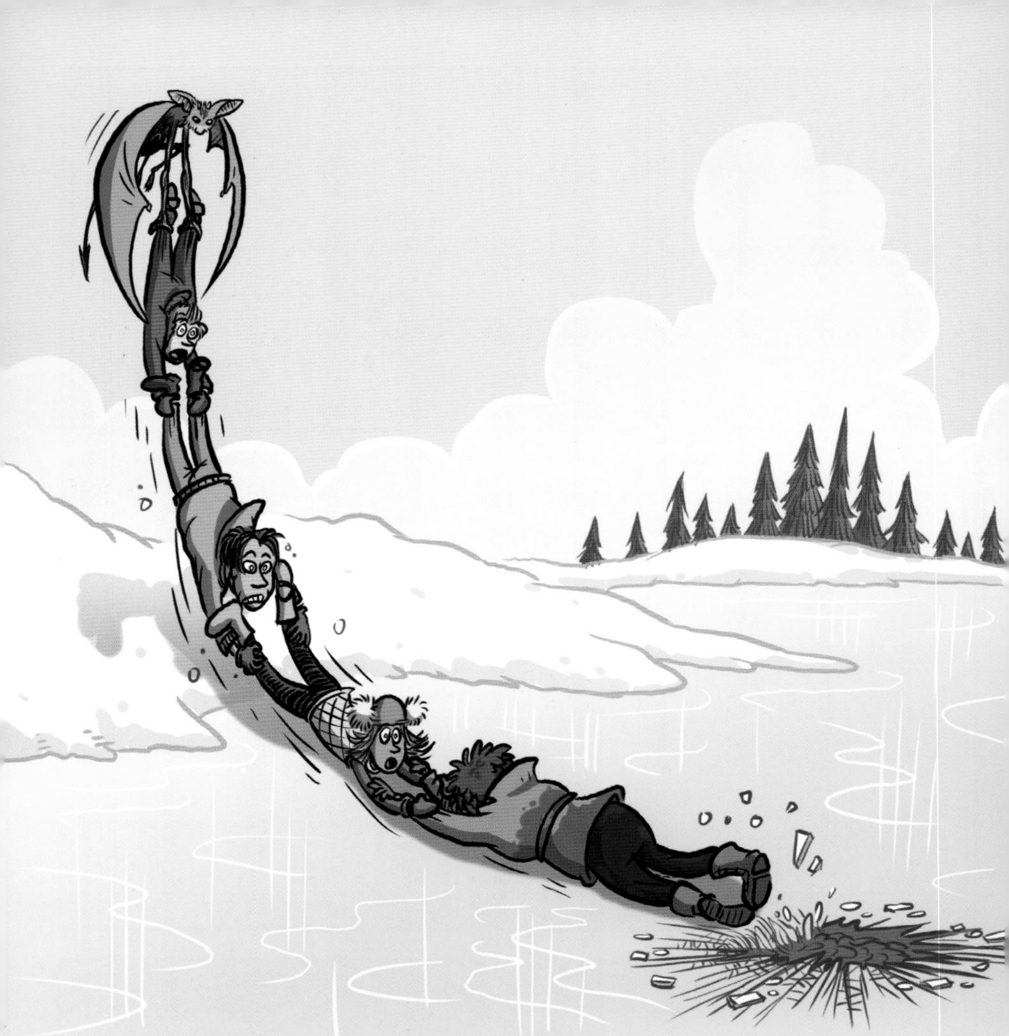

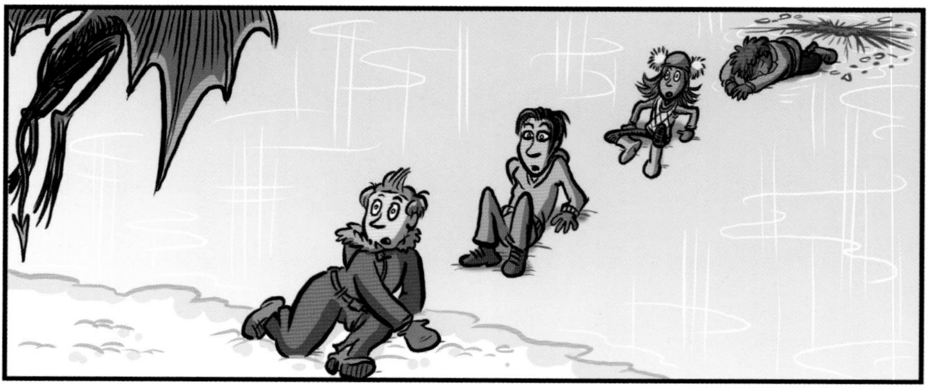

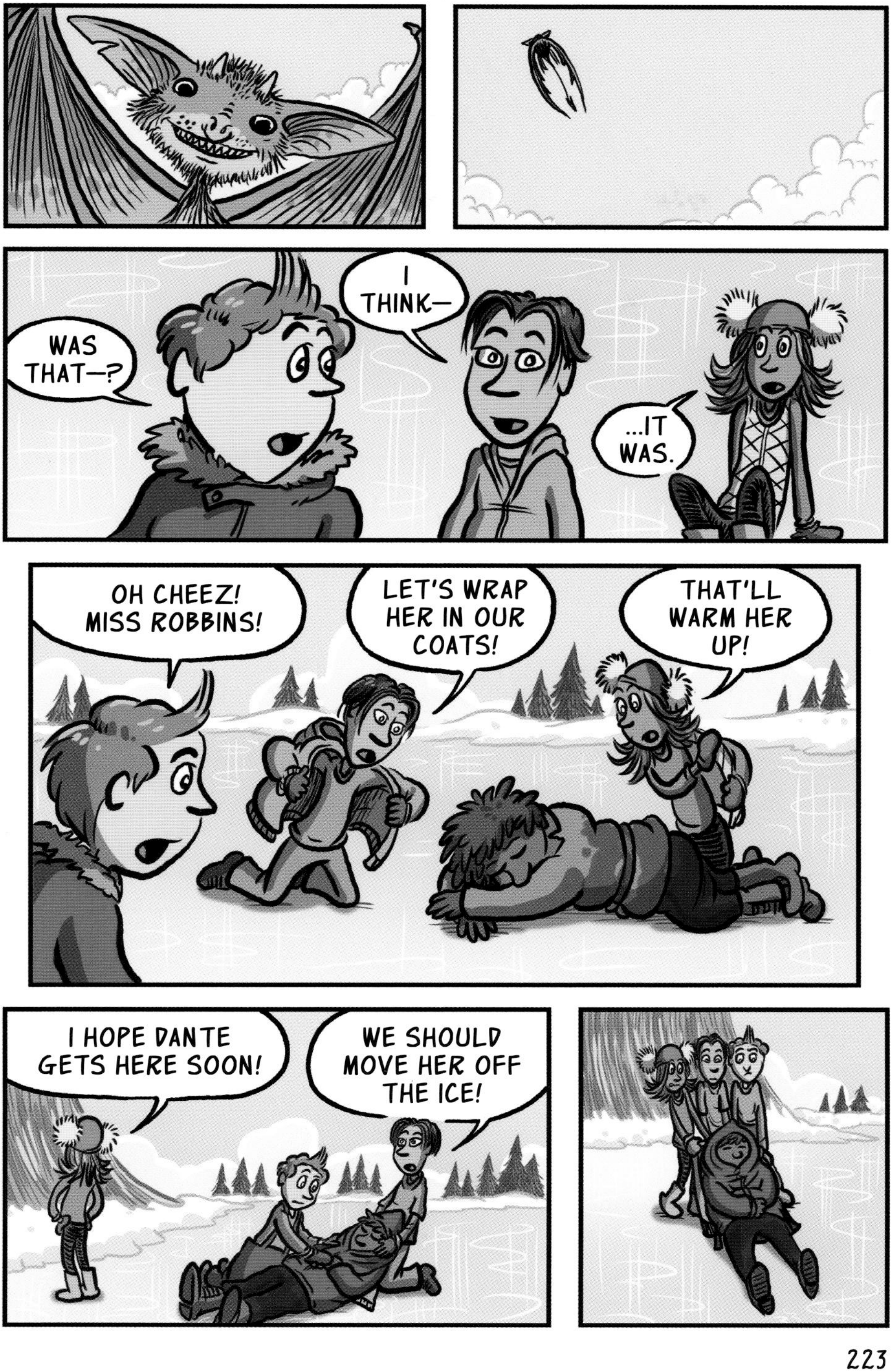
WAS THAT—?
I THINK—
...IT WAS.
OH CHEEZ! MISS ROBBINS!
LET'S WRAP HER IN OUR COATS!
THAT'LL WARM HER UP!
I HOPE DANTE GETS HERE SOON!
WE SHOULD MOVE HER OFF THE ICE!

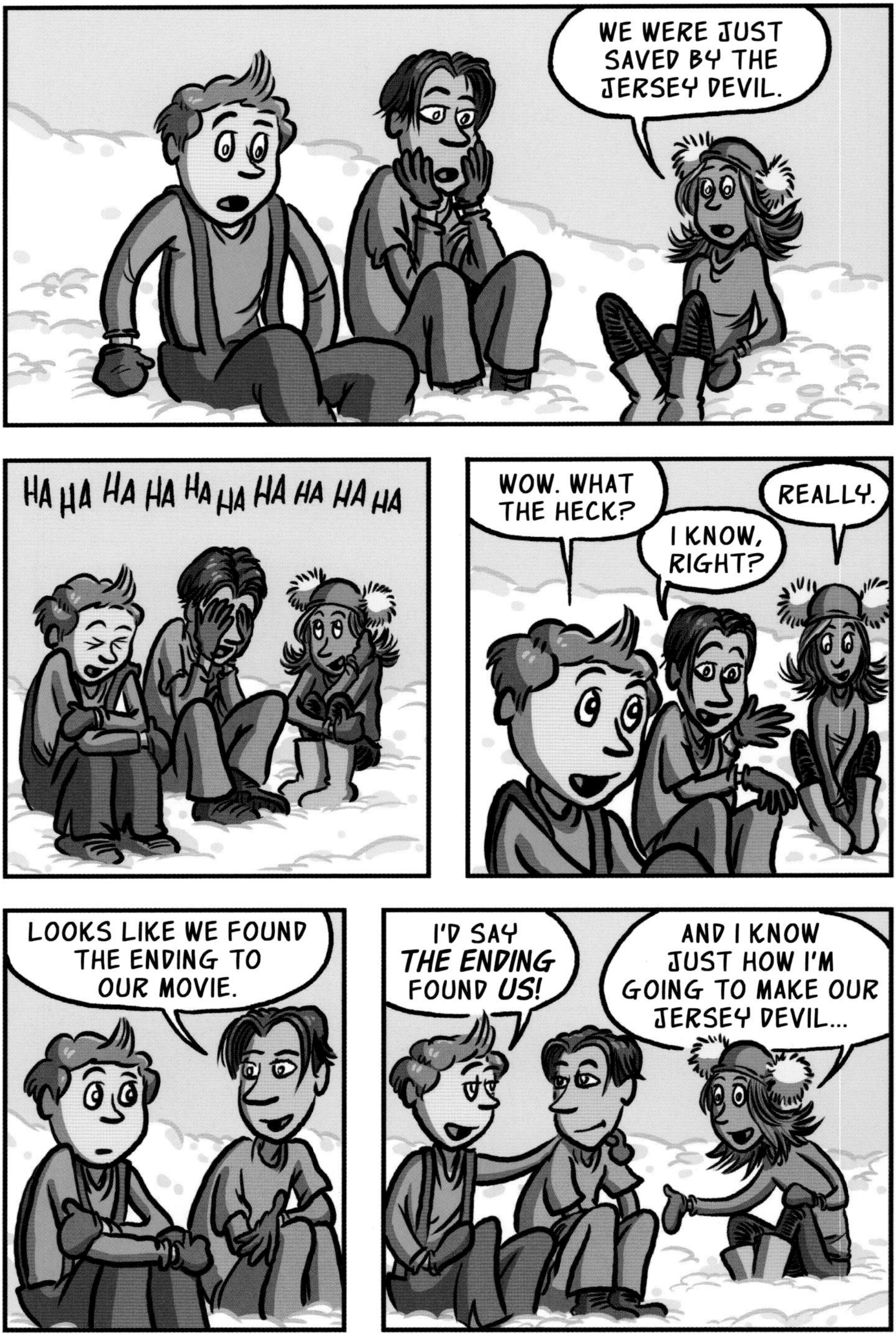

WE WERE JUST SAVED BY THE JERSEY DEVIL.
HA HA HA HA HA HA HA HA HA HA
WOW. WHAT THE HECK?
I KNOW, RIGHT?
REALLY.
LOOKS LIKE WE FOUND THE ENDING TO OUR MOVIE.
I'D SAY *THE ENDING* FOUND *US*!
AND I KNOW JUST HOW I'M GOING TO MAKE OUR JERSEY DEVIL...

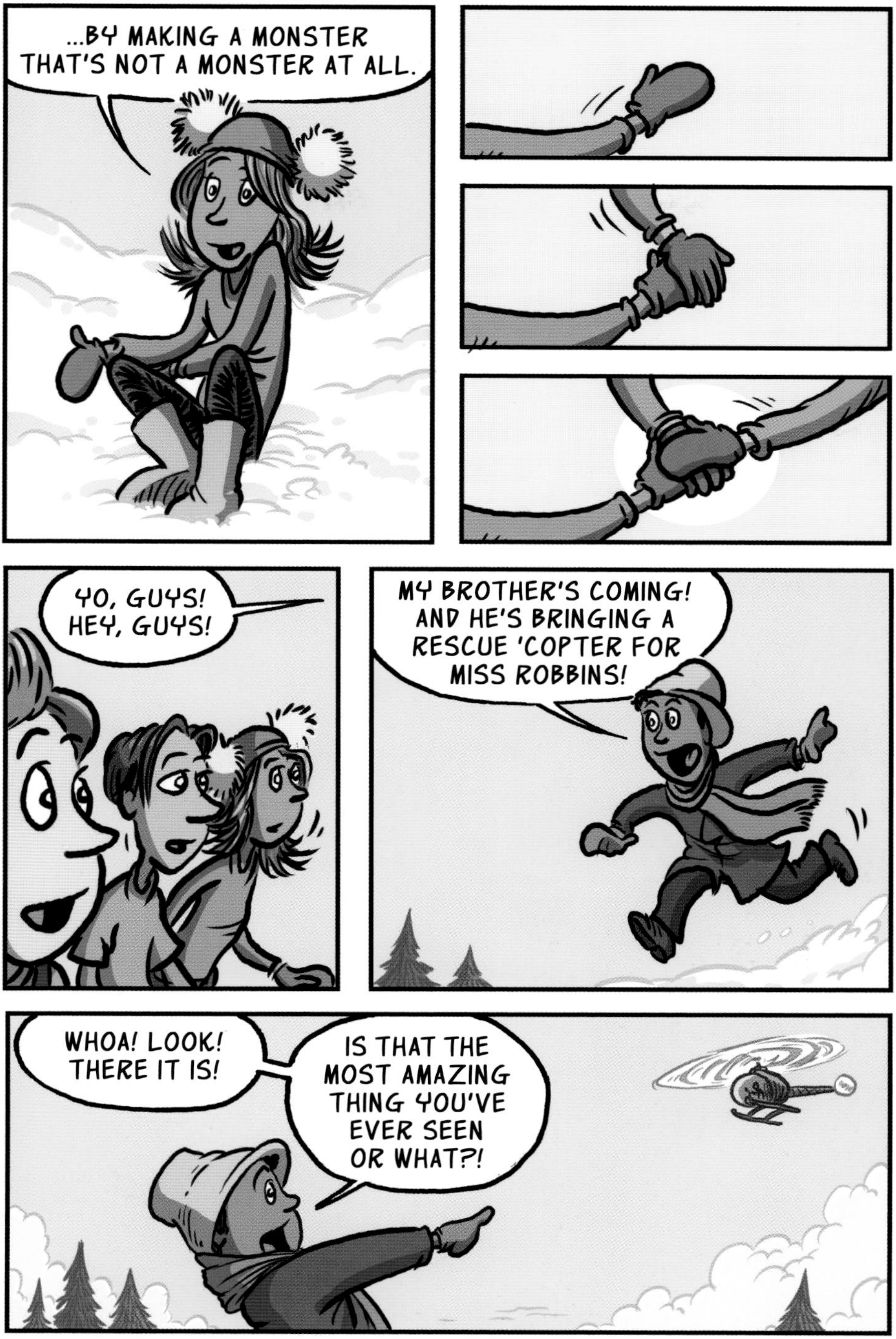
...BY MAKING A MONSTER THAT'S NOT A MONSTER AT ALL.
YO, GUYS! HEY, GUYS!
MY BROTHER'S COMING! AND HE'S BRINGING A RESCUE 'COPTER FOR MISS ROBBINS!
WHOA! LOOK! THERE IT IS!
IS THAT THE MOST AMAZING THING YOU'VE EVER SEEN OR WHAT?!

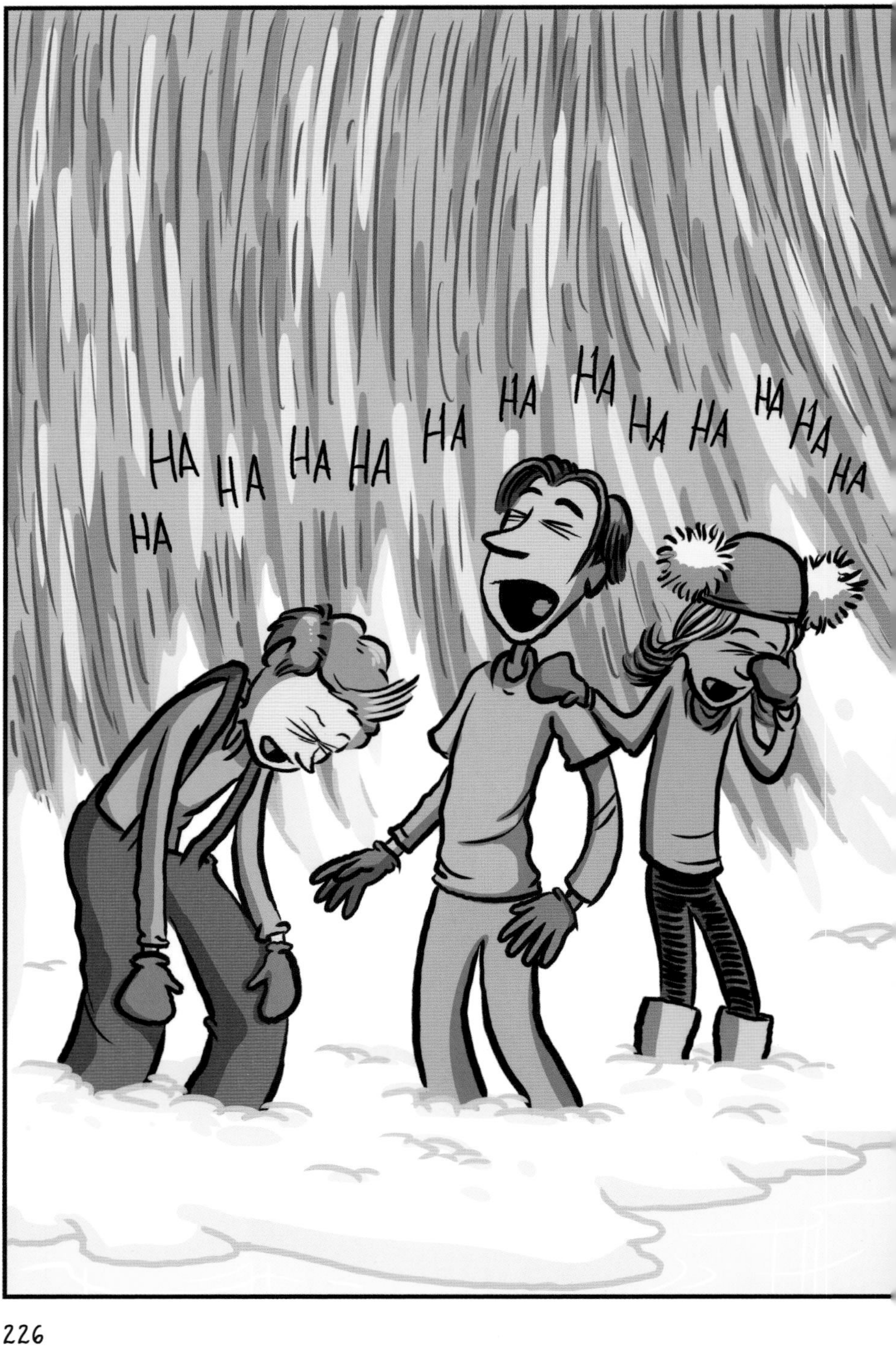
HA
HA
HA
HA
HA
HA
HA
HA
HA
HA
HA
HA
HA
HA

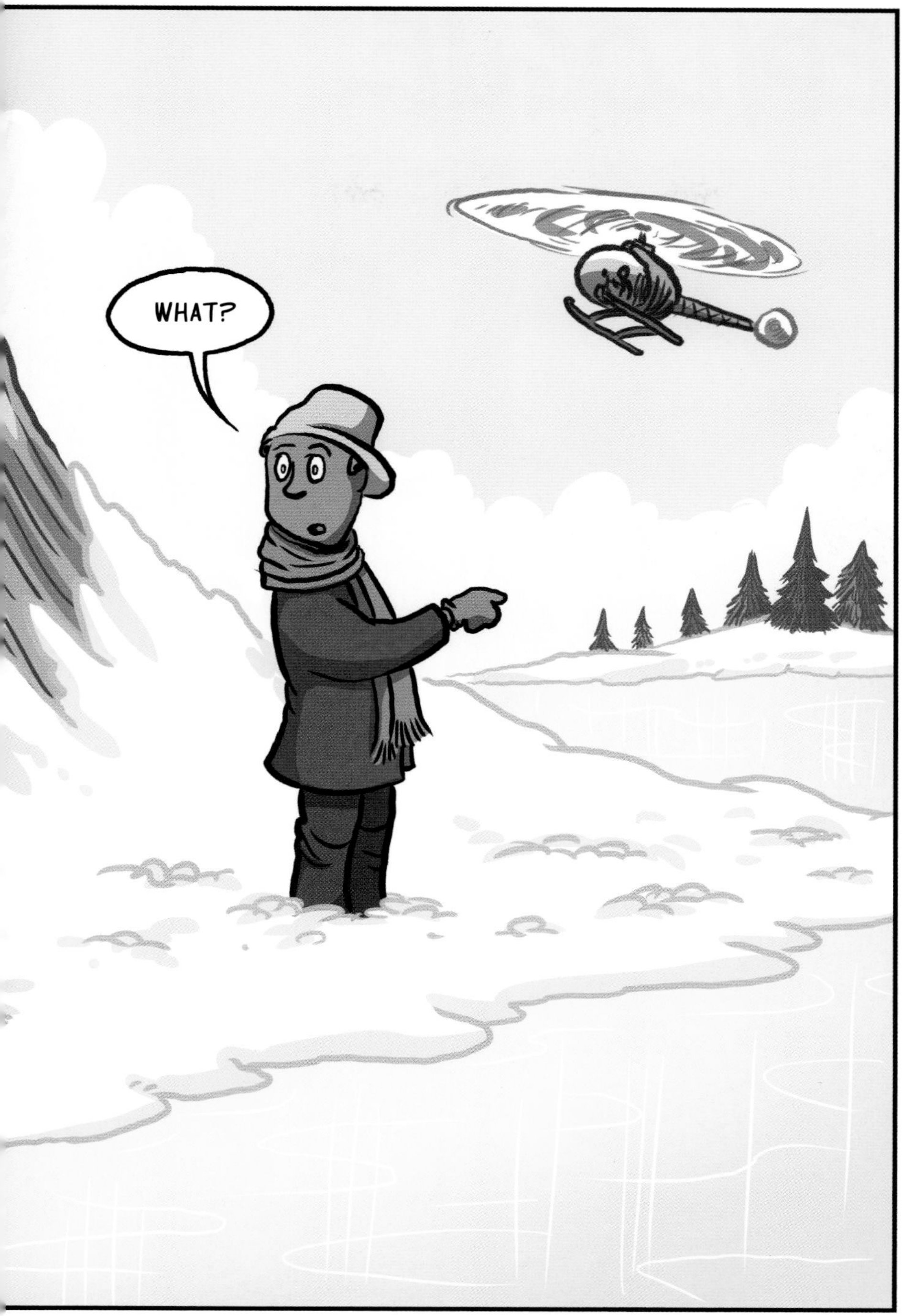
WHAT?

EPILOGUE

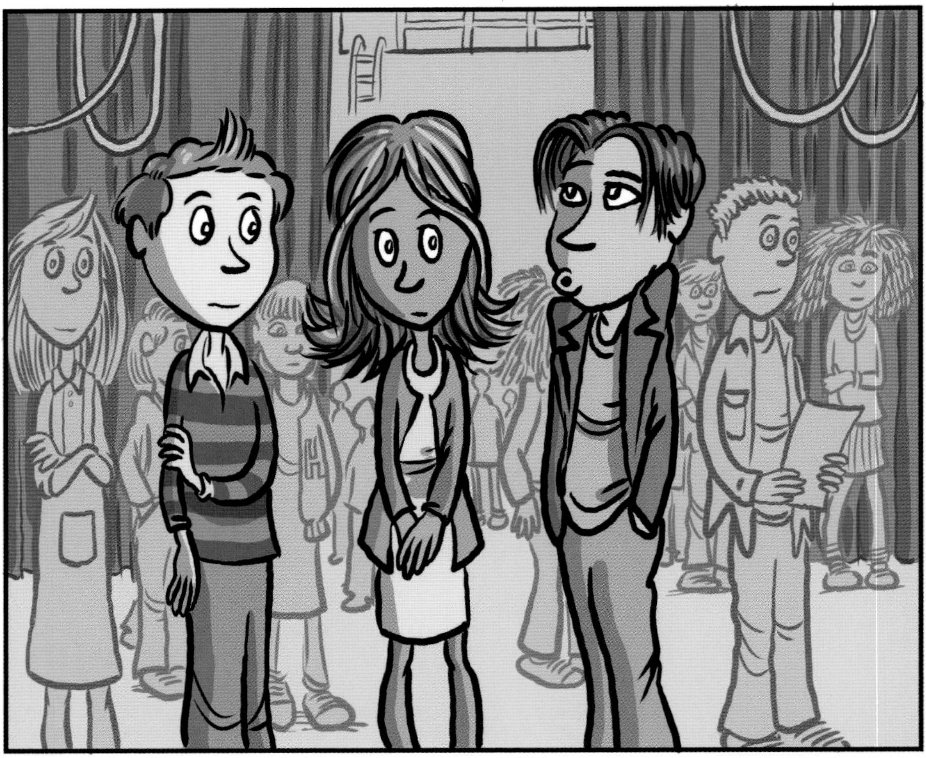

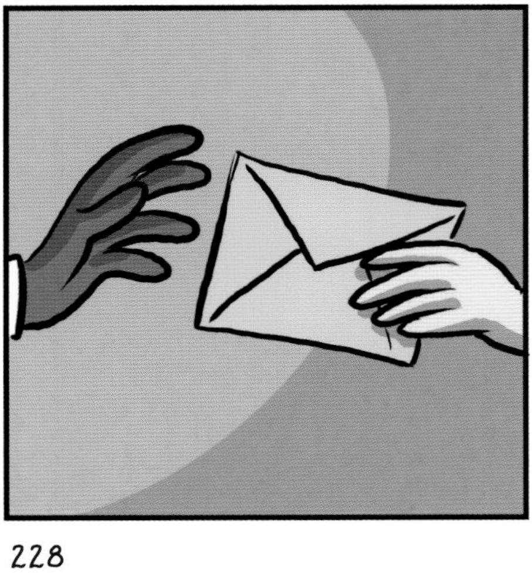

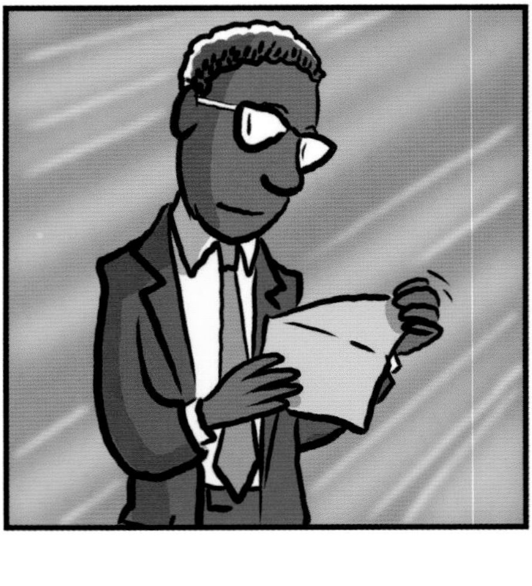

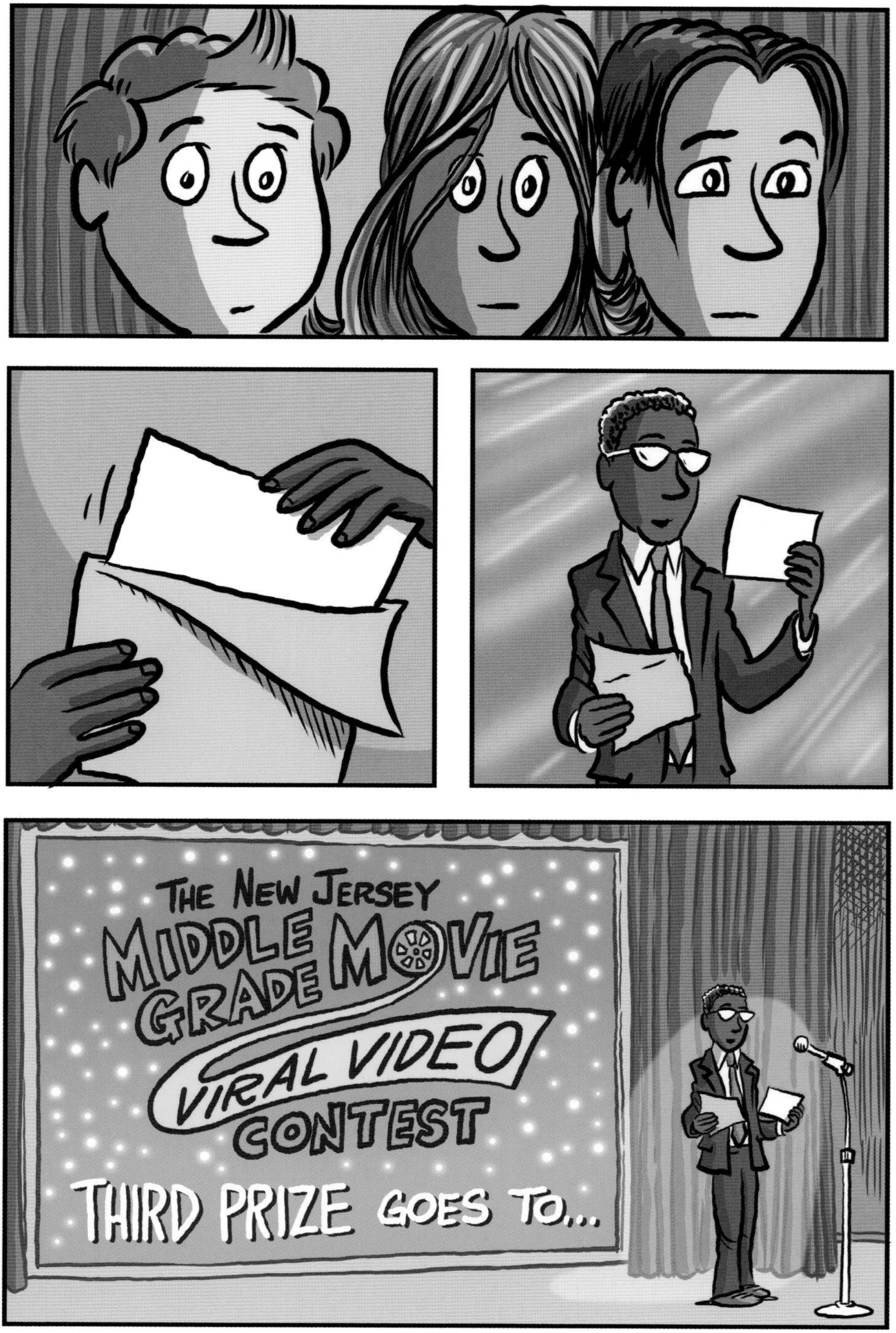
THE NEW JERSEY
MIDDLE GRADE MOVIE
VIRAL VIDEO
CONTEST
THIRD PRIZE GOES TO...

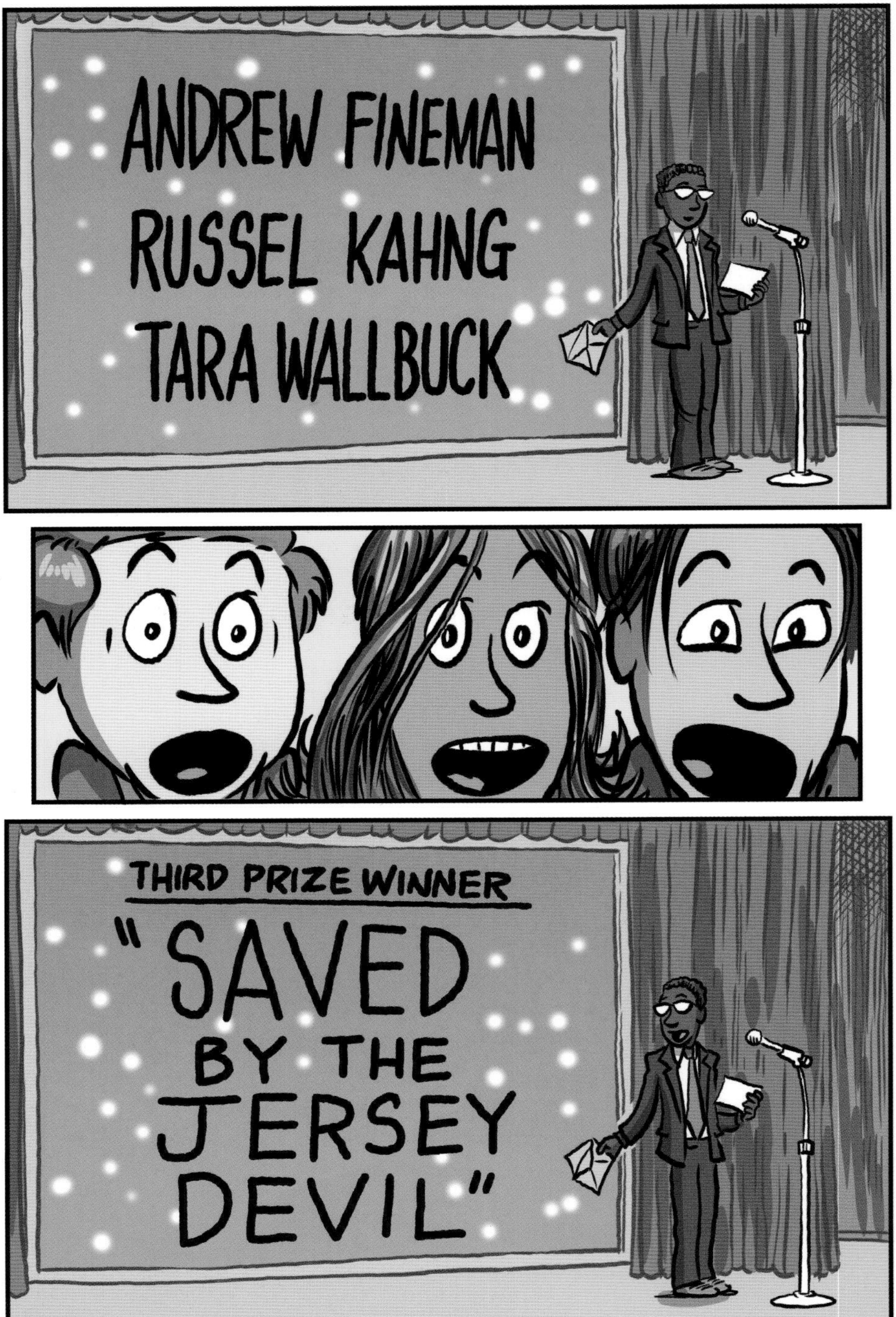
ANDREW FINEMAN
RUSSEL KAHNG
TARA WALLBUCK
THIRD PRIZE WINNER
"SAVED BY THE JERSEY DEVIL"

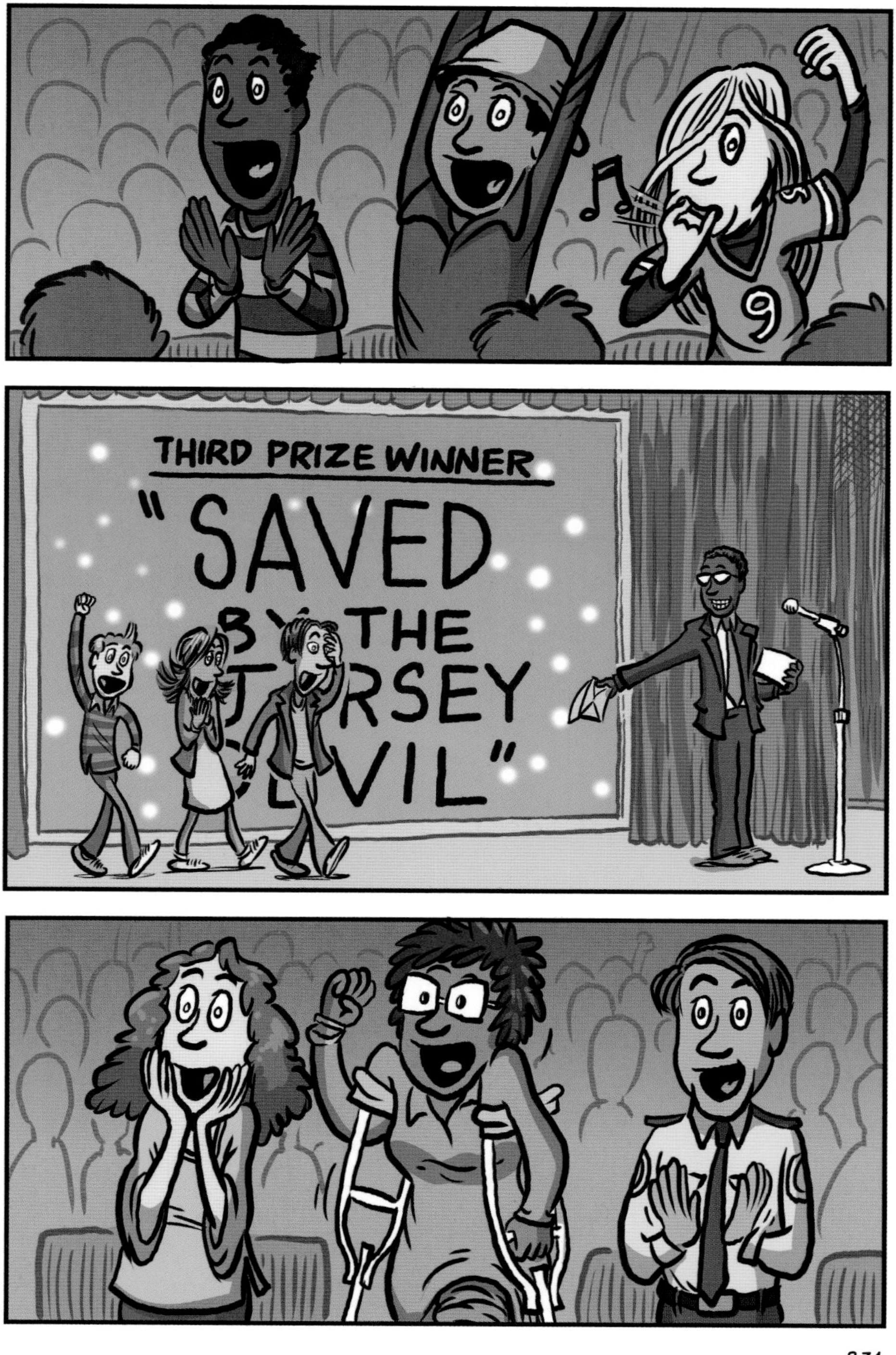
THIRD PRIZE WINNER
"SAVED
B THE
RSEY
VIL"

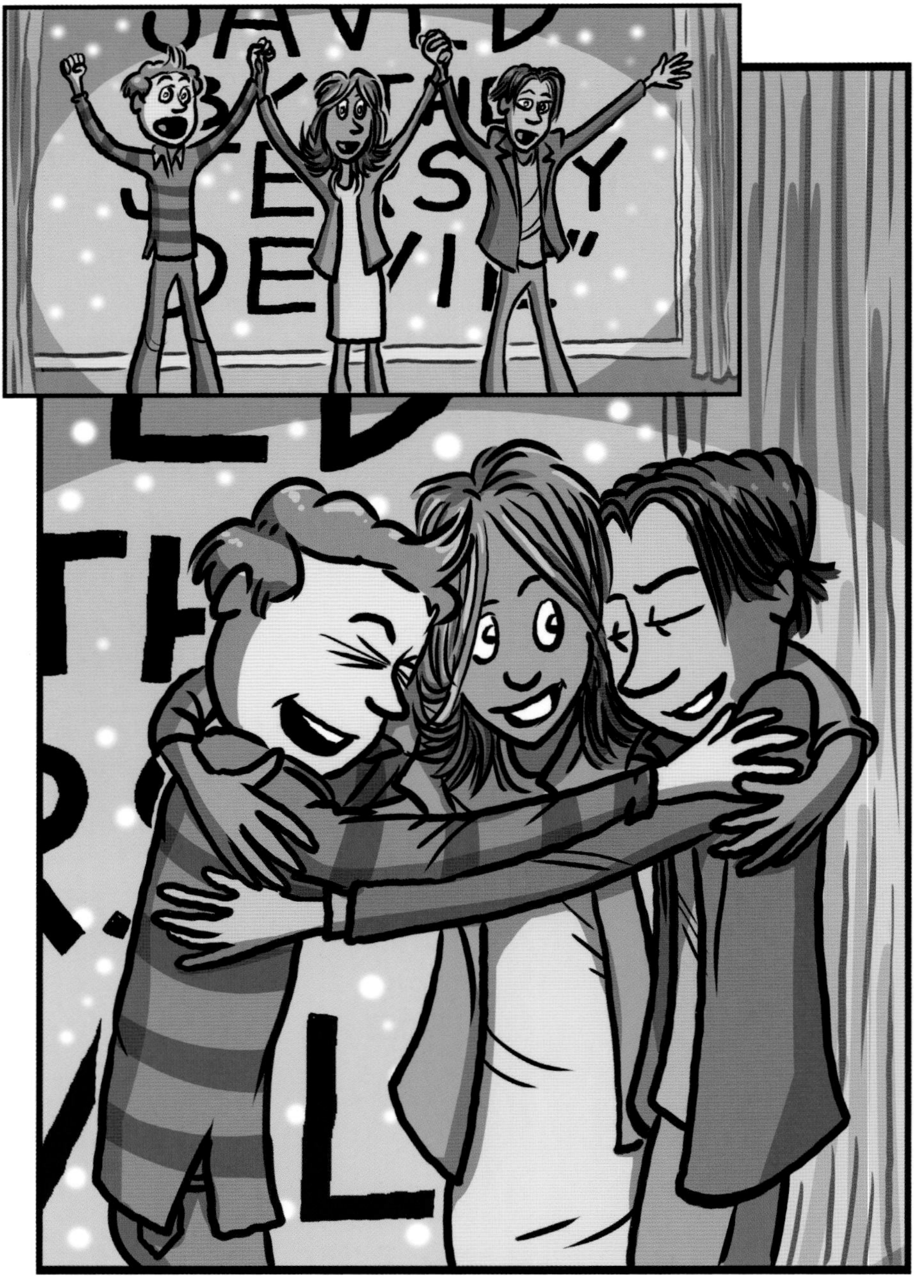

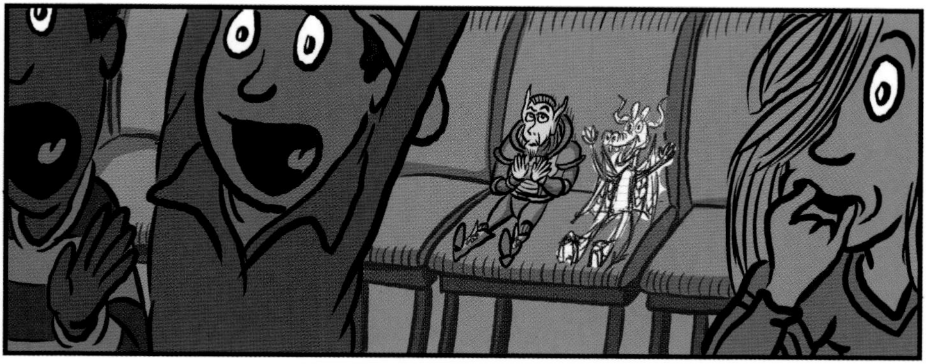

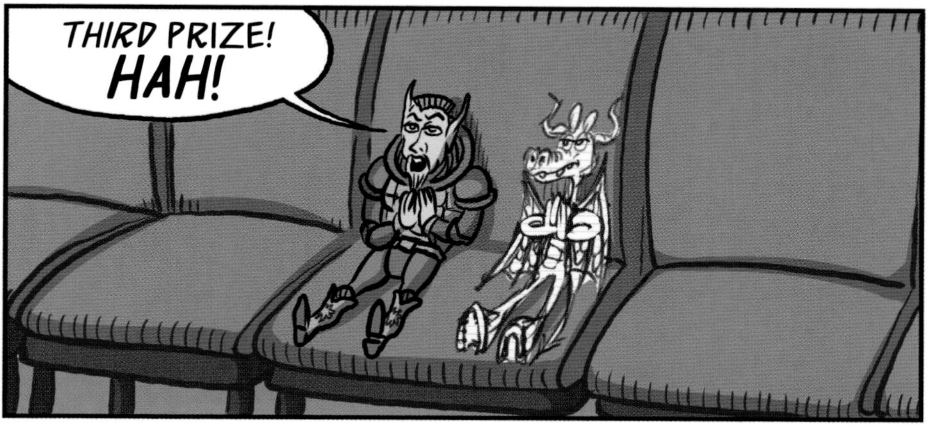
THIRD PRIZE! HAH!

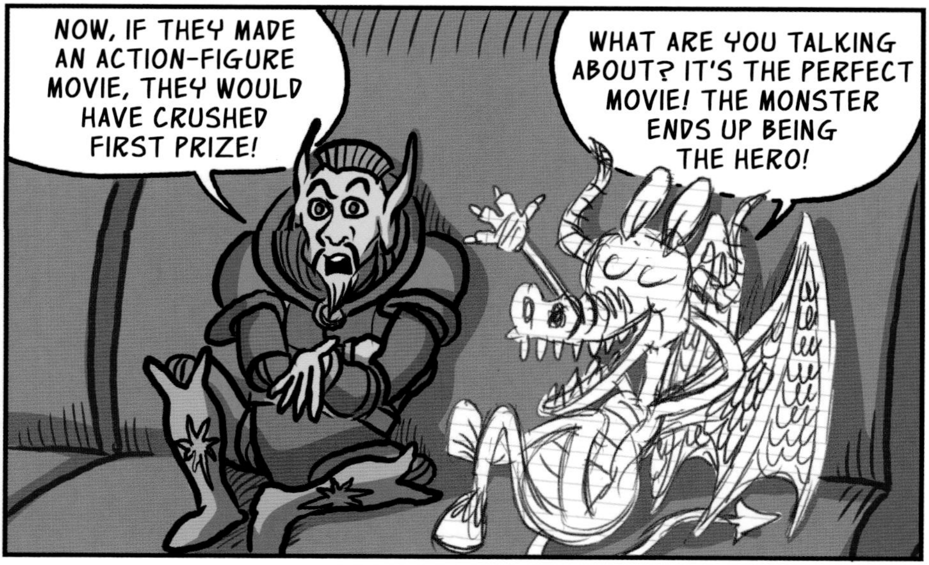
NOW, IF THEY MADE AN ACTION-FIGURE MOVIE, THEY WOULD HAVE CRUSHED FIRST PRIZE!
WHAT ARE YOU TALKING ABOUT? IT'S THE PERFECT MOVIE! THE MONSTER ENDS UP BEING THE HERO!

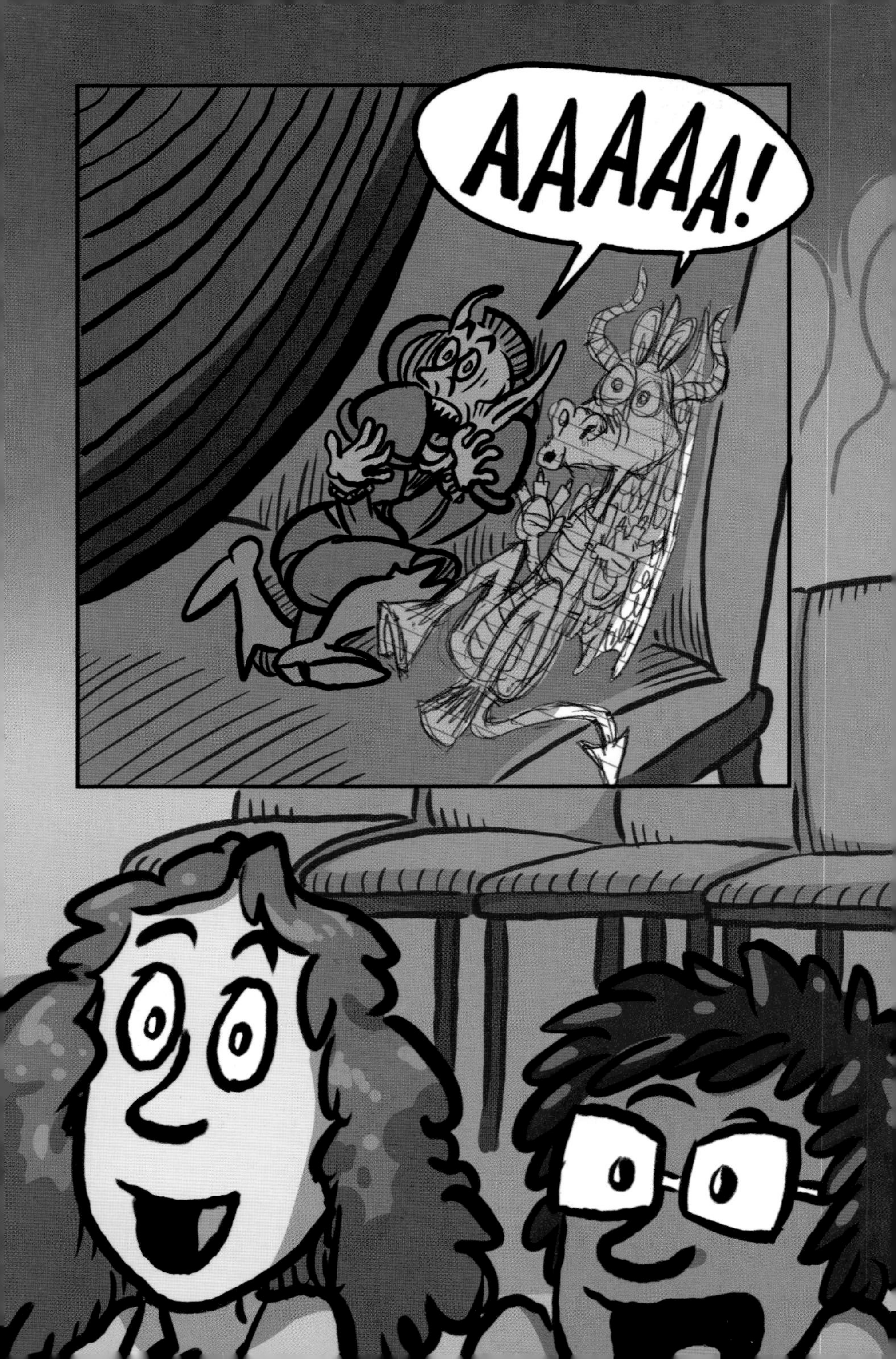
AAAAA!

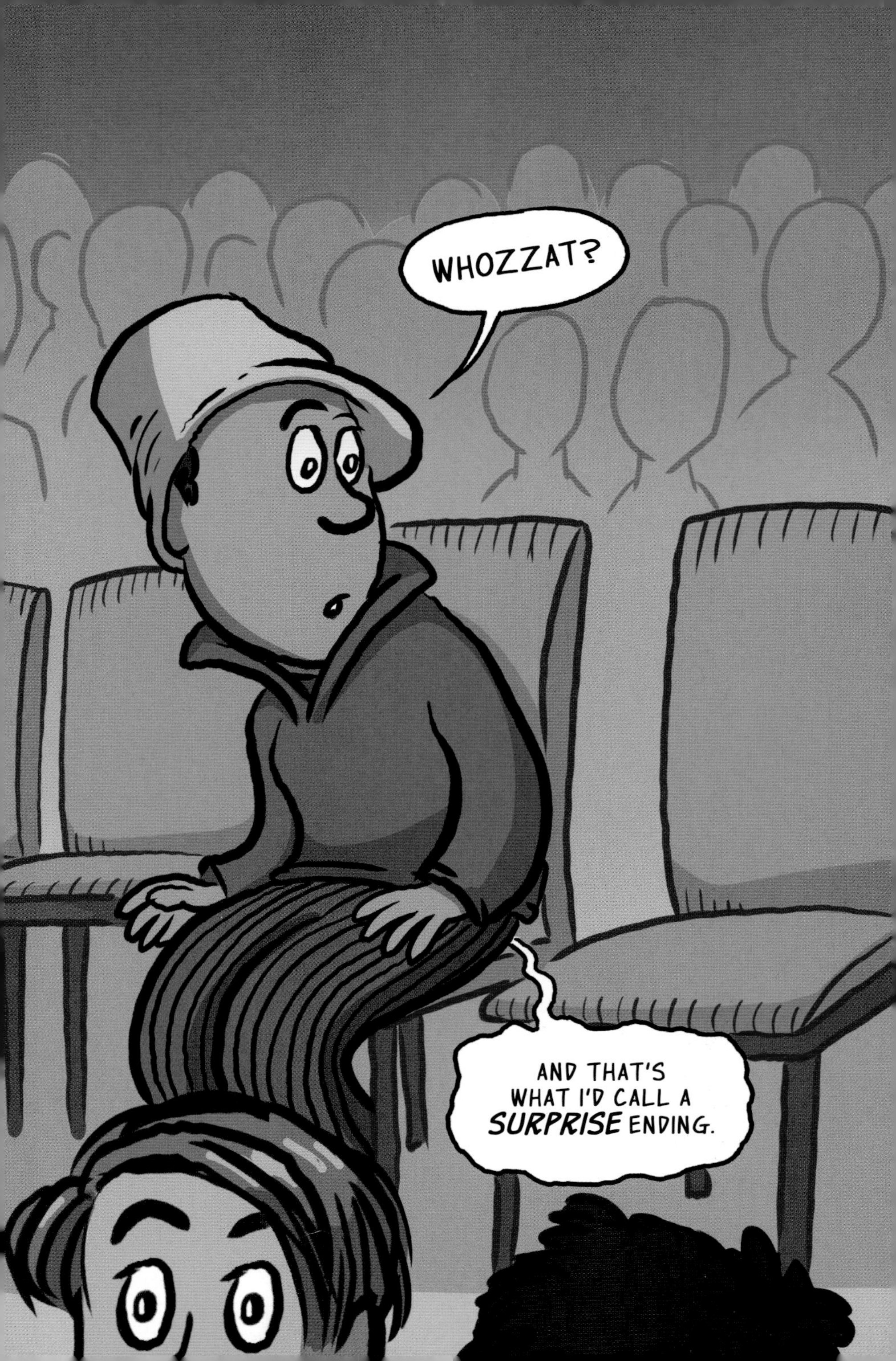
WHOZZAT?
AND THAT'S WHAT I'D CALL A SURPRISE ENDING.

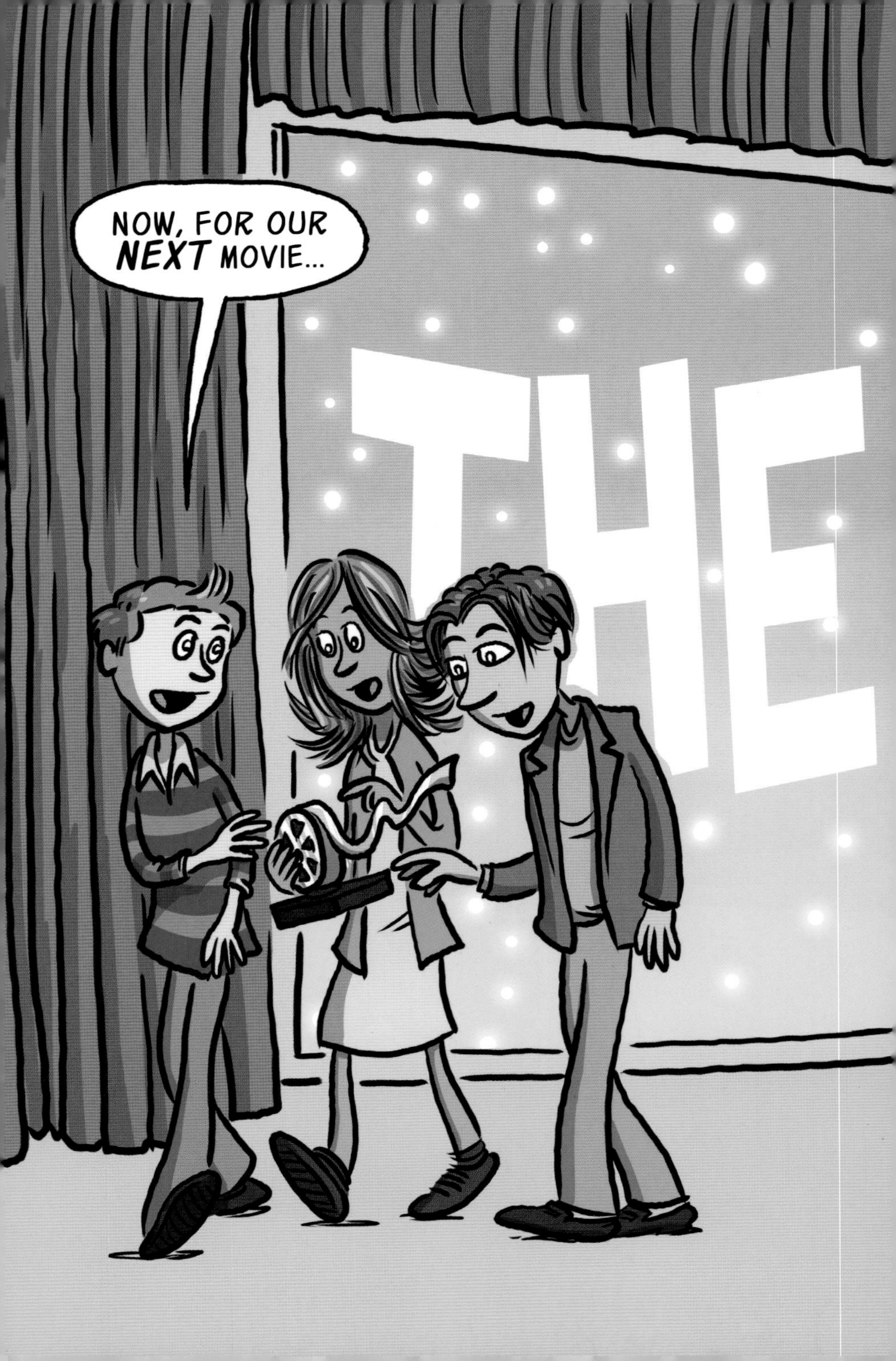
NOW, FOR OUR *NEXT* MOVIE...
THE

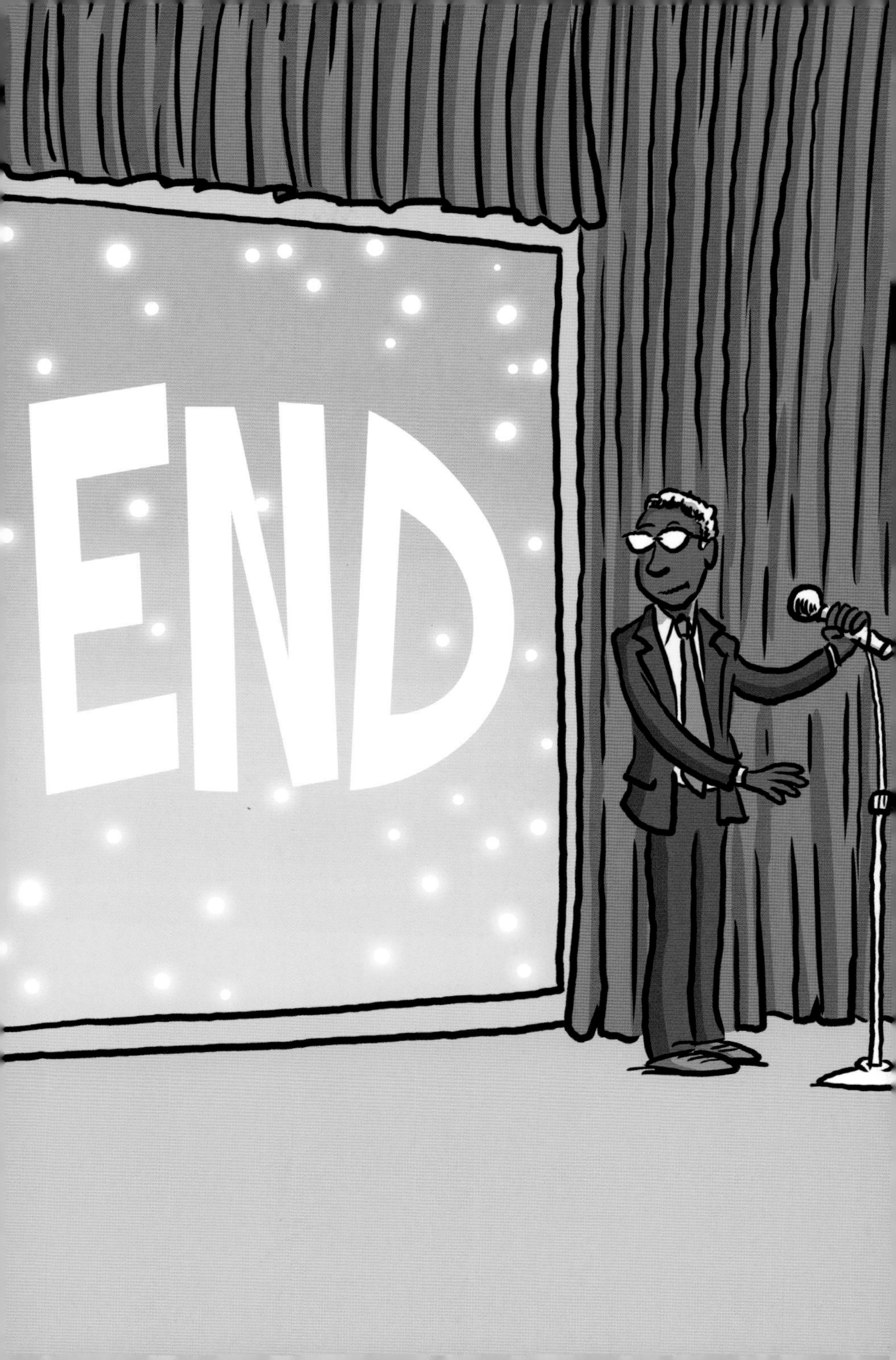
END

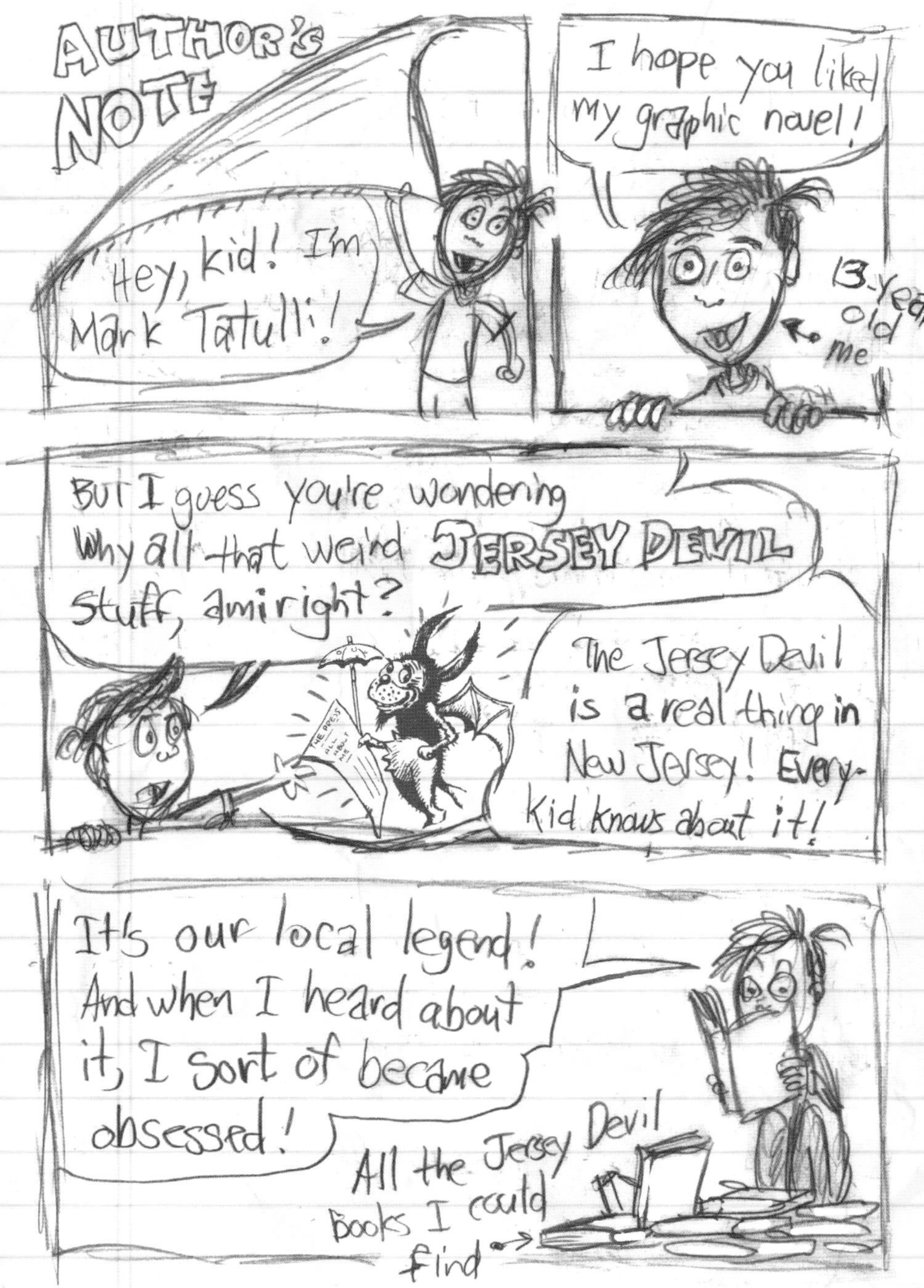
AUTHOR'S NOTE
Hey, kid! I'm Mark Tatulli!
I hope you liked my graphic novel!
13-year-old me
But I guess you're wondering why all that weird JERSEY DEVIL stuff, amiright?
The Jersey Devil is a real thing in New Jersey! Every kid knows about it!
THE PRESS
ALL ABOUT ME
It's our local legend! And when I heard about it, I sort of became obsessed!
All the Jersey Devil Books I could find

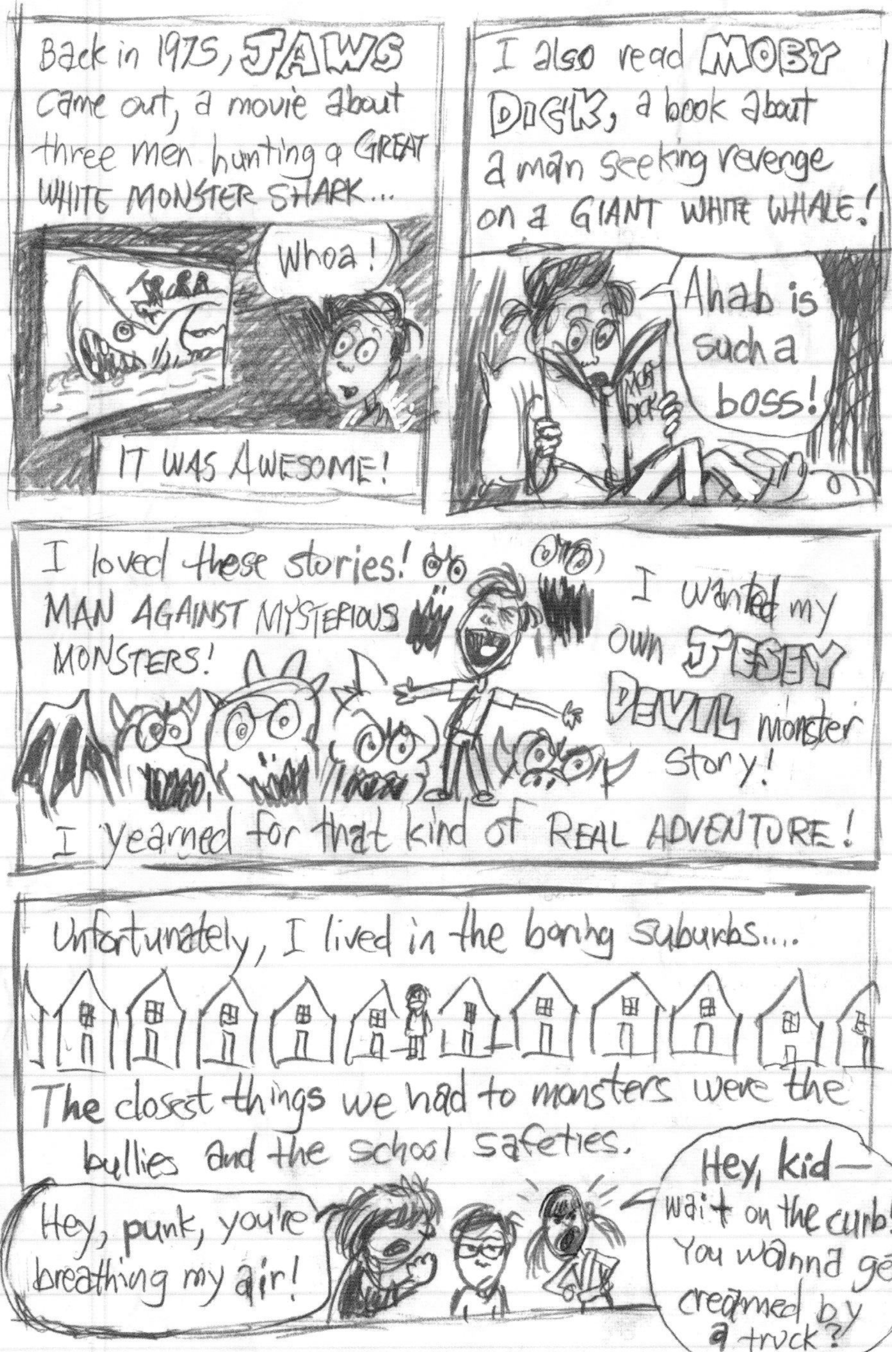
Back in 1975, JAWS came out, a movie about three men hunting a GREAT WHITE MONSTER SHARK...
Whoa!
IT WAS AWESOME!
I also read MOBY DICK, a book about a man seeking revenge on a GIANT WHITE WHALE!
Ahab is such a boss!
MOBY DICK
I loved these stories! MAN AGAINST MYSTERIOUS MONSTERS!
I wanted my own JERSEY DEVIL monster story!
I yearned for that kind of REAL ADVENTURE!
Unfortunately, I lived in the boring suburbs....
The closest things we had to monsters were the bullies and the school safeties.
Hey, punk, you're breathing my air!
Hey, kid— wait on the curb! You wanna get creamed by a truck?

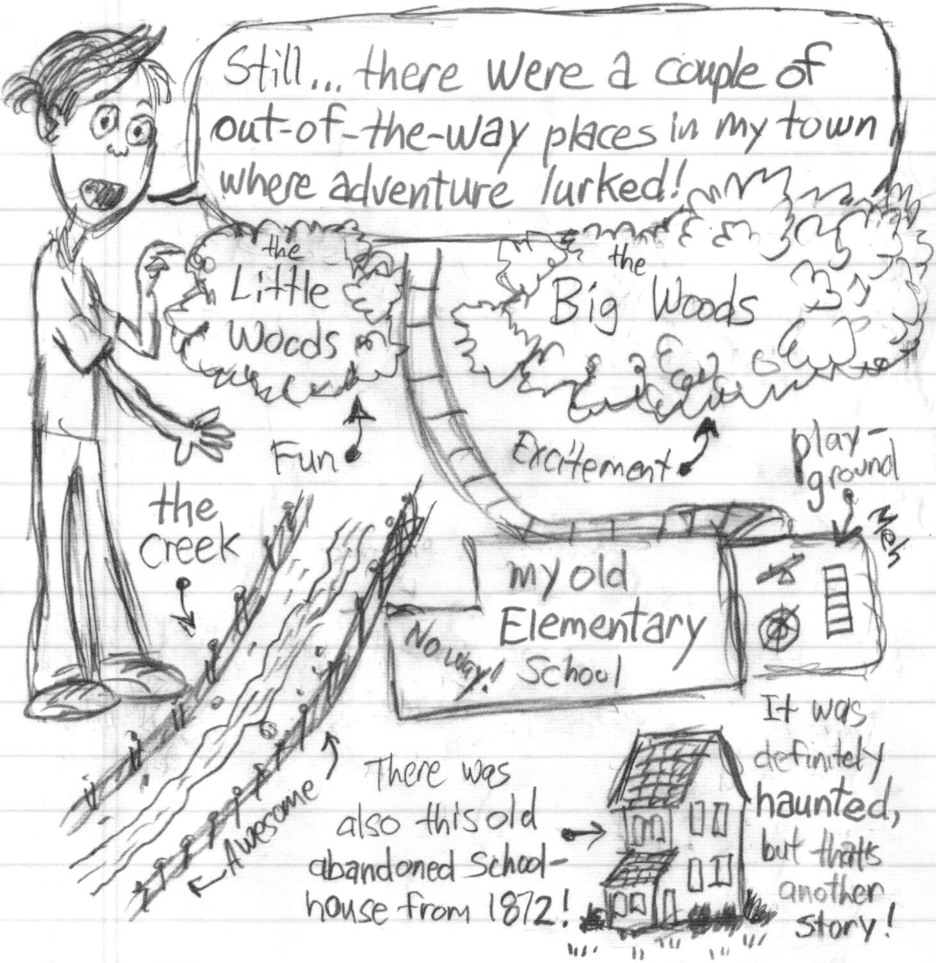
Still... there were a couple of out-of-the-way places in my town where adventure lurked!
the Little Woods
Fun
the Big Woods
Excitement
play-ground
Meh
the creek
my old Elementary School
No way!
Awesome
There was also this old abandoned School-house from 1872!
It was definitely haunted, but that's another story!

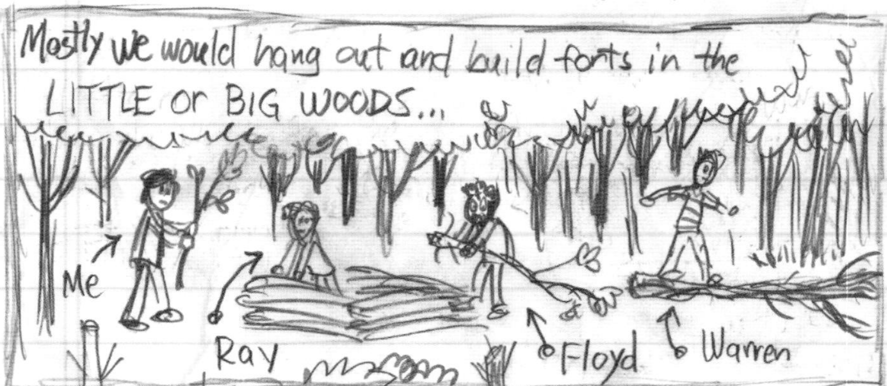
Mostly we would hang out and build forts in the LITTLE or BIG WOODS...
Me
Ray
Floyd
Warren

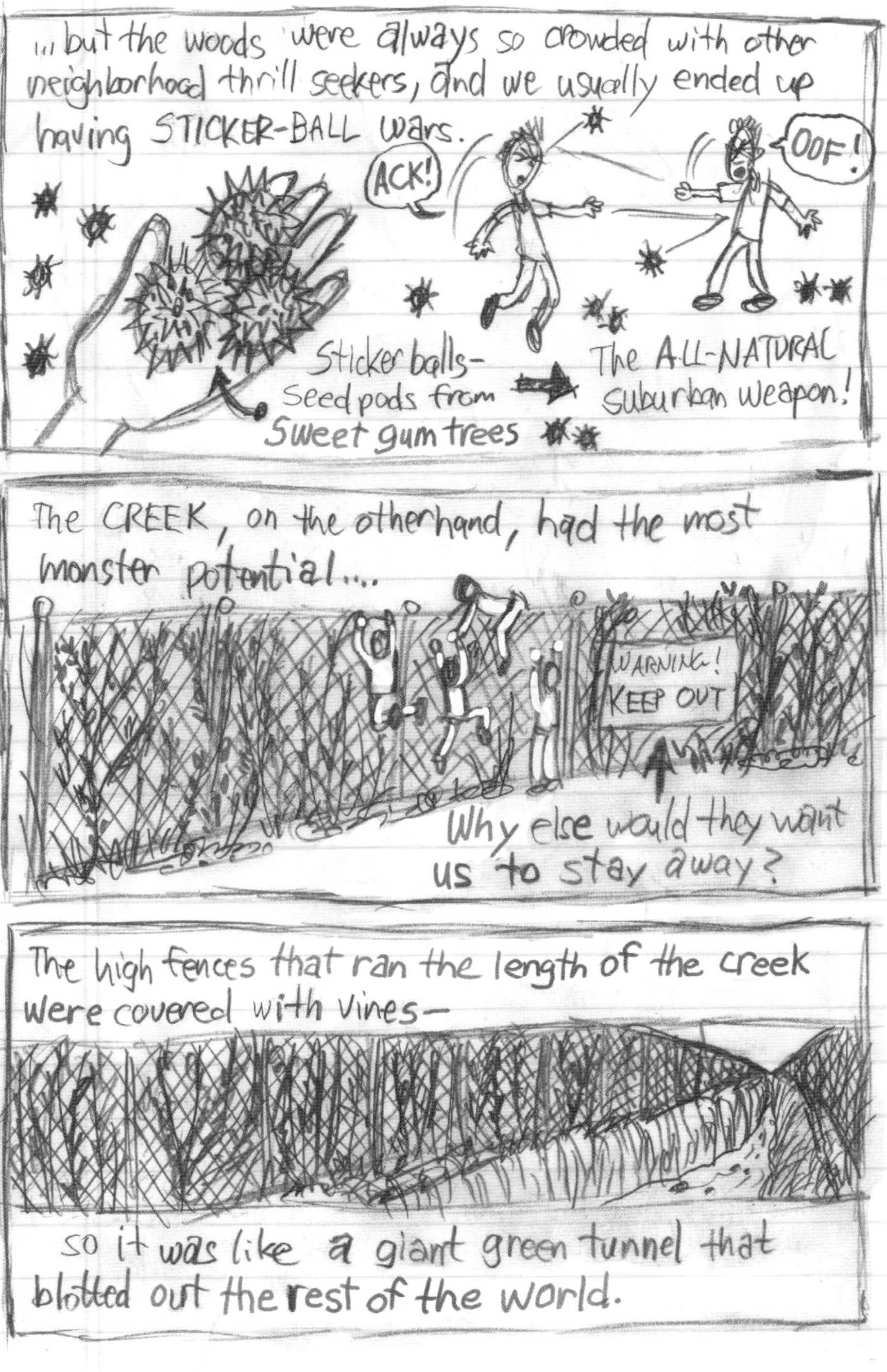
...but the woods were always so crowded with other neighborhood thrill seekers, and we usually ended up having STICKER-BALL wars.
ACK!
OOF!
Sticker balls- Seed pods from Sweet gum trees
The ALL-NATURAL suburban weapon!
The CREEK, on the otherhand, had the most monster potential....
WARNING! KEEP OUT
Why else would they want us to stay away?
The high fences that ran the length of the creek were covered with vines-
so it was like a giant green tunnel that blotted out the rest of the world.

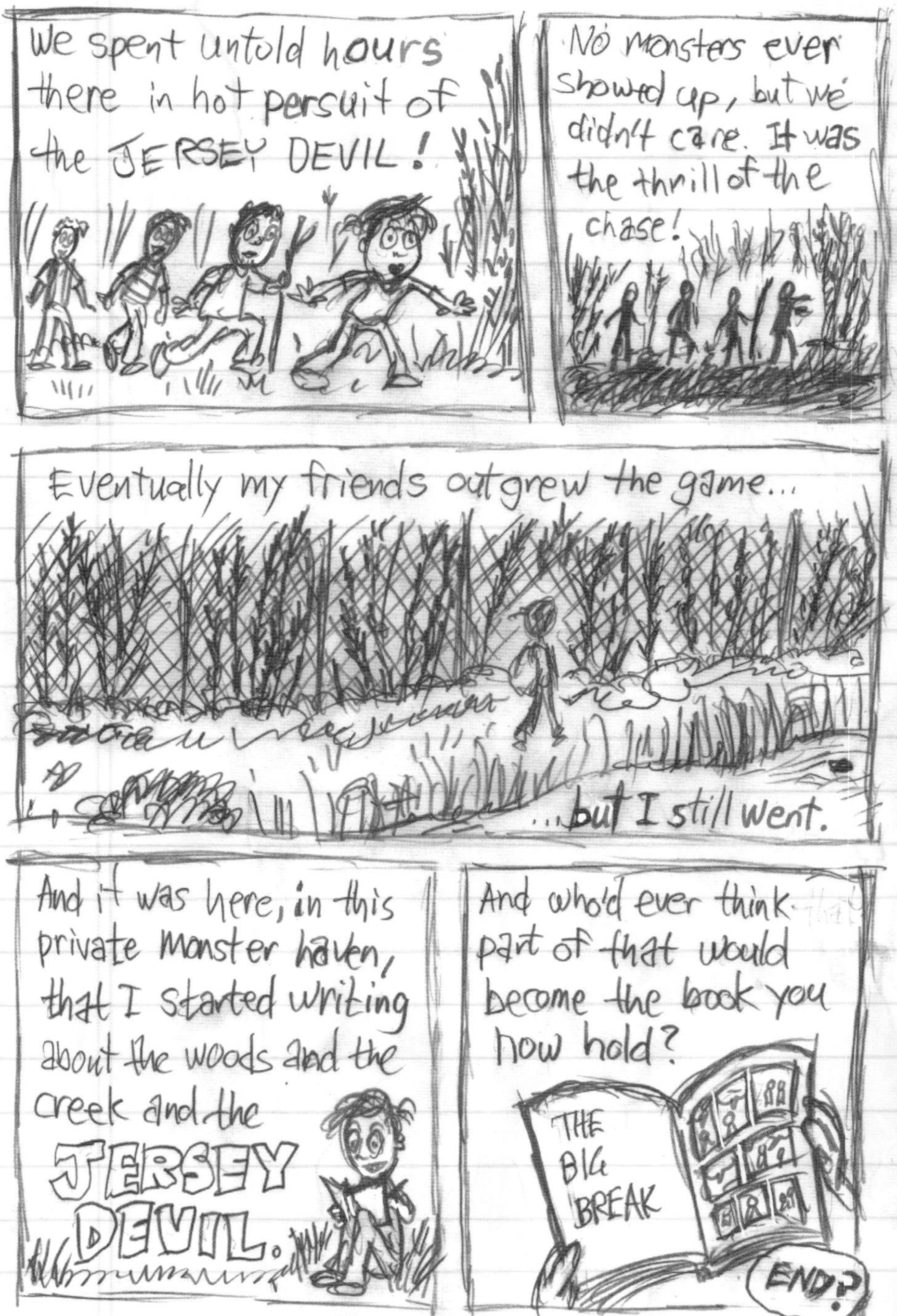
We spent untold hours there in hot persuit of the JERSEY DEVIL!
No monsters ever showed up, but we didn't care. It was the thrill of the chase!
Eventually my friends outgrew the game...
...but I still went.
And it was here, in this private monster haven, that I started writing about the woods and the creek and the JERSEY DEVIL.
And who'd ever think part of that would become the book you now hold?
THE BIG BREAK
END?

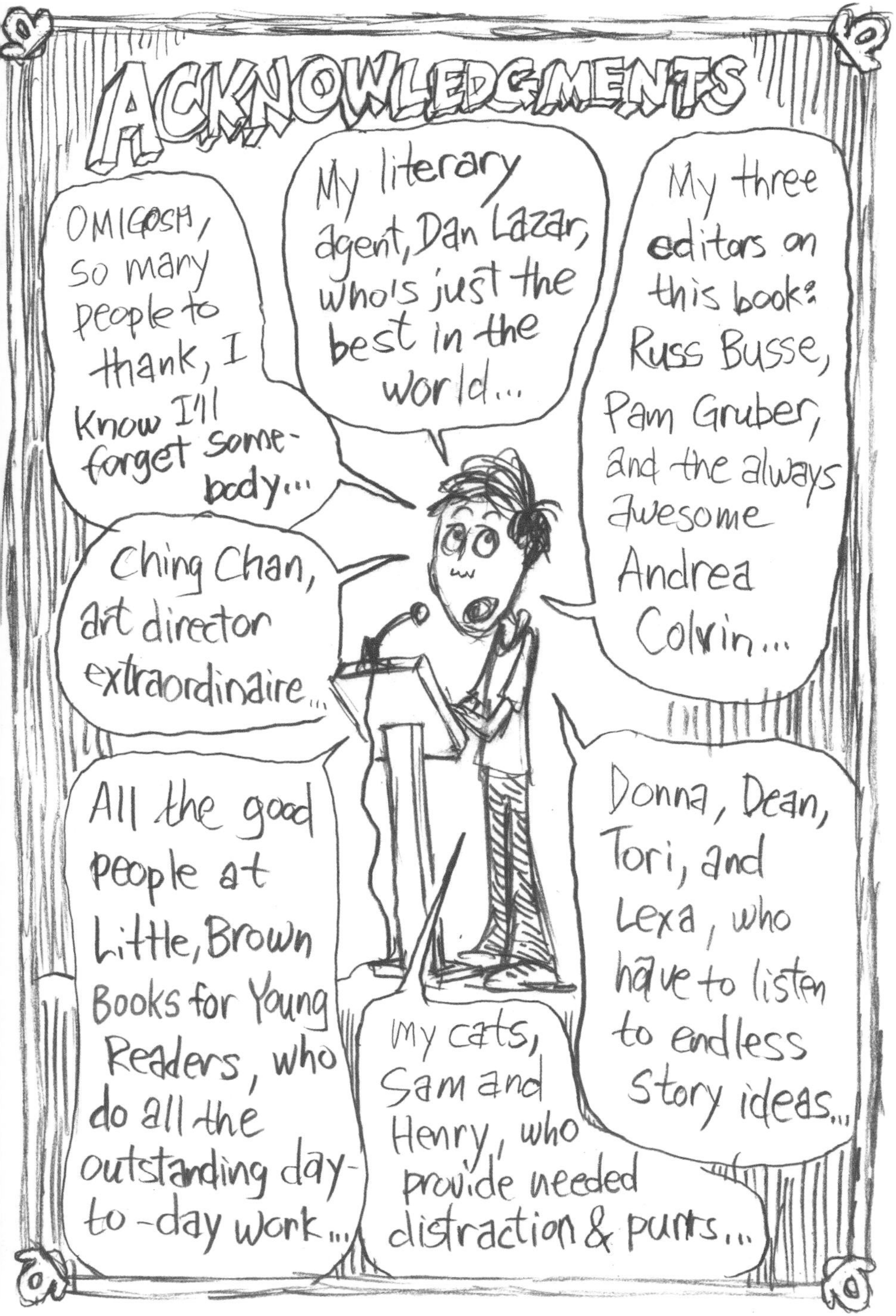
ACKNOWLEDGMENTS
OMIGOSH, so many people to thank, I know I'll forget somebody...
My literary agent, Dan Lazar, who's just the best in the world...
My three editors on this book: Russ Busse, Pam Gruber, and the always awesome Andrea Colvin...
Ching Chan, art director extraordinaire...
All the good people at Little, Brown Books for Young Readers, who do all the outstanding day-to-day work...
My cats, Sam and Henry, who provide needed distraction & purrs...
Donna, Dean, Tori, and Lexa, who have to listen to endless story ideas...

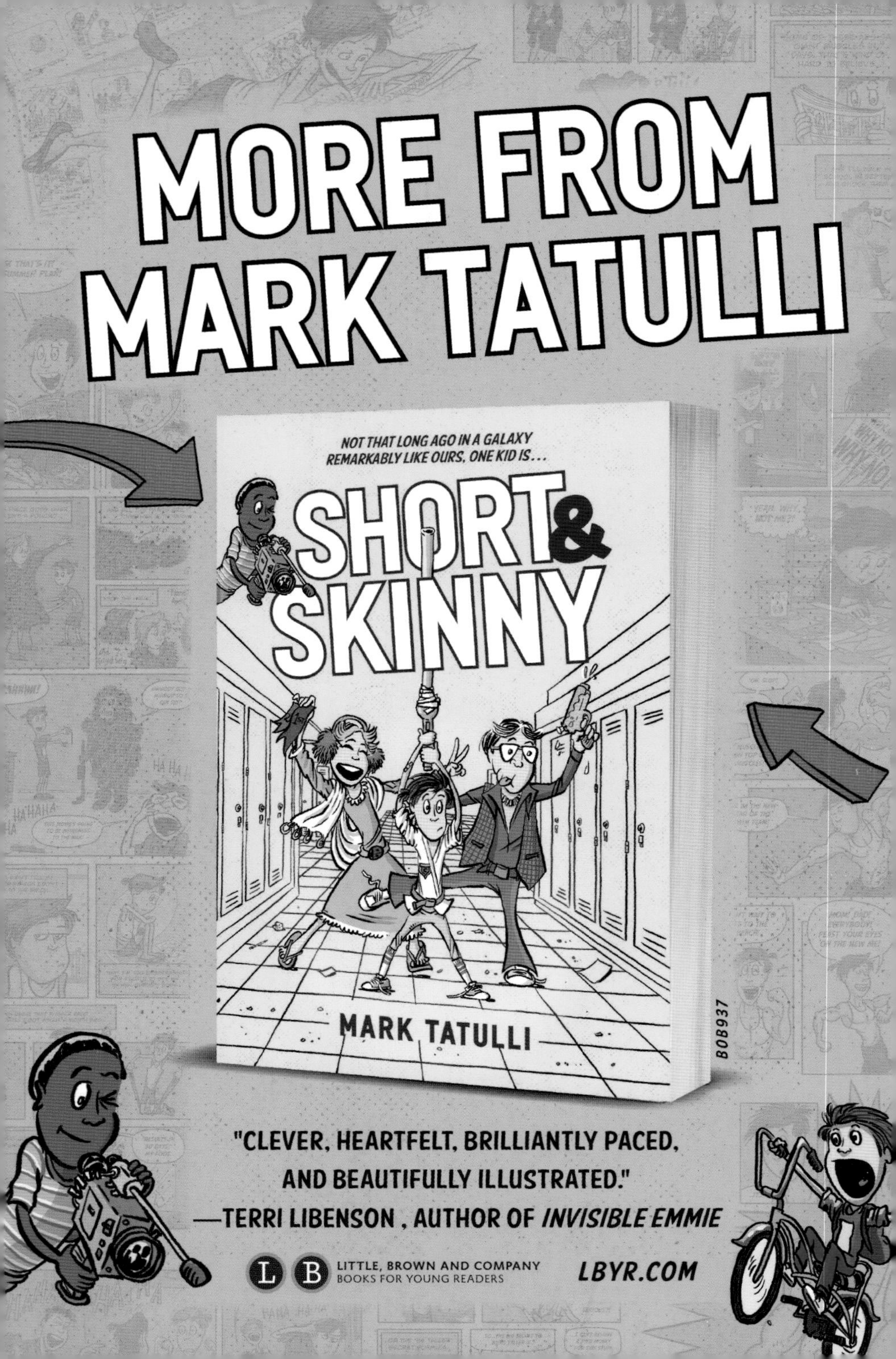
MORE FROM MARK TATULLI
NOT THAT LONG AGO IN A GALAXY REMARKABLY LIKE OURS, ONE KID IS...
SHORT & SKINNY
MARK TATULLI
BOB937
"CLEVER, HEARTFELT, BRILLIANTLY PACED, AND BEAUTIFULLY ILLUSTRATED."
—TERRI LIBENSON , AUTHOR OF *INVISIBLE EMMIE*
LB LITTLE, BROWN AND COMPANY BOOKS FOR YOUNG READERS
LBYR.COM